Northern Ways

Community Sakes

All the Best

Josh Pahm

Presented by

The Community Library

of Lake & Salem Twps.

In honor of our Open House

Thy Will Be Done

JOSEPH PALMA

authorHOUSE™

1663 LIBERTY DRIVE, SUITE 200
BLOOMINGTON, INDIANA 47403
(800) 839-8640
WWW.AUTHORHOUSE.COM

First published by AuthorHouse 3/20/06

ISBN: 1-4208-9733-0 (hc)

Library of Congress Control Number 2005911119

Printed in the United States of America
Bloomington, Indiana

This book is printed on acid-free paper.

ACKNOWLEDGEMENTS

There were many individuals who were priceless commodities in the developmental stages of writing this novel. Their insight, reaction, and encouragement were valuable tools that inspired me to continue on. To these chosen few, I will never forget: Butchie Frascone, Tommy and Julie Bruno, Marie and Paul DeFelippis, John Cavallo, Thomas Halloran, Debbie Miranda, Paula Vance and April and Terri Hernandez. I thank you all.

Special thanks to Marla Maloney and Robert Mirra. Success, if any, goes to you. Your unbridled enthusiasm, caring and true understanding of this project have touched the depths of my storytelling.

To my family, there is no special thank you; there is love. My mother Nina, sisters Michele, Nina and brother Louis, I hold all of you close to my heart, always. You are my foundation.

Ann Marie Pellini, thanks for always being there for me...Keep shining.

To my late uncle, author Chris Anderson, the eagle has finally landed.

Also, Dante the dog, for his many hours of companionship during my writers block.

To the rest of my friends, family and business associates at The New York Times, many more thanks,

If I have inadvertently left out anyone by name, I do apologize. You know who you are.

Despite all the fine advice and information given, any remaining errors and deficiencies in this novel are fully my own.

This book is dedicated to James Palma, my father You're gone, but the flame eternally burns. You have given substance to a once empty existence.

Note

The dialogues of the Apparition were taken from the book of Jeremiah. The dialogues of the prophet Jeremiah were taken from the Old Testament. The dialogues of Jesus were taken from the Book of Revelation.

Actual scriptures were chosen randomly to enhance the fictional storyline. They were used in no specific order. Nothing was added or deleted from that content.

"Whoever sheds the blood of man,
by man shall his blood be shed;
for in the image of God
has God made man."

GENESIS 9:19 VERSE 9

Prologue

THE MONTH WAS August; the year, 1908.

Alfonso Carlucci, his peasant garb white with dust, his face wrinkled by age and weathered by the sun, clawed through the mounds of rubble and debris that only days before had been a tiny village near Catania, Sicily.

A massive earthquake had leveled the quaint ancient village and all the surrounding areas. The thunderous quake, centered a few miles south of Mount Etna had killed tens of thousands and had left many more homeless.

Many had come great distances to offer assistance. Humanitarian aid from all over Europe began pouring into the area to help the hapless and bewildered survivors. The once peaceful town resembled a giant cemetery as the death toll kept rising.

Hours earlier, hope of finding survivors had dwindled. Corpses were thrown in a heap one on top of the other as tired men piled the decaying bodies in a nearby common grave. It was a valley of death as the heat intensified the decomposing process of the human body. A dense vaporous cloud of haze and dust smothered the inhabitants of this rural settlement. The smell of death cloyed at the senses and hovered above this human wasteland.

Still Alfonso continued to search. Something beneath the piles of mud bricks and broken timbers beckoned him and gave him strength to withstand the stifling 100-degree heat. Like a magnet, this unseen presence compelled him to ignore the pain of his bleeding fingers and the weariness---drove him to keep digging long after a reasonable man would know it was a futile effort. Alfonso knew that something was lying stagnant underneath him. This unforeseen presence drew him closer and closer, he felt it pulling and tugging at his inner soul.

Nearby, an injured man deliriously poked and prodded the piles of destruction with his bare hands, begging for a miracle. The devoted continued to dig on while the orphaned children searched and called out to their parents who were no longer there. Stray dogs were sniffing around the ruins for scents of their lost masters. Even they looked overwhelmed and lost by this tremendous natural disaster.

With each passing second the miracle of finding life started to fade away into the blazing sun. The situation looked hopeless as the stark reality set in.

Defiantly clawing through the hot baked bricks and shattered pieces of wood, the old man continued on. The proud and caring father did not stop until he finally found what was calling for him. His tired eyes were squinting when he noticed some human flesh underneath some of the fragments of rock and debris. With sweat relentlessly pouring down his face, Alfonso's efforts raced to a higher tempo.

Alfonso lifted a huge timber and underneath he found an arm clutching a dead child. Carefully, he moved the timber to the side and with great reverence removed the rubble from around the lifeless body of a woman. With one arm she held the dead infant close to her body; in her other hand she tightly clenched something in her fist.

Gently, he pried her vice-like fingers open to reveal the small round medal that lay in the palm of her hand. Wearily, he removed the round piece from her grip and lifted it towards him for a closer look. It was made of solid gold.

He gently folded the woman's arms lovingly around her child.

Rising from his crouched position, Alfonso blew the dirt away from the ancient relic and studied it more intensely. He was astonished to see the face of Jesus Christ engraved in the medal. He traced the lines with his fingers and a sudden numbness rendered him motionless. A strong jutting wind swirled the odor of decaying flesh and lifted the dust from the debris skyward, blotting out the sky. It was then, Alfonso knew that he was destined to find and retain this spiritual round medallion. The Gods were calling out his name; it was now time for him to answer the call.

Through the thick mass of swirling particles, a bright shaft of light opened up a seam to a majestic orange sky. Windswept, Alfonso stood frozen as the light engulfed him. He raised his arm, trying to protect his eyes and squinted toward the heavens. As he gazed up, the old man, amazed now, turns his face skyward where the shaft of light pierces the haze and seeks him out bathing him in a spotlight of heavenly mist. Blindness was all around, only he saw what waited behind it.

The magnificent wind and light reigned supreme over everything around it.

He clutched the medallion tightly in his fist. Instinctively he knew he must protect this object no matter what the cost. The earth began to shake beneath his feet, the violence nearly knocking him to the ground. To Alfonso, this aftershock would be felt for an eternity. Gradually, the mighty tremors subsided, and the mysterious light receded into the never-ending sky.

Something or someone was awakened from this terror filled act of Mother Nature. A phenomenon was reborn underneath the dirt and debris of this massive quake. It was searching for a new legacy to hear its foretold messages and commands. This remarkable awakening would span from the beginning of man into the turn of a new century.

Alfonso Carlucci had answered the call; now he must carry this sacred prodigy into the unforeseen future.

Chapter 1

RAIN WEEPS SOFTLY from a dark overcast sky. Four stories down, the passing shower spawns small pools of water on the pavement. Now, sunshine beckons, as it struggles to crack through the cumulus that races across the dark sky.

The Labor Day weekend had just flown by as the nineties and another millennium approached with its litany of unanswered questions.

Joey DeFalco stood over the small sink in his co-op apartment's master bathroom. The streaky mirror in front of him reflected the sad story of a beaten and worn out man. Though the scars were not physical, the mental anguish dulled his lifeless eyes even more. The proof was many, many sleepless nights dreading the days ahead. For Joey sleep was now a luxury and sometimes the lost peace was only in his dreams.

Dumbfounded for the past ten minutes, he woefully recollected the past accounts of the previous miserable year. Unable to deal with the insurmountable pressure, Joey reached for the rosary beads hanging from the mirror's edge. He placed the string of black beads with the gold crucifix in his right hand and squeezed tightly. Needing strength, he quietly prayed. His fervent plea seemed to go unanswered.

Unexpectedly, Joey felt something very peculiar smothering his being as it slowly entered the tiny room. With a ghastly complexion and both eyes darting, he searched the room for answers. Now frantic, he noticed an entity of thick grayish steam oozing out of an air vent below him. Trying to swallow his fear, Joey followed the gaseous matter from the duct to where ever its final destination would be. In an accelerating circular motion, the foreign vapors were quickly rising upwards. The hazy mass of vapor now formed a visible body. Effortlessly, the translucent orb hovered between his body and the medicine cabinet. Slowly, the small case started to siphon in the mysterious substance. The small cloud vanished in a matter of seconds.

Joey's perception and thoughts now wandered in and out of obscurity. With his mouth agape, his senses feeble, the terror paralyzed him.

Suddenly, a dark, translucent and muted image developed and occupied the mirror. The anomaly kept growing in proportion with the size of the rectangular sheet of glass. This ominous and eerie reproduction faded in and out as it seized control of Joey's reflection. The impression was oval, the characteristics bleak. The dark, gloomy mask concealed the true identity of this anonymous caller.

With his virtual image lost, Joey stood stunned and frightened. Stepping back some, he shivered as he rubbed his eyes in disbelief. Slowly uncovering his weary eyes, the image refused to die. Intermittently, it kept flickering in and out more profoundly with each passing second. Though petrified, Joey fought the natural instinct to retreat. Not knowing what to think, he continued to look on in awe. He was held captive to this mystical occurrence. The entity was now overpowering as an invisible emanation seized control of the room. Joey anxiously waited for the horror to subside.

The waiting seemed eternal.

Now weak kneed, Joey's scrutiny was horific as the medicine cabinet over the small pedestal sink began to tremor.

Vibrating violently, the amorphous form continued to express its coming until it peaked with intensity. Abruptly, from the combustion within, the mirrored cabinet door burst open with a fury. Joey felt a strong breeze brushing and probing against his stagnant body. The foreign gushes raced right through his bewilderment and slammed into the tiled wall behind him.

Breathing was now a problem, the gnawing presence left him gasping for air.

Whatever this was, its disembodied touches and indistinguishable presence was felt.

Whatever it came for, its message was sent.

Joey hesitantly inched closer to the cabinet and slowly reached for the opened door. Little by little, he nervously pulled it close, each inch filled with fright. Shaking profusely, he finally closed the glass door. What he saw startled him and left him stunned. The seed had been planted; he now came face to face with his destiny.

The phenomenon had withdrawn from the same mirror that gave it birth.

It disappeared leaving a visible trace of its power.

Joey examined the mirror closely. He noticed a facial expression that was embedded within the dust and vaporized film of the streaky mirror. Now edging his finger closer, he caressed the happening ever so lightly. Carefully, he rubbed his right index finger over the unusual blemish.

"Jesus Christ," he whispered, "what the hell is this?" Absently, Joey made the sign of the cross as his mirror witnessed the untold truth. "God, please tell me what is happening to me. Am I going crazy now? Please help me," he pleaded. "I don't know what any of this means. Help me get through all of this!"

No matter how hard he pleaded, he knew that this was one affair that he would try to forget. In the back of his mind, Joey also knew that this was not the end of this significant occurrence. It was just the beginning.

His spacious five room apartment was stripped bare, and the lavish furnishings were now gone. The emptiness of the place was a memorial to a once happy home. A gorgeous setting was reduced to nothing more than a squatter's haven.

The bare walls that used to boast magnificent abstracts now only exposed a badly needed paint job. Peeling paint was further testimony to the demise. Dust motes floated in the weak light and seemed to add to the sadness of the once grand dwelling. All that was left was a panoramic view of the canyons of Manhattan.

To Joey, even this prestigious sight now seemed trivial to his bloodshot eyes. In the back of his mind, he knew that he was never ever coming back to this place he once called home.

Still looking into the bathroom mirror and disgusted with what he saw, the Brooklyn born young man had a hard time accepting his demise. The more he thought of his impending ordeal, the harder he squeezed on the rosary beads. Joey's life was like a constantly boiling cauldron of anxiety.

Haphazardly, Joey opens the palms of his hands and studies the rosary beads. Again, he prays silently. Following his tears, he buries his face into his hands and grips tightly.

The string of beads dangle idly with the cross wedged in between his face and his trembling fingers.

Inch by inch, his hands slowly glide down the length of his perplexed face. With his face exposed, Joey levels a glower at himself in the tainted mirror. His paralyzed eyes uncover a face smeared with blood. He gasped.

"What the hell is this?" he shuddered.

Now daunted, Joey's eyes drop to his hands. More blood.

"Where did this blood come from?" he wondered, flipping his hands in different directions. "There's blood all over my hands!"

The consecrated blemish left him breathless.

Searching for the wounds, Joey could not find one puncture or even a pinhole in his skin. *This is not my blood,* he thought, quivering. *Whose blood is this?*

With no signs of any stigmata, he quickly ran some warm water, splashed his face and placed the bloodied hands under it. Not believing what he was seeing, the thick red substance quickly dissolved. Only the clear water found its way to the sink's drainpipe. Now free from the red stain, he picked up his hands to examine them even closer. Still nothing, his right or left hand did not have a mark or flaw on them. Joey dazzlingly gazed at the rosary beads with his mouth agape, his body trembling. Befuddled, he stood wondering what this all meant, its significance. For many minutes he just gawked at the holy beads.

"Aaaah!" He suddenly jumped, nervously reacting to the ringing telephone. Joey followed the ringing sound through the clothing that was scattered about the parquet wooden floor.

"Hello," he uttered, kicking his belongings off to the side.

"Joey, it's me Jack!" the sleepy voice said.

"What's up, Jack?"

"Listen, meet me by the coffee shop across the street from the courthouse. There are some last minute details that we have to discuss."

"Like what?" Joey asked, his voice was growing very somber. "I thought all the ground work and preparations were set?"

"They are, but before we go in I want you to know what you're up against!"

"I think I already know what I'm up against."

"You don't know all of it."

"What else is left but my sentencing?"

"That's what I want to talk to you about before we enter the courthouse," the lawyer said. "So anyway, how are you feeling?"

"How could I feel?" Joey asked, in a higher tone of voice. "I feel like shit! I just want to put all of this behind me. What time do you want me to meet you?"

"Eight o'clock sharp, make sure you pack a bag."

"It's already packed," Joey said. "See ya in an hour."

Jack Crenshaw was Joey's criminal defense attorney. Like most lawyers he lacked charisma and had little compassion. But his charm was not what he was hired for; his legal savvy was. Jack's price tag was high but he was an old hand at the criminal justice system. He was very prudent on how he handled most practical matters, especially his own. Never the fashion plate, Crenshaw looked like he plucked his entire wardrobe off the rack at a Sears fire sale.

Locking the door to his apartment for the final time filled Joey with an odd, lonely sense. All the tranquility that he once enjoyed was painfully evaporated. The merriment and comfort that once was his life was gone. But this was now the past, there was no time to rehash or start crying over spilt milk. One last glimpse was all there was time for. When the tears started to stream down his face, Joey knew it was time to leave. It was just a matter of days before the Federal Marshals would padlock the door as the bank foreclosed on his mortgage.

S truggling through the revolving door of the coffee shop, Joey suddenly realized that this might be his last meal in the civilized world. His new dining partners would surely lack the table manners that he had grown accustomed to. He knew that the food would not be too rich for his blood either. After all, the great chefs of Europe were not preparing anything on the prison menu.

"Joey!" Jack yelled, waving his arms in his direction.

Joey quickly acknowledged the call and lugged his suitcase through the narrow aisle.

"Good morning, Jack," he said, extending his hand.

"Let me ask you a question," Jack said, pointing to the oversized suitcase in Joey's left hand. "What the hell is that?"

"My clothes and some things that I need."

"I hope you have your tuxedo in there?"

"Why?"

Jack stuffed a piece of toast in his mouth and then washed it down with a sip of coffee. Joey just stared at him with a puzzled look on his face. His left hand was numb from toting the heavy luggage all around town. He rested the large suitcase between the booths and the counter stools. Every patron in the crowded diner had a hard time maneuvering around the unnecessary baggage.

"Because every Saturday night they have ballroom dancing in the gymnasium," he cracked.

"I don't find that comment too fuckin amusing."

"Lighten up; I'm just trying to tell you that you took to much clothing with you. That's all!"

"Well, then say it the next time," Joey warned. "I'm not in the mood for any jokes."

At that moment, Joey felt like slapping his lawyer from one end of the booth to the other. He had no use for humor now, especially at his expense. Joey was growing very tired of all the lawyer talk. After all, this guy was worse than having a wife. Jack was constantly up his ass asking him one question after another about his whereabouts and personal life. But most of all, he was looking for money.

"What will you have?"

"Just a cup of coffee," Joey said. He slowly slid into the booth and sat facing his high powered attorney.

"It's going to be a long day for you. Why don't you have a little breakfast?"

"Would you be hungry if you were me? Just get me a cup of coffee."

In deep thought, Jack just sat there with his hand under his square chin looking at some paperwork. He was now totally engrossed in the documentation that lay before him. Page after page, he just scanned through and shuffled the papers, creating a mess. Oblivious to everything but his work, Jack looked up as if he was in deep thought. Joey just shook his head in resignation and turned towards the large window. He was less than happy with the best lawyer that money could buy.

Outside, the rush hour traffic was bumper to bumper. Pedestrians overflowed off of the narrow sidewalks, hurrying to punch their time clocks. Like robots, their rituals never seemed to change.

"Okay," Jack sternly said, "let's get down to business. Do you know what you're looking at here?"

"Yea, I know what I'm lookin at," Joey shouted, pounding his fist on the table. "I'm lookin at a blood suckin, money hungry, fuckin leach. Let me tell you something, Jack! You're no different than me," he said. "The only difference is that you rob people legally. It seems to me that after the retainer money ran out, so did my chances. I should've gotten a legal aid lawyer," Joey spat, "he couldn't have done any worse."

"Calm down, you're making a spectacle of yourself," Jack said, noticing the gazes of the early morning diners. Where he came from, Harvard law school graduates never acted this way. Only people from Brooklyn did.

"Don't tell me to calm down. Fuck you and fuck everybody else in this place. Now at the last few minutes you're gonna tell me my fate. You knew what my sentence would be a long fuckin time ago. You knew, you cocksucker! You were just afraid that if I knew you wouldn't have gotten another dime out of me!"

Jack just sat motionless, his jaw slack. Joey could see the amazement in the lawyer's eyes.

"Listen, Joey," Jack said. "You were indicted and we copped a plea, we plead guilty for a reduced sentence. Since this would have been your first offense and felony conviction, you were probably looking at probation, a small fine and some restitution. Now given the fact that you cooperated, it weighed heavily on the court's decision. But since you have this damn drug charge," he said pausing, "well, the court and the system will not show any leniency towards you."

"So what's the verdict?"

"Eighteen months," he said in an unsteady voice. "You will probably be released in half that time."

"So I have to go before the judge so he can tell me that?"

"Its procedure, he's probably going to give you an earful and a nice tongue lashing. So be prepared for it," he warned. "I didn't tell you sooner because I was afraid you would do some unnecessary worrying."

Sitting there with his face buried in his hands, Joey started to show some sure signs of weakness. Too proud to display the softer side of himself, he regrouped and looked at his attorney. "So that's it?"

"Not exactly!"

"What do you mean not exactly?" Joey asked, running his hands through his thick black hair.

"There's just one more issue," Jack said softly, his eyes darting. "You're not going to be placed in some minimum security facility."

"Yea, so. Where are they gonna send me to, Siberia?"

"You're not going to the basic country club for high profiled white collar criminals."

"Jesus Christ, Jack," Joey began to demand. "Would you just spit it out already? Where the fuck are they sending me?"

"Because of the felony drug charges, you will be residing in a much more supervised program. Joey, you will be serving hard time."

"Oh shit," he said. "You mean to tell me that they're dumpin me in with the garbage?"

"That's right," Jack said, his tone somber. "You'll be serving time with hardened criminals."

"That's the best you could've done for me?"

"I'm sorry, Joey."

"Where?"

"That's yet to be determined."

The morning sun started to enter through the large storefront window. Jack's bad news had brought a temporary lull to the conversation at the breakfast table. Joey sat silently, before leveling a glower at his lawyer. He slowly turned his head, squinting and peering at the immense courthouse across the street. The waiting was almost over. There was only time for one last cigarette.

"May I take your order?" the good looking but absent minded waitress said with a forced smile.

"I've been sitting here for the past twenty minutes and you finally decide to take my order?" Joey grumbled, while lighting another cigarette. "Just give me a damn cup of coffee!"

"I'm sorry," she said. "Will that be it?"

"That's it. I don't have time for anything more than that."

The waitress took the order and quickly left the hostile environment. Jack just looked at his client shaking his head.

"Joey," he said. "She was probably afraid to come over here. You know with all the yelling going on."

"Why? What, does she know that I'm a convicted felon already?"

"I didn't say that."

"Let's go!" Joey said, taking a last puff from his cigarette. He then reached for the ashtray from across the table and violently snuffed it out.

"You didn't have your coffee yet."

"Fuck the coffee!" he snapped as he reached for his suitcase. "Let's get this shit over with!"

T he two men emerged at the bottom of the courthouse steps. Joey tried to blend in with the crowd, but his guilt had all eyes upon him. With the suitcase by his side, any passerby would think that he was going away for a very long, long time.

The courthouse steps stretched endlessly before him. One step after the other, the massive intimidating building brought him closer, closer to what he feared most. He started to feel the sweat seep through the underarms of his dark blue suit. Jack, noticing his reticence, reached out to put his arm around Joey's shoulder.

"Hang in there, kid."

"Please, Jack, don't baby me. All I have left is my manhood."

They hopped on the elevator to the third floor of the quiet building. Quickly they proceeded to Room 312 and opened the heavy wooden doors. Jack rushed into the courtroom while Joey just stood there trying to take it all in. Joey was not alone in crime on this sunny day. There were other criminals scattered around the courtroom awaiting the same fate as he. In the rear of the spacious room sat the spectators waiting to capture their cheap thrills for the day.

"Let's sit here," Jack insisted.

Joey would have sat anywhere just to get off of his feet. A certain presence that was alive in this building, a presence that seemed to render him senseless was overwhelming him.

"When the court calls for us," Jack whispered, "I arranged that the judge sentences you in closed chambers."

"Why?"

"Well, this way nobody gets to know your business. You never know who's sitting in the grandstands."

"You finally did something right, Jack."

Jack looked at Joey with a discouraged look on his face. He then threw his small briefcase on the long bench beside him and opened it up. Retrieving some paperwork, he turned to Joey one more time. "We want to keep as much of this as possible away from the newspapers."

The courtroom was as silent as a tomb. All the noise and confusion of the outside world was beyond the hush of the courtroom. An occasional sneeze or a flip of some pages was the gist of the morgue like atmosphere. Most strangers would take a peek at each other while trying to retain their anonymity. The feeling of the unknown was thick; the room reeked of it.

"All rise," the court officer bellowed from the front of the room. The chamber door swung open as the magistrate entered the courtroom. Everyone stood motionless while the judge took his place behind the bench.

"There he is," Jack said. "There's the man."

"Big deal," Joey retorted. "He's only big in this courtroom."

"Yea, well right now the courtroom is your major obstacle."

"No shit. I bet you when he goes home he hides behind his wife's apron."

"Sssh, be quiet or they'll add another eighteen months to your sentence."

"What the hell is the difference," Joey said. "I'll probably never make it out of there alive anyway."

"Don't say that," Jack said grinning. "You still owe me money."

"Fuck you, you raped me enough. You know you'll never see a penny of that money anyway."

"I had a feeling that you might say that."

"You may be seated," the court officer said in a softer tone of voice.

The elderly judge slowly took a seat and started to arrange the day's procedures before him. He sifted through some court documents as the stenographer got situated off to his left. The final outcome was about to be imposed by this great force that governs human destiny.

"The United States Government vs. Joseph DeFalco. Southern District Case # 28317. Please come forward," the officer demanded.

"Its show-time," Jack whispered to Joey as they rose from the long wooden bench. For Joey the court officer's words meant that his closure was finally arriving.

Both men walked in tandem one after the other. The shorter Jack led the way down the aisle towards the judge's chambers. Every step of the way produced an echoing sound that bounced off of the naked walls. All the critique and explanations expressed by Jack were about to be reiterated by a much higher authority. Shaking, light headed and sweaty, Joey walked into the private room. He felt like a weakening crack head in dire need of a hit.

It was a small room that had a very shiny and clean appeal to it. All the furniture appeared like it was buffed with some kind of commercial polishing wax. The large oval table reflected the images of those who hovered above it. Not a piece of paper or a pen was out of place. The judge's chambers with all its gloss carried the pleasant characteristic odors of a pharmacy.

Everyone took a seat in assigned leather chairs. Like a boardroom meeting, five people amassed around the spacious oval table. Jack sat right beside Joey and directly across from the judge. To the left of the judge sat a Federal agent and Joey's main nemesis.

The Assistant Attorney General of the United States was the government's avenger for retributive justice. Being a man of high stature and standards, he looked like an unbeatable rival. He had a polish, a veneer about him that suggested a winner. David Glassman was an undersized little runt of a man, but during litigation, it didn't matter. Outside of his domain you could kick sand in his face, slap him around, pull his girlfriend off of his beach blanket and walk away with her. You could commit all these atrocities upon him and he probably wouldn't do a damn thing about it. But not in a courtroom, this was his stage and he was omnipotent.

Behind Glassman and a few feet away from the table sat the stenographer. She quietly adjusted her equipment as she prepared for the testimonials to commence. Behind her, stood a stoned face court officer.

Only Joey's annoying finger tapping and a nervous knee banging on one of the table legs broke the silence. "Calm down," Jack said, reaching down to grab Joey's left knee.

"That's easy for you to say," Joey said, struggling to keep his body parts from vibrating. "You're not the one going to prison."

Basically, everything that was going to be said was cut and dry. Everyone in the room already knew what the imposed sentence was going to be. Joey's fate had already been satisfied and predetermined. It was just a matter of crossing the T's and dotting the I's. His bloodshot eyes and distressed demeanor were apparent to everyone in the room.

"Let the proceeding begin," the judge said, panning the room at everyone. "Mr. Crenshaw?"

"Yes, your Honor."

"Do you have anything to say on behalf of your client, Mr. DeFalco?"

"No, your Honor, the defense rests."

"It figures," Joey muttered under his breath. "This is what $25,000 buys for me."

"Mr. Glassman?" the judge quickly said, turning towards the Assistant Attorney General.

"Yes, your Honor."

"For the record, do you have any closing statements or arguments to be made for or against the behalf of Mr. DeFalco?"

"Yes I do, your Honor," he said with a sharp crisp voice. "It has been asserted that various rulings have been made in construing the foregoing conclusions to which I have agreed upon. The defendant was given a preferential assignment based on the allegations of his injustices. Mr. DeFalco's early failures to comprehend the consequences provided a salutary jolt to his assumption that his cooperation was necessary."

Holy shit, Joey thought, amazed by the impressive courtroom chatter. *What the fuck is this guy talking about?*

"Therefore under the profusion of information that he has provided based on his actions, was acceptable," he continued on with his flawless presentation. "The Attorney General's office now agrees that the enumerated sentence imposed upon this defendant to be satisfactory. Satisfactory to the prosecution and the United States Government, to whom I represent. Thank you," Glassman concluded.

Off to the corner the court stenographer was finishing up on the distinguished dialogue. In Joey's mind, he thought the Asst. Attorney General would tear him into pieces and destroy any self-respect that he had left. But he didn't, all Glassman did was pertain to the business matters at hand. Although there were many openings, never once did he try and shoot down the defendant's character and self-respect. To Joey, that meant an awful lot.

"Well, Mr. DeFalco," the judge said, "this leads us to you. Do you have anything to say before your sentence is handed down?"

"Yes I do, sir."

There were no cue cards to read from or scripts to rehearse by. For the first time Joey felt some sort of transformation going on inside of him. This was not about business or reading a spreadsheet. It was not about bank accounts or fancy cars. This was all about showing some remorse and compassion towards your fellow man. It was a time for this so called monster to dig way deep and try to find the inner feelings that had been stagnantly buried. This monster had been living in a shadow for the past five years; it was time to come clean. Hopefully now he would fess up to all his wrong doings and the pain that his evil had caused others.

"Begin," the judge said in a restrained voice.

"Your Honor, I was raised by parents who set established standards on good behavior. I was taught to respect others at a very young age," he said. "My adolescent years flourished with strong friendships and love. Somehow, I got caught up in a world that I never knew existed." Joey reached for a tissue on the table to wipe his eyes. "I come from a hard working blue collar family. It boggles my mind how I got caught up in this corporate web of greed. To this very day I still don't know how I got myself into this mess. This was not me! But it seems that my fondness for money lured me into a world that was once totally unknown to me. I made the choices, and I alone inflicted the pain that disrupted the lives of many others. Those choices left severe consequences based on my irrational decision making. Now I am left with nothing," he said with his head low. "I am drowning in my own shame. For the first time I am afraid of the enigma that awaits me. But I do realize that it's not about me anymore," Joey said, lowering his eyes. "It's about the others. To them, I hold the utmost and deepest remorse for. Thank you."

Was this an Academy Award winning speech or what? After his sob story, Joey just sat there lamenting about the so-called remorse that he was now feeling. He also sat there thinking about all the so-called misery that he supposedly inflicted upon others.

Did I really feel remorse or was it the right thing to say at the right time, he thought. *All the horrible pain and sorrow are true, because I'm experiencing it. Do I feel the pain of others? Should I suffer just because of another person's losses? Or did their own stupidity cause their own demise? After all, I didn't rape or kill anyone! I committed all of my crimes with a pen and a telephone, big deal. Does all of this add up to feeling remorseful? How can I feel remorseful for crimes that I never fully understood why I committed them?"*

Now it was time for the big cheese to be heard. Dressed in his black robe, his intimidation was dominant. The honorable Thomas A. McGee was a man who practiced traditional values and beliefs. His hard knocks approach was handed down from his immigrant Irish parents. A steadfast public official with a flushed complexion, he was two years away from retirement. Frequently growing tired and lacking the patience of yesteryear, long trials were very trying on his stamina. Through a lot of his recent actions he developed a nickname within the judicial system. Most prosecutors and defense attorneys called him, "cop a plea McGee." To Joey, he was nothing more than a lucky roll of the dice.

"Mr. DeFalco?" the aging Judge said.

"Yes, sir!" Joey answered.

"Well, let me start by saying that I am happy that my retirement is less than two years away," he said, drawing a slight chuckle from everyone who was not going to prison. "Deep down, way down underneath this false pretense that you call a life, I find it despicable and deplorable how you misapplied all the principals of the law. Your rules and regulations only existed in your own personal playpen. By your negligence, you fraudulently misrepresented innocent investors. The applied boiler room tactics have put a scar on corporate America and the trust that it should signify," the Judge jutted. "You are in violation of numerous sanctions and Federal regulation codes of ethics within the Securities and Exchange Commission Act of 1934. These findings of section 11-A of the commission by laws, institute these public proceedings against you."

Judge McGee then removed his wire rim glasses and looked straight into the eyes of the disgraced defendant. Shaking his head with a repugnant look on his face, he took a deep breath. The man of justice was about to bear down for another round of discipline. This tongue-lashing had no mercy, and it was about to continue.

"Pursuant to sections 15-B, 15C 1-2 and 21-C of the said Act and under the general construction of the laws I uphold and comply to. You," he sternly said, "Mr. DeFalco, are being charged as a member of a conspiracy to commit bank fraud. You also pleaded guilty and were in violation of breaking the insider trading statutes. Both are class four felonies that carry a fine and restitution. The charges of possession and solicitation of an illegal controlled substance carries a class two felony conviction."

"Oh Jesus," Joey said under his breath while looking at Jack.

"Mr. DeFalco, I have come across all types of cases involving white collar crimes. I have dealt with many defendants from all walks of life. But you are in a class all by yourself. Never have I ever encountered such an extreme mixture of illegal activities. It was amazing to me how you still found time to solicit cocaine to some of your clients and working peers. Your premeditated design for the law can not go unpunished in my courtroom. These are acts that I will not condone and will not tolerate." For the first time Judge McGee became irate, his face was actually changing colors. "I hereby sentence you to 18 months at the Federal Penitentiary in upstate New York. You will serve no more than 18 months or no less than nine months. Of course, that all depends on your conduct while incarcerated. I will also impose an incidental demand for equitable relief to your clients," he continued, while reading from his paperwork. "Starting with your assets and not to over exceed the imposed penalty of restitution, you are also fined $100,000 and the method of payment will be notified your way. Good luck, Mr. DeFalco. You're going to need it. This case is now adjourned," he said slamming the hard wooden gavel to make it official.

Everything that came out of the Judge's mouth was true. Justice was just served and to Joey the taste was very bitter. By the time they finish the liquidation of Joey DeFalco, he thought, he will be worthless. Joey wasn't a smart thief; everything that he owned was in his own name. For the government, this would be a very easy confiscation. There are some people like Joey who never think about the future. For these certain few, tomorrow never, ever, comes. It seemed that someone or something already had Joey DeFalco's future secretly planned for him. Whoever that is still remains anonymous.

Joey was remanded to custody as the handcuffs were slapped tightly around his wrists. For the first time he felt his life and freedom being taken away from him. It was more painful than anything he had experienced before.

Now it was finalized, Joey DeFalco was 100% United States Government property. He painfully awaited that long scenic countryside ride to his new home.

Jack wished him well.

Chapter 2

AFTER PROCESSING AND an hour-long stint at a detention center it was now time to get ready for transport. Joey slipped into his bright orange jumpsuit and heavy leg irons and handcuffs were applied. The luminous state issued uniform would stick out like a sore thumb if a prisoner managed to escape. The blinding color made it almost impossible to blend in with the law-abiding citizens of the world.

Upon boarding the bus, Joey was told to take a seat to the rear. The composition of the seating arrangements suggested a very familiar scenario. The men were being separated by the color of their skin and ethnicity. Blacks were in front, Hispanics and Mexicans were situated in the middle of the bus. Whites and whatever else was left occupied the rear. Even on a bus, it was the Corrections Departments way of controlling race relations and the peace.

Two heavily armed guards policed the front of the long yellow vehicle, while the other sentry alertly patrolled the rear.

The bus crawled through the New York City traffic as the sunlight found ways to send shafts onto the streets through the canyons and tall skyscrapers. Each prisoner sat stone faced as he would experience the tension all around him. In silence, each one of them had an impulse to take a peek at a counterpart. The prisoners didn't look the same physically, but their common plight separated them from the free society.

Inside the bus, besides some idle chatter, the only sounds were coming from the worn out and squeaking brakes. The badly tuned engine and rotted exhaust provided the other glorious tunes for the long and hot bus ride. Most of these born criminals sat quietly, not ready to make any new friends.

This crop was a seedy looking band of misfits. The faint of heart did not belong with this rancid smelling bunch of losers. Where they were going the stench really didn't matter, they were considered all the same now. Every face on this bus told the story of another life in ruin. They all crossed that fine line between right and wrong. For some, it was their emotions that pushed them over the edge. For others, they really didn't know any other way of life. Depending upon how severe the breaking point was, some would make it back. The others would either die or call prison their home for a very long time.

The bus picked up some speed as it entered and headed up the F.D.R. drive. A lukewarm breeze meandered through the half opened safety windows. Joey's mind was racing at uncontrollable speeds. These thoughts were very common for the first time offender, most of the time the heavy load would fatigue a prisoner to sleep.

"What are you looking at?" Joey said to the neighbor sitting next to him.

"Hey, my name is Justin," he said. "Justin O'Leary."

"Joey DeFalco."

"First time?" Justin asked, trying desperately to get acquainted.

"Yeah," Joey said. He then turned his head to look out the window. Joey was not going to offer anything in the way of conversation. Keeping to himself was his number one priority. Playmates, companions or any sexual activity were not part of his prison agenda.

"Me too," Justin said, almost proudly boasting, yet in a simpering manner. "Drugs, man, I got bagged selling shit to an undercover cop. Fucked up, right? I got three to six." Justin just sat there waiting for some sympathy, which was not about to come.

"That's too bad."

"I know, I'm fucked for at least three years."

Raised on the streets of Flatbush, Brooklyn, Justin O'Leary was the product of an Irish father and a German mother. He had a hard time adjusting to family life and values. His father's alcoholism and his mother's substance abuse forced Justin to stray from his family's grip. Before his sixteenth birthday, delinquency became a major part of his life. He haphazardly abused his studies and whatever home life he had. Lost and confused he hit the pavement for the fast buck. The nearest street corner became his new home. His dossier included all the hot selling drugs that could be found in a dime bag. Justin made a decent living until something happened that was beyond his control. After a couple of years the complexion of the neighborhood started to change, so did his luck. With reddish blonde hair and a milky white pigmentation, his physical attributes created a huge dilemma for him. They were not the perfect setup for a small white street dealer in an all-black neighborhood. At 5 foot 8 and weighing not even 150 pounds soaking wet, Justin lost the turf war for his survival. Forced to relocate he would take more risks to make a sale. Eventually he would make the one sale that would cost him dearly.

"What about you?" Justin asked, looking eager to hear Joey's sob story.

"You don't want to hear my shit."

"Hey man, it's a long bus ride. Could you think of anything better for me to do? Come on, man, open up, it might do you some good."

After a long pause, Joey decided to open up a bit. "I don't know," Joey started to say. "Getting in this mess sucks, but I keep thinking of my family."

"Why's that?"

"My poor mother has no clue what's going on with me."

"You didn't tell her?"

"No, it would have broken her heart."

"Shit, my folks went out and bought a bottle of fuckin champagne when I got busted," Justin said. "They partied all night long."

"With me it was a little different," Joey sadly said. "When my father passed away, the bond between me and my mother grew stronger. She has two other children, Michele and Louie, but the relationship we shared was something special. I was always so handsome to her and she was always proud of my success. The only thing left for her was to see me get married and have some kids. Boy, did I fuck that up."

"How long are you in for?"

"9 to 18."

"Years?"

"Nah, months."

"That's nothing!"

"Maybe to you it's not," Joey shot back. "But to me it's a lifetime. Growing up I was always cautious. I don't know what the fuck happened to me. I never stuck my neck out for anything or anyone. But I fucked up big time. To this day I still don't know how the hell any of this shit happened to me. I don't know what possessed me to get into this mess. This is not like me. I don't belong here."

"Yea right," retorted Justin. "That's what we all say."

"I know, I guess you're right." For some strange reason, Joey felt comfortable telling his life story to Justin.

The bus maintained the steady speed of 55 miles per hour. Prisoners were bouncing up and down with each bump of the outdated vehicle. The engine roared as the bus whisked through the mountainside that bordered the New York State Thruway. Most of the occupants were so tired that even an avalanche would have a problem waking the sleeping ones up.

Now eyeing Joey up and down, Justin asked, "Are you tough?"

"Let's just say that I have pretty quick hands for a white boy," he answered smiling.

"That's good to know," Justin professed. "Because where they're taking us, you're gonna need them."

"I plan on staying clean in prison."

"That's gonna be a hard thing to do."

"I know it is," Joey said. "But I have to make it out of there. It might sound strange to you, but I feel that there is something waiting for me on the outside. I don't know what it is, but it's there. Just like I know that there is something waiting for me inside this prison that we're going to."

"What is it?"

"I only wish I knew," a wide-eyed Joey said. "But it's in there."

"This is spooky shit, man," Justin whimpered. "How do you know this?"

"It might sound supernatural and ya might think I'm a fuckin nut but I just have this strange feeling about all of this," Joey quietly said. "But trust me, whatever it is that I'm looking for, I know I'm gonna find it. I can feel it tugging at me and pulling me in."

After a short pause. "You still never told me what you got busted for?" Justin asked.

"I got nailed on some white collar crap on Wall Street."

"So what are you doing on this bus? This is for violent offenders."

"There was also a drug rap that they hit me with," confessed Joey. "It's funny, but at the time I was in way over my head trying to support my bad habits and expensive lifestyle. The more I spent, the harder I had to work just to make ends meet. That was the start to my demise."

"Were there any other guys in it with you?"

"Yeah, man. That's when you find out who your friends really are," Joey said. "But I won't miss them. They weren't friends, it was all about competing and using one another. I won't be losing any sleep over them, that's for sure. Well, Justin, the rest is history!"

"So here you are!"

"Yep, here I am!"

Justin seemed to thrive listening to Joey's misery. Besides that, Justin probably felt like he had made a friend. Both men knew that where they were going friendships would be hard to come by. Joey knew that Justin was needy for something; it was more than a friendship that he was searching for. He just wanted to be accepted.

After the long conversation, the two men drifted off into a much-needed sleep. The bus was now only an hour away from its destination, but everyone wished that the hour would last forever.

"Wake up!" the huge Corrections Officer growled, poking his nightstick into Joey's ribs.

"I'm up, I'm up." Joey quickly answered, awakening from a short sound sleep. "Where are we?"

"Hell," he intoned. "Your worst nightmare."

Joey looked around and peeked out of the dirty window. He stared, stunned, his eyes and mouth wide open. "Jesus Christ, please help me," he whispered to himself.

His astonished eyes gawked at the surrounding forty-foot walls and their intimidating gun towers. In between the great walls was a huge steel entrance gate. Joey looked on in awe as the bus slowly approached the front gate. The overheated vehicle started to make its way inside.

"Shit!" Joey said, loud enough for the Corrections Officer to hear. "I know this isn't Buckingham Palace!"

"That's right boy," the officer replied. "And I ain't the fuckin Queen of England."

This was the big house, the slammer or whatever else one wants to call it. But it was one thing for sure to all of the prisoners surveying the intimidating surroundings. This was no nightmare or illusion. This was their new home.

Chapter 3

$\mathfrak{I}$T WAS NOW 2 p.m. as the sun was transmitting its radiance up the walkway to the large gray building. The yellow bus finally came to a halt inside the prison walls. The prison guards lined up on the steps of the administration building. One by one and in single file, they started their march down the wide walkway. The sounds of their stomping feet echoed throughout the large front courtyard. With each step they trampled the summer weeds that found their way through the cracks of the sun drenched pavement.

The new inmates sat patiently and sweltered in the oppressive heat. With his body sticking to the cheap vinyl seats, Joey wondered what tyrannical beings waited for him on the inside. All of nature's elements were easily tolerated. It was the unexpected that weighed heavily on his mind.

"Listen up!" the Captain of the prison guards shouted after he hopped onto the front of the bus. He then pounded his nightstick into the palm of his callused hand. The show of discipline was evident while the new convicts waited for their instructions. "In groups of four you will exit the bus. Then you will meet some of your new caretakers." The no nonsense voice spoke adamantly with each assignment that was given. "You better calm down over there, Buckwheat, or I'll loosen up your fuckin braids!" he screamed at the chattering black man who was totally ignoring him. "You don't want a piece of this, I ain't your Mama," the Captain shouted. "Now, before I was rudely interrupted. The guards will slowly escort you down the walkway to the front of the main building. Then you will simultaneously be frisked and administered a complete shakedown. After these procedures, some of you will enter the building for the first time. I see that there are a lot of familiar faces here. Welcome back, Gentlemen," he said with a grin. "I knew that some of you would be back sooner or later. So stay seated until you are called upon. And remember, if anybody tries anything foolish, this will be a stint that you will never forget!" The neatly groomed Captain began to wipe the perspiration off of his forehead. The torrid heat looked like it was getting to him also. "You two, up!" He pointed with his nightstick to the two black men seated in the front row of seats.

The two men exited the bus as he repeated the process with two other black guys who were behind them. The four men were quickly swooped up and escorted to their destinations. They walked one behind the other and in between four guards on each side. The orange jumpsuits were overwhelmed by the sea of blue surrounding them. There were 16 prisoners remaining on the sun baked bus. This procedure had to be repeated four more times.

The clock was ticking down while the last four convicts made their way off the bus. The walk was more like a crawl. From their feet came the instrumental music of a chain gang. With each short stride the heavy leg irons would play a different tune. The melodies only subsided once the foursome reached the front steps of the administration building. One at a time they started to climb the steps to the entranceway of the institution.

Joey and Justin paused and waited for the first two felons to be patted down. They looked at each other and then were motioned to continue up the concrete steps. The rituals to become an inductee of the New York State Federal Penitentiary were about to begin.

The penitentiary was a U shaped structure, three stories high. It was erected after World War II to alleviate some of the overcrowded conditions at other Federal prisons. This institution housed prisoners from up and down the East Coast. The 390-foot main building had two wings that ran approximately 250 feet deep. It was the home to 1,200 inhabitants, set on 85 acres. The dark gray building overlooked some of the most ravishing countryside in the state. Majestic mountain peaks provided a backdrop of beckoning autumn foliage.

The men had their commitment papers handed over to the Records Office for processing. In a receiving cell they were harshly lectured and released from their chains. A needed shower was the next itinerary on the prison's checklist. Authorities had to make sure that no one brought in any unwanted parasites such as lice or any other vermin.

All the new inmates just looked at each other as they started to peel their sweat stained clothes off. "This fuckin place stinks, man," Joey said, looking down at the hard dull floor. "It stinks of piss!" He looked all around the receiving cell and then into the eyes of the man across from him. Joey's eyes became glued in between the man's widespread legs. It was then that he noticed a small drip that was forming a puddle underneath his seat.

"He pissed his fuckin pants," Justin jubilantly screamed. "Joey, look, he pissed his pants!" he repeated, laughing hysterically at the embarrassed Hispanic man.

"Fuck you, you fuckin faggot!" the man sneered as he stood up to issue his challenge. "Get up, you little piece of shit!"

No, not already, Joey thought, his mind racing. *We just fucking got here.*

Justin, looking around the room for encouragement, received none. Even Joey knew better to keep his mouth shut. In this place if you're going to make statements or gestures you better be able to back them up. Justin, looking confused and frightened, stood up to face the man. The challenger then lunged at his opponent and wholeheartedly rammed his shoulder into Justin's midsection. The two men fell to the piss stained floor with a thud. Their inane grappling soon turned into an uninspired wrestling match. Hair pulling and finger gouging were the highlights of this cat-fight. Suddenly, through all the commotion and screaming, four prison guards burst upon the scene. With a couple of swings of their clubs, this uneventful bout came to an end. Then came the barrage of verbal insults, which packed more of a punch than the fight did. The two men were dragged out of the cell kicking and screaming at each other. They would be left abandoned in a secure unknown dark location.

Joey sat with his face buried in his hands wondering if this was just the start of things to come. He knew that if this was a sneak preview, he was in for a very long stay. *Mind your own business and keep to yourself,* he said in his mind. *Just mind your own business. I have to make it out of here.* His goal was to make it out of this hellhole as quickly as possible and in one piece.

Theither lukewarm water was bouncing off the flat tile surface. Steam and dirt had left a grayish film of mildew on the white ceramic walls. The shower facility was massive with thirty stations on each side. In the middle of the room a little closer to the toilets, stood a large round basin. It contained a tire-sized fixture that supplied water to all dirty faces and hands. There was no privacy at all, it didn't matter if you were on the can or showering, and everything was exposed.

Joey and the rest of the inmates scrubbed furiously as instructed. They each had a bar of some limed base soap that was provided by the prison. The lime acted like a disinfectant against lice, crabs or any other parasite that inhabits the unclean body. The last thing anybody wanted was a filthy epidemic running loose around the general population of the prison.

"Rinse the soap off your bodies now," the bathroom attendant shouted.

The time limit was up as the water was about to be turned off. It was just a matter of going through processing procedures and seeing the prison doctor. Finally it was off to get your new prison attire and some linen for the cell. In an hour or so, the newly inducted felons would be introduced to their new playmates.

Back in the records office, two clerks, a typist and a secretary were about to tackle the paperwork that was just submitted. The personal data was about to be inputted into the outdated computer.

"Red," the aging secretary said. "Bring me the first batch of documents!"

Sarah was the typical prototype for prison administrative office work. The wrinkles on her frail body offered no temptation to anyone who strolled through the front door. Her gray hair and drab attire fit her dull personality to a tee. Typographical errors were common as she struggled with her faltering eyesight and shaky hands.

"Here!" Red said, handing her the large yellow envelope.

It was customary for Red to take a quick peek at a rap sheet before it gets tucked away. The central file or C-file was a filing system that contained critical information on each inmate. Dead or alive, incarcerated or released, if you ever served time in this institution you were a part of this fallible system.

Red started to file the completed paperwork away. Pulling open the drawer marked with the letter D, he paused. He seemed to take a particular interest of the rap sheet titled, "Joseph J. DeFalco." Looking around and behind his shoulders, he quickly scanned over the government document. Instead of following the usual procedures, Red placed it at the bottom of the batch. Nonchalantly, he waltzed over to the copy machine to duplicate the private information.

"Pssst," Red signaled to his buddy in front of the counter. His friend failed to respond to his light murmur. "Yo, Paulie," he whispered, slightly bending over the front counter.

Paulie looked up to check out the identity of the familiar sounding voice.

"What?"

"Keep mopping, but listen to me. Tell Vito that I have someone coming through reception that he might have an interest in."

Paulie just shook his head and continued his work detail. Sometimes a nod of the head or a twitch of an eye says it all. Bodily gestures were the most common form of communication amongst the inmates. In prison, the less said the better off you are.

The prison janitor began whistling a tune as he wheeled his mop and bucket out of the office. Paulie then entered the maintenance closet to unload his cleaning implements. He then began his short excursion to see Vito.

Standing by the railing half way down the second floor tier, stood Vito. He was puffing on a cigarette while examining the activity below. There was always something happening on another floor or someplace else in the cell block area. There was never a dull day in sight; most inmates would have a fight or an argument over a stick of chewing gum.

"Vito," Paulie blurted out. "Another paisan has just come through reception."

"Did you see him?"

"No, Red just told me to tell you."

"Tell Red to pull his sheet and then you bring it right back to me," Vito demanded, throwing his finished cigarette to the floor. "If this guy pans out, make sure he gets put close by."

Red knew exactly what Vito wanted, so he always stood a step ahead of the game. The rap sheet was already photostatted and ready to go. As long as the applicant wasn't a fag, pedophile or rapist, Vito wanted to see him. But he had to be Italian; there was no substitute for that. The guy had to be 100% grade A grease-ball. If he was Sicilian, that made it even better. Red knew all of this, besides, any chance he could stick it to the system, he would. Known as a standup guy, he remained very bitter over his controversial conviction.

Dennis, "Big Red," Trapani was a tall good-looking man with salt and pepper hair. He was serving 5 to 10 years on a self-defense homicide. At 45, Red had 2 years left before he will be eligible for parole. How he got the nickname Red was something that he would never be able to live down. On his 25th birthday at some nightclub, Dennis went down on some broad during her menstrual cycle while fooling around in his car. It was only when he went back into the bar that his friends discovered that he had a face full of blood. That name and color would remain with him for the rest of his life.

Joey entered the cellblock area dressed in his new prison apparel and holding onto his bedroom linens. Walking slowly and visibly shaken, he just stood frozen checking out the new surroundings. He was escorted every inch of the way by a prison guard.

"Welcome to the neighborhood!" said the guard while showing the block to Joey for the first time.

The newcomer slowly looked around as he felt his knees start to buckle with fear. The place looked like Times Square during rush hour. The only difference was that this crowd was filled with killers, junkies and thugs. There weren't any tax paying citizens among this group. The noise was almost unbearable. In this dungeon every unexpected and unpleasant sound would reverberate off the high ceilings and down every concrete slab in the building.

"I never saw a place where everybody dressed the same could look so different," Joey said to the prison guard.

"But they are different," he said. "Each one of them is different in their own sad, sadistic way."

The block was huge and it had a weird cryptic feeling to it. Welcome to the neighborhood of boredom, frustration and many hours of pointless existence. Welcome to the neighborhood where every inhabitant wants a piece of your ass, dead or alive. Welcome to the neighborhood where even your identity will change to some eight-digit serial number. Welcome to the neighborhood of the convicted felon, branded for life like a piece of livestock on some cattle ranch.

Joey stopped walking and turned in the direction of his temporary escort. "I bet Mr. Rogers doesn't live in this neighborhood?"

"Nope."

"And it's not a beautiful day either," Joey said in disgust.

Chapter 4

DRESSED IN HIS light blue prison garb, Joey started his long climb up the steps to his cell. Stopping to look around with each scream was common. There were inmates everywhere, on the steps, by the railings, in the cells; they looked like ants running amok. It didn't take the rest of the population long to spot the new kid on the block. With sharp eyes and a thirst for fresh meat, they suddenly serenaded Joey with a chorus of prison greetings. Everything from racial slurs, threats of violence to sexually explicit taunts and whistling were vulgarly thrown his way. Being a good-looking first time offender, almost everyone wanted a piece of Joey's virgin ass.

Walking down the tier trying to get to his cell was an effort. "Excuse me," he kept saying. Either they were hard of hearing or their mother never taught them any manners, nobody moved out of the way. Trying to exit a crowded subway car was a much easier task.

"That's him!" Paulie said to Vito, while they both watched Joey walk by. "In a little while do you want me to bring him back here to see you?"

"Nah, let him settle in for two or three days," Vito said. "He has to get his own feel for this shit hole. Besides I didn't even look at his sheet yet. In the meantime, tell Dutch and Red to watch every step that this kid takes."

"Will do."

"If he falls into the wrong hands he'll never get over it. We're a dying breed in this fuckin place, so this is important," Vito warned. "Even if it was just the two of us we could still control these animals. But because this kid's Italian, they would fuck him up just to stick it up our asses."

"Don't worry, Vito," Paulie promised. "We will take care of the situation."

Most Italian people are full of self-respect and always proud of their heritage. They want to be highly respected and honored by everyone around them. The respect they desperately seek for themselves sometimes lacks the esteem that should be given back to others.

"What's this kid's name anyway?"

"Joseph DeFalco," Paulie said.

"What?"

"I said Joseph DeFalco. Why?"

"No, nothing." Vito put his arm around his confidant's shoulder as they both walked into his cell. Paulie reached into his pocket and pulled out a piece of paper.

"Here's his rap sheet," said Paulie. He then handed over the government information to Vito.

Vito examined the document closely and shook his head, looking confused. There was something much different about this rap sheet from all others. It seemed that a sad part of Vito's unstable past had come back to haunt him.

"Is everything alright?" Paulie asked, noticing something strange on Vito's face. "You look like you just saw a fuckin ghost."

"What?" a discombobulated Vito said, still looking at the rap sheet.

"I said is everything alright?"

"Yea, yea, everything's fine."

"Do you know this kid?"

"No," Vito lied. "His last name just rang a bell for some reason, but it's nothin."

"Are you sure?"

"Yea, now go tell the boys to keep an eye on this kid. Tell them to make sure nothin happens to him."

Besides Vito's strange behavior, all the other pretentious prerequisites had been satisfied. His criterion for grading an inmate had been precociously fulfilled. Now he would sequester the data and keep everything copasetic.

Without hesitation, Paulie raced out of Vito's cell to tell his comrades their instructions.

Paulie B. was a soldier for one of New York's bigger crime families. He was serving 10 to 15 years on Federal gun charges. Running guns from Florida to New York was no problem for the ever so reliable gangster. The East Coast drive was a breeze, except for one undetected problem. He was unexpectedly pulled over on Interstate 95 for a busted tail-light. Never the smooth talker, Paulie always had a problem getting himself out of tight jams. This stroke of bad luck would be no different for the high school drop out. To this day, he never forgot the look on the State Trooper's face when he opened the back of the small truck. Paulie was caught with his pants down trying to comically explain what he was doing with $750,000 worth of firearms. The idiot told the astute trooper that his family was into hunting. In a way he was right, but his family never hunted for the four-legged type animals. They preferred the two-legged creatures that roamed the city streets. Known as a straight shooter, Paulie would die for his loyalty. Repeatedly beaten up, stabbed and with his face badly marred, he would never be confused with a Calvin Klein poster boy. The honorable foot soldier was the liaison between his boss and trouble.

Joey finally settled into his cell and was putting the finishing touches on his once bare pillow and mattress. He looked around his cell in disgust at the stench and filth. Housekeeping was never a top priority for the subdued lawbreaker. Fluffing up a pillow or spreading out a bed sheet was the extent of it. Prison cells were not equipped with disinfectants or room deodorizers. It was strictly up to the inmate to bring out that homey feeling without all the modern conveniences.

It was an 8 by 10 cell with thick steel bars horizontally running across the front. A urine-stained toilet and a sink barely big enough to wash your hands in were against the back wall. Cinder block from top to bottom was the makeup of the surrounding walls. Scotch tape was the only method that was permitted in order to hang a picture of a loved one. In this dump, there was no such thing as a hammer and nail. The only hammering that was ever done was when someone carelessly bent over while taking a shower.

The furniture consisted of a four inch worn out mattress with no box spring and a small medicine cabinet above the sink. Toothpaste, a toothbrush and maybe a few Q-tips were the extent of the dingy cabinet's holding capacity. Hygiene must not have been a top priority for prison officials.

Occasionally you might find a tiny chest of drawers, but not if you were a new inmate. The new inmate just received the minimum essentials to survive. The only thing you could do about these horrible living conditions was to just grin and bear it. You had no other choice.

This was not the Waldorf Astoria; there were no bellhops or chambermaids roaming the premises. Room service consisted of visits of a much different, perverted manner. The imposingly fashionable or elegant dweller would not want to sign in at the front desk. This was a barely furnished one-room rat hole with no view of Central Park.

High society socialites and debutantes did not reside at this up state asylum. The tenants here were the lowest element of worthless impure matter that only an unbalanced society can breed. To put it bluntly, these inhabitants were no better than pond scum. But with all the imperfections that this institution had, it sure beat two things. It beat being homeless and sleeping on the cold winter streets.

While packing away some of his belongings, Joey heard a disturbing eruption taking place on the floor below. Inmates from both sides of the prison wing raced to see what the violent uproar was all about. Every cell emptied out as prisoners were hanging over the railings to see the action.

Shaken up by the commotion, Joey contemplated whether to leave the security of his confines. His curiosity got the best of him as he wandered out of his cell. What he saw was like a standing room only crowd at the seventh game of the World Series. Two Black combatants below were starting to square off in a show of strength. A circle of cheering convicts surrounded them. The two men looked like a couple of gladiators ready to do battle at the Roman Coliseum.

"What are they fighting over?" Joey asked the stranger standing next to him. "This is crazy!"

"This is prison," he snapped back. "They're fighting over turf," the balding man replied as he was leaning up against the metal railing.

"Oh," Joey said, acting like he knew what the hell the stranger was talking about. *Turf? What turf,* he thought. Joey was right; there was no grass in sight. If it were property the two men were fighting over, who the hell would risk his life to own a piece of this fucking joint? But Joey would soon find out that in some cases, prison life had a lot of the same stubborn characteristics as the outside world. Even in prison, there just were certain places that you could not venture into. In each different neighborhood of this shit hole, every piece of property had a different asking price. In order to gain access you better have something good to offer or you will never make it out alive.

"He's got a shank," someone yelled from the crowd below.

What started as a boxing match slowly escalated into a more serious affair.

Brandishing a sharp object, the smaller but more boisterous man kept shouting, "I'm holdin it down, I'm holdin it down."

"I'm gonna take that knife and fuck you with it," the taller and larger gang member yelled.

"Fuck you, come and get some, bitch," his nemesis snapped back.

The movement was circular inside the wall of screaming spectators. The attacker kept wielding the pointed homemade knife in the direction of his much larger opponent. Each new jab of the sharp knife drew blood from his enemy's body. Like a pin-cushion, each poke exposed another laceration on his blood stained shirt. Now bleeding profusely, the bigger foe was missing his quicker and smaller opponent with every telegraphed punch that he threw. His roundhouse punches flew wildly and kept missing their intended target. Gasping for air with diminishing endurance, his futility was apparent. Facing a sure defeat, the weakening big man released one final lunge out of desperation. Coming to an embrace, the two men crashed to the concrete slab. Witnessing this minor occurrence, the crowd came to a silent hush, waiting for the final outcome.

"Let's book, the bulls are comin!" a gang member warned his buddies.

The charged up convicts started to scatter in all directions, clearing an easy passageway for the prison guards in their full riot gear. The two warriors lay pasted one on top of the other on the blood smeared floor. In a defensive posture, the guards proceeded to peel the larger man off of his rival. Turning him over, they exposed the homemade knife that was buried deep into his chest.

With his eyes wide open and his mouth begging for precious air, it was just a matter of time until death. The beaten man clutched onto the instrument that was brutally inserted into his torso. His pearly white teeth were chattering from the shock his failing body was putting him through. The smaller but now victorious foe was whisked away, while the beaten man lay lifeless and drowning in a pool of his own blood.

"I told you so," the winner said to his boys. "That's right, man, I told you so. I'm holdin it down, man. I'm holdin the motherfucker down."

The rest of his gang-bangers were celebrating in a show of respect for their defiant leader. Their turf was now protected by the color of a dead man's blood. It didn't matter to them that a human life was just snuffed out within thirty seconds. All that mattered was that something that did not even belong to them was won. Whether it was an inch of land or an acre, they would fight for it. These must have been the laws of the ghetto, and most of them were willing to die for the turf that they thought was theirs.

This conflict was not the product of racial disharmony. It was a rivalry of two known enemies outside the forty-foot walls. They both operated two illegal and prosperous enterprises, both within walking distance from each other. Their borders were governed and protected by the same homeboys who were born and raised on those same crime infested streets. Living large with the potential to expand, it was not uncommon to step on some unfriendly toes. Growing up childhood friends, the two men would soon be competing for the stranglehold of their money-starved community. Arrested and convicted for all of their crimes, both men would bring their street mentality inside these prison walls. But the conditions here were severely different. Race rivalries, overcrowding and every other kind of deprivation imaginable were the major obstacles. With nowhere to run, this life and death confrontation was inevitable.

Joey was rendered senseless by the horrific events that had just taken place. The energetic crowd started to thin as the mood grew somber. For even the most cold-blooded animals would realize that a human life was just lost, or would they? Any man with a conscience that could differentiate morality from the tangible effects of evil had to feel some sort of compassion. For the compassionate man's life will always be in jeopardy from the evil that dwells all around him. In prison, the weak must feel the growing concern for their slowly dying safety. To show compassion in prison is an open invitation to weakness. In prison the rules are very basic; there are none. Barroom brawls and kicking the shit out of an unfriendly neighbor was one thing. But to lose your life over a bar of soap or a tube of toothpaste was another. On the streets of the outside world you can dictate your fate or predicaments. Inside of these forty-foot walls it dictates to you.

"I've been here for five years, and after a while you kind of get used to it," the stranger said to Joey. "Every day that passes brings on another day of bullshit. If it ain't the Niggers, it's the Spics. If it ain't the Spics it's the white trailer trash. In this place they harass you for minding your own damn business. You have to belong or else you're in big trouble," he warned.

"Belong to what?" Joey asked, looking more confused than ever.

"A group, a gang or anything in numbers," he said. "And it better be a group of your own kind. Or you'll be running errands and will become the topic of some animal's favorite bedtime stories. The breakfast table will be full of laughs at your expense."

"Why are you telling me this?"

"There are certain things you have to know in here in order to stay alive. You don't have to take my advice and you can do what you want. But unless you have a Messiah, a Rabbi or a fuckin Godfather you can be in big trouble."

"My name is Joey," he said. "Joey DeFalco." Joey then extended his right hand out for a friendly handshake. Now afraid and with the feeling of total ineptness, he was in dire need of a friend. It took no more than a couple of hours before he started to feel the full effects of prison life.

"Never mind the introductions, just take my advice," the jailhouse prophet said. "Look around this place, race is used by convicts to protect themselves, their possessions and their fuckin lives. It's also the easiest way for the authorities to control the population here. Everything in here is labeled by race," he went on. "From barbells to basketballs, it's all one color. Don't touch anything that don't belong to you. But always stand up if someone tries to take what is rightfully yours. Once again, stick to your own skin color and go on from there." The stranger then took a position leaning over the railing that separated him from the bottom floor.

"Who are you with?" Joey asked, following him over to the railing.

"It doesn't matter who I'm with. Anybody fucks with me and it's their life. They know it," he said as he started to point at different groups that congregated around the cell block. "They know it, and now you know it. You can try goin at it alone, but unless you're Godzilla or fuckin King Kong, you will lose. I don't make or enforce the rules in here, but sometimes you have to abide by them. You're new in here and everybody knows that," he continued. "According to the Niggers and Spics there are no rules when it comes to fresh meat, it's first come first served. If you weren't a racist when you entered prison, you sure as shit will become one before you leave."

The stranger with all the encouraging advice pushed himself off of the four-foot high barrier. Wiping his hands on his pants, he started to walk away. About ten feet from where he had given his speech, he decided to turn around. "Always remember what I told you." He then disappeared with his shadow following him down the long row of cells.

With the rosy complexion now withdrawn from his face, Joey wondered who the man full of prison advice and knowledge was. What was he preparing him for? How long will it be before the unknown makes its presence felt? What would it take for him to defend himself? From around what corner would danger lurk and pounce on him? These were all the questions that Joey wished he had the answers to. He also wondered what he had that everybody else wanted. The inexperienced prisoner did not realize that his services were worth more than his life was.

The inmates would soon find out that the stabbing death of a neighbor would put a temporary freeze on their freedom. For the next week, the entire block would be put into a lock-down mode. Nobody could venture out of the confines of their own cells. The whole population had to suffer because of the actions of a certain few. It was the way prison officials eased tensions from boiling over into explosive situations. Twenty four hours a day for the next seven days gives a man plenty of time to think. Like a canary surrounded by the bars of his cage, the singing was sure to be much more intensified. The sounds of the jungle were sure to be very tropical for the next seven days. All the violent predators would be locked up like pit bulls after being picked up by the A.S.P.C.A. Being part of a lock-down was like living in a prison inside of a prison.

Tasteless tidbits of food twice a day was the only source of nourishment. Back and forth, back and forth, the pacing in the tiny cell never ended. All the walking only got you back to where you began.

During the daytime, there was a feeling of being in an incinerator as the still hot air smothered your senses. The prison cells were so hot that the sweat would evaporate as soon as it dripped off of your saturated body. No conversations or visitors, no radio or television... just the intense feeling of going out of your mind. Besides sleeping, writing a few letters and self-satisfying a few of your sexual desires, there wasn't much to do. New prisoners sometimes cherished the element of seclusion. To them, there was a warm feeling of safety when under lock and key. Like watching fine sand trickling through the pinhole of an hourglass, the days seemed to last forever. A week in confinement could feel like minutes to some, and a lifetime to others.

It was dinnertime; the lock-down was finally over. Prisoners were swarming like buzzards circling a decomposed corpse. It was a beehive type atmosphere where everyone was buzzing with chatter. Confinement has a way of turning a hermit into the town crier.

The chow hall resembled a huge picnic area with long tables and benches all over the place. The only thing missing was some oak trees and a soft picnic blanket. Like a large buffet, everyone waited on line for the delicacy of the day. The menu only consisted of one choice, gray hamburger meat and raw French fries. Most of the time the cooks served up such crap that even a Cocker Spaniel would not be too envious of.

Finding a seat to shovel down this puke was not rocket science. Blacks to the left, whites to the right and all the Hispanics and Mexicans hung out in the rear. Whatever other race was left, they just tried to peacefully blend into a corner somewhere. Most guys would sit in a group of three or more.

Talk about segregation, the public school system would not be too proud of this setup. Any integration going on in this district was surely against the passenger's will. The only integrated groups were made up of homosexuals. White or black, they were easily detected. For some gay men, being in prison was like living in the Garden of Eden. Getting fucked or sucked was just the blink of an eye away. To them color didn't matter, looks didn't matter, height, weight, not a problem. To the gay men in this prison, any welcome hole made a new friend. They were a non-discriminating organization with no special qualifications needed to enlist. Many nights off in some secluded corner you could hear their screams of ecstasy. They didn't really care who heard their cries of passion. To the idle homosexual, these sounds of desire induced an easily excitable erection. To the straight inmates, these sounds could destroy a good wet dream. For sexual pleasure, prison life was definitely a gay man's paradise, especially to the hardened criminal homosexual with many years of experience. In prison they got what they wanted, whenever they wanted it.

Looking around at the many angry faces, Joey quietly settled in amongst the company of his own kind. Even though he tried to blend in with his own race, he never felt so alone. For Joey, there was no hunger to feed or thirst to quench. His anxiety and nerves took care of all of that. Besides, the aromas made him sick to his stomach anyway.

After the not so well balanced meal, it's off to the prison yard. The only good thing about this was the fact that maybe some activity would make you shit out the crap that you just digested. But for most inmates it was a place to mingle and catch a good breath of fresh air.

The prison yard was quite an intimidating sight. This playpen had rolls of barbed wire running across the top of a twenty-foot high fence. There was only one way into the yard and only one way out.

The only entrance was through the rear of the main building. If someone luckily found his way past the barbed wired fence, he would still have the forty foot brick wall to contend with. Even Spiderman would have a hard time leaping over these obstacles.

For the sports enthusiast, basketball and weightlifting were just a couple of the many activities at your disposal. Many inmates always felt the need to strengthen their bodies to protect them from their surroundings. A lot of trouble-makers would shy away from someone who looked too intimidating. But if you were really smart, it's best to look like Charles Atlas before you enter prison.

If an inmate was not the outdoors type, he had the option of attending special program classes. The main themes were anger management, substance abuse and religious services. So take your pick, there was not a convict in the place who was not suffering from one of these symptoms.

Anyone with any type of compulsive disorder was welcome to attend the anger management classes. Some characters were even encouraged to attend these worthless courses. But on most nights there wasn't an inmate to be seen in attendance. Since nobody was held by the hand and dragged into the classroom, nobody went. There were no behavioral problems amongst this group of convicted felons? Not one prisoner thought he had the irresistible impulse to act irrational? So much for anger management, most of the time the instructor just stood around looking at the four walls.

If you had any dependencies that were bad for your health, help was not to far away. This program catered to ex junkies and alcoholics who had supposedly recovered from their unfriendly vices. These burnouts would sit in a comatose state trying to comprehend the ill effects of substance abuse. A nuclear bomb could detonate without sparking the faintest of a reaction from any of them. But if you threw a crack vial and a pint of Southern Comfort in front of this recovered bunch of addicts, men would be diving all over the place to retrieve the temporary high. You could probably find the next Greg Louganis from this sad lot of Olympians.

Religious services, was another story all in itself. Whether it was Jesus, Allah or Buddha, hopelessness always reaches for the Supreme Being. Criminals always repent and find God when they are trapped behind bars. People, especially convicts, always reach for God in times of desperation. In times of prosperity, He is the furthest thing from their minds. All of the inmates who went to these classes were most definitely hypocrites. They would sit quietly acting studious, rummaging through their Bible. Throughout the entire class, they would recite and listen to Scriptures from the holy book. Some of these jokers even wore shrouds or robes to express their faith even more. They stood tall acting like some Biblical character with all of his powers. If you threw a new Penthouse magazine and a Holy Bible inside the cell of one of these reformed God loving creatures, what piece of reading material do you think he would pick up? This place was loaded with wannabe evangelists. Basically, "I'm reformed now because I found God!" Jim Baker would have nothing over this group of common believers. Except maybe Tammy Faye and who the hell in their right frame of mind would want her anyway?

The bright yellow sun was setting behind the west wing of the building. Dark storm clouds could be seen approaching from the same direction. The prison yard was lively as contraband exchanged hands in total secrecy. Anything from cigarettes to condoms could be had. Somewhere inside these enormous walls was a leak the size of Niagara Falls. This was like business and industry in a cloistered world of commerce. The commodity brokers were evident as raw goods exchanged hands for something of need.

The burning smell of marijuana leaves was drifting through the evening air. Certain groups could be seen puffing away as they were huddled off from the rest of the crowd. Plotting and scheming were their main topics of conversation. The prison guards oversaw everything from up above. Some of them only saw what their lazy eyes wanted them to see. But no matter what, they were all armed with semi automatic rifles.

"Hey man, got a roll?" a huge looking man said to Joey.

Leaning up against the gray brick building, Joey just looked at him and decided to vacate the premises. As he tried to walk away, the intruder grabbed at his left arm. The sudden jolt spun Joey around and he found himself looking straight into the eyes of a heavyset Afro-American man.

"Don't fuckin dis me, motherfucker," he said.

Joey just looked at him and tried to pull his arm away from the aggressive inmate.

"Get your fuckin hands off me! I already know how it is in here and I know what you want. And you're the last person that I would look at if I wanted a playmate."

"What's the matter, I'm not your type?"

"No," Joey snapped. He was deathly afraid of this character, but there was no way he was going to tip his hand. "Tell me, what's your name?"

"Bootsy!"

"Well, Bootsy," Joey brazenly said. "I prefer the blue eyed slimmer version with not so much ass."

Bootsy's face started to lapse serious. The loathsome thug grimaced.

"Man, when the time's right, I'm gonna take my fist and bury it in your ass."

"Is that so?"

"Yea, that's so. You see my boys over there?" Bootsy said, pointing in the direction of his prison crew. Steadily, Joey took a quick gander at the unattractive group. "We're gonna pass you around like a bottle of cheap wine. Each one of us is gonna have his fuckin turn. But don't worry, I'll lubricate it real good so it won't hurt that much."

"Really," a frightened Joey said.

The oversized man had a fist the size of a bowling ball. He began to spit and spread his saliva all around his tightly clenched hand. "Yea boy, really. Eventually, after you had enough, you'll start to see things my way. So don't make this too hard on yourself. Come on, man, give me a cigarette and let's be friends. You will see that we have a lot in common."

Bootsy then proceeded to run his huge right hand up the side of his potential conquest's face. Joey lunged back to avoid the love stroke of this man about town. His obscurity left an open invitation to his manhood. With nowhere to run and nowhere to hide, it was decision time. Before Joey knew it, he had to stand up and face the music.

"Okay, Bootsy," Joey facetiously said as he prepared to pounce on this unbeatable looking foe. "You win. I guess it's time to make a few friends in here anyway."

"Good, that's real good thinking, my man," he said smiling. "I knew you would see it my way. Now go on and I'll catch up with you later. I got other business to attend to."

"What about the cigarette?"

"Changed my mind, it's bad for my breath." He then blew the unpleasant odor into Joey's face.

Bootsy started to walk back to his circle of punks with a pompous smile of victory all over his face. His ghetto strut was well received by each cantankerous thug who saluted him with a high five. He seemed to believe that his mission was accomplished.

"He's ours," he boasted. "That white boy will be runnin' errands and suckin' all of our dicks by the end of the week."

To Bootsy and his boys it didn't matter what the resume of another inmate read. From a pedophile to a serial killer, these hoodlums had no morals. The more perverse the offender, the more they wanted him. They would take on anyone and desecrate the sacredness of their total existence to get what they wanted.

To hook in a person of another color was a major coup. To them it was a maneuver for power against their enemies. It was a dangerous position for a physically and mentally weak person of another race or color to be in. Just walking to a location with someone of a different ethnicity could be dangerous. It could turn the most passive of prisoners very hostile, prompting stares, taunting and violence. Based on the averages, most of the time the powerless tended to succumb to their abusers. They allow their total impotence to be governed by a roving pack of marauders.

Every race has their self-standards for acceptance. If an inmate is shunned by his own kind, others will be waiting with open arms. To put it bluntly, the lost soul would be better off dead. If suicide were not an option, he would be quickly learning the culture and customs of his new friends. Unfortunately most of it would be against his will. For this is prison life, so get ready to die for your dignity and pride. Or be prepared to get some Vaseline or a good pair of running shoes. If you are not a marathon man, you will be taken for the ride of your life.

Joey stood glued to the pavement and nailed to the wall behind him. Surprised by Bootsy's departure, his leaving only prolonged the inevitable.

Joey was very disappointed with his own actions; they should have been quick and decisive. Win or lose, his stance would have at least been recognized. The romance should have ended right then and there. There would be no Valentine's Day celebration for this budding couple. There would be no Hallmark cards or Godiva chocolates exchanged. This dance would have to continue on another occasion. The situation had just begun to percolate.

The overcast sky created a dome on top of the prison yard. Charcoal colored storm clouds stood poised with the mighty roars of thunder. Lightning began to light up the skies with each crackle of its repertoire. The prison yard started to slowly empty out from the outbreak of rain.

Chapter 5

BEING THE SON of a painter, Joey was given the dubious distinction that comes along with a brush and roller. Unsuspecting prison officials did not know that this process of art was right up his alley. Whether on canvas or an unpainted wall, the task was performed with the greatest of ease. It was a special trait that was shared by most of his family. All the men in the family were born with that special gene; they had magic in their fingertips. This artistic flair was explicit with each stroke that surfaced from a paintbrush. Always detesting the occupation of painting, this time Joey gladly accepted his new chore. To him, he figured that he scored big time. Painting sure beat cleaning shit stains out of heavily used toilets. Besides, anything that he painted in this dump would make him look like Michelangelo.

Three days went by and all was quiet. The long narrow hall connecting the two wings to the main building was in dire need of a paint job. One side of the wall contained doorways that led into some small offices. The other side showcased windows that looked out into the front yard and its insurmountable forty-foot barricade. The paint-starved walls hadn't been coated with enamel for at least ten years. The neglect was obvious as the paint was peeling off of the dirty white walls. It would take a day in itself to scrape off all the unwanted debris. The ceiling was no better; an annoying discoloration was the product of an overflow of water from the damaged rooftop. The leaking roof left an aftermath of orange blemishes running in long circular streaks. It was a lot of preparation, but for convicts who had nothing but time to kill, it didn't matter.

This work crew consisted of two people, each a stranger to each other. After a day of scraping and sanding, it was time to paint. The two men started at opposite ends of the long, lackluster corridor. Joey got started right away, knowing exactly what to do. For him, there was no need for any drop clothes or tape. Paint never dripped from the bottom of his paintbrush. No matter how cheap the paint, the floor remained spotless. He had the technique down to a science. His so-called counterpart was another story. The Puerto Rican guy didn't have a clue, and even had problems opening up his five-gallon can of paint. That was when Joey knew that three quarters of this paint job would be his. From a distance the short thin man looked like the Karate Kid with his unorthodox and clumsy strokes. He definitely lacked the touch.

A strong September sun started to engulf the shade-less hallway. The windows seemed to magnify the heat coming from the sun's powerful rays. Extreme heat would only prolong the drying process of the oil- based paint. The paint fumes grew with each application that was applied.

Still feeling jittery, four days had elapsed since his unforgettable tryst in the prison yard. Joey was constantly looking over his shoulder for any unexpected visitors. He knew that his day of reckoning with Bootsy would soon be upon him, it was just a matter of when. With every dip of his cheap plastic paintbrush, he took another peek. One eye would be on his work detail, while the other was looking out for unruly pedestrians.

The clock had struck 3:00 p.m. as the painters retired their hardware for the day. Certain liberties and so-called luxuries were given to inmates pertaining to their jobs. Joey and the Karate Kid were blessed with an afternoon shower after every day of hard work.

The warm water felt good against his paint free body. Each soothing drop of the tranquil water seemed to wash away his distress. Joey kept his distance from his paint-covered partner. The two men had worked together for almost a week, not even speaking a word to each other. They had almost nothing in common. The only thing that they shared was the shower facility, nothing more.

Approximately five minutes had gone by before another bather had entered the shower. Undaunted, Joey didn't seem to mind after he glanced over at the newcomer. Even if trouble would arise, he was sure he could handle this guy. Besides, with a guard stationed right outside the room, any disturbance or unfamiliar sounds would be easily detected.

In a sneaky way, the newcomer started to show some inconsistencies in his bathroom behavior. With snail like characteristics he slowly inched his way towards his prey. Unaware of the light-footed predator, Joey continued to scrub his body with a bar of unscented soap. The heavy lather started to stream from his hair and into his now burning eyes. While rubbing his eyes the bar of soap slithered from his foamy hands. Skidding across the tile floor, the soap landed a few feet away from his naked body. Looking around, Joey finally spotted it and bent down to pick it up.

With cat like quickness, a long fingered hand enveloped his wrist. With both men on one knee and staring into each other's eyes, a move had to be made.

The Karate Kid made the first move, streaking towards the open door. If he painted as fast as he ran, the hallway would have been finished in a day. His bare ass was the last visible indication of his fleeing body.

The agile and nimble outsider started to gently rub his free hand up the side of Joey's thigh. "What's up, precious?" he said with a soft voice and an even softer touch. "Do you mind if I join you?" He then started to make loud sniffing noises. His head started to bend forward with a large pinkish black tongue protruding from his foul smelling mouth.

All the tension, stress and anxiety that were building up from many months of frustration, were about to be released from Joey's body. All the tension of his short prison life was about to erupt. Suddenly all the fear had disappeared as the Italian flew into a violent rage.

With a quick thrust of his right knee, he caught the assailant right under the chin. The man's head was now vibrating from the fierce impact of the swift and precise blow. He then fell backwards, landing face up and flat on his back.

In an uncontrollable fit of anger, Joey started screaming. "You black cock suckin' son of a bitch! I ain't gonna be nobody's bitch." He then pounced on top of the dazed man, looking to finish him off. With his fury still racing at a high tempo, he cried out, "You want to fuck with me, you sorry ass piece of shit?"

He began to throw short right-handed punches into the head and face of the already beaten opponent. Like a jackhammer drilling to break up a concrete pavement, the steady barrage of punches cracked through the tight facial skin of the now disfigured thug, rendering him senseless. A spate of blood soon followed. The outpouring was slowly finding its way to the shower's drainpipe. Joey's knuckles started to bleed and swell with each direct hit. The indentation of his rival's teeth on his fists left reminders of the severe blows that were coming from his right hand. But Joey's rage would not let him stop; he continued his savage assault. He began to pick up his attacker by the hair and bang his head repeatedly off of the hard tile floor. One after the other, the thumping sounds echoed throughout the shower facility. What started out as drops, an opened gash behind his head produced a river of blood.

Without warning a loud burst of applause echoed throughout the large bathroom. Bootsy and two more of his molesters had entered upon the scene. Still clapping with a smile horizontally running across his big round face, Bootsy looked impressed. His adoption of Joey was going to be a little tougher than he had originally thought. To him, looking down at his badly beaten and bleeding homeboy was a sure sign of defeat.

"Man, you really fucked my boy Jamaal up," he said. "But now it's time to play with the big boys."

He continued to slowly walk forward until he got to within three feet of Joey. His huge partners started to slowly surround Joey from each side. The two black sidekicks looked like monsters; they were both waiting for their signal to start the exploitation. The list of dishes on their serving table included rape, robbery, oral sex and severe beatings to the unwilling. Every time an advance was rebuffed a beating was sure to follow.

"What the hell do you want now?" Joey asked, looking up at the three intruders from his hands and knees. "I didn't know that this guy was with you!"

"A lot of these brothers are with me," the pugnacious felon said, "and you're gonna get a taste of their hospitality real soon."

"So you sent this asshole in here to soften me up?" he said, pointing at Jamaal.

"This was a setup, punk. This way you should be going down a little easier. But I gotta hand it to you, you a little tougher than we thought."

"But why me?"

"Because you're a white boy, and we kinda fancy white meat. Especially the Italian kind. Let's just say I owe somebody a pay-back."

Bootsy reached into his pocket and pulled out a latex surgical glove. He started to stretch the light rubber material with a sign of impunity. His corrupt, immoral mind expected immediate and unconditional surrender.

Joey started to rise with caution from his hands and knees. He knew what that surgical glove was intended for. But the proctologist administrating this examination was not too much of his liking. Like a cornered cat, his curiosity was now very distinguishable. Standing stagnant with his body immobile, he focused on the uninvited trio. His heart raced, and the room was silent.

Now getting ready to prepare himself for battle, Joey braced his body for war.

"You're going to have to kill me first, nigger!"

Bootsy's face seared with anger. Nobody would talk to him that way, especially an unseasoned white inmate. "Get that motherfucker and bend his white cherry ass over," he ordered. "I wanna hear this white boy recite my Pledge of Allegiance."

Bootsy blasted out his demands while slipping the white glove over and around his large fingers. His two cohorts rushed towards their retreating opponent. The fists started flying and Joey was overwhelmed by numbers. The punches started to smash down on top of Joey's face and body like a battering ram; he never had a chance. Reduced to a helpless punching bag and trying to fight back, the battered victim was falling silently to the barrage.

An opening appeared above Joey's left eye as the blood was finding its way down his face. One after the other the punches were thrown, each one finding their intended target.

"You're gonna see things my way, sucker," insisted Bootsy.

This beating went on and on until Joey's pulverized body gave in and fell to the floor. But the onslaught continued, with each man taking his pot shots at the limp and tired body. Joey's whole body was an open target for whatever came from his oppressor's arsenal.

"Had enough?" a relentless Bootsy asked. "Or do you want some more?"

Joey looked up at the aggressive pugilist with one eye practically closed. "Fuck you," the defiant Italian said. "And fuck your mother."

After that exchange, sharp kicks to the midsection were endured as Joey desperately tried to cover up his fallen body. His beaten and pain wracked body curled into a fetal position on the musty smelling floor. With the flavor of blood everywhere, the shower facility was now the scene of a cruel and wanton blood bath.

"Ahhhh," Joey moaned, twisting in pain, clutching his abdomen. "Ahhhh."

"Now stand this motherfucker up," Bootsy demanded, his body now breathing heavy.

Both of his musclemen grabbed Joey underneath each armpit and stood him up on his knees. With one final thrust, Bootsy connected with a thunderous kick right to the face of the finished Italian. Joey's head jerked backwards from the crushing blow. But the rest of his body stayed put, the strong hold by both of Bootsy's men made sure of that.

"Get him to his feet and bend him over," Bootsy mercilessly snarled. "It's time to start ripping this dude's ass wide open. Now you're gonna get a taste of what prison life is all about."

"Bootsy," a loud voice commanded. "Let him go!"

With his hormones still running at a feverish tempo, Bootsy turned his head to identify the anonymous caller. "This ain't your business, stay the fuck out of it."

"Let him go," the voice repeated.

"Fuck you, man!"

"I said, let the fuckin kid go, he's with Vito." The three savages suddenly began to back-pedal away from the battered body. All it took for the destructive trio to back off was to hear the reciting of one short name. "Consider this one on the house," Joey's savior then said to Bootsy. "But there will be a payback," he warned. "And it's gonna be a bitch!"

"Fuck you, Dutch," Bootsy said, with his back facing Dutch. He then continued to walk towards the exit door of the large room. "Fuck you!"

"Fuck me," Dutch echoed, he then looked down at Joey. "Did he say fuck me?"

"Well, thanks to you," Joey struggled to say, "he didn't fuck me. So I guess he must have said it to you."

"Hey, turn around and look at me. Turn around, you fat bastard," he screamed at Bootsy. The three men then turned around. "Remember this, Vito now owes you one. And it's comin' real soon."

"Bring it on, Dutch," challenged Bootsy. "You and Vito can kiss my big black fuckin ass," he said as he turned back around and swaggered out the door.

Bleeding and looking befuddled, Joey looked at the conquered Jamaal still lying in his own blood. His mentally defeated comrades hung him out to dry. Jamaal had fulfilled their purpose like a piece of bait dangling from the end of a fish-hook. After being used and beaten, when he regained his senses he would go running back to his leader. His next mission awaited him, as he would always be ready and able.

Dutch looked down at the fallen Joey and threw him a clean white towel. "Here, clean yourself up! Are you alright?" Joey shook his head in a positive direction.

"Can you tell me what the fuck is going on here?" a confused looking Joey said, wiping the blood from his battered and ruptured face. "Are there anymore surprises comin' through that damned door?" Joey shakily managed to get to his feet to ask some more questions. "What about you, are you finally going to tell me who the hell you are?"

"My name is Dutch!"

"I already know your name," he said. "It's more than your name that I want to know."

"What do you want to know?"

"First you lecture me for about ten minutes in front of my cell and then you disappear. Then you show up like some fuckin knight in shining armor while I'm getting the shit kicked out of me. Why?"

"I'll tell you what," Dutch replied. "I was told to watch over you for a couple of days."

"By who? I don't know anybody in here!"

"You will soon find that out. We had to let you get a feel for this place. This way you can find out for yourself what it's really like in here."

"It's just like Disneyland," Joey said, his voice devoid of mirth.

"Well now you know. I saw everything that went on in here." Dutch pointed to the far corner of the enormous room. "I was hiding behind that wall by the shit toilets."

"Why didn't you stop it sooner," Joey asked. "Look at me, I'm a fuckin mess."

"Because it's like I said before. You had to get a taste of what prison life is really like."

"It don't taste too good."

"Yea, but at least you got your feet wet."

"My feet wet! I'm drowning in blood!"

"But you proved a point," he added. "The odds were against you and you never backed down."

"That prick wasn't gonna stick anything up my ass."

Dutch laughed and shook his head. "You're a pretty tough kid, you know that. You stuck to your guns and I like that. You showed me what you were made of."

Searching for some reasoning out of all this insanity, Joey picked his head up from behind his once white towel. "Well, I thank God you stopped it when you did. Thanks."

"Look, this had to be dealt with at one time or another. As soon as I felt that it was getting totally out of hand, that's when I decided to step in." Looking neat and well groomed in his prison attire, Dutch walked over to the leaky shower. He spotted a bar of soap on the floor and picked it up. "This shit with Bootsy isn't over yet. He won't bother you anymore, but we now have some unfinished business to take care of with him. He's the one with the fuckin problem now," threatened Dutch. He then started to ring his hands free of any excess water. Looking for something to dry his hands with, he came up empty.

"You don't want this," Joey asked, holding out the blood stained towel in his hand.

"Why not, we're going to be blood-brothers anyway."

Joey tossed the dirty towel in Dutch's direction along with his extended right hand. "I'm Joey DeFalco."

"I already know your name kid."

"I wish I knew what the hell is going on here?"

"Soon," promised Dutch. "You will find it all out very soon."

The two men interlocked right hands as a new friendship was born. Still naked, Joey took the towel back from his friend and wrapped it around his waist.

"You want me to see if I can get the shower turned back on," Dutch asked. "You got that nigger's blood all over you," he said pointing to the comatose man on the floor.

"I just want to get the fuck out of here."

"Alright, get dressed then. There's someone I want you to meet."

"Hey, Dutch," Joey said. "Who's Vito?"

"Come on, let's go."

"What ever happened to the prison guard by the door?"

Dutch ignored the last of Joey's questions. All of his questions would soon be counteracted with the antidote for his state of confusion. The two men walked slowly to the exit door.

Dutch looked back and said, "Wait a second." Without notice, he turned around and abruptly walked back to the scene of the crime. He then positioned himself over the body of the beaten loser. The wretch was finally starting to show some signs of life. His sprawled out body showed movements like an old man awakening from a sound sleep. "Here's one for the road, you fuckin hard on." With a tightly closed fist, Dutch bent down and hammered the face of the awakening lethargic body one more time. "By the time this low life regains some of his senses he'll be eligible for Social Security. Let the cleaning crew clean up this fuckin mess."

Both men smiled at each other and started to walk away in a stately, pompous manner. The remnants left behind gave them a surviving trace of victory against a hated prison rival. To Joey this meant everything in the world, to Dutch, it was just another day in prison.

The walk back to the cells was easy and fluent. For the first time Joey felt some of the security that he had been yearning for. Walking side by side with Dutch would sure raise a few eyebrows around the cell block. All of a sudden, people started to step aside as he walked past them. Like a soldier marching with pride, Joey's steps had a lively and perky bounce to them. Still feeling battered and overly exhausted, it was the drastic turn of events that kept him energized. Little did he know that he was walking in the shadow of the respect that was earned by Dutch.

"Go to your cell and I'll talk to you later," said Dutch.

"Dutch, I don't know how to thank you enough. You probably saved my life," Joey sincerely said.

"Go get some rest, you look like you need it."

"Yea, you're right, I feel like shit. The pain is starting to seep in."

"It will hurt for a few days and then it'll be all over. But whatever you do," Dutch warned. "Don't tell the bulls a fuckin thing on how you got those bruises. They're going to be asking you all kinds of questions. Just tell them you fell down the steps."

"I've been here less than two weeks and I think I know how things are run around here."

"Good, now go get some rest."

Joey proceeded another twenty feet towards his destination. Dutch just watched him as Joey made the right hand turn into his cell. He then stepped into the home of Vito Carlucci. Sitting down reading a newspaper, Vito glanced at the shiny pair of shoes before him.

"Well, the shit just hit the fan in the shower," said Dutch.

"What are you talking about?"

"Bootsy and a couple of his spooks just jumped the kid. He got banged up a little bit."

"What happened and where the hell were you?" asked Vito as he threw his newspaper to the floor in anger. "I told all of you guys to watch over this kid!"

"I was right there. I just waited a little to see what the kid was made of. We got nothing to be ashamed of; he handled himself pretty well. But most of all, he didn't give in to those scumbags one fuckin inch. You know Jamaal Walker?"

"What about him?"

"You won't be seeing him around for a while. Your boy kicked the living shit out of him. A few minutes later, Bootsy and those other two clowns came in and then it wasn't too funny to watch any more."

"Funny?"

"Well, things started to change and it got a little rough for the kid. That's when I jumped in and broke it up."

"How's he feelin? Does he have any broken bones?"

"He's got some lumps and bruises, but he'll be alright. You got a keeper here, Vito, the kids got some balls. Do you want me to bring him in here?"

"No," Vito chided. "He had a rough day, let him rest up for a while. After dinner have Paulie bring him to my table in the courtyard," he said in a more profound tone of voice. "I want the meeting to be visible. I want every animal in this place to know that this kid is with me!"

"Vito, why are you showing so much interest in this kid?"

"Because he reminds me of the son that I once knew," he softly said. "He also reminds me of myself when I was his age. One day I will tell you more Dutch, but not now."

"What about Bootsy?"

"Don't worry about that motherfucker. His downfall will come very, very soon. He is goin down in front of the whole prison population. And I will make sure that everyone in this fuckin cesspool sees it. That piece of shit's destiny is already mapped out," he said.

"When is this?"

"When the time is ripe."

"How?"

"You leave it to me, but that kid Joey is going to get his revenge. He will have his day in the sun, I can guarantee you that! I hope you told Bootsy that I owed him one?"

"Yea, I told him!"

"And?"

"He told me to bring it on and that me and you could kiss his big black fuckin ass."

"That's what he said?" an angrier Vito asked. "Mark my words, Dutch, every nigger and every other piece of shit in this dump will know. They will all know where and when Bootsy's demise is going to take place. When it's all over with, they will all know that it came from me. This is a promise that I will keep to you."

Vito Carlucci was a chain smoking itchy fingered Captain for one of the most notorious crime families in the city. Committed and often bewildered by his profession of choice, his family ties did not run too deep. Through dedication and brutality, Vito quickly climbed to the top of his occupation. Always a top earner, he was relentless in his pursuit up the family ladder. Tough as nails and with no hope of ever being reformed, he was awaiting his release on extortion and racketeering charges.

Originally from Sicily, his family migrated to the United States when Vito was just eight years old. The Carlucci's settled down on Mott Street in Little Italy to raise little Vito and his younger sister Carmella. Dropping out of school at a young age forced him to take to the streets. Eventually he started to mingle and hang with the wrong set of people. Wheeling and dealing would soon become his way of life, as did prison. His tightly closed lips and cocky attitude made him a winner with all of his associates. Dedication, street savvy and astute business deals won Vito a promotion within his ranks very quickly. He was now a Captain of his well-known family of organized crime. It took many years of patience and illegal activities to climb up the ladder from just being a made man. His slicked back hair and ruggedly handsome looks drew a certain respect from everyone. Always looking neat and dapper, Vito loved the image, but shunned the spotlight. If you lived in Vito's neighborhood, you knew Vito. For better or for worse, you still knew him. Even if you never saw him before, you knew of his stone cold reputation. Now he ruled in a different world, a world where the people were different but the stakes were still the same. A world where having ice-cold blood was the key to survival. This world is unknown too most, but a way of life for the men behind these prison bars.

Joey entered the chow hall late, his aching body slowing him down. He painfully waited on the diminishing food line. The small line moved swiftly as the slop was plopped onto the rectangular plastic trays. Spaghetti and meatballs was the big highlight. The food looked like it was just scooped out of a can. But most of the inmates did not seem to care at all. Their plastic knives and forks were rubbing together so hard they were practically melting.

Still dining alone, Joey's enemies were just a first down away from where he was sitting. He could feel the common stares of each set of evil eyes that bore down on him. The bruises on his battered face and body easily identified him; they were darkening with each passing second. Joey winced in distress with every movement of his agonized body.

Without even noticing, two hands found their way onto the edge of Joey's table. Just picking at his meal, Joey struggled to pick his head up. Standing before him was a face that looked like it took a beating for a living.

"Dutch wants you to meet him by his table in the courtyard," the rugged looking man said.

"Who are you?"

"Paulie," the man replied.

It was evident to Joey; he was about to meet his prison maker. Vito loved the element of exposure, especially in prison. He liked being recognized and being in the limelight. But in the outside world, he was quite the opposite. The whole place had to know that Joey was to become a new member of his crew. That's why Paulie relayed the message, not Dutch. The cell block had already seen him with Dutch. Now the chow hall gets to see Joey with Paulie.

"Just follow me out," Paulie said. "We're sitting three tables behind you."

"Okay," Joey faintly said. "I'll look for you on the way out."

While finishing his dinner, Joey decided to turn around to see where Paulie was seated. There he saw Dutch, Paulie and two other unidentified characters. He knew one of them was Vito. He could tell these men were something special. Everybody sat at least ten feet away. They had a ten-foot table all to themselves in an overcrowded dining hall.

"Joey, hey Joey," the voice from behind squeaked. "What's up?"

"Who the fuck is it now," Joey whispered to himself. Joey slowly turned around and saw Justin walking towards his table. Looking pale and frailer than ever, Justin acted like the two had a long-standing relationship going on.

"What's up, buddy," Justin said.

"Hey, how are ya?" Joey asked, pushing his tray of food away from him. Two mouthfuls of this crap and he had had enough. "Where have you been?"

"They threw me in the box for a while because of the shit that went down when we first got here."

"What's the box?"

"It's a six by six padded cube with a little peephole in it. No lights, no sinks no nothin," he said. "I went out of my fuckin mind after a while. Out here is like a country club compared to that."

"Shit," a wide-eyed Joey said.

"Hey man, what happened to your face?"

"I had a little problem with some inmates."

A few minutes had passed by and the chow hall had started to empty out quickly. Most of the inmates had already filed out of the room. Looking around, Joey had lost sight of his future associates. He stood up quickly and grabbed his food tray. "I've got to go!"

"Where are you going?"

"I have to meet somebody in the prison yard."

"But wait a second," Justin pleaded to an empty seat. "I just wanted to talk."

"I'll catch ya later," Joey said while dumping his food tray and running for the exit door. "I just gotta go."

Dutch and Vito took their usual table by the high courtyard fence. The fence acted like a holding pen that separated the prisoners from the other outdoor facilities. The prison yard and the courtyard were one and the same.

When making an appointment, inmates liked to use the word courtyard because it sounded more professional. To certain other kinds, it sounded much more romantic.

"Dutch, there's something I've been holdin back from you," Vito said.

"What's up, Vito?"

"You know a lot of things I keep to myself," he started to confess. "There's certain information that I don't share with nobody. But this is a little different. In my cell you asked me why this kid Joey was so special to me?" he said, playing with his pack of cigarettes. "The answers I gave you were true, but there's just one more thing. This kid is my godson! I baptized him when he was just an infant. I'm his fuckin godfather, Dutch!"

"Are you shittin me?"

"No, me and his father were the best of friends many years ago. Then certain situations pulled me away from the both of them. You know how good I am about runnin out of relationships."

"That I know!"

"Well, this is no different; I haven't seen either one of them in twenty-five years. For Christ sake Dutch, this kid doesn't even know who I am! I knew who he was as soon as Paulie told me his name. When I read his rap sheet, it was confirmed. I feel like I betrayed him and his father."

"Vito, if you would have told me this," Dutch said. "I would have stopped the beaten that he got from Bootsy a little sooner."

"That's alright, that beaten probably taught him something. But never-mind that. These are the reasons why this kid is so important to me." Vito then paused for a second, his eyes started to wander around the crowded courtyard. "It seems like every time I turn around some part of my past is comin through those prison doors. It's just fuckin unbelievable, like this is some sort of plan or something. First you, and now Joey."

"Don't worry about it," Dutch said in a consoling voice. "Sometimes strange things happen that are out of our control."

"You know, life is funny. After twenty-five years the both of us are reunited behind bars," Vito continued. "But when it comes to you it's a little different, I always had a feeling I would see you in here."

"Why's that?" Dutch said, with a little knowing smile.

A slight and gentle breeze effortlessly stroked both inmates.

"Because you and me were broken out of the same mold. We're both no good pieces of shit," Vito professed, joining his old time friend in a little moment of humor.

"It's called destiny, sometimes it spins in mysterious ways."

"Well whatever it's called, I don't want you to mention a word of this to anybody. Whatever we speak about in privacy stays private. It's just between me and you. Don't even tell Joey. Somehow, sometime down the road I will find a way to explain all of this to him."

Vito and Dutch locked hands as a solid bond of true friendship and loyalty. For both men their word had always been the cohesion that solidified their relationship. And this was one of the few times that Dutch had seen the sincerity in Vito's eyes. Was this an omen of things to come? Was there something that was lacking in his life? Whatever it was, he sure showed a side of him that not too many people get to see.

Throughout the scattered crowd that had congregated inside the broad courtyard, Red and Paulie were making their way back to the rectangular table. Funneling trough the crowd, both men failed to bring back what Vito was waiting for. "Where's Joey?" Vito asked in the direction of Paulie.

"I told him to follow me out of the chow hall."

"I told Dutch to tell you to bring him here," an angry Vito said. "Is he under this fuckin table? Vito mockingly crouched down to take quick peek. "Nope, he ain't there. I don't see him. So tell me Paulie, where the fuck is he?"

Paulie looked throughout the surrounding area and came up empty. He expanded his arms to telegraph his confusion. "I don't know."

"Well go find him!"

Vito's gopher started to sift through the crowd with no success. Five minutes had elapsed before he spotted Joey sitting off in some secluded corner. In his hands was a small booklet that kept his mind actively in motion.

"You were supposed to follow me, what happened?"

"I got caught up talking to someone and when I turned around you were gone."

"What are you a fuckin celebrity already," Paulie cracked. Showing disrespect to Paulie, Joey then planted his eyes back into the insignificant looking book. "What's that you're reading?"

"It's a pocket Bible," Joey said while flipping the page. "In this place everybody else finds God, why can't I."

"Come on get up, let's go," Paulie said, gently tugging away at Joey's blue shirt. "That shit ain't gonna help you in here. Where I'm takin ya is your only source of salvation." He kept grabbing at the cotton material until Joey was off of his feet. "Save the Bible for when you're locked up in your cell."

"Where are you taking me to? Jesus?"

"No, but he's the closest thing to Jesus in this place."

Vito sat with Dutch and Red waiting for the arrival of their inductee. After the introductions it would be time for a no-nonsense talk between Vito and his new student.

"Red, did the cigarettes come in," Vito asked.

"Yea, they came in right on time," the quiet member of the small group said. "I'd say about eight this morning. They're resting in the usual spot."

"Well see to it that the right people get their palms greased," Vito ordered.

"Will do."

"Give that blood suckin Mick bastard by the front door an extra carton."

"Who? McCauley?"

As he unwrapped the plastic off of a fresh pack of cigarettes, Vito nodded. "Yea, we got some more shit comin in by the end of the week," he said. "We don't want any more problems comin from the prison guards. When you throw those cocksuckers a bone, they all look the other way."

"That piece of shit would sell out his mother for a freebee. Don't worry about him, Vito. Every one of these cocksuckers can be bought in one way or the other."

"You know, Red, when I get out of here in a couple months, I'm gonna miss ya."

"Don't worry, Vito, I only have a couple of years to go."

"I know, but nobody runs my business the way you do."

"I'll be back, Vito," Red vowed. "I'll be back."

Vito nodded. Red had always been a very important player on Vito's team. Out on the streets, the two men never parted when it came to business deals and decision-making. In prison, these small enterprises were like child's play compared to the real world. Cigarettes were just a part of the import export business in prison. Goods are imported or smuggled in, then exported out to inmates at a profit. The fee depended on the buyer and the buyer alone. It didn't matter whom he was with or what he stood for. It was all about personalities and your prison mannerisms. It was very simple, the more you were hated, the more you would pay. This way, it forced a lot of prisoners to be very cordial. A cold-blooded killer would turn into Alice in Wonderland if he had a nicotine craving. Goods were swapped for money and sometimes favors. But the favors came at a much higher price. Everyone was on the take and everyone ran with the program. Vito had this barter system down to a science. This science worked to a dictatorial perfection in the underground black-market of the prison complex.

Overlooking the activity of the interracial prison yard, Dutch spotted Paulie and Joey making their way to the table. This time Paulie had a firm grip on his guest. "Here they are," Dutch announced, pointing at the two expectant visitors.

"Listen, when they get to the table you guys get lost somewhere. Take Paulie with you but don't stray too far," Vito directed. "Jesus Christ, look at this kid's face. Dutch, I thought you said that he just had a few bumps and bruises?"

"I did, but they seemed to get worse."

"Worse," Vito said, his facial expressions told the whole story. "He looks like he got hit by a fuckin bus."

"He'll be alright," the Irishman predicted. "We both took much worse beatings than that."

"Yea I know, but not in a shower. That's what makes it even more sickening. Those motherfuckers were probably going to get off on him," a seething Vito said. "Am I right?"

"They were just about to bend him over before I stepped in."

"Those dirty bastards!" Vito said, shaking his head in a negative direction. "Hey, here they come, so let's forget about this shit for now. The damage is already done."

"Joey DeFalco, meet Vito Carlucci," Paulie said. "And this other gentleman is Dennis Trapani, but we call him Red. The other guy over there you already know," Paulie said, pointing to Dutch.

"Why do they call you Red?" an inquisitive Joey asked, looking for some characteristics to match with the name. "You don't have red hair."

"I know," Red said laughing. "A long time ago I ate some bad pussy while she was having her period. The fuckin name and the smell stayed with me forever."

"I could smell it from here," Paulie said.

"You ought to recognize the smell, Paulie," Red shot back.

Paulie glared at him.

"It was your sister's pussy I was munchin on. Tell her to douche once in a while."

All the men laughed hysterically as they all got to their feet for the introductions. Joey was shaking like a leaf, he did not know what to expect. His uneasiness left him struggling to keep his hands moisture free. Perspiration started to trickle down the side of each temple. All of his sweating just highlighted the destruction that was on his swollen face.

The handshakes were well received by the distinguished looking group. Vito, focusing more than ever on Joey, noticed his uncomfortable and sporadic behavior. "Relax, relax," Vito said as they finished shaking hands and ended the introductions. "You're all sweaty, calm down and take a seat over here."

The two men took seats sitting across from each other. The rest of the unit wandered off into the center of the yard. Slowly, the fading sun was disappearing behind the right wing of the enormous building. The mood darkened as nighttime encroached.

Vito offered Joey a cigarette to try and break the ice between them. "Cigarette?"

"No thank you," Joey said. "I'm feeling a little lightheaded."

"I heard your first couple of weeks here were pretty rough."

"This past year has been a disaster for me. Coming here it just seemed to get a little worse," Joey said. "From the mental anguish to the physical pain, they both seem to break you down the same way."

"I know, it can leave you feeling hopeless at times."

"At least the physical pain fades away. Unless I keep getting the shit kicked out of me once a week," he winced, while repositioning himself on the bench. "It's the mental shit that's hard on you. It eats away at your brain. I still can't get over that shit that happened to me in the shower this afternoon."

"Listen to me, forget about that nigger. I will promise you that he won't come ten feet near you ever again. Besides, in about a week or two you're gonna fuck his fat ass up big time. You're gonna be the head surgeon dissecting that elephant in a public forum. To me, this beaten that he's going to get is long overdue. Best of all, every rotten rat bastard in this place will have a ringside seat."

"Why?" Joey asked, looking more confused than ever. He just got the shit kicked out of him and this guy wants to send him back for more? "Why me?" Joey asked, holding his hands apart.

"Because I'm gettin out of here in about four months. These morons in here know it. They'll start feasting on you all over again."

"Why, Dutch will still be here, won't he?"

"Yea, he'll still be here," Vito said. "But Dutch does not command the respect that I do. Nobody fucks with him, but they don't respect him the way that they do me."

"Isn't there another way?"

"No, we have to make a statement. A statement for you, for me, and for the rest of the boys. Everyone knows what went on in the shower," Vito said, then paused, reaching for a cigarette. He flipped open the lid and removed the long white roll of tobacco. "You can't show that you're hiding behind me for protection. No one will touch you, but no one will respect you either. You got the balls, son, but now it's time to stand up and start bouncing them."

"That guy in the shower was nothing. But this Bootsy character is another story. He's twice my size! He's twice my damn size!" Joey pleaded hoping that Vito would change his mind. "He'll fuckin kill me."

Vito lit up his cigarette and took a long drag on it. Trying to console his pupil, he reached over the table and put his hand on Joey's shoulder. "Did you hear Dutch tell Bootsy that Vito owes him one?"

"Yea, so what!"

"Well, those words are the law of the prison. By fuckin with one of my own, means that I owe him one! We have to fuck up one of his. But it's not going to be one of his hamsters. It's going to be him!" Vito warned, flicking his half-smoked cigarette among the rest of the clutter on the floor. "The best part is that the asshole ain't even gonna know what hit him."

"What about that guy I banged out in the shower or the rest of his crew?"

"What about them? That schmuck wants no part of you after you gave him the beaten of his life. You earned his respect the hard way. Unfortunately violence is the only way to earn anyone's respect around here."

"Bootsy had two other gorillas with him, what about them?"

"Don't worry about the rest of his boys, they don't want to fuck with us. They just follow him around and do what he says. It's just him that we're after."

"How we gonna do this?"

"Back in my cell, hidden inside a wall, I have a plastic bag filled with sedatives. They are already crushed into a fine powdered form. I'll pull some strings in the kitchen and I'll have some of that shit put in his food. That stuff could knock out a fuckin hippopotamus. It will take about twenty minutes for the drug to kick in. So one night after dinner you're gonna start a fight with him in the prison yard."

"I don't know about this," a troubled looking Joey said.

"Listen to me," Vito sternly said before calming down. "He'll be so tired and fucked up that his mother could be giving him a blow job and he wouldn't even know it was her. Then you will have your way with that scumbag by kickin the living shit out of him. And then you're home free," Vito said making everything sound so easy. "Only then will you have the respect that you deserve. You'll have it when I'm here and you will have it when I'm gone."

"What about his boys, won't they get involved?"

"Nah, half of them despise him and the other half wants to assume his position. Any sign of a leader faltering is a sign of weakness. Whoever is second in command of that tribe is chomping on his chicken wings to take over. But his successor we will have in the palm of our hands."

"Who is it?"

"I don't know, probably one of the two guys that jumped you. But I do know that you will never have to prove yourself more than once. This has to be done!" Vito vowed as he banged his closed fist on the face of the table. "This has to be done!"

"If that's the way it has to be, then that's the way it has to happen. But I have to be honest with you."

"What is it?"

"I'm scared shit!"

"It's okay to be afraid. But after the first punch is thrown, all the fear will filter out of you. You know what you're up against and you know what has to be done. Do you have any more questions?"

"Yea, after this goes down, that's it, it's over?"

"No, there is one other downside to all of this," warned Vito. "You're probably gonna be sent to the box for a couple of weeks."

The Box, the little Joey knew about this enclosed cavity, scared the hell out of him. Impatient and claustrophobic, he wondered if it was all worth it. But on the upside of it all, if Justin could survive it, he could too.

"No problem," Joey sternly said while feeling very tentative.

"Your face don't look too good. How are ya feeling?"

"I'm okay, my ribs just hurt a little bit and my face feels like it's gonna explode. It keeps throbbing every time I put my head down."

"You'll be alright in a day or two. Once you heal up a little, then we will take care of business."

"Oh boy," Joey cutely said. "I can't wait."

"Giuseppe," Vito said. "You have a choice to make. Either you're with me or you can rot with the rest of the vermin in this joint. I've been sizing you up for the past week and I have a good feeling about you. If you're in, then you do what I tell you to do. You must do nothing else than what I ask of you. Any personal problems you have, you must always tell me. You must promise to respect and honor certain vows and stay faithful to the loyalty that will bond us."

"Okay, Vito," Joey pledged as both men stood up. "Okay."

"You're with my crew now. You will stay with my crew for as long as you're in here." Vito then grabbed Joey by both sides of his head. The two sets of eyes were engrossed deep below the surface of their reflections. Like a vice, Vito's strong hands made sure Joey's face was in a firm and unfaltering position, looking straight at him. "Always stay loyal," he said. "Don't you ever break that vow."

Gangster style kisses were exchanged before the embrace of acceptance. Peering eyes were in full bloom at the site of the small but significant ceremony. Other inmates sensed that the ritual would deem the new member of the organized group very untouchable. Like Western Union, this message was telegraphed to its recipients in a hurry. When the private talk was over, all the boys returned to the table to offer their congratulations.

Scampering through the courtyard in an oblivious manner was Justin. Walking in between Red and Dutch his progress was impeded. "What the hell do you want?" asked Red, pulling at Justin by the arm.

"Let me go!" Justin said, while trying to break free from the traffic cop. "I wanna talk to Joey!"

"I'll let you go, but you'll be going in the other direction."

"Joey," Justin said.

"You know this guy?" Vito asked Joey.

"Yea, I met him on the bus ride up here. Why?"

"Stay the fuck away from him, he's bad news. Now get this douche bag out of here!" Vito ordered to Red. "Now!"

"Come on, you little prick," Red ordered. "Let's go."

"Why should I stay away from him?" Joey said, trying to reason with Vito. "He's harmless."

Dutch and Red grabbed one arm apiece and started to escort him to another part of the courtyard. Resisting and squirming to break free, Justin battled with his abductors every inch of the way.

"Listen," Vito warned Joey. "Everyone in here is bad news. But this idiot raped his twelve-year old stepsister. Don't ask me how I know all of this. But when you start to learn the ins and outs of this prison, you'll understand how and why I know everything."

"He told me he got busted selling dope to a Narc."

"That's true, but what he didn't tell you was that a few years before that his family threw him out of the house. He got picked up and spent two years in a juvenile hall for his incestuous behavior. That poor little girl got knocked up and had to get an abortion before she was even thirteen years old."

"Damn," a shocked Joey said.

"Once this news gets out, he's gonna wish that he kept his little dick in his pants. Every low life in here is going to be standing on line to drill him. His asshole is going to be the size of an oil well. He's too erratic and dangerous for you to be around. And you can't trust a guy like that. So for the last time stay the fuck away from him," Vito strongly warned. "Do you hear me?"

"Yea, I hear you."

For some warped reason Joey felt sorry for the discombobulated castaway. He saw Justin as a person always reaching out for acceptance and love. But his demented demeanor sent out smoke signals to those he tried to forge an alliance with. Besides the criminal element in his life, you never knew what kind of crazy rhetoric was going to come out of his bumbling mouth. His crazy characteristics orphaned him from society and the friendships he tried to maintain. In society, there aren't many second chances. The same is true in prison, where everyone is always considered a misfit. To the outside populous, some of these same misfits could not blend in anywhere. In the case of Justin, he was the perfect subject for that sad rule.

Watching Justin get dragged away, Joey turned to Vito and said in a melancholy voice, "Alright, Vito, I'll keep away from him." Those words were hard for Joey to spit out of his mouth. After all, Justin was the one who heard his whole life story on the long bus ride to prison. Now it seemed in order to protect his own ass, Joey had abandoned him. He just stared out into the open courtyard, wondering what would happen to Justin. Joey knew that in time Justin would succumb to the prison scum that dwelled all around him.

In the middle of the yard Dutch was having a heated discussion with a couple of Hispanic men. Hand motions and arm waving were visible through the surrounding crowd. The commotion brought out the rabbit ears on Joey. "What's going on over there?" he asked, maneuvering his body to get a better peek. The crowd had impeded his vision, but he kept on looking.

"It's nothing, they owe us some money and they're probably giving him some bullshit excuse why they didn't pay up."

"You're not worried?" Joey asked while stepping up on the bench to get a better view. "There's a few of them over there."

"Let me tell you something about Dutch," the Boss said. "He might not be the biggest or strongest guy in here, but none of these buffoons would ever go up against him. He's got balls the size of grapefruits, and I trust him with my life. In fact, a long time ago he saved my life from members of his own gang. You see this?" Vito then showed Joey his left index finger that was amputated down to the knuckle.

Joey jumped down from the bench to get a closer look at the disfigured hand. "How did that happen?"

"Never mind," Vito shot back. "But if it weren't for Dutch, it could have been my head instead of my finger. Some things need to be put to rest. All you need to know is that I got his back covered, and he's got mine."

For the first time Joey sensed some vulnerability in Vito's dignity and pride. This was a subject that was put to sleep many years ago, by Vito anyway. "How did he save your life?"

"It's a long story that I prefer not to tell. But I will tell you that he is one sick bastard."

"He seems so calm and logical."

"Don't let those characteristics fool you. Underneath all of that shit lays one callous and ruthless son of a bitch. If he likes you, you're in. If not, he will get you. It might take time, but he never forgets."

"That's unbelievable!"

"Years ago on the Upper West Side, some turncoat was sniffing around in his business. He actually bit the fuckin guy's nose off and delivered it to whoever the rat was working for. It turns out the guy was a wired informant working with the Government. Dutch carried the nose in his mouth and spit it out all over the agents sitting in the car down the street."

"Holy shit," a laughing Joey said. "That's a great story."

"But I will tell you one other thing, that poor guy won't be sniffing around in anyone's business ever again."

"Did Dutch get busted for it?"

"What do you think he's in here for, to visit me? Dutchie and his boys were very big on dismemberment. If it was up to them every enemy would have been gelded," Vito said.

"Why gelded?"

"So they wouldn't be able to reproduce."

"When did you first meet Dutch?" Joey asked as the questions just kept pouring out of him.

"Me and Dutch grew up in the same neighborhood. We ran the streets together as kids. Through the years our different heritage pulled us apart. My grandmother died and left my father her house in Brooklyn. We moved away from the neighborhood and Dutch started to hang with a group from the West Side of Manhattan. Years later, with a twist and turn of fate, we are back together in this nut house."

"You met him again in here?"

"Yea, you should have seen the look on our faces when we reunited for the first time in the chow hall. That son of a bitch was standing right behind me on the chow line." Vito's smile grew wider with each word of his reminiscing. "Our food trays went flying as soon as we recognized each other. There was slop all over the place and all over the both of us. With all the hugging and screaming going on the prison guards jumped in to separate us. Those pigs thought we were having a fight. That was five years ago. In all my life I never associated myself with many Irish people. But this guy is like my brother. If you cross him he's like a cold-blooded animal. But to me, he's loyal without a trace of greed running through his whole body. Certain qualities that some people possess you can't buy, they're born with them. If greed is in your blood, then that greed will flow through your body for the rest of your life. Sometimes for better or for worse, you can't get rid of it," Vito said. "It's like a fuckin cancer running amok throughout your whole body. It spreads and spreads until it kills you. If the greed don't kill you, then somebody will because of it."

"I guess true friendship comes before all," Joey said.

"I couldn't of said it better myself," Vito agreed while shaking his head.

With all the sincere dialogue going on Joey became very uncomfortable with Vito's closing statement. He started to ponder it. *Why did he have to end his talk on the topic of greed? After all, aren't all of us a product of greed? Don't we all want to take a little bit more than what's given?* He was sure that once Vito heard his story he would definitely be thrown back out to the hungry wolves.

It was obvious that Paulie and Red were soldiers in Vito's small army. But Dutch was something much more. In prison they were tight, but would the conditions be the same on the outside? Or would their huge egos make them part their ways again? In prison, Vito was the boss and Dutch was his under-boss. When freedom finally calls, Dutch could never be anything of importance with Vito's circle of friends. He lacked the one thing that he needed for success: the Italian bloodline. The family tree had to have its seeds planted somewhere in Italy. All ancestries had to possess the pedigree of being 100% grease-ball. In some cases you had to show the papers to prove it. It was nothing different than breeding a dog. The paperwork meant more than the sperm itself. Any mixed origin of another descent was totally unacceptable. Under confinement some of the rules and orientations are bent to fill certain needs. In the real world, it's a totally different story.

"Come on, let's go watch some television," Vito said.

"I'm going back to my cell," Joey said. "I have a letter that I have to write."

"Alright, tonight at eight o'clock meet me in my cell. We're gonna play some cards!"

They walked to the rear entrance of the building as a pair. Together they met up with the rest of the crew and entered the building. For Joey a long and drawn out day was coming to a close. This day could not end quickly enough for him, his bruises could attest to that.

Chapter 6

THE MONTH OF October was creeping in. A slight chill started to hug the fresh rural air. Autumn received a very pleasant welcome from most inmates. The cool breezes provided needed relief from the summer torment. With the brisk weather hovering down on them, prisoners were supplied with heat and blankets. The blankets weren't goose-down comforters, but they were sufficient. In the summertime you were basically on your own. Prison cells were not equipped with central air conditioners. But through the fall and winter months ahead, some amenities were provided so an inmate would not freeze to death.

Days went by and it was business as usual, the routines never changed. Being hooked with Vito's crew added new responsibilities to Joey's agenda. A little distribution and a once a week collection had some very rewarding fringe benefits. Everything started to feel and taste much better. If a problem would arise Joey went to Red or Paulie. If they couldn't handle the issue it would wind up on Dutch's lap. Dutch always had the green light to handle all situations on his own…sometimes creating even bigger problems. In prison there weren't too many places to hide dead bodies or their dismembered parts. When the problem went anywhere past Dutch, it became a five-alarm business complication. Hence forth, Vito Carlucci.

Any crew-member who had a personal problem would go straight to Vito. From depression to a personal conflict with another inmate, you had to go to him. All four men obeyed the rules and regulations as their codes of conduct. If any secrets were shared they would fall under a code of silence. The structure was laid out; it was up to his men to protect it. Vito's henchmen ate better; the drinks went down smoother and even their laundry smelled cleaner.

The one thing Vito could not furnish was a woman, the most powerful vice known to the human male. Those were the same women that gave most men the desirable craving that flows through every passionate vein in their body. Vito's pipeline ran deep, but women were not a part of its supply. The only ladies to be seen were strictly out of a published syndicated monthly magazine.

After eight o'clock everyone had to return to the cell block area. Time was consumed in or out of the cell. Some convicts used the three hours to write letters or to catch up on some reading. Others just hung around or played some cards with their neighbors before the lights went out. With the cell door open it gave prisoners the option of going in and out at their own leisure. But for most it gave them time to think. Time to think about loved ones, their misfortunes and their futures. The clock keeps ticking, but for most it couldn't tick fast enough.

"What the hell are you doin?" Paulie said to Joey. His body was extended on the floor moving in an up and down motion.

"Thirty six, thirty seven, thirty eight, I'm doing pushups. What does it look like I'm doin?"

"You're supposed to be in Vito's cell. We're all waitin for ya."

"Forty eight, forty nine, fifty. Tell him that I'll be right there," a huffing and puffing Joey said. He then reached for a towel to wipe the perspiration from his forehead.

Paulie picked up an envelope that lay on top of Joey's bunk. "Hey, who do you know in Houston, Texas?"

"I'm writing a letter to my mother."

"Your mother lives in Houston?"

"No, my friend does."

"Your mother lives with your friend?"

"No, my mother lives in Brooklyn."

Joey kept up the game until Paulie would either hit him or solve the problem. But to Joey, this guy was not the sharpest knife in the drawer. He then figured that he better eventually tell him or he would be at it all night long.

"Is your mother vacationing in Texas?"

"My mother doesn't go on vacation."

"Alright, wise guy," Paulie said, rubbing his chin. "If your mother doesn't live in Houston and she's not on vacation that means either your friend is banging her or she's on tour with the fuckin circus."

"Nope."

"Alright, the fuckin game is over," he fumed. "For the last time, why are you writing her a letter with a Texas address on it?" his unyielding voice said, growing impatient.

"Okay Einstein," Joey teased. "My mother does not know that I'm in prison. She thinks I had to relocate for business reasons. So I write and send the letters to my friend. He just removes the smaller envelope from the larger one." Joey held up the contents of the larger envelope. "He then drops the envelope addressed to my mother in the mailbox. Then she receives the letter from me with a Houston, Texas postmark on it. And like magic, I'm in Houston, Texas."

"Oh, now you live in Houston too," Paulie said, still acting confused.

"Do you want me to explain it to you again?"

"I get it, I get it," he said. "I was just breakin your balls."

"Thank God, for a minute I thought you were retarded."

"I was just testing your patience, kid. I wouldn't have made you go through it again."

"I have no patience. I was gonna tell you to go fuck yourself," Joey jokingly said.

The two men started sparring in a playful boxing match. There was plenty of bobbing and weaving with each harmless jab that was thrown.

"Come on, let's go play some cards," Paulie said.

"Tell Vito I'll be there in ten minutes. I want to finish writing the letter to my mother in Houston," Joey said smiling.

Paulie gave Joey a light slap on the back of the head. "Hurry up, I'll tell them you'll be right in."

"Paulie, if my mother knew I was here, it would kill her."

Playing cards was the furthest thing from Joey's mind. His thoughts were focused on the family he'd temporarily lost. That, plus the fact his girlfriend had departed, stayed cemented in his mind. Only his sister and his ex girlfriend Diane knew of his misfortunes.

Diane was a stunning blond with a dark Californian complexion. Class, grace and lies were the makeup of her false foundation. Her lavish lifestyle included the best of everything. Furs, diamonds and exotic vacations were all in her catalogue of pleasures. All the I love you sayings and all the good times ran out when the money disappeared, and so did Diane.

How can some women have their total being governed by the power of the all mighty American dollar? How can they live with themselves knowing that they used and violated others because of their selfishness? Some men can never put these horrific egocentric acts behind them. They can never forget the past as they bring the resentment into future relationships. Trust in all aspects of life is the cornerstone to any aspiration. When trust is tainted it brings a reversal towards failure. But like most setbacks we try to pick ourselves up, dust ourselves off and move on. All of Joey's crimes found a way to ricochet back to him from the woman he loved.

The cell block was quiet on this Wednesday evening. Joey took the short walk over to Vito's cell. The social club atmosphere was indicative of its inhabitants. Secondhand smoke filled the air from the burning tobacco. The thick vapors hovered over the smokers like storm clouds ready to erupt. Joey just stood silently by the entranceway before he was noticed.

"Oh, let's go, you're holdin up the game," Vito said while holding the deck of cards. "What the fuck are you doin?"

"I don't feel like playing."

"You got to play, we need four guys. What's wrong with you?"

"Nothing."

"Nothing! You're doing pushups and reading the Bible and you're telling me there's nothing wrong."

"So, you never did a pushup before?"

"Don't get smart. It's Bootsy isn't it?"

"No," Joey said afraid to admit to anyone that he was right. Bootsy was the major player in his composition of issues.

"After the game hang around, I want to have a little talk with you," Vito ordered as he started to deal the cards. "Fuck it, we'll play with three men."

The game lasted for about an hour and a half. Cards were strewn all over the bed. There were no winners and losers with each hand of poker that was dealt. Business was the topic of conversation for the duration of this get together. Vito handed down his instructions and orders for the upcoming tasks that needed to be tended to. Most of the information was filtered to the streets where its destination was intended to be. The business that went on behind bars was menial compared to the rocking and rolling of the city streets. The power never diminishes from Bosses who are incarcerated. Where there's a will they somehow find a way to get their messages to the awaiting streets.

"Relay all the instructions to Red. The poor guy has been shiting and throwing up all day," said Vito. "He's probably lying down in his cell."

Dutch and Paulie shook their heads in agreement as the duo left the cell. These guys never had to be told the same things twice. Sometimes Paulie tended to get a bit lackadaisical, but it was nothing that a slap behind the head could not correct. If that didn't work, a good swift kick in the ass was sometimes needed to get him moving a little faster.

"Alright, now you," Vito said, "get in here and stop holding up the door. What's going on inside your head?"

"Nothing, I'm just feeling a little down," he said, slowly entering the small cell. "I feel like I have nothing left."

"Why?"

"I'm totally drained, mentally and physically. I'm just doing way too much thinking."

"About what?"

"About life and all things that I lost."

"The thinking that you are doing is only normal."

"Normal! I lost everything, from my assets to my girlfriend. I miss my family and I feel terrible that I let them down this way," Joey confessed. "My mother thinks I live in another damn state. What kind of future do I have with this felony conviction on my resume? It's all starting to hit me all at once. I fucked my whole life up."

"You're young," Vito lectured. "This is just a temporary setback."

"Temporary, what the hell am I going to do when I get out of this place?"

"Once you clear your head up it will all come back to you. Yea, you got into some trouble on Wall Street, so what! Do you think that anybody can pull off what you did? It takes some brains and a pair of big balls. You took a shot and you got caught with your pants down. Just concentrate on getting out of here," he said while gathering up the playing cards from his bed. "You'll find something to do."

"How did you know I worked on Wall Street?"

"I took a look at your rap sheet."

"So you know everything?"

"I know more about you than you want me to know."

"Like what?"

"It's all water under the bridge. It will soon be time to start swimming in the right direction."

"Well right now I feel like I'm drowning, so I'm not swimming anywhere."

"What you seen and experienced at a young age some people don't see in a lifetime. You got what it takes, but the next time, think ahead and be smarter. Stop going for the quick buck. The next time, stay clean and go legit," Vito said in a father like manner. "I know you miss your family, but they will always love and be there for you. Your mother would still love you even if you blew up a bus full of praying nuns. It's a love without conditions or reservations, it's genuine."

Joey just stood there shaking his head in agreement. Every word of Vito's sermon seemed to be swallowed like a little boy with a hungry appetite.

"Women," he continued. "Fuck women, they come and go. Some women stretch your dollar as far as it will take them. When the free ride is over, they never look back. In a day or two they hook up with some other sap and they start suckin the life out of him. Day after day after day they keep on suckin, until the poor bastard is finally dry."

"Diane wasn't that bad."

"Did she leave you when things turned sour?"

"Yea."

"Then she's a pig," he said. "And she is no better than a whore off the street. That woman never even loved you to begin with. You're better off getting rid of that bitch now. She just hopped on board for the free ride. If she gets pregnant with your baby, then you're really fucked. You're either buried up to your eyeballs in alimony and child support, or you're forced to grow old with the bitch. And every day for the rest of your life you would have to stomach her, knowing all the while what she is really made of. When and if you ever see her again, thank her. She did you a big favor by leaving you."

"I never thought of it that way," Joey said.

Vito was acting relentless with his choice words about gold-diggers. At one time in his life he must have gotten burned real badly. It seemed like Joey's misfortunes had opened up some serious wounds. Vito continued on with his sermon in a non-stop fashion.

"If you fall in love with a bitch she will ruin you. You'll always be wondering what you did wrong and what more you can do for her. They are so good at it that you're the one who will be left with all the guilt. She will act like she is doing you a favor just to get into her pants. There is nothing worse than a woman that always wants. Most of the beautiful ones are like that; it's called high maintenance."

Vito lectured on, rolling like a bus on a cross-country tour. You would figure that his many years of experience with the opposite sex seemed to fit his lifestyle of hit and run. But it somehow left an open warfare with most of his failed relationships.

"If you have to get laid, take a hit for a night," he said.

"What do you mean take a hit," said Joey. His fatigued body was starting to act up. He then walked over to Vito's bed and took a seat on the thin mattress.

"It means get a hooker, a prostitute, or a fuckin whore. It's easier and she takes care of the business that she was hired for. When you get your rocks off you pay her and it's over with. There's no bitching and complaining, and in the long run it's much cheaper. You don't even have to leave your apartment. There are no flowers and five star restaurants to deal with. Some men go for it all, from limousines to fine champagne and they still go home to jerk off. Jesus Christ, I spent a fortune on women when it wasn't even appreciated. Don't be an asshole like me."

"But how do you know if someone really cares about you?" asked Joey. "Not all women are like that."

"When the right one comes along, you'll know it. Everything becomes us instead of me. For the both of you, the butterflies will be spreading their wings right after you first set eyes on each other. The hand holding will never stop, even in times of trouble. She will become your best friend as well as your lover. You will find yourself doing things you never thought you were capable of doing. It's a totally different feeling, when it hits you believe me you will know it. The biggest difference is that the woman who truly loves you can never do enough for you. But always remember one thing," he said while pointing in Joey's direction. "Always stay with your own kind."

"What does that mean, my own kind?"

"What it means is that if you stray and venture into another race or color, you will forever have problems. The trouble starts right after your first date. It keeps brewing as you're walking down the aisle to get married. It even affects your children who sometimes don't even know who or what they are. Society can also be very cruel to situations that it is not accustomed to seeing."

Vito knew that he had to tackle one problem at a time. Certain things were far more important than the shit that went on behind bars. He also knew that his godson was very naïve when it came to worldliness and sophistication. He started to feel that Joey could be easily seduced into situations that were not good for him. He was a sucker to any smooth talker who offered him the world.

"Listen, kid, I might not know about a lot of things. But the little I know, I know a lot about," said Vito.

Vito Carlucci was quite the skilled orator for a street-smart gangster. He possessed the ability to elevate or descend his elaboration in the art of speaking. Whatever the obstacle or confrontation, he had a certain way of leveling off his form of communication. Whether speaking in a courtroom full of complex lawyers to the fleecing of a small time street peddler. No matter what, he would always get his point fluently across.

"Vito, the other day when you were telling me about Dutch, you mentioned the word greed. It bothered me because everything he's not when it comes to greed, I am. I always had that selfish desire for more," confessed Joey. "It got to the point when more was never enough. Now that I am reduced to nothing, that feeling is still there. It takes you places where you meet people that are just like you, and worse. For every greedy person out there you know somewhere, someone else is getting fucked. I was supposed to be a symbol of trust. But basically I was just a symbol of my own greed," Joey said as tears started falling from his tired looking eyes. "This addiction has put me here. But the funny thing about all of this is that I don't know what came over me. Out of nowhere I became this other person."

"Who caught up with you, the Feds?" asked Vito.

"Yea, for almost a year I've been exposed like a cheap hooker trying to turn a trick on a street corner. They wired me up, bugged my home and tailed my sorry ass all over town until they got what they wanted." Joey started to rub his watery eyes with his right hand. But he knew that he had to continue on. "Intimidation, isolation and a bombardment of questions were their best weapons. They hoped that I would slip up or crack under the intense scrutiny of pressure."

"I know, Joey, if you don't slip up," Vito said, "those assholes are too stupid to figure anything out for themselves."

"You are so right," he said while looking down at the floor. "They don't know much about white collar crime. They feast on your intelligence and how much you know. Then the idiots threaten you with life in prison, restitution and big fines."

"I've been there before, Joey. So I know what it's like."

"I only cooperated because some faggot ratted me out. The fuckin pussy bastard cracked under the pressure. If I didn't cooperate, I probably would have taken a bigger hit. After that prick gave me up, they came down on me even harder. So I just gave into their demands and copped a guilty plea. I had no other choice. The Feds had me all on tape, that's when I knew that it was all over."

"Sometimes if you don't give them what they want this shit can go on for years," said Vito.

"I know, but in my case I just gave them enough. I had enough of the probing and groping with the uncertainty of always being at their beck and call. I needed closure. When they finish chewing on you, they spit you out like a tasteless piece of gum on a dirty subway platform."

"You would have never been in this prison, if it was not for the drugs that were found. You would have been on some luxury farm somewhere with all the rest of those corporate bastards."

"I know, but Vito, I never even knew that the cocaine was in the house. That bitch Diane had it hidden in some closet. She had her own personal stash. Yea I was dealing a little, but not for the money. They made me out to be some sort of drug lord."

"Listen, it's over and you handled it. Just thank God that your heart is still beating. Stop feeling sorry for your self," he insisted. "Do you think that anyone is losing sleep over what happened to you. Nobody gives a fuck and nobody cares. You're not depressed because of your greedy actions. You're depressed because this shit caught up with you." Picking up an ashtray, Vito then walked over to the trash basket and emptied it out. "Look at me," he said pointing to himself. "I'm the greediest son of a bitch on this rotten earth. I take, take, take and take and then I take some more. But I don't take from one of my own. And one of my own dare not take from me. That's what I meant when I said that about Dutch. No matter what the temptation might be, it isn't big enough to ever break the bond between us."

"So what are you saying that it's alright to rob people as long as they're not one of your own?"

"For you its not, but for me it's a way of life. You're young and there is plenty of opportunity for you. For me it's too late, I'm already into this lifestyle way too deep. In reality you're no different than me and I'm no different than you. We just did it in different ways. You used manipulation and a fountain pen. I used a baseball bat and fear."

"I guess you're right," Joey said. "There are different ways to express your greed."

"Just take all this so called greed and focus it in a positive and legitimate way. It will all come to you, and when it does you will say that Vito was right. When you get out of here just make sure you don't make the same mistakes twice. If you ever wind up back in here then you would be a major disappointment to everybody. In this day and age to make an honest living sometimes seems like the hardest thing in the world to do. But you have no other choice. It's what you have to do. When you leave this fuckin place, you will be on your own again. So don't ever let me down. Make me proud."

"It's almost eleven o'clock already," Joey said, after looking at the watch on his wrist. For some reason he did not want to hear those words coming from Vito's mouth. In the back of his mind, he already knew this was going to be nothing more than a temporary friendship. The future groundwork was already set in stone. Once his prison stay was over he would not be entering the dark side of the underworld. Organized crime would not be a part of his updated resume.

"Yea, get the hell out of here before you get locked in for the night. That's all we need is a rumor spreading that we're two fags," a laughing Vito said.

"Thanks, Vito."

"For what?"

"For taking the time and having this talk with me. It meant a lot to me."

The two men then hugged with the show of an affection that was growing with each passing hour. Joey started to exit the room feeling a little different about his life and his future. He knew that outside of prison he would be on his own. This was the only way that it had to be.

"Hey Joey, I didn't forget about Bootsy," he reminded him.

Joey just nodded and returned to his empty cell.

At eleven o'clock the festivities are over for the day. It's lights out and all the units are locked up for the night. The pace and the tempo are limited to the confines of the 8 by 10 cell. At night there is no roaming on the prairie. There are no night-lights to read a good bedtime book by. There are no televisions to watch your favorite late night shows. All you are left with is apathy. For the lucky few who possessed the more vivid of imaginations, the coming of darkness was more bearable. Self-sexual activities and their perpetual dreams got them through the night. The rituals of prison life can become very lethargic. Especially when you are locked in that concrete can that they call a prison cell.

Vito worked the best job in the house. He was the custodian for keeping all the literary and artistic materials in place. The library was the place where one could enhance his learning capabilities. Quite frequently it retained the ambiance of a desolated grave-yard. Most prisoners would rather spend their free time in the company of trouble. Just a certain few understood the benefits and solace that can be rewarded by stimulating the human mind. Illiteracy springing from the lack of a formal education was common. Their elementary thinking feeds the brain with childlike thoughts. These infantile thoughts are the main reasons why most inmates wind up behind bars. The unattained knowledge that most prisoners lack would only enhance their mental and physical behavior to respond in a more positive way. Very few inmates realized the difference between the two.

Vito had a strong fascination for true crime literature. The sick and perverse thinking of the twisted human mind was his favorite topic of reading material. From Ted Bundy to the Boston Strangler his free time engrossed it all. He sometimes would read for hours with a detachment from his physical surroundings. His reward was to attain the thoughts and patterns of the devious mind and what makes it tick. Over the years he developed an analytic technique on criminal behavior and disorders. Was he a psychopath or did he miss his calling to become a psychotherapist? The bottom line was that Vito always had to stay one step ahead of people just like him; the hard core, heartless criminal.

This criminal was capable of love but did not trust to many people. If you gained access into his cold-blooded heart, the conditions and consequences were pretty basic to stay there. His undying love required one thing, loyalty. If you swayed from that allegiance, the alliance was dead. There would be no place on earth to hide from his wrath. It might take time, but he would find you. Whether it was love or business, in Vito's mind it really didn't matter. Loyalty, respect and trust were the three words that he etched in stone. Those three words walked in every direction that life would take him. In his eyes those same words separated the good from the evil, success from failure and love from hate. The great motivational speakers had nothing on him when he had to get his point across. But he did have one thing in common with most of the general prison population. He lacked a conscience and the ability to feel remorseful for his actions. For Vito there was no difference between right and wrong. If it was to his benefit, it wasn't wrong. Every decision that he made was always the right one. The infliction of vengeance or the reprisal of justice, were methods of retaliation that meant nothing to him. There was no fear in his life and he was never afraid of any consequences.

The following morning Vito was sifting through a box filled with hard cover and paperback books. Part of his detail was returning the books to the appropriate section from which they were taken. The other part was to keep the library neat, tidy and orderly. Books lined three surrounding walls about seven feet high and forty feet deep. Six bookshelves lined up in rows of two divided up the room. Compared to the standard size public library, this place was not that big at all. There were so few studious visitors that you could hear a pin drop. In prison, the library was the only place where peace and quiet could be found.

Outside the library doors, footsteps echoed down the narrow hallway. The squeaking sounds of untreated wheels accompanied the stomping footsteps. Paulie entered the room pushing a wash bucket by the long pole that was attached to his mop.

"He'll be here in about ten minutes. He just has to finish cleaning up the breakfast mess," Paulie said.

"Did Nat ask you any questions?" Vito inquired, looking a bit suspicious.

"Vito, whenever you ask to speak with anybody they know something's up. Of course he asked me a few questions."

"What did you tell him?"

"I told him I had no idea what it was all about. But I also insisted that he don't tell anybody else that you called for him."

"Good, this is important."

"So what's going on, why did you ask to see him?"

"Don't worry about it, go back to your job," Vito demanded while picking up a copy of War and Peace. "Hey Paulie, get a load of this fuckin book. Only a lifer would have time to read this monster."

Vito started to walk away with the thick book in his hands. Paulie just shook his head and wheeled his mop bucket out of the room. Always being the messenger, Paulie's work detail gave him access to most of the prison facility. Whenever prison guards saw some suspicion, he would just dip his mop into the pail and make it look like a work related visit.

"Nat, how are you," Vito politely asked with a smile.

"Alright, Vito," he said while standing in an erect position.

"You're probably wondering why I asked to see you."

"Yea, it has crossed my mind. So what's going on," Nat nervously replied. "I know you didn't ask me here for some recipes."

Nathaniel Johnson was a Black man who managed some of the work detail in the kitchen. He helped plan the menus before they were cooked and served to inmates in the chow hall. A polite gentleman with Southern roots, he was serving ten to twenty years on an armed robbery charge. The sixty-year old graying man had respect for all guys who showed respect to him. Vito and Nat shared a cordial relationship, exchanging menial favors. Anything coming out of the kitchen was always specially prepared for Vito. He got the best cuts of meats and the freshest of fruits and vegetables. Any imported goods that were smuggled in, Nat would surely whip up something very creative for him. Everyone knew it but no one said a word about it. Nat's end of the deal was some cigarettes and some homemade booze.

"Sit down," Vito said pulling out a chair. "Listen, I need you to do me a very special favor. You see this?" he said, holding up a small vial with white powder in it. "Tomorrow at dinner time, I want you to mix this shit into Bootsy's food. Make sure you prepare something where it blends in nicely. It will probably dissolve, but let's not take any chances where someone gets suspicious."

Nat just sat there observing the small glass vial. He picked his head up and looked straight into Vito's eyes. A bright smile appeared on his rough unshaven face. "Yea, yea," he said. "I get the picture."

"Please, Nat, don't ask any questions and do not converse with anyone about what's going on." Vito paused while looking around the empty room. "Do you have any problems doing me this favor?"

"Look at my neck," Nat said while pointing to a spot below his Adam's apple. The scars that were left from the scalding bath were quite visible. "That motherfucker threw a bowl of chicken soup back at me because it didn't have enough white meat in it. Do you think I would have any problem doing this for you? Come on, Vito, give me some credit."

"Excellent, I've been watching that fuckin loser since he came in here. Once judgment day smacks him in the face, he will be reduced to nothing. He has been having his way in here far too long. At about 6:30 tomorrow night it will all come to an end," he warned.

"That fat boy loves cream of mushroom soup. Tomorrow he's going to get it nice, thick and creamy," Nat promised. "Just the way he likes it."

"I will arrive in the chow hall early. You keep your eyes on your business and don't be too conspicuous. Let's keep everything nice and quiet."

"I will keep a special bowl on the side for him with this stuff already in it. Vito, please stop the worrying. I will make sure he gets it."

Nat was a very special man when it came to honesty and trust. He would hide your life savings underneath his bed pillow while never touching a dime. Most people forgave him for his wrongful acts. They find it very forgivable when someone robs in order to feed his family.

"Thanks, Nat."

"I just wish I could see what you really have in mind."

"Because you are a good friend and I could trust you, I will tell you this, be in the prison courtyard tomorrow after dinner. The fireworks should start at about 6:30. You're gonna love what you see," Vito vowed. "But once again, Nat, make sure you keep this quiet."

"You know it, Vito. I see and hear nothin."

"Good, that's about it then."

"My man," Nat said while getting out of his chair. "Let's do it up."

"For any reason that this does not go down, I will let you know sometime tomorrow afternoon."

Vito then handed the small potent vial to Nat.

The only thing left on Vito's agenda was the preparation of his star player. Being a young man with only three weeks of incarceration, Vito was asking a lot.

Later on that same day, Vito summoned everyone to the dining hall early. Red, Paulie and Joey were carrying their food trays back to the table already occupied by Vito and Dutch. The whole crew knew about the plan. They just didn't know how and when it would happen. Only Joey, Nat and Vito knew that it involved the little white powder. Vito instructed Joey to sit next to him. The other three sat across from them, tightly together.

"It's all taken care of. Tomorrow night after dinner is Bootsy time," Vito declared, while looking at Joey. "The three of you will scatter around the yard, always keeping one eye on me. Your other eye will be focused on that fat fuck's table or wherever he is. When the fight goes down, stay apart, but inch your way closer to each other and to the fight. Don't get involved unless I motion you to do so. Just observe and make sure everything goes according to plan. If we have to mix it up, that's when you guys will know what the high sign is."

"What's the high sign?" asked Paulie, dumbfounded.

Vito rolled his eyes and said, "I'll grab my fuckin balls. What's the high sign? If things go sour and you see me running into the fracas then you should know what the high sign is. Come on, Paulie, use your fuckin brains for a change."

"I just thought…," he started to say, while being cut off in the middle of his sentence.

"Never mind what you thought or what you're thinking. You will know if and when you have to get involved. I just used this high sign shit as a figure of speech."

"Paulie, just shut the fuck up and listen," Dutch ordered. "Jesus Christ, Vito, this guy has a question for everything."

"Never mind him, let's get back to business. One of the main things is to always expect the unexpected. If the kid is gettin his ass kicked or some of Bootsy's monkeys jump in, then and only then do we have to get involved in a hurry. But if things go the way I perceive them to go, it should be a cakewalk," Vito guaranteed.

"Yea, a cakewalk," Joey sarcastically said. Vito gave him a sneer and continued on.

"When the prison guards start comin in you guys nonchalantly start retreating from the scene. As long as Joey is kickin his ass, the guards will be taking their sweet time. I covered all aspects of this. I will let Joey know when to start and when to finish the fight," he said while his attention averted to Dutch. "Hey, Dutch, what's the matter? You're not saying much."

"I'm just taking it all in."

"Is there something that you have a problem with?"

"Nah, it's nothing important. We'll talk about it later."

"There is one more thing. If there is any reason that this thing doesn't go down. We will save it for another day. If it doesn't look right it's not going to happen. But only I will make that decision." Vito then turned his attention over to Joey who just sat there quietly. "Joey, you meet me in my cell at 9: o'clock tonight. There are a few things that I have to go over with you."

"Okay, Vito," he said looking uneasy. "I'll be there!"

"Alright, enough of this shit, let's eat," he said while picking up his utensils.

Joey just sat there barely picking at his food. His meals had gotten much better since Vito sanctioned him in. But the impending battle had just eaten away at his appetite. The rest of the crew was chowing down without a care in the world. Why shouldn't they eat, they were not the ones getting thrown to the lions. This fight was really no big deal to them; it was the outcome that they feared the most.

Looking around the dining hall for his antagonist, Joey spotted Bootsy. The two made eye contact and Bootsy blew him a kiss. Not a day went by that Bootsy didn't make some kind of obscene sexual gesture or overtone at Joey. All of his boys seemed to get a big charge from this indecent exchange. They knew that Joey was still intimidated by them. Vito was right; although Joey was labeled untouchable he still lacked the respect that he needed to earn. In prison the options of gaining another's respect are very limited. Out on the street admirable deeds or good-natured dispositions earned respect from most. In the Joint, fisticuffs and violence are the only answers to any aggressive threats. In this place two wrongs do make a right unless you stand up to them with an act of physical force. Any exertion of physical force usually put a conclusion to all intense discrepancies. Of course, that all depended on if you win or lose the battle.

In this battle, there would be no umpire or referee. There would only be a bunch of fanatical screaming spectators. This contest would be between a pugnacious street thug who preys on the vulnerable and unseasoned, and a street-smart criminal, fighting for his dignity and his right to simply exist. Whatever the outcome, all the bystanders would be gratified as soon as they saw the first drop of visible blood.

About 8 pm. that same evening, Joey was standing in front of the mirror. The razor in his right hand did not slide down the side of his face in a fluid motion. Joey's unstable condition was responsible for the little nicks that were quickly left bleeding. Besides the little nicks and cuts, his face was still a little sore. The pain of the past, however, now had to all be put behind him. For tomorrow shall be the biggest day of his young prison life. No pocket Bible and prayers to God would make this situation disappear. Joey had no choice but to put all his faith and trust in this gangster he barely knew. Vito might know Joey from baptism, but Joey had no idea if his godfather ever existed.

Walking into Vito's cell with his hands in his pockets, Joey raised his voice over the sounds of the cell block. "Vito," he said. "I'm here!"

"Here, drink this," Vito said, handing him a plastic cup.

"What is it?"

"Just drink it," he said as he watched Joey sniffing the contents of the cup. "Go ahead, it will calm you down. You look like you're gonna get a heart attack before tomorrow even comes."

Vito picked up an empty cup and poured himself a shot of the homemade whiskey. This comforting delectable liquid was the product of water, potatoes, some orange peels and a touch of yeast. This concoction would be placed in a big heavy plastic bag that was tied up nice and tight. The makeshift bootleggers would then dig a hole adjacent to an outside wall that was exposed to the most sunlight. The aspiring bag of alcohol was then placed inside the wall as the intense heat from the afternoon sun baked its ingredients to an acceptable distinction. At night the bag was then taken in and placed under the nearest bed. This process had to be repeated every day for about eight weeks. The best brewing results were always attained in the hot summer months. A couple of shots of this stuff could knock some of the most accomplished drinkers off of their bar-stools. In prison, this mixture of elements was considered top-shelf.

"Salute," Vito said. The two men tipped cups and chugged down the almost lethal drink.

"Ugh, ugh," Joey choked. "This shit tastes like poison!"

"Ha, ha, ha, ha, ha," Vito laughed. "You should see your fuckin face? You're as red as an apple. Ha ha, ha."

"What is this shit?"

"Just drink up and tell me how you feel in a minute."

Within the minute, Joey was feeling no pain. This so-called potable drink was better than morphine. In time, it killed everything from your pain to your memory. Feeling a bit more relaxed, Joey took a seat beside Vito on his bunk. Out of a small carafe Vito proceeded to pour another dose of the potent whiskey.

"Vito, I don't know how to tell you this," Joey said, and then paused for a moment as he stared into the empty plastic shot glass. "I'm afraid. My whole body is trembling with fear. How do you know if that drug is going to work?"

"Don't worry about it."

"What if you don't give him enough?"

"I said, don't worry about it."

"What if you give him too much?" All of a sudden his questions were filled with a bunch of what ifs. His rambling voice was racing faster than a rush hour commuter train.

"For the last fuckin time," Vito sternly said. "Read my lips; don't worry about it."

"I don't know if I have the balls to do this," Joey confessed. "It just seems like it's too much for me to handle."

"Shut up," Vito brusquely said. "Do you think I would put you in a situation where you would get your ass kicked and I would be totally humiliated?"

"No."

"Then don't ever question or second guess my authority or know how again. I would never put any of my men in a precarious situation. Sometimes it don't always seem right, but when it's over they always realize that my way was the best and only way. If I didn't take you in, you would have already been on that scum bag's dinner table. We wouldn't even be talking about this shit right now."

"I know."

"So you know that I saved your ass?"

"Yes, I know you did."

"Good, so show me the respect that I think I deserve. I know you're afraid, anybody would be. Just trust me. I would never let you down."

To second guess Vito was a show of disrespect to him. To disagree with him was a sign of insulting his intelligence. Like the Chairman of the Board, his decision-making and the way he delegated things were non-negotiable.

Joey just sat there and nodded. He knew that Vito was right. If not for him he would have either been dead or somebody's late night snack. Without Vito the cards were stacked totally against him, each time turning up the ace of spades.

"Bootsy," said Vito. "He's like a scavenger. He just picks up all the leftover pieces that nobody else wants. He just feeds on the decaying lives of others. He circles around his prey until he feels the time is right to strike. Age, sex and color are all the same to him. The man has no dignity. He would desecrate the life of a newborn baby if it were to his advantage. Everyone is a pawn in his little world of deceit and destruction."

Rising to his feet, Joey reached into his pants pockets to retrieve a pack of cigarettes. He then offered Vito a smoke as the older man poured another shot of whiskey. Joey lit both cigarettes, and then returned to his seat on the uncomfortable mattress.

"Bootsy was dealing drugs around every fuckin school in his neighborhood. He had ten-year old kids running dope from one block to the other. On every street corner he provided young girls who offered sexual favors for the right price. These kids earned more than their parents did. Do you know what it's like when a ten year old kid has a couple of hundred dollars in spending money in his pocket?"

"No, I don't"

"Well I do," Vito said. "Some of their parents were afraid to stop the association their kids had with Bootsy. They were always thinking of the retaliation factor. Then there were the other families that just enjoyed the extra income. Those greedy bastards never said a word, while their little children hustled the streets." Vito took a long drag from his cigarette and watched his exhale float to the top of the tiny room. "Most of these kids were hooked on the shit they were selling within a few months. So their money went right back into that bastard's deep pockets. Everyone did his running for him while he drove around in his BMW."

"Where were the cops?" asked Joey.

"Cops, what cops? Most of the times there is not a cop to be found in these neighborhoods. If there are, then they're lookin the other way. Sometimes the temptation of money can turn the most honest of cops into a piece of shit on the take. They fall victim to the streets that they are paid to patrol. It's like a disease that can't be stopped. Everyone knows where it is, but nobody does anything to stop it. There is too much money involved, so it goes on and on, like a broken record. From the little ten years old kid all the way up to the men in blue. Everyone is gettin a piece, unfortunately sometimes at the expense of a young innocent life."

"What makes those people so different than anybody else?"

"Are you referring to me?" Vito asked.

"Not really," Joey nervously replied.

"Well, if you have any doubts, which I'm sure you have, let me tell you something. I pick and choose who I associate myself with and I'm very particular about it. Forget about what you see in this place, this is all bullshit. I can shut this whole fuckin place down with the blink of an eye. Nobody would see a fuckin candy bar or a stinking cigarette if I tightened my grip on things. Having all this shit in the place just makes my life a little easier while I'm here. A lot of people owe me favors because of it," he said talking about all the contraband smuggled into the prison. "So I use everything to my own advantage."

Joey just sat in silence as Vito tried to separate his life of organized crime from Bootsy's. Vito seemed to have an urgency to get his point across to the young inmate. Since learning of the identity of his godson, he spoke as more of a father figure. He knew that sometimes his lifestyle could appear to be just as cruel and ruthless to others. But there were always set boundaries that had to be obeyed. In his book there was always a list of the do's and the don'ts of criminal behavior.

"We might do a lot of bad things," Vito said. "But these bad things are never at the expense of women and children. There are certain things that I am dead set against. Drugs and prostitution are just two of them. Those two money-makers destroy young life in all shapes and forms. They are both controlled by fat cats who will go to any extent to get what they want."

"What about the other Italian families, do they have the same beliefs?"

"What the other families do is their business. But we usually follow the same general rules and principals. I'm just trying to show you the difference between Bootsy and me. I am not saying that what I do is right. But on the other hand I don't ask or force anybody to be a part of something that may seem wrong. All of my guys are willing participants, nobody is held against his will. It's like anything else in life, you have to know where to draw the line."

"What line is that?" asked Joey.

"The line which separates immorality from morality. Every system has a rule of conduct based on certain principals of right and wrong. No matter how corrupt and vicious this fraternity may be, rules are rules. All of my boys know where and when to draw the line based on my set of rules. When it comes to Dutch and his old crew, the higher command was much more lenient. If anyone done them wrong, from family members to family pets, nobody was safe. Once in a while I have a problem trying to break Dutch out of his old habits. In the old school that I come from, harming family members for the wrongdoing of relatives was off limits. We never held anyone for ransom based on other people's actions," he said.

"I'm starting to understand it all," Joey said, nodding. "I'm sorry if I doubted you."

"When you don't know about something, that's okay. But make sure that you never ever assume. Because that's when you will get yourself in a pile of shit that you can't crawl out of. Take everything for what it's worth and what you see. Do you understand me?"

"I think so."

"That motherfucker Bootsy put some eighty year old grandmother of one of his dealers, on her deathbed. The old lady flushed ten ounces of pure cocaine down the toilet. The poor woman thought she was doing the right thing for her grandson. When the kid couldn't come up with the money or the dope, he was beaten until he gave up his own grandmother. That prick sent two goons up to see her and they beat her into a coma in which she never awakened from. The grandson is now in prison serving a life sentence for the murder that Bootsy committed. The authorities think that he killed his own grandmother. The dumb bastard was so afraid that he pleaded guilty for another man's crime."

"So why didn't he just tell the cops the truth?"

"I guess he just feared for his life. He must have figured that he was safer in prison than being out on the streets. Fear sometimes does that to a person. That's why the word fear does not exist in my dictionary. For such a small word the meaning of it can last a lifetime. It makes people tremble never looking forward to tomorrow. They start drinking and sticking needles in their arms trying to forget about today. When the shit wears off the fear reenters their body and it can linger on forever. That's why you always have to face your fears. Or else you will be looking over your shoulder for the rest of your life. If you have to live your life in fear, you are better off dead."

Vito's aggravation was apparent. If he was trying to paint an ugly picture of Bootsy, and fear, his talk worked. Joey was starting to feel Vito's anger, but his fears still lingered aimlessly over his tired body. At times Joey wondered if he was being sent out to settle a personal vendetta between Vito and Bootsy.

He then figured he would do it for Vito as well as to rid the fears that have possessed him. Joey now knew that this problem with Bootsy would never go away unless it is confronted and severely dealt with.

"Vito, I am ready to face my problem," Joey said.

"That's wrong, kid," he snapped back. "You should have said you're ready to face our problem."

"I won't let you down."

"I know, son, if I wasn't getting out of here in a couple of months I would have taken him out myself. I know you won't let me down. Make me proud."

Vito knew that time was not on his side with this up and coming encounter. His godson's reputation and respect had to be protected before he was released from prison. No matter what it might take, he felt he had to install the confidence in him to get the job done. If his plan faltered, then it would be time for much more extreme measures.

"Vito, what kind of world do we live in?" Joey said, wondering what life was all about. "Why did it have to come down to this?"

"Because it's a fucked up world that is reduced to the confines of this concrete jungle. If you survive in here, then you must face all the assholes that await you on the outside. There is no escaping from it, but in your case I know you have what it takes to make it. The next time we meet up let's hope it's under better circumstances," he said while putting his left arm around Joey's shoulder.

"Yea let's hope so," Joey said with a smile. "Let's hope so."

"How do you feel physically?"

"I feel fine," lied Joey. "I'm ready to go," he bravely said. What he failed to tell Vito was that he still felt soreness around the face and on the left side of his ribcage. His bruises were easily perceived, even underneath his white tee shirt. But it didn't seem too matter much, as all the upcoming drama seemed to override the pain. It was time to put this baby to rest. "All of my pain is gone," he said in vain. "All my pain is gone."

"So tomorrow when we are in the yard, you follow my lead. Look at me," he sternly said as he grabbed Joey's face and turned it towards his. "When I tell you to go, you go. Don't look around and don't say anything. Just start walking towards him. Block out everything that is on your mind and take care of business. All the days and nights of worrying will be over within a minute or two," declared Vito. "Once you get started with this, don't ever look back."

"What should I say to him?"

"Anything, tell him his mother sucks horse cock. I don't know, just get him mad and challenge his manhood. Joey, just believe me, he will bite. That fat prick bites everything else. There's no reason why he wouldn't want to take a bite out of you."

"Alright."

"When you get him down, don't kill him. You have to know when enough is enough. If he is comatose and you're still banging away, ad-lib a little bit. Don't ever show any sympathy and never let your emotions get the best of you. In this place if you show any signs of remorse or sympathy, you're as good as dead. Remember, you are doing this in front of everyone, so do not kill him. Do you understand me? Do not kill him!"

"Yea."

"Do you understand me," he then repeated in a clear cut no nonsense voice. "Repeat it to me that you understand!"

"Yes, Vito, I understand you," Joey said.

"Good, and don't give me none of these yea answers. It makes you sound like the rest of these illiterates in this joint."

With each drink that was absorbed, the contagious terror that captured Joey's emotional nature seemed restrained. Alcohol has a way of deflating any major issues. It's when you wake up the next morning that you find out that nothing has really changed.

The distance was growing shorter with each passing second leading up to the main event. Vito understood the consequences of hurting Bootsy anymore than what the plan called for. Eighteen months could turn into eighteen years with the strike of one final devastating blow. A long stay in a hospital bed was the intention, not a pine box in a cemetery.

"Let's have one for the road!" suggested Joey.

"Before we do that there's just one other thing."

"What's that?"

"When the prison guards step in to break up the fight, don't resist. Just step back peacefully and do not show them up," Vito warned. "Remember, timing is everything, so always try to time your next move. Don't stop beating him until the guards break it up. If you show any compassion for that nigger, it will be all for naught."

"Vito, I now know what life would be like in here without you. I'd rather live a life in hell than to be stalked by that animal. I promise you that

I will take care of business," he vowed. "I will not embarrass you by letting you down."

"I know you will not let me down. Joey, no matter what happens; you will never be an embarrassment to me. But remember, your life for his is not an even swap. And do not ever make it an option. So you must do it my way."

"Are you ready for that drink?" asked Joey, holding his cup out.

"Pour away my good son."

"Too us," Joey toasted as both men stood up and raised their glasses. There was no hesitation at all; the flaming homemade remedy was going down much more smoothly.

"You know, I think you can kick his ass without spiking his food with drugs," Vito said. "Am I right or wrong?"

"You're wrong," said Joey. "So don't even think about it. I need all the fuckin drugs I can get. But I'm ready now."

"Remember, don't kill him," he said with his last warning. "Just bring him down to his fuckin knees and then put him on his back."

The two embraced with confidence written all over their faces. Vito had the confidence of a battle-tested gangster. Joey's confidence was coming from the homemade booze that he guzzled down his throat. For a good 30 seconds, they hugged and pounded each other's backs with their clenched fists. For Vito, his mission was accomplished, his degradation of the enemy worked to perfection. For Joey, he was going deep-sea fishing. He had to reel in and filet a 325-pound whale.

Chapter 7

THE NEXT DAY started out no different than any other day. In prison a Monday is just the same as a Friday. All the inmates just tended to their usual work detail, while nothing changes. The only things that change are the X's that mark off the days on the calendar wall. To some lonely inmates counting down the days to freedom is their only feeling of pleasure. Another day gone by is another day of survival.

Autumn weather had settled upon the northeast part of the country. The blaze of color in the foliage enhanced the view. Cool brisk winds scattered about the falling leaves along the wide countryside. Inmates were forced into their very limited wardrobes for their fall attire.

"What's the odds?" asked Dutch, as he took a seat in the prison library. Vito kept making these sniffing noises with his nose. He kept looking around from his seat until he found the smell that was bothering him.

"Must you bring that fuckin filthy basket in here, it stinks like shit."

"What do you want me to do with it," asked Dutch referring to the laundry basket filled with dirty sheets and towels from the infirmary.

"Roll it over there before that stench seeps into our clothes," ordered Vito in a stern voice. "You never know what the fuck might pop out of that basket."

"Come on Vito, its only dirty laundry."

"If it's only dirty laundry, why are you wearing those rubber gloves?"

"Now that's a good point!"

"So get it out of here before something creeps into our pores. That's all I need is a venereal disease."

"That might be a good thing."

"Why?"

"People will use your name in the same sentence as Al Capone. He died of syphilis didn't he?"

"Yea, I think he did," Vito answered. "But he got it from banging women, not from a fuckin laundry basket." With a look on his face like he just stepped in shit, Vito motioned to Dutch to remove the foul smell. "Never mind Al Capone, just get rid of that fuckin thing. It's making me puke."

From a sitting position and using his feet, Dutch pushed the hamper on wheels about seven feet away from the table. The stale damp smell still lingered around the large table for a couple of more seconds.

"Let's make Bootsy a 3 to 1 favorite," Vito said looking across the table. "I think that should do it."

"Don't you think that Bootsy should be a heavier favorite?"

"Probably, Joey should at least be a 7 to 1 dog or more."

"So?"

"So what?" Vito said. "This way, we'll see more money, and don't forget we're not telling too many people. With these odds they will all take Bootsy hands down. Our take won't be as much, but it will be guaranteed."

"What kind of guarantee can you give when you send a young calf to the slaughterhouse?"

"It's not like that, and I don't want to hear about it anymore!" Vito sternly said while rubbing his fingers through his now disheveled hair. "I know what I'm doin."

"How many bets do you want me to take?"

"Just take action on 20," he said. "No lower than a hundred, no higher than five. Make sure you get all the money up front. We don't want to be chasing these assholes all over the cell block for our cash. Dutch, this is a cash on cash bet. No money, no bet."

"I'll get started on it right away," Dutch said. "I just hope you know what you're doin."

"Make sure everybody keeps quiet or nothing will go down," ordered Vito. "Be sure to keep this a secret from Joey. That's all the kid has to find out is that we're taking bets with his ass on the line."

"Don't worry, I will make sure everyone has a tight lip on this one."

"Go to those two schmucks in the infirmary, they're always good for something big. Oh, there is one other thing, put Nat down for five hundred on Joey."

Dutch looked at Vito as if he was nuts. "Nat that works in the kitchen?"

"That's the one."

"Does he have the money?"

"Yea, he has the money."

"Where the hell is he gettin the money from?"

"I'm fronting the money for him."

"I wish I knew what the fuck is going on here," asked a very confused Dutch. "You got me all fucked up on this one."

"Let's just say I owe him a favor."

"So Nat's the only one that's gonna win money?"

"You got that right," assured Vito. "He's the only one! You might get a few bets on the kid here and there. I don't expect much money to be dropped on Joey. If there is, just take a little more action, that's all. You have to be a complete moron to bet with Joey in this fight."

"If the kid loses, we are going to lose a small fortune."

"You're right, if he loses we will lose a lot of money. But you're forgetting one thing," he said.

"What's that?" asked Dutch.

"He ain't gonna lose."

"Again, I hope you know what the fuck you're doin."

"Just leave it all in my hands. I know what I'm doin."

From prison doctors to prison guards, all the thrill seekers are easily exposed. The addiction called gambling lured them to place a bet on this lopsided fight. The odds made the bet that much more irresistible for them to bet their hard earned money on. Only the professional employed dwellers of this institution had the money that was any good to Vito. Vito was only interested in dipping his long greedy fingers into the working man's wallet.

Prisoners would only want to nickel and dime the action to death. That would cause too much confusion and wasted time for the prison bookmakers, especially when it was time to pay the piper. When making a wager, most inmates did not have the money to put up front anyway. If an inmate couldn't pay his debt, then it would be taken from him in favors. Vito's little black book was already filled up with enough favors to last him a lifetime. So favors were strictly off limits on this one, it was cash or nothing.

"Vito are you sure about this?" asked Dutch. "I mean Bootsy is a pretty tough guy, you seen him rumble. You know he ain't no pushover."

Dutch looked worried about the upcoming event. He was never the one to question Vito's business tactics, but this one made him feel very uneasy. The thought of Vito sending his godson to do battle with King Kong did not sit right with him. After all, Dutch was growing a strong fondness to Joey also. With all feelings aside, he had every right to worry. He was totally unaware of the one reason why this bout was taking place anyway. Dutch knew nothing about the powerful sedatives that were going to be placed into Bootsy's food. Speaking for the whole crew, they all thought it was a lose and lose again situation. But in the back of his mind he knew that Vito was hiding something from him.

"Not only am I worried about the spread, I'm also worried about Joey. We might be asking too much of him. Vito, I think he's in way over his head. This guy will murder him," warned Dutch, raising his voice a bit. "You have to know this!"

"Dutch, please, he ain't murdering anybody. Please trust me," he pleaded quietly. "I have everything under control,"

"If it's about respect, there are other ways that we can go about this."

"It's about more than respect. The kid has to be able to fend for himself when we are not around anymore."

"When you get released I'll still be here to watch over him," offered Dutch. "Joey will get out of here a couple of months before me. So there's no need to worry about him."

"I know, Dutch, but he has to face up to his problems and become a man. I do not want to make the same mistakes twice. I made them with Eddie. I'm not going to make them with Joey."

"But with Eddie it was a totally different situation."

"Eddie is my son and he always leaned on me to bail him out of whatever crap he got himself into. He never learned how to fend for himself. Take a look at him now. He's a fuckin crack head who steals loose change from the bottom of his mother's pocketbook. I have not seen him in over six years," Vito confided. "To make this little story perfect, he'll be the next one to walk through those prison doors."

"That would be a trip," Dutch joked. "Then we can all be one big happy family."

"Dutch, stop fuckin around. All I'm saying is that there comes a time in a man's life when he has to start growing up. For Joey the time is now. What happened to Eddie is not going to happen to Joey. Please, Dutch, as a man who failed at being a father, please trust me on this one. I do not want to make the same mistakes twice. This kid is the son of one of the best guys that I have ever met in my life. May his soul rest in peace," Vito continued on while making the sign of the cross. "I feel like I am taking on his responsibility as a parent. That's the least I can do for him. But you know as well as I do, that once I leave here it's all over. I do not want him to be a part of my corrupt lifestyle."

"So what are you going to do, give him temporary love," asked Dutch.

"That would be the best kind of love for the both of us."

"You know it is possible to keep business and your personal life apart from each other," said Dutch.

"Come on, Dutch, give me a fuckin break. We have both killed and we probably will kill again. Revenge these days has a funny way of finding loved ones to settle personal vendettas. Things are not like they used to be out there."

"How so?"

"Because these new groups of wannabe gangsters have no respect for the old traditional values. They would stick a knife in their own mother's back if it benefited them. I don't want anybody to get killed as a pay-back for something that I did."

"There, I agree with you."

"Every time I look at what's left of my finger, I consider myself very lucky. The only thing that bothers me was that they had to do the same thing to my son Eddie. I was responsible for his actions because I was his father. I didn't do a good job raising him, Dutch. They should have just held me accountable for his actions."

"I should have gotten there sooner. When I told you that your kid was in trouble, you were supposed to get back to me. I would have walked you in the bar and maybe none of this shit would've happened," Dutch said. "But before I found out, it was already too late."

"At the time I felt it was something that I had to take care of myself. I thank God you came in when you did. They probably would have killed the both of us. Instead of our fingers," Vito then held up his amputated left index finger as both men looked at it. "They probably would have taken our fuckin heads off."

"The boys up in Hell's Kitchen have no conscience and neither do I. Everything they do when it comes to their brand of justice is unethical, you know that. You came to them in good faith, but to them that wasn't enough. If they had to come lookin for you, you and your son would surely be dead."

"Dutch, you know I could have gone to my people for help. But I didn't want to start a war with you and your boys. I'm so humiliated by Eddie's actions that I felt that I had to go at it alone. He's a disgrace to me."

"But look at the brighter side of all this," said Dutch.

"What brighter side?"

"At least they didn't cut off your trigger finger. If they did you would be useless to everybody," he said laughing. "You wouldn't even be able to wipe your own fuckin' ass."

"That's what I love about you, Dutch, you don't take a thing on this Earth seriously. Nothing seems to bother you," Vito said. He then paused a few seconds as he was writing down some notes. "But I remember that night like it was yesterday. Nothing felt right. I smelled trouble as soon as we walked through that front door. You had to see the fear in Eddie's eyes. He looked like he just saw the devil himself," he said while thinking back to the point of almost no return.

It was a cold dark winter night that smelled like snow. The freezing winds from the Adirondacks were whipping up fiercely. The blistering conditions were gustily blowing from the traffic free waterways of the Hudson Bay. Up and down the West Side Highway venders scurried to retrieve and salvage their offerings from the brisk choppy winds. The smell of pine was evident with each fresh cut tree that lined the desolate streets. These seasonal conditions forced most Christmas shoppers into the warmth of their humble abodes. Unbearable sub zero temperatures and the threat of frostbite were too much for most city dwellers to endure. The holiday spirit that the outdoors can bring would have to be saved for another day.

The Black Dove was a small dimly lit tavern up on the West Side of Manhattan. The seedy looking watering hole was the meeting place for a gang of unruly and ruthless roughnecks called the "Westies." This place was not on the city's list of the top ten tourist sites in New York. Even the locals would walk out of their way to avoid this very dangerous hangout. The rundown tenement that was the landlord to the infamous pub was all but vacant, with only a second floor apartment occupied, by an aging and sick sentinel.

This retiree's eighty-year old eyes watched all the activity on the streets below from his dirty bedroom window. Living on a fixed income and rotting away from terminal bone cancer, his time was limited. He was the last survivor in a building that holds six apartments. Every other tenant relocated as soon as they heard the screams of the first victim. Even the landlord vacated the premises in fear for his life.

Tommy Whiskers ran the show for this powerful Irish organization. His strength spanned throughout the metropolitan area. Everyone knew how ruthless he really was, everyone but Eddie Carlucci. They say that Tommy Whiskers cut up more body parts than Frank Perdue, the chicken king.

The little dining room in back of the dull cherry wood bar was his home for all business matters. All money laundering ran through the Black Dove and some other enterprises that the gang controlled. Behind the small dining room was a grease pit they called a kitchen. The kitchen held an arsenal of utensils for butchering and dismemberment. Some of the screamers, in order for them not to be heard, were taken to the top floor of the building.

Devoid of any matter, this room acted as a butcher shop for the slowly dying victims. This empty and blood stained apartment left reminders of the gruesome rituals that were performed there. The oversized room had a distasteful smell of foul blood and death. A couple of cheap room deodorizers were overwhelmed by the stench coming from this torture chamber. In the middle of the bizarre room, duct tape and some black plastic bags lay beside a broken down wooden chair. Like a check out counter at some supermarket, the body parts were quickly bagged and ready for disposal. Whatever morsels of human flesh that were left behind, packs of hungry rats quickly devoured them when the lights went out. For the victim who could take his punishment like a man, climbing the steps to the top floor was not necessary.

This was the macabre setting for Vito and his young son Eddie. They came to settle a score for the proceeds from illegal drugs. Eddie happened to be Johnny on the spot to a car that was left unattended with the engine running. The quick and mischievous Eddie decided to perform grand theft auto and go for a long joy ride. Little did he know that the car and its contents belonged to Donny Morrison. It didn't take Eddie to long to find the 10 grand buried inside the glove compartment of the 1980 Impala. The money was from drug sales. But to Eddie it didn't matter, as he then made one of the biggest mistakes of his young wasted life. Donny Morrison just happened to be one of Tommy Whiskers' right hand men.

A day later, Eddie got bagged by Donny's friends copping dope off of a drug dealer. The asshole was still driving around in Donny's car. Luckily, after he was spotted, Eddie somehow managed to get away on foot. If not for his quick feet, he would have surely lost both of his legs.

Eddie was a regular drug buyer at this West Side location. He was well known by all the dealers and junkies who ran these streets. Donny was the protection and the pipeline for these same street corner dealers. The money just happened to come from the same location Eddie was copping his high from. Going through withdrawals and bugging out, Eddie was not too particular where his next fix was coming from. Finding ten grand was like hitting the lottery for a drug addict who carries his bankbook in his not too deep pockets. With a "live for today" attitude, the consequences of what tomorrow brings was the furthest thing from his drug polluted mind.

Word soon got out that the Westies were looking for Eddie. Roaming the streets in fear for his life, he then turned to his father to bail him out once again. The ten thousand dollars was well spent by Eddie and his dependent drug habit. The price for revenge was two left index fingers at five thousand dollars apiece. This was the only belated birthmark that links the two as father and son.

Vito looked thoughtful. "Believe it or not, to this day that stupid kid still blames me for not bailing him out of that situation. I mean, he lost a finger, but he's still alive!"

"How could he blame you for that?" asked Dutch, shaking his head.

"Because he's a moron! He doesn't realize that if it weren't for you and me he would be dead right now. It's in the breeding, Dutch. I should have never banged that spic bitch. One night of drunken passion is making me pay for the rest of my life. The only thing that Puerto Ricans and Italians do well together is making beautiful babies."

"You can't blame that."

"Yes I could and I'll prove it to you," Vito said. "Linda had two more kids with some Puerto Rican guy and both of them went to college. To this day, they are both professionals with good jobs. Look what I got stuck with, a junkie who roams the streets to nowhere. He's a crack head who hates his own father because I won't support his drug habits. I tell you, Dutch, I think it's in the blood. When the blood is not pure, I think it taints the mind with madness. That's why it's so important to stay with and marry your own kind. Because at the end it's the kids who suffer. And through their suffering the parents are the ones who pay the ultimate price," Vito said with a voice that was filled with heartbreak. "Do you understand what I'm saying to you?"

"I do, Vito," he said. "Is he living with his mother now?"

"His mother moved out to Long Island years ago when she first got married. She has a whole new life out there and she seems happy. Eddie visits her once in a while and she gives him some money just to get rid of him. Her husband doesn't want him anywhere near the house. A junkie in heat is never welcome for a Thanksgiving dinner. So basically he has a mother who disowned him and a father he can't stand. Dutch, I am embarrassed to say it, but I gave up on him many years ago. He is just no damned good. The next time I see him will probably be at the morgue." Vito then buried his head into the palm of his hands. Dutch just sat in silence as his childhood friend percolated in his own pain.

"I'm sorry, Vito, I knew the boy made a few mistakes but I didn't think that it was that bad," Dutch said.

"You see this!" Vito said, while picking up a round medallion that lay upon the top of his chest. The eighteen-karat gold decorative tablet was approximately one inch in circumference. The Head of Jesus Christ adorned the heavy gold piece that was hanging from a thick link chain.

"Yea, I always noticed that hanging around your neck."

"Anyway this is the only thing I have left that attaches me to my old man and the rest of my relatives. It's been in my family for more than three-quarters of a century. My Great Grandfather Alfonso found it on a rescue mission during an earthquake.

"That's unbelievable," Dutch said. "It is very special."

"I know," answered a proud Vito. "Before we came to this country, my Father and I went to the Citta Del Vaticano in Rome and had this blessed by the Pope. Since that day, my father always knew that this medallion was very special. I think he even knew before then, but he never told me anything until many years later. So anyway, he whispered a few words into my ear and slipped it around my neck. I'll never forget the chills that ran up and down my spine when he put this medallion on me."

"Why did you get that feeling?"

"I don't know, but it was like the thing was alive. This medallion didn't want to be around my neck! It was like it knew what type of person I was going to become. When I put it around Eddie's neck for the first time, he complained of the same symptoms."

"That's nonsense!"

"To you it might be, but to me, I just sensed a rebellion coming from it. It was defying my body and my body knew it. I was only eight years old at the time, but I knew that this medallion did not belong around my neck. And it still don't. A couple of months later my father moved the whole family to America. Over the years, many strange things have happened to me. I have weird dreams and in them I see things that I just can't explain. Biblical things. Now I know that this medallion is responsible for all of it."

"This all sounds crazy," Dutch responded. "What did he whisper in your ear?"

"He said, this medallion is special so make me proud, son, and never disgrace me. Many days have gone by where I feel that I am not honorable enough to wear this medal. Maybe that's why I got those strange feelings when he put it on me. This piece means more to me than life itself. When Eddie became eight years old, I gave the medallion to him and whispered those same words. Well, the rest of the story is ancient history."

"Well, what happened?"

"Years later the son of a bitch hocked it at some pawn shop in the Bowery. He sold it for a hundred bucks so he can get high. You don't want to know what I had to go through to get it back. In time, I knew I would have ripped the thing off his neck anyway. Me and Eddie have both disgraced our families in different ways, but I always loved and respected my father. This piece of shit couldn't care less if I lived or died. He gave away the two things that meant the most to me, his love and this medallion. My poor mother and father must be turning over in their graves."

"Okay, pal, I'm starting to see the whole picture. I think I understand now," said Dutch as he threw one of the library books into a pushcart piled with books. "Maybe, just maybe, one day he will turn around for the better."

"I doubt it, Dutch, his fate is all set in stone," lamented Vito. "Dutch, I know you have a problem dealing with this fight, but there's one thing that I failed to tell you."

At that moment footsteps and the sound of keys hanging from a belt buckle came from the outside hallway. A prison guard doing his rounds was about to peek his head in for one of his daily checkups.

"Does the infirmary miss you?" asked Vito.

"Nah, they don't even know that I'm gone," answered Dutch. "I just have to go to the laundry room and drop that shit off and pick up some clean linen and towels," he said as he pointed to the basket with the ill-fated aromas.

"Good, go hide behind the bookcase before this prick sticks his head in."

"Fuck him."

"Come on, Dutch, they'll think we're scheming or plotting something."

"But we are!"

"Yea, but this jerk-off don't have to know that. Hurry up, he's coming, and take that basket of cheer with you."

Dutch gingerly walked over to retrieve the canvas container and slipped behind one of the seven foot high shields to avoid the confrontation. Vito started to tend to his daily work routine as if nothing was going on. During working hours prisoners were not allowed anywhere away from their work detail and its related work site. Sometimes, a day in the box was the severe penalty a wandering inmate would have to pay for being absent minded.

"Is everything alright in here?" the burly officer asked, while scanning the room.

"Yea, I got two naked broads hanging out in the back. You care to join me?" Vito asked. Vito then started to push the cart that was loaded to the top with books. "You look like you could use some head?"

"Shut the fuck up, Carlucci, and put your books away," he ordered.

"Yes, sir, but if you change your mind you know where to find us."

"You're an asshole," he said as he turned around and started to walk the remainder of his beat. Vito took a peek outside the doorway to make sure that the coast was clear.

"Dutch, you can come out now, he left." Dutch reappeared and Vito continued on with his confessions. "Now, before that asshole interrupted us I was about to tell you something."

"What is it?" asked Dutch.

"I know how much you have grown to like Joey."

"Vito, he's a good kid and he is one of us," he compassionately said. "I just can't see why you would throw him to the wolves like this. Like I said before there are other ways to take care of this problem."

"I know there are, but," Vito said before he was interrupted.

"Why don't you let me take care of this, I will chop that nigger up into a million pieces. I know there are issues with respect and the kid should always have to fend for himself, but this is different. I don't think you should consider this a situation where you would be bailing him out. This is a thoroughly new world for him. Out on the streets I know he would be just fine, but in here it's a totally different story. I know this problem has to be confronted with, but I think that we should handle it."

"Dutch, when the fight goes down we will be there for him in case anything goes wrong. But there is one little intangible that you are unaware of. You know that little bag of miracles that I have hidden inside my cell?"

"What the booze?" asked Dutch.

"No, the pills that I have in that little plastic bag."

"What about them?"

"Well guess what Bootsy is getting in his dinner tonight?"

"You son of a bitch you," said a smiling Dutch. "You motherfucker, I knew you were up to something. I knew you had something up your fuckin' sleeve."

"Did you really think that I would throw my godson into the fire like that? There is still some risk, but I think we will be alright."

"Is the kid ready?"

"He is as ready as he will ever be. I got him primed real good."

"At least I feel a little better now, now it's seems like it's almost a fair fight."

In Dutch's mind the narcotics would equalize the severe weight advantage that Bootsy had on their boy. In his eyes this was the handicap that he was looking for. These pills acted like the neutralizer and compensation that was given to Joey in order to counterbalance his chances of winning. Now everything seemed to fit into place, the fight, the bets and the odds. They were all looking like a very winnable speculation to Dutch.

"Now I know how Nat fits into all of this," said Dutch.

"Nat's the man who is going to sprinkle the magic into his food. About a half hour later its lights out for that big fat fuck," vowed Vito. "You're gonna love this one, Dutch. I can promise you that!"

"Why didn't you tell me about this plan sooner?"

"I was gonna, but I figured the less people that knew about it the better. But now the time has come and I did not want to hold it from you any longer. Whatever you do, do not tell Paulie about the drugs. Once that clown gets on his loud speaker, the whole fuckin place will know about it."

"What about Red?" asked Dutch.

"You can tell Red; that guy doesn't say much about anything."

"Alright Vito, let me get going. I have a very busy day ahead of me. After I'mfinished in the laundry room, I'll go back to the infirmary and start taking the action on the fight."

Dutch stood up off of his chair and walked behind the bookcase to fetch his work detail. He then was about to start his short journey to the laundry room.

"Dutch, did you ever think that I was going out of my mind?"

Dutch then stopped pushing his laundry cart and turned around to look at his partner in crime. "No I never did, I just thought that you were in the early stages of some mental disorder. I think it's called Alzheimer's disease."

"Get out of here," said a smiling Vito as he picked up a paperback book and threw it at him. The book missed Dutch and bounced off of the wall adjacent to the exit door. As Dutch left the room, Vito walked over to pick up the small text from the floor below his knees. To his surprise the title that was printed on the cover was called, "One Flew Over the Cuckoo's Nest."

"Son of a bitch," he said to himself while walking back to continue his chores for the day. "What a crazy and fucked up life this is."

Chapter 8

THE CHOW HALL was still empty as Nat Johnson was putting the finishing touches on his famous cream of mushroom soup. In a small soup bowl he then emptied the contents of the sedative medicine from the little glass vial. While always looking around for suspicious eyes, Nat placed it under a long metal preparation table for safekeeping. Soon the food lines would be forming in front of the steam table that kept all his delicacies piping hot. The hot water was now exposed to steam as the small clouds of vapor were slowly rising in a circular motion. The glass partition and countertop that separated the food selections from the diners was covered with the light mist emitting from the scalding water. The prepared food was placed into the metal serving trays that floated on top of the electrically heated steam table.

Vito and the rest of his crew arrived at the dining hall before most of the other prisoners. The only person missing was their star performer. It was customary for a combatant to say his prayers or to do some last minute loosening up before a major fight. To some others, it was a way of delaying their moment of truth. When fear sets in, the sound of the ringing bell that signals round one alarms the awareness and the expectation of danger. Only Joey knew what was going on in his own mind. For he was the one to be showcased before the whole population of this madhouse they called a prison.

A loud verbal exchange erupted behind the table of seated gangsters. Bootsy and his conglomerate of thugs had just come into the eatery. They entered in the only fashion that was known to the rest of the prison inhabitants, uncivilized. This gang of unruly guests unraveled all of the elements of mystery. When they were about to embark upon a room, you knew they were coming minutes before they had actually arrived. Their mannerisms were appalling; each one of them had no regard or respect for their fellow inmate. When it came to standing on line to satisfy their appetites, there was no line. To them, there were no chow hall rules. Whoever was standing in front of them was quickly cast aside so these animals could have first digs on whatever garbage was on the menu. This pack of a half a dozen jungle dwellers ruthlessly ruled with their fierce intimidation. These badlands, with its dense population were a haven for them and a struggle for survival to others. A rendezvous with this pack of wild predators was like dangling a piece of raw meat in front of a hungry lion. In their minds and in the minds of many others, they were the kings of this savage jungle. As far as Bootsy and his crew were concerned, there was only one obstacle standing in their way. He was an Italian who ran by the name of Vito Carlucci.

The Italians watched as the six hovered around the food line in search of their dinner. The chow hall started to assume its natural ambiance of classless convicts. Masses of bodies started to fill the room to capacity. Vito carefully surveyed the activities surrounding Nat as he kept spooning the slop into different serving trays. Suddenly Nat disappeared under the counter to retrieve a stack of soup bowls.

"I got fresh cream of mushroom soup today," he said to the waiting recipients. Bootsy just nodded with approval as the thick soup was poured into his tainted bowl. The cloudy glass obstructed his vision from the small white bowl that blended in nicely with the powdery substance.

"Sounds good, old man," Bootsy said. "Hook me up."

"I put some extra mushrooms in yours, Bootsy, cause I know that's the way you like it. Here you go, nice and hot," Nat said as he blended the brown vegetable thoroughly with the creamy mixture. "Be careful now!"

"It better be good or else you'll be wearing it," he warned. "You wouldn't want another bath with this shit would ya?"

After his threatening words, Bootsy blew the Southern gentleman a kiss with his thick oversized pink lips. His serving tray was now full of essential vitamins and nutrients that a growing boy needs...plus a little bit more.

"It better be good," he said again to Nat. He then turned around to start his walk over to the usual dining spot. "That motherfucker knows better," Bootsy said to his buddies.

"Oh, it is good, my brother," Nat shouted. "You will notice the difference right away. You will feel like you died and went to heaven."

Bootsy just shrugged and rumbled down the passageway that was lined by the row of tables. With each step his big brown eyes canvassed the large room filled with onlookers. It was not uncharacteristic for him to tip a tray onto someone's unwelcome lap as he walked by. When this fat piranha strolled by, nobody's dinner plate was safe. If he were excessively hungry, he'd quickly snatch up whatever looked appetizing to him in his giant sized paws. Within seconds, the food was plucked off of someone's dish and then engulfed into his waiting tunnel of love. Bootsy felt that he had a free reign to everything and everybody around him.

Off to the other side of the room Vito looked in the direction of Nat. Nat nonchalantly gave Vito a quick nod signifying that his mission was accomplished. So now the table dressing had been set. It was now up to the wonder of medicine and its quick acting ingredients. It was also up to the patient who seemed to have no problems consuming his dinner with its dose of stupefying drugs.

"Where the hell is Joey?" Vito angrily asked, waiting impatiently for Joey to arrive. "I hope he's not having second thoughts about all of this."

"I caught up with him about an hour ago heading for his cell," said Red.

"Go get him," Vito said while rubbing his eyes. "Jesus Christ, I hope he's not turning chicken shit on me."

"Calm down, Vito, I'm sure he'll be here," said Dutch. "He's probably preparing himself for battle."

"Holy shit, what the fuck is that?" said an astonished Paulie. "Look!"

Paulie and Red stared in disbelief as Vito and Dutch turned around to look at the sudden surprise.

"What the hell did you do to yourself?" Vito said in a very disturbed manner. "Look at your fuckin' head!"

"I shaved my head a little, why?"

"You look like a fucking skinhead, that's why. You look like you belong to the Aryan Nation. Look at them over there," Vito pointed to the group of white roughnecks. "They're even looking at you. And what's that shiny shit all over your head and arms?"

"Grease," said Joey. "I greased up a little so Bootsy would have a hard time grabbing a hold of me."

"Hey, Vito, he looks like a fuckin' cue ball," said Paulie in an uncontrollable laugh. "Red, rack em up, I feel like shootin' a game of pool."

"Paulie, leave the kid alone," chided Dutch. "He's doing what he feels he has to do."

"Hey, Red, eight ball in the corner pocket," Paulie teased again.

"Yea, Paulie, shut the fuck up," Joey shot back. "You should be the last one to talk about looks. You look like the last shit I took."

"Will everybody just shut the fuck up. I had enough of this cue ball shit already," said Vito. "You guys are drawing too much attention over here!"

"How you doing, slugger?" asked Dutch.

"I feel good, but I'm starving. I got to get something to eat," Joey said.

"No, you're not getting anything to eat," ordered Vito. "The food will only slow you down. You have to stay light and limber. Come over here and sit down."

"But I'm hungry."

"Never mind the food. Just get over here!"

Joey took a seat next to his school-yard trainer. Vito quickly took his hand and started to message the top of Joey's back. The clock was ticking down with each spoonful of soup that was shoveled into Bootsy's mouth. Vito only had a few moments for some last minute instructions.

"Your best attribute in this fight is going to be speed," Vito said. "Always keep your jab active to keep him away. If he grabs you, all that jelly all over your fuckin body won't mean a damn thing. Just keep sticking and moving, sticking and moving. Wait for an opening and then give it to him with everything you got. The drugs are going to help you out a lot, but in reality it's all about you. Just stay focused and get the fuckin job done."

"What drugs?" asked Paulie.

"Joey," whispered Vito. "Are you ready?"

"I've never been so ready for anything in my life," lied Joey. Underneath the tough talking bravado, fear clawed at his belly like a bear trap. But he could not let anybody else know that. "I'm going to fuck him up good, Vito."

"What drugs?" Paulie annoyingly repeated, this time looking at everyone for an answer. "Will somebody answer me!"

"Red, take Paulie into the yard and explain to him what's going on. The rest of us will be out in about ten minutes," the boss said.

"Paulie, let's go," Red said as he stood up from the dinner table. "Good luck, kid!"

"Thanks Red," Joey replied.

The two then walked away to take their positions in the prison yard.

"What drugs?" About four or five feet away from the table you could still hear Paulie asking that sacred question.

"Paulie, shut the fuck up," Red said as the two men were leaving the chow hall. "I will tell you when we get outside."

"That guy has to be the stupidest motherfucker that I have ever met. Dutch, we have to find a way to wire up his jaw permanently," Vito said while scratching his head. "One day he's gonna get us all in trouble."

"Yea, but you know you still love him."

"I know, but he just doesn't think before he opens his mouth."

Joey just sat there in silence while his cohorts conversed about Paulie. Every so often he would take a small peek over at his rival to check on his behavioral patterns. So far the tarnished soup did not seem to have any adverse effects on his physical condition. After all, this was a big man with the propensity to digest anything at an alarmingly slow rate. He possessed these essential characteristics at birth. His whole family shared the genetic trait of obesity.

"Vito, are these drugs that you gave Bootsy generic?" asked Joey.

"What do you mean generic?"

"Who's the manufacturer?"

"What the fuck do I know," barked Vito. "What's with this generic crap?"

"It means that when a specific product has its patent expire, another company can reproduce a similar product by using just about the same ingredients. These reproduced products are not protected by any trademarks or trade names," Joey continued to explain. "Therefore they are called generic products. They are facsimiles of the real thing. Sometimes they are just not as potent as the original manufacturer's product."

"Dutch, do you know what the fuck this kid is talkin' about?" a confused Vito said, shaking his head with bewilderment. "Because I don't."

"I think what he is saying is that he don't think these drugs are strong enough."

"Bingo," Joey said.

"Bingo my fuckin' ass," said a furious Vito. "Would you like to call my pharmacist? All I know is that those pills can bring down a fuckin' blimp.

Forget about this generic shit and all this Wall Street mumble jumble. If it wasn't for Wall Street you wouldn't be here in the first place. Now I am your fuckin' stock analyst and I say that the shit is going to work. So after the drugs kick in you bring that motherfucker down to his knees. You're thinking too much. Like I said before just stay focused on that fat bastard over there," he pointed towards Bootsy. "For the last time, just concentrate and stay focused," Vito demanded. "Are you ready?"

"I'm ready," a contrite Joey said.

"As soon as he gets up to leave, we will follow him out. Make sure you take care of business or I will get a gun and cap that motherfucker myself."

A few more minutes went by before there was any movement at Bootsy's table. Half of his gang had picked themselves up and started to embark toward the prison yard. Slowly but surely, Bootsy removed himself from his seat and started to follow his comrades out the door. Vito watched carefully as the big body was moving in an unstable and staggering slow way. With each step his heavy legs were having a hard time holding up his large torso. Then all of a sudden the inevitable started to happen, his body started to lean to one side like the Leaning Tower of Pisa.

"Look, look, I told you this stuff was gonna work," Vito said while jabbing his elbow lightly into Joey's ribs. "Don't ever doubt me or my know how ever again! What did you think, that this was the first time I ever used this shit? I know how much to apply and how long it takes to work. My pharmacist taught me everything and my pharmacist knows for sure," he said with a smile.

At that moment Vito felt like a little kid who was left loose in a candy store. His emotions were running amok with enthusiasm. Part "A" of his ingenious plan seemed to work to pure perfection. It was time to spring plan B into full gear. From about twenty feet behind the now guinea pig, the trio followed their mark out of the chow hall.

The walk down the long corridor to the prison yard was flooded with anticipation. Joey's walking steps were forestalled with his precautionary thinking. Vito stood by his side to move him along as he kept whispering words of encouragement into his ear. No matter how hard Vito tried to instill the warrior mentality into his pupil, something was missing. He knew the kid was lacking aggression and the killer instinct needed to win this fight. He also knew that Joey was at his best when he was cornered and had to fight for his life. Asking him to be the aggressor with the spotlight on him was against his nature. But it was too late to turn back.

"Vito, I'm going to go through with this, but I'm shitting in my pants."

"Listen," he said while the two came to a halt. "Whatever happens out there, I will be there for you. When it is going down you might feel all alone and thirty seconds might seem like an eternity. But I will be right behind you in case things don't go according to plan. You can do this if you stay strong and focused, I know you can. If you feel that things are out of control, give me a nod and I'll step in. Listen, in the short time that we know each other, I feel like I know you forever. You're like a son to me and I love you."

"I know, Vito, I know."

"There's just one other thing I forgot to tell you."

"What's that?"

"When you're baiting him into the fight, make sure you lure him into the center of the yard."

"What's the difference where it happens? Now you're being particular on where I get my ass kicked! You're unbelievable!"

"There's a big difference," said Vito. "I want everybody to know who the fuck you are. And your position makes it a lot easier for me and the boys to keep an eye on you."

There was one thing that Vito failed to tell his fighter. He didn't tell him that all his betting clientele had to get a full view from any window they were watching the fight from. To Vito every window had to be a ringside seat. He didn't want to disappoint his betting customers.

"No problem, the middle of the yard is where it will be," a not too confident Joey said. "Is there anything else?" he sarcastically said, knowing that Vito was asking for a lot.

"No, from here on in, you're on your own."

Joey looked down at the medallion dangling around Vito's neck. He stood mesmerized as the medallion reflected its image out of his gaping eyes. Still frozen, Joey felt traumatized by this sudden connection. Now shaking his head back and forth while flapping his eyelids, Joey was having flashbacks of the image he saw in his bathroom mirror a few months back. In and out, the intermittent bursts were sudden and intense as they shot before his eyes. Trying to shake free from the ambiguous perception, the illusion stayed defiant. Its gripping powers raced through Joey's body. Vito looked on confused.

"Would you snap out of it already," barked Vito. "It's show-time."

"What?"

"What's wrong with you?"

"Huh? No, nothing," Joey responded, waking up from this semi trance. "Let's do it!"

With those parting words they finally stepped out into the chilly yard. The feeling was that of a prizefighter walking down the ramp at Madison Square Garden. Joey walked cautiously as he picked his head up to survey the surroundings. Aside from the inmates, everyone from the medical staff to the administrative crew seemed to be waiting with anticipation. There were people everywhere. Each and every window of the immense building that looked down into the crowded prison yard was filled to capacity with peering eyes. Those eyes appeared to have a craving for violence. Anxiety was floating above the building. For a fight that was supposed to be kept quiet from most of the inmates, word sure got out in a hurry. Joey's apprehension grew stronger by the minute. But now was not the time to turn back, his not too distant future was calling for him.

Vito took Joey to their usual spot in the prison yard. He looked around for anything abnormal, but saw nothing. They were all just going through their normal routines. Inside the building was another story altogether. The news of the upcoming fight was spreading like wildfire. People were jockeying for position at every available window with a good view. It was only a matter of time before the news would trickle down into the prison yard. Vito knew that Joey had to strike now as the sedatives were about to kick into full gear. He then gave the nod to Dutch to disperse himself within the crowd. Red and Paulie were at their assigned positions, about one hundred feet away from their leader. Everything was in place as Vito turned his attention in Bootsy's direction.

"Look," he said. "He's starting to yawn."

Joey looked in the direction of his mammoth opponent, his lips tight, his eyes darting. The fat man was showing sure signs of grogginess. His huge hands were constantly rubbing his eyes as he struggled to stay awake. The move had to be made before he dozed off into dreamland.

The wind started to kick up and loose debris flew in every direction. The sun was setting earlier as daylight savings time was about to arrive. Darkness was approaching with each ticking second. It was a typical autumn evening and the temperatures were stabilizing in the upper fifties.

The war drums were starting to beat without a smoke signal in sight. For the novice, Joey, it was time to take his final vows and gain the respect that Vito thought that he needed.

"Okay, the time is now, go," ordered Vito.

"Now?" a hesitant Joey asked.

"No, next fuckin' Christmas. Now, go, go, go, go," Vito ordered. "The time is right, we came this far so don't blow it. Go, God damn it, go!"

"I'm going, I'm going," said a slow moving Joey.

Vito then gave his godson a stern shove in the back. Joey started his short journey over to the man who had the blood of Satan in him. His eyes were fixed in one direction and one direction only. His steps were short with a steady pace as he approached his mission in an unyielding fashion. Suddenly the whole yard seemed frozen while he filtered through the crowd. There was an uncomfortable portent in the air. Most inmates felt it as they watched each other's backs for the purpose of safety. The different groups huddled closer together, showing strength through numbers. It was so quiet that you could hear an unlit match that was being rubbed against its striker.

The horizontal table grew larger as the distance between the two diminished. Sitting there undaunted and unaware of the things to come, Bootsy's interactions were minimal with no engaging conversation. Daryl Baker and Roland Harper sat directly across from the immovable object. These were the two who had administered the beating to Joey in the shower. These two guarded the fortress that led to the gate of jailhouse misconduct and Bootsy. To get to their boss you would have to get through these two physical specimens. Both men and their inflated biceps were heavily into pumping iron. They were no strangers to the weight room.

Jamaal Walker stood as the watchdog at the far end of the table. His bruises were easily recognized with contusions running rampant all over his face. For Jamaal, the sight of Joey approaching the table brought back too many distasteful memories from the shower of pain.

"Hey, look who's comin our way," a statuesque Jamaal said. "Bootsy, he's comin' in your direction!" Jamaal stood staunchly while his warning reached the ears of his cohorts. His companions turned around and looked into the eyes of the emerging Brooklyn brawler.

Bootsy sat there fixated with an unhealthy look on his face. Daryl Baker arose from the bench to confront the oncoming perpetrator. "Well look who it is," said Daryl. "It's Al Capone." The well-built man began to flex his chest muscles with a show of intimidation. His many years of training were apparent as his rock hard foundation was busting out of his tight gray sweatshirt. The man looked like an NFL linebacker.

"I got no problem with you," a shaky Joey said.

"Man, you had a problem with us as soon as you came into this joint."

No sooner than a second later, Roland Harper stood up from his seat to join his playmate. Now standing side by side with Daryl, the two looked more intimidating than The Great Wall of China. Together they resembled perfectly matching pillars of steel.

Vito stood in the far background with grave concern as he wondered if his boy was smart enough to talk his way through the bodyguards. Time was of the essence with each passing second that ticked off the clock. The medication was now steamrollering through the system of the enemy. His blood along with his mind was now tainted to the right proportions that the doctor had prescribed.

"My problem is with that piece of shit over there," Joey said while pointing in the direction of Bootsy. "What's the matter, the pussy doesn't have the balls to handle me himself?"

"Oh shit, man," a laughing Daryl said. "This dude is fuckin' crazy."

"Now let me through."

"Just because you been suckin' Vito's dick, you think you a tough guy. Well, all that Italian crap don't mean shit to us. I'll beat you right in front of his Mafia ass and he won't do nothin' to help you."

"You might beat the living shit out of me," Joey said, then challenged and pointed to Bootsy. "But I will keep comin' back until I get my hands on that piece of shit over there."

With his ears slightly perked and somewhat receptive to the conversation, Bootsy struggled to a standing position. Even though his senses were dulled, his crew was oblivious to his sedated behavior.

"Hey, what's that, that dumb fuckin' Dago bullshittin' about?" a somewhat rejuvenated Bootsy said.

"He say he got a problem with you, Bootsy," Daryl said. "He say you a fuckin' pussy!"

"I don't need no, no, nobody doing my jawing for me, let that motherfucker through," Bootsy said with a slight stutter.

Joey tried to sidestep around Daryl and Roland and was met with a hard and vicious shove. Maintaining his balance he then proceeded another ten feet towards the anxiously waiting Bootsy. The young man's moment of truth had arrived. It was now or never as he stared into the evil eyes of this mountain of a man.

"So you got a pro...prob...problem with, with me, punk," he said. Bootsy stuttered again as his words were having a hard time leaving his mouth. His jaws were getting heavy as his brain was starting to ease up on him.

"Yea, me and you have some unfinished business to tend to. But this time I'm gonna bend you over and fuck you in your big fat ass. And when I'm done, I'm gonna go up to Harlem and give it to your momma real good too."

"What, what, what the..." he stuttered.

"Your momma likes Italian food, right? Well I'm gonna make sure she gets a nice fat Italian sausage jammed right up her big black ass," Joey chided, while clutching his genitals. "I figure she could take about seven or eight inches, don't you! But don't worry, I'll make sure I lube her up real good. I know, I'll use the same stuff that you were going to lube me with."

Bootsy and his comrades just stared in disbelief.

Without a moment's notice you could hear the sounds of Joey's gurgling throat. His mouth was calling for the mucous membrane to muster up and deliver all of its lubricants to the tip of his tongue. With a mouth full of saliva and any other unwanted solid or liquid, the secretion process was finalized.

Within the blink of an eye Joey took one step forward and showered Bootsy with his bodily fluids. The large quantity of saliva caught the unexpected opponent right between the eyes. For spitting purposes, this was considered a bull's eye. In a split second the thick liquid was slowly finding its way down Bootsy's large round face.

"I do believe that this is the stuff that will take away all of your momma's pain," a wise cracking Joey said. "I'll make sure she gets it the same way that you did, nice and wet."

"Man, that's some nasty shit. This motherfucker is crazy!" a stunned Daryl said. "This motherfucker is crazy!"

"Shit, Bootsy, kick his white fuckin' ass," chimed Roland.

At that moment he tried in vain to wipe away the embarrassing liquid from his face. Like an enraged bull, his nostrils started to flare up. His matador stood before him, waiting for his upcoming stampede. But for Bootsy it was too late, Vito had him right where he wanted him. The once boisterous man from the loud streets of the city was reduced to nothing more than Little Bo Peep.

"Man, I'm, I'm, I'm gonna kill you," said the enraged Bootsy. "I'm gonna fuck you up, white boy!"

Joey started to back-pedal as the Sherman tank followed in a slow rumbling motion. He proceeded to back his way into the middle of the prison yard. Inmates cleared the passageway to the center stage of the upcoming fight. The crowd buzzed with excitement as chants for both combatants wafted through the air. The cheering grew louder and louder while the inmates formed a circle around the determined duo.

"Come on you want some, you fuckin' eggplant? You've been breakin' my balls since I got here. So here I am, now let's dance!" a more confident looking Joey said. "Come on you piece of dog shit, come and get me!"

"You gonna die!" threatened Bootsy.

"Come on, come on you son of a bitch," Joey said. "Let's see what you got."

The hatred and anger in Bootsy's eyes drew him to Joey like a force that was exerted by a magnetic field. The pull was so powerful it seemed to supersede anything that would stand in his way. His huffing and puffing proved that he was fighting against his own body and the drugs that Vito had installed in it. His defiance was saying go, but his body was saying no.

Joey knew it and he also knew that he had this monster right where he was supposed to be. He knew he had him in mind, body and soul.

Vito looked around the yard to make sure that everything else was in place. The rest of his crew was positioned exactly where he wanted them to be. Each member of the opposing gang was accounted for under intense scrutiny. He then took a quick peek up at the gun towers and knew things were going the way he had planned them. The prison guards were looking away from the commotion, and among the crowd there was not one in sight. The iron was smoking and now it was time to strike. Vito then took a step up onto one of the benches so he could see over the fanatical crowd. He then locked his calculating eyes on his godson. Joey looked up at his mentor and was given the nod to proceed. They both put their left fist in the air as a prescribed gesture to honor their friendship and the proceedings that waited ahead.

The two adversaries started to square off inside the large man made circle of screaming felons. Two sets of eyes were converged on each other's first point of attack. Bootsy's fighting stance looked awkward, he prepared himself with a drooping and unconventional style. The lazy and incompetent slouch resembled a punching bag just waiting to be beaten to a pulp. He kept moving slowly and forward like a steamroller.

Still retreating and waiting for an opening, Joey finally saw his window of opportunity.

With lightning quick jabs, Joey's tight fists were finding their way through Bootsy's bad defense. Again, again and again, his sharp, straight, left- handed jabs were finding the landing pad on Bootsy's face. Every so often a hard right hand punch would follow the devastating barrage of jabs. The chilly prison yard air made the punches sound crisp as the popping sounds were evident to all. Like a springboard, Booty's head was rocking back and forth with each punch that was absorbed. Round welts started to protrude from underneath his eyes. Sticking and moving, sticking and moving, Vito's advice was working with pure precision.

Through all the rapid jabs that were inflicted from Joey's lightning quick hands, Bootsy kept coming and coming in a slow forward motion. Trying to initiate an offensive attack was futile for him. His punches lacked the element of surprise; you could see them coming from a mile away.

Showing signs of sure desperation he started to lunge forward trying to connect with one of his flailing roundhouse punches. Joey just stepped to the side, easily avoiding the misguided punches. The medication had slowed him down so much that his punches were sluggish and way off of their intended targets. Every missed punch that he threw produced a loud grunt from his exhausted body. Beads of sweat started to pour off of his bruised and swollen face. The fight was not more than a minute old and already Bootsy looked like a beaten man.

"You're all mine now you big fat fuck," said Joey, while continuing his assault. "I want my respect, God damn it. I want my fuckin' respect!" The onslaught raged on. Rap, rap, rap were the sounds bouncing off of Bootsy's face. Joey kept circling around his opponent, now taunting him even more. "What's the matter? You don't look so tough anymore."

The assault continued.

Bootsy never said a word, as his embalmed body was absorbing the brunt of this one sided violent attack. With a left eye that was swelled shut, his vision was limited to shadows from the right side of his face. His facial wounds were about to burst open with each throb of pressure that pounded against his now sensitive skin.

The crowd stood stunned in silence and wide-eyed. The unexpected was happening and it seemed to shock the emotions of the inmates. Inside the building, the bettors were screaming while the return for their wagers looked nil. For this was the art of boxing in its truest form. The big underdog looked like Muhammad Ali as he sliced and diced his opponent into chopped liver.

One man stood tall and proud, with a smile on his face that could span across the Atlantic Ocean. Vito was still perched on top of the bench observing the scene before him. With his arms folded, even he was a little surprised how well things were going. Dutch and the rest of the crew remained stagnant with their eyes looking for any third party participants.

There was a slight pause in the action. Joey retreated while sizing up the situation. Five feet separated the combatants. For Joey it was now time to really seize the opportunity in this do or die situation. It was now time to throw all the techniques and patience out the window. It was time to revert to a street brawling style of fighting. Everything he had in his physical arsenal had to be thrown in the direction of Bootsy. The time had finally come to put this situation and Bootsy behind him forever. It was time to put him away. It was time for the kill.

Hunched over with his large hands enveloping some shaky knees, Bootsy looked dazed. He knew that a loss to the Italian would topple him from the power he held over his gang. Never the one to surrender, Bootsy now waited for his adversary's next move. Defeating the smaller and more agile opponent seemed to be a much greater task than he had thought. It never even dawned on him that his body was polluted with stupefying drugs. It was made clear in his mind that he had to fight to the finish.

Joey started to move forward to continue the onslaught. He became much more aggressive with his approach. Not looking for anymore openings in Bootsy's defense, he started to bang away. Lefts and rights were flying as they were connecting to the arms and upper body of his opponent. Bootsy tried to cover up his face with his large fatty arms, but the barrage of punches was too much. His tired and bruised arms were falling from the beating, exposing his face. Suddenly a hard right overhand punch found its way above his left eye. The impact ruptured and opened up a huge gash about one inch !ong. The first drop of blood was spilled as it was finding its way into the eyes of the beaten black man. With one eye shut closed and the other practically rendered blind by his own blood, Bootsy was helpless. One by one his faculties of self- perception were disappearing.

The scent of blood and the feeling of death in the air whipped up the frenzied crowd. All the cheers were for Joey as the inmates enjoyed the display of sadistic punishment. To them it did not matter who the winner was. To them they were the winners as their fanatical whims were satisfied by this excessive and irrational zeal.

Somewhere inside the crowd, Roland Harper was prancing and bobbing as if he was a fighter himself. He seemed ready to jump in and help his faltering leader. His erratic behavior was under surveillance by a pair of roving eyes.

"Things aren't going your way," Dutch said to him, while brandishing a sharp and narrow ice pick. "If you're thinking about joining your buddy, don't even think about it," he snarled. "I'll stick this thing right between your fuckin' eyes."

"I ain't goin' nowhere!"

"I know you're not," Dutch said evenly. "I'll be watching you."

Roland just stood there realizing his position was put in a checkmate. Any move from him or anybody else in his crew was monitored very closely. This was a thought out plan with the enemy caught way off guard.

With his head now leaning forward and the aroma of blood everywhere, it was just a matter of time. Within the blink of an eye, Joey unleashed a vicious straight uppercut that connected right under Bootsy's jaw. The blow rocked him as his large body was sent staggering backwards into the crowd. Still, the massive man refused to get knocked off of his feet. Fighting basically untouched, Joey was starting to wonder what it would take to soundly defeat this man. He then followed Bootsy to the wall of spectators to continue the offensive. Now lacking discipline, he grabbed him by the shirt on top of his right shoulder. Trying to restrain Bootsy's head in an upright position, the turbulent savage assault was about to show no mercy. In a wild and out of control manner, Joey unleashed a furious bombardment of short but sharp right-handed blows. One after the other the high-energy barrage of punishing punches bounced off the head and face of the submissive man.

Then the unthinkable happened, Bootsy dropped to one knee. With his face covered with blood, his head was bent over facing the pavement below him. Joey retreated about three or four steps, and then looked down at his beaten opponent. Standing above him like a victorious warrior was very gratifying to him. His battle scarred hands proved victory as they were covered with cuts and abrasions. To Joey the fight was finally over.

Joey then turned around and looked beyond the crowd for Vito. Searching for advice, he then noticed his friend shouting the words that he had been hoping for. But the loud screaming crowd muffled Vito's words of wisdom. Acting confused Joey was put at a standstill. His inexperience caused him to lose total focus of the enemy. He was now in a very disoriented and discombobulated state of confusion. Vito knew it and more important than that, so did Bootsy.

"Finish him! Finish him, God damn it," Vito yelled in desperation from atop the bench. But the frenzied crowd muted his hysterical cries. "What the hell are you doing? Joey, it's not over! Don't let up on him!" Time after time his loud voice was falling upon Joey's deaf ears. Standing on level ground behind the crowd, Dutch saw Vito's panic. He started to race towards the inside of the round circle.

"Shit," Dutch said under his breath. "I knew this would happen."

"Finish him off, he's going to get up," Vito screamed again at the top of his powerful lungs. "Damn it, Joey, what the fuck are you doing? He's gonna get up! Turn around, kid, turn around!"

It was useless; all of his yelling and screaming was to no avail. Suddenly Vito spotted Bootsy reaching down into a sock underneath his pants. He slipped the weapon inside the palm of his right hand as he clenched his fist tightly around it. The object was unknown, but now there was a major cause for concern.

"Jesus Christ almighty," Vito said to himself as he jumped off the bench to get closer to the melee. "Turn around, turn around," he yelled. Over and over, all of his instructions were not heard. That's when Vito knew that his boy was in big trouble.

Vito and Dutch raced towards the crowd as Bootsy slowly had risen to his feet. It was a foot race to the subject who was totally unaware of the danger that lurked behind him.

Walking slowly and very nimble for a man his size, Bootsy was now within striking distance. The crowd was no help to Joey; to them it was time for pay back. Besides, the longer the action lasted, the longer their uncontrollable thirst for blood would take to be quenched.

Joey then felt Bootsy's presence, but by that time it was too late. He got hit with a wild right hand that felt like a sledgehammer. The blow caught him right on top of his left cheekbone, shattering facial bones and opening up a large gash which was gushing his own blood. Staggering ten feet backwards, the heavy punch knocked Joey flat on his back and left his senses in total disorder and confusion. The fierce impact throttled his brain into a temporary loss of activity from his central nervous system.

Vito and Dutch rushed to the fracas, struggling to get through the hostile crowd. It was total chaos as they finally found their way inside the circle to get a full view of the drastic turn of events. What they saw was not supposed to be taking place. Joey was still on his back struggling to regain some consciousness. A revitalized Bootsy was slowly approaching, ready to pounce on the easy prey. In his right hand he was brandishing a set of brass knuckles. Vito knew that if Bootsy was to ever get on top of Joey it was all over. One more strike from that weapon could be lethal.

"I'm goin' in," Dutch said. "I've seen enough of this shit!"

"Not yet," answered Vito as he grabbed Dutch around the wrist. "Wait a second or two. I just know that the kid will pull through this. If we go in now all hell will break loose."

"Vito, the medication is starting to wear off. You could see it in his movements."

"That son of a bitch is a fuckin' monster. I should have put enough in there to kill him. Fuck me," Vito screamed. "Get up, kid, get up." He continued screaming, hoping that Joey could hear his calls. Vito knew that if he would intervene it was sure to cause a prison riot.

Struggling to get to his feet, Joey's head was still vibrating. His vision was blurry and his balance lacked the stability to stand on firm ground. Rising to one knee, Joey saw a huge, fuzzy shadow hovering over him. Still unaware of his surroundings and feeling dazed, he somehow managed to get back on his feet. Not more than a second later he stood face to face with his nemesis and the pain that was sure to follow.

In an instant, Bootsy delivered a sharp quick blow into his half-dazed opponent's midsection and ribs. The punch sent the top part of Joey's body forward and right into Bootsy's arms. He quickly wrapped both of his tree trunks around the smaller foe. With a show of strength, he easily picked him up and started to squeeze the life out of him. He squeezed and squeezed as his strong arms performed like a powerful grip from a vice. Gasping for air and in excruciating pain from his badly damaged ribs, Joey needed a miracle. The compression made him feel like a grapefruit on somebody's breakfast table.

"Ahhhhhh," Joey cried out. He could feel Bootsy's heavy breathing running down the side of his neck. "Ahhhhhh, I can't breathe!"

"You want your respect?" Bootsy laughed, fastening his grip on his struggling victim. "You have to earn that, boy. Now it's my turn," he said. "Who you think you fuckin' with? You could never put me away. Now you gonna die!"

"Fuck you," Joey eked out, struggling with each word that was coming from his mouth. "You're gonna have to kill me!"

With each passing second the embrace from the suffocating bear hug got tighter and tighter. Numbness started to creep through Joey's body as the flow of blood was being stopped from its circulation. A move had to be made to defuse this wrecking machine, or Vito would have to step in and try to stop this carnage.

Joey extended his arms outward, arched his back and looks upright, towards the sky.

"Help me," Joey deliriously cried. "My dear Jesus, please help me!"

Something or someone heard his perilous pleas for help. A sudden calm reigned. Overhead, the aroused clouds condensed, spinning violently. The swarming mass darkened as it pitched an enormous shadow over the prison yard. A brisk and mysterious wind caressed the inmates.

Everyone looked skyward. Stunned.

Deafening thunder rumbled and a shaft of blazing lightning cracked through the agitated cumulus. Snakelike, the radiant discharge spiraled downwards, dancing with enthusiasm. With a loud explosion, it crashed behind Bootsy, leaving a cloud of smoke.

The happening sent a massive jolt through the prison yard.

Bootsy, turned around, bewildered, but still holding onto Joey.

Never rising, the smoke loomed. Seconds later, the unearthly matter started to rotate, forming a column of air. A whirlwind.

Horizontally, the agitation gathered steam and aggressively moved forward dragging dirt an debris with it. It passed right through Joey and Bootsy before it disappeared.

Bootsy started to wilt. His once rejuvenated body was withering.

Still struggling to break free, Joey looked skyward, never saying a word.

"What the hell was that?" asked Vito. With wide eyes, he looks at Dutch in disbelief. "Dutch, what the fuck is going on here?"

"Shit…I don't know," he answered, while still focusing on Joey. "But look!"

Vito eyes slithered back towards the fight.

Joey desperately tried to seize the moment.

With his feet still dangling about a foot off of the ground, Joey went into action. He molded his hands into the shape of a cup. With all his exertion and whatever strength he had left in his faltering body, Joey let loose. His hands came together on both sides of Bootsy's head and ears. Both of the hearing organs were hit simultaneously and straightforward with a loud bang. Bootsy, obviously stunned, staggered like a drunk but still holding Joey.

Joey grabbed Bootsy around his head and sunk his white teeth into the large nose of his enemy. Like a hungry lion in search of food, he gnawed away and shook his head side to side, violently tearing at the black flesh. Digging and gnashing his teeth, Bootsy screamed and unlocked his grip from the once mighty bear hug. Joey fell to the ground free of the certain death lock. On the way down he took a piece of Bootsy's nose with him.

"Yea," Vito screamed from the sidelines. "Yea, now kick his fuckin' ass. This time finish him off." He then turned to Dutch and stuck his elbow into his buddy's ribs. "Dutch, did you teach the kid that move? The kid bit his fuckin' nose off!"

"Nah, I would have swallowed the nose so they can't sew it back on his face. He still has it in his mouth."

"Go, kid, go" Vito screamed. "Get after him, but this time don't let up!"

Positioned on all fours with the tip of Bootsy's nose in his mouth, Joey looked up at the stationary enemy. With a face full of blood he quickly spat the flesh from his mouth. He looked up and saw Bootsy's face contorted in agony.

Joey took a few seconds to regroup his thoughts. Then the opening he was looking for appeared right before him. With an abrupt and hard sudden thrust, his right arm came flying up through the opening between Bootsy's legs. In between his forearm and his bicep, Joey's arm caught him right in the family jewels.

"Damn," he cried. "Ohhhh, man, my fuckin' balls!" Bootsy screamed as he started to bite on his bottom lip. Bootsy stumbled backwards, reeking in pain

The whole prison went silent as the waves of distress resonated silently through the yard. The big black man tried to ease the pain by holding his genitals. The white-hot pain clear on his face. Bootsy looked like he was going to regurgitate his balls as he stooped over in pain. Grasping and clutching at his private parts, his scream was primordial. Then he went down to both knees. The crowd gasped.

With no time to waste and learning from his past experience, Joey continued the massive offensive. He quickly got to his feet and rushed over to the fallen man. Pulling Bootsy's head forward with both hands, Joey drove his knee into his skull. The force had driven him backward with such speed that the back of his head bounced off of the pavement behind him.

Joey then pounced on top of the man who now resembled a beached whale. Spotting the brass knuckles, Joey removed them from the black man's right hand. Still enraged and acting like a man possessed, he slipped them around his fingers. Then the final barrage, now in brass, began. The punches were as pounding as a piece of pneumatic equipment. Pop, pop, pop, were the sounds. Every blow brought out a new laceration. Skin was now molting from the face of the disgraced felon, exposing bone. The whole battlefield was a mess, there was blood everywhere.

"Joey, enough," a voice shouted from behind. "Enough, you're gonna kill him. It's over for Christ sake, he's had enough!"

This time he heard his jailhouse mentor. Joey took one look back and spotted his general. He managed to spot Vito standing within the large crowd. Joey looked at Vito and Dutch and they all shared a grin. All shook their closed fists in victory. For Joey, it was finally over. He had gained his respect.

"This kid is really something," Dutch said. "He's something really special."

"You got that right," answered Vito. "He certainly is."

Gunshots then echoed through the prison yard, and the fight crowd scattered in all directions. Some inmates hit the floor and covered their heads.

Joey just stayed on his knees, which were planted right on top of Bootsy's body. He just stared into Bootsy's closed eyes with regret. "It didn't have to come down to this," he said to the unresponsive body. "It didn't."

About a half a dozen prison guards raced to the scene. Silence now reigned. The blood-fest had finally come to an end. Joey felt a hand on one of his shoulders.

"Come on, DeFalco, it's all over," the officer said as he took the brass knuckles in his possession. The weapon was quickly placed into his pants pocket never to be seen again. "Come on, get to your feet. The party's over."

The prison guards were more lenient with this altercation. For them, getting rid of Bootsy was like getting rid of a terminal cancer. With guys like Bootsy around, even they had to watch their backs from getting jumped or stabbed while trying to break up a melee. Many prisoners would even stage a fight just to get an opportunity to fleece a prison guard. Most of the time, their punishment was a short stay in the box or the loss of some privileges. The penalty in most cases was not severe enough, so to some prisoners it was open season on the men in the blue uniforms.

For every Bootsy there were fifty more gang leaders just like him in this prison. Every ethnicity that was represented in this melting pot of scum had a Bootsy controlling their gang. Each gang had their own distinction, their own colors and their own bandannas.

Joey just looked up at the officer and shook his head. He slowly got to his feet and started walking in the custody of the prison guards. Stone faced, he then turned around to look at Vito. The two locked eyes that were all-knowing. Tears started to fall from the young man's face as the tension and fear drained off. He was now going through the beginning stages of some sort of a mental breakdown. Joey was not the hardened criminal type and these symptoms of withdrawal proved it.

The walking was slow but the respect that he gained was immense. Joey had earned his reputation the hard way; he had taken down a notorious prison gang leader. You could feel it and see it in all the eyes of every prisoner who witnessed this tremendous backyard brawl.

What awaited Joey was a trip to see the warden and probably a short stint in the prison's hospital. After that was a long stay in the dungeon of doom and twenty-four hours a day of solitary confinement. This was the final chapter to his survival of prison life. After this, the rest of his stay would seem like a walk in the park.

For Bootsy, his grave condition looked much more severe. He was waiting for the paramedics to arrive and supply emergency medical treatment. His large body lay lifeless soaking in his own blood. His destination was yet to be determined. A transfer to another prison was likely; to reunite him with his school-yard pals would be a big mistake. His falling from grace would mark an ending to his status of leader. By losing this battle, he had disgraced his gang members and the symbol of brutality that they had stood for. Soon it would be time for him to become accepted at some other institution where his former reputation meant nothing. He would become some other prison's big headache. It was time for Daryl Baker to hop into the pants of his shamed leader and assume his responsibilities. Right after the last punch was thrown, Bootsy became a distant memory to his former gang of roughnecks.

After the commotion finally settled down, Vito and the rest of his crew gathered by the entranceway into the large building. All of the men had smiles on their faces exposing them from any hidden feelings. This was a moment of great conquest for the Italians. They conquered the impossible and bucked the odds with a young kid from the Financial District of Downtown Manhattan. The Wall Streeter had proven that it's impossible to judge the toughness of a man just because he wears a suit and a tie.

"I have never been so proud of anyone in my whole life," a pumped up Vito said. "Did you see that kid in action? He was unbelievable. I told him to bring him down to his fuckin' knees and he did. That shot he gave him to the balls was brutal. Man, he hit him so hard I felt the pain myself."

"Yea but for a minute it didn't look so good. I thought we were going to have to go in there," said Dutch. "Vito, I guess the kid might have been right."

"What do you mean?"

"Those drugs must have been generic, they didn't work too good."

"Bullshit, it's just that he was such a big bastard. I guess I just underestimated his size. When he started to come alive I realized that I should have given him more."

"But it all worked out anyway, Joey performed like a champ," said Dutch.

"Did you see when he bit off his fuckin' nose and then spit it out," asked Vito. "I wonder if they're gonna try and put the tip of his nose back on?"

"Well if they do, they're gonna have a hard time finding it," said Red acting like he knew something special.

"What are you talkin' about?" asked Vito.

Red reached into his pocket and pulled out the large round tip of Bootsy's nose. The piece of flesh contained the tip and a part of the left nostril. The repugnant and gory chunk of skin was still moist with blood. Red just held it in between his thumb and index finger as he displayed it to his buddies.

"Holy shit, you sick bastard," Vito said in astonishment.

"I guess Bootsy won't be sniffing around in anybody's business anymore," a smiling Paulie said.

"Hey Red, give it to me. I want to wear it around my fuckin' neck," Dutch said as he went to grab at the small piece of meat.

"Why, do you want to put it with the rest of your collection?" asked Red.

"Yea, all I need now is a tongue and maybe an eyeball."

"Well if you want some balls and maybe a piece of his cock," said Red laughing. "I'm sure you can find them splattered somewhere in the yard. In fact I think I know where we could find them," he joked.

"Those parts I think I'll pass on," Dutch said laughing.

The foursome then burst out into a loud roar of laughter. For them it was a joyous occasion marked by the victory of a young man struggling for survival. The Italians took it personal; for them it was another notch on their bedpost. They were definitely outnumbered, but in prison to survive you had to strike fear into your opponents. With the element of fear you can keep a whole army at bay. This triumph in front of more than a thousand pairs of eyes just reinforced this belief.

One by one the men started to enter the building. They too would have to suffer because of the activities that took place in the prison yard. A day or two locked up in the luxury of their own cells was the extent of it. To lose some privileges for a couple of days was no big deal. What they just witnessed was well worth the price of seclusion.

Chapter 9

"JOSEPH J. DEFALCO," the Warden said. "You're not looking too good. Tell me? How does a nice kid like you get tangled up in such a mess like this?"

Joey just stood there shrugging awaiting his punishment. Any information that was to be given was not about to come from his mouth. Besides, the shot he took from the brass knuckles made it almost impossible to speak. He was in desperate need of some painkillers.

Warden Sweeney was a tough ex police sergeant who rose through the ranks of law enforcement. His office seemed to signify his personality and attire. The drably decorated looking place had an aura that resembled a home for the elderly. Just the bare essentials needed to perform office duties were represented. The plain looking man spent four years with the United States Marine Corps before moving on to the New York City Police Department. He served about ten years working both uniformed and plain-clothes units in grand style. He received the Medal of Honor and the prestigious Medal of Valor awards for his heroic public services.

"So DeFalco, tell me something?" the Warden said. "Did Carlucci have anything to do with this?"

"Carlucci had nothin' to do with anything. I was just taking care of my own ass."

"You do know that Carlucci is getting out of here in about three months. When he leaves it might be open season on you," he threatened. "Right now you might think that you are some kind of bad ass. But let me tell you something, this place will eat you up and spit you out like a piece of chewing tobacco. Hell is a better alternative. Your protection is going to have to come from somewhere. So if you cooperate I'll make sure that nobody lays a finger on you for the rest of your stay."

"And if I don't?"

"If you don't I'm going to make the next few months of your pathetic life a living hell. Where you're going, regular prison life will seem like Breakfast at Tiffany's to you. Compared to this place, Darius Jackson will seem like going on a date with Mary Poppins."

"Who the hell is Darius Jackson?" Joey asked with a bewildered look.

"Bootsy, that's who he is," the Warden shot back. "That's another thing, right now his condition is stabilized. But if he takes a turn for the worse and doesn't make it, your prison sentence will have to be reevaluated."

"Do you think I give two shits about what happens to Bootsy? If you really want to know the truth, I think I did you a major favor by getting rid of that piece of shit. You should be rewarding me, not condemning me," Joey said.

The four prison guards in the room were absorbing the verbal exchange. Two could barely hide their grins.

"In this place you are not rewarded for taking matters into your own hands. In here I am the judge and the jury, and only I dictate the imposed penalties. What happened in the prison yard was instigated by your aggressive actions. I believe that a certain third party induced you into such behavior. Are you going to come clean?" the Warden demanded. "Or are you going to force my hand?"

"I acted alone!" Joey firmly said. "I know how things are done in here. And now I also know what it takes to survive in this cesspool. I've been beaten and fucked over since I got here, so now it's your turn. Everybody tries to take a turn to ride your ass. It started with my lawyer and it worked its way all the way down the system to you. So go ahead, take your turn, take your best fuckin' shot."

"Since I am not getting any cooperation, you leave me with no other choice. I'm throwing you in the hole for three long months. In less than one week a guy like you will be crying for his mother. From what I see of you, you will never make it."

The Warden stayed seated throughout his tongue-lashing. His temperament was mostly composed throughout the short hearing. To him this was just another day at the office. This case was no different than any other one. But there was one thing that was hindering his judgment. He would have liked nothing better than to throw a noose over the head of Vito Carlucci.

Joey just stood before the Warden with the after effects from the brutal battle. Still bleeding with a face that was starting to turn colors, he stared in disbelief. The two weeks he assumed that he was getting as punishment, turned into three months. He then started to wonder how much more of this punishment his body could take. Joey bent down and placed both hands on top of the desk of Warden Sweeney.

"Now let me give you one word of advice!"

"What's that?" the Warden asked.

Through tight teeth Joey said, "You just said that I will never make it out of solitary, well don't bet on it! There's not a damn thing in this place that scares me anymore. That includes you and that rat hole that you're sending me to."

"Get this fuckin' guy out of here," the Warden then demanded. "He's starting to get me sick. First take him over to the infirmary to get those bruises looked at. Then right after they bandage his sorry ass up, throw him right in the hole. Let his wounds heal in there."

There was no mercy, a couple of cracked ribs, a badly swollen eye and a fractured cheekbone was not enough to delay the sentence. Dogs that were picked up by the A.S.P.C.A. were receiving better medical attention. The only therapeutic relief came from a mild pain-killer that couldn't silence a toothache. Every wound had to depend on Father Time and his curative healing powers.

The rigors of the box, the hell-hole, the dungeon or whatever else they call solitary confinement was understated. Many a man in this punitive cavity of isolation had come to terms with the demons buried deep inside of them. Prison privileges were just an afterthought as the human body was suffocated with impurities and unsanitary living conditions.

Contamination lingered in every crevasse of this immoral and obscene six by eight foot coffin. Everything from tears to semen covered the black padded walls surrounding the front door and the urine stained toilet. Human feces hovered above the water of the disposal apparatus. The defecation left embedded rings of filth around the inside of the bowl. The stench was appalling, digesting or breathing anything was almost impossible. Vomiting and choking on the distasteful odors was not uncommon upon arrival. Many a night inmates could be found sleeping in their own waste. The cold concrete slab below them spawned puddles of any kind of human waste that the body disposed of.

Spider webs controlled the corners of the bare ceilings above. The eight-legged arachnids dangled from their own creations in an attempt to snare the insects that infested this chamber of horrors.

Nighttime brought a different cast of furry little creatures. Many nights the long tail rodents could be felt crawling and pecking on a sleeping body. The rats and mice would come out like armies in search of any unwanted food and garbage. After a couple of weeks the sleeplessness would overpower the horror as the human body succumbed to these dreadful living conditions. The highlight of the stay was when a prison guard slipped your meal of the day through a little opening in the door. The food was pretty basic, shoe leather meat, some diarrhea-mashed potatoes and a piece of leftover green molded bread. All washed down with a paper cup filled with room temperature water. There were no lights, no windows or voices, just your own screams and the inner thoughts that contemplated many things, including suicide. Demons, panic attacks and claustrophobia were some of the obstacles one must overcome. These innate terrors seemed to do the most damage when the sunlight went down and the true darkness set in.

Sometimes death was welcome as the depression formed a chemical imbalance too severe for life to exist. This place left you broken and separated with the feeling of complete hopelessness. It turned dreams into nightmares and many hearts into stone. One needed to find the strength that's buried deep inside of his soul to survive this torture. Then and only then could one hope to find his way through this eternal black abyss they called solitary confinement. Then and only then, one could come to terms within himself and find that flickering glimmer of light.

"Get in," the prison guard commanded.

Joey paused as the horrific elements of this cell were brought forth. His whole body trembled with fear; the unknown had surfaced with a superior force. Suddenly his body broke out into a cold sweat. Numbness possessed every limb of his now shaking being. Lightheadedness and nausea started to set in as he was pushed into this man made womb. Barely able to stand, Joey stumbled towards the nearest corner.

The heavy metal door was slammed shut behind him. This would be his home for three long months without a chance to see sunlight.

"Nooooo!" Joey screamed out from the top of his lungs. "Nooooo!. I can't take it anymore. Please, God help me!" he continued to plead. "Take me now," he cried. "I wanna die!" Now sobbing painfully, he repeated, "I wanna fuckin' die."

For the next several minutes Joey was conversing with himself, wondering how he had arrived in this dreadful situation. The conversation was filled with what ifs and should haves. The internal voices echoed throughout his brain with guilt of past misdeeds. Sometimes the guilt would turn to hate as the demons wiped out any remorseful feelings that he might have had. Still in massive pain, he would soon slide down the padded wall, curl into a fetal position and stare into the darkness. He felt his mind slip into some new dimension.

This spatial state swept him to a place of great magnitude. Someplace very far away.

Moments later, underneath Joey's body, beneath the concrete bed, something unexplainable was happening. The small solitary cube began to give birth to something unfathomable.

Vibrating with frenzy, the stone slab started to tremor.

The accumulated stress created a hissing sound. The breathing was erupting like a volcanic surge. The sounds grew to that same nature. A powerful force was pressing against the inner walls of the concrete, trying to break through.

With incredible power the force broke free.

Miniscule pores opened in the jolted pavement.

The outbreak emitted a haze of supernatural and surreal effect.

Like rising smoke, an unsettled and untamed apparition surrounded Joey while passing right through his being. Now violently rotating, the coming kept rising and rising, spiraling upwards as it coalesced into a hoary bodily image.

With wide red rimmed eyes that lacked total awareness, Joey just stared into space, oblivious to everything around him.

Something unknown, something not of this planet, hovered over Joey. It stayed defiant for a few seconds, intently peering down on him. In a flash, the juggernaut dropped towards its purpose. The orb quickly penetrated the immobile body as it disappeared. Now internally a part of him and gaining total control of his senses, the sphere started to speak to the mind beneath the depths of Joey's conscious perception.

"The days are coming," it said to his lifeless body. "See, the storm of the Lord will burst out in wrath, a whirlwind swirling down on the wicked."

Joey's head started to throb with pain. The vibration from this message was spellbinding. Still incoherent, his hands now clutched both sides of his head as he bellowed aloud from the afflicted distress.

The cloistered voice continued on.

"I will bring disaster on them in the year they are punished. They will be banished to darkness and there they will fall. I will make my words in your mouth a fire and those people the wood it consumes," the mysterious voice said. "In days to come you will understand it clearly. So do not fear, do not be dismayed. I will surely save you out of this distant place. I will build you up again. I will restore you to health and heal your wounds. I have drawn you with loving kindness. I am with you and will save you."

Slowly, the mass started to emerge from Joey's body and dipped back into the bed of concrete that gave it life.

With the pain now subsided, Joey just laid there, not knowing or remembering what had just taken place. His brain was not the intended target of these powerful messages, his soul was.

These words will stay with him forever.

Back in the cell block, Vito sat on his bunk worrying about his godson. Word had just filtered down that Joey had received three months in the hole. He thought that was too much for any man to survive. Vito started to have second thoughts about the fight and its consequences. He knew what the hole was all about and the toughness it took to beat it. This was one subject he failed to discuss with Joey, and it weighed heavily on his mind.

"Here!" Dutch said as he entered Vito's cell and threw a white envelope on top of the bed.

"How much is it?"

"A little over sixty five hundred."

"I'm starting to ask myself if it was all worth it," said Vito as he shook his head. "This feels like blood money to me. I never felt this way before after collecting on some bets. Jesus, I hope he's alright."

"Vito, the kid's gonna make it. Don't underestimate him," Dutch responded. "He's one tough bastard."

"If anything happens to him I will never forgive myself. They fucked me, Dutch, they told me he would get two to three week's tops. The bad thing is that we can't even get to him to help him out."

"Vito, in the long run it will all be worth it. He gambled in the game of life and he lost. He's a smart kid; he will come out of there tougher and wiser. And I guarantee you one thing."

"What's that?"

"Nobody, and I mean nobody, will ever fuck with him again. Whether it's in here or out on the streets," Dutch said. "Even if the both of us left this place tomorrow, nobody wants a piece of him. Jesus Christ, they all think that he's fuckin' crazy."

"Why, have you heard anything?"

"The whole place is talking about the fight. When Joey comes out of the box they'll all treat him like he's royalty. He now commands the respect that you sought for him."

"That's good, but I swear on my mother's grave," Vito threatened. "If anybody ever goes near that kid again, I'm gonna chop them up into little pieces and bury them in a fuckin' shoe box."

"There's gonna be no need for that," Dutch predicted. "At least in here anyway."

"You're probably right, but I still feel kind of guilty. I can't help it."

"Listen Vito. If he didn't meet up with us in here he probably would have been somebody's bitch already. Who knows what would have happened to him? At least we isolated him one on one with Bootsy and he came out on top. For the most part he did it without the help of those drugs. Between me and you that shit wore off of him pretty fast," said Dutch. "So stop feeling guilty, everything worked out for the best!"

"Yea, I guess you're right," Vito said, as he took the large sum of money out of the white envelope. "Here, here's five hundred. Do me a favor, before breakfast tomorrow, run this up to Nat. Here's another fifteen hundred, split it up between you and the boys." Vito then sealed the envelope and placed it inside a hole in the wall behind his bed. "Dutch, go get some sleep, it's been a long day," he said while rubbing his tired eyes. "It's been a long day."

The next couple of months flew by in irreversible succession. Prison never stops beating its ugly heart for anybody. Every day there are some poor victims taking some kind of abuse and it seems that there is nothing that anyone can do to stop it. Inmates come and go, some make it and some don't. For every rape and beating that takes place, there is always another victim coming through the front gates. Prison officials have their hands full, but they are constantly caught looking the other way. The inmates run the prison and they know it. The gangs ran the place in the same fashion that they terrorized the city streets.

On November 21st, three days before Thanksgiving Day, Justin O'Leary was found dead in the toilet facility. His frail and limp body was discovered suspended, hanging from a water pipe above the toilet. Two large towels made up the noose that had choked the life out of him. Rigor mortis had set in as his stiff body was exposing a pale blue color. With his eyes wide open and blood dripping from the corner of his mouth, death was his self-induced destination.

Justin's young life was cut short because of the constant heckling and abuse he took from the older inmates. Always in constant fear for his life, he reached out for protection and was repeatedly turned away. The authorities felt that his abuses failed to meet the emergency grievance criteria for protective custody, so his pleas were in vain. For two months he was beaten, robbed, raped and forced to perform oral sex against his will. On many nights, thugs would stand on line waiting for Justin to perform his forced sexual duties.

Time and time again he was passed around like a cheap hooker at someone's bachelor party. The Warden denied his requests for segregated protection every time. Growing tired of living his life in constant terror and pain, Justin gave up the desire to live and took his own life. An autopsy revealed numerous tears in his rectum caused by forced entry. His abusers were never found. They still wait salivating for a chance to prey on the next poor victim. In a day or two Justin O'Leary was a forgotten man.

The clock was ticking down as Joey's impending release was approaching. His dark sunken eyes and pale complexion yearned for the radiance of sunlight and some fresh air. Now tipping the scales about ten pounds lighter, he managed to maintain his strength with a daily rigorous routine of pushups. With a more chiseled and defined physique, his body showed no ill effects from the battering it received. But with each passing day his hope would increase as his will to survive grew stronger. It was now apparent that he would make it through this terrible ordeal. Leaving the box would feel like being reborn all over again.

It was a little bit after 5 p.m. on the 22nd of December. Christmas was just a couple of days away as another year was about to come to an end. The first snowfall buried the upstate community with 18 inches. The blizzard caught the rural population by surprise, bringing businesses to a temporary standstill. Picturesque quartz mountainsides were blanketed in snow.

He heard the cylinder turning in the direction to open the heavy door. A sharp light shot through the crack of the opened entranceway. The total darkness evoked the light. Joey started to squint as the foreign ray of light blossomed and left him momentarily blind. The forgotten brightness forced his body to react in a repelling way. He partially covered his eyes as a large shadow appeared before him with a welcoming gesture. It was not Santa Claus, but to him it was someone even better.

"DeFalco, come on," the voice from heaven said. "You're out of here!"

Joey sat frozen, thinking that it was all a dream. He welcomed the sight of the prison guards with open arms. A half-assed physical and a quick shower were all that stood in his way before entering the cell block arena. Joey actually yearned to see his cell again. To him it was paradise compared to his living quarters for the past three months.

On both knees, he placed his head in an upward position. "Thank you, Lord, for seeing me through this," he silently said while performing the sign of the cross.

The long walk back to his cell was uneventful. Prisoners would back up pressing on the walls behind them to let him through. Their eyes stood focused as little tidbits of gossip were exchanged. No one even wanted to make eye contact with him. To them, Joey was a walking time bomb ready to explode. Nobody wanted anything to do with him - this was the respect that he had gained through fear. They knew his plight and they also knew that he did not have to hide behind anybody's skirt anymore. In their eyes on this day, another bad ass was born into the society of life behind bars.

The sight of his cell looked like a penthouse suite at a luxury hotel. His four inch thick mattress would seem like sleeping on a soft white cloud. Joey's scarred body showed the lingering effects of solitary confinement. Many nights of sleeping on a cold concrete floor left stains and abrasions running across the front and back of his broad shoulders. Entering his cell for the first time, a good night's sleep was all that was on his mind as he sat down on his bunk. In a matter of seconds his head touched the pillow. His heavy eyes started to close and a deep sleep was sure to follow. All the sounds coming from the cell block were irrelevant.

Red raced through the crowd to tell Vito the good news of Joey's release. By some technical error Joey was let out a day early. The whole crew was expecting his release on Wednesday the 23rd of December. Prison officials liked to confuse the inmates on when certain prisoners were reunited with friends. They called it a technical error, but in reality it was just a way to sneak a prisoner back into the population without a major uproar.

Vito was sitting down watching the evening news with Dutch and Paulie on each side. With a cigarette burning in his hand, he focused intensely on this special news report. It seemed that the underboss of his crime family was executed gangland style. His bullet-riddled body was left for dead in front of an Italian restaurant in Brooklyn. The gruesome video exposed the blood pouring out of his tailor made suit. Most gangsters die the same way they live, alone. The police had secured the scene as the yellow tape kept the rubber-neckers and nosy pedestrians away.

A growing fear loomed as a potential mob war was imminent. This was the fifth mob hit in the last four weeks involving two different factions of the Mafia's two biggest organized crime families. Vito knew that this killing would bump him up a notch to a position near the top. It was he who would now walk in the shoes of his dead underboss.

"Vito," Red said.

"Not now, Red," said Vito in a threatening tone.

"But I have to tell you something."

"Shut up and tell me later."

"Dutch, what's eating him, all that I wanted to tell him was that Joey was out."

"What?" Dutch screamed. "Joey's out! Vito, Joey's out!"

"Holy shit, Red, why didn't you say that in the first place?" asked Vito.

"You didn't give me a chance to, that's why."

"Well, where is he?"

"He's in his cell."

"Vito, what about the news on the television?" asked Paulie.

"Fuck the news, let's go!"

Like women running to a fire sale at Macy's, the four men bolted from the room and ran towards the cell block area. They all stampeded their way through any impeding traffic. Climbing up the steps they were stumbling and bumbling all over each other. The dangerous foursome could not wait to see their battle tested comrade. Over the past three or four months, each one of the mobsters grew to love the kid in his own different way.

They all stood by the opening of Joey's cell staring at him sleeping. He seemed comatose.

"He looks like he's dead," remarked Paulie. "Look at his eyes."

Paulie was talking about the large brown circles that had formed around his eyes. The dark rings and the bags under his eyes cast his face into a hollowed skeleton. His pale complexion seemed appropriate.

"You would look dead too if you spent three months in the hole," Dutch replied. "I don't think he looks that bad."

"Let's wake him up," Paulie said.

"If you wake him up I'll break your fuckin' neck!" warned Vito. "Let him sleep, come on, let's go."

The following morning after the daily head count, Joey would soon be reunited with his friends. The prison staff would count bodies over and over throughout the course of the day. Any missing body would throw up a red flag and bring the prison to a standstill. Inmates would be forced back into their cells until the missing person was accounted for. At 7 a.m. the march towards the breakfast table would begin.

Walking down the tier, Joey spotted all of his buddies anxiously waiting to greet him. Slaps, kisses and hugs were propelled through the air to welcome him back. Vito, acting like an Emcee, quickly had to calm his crew and their emotions down.

"Calm down," he said pulling Paulie off of Joey. "He's been mugged enough in the last couple of months." He then turned his attention over to Joey. "How ya doin', kid?" he said while embracing him.

"I'm good, I'm just glad it's all over with," he said with a big smile. Joey's words flowed smoothly, as all the tension seemed to have eased from his body. He was a world apart from the man who entered prison back in September. "It feels good to be back."

"Well, you've been baptized the hard way and now it's all over," Vito said, placing his hand on top of Joey's shoulder. "Bootsy survived the beating you gave him and they shipped him out to another prison."

"Thank God for that," Joey said. "I'm too fuckin' tired to have to deal with that asshole all over again."

"It's done, finished. You made a statement and your presence is felt by every jerk-off in this place. You look exhausted!"

"I do feel a little bit more at ease. But to tell you the truth, I could have used a couple of more days of sleep."

"In a couple of days you'll be fine. Did you hear what happened to Justin?" Vito asked Joey.

"No, why? What happened to him?"

"He was found hanging over a toilet seat in the shit room right before Thanksgiving."

"Is he dead?"

Joey just stood there with a blank expression on his face. He knew that Justin needed some help to survive in this place. He kept reaching out, and reaching out, but nobody seemed to care.

"Yea, he's dead."

"He committed suicide?"

"It looks that way, that's what the Medical Examiner said. But for some reason I have a feeling he was lifted up to that water pipe."

"What do you mean?"

"Sometimes life has very suspicious ways for pay-back. These punks found out about his past. They also knew that you and him had some kind of relationship going on. You might have not been the best of friends, but to them, killing Justin was their retaliation against you. They passed that kid around like a fuckin' blow up doll, with each one of them taking their turn. I think the prison officials just listed it as a suicide and swept it under the table."

"Those motherfuckers! Who did this to him?"

"Listen Joey, I could be wrong. But whether I'm right or wrong, you must let it go."

"But I…"

"Listen to me, let it go!" Vito ordered. "Do you understand me?"

"I know Bootsy and the rest of those pricks had something to do with this.'

"You're probably right."

"Couldn't you do something to stop them? All he ever wanted to be accepted as a friend."

"What the fuck do you think that they had their orgies in my cell? I told you about his past, even I stand clear and avoid certain people. So don't even think about trying to hold this shit over my head. Sometimes these perverse things that people do, catches up with them. It's like that old saying, if you live by the sword be prepared to die by the sword."

"Jesus Christ, Vito, it could have been me hanging up there."

"Just count your blessings that it's not and let the fuckin' thing go."

"I will," Joey said.

"It's not worth it, so promise me that you will do as I say. You lucked out with Bootsy. If you fuck one of his niggers up, you will die of old age in this place. So promise me that you will forget about this."

"I promise."

"Come on, let's go have some breakfast," Vito said. "You must be starving."

"You don't know the shit that I have been shoveling down my throat for the past couple of months."

"Oh I know, kid, I know. Believe me, I've been there before," he said smiling.

At that moment Joey's bond towards Vito grew stronger. He now realized how important Vito was to his existence behind bars. This man had saved his life from the degenerates who populated most prisons. All the beatings along with the pain and suffering were well worth it. Seeing Justin flashing before his eyes convinced him that Vito was his savior.

About another four weeks had just disappeared with time. Christmas and New Year's came in through one door and out the other. Inmates tend to want to forget these special times of the year. Even they shared some tender moments with loved ones at one time or another. To them it was the season of thought and forgotten memories. The best they could hope for was a phone call to hear some familiar voices from the past. Sometimes even the closest of families forget a certain member who has caused them pain and humiliation. After the first couple of months, visits were not that common anymore. Only the lucky ones who found true love experienced the feeling of being wanted. For Joey he was too proud to have anyone in his family see him in such a position. Deep down he knew that he would never return to this place. Living a life of total poverty was even better than this. A life in some trailer park struggling to raise a bunch of kids was a better alternative. To him, there was no excuse for ever returning.

On the night of January 15th Joey was called into Vito's cell. Deep down he knew what the meeting was all about, so it just had to be confirmed. The following day he would be losing someone very close to him. He was happy for Vito, but sad that his friendship was coming to an end. Judging by his previous conversations with Vito, he knew that it was all over.

"Vito," Joey called.

"Sit down and have a drink with me," offered Vito.

Joey took a seat on Vito's bunk as a plastic cup was filled up with the homemade whisky. He looked up into the older man's eyes. The sad inmate had a hard time accepting the fact that he was about to lose a friend and a father figure. Not to mention the man who saved his life.

"You know tomorrow I'm leaving."

"I know, but won't I see you when I get out of here?"

"We already discussed this, and it would be better for the both of us if we part ways."

"No, I won't accept that. You mean too much to me for me to just forget about you," Joey said, getting to his feet. "I won't let that happen!"

"There's no other way around it, I'm caught up too deep in other shit and it just won't work. In here you needed me to survive. Out there I would only hurt your chances of bettering your life. You don't need me out in the streets; you'll do just fine without me. Just remember all the talks that we had and apply them to your life. In the long run you will be better off. My life is too corrupt to be dragging you down every time I take a fall. Sooner or later somebody might take a pot shot at you for something that I did. Trust me when I say this, I don't want that happening to you. So get on with your life and promise me one thing," he said.

"What's that?"

"I want to be invited to your wedding," he said as he extended his hand.

"Are you kidding, you're my best man," Joey boasted. The two men then exchanged handshakes as Vito pulled Joey towards him. The sudden jolt emptied some of the contents from his plastic cup.

"Come here," Vito said as he embraced his godson with tears in his eyes. "I love you, kid, don't ever forget that. This hurts me just as much as it hurts you."

"I love you too. I just wish it didn't have to end this way."

"Here, take this phone number, don't ever use it unless you are calling me up to come to your wedding. If I relocate I will find a way to indirectly get in touch with you," he said while handing Joey a business card with his name and phone number on the back.

"Fred's car wash?" Joey said staring at the white card with blue printing on it. "What, are ya gonna be running a car wash?"

"What car wash?" he said. "Turn the card over, my number's on the back of the card."

"Oh, for a minute there I thought I would be able to get a job when I get out of this place."

"Joey, I meant what I said about not calling me!"

"What if I'm dying?"

"Don't be a wise ass. If you're dying make sure you reach out to me before you're dead. I'm good at sending flowers. I've been to enough damn funerals in my life. Joey, I'm serious when it comes to this. Only use this number if the situation is absolutely dire."

"Okay, okay."

"There's just one other thing."

"What's that," Joey asked.

Vito began to fumble with the clasp that was holding together the chain around his neck. His big hands were awkwardly trying to open the fastener on the 18-karat gold piece.

"Here, I want you to have this," he said as he held the medallion in his hand. The piece was sparkling with glitter as the gold chain was draping from the palm of his hand. He then placed it in Joey's possession and squeezed it into his awaiting grasp.

"Vito, I can't accept this," he said trying to place it back into his hand. "It's too personal."

"You must take it and always wear it around your neck. This marks the heart that makes me and you beat as one. My father handed it down to me when I was a kid, and now I am handing it down to you. Someday I hope you will be proud and hang it around the neck of your own son. By giving it to you I know that this medallion will have a long legacy of love. With me keeping it, I know now that I will die with this thing hanging around my neck. Then some fuckin' undertaker will grab it before I hit the coffin."

Vito retrieved the medal from Joey's giving hand and put each end of the chain into separate fingers of his expanded arms. He raised his arms and placed the medallion around the neck of his Godson. Joey gracefully accepted the gift from the new Underboss. With two lives going in different directions this was the only symbol of remembrance. There were memories, but you could never put your arms around them.

"It looks better on you," Vito said.

"You think so! I will promise you one thing, I will never take this off from around my neck," Joey said as a chill ran through his entire body.

"I know you won't. What's the matter?" Vito asked, noticing an odd look on Joey's face. "Are you okay?"

Shrugging he said, "I just got a strange feelin' running through my body."

"Like what?"

"I don't know," he said with a peculiar look. "I never had this feeling before. I feel like something has entered inside of me. All of a sudden I feel very shaky. Vito, what could it be? I feel numb! My whole body is shaking. Look at me." Joey held out his trembling hands. Vito studied Joey's uneasy appearance.

Joey's eyes opened wide. Suddenly, he dropped his head. Mind boggled, Joey looked down at the medallion. Simultaneously, bright flashes of biblical images and events raced before his sub-conscious mind. Chanting, cheers and jeers resounded loudly inside of his head. Beneath the threshold he saw himself standing in a courtyard, almost 2000 years ago, amongst a group of common peasants. With tears streaming down Joey's saddened face, he watched a man being ridiculed and severely punished. Crack, crack, crack were the sounds of the repeated strokes from the heavy leather whips. Defiant, the valiant man continued on. From head to toe, he was covered with his own blood. On his back he was carrying a large wooden cross.

The man stopped for a moment and looked over at Joey.

A teardrop fell.

Tacitly, the man turned away and proceeded onward. Thump, thump, thump were the sounds of the heavy cross as it dragged across the cobblestone walkway. In its aftermath, a long trail of blood.

"Nooooo," Joey screamed, while putting his hands to both sides of his head. Now raising his head he just stood numb and gazed at Vito.

"What the hell is wrong with you? Vito asked, and then developed a surprised look on his face. "Joey, look, blood! Your nose is bleeding."

Joey wiped off the blood from underneath his nose with his fingers. Now rubbing the stained fingers together, he looked at the blood. "This is not my blood."

"What the hell are you talkin' about? Whose blood is it?"

"I don't know."

"Stop talkin' like an idiot. It's nothing," said Vito. "It's just a nose bleed. You just been through a hell of a lot lately. Ya know, solitary, stress and all the other shit."

"No, no you're wrong, this is something different. I'm starting too see things and my whole body feels all fucked up. I feel like I'm someone else. Something or someone is inside of me, Vito."

"Will you cut this shit out," Vito said. "It's all in your mind, nothing more than that."

"I don't know, but I hope you're right," Joey replied. "Maybe I just need some sleep."

Was Vito right? After all, Joey had been through a hell of a lot. Anybody in their right mind would feel different. If they didn't, then they would have not been considered human. But Joey was also right, the medallion seemed to come alive as soon as it was placed around his neck. There were no explanations for this. Whatever Vito knew about the medal, he was not about to reveal, not now anyway. This Medallion with all the past generations of hardships, prosperity, heartbreak and love was now inherited by new blood. Joey DeFalco was the new generation with the same intentions of stabilizing the love that it should represent.

As Joey was exiting Vito's cell he turned around to face Vito's parting words. He looked at him and the moment was very touching. After all, these were two grown men who formed a remarkable bond in a matter of a few months. The parting of the two was sure to be painful for both.

"You're gonna make it, kid," he said. "Always remember to stay pure and make me proud."

Those were Vito's parting words. He was always thinking and practicing these laws of purity. Any interracial marriages or relationships were against his will. In his eyes it was always about the blood and preserving the uniformed composition of it. For Joey to be with anyone else other than an Italian would be breaking his laws of moral conduct. He felt his reasons were justified since the birth of his son Eddie.

Vito did not like to hear anybody's disappointments. When somebody failed to satisfy his hopes and expectations he indiscreetly kept his distance from them. He was very prudent in regard to his own interests; failure was not a part of his comfort zone. Everyone had to make him proud and he loved the feeling of the people who actually did it. To Vito the words, "make me proud," were words full of self-respect and independence. Those were the three honorable words that would put a person on his majestic pedestal.

At 11:00 a.m. the following morning, Joey ventured away from his work detail and walked into Vito's cell. "Vito," he called.

The cell was empty; all there was left were a few personal belongings strewn across the top of his neatly made bed. Joey could not help himself but to rummage through the small mess. What caught his eye were a couple of photographs of Vito with his arm around a young man no more than twenty years old. But there was something peculiar about this photo as he picked it up and examined it closely. What came to his attention was that the kid in the picture was wearing the same medallion that was now in his possession. Vito and the unidentified young man wore huge smiles running across their faces. Whoever this mystery man was, Joey would make it his top priority to find out. He quickly stuffed the small Polaroid into his back pocket and turned around to leave Vito's cell.

"What are you doing here?" Vito asked as he entered his cell.

"I was lookin' for you. I wanted to say goodbye to you before you got escorted out."

"Well, I'm glad you're here, I have to give you something." Vito then jumped on top of his bed and started to stick his left arm between the bed and the cinder-block wall. Struggling to find what he is looking for, he finally pulled it out. "Here," he said as he flipped the white envelope in Joey's direction.

"What's this?

"Open it and find out!"

Joey opened up the sealed envelope and looked inside. The expression on his face alone said it all. The surprised look was transmitted to Vito in a hurry. "What's this for?" Joey said, confused.

"Just take it, it's yours."

"How much money is here?"

"It's a little under five thousand."

"I can't take this!"

"Why not, you won it."

"What the hell do you mean, I won it."

"It's from the fight, I took a few bets on it."

"You took a few bets on the fight? You mean to tell me as I was bustin' my ass out there you were running a fuckin' casino?" Joey snapped. "What are you, the Bugsy Siegal of this place? Why didn't you tell me?"

Vito started to laugh hysterically as he tried to control his emotions. He then took a second or two to regroup before he hopped back into the conversation. "Wait a minute, I can't stop laughing."

"Take your time, I have another five months left!"

"The only reason why I didn't tell you was that I felt that it would have put more pressure on you."

"Well, whatever the reasons are, I'm not taking it."

"This will help to get you through the next five months."

"You're the one who always tells me to do things right and stay straight. Now you want to give me this money that I almost died for. I don't want it!"

"Listen, you earned this damn money. I just wanted to set you up with a little cushion for yourself in here and when you get out of here."

"I just can't believe that you would take bets with my life on the line."

"You don't understand, I had more faith and trust in you than I have had for anyone in a long time. Deep down I knew that you would pull through, and you did. Believe it or not, I did it all for you. I would never steer you wrong, kid."

At that moment Joey felt like whipping out the picture and asking Vito the million-dollar question. But his better sense of judgment prevailed. After all, he figured that he had gotten away with enough of the second-guessing.

"So here, take the money," he said as he folded the envelope and stuffed it into the front pocket of Joey's pants. "I know it's not much, but it will help you."

Within a couple of minutes all the boys would crowd into Vito's cell to say their good-byes. For the rest of the crew these good-byes were only temporary, they would somewhere down the road of time be reunited. They would all pick up on all the business that prison forced them to leave behind. On the outside more corruption awaited them, especially with Vito's new position of a Mafia Underboss.

But for Joey this might be his final farewell to a man whom he will never forget. It still escaped him that the man who was ready to walk free from the forty foot walls, was his godfather. The well-kept secret was hidden safely in the minds of a powerful friendship between Vito and Dutch. Not telling Joey only made it easier when it came to saying goodbye.

"Well, that's it," said Vito. "It's time to get the hell out of here," he said while looking around his cell for the last time. "I'm as good as gone!"

"You got everything?" Dutch said.

"All my belongings are in this bag, and my release papers are in my back pocket. I think that's about it."

The men started to go through their final hugs and handshakes. Some parting words were overheard in the background. It was now up to Dutch to assume all the business and leadership roles left behind by Vito.

"Joey," called Vito. "Wait outside the cell, I want you to walk me out."

"Okay," he said as he went to assume a position against the railing outside the cell. Joey was soon met by an approaching prison-guard stationed right by his side. His intentions were to usher Vito out of the cell block area in a peaceful manner.

"Dutch," Vito said. "Promise me that you'll watch over this kid. He's still not a seasoned vet, you know. He has to make it out of here."

"You got it, Vito. You know you didn't have to ask me that."

"I know, Dutch, I know. Deep down, I'm really going to miss the kid a lot. This is killing me."

"I know it is, but it's time to move on. Now get out of here," Dutch said. "Freedom is calling!"

"I'm out of here," he proclaimed while walking out of his cell for the final time. "Joey, let's go!"

The two men then started to walk down the second floor tier side by side. The guard followed up the rear about six feet behind the duo. Cheers and jeers were overheard from every floor of the cell block. Each step brought on different catcalls derided with hate. Vito walked proudly as the messages of detestation were a sure sign of victory to him.

"Ignore all this shit," he said to Joey. "Stand proud and smile."

"Vito, in a sick way I'm kind of enjoying it."

"These assholes know I'm leaving so they have to take their last parting shots at me. In a way it makes me feel good."

"How's that?"

"That my presence was felt and they feel relieved that I'm leaving. But they are so wrong!"

"Why?"

Vito's walking came to an abrupt halt. He looked into Joey's eyes with integrity. "Because you're still here!" he said with authority. "My presence will be carried on through you. But you have to promise me that you will make it out of here in five months."

"You've got my word."

"I want you to hang tight with Dutch. You should be gettin' out before him anyway."

"I will, don't worry. I'll be alright," Joey assured him. "But you do the same."

The men descended down the steps and proceeded to walk out of the cell block area. Joey walked Vito as far as the system would let him. A whole wall of steel bars now separated Vito from his impending freedom. A large electronically controlled gate swung open waiting for him to step through it. Vito stopped before the opening and turned in the direction of Joey. Joey just looked at him, waiting for his departing words.

"Somewhere, somehow, some way I know we will find each other again. But it has to be under the right circumstances," Vito said. "Let's just see what life has in store for the both of us? Only God has the answer to that question."

The over sensitive Joey just looked at him as his eyes started to water. Somehow he had a feeling that this was the last time he would see Vito's face again. He was facing the reality that Vito was afraid to tell him.

"Come on, kid, don't do this. It will ruin your image."

"I'm alright, get going before they lock you in here again."

Vito then dropped his small blue duffel bag and with great force wrapped his arms around Joey. The embrace was very powerful as both men were squeezing with strenuous exertion.

"Remember one thing," he whispered in Joey's ear. "I love you."

"I'm gonna miss you, Vito!"

"I know, kid, I'm gonna miss you too. Make sure you stay tight with Dutch."

"I will."

"Make me proud!"

With those parting words, Vito picked up his duffel bag and embarked through the steel bars towards his freedom. Joey watched as he slowly disappeared down the narrow corridor. Vito turned around for one last time. He looked at Joey, raised his right fist into the air and shook it in Joey's direction. Joey did the same as he cracked a small smile. Vito then slowly turned his head and walked away never turning back again.

The next few months went by smoothly without any problems at all. Joey's nasty reputation had gotten him past every day with ease. Vito had been right all along; nobody wanted a piece of him. What other prisoners thought was their own business. Deep down Joey knew who he really was, and he was not the person that all other inmates thought he was. But for his own safety, he wanted to keep the image of being a cold-blooded animal.

Joey stood by a calendar hanging from a wall adjacent to his bunk. The bright red X's marked off the pending days towards his release. Prison life in some way became like a ritual as he grew more accustomed to it. The customary procedures start to sink into most prisoners as a way of life. After a while you start to learn how to put up with it.

"What are you doing?" Dutch said as he entered Joey's cell.

"Nothing much, I'm gonna hit the sack early."

"I feel kind of tired myself," he said. "You know you're out of here in a week or so!"

"I know, I still haven't figured out what the hell I'm gonna do with myself. My whole fuckin' life is turned upside down. I'm worried about this, Dutch."

"There's always painting!"

"Are you kidding me, after this place I never want to see another fuckin paint brush for the rest of my life."

"Don't worry, something will break open for you."

"Do you think the parole board is going to turn me loose?"

"Are you fuckin kidding me!" he said. "The other day they let a minister go who was convicted of molesting young boys. That scumbag didn't even serve his full sentence. Just make sure you tell those idiots what they wanna hear. You must act like an altar boy when you go before them. Tell them there is tons of work waitin' for you when you get released."

"Okay, I will," Joey promised. "Dutch, there's something that I have been wanting to ask ya."

"Shoot," he said.

Joey then picked up a yellow envelope and opened the flap. He reached inside and pulled out the subject matter. "Can you explain this to me?" he said as he handed it to Dutch.

"Where did you get this?"

"It was layin' on top of Vito's bed the day he got released."

"I suppose you wanna know who the other person in the picture is?"

"It's not only that, Dutch, he also happens to be wearing this around his neck," he said, lifting the Christ head from off of his chest.

"I shouldn't be tellin' you this, but whatever I tell you stays here. Do you understand me?"

"I swear it will go no further."

"Don't even say anything to Red and Paulie."

"I won't, you can trust me."

"For some reason I have a feelin' that you have a right to know. But if Vito ever finds out that I told you, he would probably put a bullet in me."

"Come on, Dutch, you know that's bullshit."

"I know, but it might put a strain on our friendship."

"Dutch, from my lips to your ears, I swear to God I will not say a word to anyone."

"That's Vito's son Eddie!"

During the next fifteen to twenty minutes Dutch related the whole story. From the time little Eddie was born, all the way up to the dismemberment of his left index finger. He even threw the long history of the medallion into his heartbreaking story. More than that he could not tell him, for even Dutch did not know Eddie's present whereabouts.

In Joey's mind there were a lot of questions that remained unanswered. Obviously there were a lot of problems between Eddie and his father that would never surface. In this day and age it is not too uncommon to hear problems coming from dysfunctional families. With this relationship it does seem too late for Vito to recapture the heart of his wayward son. Drugs and many years of wrong doings by both father and son would keep these bitter feelings alive. As far as Joey was concerned this issue was dead and buried.

"Make sure you get rid of that picture," Dutch ordered while leaving the cell. Joey then disobeyed his pal's orders and stuffed the picture back into the yellow envelope. He then hid the envelope in a safe resting-place.

Joey's sentence was dwindling down to a matter of days. With nowhere else to go, he started to make some plans to return to his mother's home. It would soon be time to explain all of his failures to her. Little did his mother know that this little visit was about to become permanent. But, after all, this was her son, and like most Italian mothers she would welcome him with open arms.

All that was left was a meeting with the Parole Board and its left wing members. His freedom was pending, but their stamp of approval was an absolute necessity. These days the parole board was much more lenient. Prison overcrowding would sometimes put a murderer back on the streets before his full sentence was served. Most of the time these die-hard liberals were a hardened criminal's dream. To them, everyone had a shot at rehabilitating themselves; even Charles Manson had the potential. This was the sick thinking of these freedom makers as the filth was always thrown back onto the streets.

Joey quietly closed the office door behind him as he exited the room. Silence occupied the hallway of the second floor of the administration building. With his head bent down, the young man took a few moments to reflect on his current situation.

"Yes!" Joey screamed from the top of his lungs. The short loud thunderous sound rumbled down the hallway with great intensity. It turned down every corner of open space as the echo started its repetition. He started to pump his fists with jubilation. The happy inmate had just received his walking papers.

All that was left for him to do was to say his sad farewells to Dutch and the rest of the boys. It was a warm day this June 6th, 1990, and it would start a new beginning to his emerging independence.

Chapter 10

THE MODEST TWO family brick house was a long way from the ultra modern high-rise building where he once resided. The cozy tree lined block was very peaceful. Besides some passing vehicles and homeowners tending to their everyday activities, there wasn't much going on. Over the years the neighborhood seemed to thin out a bit. Most of Joey's childhood friends either got married or simply moved on with their lives.

It was still a predominantly Italian neighborhood in the Bensonhurst section of Brooklyn. You just know that Italians live here just by the texture of the community. Every Sunday the sweet smelling aroma of a hearty meat sauce lingered above the many rows of houses. A weekend never passed when you wouldn't see a senior citizen walking down the street with a loaf of Italian bread in one hand and a box of their favorite pastries in the other.

You name him, from Saint Anthony to Saint Joseph the front gardens were like a Nativity set. Statues of the holy were everywhere. These shrines took up every square foot of space in the front yard. Even the grass had a hard time finding some sunlight with all the marble and stone hovering above it. It was like these people were trying to keep some kind of evil from entering their homes. To them these symbols of faith offered more protection than steel bars covering the windows of their homes.

The back yards were the domain of fruit trees and vegetable gardens. These urban farmers grew everything from squash to tomatoes. Every square inch of dirt was sprouting up something. Sometimes even the cracks in the walkways would sprig a basil leaf ready to be plucked. If you looked up, you would find grapes and figs covering the skies. The man made props kept the growing fruits from falling to the ground below. Every space was utilized, whether it was under your feet or above your head.

The remainder of the backyard resembled a launder-mat during a hurricane. When the wind blew it seemed like there were clothes flying everywhere. Clotheslines were stretched out from every available window to every telephone pole in the neighborhood. On a nice sunny day you could always see what your neighbor's bed sheets looked like. If you were really lucky you could see Gina Petrillo's sexy undergarments hanging from the clothesline a couple of houses down.

Everything you do in an Italian neighborhood gets noticed. Sometimes nosy neighbors even know what time you smoke your first morning cigarette or take your first shit. Nothing is ever kept under lock and key. They know what time you wake up and the time you go to sleep. What time you eat your dinner and what you're even eating. Many times you would catch a nosy neighbor staring at the contents of your own garbage pail. When you take out the trash, they're there. When you water your lawn, guess what? They're there! When you're coming home from work they are outside to greet you. Some of them even know your agenda for the day better than you do.

They also had a warped sense of morality. If a young lady returned from a date after midnight, she was branded a whore. It really did not matter where she was or what she was doing; she was still a whore. If she wore makeup, she was a slut. If her pants were too tight, she was a pig. It was not good to be a growing young lady in this neighborhood. If she had a life she never had a chance.

Some of these people could hear footsteps before they even turned the corner to come up the block. It was a common sight to see a pair of peering eyes peeking through the Venetian blinds at all hours of the day. It was so bad that you could feel their eyes running right through your body. Even if you were just strolling on the concrete walkway while passing their homes, there would be a careful eye watching you.

God forbid if you would block any part of their driveway with your vehicle. The cops would be there before you even stepped out of the car. All of the residents of this Italian neighborhood acted like they were protecting a sprawling estate in Beverly Hills. It seemed like these nosy bastards would never sleep. No wonder their houses were never burglarized, these people stayed awake for most of the night. They knew that you saw them looking, but they didn't care. These snoops had their noses in everybody else's business but their own.

Joey's old 2nd floor bedroom still held some of the mementos and many reminders of his youth. Even the wallpaper was the same, the ugly pattern screamed at you every time you walked through the bedroom door. The once white walls and ceiling were in dire need of a paint job. It was last painted a year before Joey left the house for good. In the corner of the room there was a 19 inch television set that sat on top of a small stand. Everything was left basically untouched throughout the years. You could tell that the room was untouched just by the smell of it. Only an occasional dusting prevented the room from being walked into at all. This emptiness was all about to change, for Joey DeFalco was coming home.

The whole neighborhood knew about Joey's misfortunes and so did his mother. After all, the story was printed in every major newspaper in the city. If it wasn't the tabloids breaking the news to her, she was sure to hear it from family or friends. She never let her son know that she knew anything about his past. The mother of three didn't want her son to do anymore worrying than he had to, especially when it came to herself. The strong woman kept it all inside to protect whatever dignity her son had left. But deep down his criminal convictions were slowly killing her. No matter what, she always held her head up high, even though her son had disgraced the family name.

Once he got settled in, a few minor changes had to be made. He still had over forty five hundred dollars left from the money that Vito had given him. A new 27 inch color television set and a black leather recliner had to be added to the old fashioned décor. A stereo, cable hookup and a video cassette recorder were soon to follow. It did not take Joey long to get settled into his old bedroom. It was the outside world that left him with the feeling of hopelessness.

For the first couple of days the phone was ringing off the hook from people and some so called friends he had not heard from in years. Some were truly sympathetic while others were oh so happy to hear about his fall from grace. At the ripe old age of 27 Joey was old news as most acquaintances stayed clear of the now convicted felon.

The next few months brought severe bouts of depression and loneliness. These two sicknesses developed into something a bit more extreme. He was suddenly hit with this overpowering bout of panic-stricken terror. The attacks would sometimes strike two or three times a day. Accelerated heartbeat, light-headedness, severe stomach cramps and the uncontrollable feeling of dying were just a few of the symptoms he had to deal with. Even his blood pressure was shooting through the roof from all the stress in his life. Several trips to the doctor were futile and a waste of money. From Prozac to Paxil, you name it and Joey was on it. It got so bad that he did not even want to leave the confines of his own bedroom anymore. Hour after hour and day after day, he just sat in front of his television set lamenting about his past. Even though he was out of prison, the feeling had gotten worse. He was a free man but still unable to function in the civilized world. After only nine months behind bars, the sentence left a lifetime of shattered dreams. His drive and the will to live had disappeared in the courtroom. He took these symptoms to prison and then when he came home they spilled out all over his bedroom. Talking to people was useless, because they could never understand the pain and suffering involved with these mental diseases. With no self esteem and stricken with depression and anxiety, his mental condition had decided that he spend his remaining life in the safety of his mother's home.

It was an early August afternoon; the summer sun was so brutal that it smoked the tar roof of his home. All summer long the city was subjected to high humidity and intense heat. The heat wave with its 98-degree temperatures had every fire hydrant in the neighborhood supplying temporary relief. An automobile would receive a free car wash as it passed through the pleasurable blast of cold water. Little children frolicked around in the cascading water. For parents who could not afford a pool or get to the city beaches, this was the next best thing.

Joey was sitting in his recliner watching a ball game on TV. His five thousand BTU air conditioner barely put a dent in cooling off the overheated bedroom. The sweat was pouring off his unkempt body. His undershirt had yellow stains of perspiration underneath both armpits. Looking seedy and dirty, Joey resembled a bum taking residence on a public park bench. Greasy and filthy, his hair looked like a matted mess with its thick and tangled style. The once good-looking face had not seen a razor in weeks. His beard covered most of his face; the other part was not worth looking at. The only thing that stayed the same was his weight as his stress and nerves kicked his metabolism into full gear. This self induced tragedy had definitely taken him down, way down to where he was almost a hopeless case. Help would have to come from somewhere, even if it took a miracle.

His mother was shocked by the disintegration of his life. After a while the poor woman did not even recognize her own son. The best she could do was clean up the messes that he left behind. Joey was too old for her to throw into a bathtub and start bathing. The best she could do was just recommend one. A mother's love is unconditional and slightly irrational, so his pain was hers too. Every day the lady took her rosary beads to church hoping and praying that her son would snap out of this living coma.

L ater that same evening, the telephone was ringing and ringing. Joey didn't move. Finally he decided to pick it up only because the person on the other end was so persistent.

"Hello," he said, annoyed.

"Joey! It's me Tony."

"Tony, Tony who?"

"You forgot about me already," the voice answered. "It's me, Tony Salvo."

"What's up, Tony?" Joey said, taking a sip from a cold can of beer.

"How are you feeling?" Tony said, standing at a public pay phone.

"I'm getting by."

"I was thinking about reaching out to you a couple of months ago, but I knew that you needed some time to think things over."

Tony Salvo and Joey had a friendship that was approaching its twentieth year. Even though the relationship was never a steady one, they always managed to keep in touch with each other. From grade school to each guy's first blow-job, the two shared a lot of fond memories. Over the years, the two men had some major disagreements with each other, but there would always be something that would unite them back together.

Tony owned and operated a major food distributor in the Tri State area. He supplied restaurants and pizzerias with everything from pizza sauce to paper cups. Business was very good for him as his fleet of trucks grew from 3 to 13 over the last five years. From a small business that his father handed down to him, he expanded outside the 5 boroughs and into the surrounding states. Living high and large Tony never helped anyone without expecting something in return. He never did anything for anybody unless he was the major beneficiary.

"Listen, Joey, what are you doing right now?"

"Nothing, why? Where are you?"

"I'm in your neighborhood so I thought I would give you a call. Why don't you take a ride with me?" he said, peeking out into the busy street at his double-parked car. The sounds of the busy Brooklyn streets droned on in the background.

"Why, where are you going?"

"I got a business proposition for you and I want you to check it out."

"What kind of business?" Joey asked while lighting a cigarette.

"It's a pizzeria," Tony answered, making these clicking sounds over the phone.

Whenever he discussed business or got stressed out in any way, Tony had this nervous twitch that rocked his head from side to side. The twitch would somehow start at his shoulders and the tension would slowly work its way up to the top of his head. Slowly but surely the nervous reaction would find its way down from his head and into his mouth. The sounds were reminiscent of a grandfather clock clicking the seconds away. For a person who knew him well, these sounds were all too annoying and all too familiar.

"Tony, if you think I'm going to start flipping pizzas around you're out of your fuckin' mind."

"No, it's nothing like that."

"Then what the hell are you talking about?"

"I have this account that owes me a lot of money, the guy had a gambling problem and he couldn't pay his bills. So through Bankruptcy Court I inherited this place," he said as the clicking continued. The weird bodily noises would continue throughout the conversation.

"Why did you overextend yourself on his line of credit," Joey said as his Wall Street knowledge was starting to surface.

"He was a good friend of mine. He told me that he was renovating the place and I believed him. So I gave him more stock and extended his line of credit. Little did I know that he was gambling everything away."

"Why don't you try to sell the place or liquidate the equipment?"

"The store has only been empty for three months. If I sell the equipment I will only get back pennies on the dollar."

"So how do I fit into all of this?" Joey asked, his curiosity piqued. There was something that Tony was not telling him.

"I want to make you a fifty-fifty partner. I want you to become the working partner and operate the place. I know you have great business savvy and I think you can make a go of the place"

"I don't know a damn thing about running a pizzeria. Besides, I don't have the money to do it even if I wanted to."

"That's the beauty of it as far as you're concerned. It's not going to cost you a dime," Tony said while adjusting his wire-rimmed glasses.

"What's the catch then?" Joey said. "I know you and I know you wouldn't be offering me fifty percent of anything that was making money."

"This place was making money, I just need someone that I can trust. You know, like watching my back."

"I don't know, I have to think about it," Joey said already knowing that he was not the man for the job. "I need some time to think about it."

"Well what else do you have going for yourself right now?"

"I got a few other things in the works. One of them has to come through for me!" he said, hurling lies over the phone. Joey defended himself from the demeaning position that he had put himself into. He was not a top prospect on anybody's list of eligible employees.

"Well, will you do me a favor then?" Tony asked, putting another dime into the pay phone.

"What's that?"

"Just promise me you'll think about it."

"Alright, I'll think about it. Give me a couple of weeks and then get back to me."

"Good, and remember it's a good opportunity for you. At least you know that I'm thinking about you."

"Thanks, I feel a lot better knowing that you care," Joey said.

"Why don't we get together one Saturday night for dinner and maybe hit a few nightspots?" Tony said as he reached into his pocket for his car keys. "You have to start getting out there again."

"Yea, maybe in a couple of weeks we'll get together."

"I'm sure you could use a nice piece of ass."

"Yea, it's been a while, jerking off just don't cut it anymore."

"Yea, I know what you mean, but don't forget what we talked about."

"I won't, I'll keep it in mind."

"Alright, I'll talk to you in a couple of weeks."

Joey put out his cigarette into the overloaded ashtray. "Talk to you then," he said before he hung up.

Joey sat and stared at the white trim-line telephone. Deep down he knew that a move had to be made sooner or later. Vito's money was rapidly dwindling down to nothing. His daily ration of beer, cigarettes and whatever junk food his sometimes appetite called for were quickly eating away at his pocketbook. But like everything else in the last couple of months, he pushed it aside and saved the worrying for another day. Everything seemed to be pushed towards the future, for in his mind he wished the future would never come.

T he states of North and South Carolina were about to be hit with a major tropical storm. Heavy rain and high winds were expected as the summer depression picked up steam over the Atlantic Ocean. Hurricane status was expected as the winds were approaching the shoreline with 100 MPH gusts. Up to ten foot waves would soon pound the beaches, possibly leaving erosion and heavy damage. The forecast called for the dangerous weather to slam into the Carolinas and rumble north up the East Coast in intensifying fashion. Hour after hour it gathered more strength as the balmy high seas fed the fuel to its enormous appetite. September was here and the hurricane season would start off with a thunderous bang.

In the Northeastern states people were sitting on pins and needles hoping for the best. For only an act of God could save them from this dark apocalyptic type weather. In a matter of twelve hours, New York City was about to be hit with one of the worst storms in recent history.

Joey and his mother had just finished dinner. The kitchen television was working overtime monitoring the upcoming storm. The saintly looking woman was glued to the set praying for a miracle. In a way Joey was pleased that his mother felt some comfort by having him close to her. It was times like these that widowed parents needed the security of having one of their children around. Sleeping would become easier for her. All loving mothers welcome the return of their children, no matter what circumstances have brought them home.

The clock struck 10 p.m., and it was bedtime for the middle-aged woman. She then started her journey up the short flight of steps to her bedroom. For her, six o'clock in the morning rolled around pretty fast. Her routine was pretty basic, it seemed that she did the same old things day in and day out. It never changed for her, most things that were important at one time or another became irrelevant. The short, slightly overweight woman lived for two things, her children and her home. After the death of her husband those basic things just became her way of life.

Feeling tired, Joey decided to retire for the night around eleven. Sometimes mental stress is more tiring than any physical activity could ever be. It was not uncommon for him to be tossing or turning for several hours, before finally falling asleep. This night would be no different, sleeping was an hour or two away. This trend became habit forming for him, too much time and stress made sleeping an almost impossible chore.

The only light came from a bedside clock radio and a night-light that dimly lit the other side of the large room. The half-opened window, with the shades a quarter up, provided a glimmer of brightness from the moon. On this night the moon was full and bright, overpowering everything in the nighttime sky. The summer scene was picture perfect. The setting was serene and peaceful as the clock struck midnight.

Lying flat on his stomach and facing away from the window, Joey had tucked himself under a light gray bed-sheet. A newspaper that sometimes made sleep more attainable was by his side.

Suddenly, Joey felt a powerful breeze hitting his sprawled out body. The peculiar gust of air had awakened him out of a semi conscious sleep. Thinking that the storm had arrived early, he picked his head up astonished at what was going on before his eyes. The wind grew stronger. The thrust was rattling his windows and flapping the shades. The window covering then suspended in an extended position, like it was floating on air. Everything from bottles of medication too knick-knacks went flying off the night table beside the bed. The debris was spiraling upwards and crashing into the ceiling above.

Still gusting, the powerful breeze just kept coming and coming, like it was being sucked into the room. His newspaper was inhaled by the strong wind and strewn about the room in a circular motion. The hanging light fixture was oscillating like the dervish. Joey started to squint as the room turned bright. A great bright light followed the untamed winds through the opened window. Joey was sightless by the streak of fire like light. Blindness was everywhere. Like a flume, the conduit rays circled the room at accelerated and uncontrollable speeds, emitting fusions of intense heat.

Then out of nowhere, the powerful breezes and intimidating light subsided. There was calm and darkness again.

Sitting numb for a few seconds, Joey slowly and cautiously climbed out of bed and walked a couple of feet to the window that faced the backyard. Bending down and then looking out of the opening gave him an eerie feeling. Outside the movement was still, not a leaf was shaking on the pair of maple trees within his view. The atmosphere was unruffled and smothered with dead silence.

Looking around he could not find any answers for this strange phenomenon.

Am I dreaming? he thought. *Will these prison nightmares ever end?*

After a couple of minutes he just pondered the moment, shook his head in disbelief, shut the window and returned to bed. The mess was left where it fell; tomorrow was another day.

Left visibly shaken and somewhat daunted, Joey clutched his pillow and gently closed his eyes as if nothing ever happened. Then, out of nowhere the bedroom started to erupt with earthquake like tremors. Joey was jolted and bounced to an upright position. Side to side, up and down, the room shuddered. The fury was steadfast. Open fissures started to run up and down the surface of his bedroom wall. Clinging picture frames fell to the floor. Chaos was evident. This time Joey looked on horrified. Then the tremors subsided.

Something unexplainable had entered the room. But this time, Joey felt it as it surrounded and touched his entire body. The undisciplined force had brought his senses to a standstill. Stunned, he just stared into the darkness and rubbed his eyes.

For some strange reason Joey's apprehension and fear had disappeared. He felt bewildered, but unafraid as the presence engulfed the room.

Little by little a glowing figure started to coalesce right before his eyes. A ghost like creature started to submerge from the ceiling above. The entity dipped lower and lower, never divulging its true identity. The large shadow, though translucent, was thick in density as it hovered over the darkness.

In Silence, the bedroom started to light up with flashes of reflecting light, each beam of a different color. The incandescent source created radiance, emitting a broad sequence of wind, heat and light.

The shining was fading in and out as the figure slowly transformed. With still unidentifiable features, the amorphous loomed above his bed, an enigmatic apparition. The features of this alien were formless to the human eye. Long dark hair and broad shoulders were the only characteristics that he could distinguish. The outline of the upper torso was massive and very hypnotizing to the sub-conscious mind.

"I can't believe what I'm seeing," Joey whispered to himself.

A cloak appeared to cover the body all the way down to below its knees. The loose fitting garment was flowing through the wild breeze that occupied the room. Suddenly the specter from another world extended his arms in a welcoming fashion. This gesture spanned across the room with one effortless motion. It was ready to speak.

"Will you come with me?" it said, in a foreign language. Somehow Joey understood the extraneous dialect. Joey sat motionless, but attentive. "Will you come with me?" it repeated with the same deep and powerful tone of voice. Each word created an echo that reverberated off the walls.

"Who are you?" Joey asked, frozen with awe.

"Before you were formed in the womb, I knew you. Before you were born, I set you apart. You must go to everyone whom I send you and say whatever I command of you. Do not be afraid of them, for I am with you and will rescue you," the mighty voice said. "Today I appoint you to uproot, tear down, to destroy and overthrow, to build and plant."

"Who are you?" Joey asked again, looking up at the massive and dark figure.

"Get yourself ready and do not be terrified by them or I will terrify you before them. They will fight against you but will not overcome you," the spirit said. "For I am always with you and will rescue you. Now I have put my words in your mouth. You must go where I command you."

"Go where?"

"I, and only I, have the power to guide you," the consuming voice said. "Out of the North an evil breaks forth upon all the inhabitants of the land. You will utter my judgments against them, touching all of their wickedness. Withhold thy foot from being unshod, and thy throat from thirst. Love thy humble stranger, but be aware of the evil that dwells among them. Will you come with me?"

Joey started to obtain a feeling of peace running through his being. All of the stress and anxiety started to drain away. This transformation was felt right away as the pain was lifted from him. Now feeling more at ease within himself, he looked at this great presence to speak.

"Yes, I will come with you," he said, as he lowered his head.

Then with great force, the messenger from another galaxy started to retreat. There was a powerful suction that was pulling Joey with him. The vacuum kept pulling and pulling as if it was trying to draw something from his internal body. The massive pull started to leave a feeling of emptiness to his unwilling being. His gold medallion was practically yanked from around his neck by this urgent and powerful force. The medal was glowing in the night, the colors intense and vibrant. Sparks and flashes were thrown from the radiant relic, touching its visitor. Like minuscule bolts of lightning, the discharge was electric.

Holding on for dear life, Joey then grabbed onto the headboard of the bed, refusing to let go. The tugging continued as the suction started to drag the bed along the carpet below it. Joey, fighting every inch of the way, stayed defiant. The bedroom air was thick and he started to gasp for air. But the creature was relentless, never letting up; it continued to exercise its choking powers. Joey fought on and never gave up; it was not time for him to give up his life. It was not his time to die.

Suddenly the cosmic spirit started to relinquish its almighty clutches. Like drowning smoke, the gray amorphous casually started to disappear into the wall behind the black leather recliner.

There was a smell of smoldering remains from a mighty fire.

Still gasping for air, Joey fell back as he was released from the powerful grip of the unknown. The sudden thrust backwards temporarily left him dazed. At that moment something was taken from Joey, never ever to return. But the presence will linger on forever.

Flapping his eyelids, he then jumped off of the bed hurrying for the light switch on the wall. To his amazement the light gray wall behind the leather recliner was discolored. The departure left a silhouette in the paint covering the wall. Joey slowly walked over to the blemish, staring with every step. Never retreating, he studied it and looked close enough so he could see an image of something surreal. It was an optical image in the embryo stages of exposing its true identity.

"Damn," he whispered. "What the hell is this?"

Placing his hand over it, he lightly ran his fingers over the outline of the figure. To his surprise, this optical imprint had a great sensation of warmth running through it. Light smoke or steam seemed to be running from the pores of the stain and into the air it once possessed. This extraterrestrial being was either a visitor from the heavens above, or the depths of the darkness below. There was no logical explanation to all of this madness, just a sigh of relief that it was gone. At least for now.

The next morning Joey was very tentative in his assessment. He looked around the room and realized that this was not a dream. The mess from the windstorm was very real. Everything from newspapers to hanging pictures lay scattered about the room. The light shadow in the wall was no mirage; it was still there and still warm. This deviation from the normal was definitely a message coming from somewhere.

Who the hell would believe this? he thought.

Around 5:00 pm. Joey was pasted to the television set in his bedroom. The New York winds were picking up heavy steam with each passing hour. Light rain started to fall as the storm began to hit the southern Jersey shoreline. Every channel was broadcasting this event throughout the day. Then an unexpected twist of fate took take place. A meteorologist on one of the local stations reported a sudden shift in the hurricane's path. The storm made a miraculous right hand turn, and started to veer out to sea. Mysteriously it had lost a lot of its impact as it was reduced to a tropical storm. The meteorologists didn't even have an explanation for this odd turn of events, nobody did.

It seems that New York, northern New Jersey and the rest of the eastern seaboard were going to be spared the devastation. Thunderstorms and heavy rains were going to be the forecast for the long night ahead. Joey sat wondering as he looked at the wall to the right of him.

Jesus Christ, he thought. *How the hell did that happen?*

The storm kicked into full gear at about 8:30 that evening. The heavy rains pounded the back of his house as a continuous pitch forking of lightning split the dark skies and were followed by crashing claps of thunder. This vestige of weather was just the outer fringe of the hurricane as the weakened eye was heading out over the roiling Atlantic.

With his mind released from the pressures of the hurricane, Joey started to relax and flip through the channels of his television set. Unexpectedly, the sky's fury sent a visible flash and a loud cracking sound hit the brick wall behind him. A roar of mighty thunder followed right behind it. An atmospheric discharge of lightning had struck his house and started to run its high-powered electrical flow throughout the room. The intense electrical surge had settled inside one of the walls looking for a place to land its natural current. The voltage ran from the outlet, through the wires, in and out of the video-cassette recorder and right into the television set. Its final resting place. The undisciplined current produced an image on the televisions screen. Looking intently, Joey saw a face. Now his focus turned to the blemished wall. Back and forth his head turned to make a positive identification. They were twins! The apparition still loomed.

From the oxidation, accompanied by intense light and heat, a chemical reaction was formed. The infusion blew out the television set as the smoke started to escape from the air vents.

"What the fuck is going on here!" Joey screamed. He then stood to his feet and looked around the room. A large crack had run its way up the wall and right through the image that was left the night before. His mother was screaming and running up the flight of steps.

"Joey, what happened?" she said with a worried look.

"Nothing, Ma, it was just some thunder and lightning."

"What's that smell?"

"It's just the television set, it's not working right. The cheap piece of shit just blew up. Don't worry about it," he said. "Come on, let's go downstairs and have a cup of coffee."

There was no way that he was going to tell her of the unbelievable events that had taken place under her roof. The poor woman would have run right to the church up the corner. His mother would have sworn that all of these happenings were really true; she was that much of a believer. But these supernatural occurrences would have to be kept under lock and key for now. If anything, a trip to the local parish for Joey might be the next best thing to do.

The birds were chirping and singing, it was a beautiful morning to the start of another day. Robins were nurturing their young with the outpouring of worms from the saturated earth. Dogs, everywhere, after being let out after the storm, barked with enthusiasm. The call of the wild and all of its beauty had returned to the great outdoors.

The raging weather had passed with only some local flooding and a few outages of telephone and electrical services. That was the extent of it as everyone almost flirted with disaster. The damages were minimal and life reverted back to its normalcy. But in Joey's mind there was a logical explanation to all of this. It was an explanation that nobody would ever understand or believe.

"Joey, Joey, come down here," his mother yelled.

"What?" he yelled back, sounding very annoyed. The abrupt screaming had awakened him from a sound sleep. "What do you want?"

"Come on down here," she repeated. "I want to show you something."

"What is it?" Joey had gotten out of bed and was now standing at the top of the steps. "What do you want?"

"Come outside and look up at the sky."

In his boxer shorts he ran down the flight of steps and went through the front door. Only in his underwear, Joey stood on the front terrace waiting for his mother's directions.

"Go put something on," she said. "You're embarrassing me!"

"The hell with neighbors," he snapped back. "I could give two shits about what they think. They should all mind their own business anyway. Now what is it?"

"It's a rainbow," his mother said. "Look how beautiful it is."

The awning that covered the front porch forced him out to the steps. From there he looked up into the sky and discovered something absolutely gorgeous. She was right, it was breathtaking.

"Wow," Joey said.

"Isn't it beautiful?"

"It sure is, Ma, it sure is."

The rainbow with all the prismatic colors of a piece of shining crystal was arched right above the house. To his mother it represented a stroke of beauty. But to Joey it meant much more than that. This sighting would start the first day of the rest of his life. He then turned to his mother and looked into her endearing eyes. Church bells started to ring from the building of public worship on the corner. The steady pleasant sounds seemed to bring everything into a proper perspective. For the next couple of seconds, Joey recollected his thoughts. It was then that he felt that everything was starting to come together.

"Ma, I had enough of this shit."

"What do you mean, Joey?"

"I had enough of feeling sorry for myself. I'm going to go out there and make something of myself again. It's not going to be easy, but I'm gonna die trying."

His mother's face lit up like a Christmas tree in a dark room.

A fter a hot shower Joey got dressed and walked up the block to the church rectory. The small building was located in the back of the parking lot that belonged to the church. This house of worship had a beautiful architectural design to it. The design stretched from the massive wooden doors all the way up to the tall tapering tower rising from the roof of the building. Beautiful etchings of the patron saints were sculpted into the granite walls. Stunning colors of the stained glass windows ran up the sides of the building into the projecting eaves of the roof.

Sinners of all ages would come here to repent. Many a bride would stroll down the aisle towards the altar where her future husband anxiously awaited her. This holy structure was a landmark in this closely-knit Italian community. Everyone in the neighborhood would visit it at one time or another. They all had different reasons for visiting, but they all searched for the same conclusions.

"Father Pasquale," Joey called as he kept ringing and ringing the rectory doorbell. "Father, are you there? Father!"

"I'm coming, I'm coming," the mature sounding voice said in broken English. After unfastening the lock, the rectory door was slowly opened. An aging head peeked out.

The senior priest had a hard time recognizing the visitor at the door. He squinted and struggled to place where he knew the person before him. It had been about eight years since Joey had last visited the neighborhood parish. The aging man of the cloth had no idea who he was. "Yes, can I help you?"

"Father, it's me Joey!"

"Joey?" he asked, while studying the face of the young man. "Joey who?"

Looking down at the slightly built man, Joey then grabbed him by the arm and said, "It's me Joey DeFalco, from up the block! My mother is Nina!"

"Oh, Joey," he said. "Joey, it's been a long time. How is your mother?"

"She's fine, thank you. She sends her blessings."

"I seen her a couple of days ago and she looks like she has a lot on her mind."

"Yea she does, that's why I came to see you."

"Is she okay?" the priest said, while holding onto the front door.

"She has been worried about me."

"Come in," the Father said as he invited Joey into the rectory. "Come on in."

Joey took a seat on a sofa in the reception office. Father Pasquale took a seat right by his side. The relationship between the two went back at least twenty years. After all, Joey was the star player on one of the church's baseball teams. That plus a short stint as an altar boy brought back fond memories for both.

"So, Joey, what seems to be troubling you?"

"Father, the other night something very strange happened to me."

Joey proceeded to tell him the events that had occurred in his bedroom. The holy man just listened and occasionally shook his head in silence. Word for word for about fifteen minutes, Joey rambled on and on about that unforgettable evening. He also told the understanding priest everything that happened over the past couple of years. Even the church knew of his misdeeds. In this bedroom community, everyone knew everybody else's business.

"Father, there is just one more thing," Joey said. "These words that were spoken to me were of another language and I understood it all. I never studied another language before in my life but I somehow knew this one. What do you make of it?"

"The language was Hebrew," the Priest said. "You were meant to understand it all. It seems that the good Lord is reaching out to you to provide some direction. These sightings are sometimes common in people who are reaching out for help. God wants you to become closer to him so he can show you the way. Follow him, my son, he will lead you out from under this darkness that you have succumbed to."

"How do I do that?"

"Just keep him in your prayers and always have faith. No matter what happens, never lose your faith in the Lord. He has chosen a path for you, follow it and you will be rewarded," the priest continued. "It will not be easy, for there will be many obstacles and hard times ahead. But in the end you will be in the arms of our Lord and savior, Jesus Christ."

Joey just sat there as the passionate priest spoke his words of wisdom. Never the one to attend Mass every Sunday, he felt like a hypocrite reaching out for the Lord only in his time of need and despair. But to the Church this was very understandable and common; it seemed like this was a way of life for them.

"Father, when the voice said will you come with me, I thought that he was going to take my life now, and I agreed."

"What you are getting from him is a message and a chance to make things right. True, he would have taken you now. But your fight for life showed him that your mission on earth is not fully completed."

"But why me?"

"Listen, we are all God's children. But you, my son, have been chosen. You are a chosen one," he said while putting his hand on top of Joey's shoulder. "When your mission on Earth is completed, then and only then will you be reunited with your creator."

"I still don't understand!"

"Because, Joey, many are called upon by the Lord, but few are chosen. As water reflects a man's face," the priest passionately said, "so a man's heart reflects the man."

"So what happens now?" Joey asked, staring down at the beige carpet.

"That question remains unknown, but fate will dictate to you. Just make sure that you make the right choices."

"I will, Father Pasquale, I will."

"Amen, my son, may you always travel in peace."

"Father, could you do me one other favor?" he said, grabbing the medallion that was hidden underneath his shirt.

"Sure, what is it?"

The two men slowly arose off of the sofa and onto their feet. Joey then held out the gold piece and pointed in the direction of the priest. "Can you bless this for me?"

The Father carefully examined the gold medallion. He turned it every which way to get a better look at it. Father Pasquale noticed something very alarming about the medal. The soft-spoken priest then looked at Joey strangely.

"This explains it all," the good priest said. "Where did you get this from?"

"A good friend of mine gave it to me, why?"

"Who is this good friend?"

"He was just someone that I met in prison."

"Does he know the history behind this piece?"

"I don't think so, he never said anything about it. Why?"

"Because it is a very unusual piece, it is very unique."

"How so?"

"This piece is hundreds and hundreds of years old."

"Really?"

"Yes, I have only seen one other medallion like this one in all of my years."

"Where, Father?"

"I last saw it in Italy, many, many years ago. It was brought to the Vatican to be blessed by a man and his young son. I along with many stunned priests witnessed that blessing. And this, my son, is that same medallion."

"How do you know that?"

"You see these markings on the back of the medallion?"

"I thought they were scratches," Joey said. "But anyway, what about them?"

"They are not scratches," he sternly said. "They are engraved letters of the Hebrew dialect. Over the years they have worn out some, but they are still legible to those who know what they represent."

"So what's the big deal?" Joey brashly asked, as he looked straight at the shaking priest. "You look like you just saw a ghost!"

"No, my son, not a ghost," he responded. "These are the initials or markings of the 12 Apostles of Jesus Christ." The elderly priest took a moment to reestablish his composure. Joey stood frozen with his mouth wide open. "All I will say that it is very special, keep it close to you at all times. Never take it off from around your neck."

"Why?"

"Because it has powers and it will protect you until your mission is satisfied. Eventually, you will find out why."

"What mission?"

"The mission that was commanded upon you," the good priest said. "That same mission that you vowed to fulfill."

"Does this have anything to do with what happened in my bedroom the other night or what happened in my bathroom before I went to prison?"

"Yes, and that's all I am permitted to say," the priest faintly said. "This medal was not supposed to be worn dangling from around one's neck. You see this loop over here?" The priest then pointed to the gold loop where the chain was inserted through.

"Yea, what about it?"

"Well, it was put on many years later and used as a necklace."

"So what are you telling me?"

"I have said enough already, I will say no more. You will find out everything on your own."

"How?"

"Through the medallion! It will guide you."

"How?"

"In time, Joseph," he said, his very voice an enigma. "You will find out in time."

Father Pasquale then performed his magic in the language of his homeland. His hand movements and dialogue were foreign to Joey's eyes and ears. But deep down he knew the message that was being sent. The session soon ended after he was splashed with holy water, the holy water that represented the tears of Jesus Christ. Joey left the rectory scratching his head, he did not like the look on the priest's face after he saw the medallion. Nor did he like the fact that many of his questions were left unanswered. To Father Pasquale, it seemed like the medal had a mysterious past, a past that he was not willing to reveal.

The elderly priest quickly shut the rectory door behind Joey. Acting a bit irrational, he raced to the nearest telephone in the rectory's office. Picking up the receiver, his wrinkled and unstable hands trembled with each touch of the buttons on the telephone's keypad. Finally completing the call, he waited impatiently for the ringing to end.

"Hello," a voice said.

"Father Catrone?"

"Yes!"

"This is Father Pasquale."

"How are you, Frank?"

"I'm okay," he said. "But this isn't a personal call about me."

"What's troubling you my good friend?"

"The Medallion of Nazareth has resurfaced."

"Where? Over by you in Brooklyn?"

"Yes, it has reappeared before me. I just held it in my hands."

"Are you absolutely positive?"

"Yes, I am," Father Pasquale boldly stated. "All the markings and signs were there. Father Catrone, tell me something. I know of this medallion and what it represents, but please educate me of its ancient past and the mysteries behind it."

"Well, Frank, since its path is now at your doorstep," Father Catrone said, "you have the right to know." The high ranking Roman Catholic clergyman took a sip of water and continued on. He was about to reveal some dark secrets that only the higher echelon of the priesthood knew. "After Jesus was crucified and died for us that is when it all began. When his body was resurrected, that medallion was made in his image. His twelve apostles sat around campfires praying endlessly for countless days and cold nights for his return. Each one of them took turns holding the medallion until the voices and powers of Christ were heard and finally felt. That medallion has retained those same powers ever since," Father Catrone said. "Once Jesus walks the Earth again, then and only then, will those powers be released from the medallion. For centuries, God and his Son speak through the relic to fulfill their commands here on Earth."

"I see, Father," Father Pasquale answered, shaking his head lightly. "Now it is this DeFalco boy's turn. He is the next chosen one!"

"Is that the name of the person whose possession it is in?"

"Yes, Father Catrone."

"Well," Father Catrone said, but then added a word of caution. "He will not speak the words of the Bible, he will perform them. He is not a Prophet or an Apostle who preaches the Gospel. But he is a Disciple chosen at birth. You know, Frank, this medallion has not been active in over forty years."

"I know. The last time was in Palermo, Sicily."

"Yes," Father Catrone agreed, but added. "The last occurrence before that was 1908 in a tiny village outside of Catania."

"Wasn't that during that devastating earthquake?

"What do you think caused that earthquake, Frank?"

"My God," Father Pasqual uttered.

"That's right, it was another calling. Her name was Anna Marcelli. The young woman was another chosen one. She died underneath the destruction from the mighty quake with her baby in her arms. Some callings are much more severe then others."

"Divine retribution," Father Pasqual whispered to himself, but not loud enough for Father Catrone to hear.

"What was that, Frank?"

"Nothing, Father, I was just mumbling to myself. Who was the Prophet in 1908?"

"Micah! But now let's get back to your situation. Whose possession is the medallion in again?"

"A young man by the name of Joseph DeFalco!"

"How old is he?"

"26 or 27 years old."

"Tell me a little bit about him?"

"I know his family for a very long time. The boy just had a series of bad misfortunes that had just happened to him. He got into some trouble that was associated with his profession."

"Has anything happened to him yet?"

"He had a sighting in his bedroom the other night and another one about 11 months ago before he went to prison. That is why he came to see me. The young man had a personal visit from the spirit of the prophet Jeremiah. To me it sounds like the Scriptures of Jeremiah were spoken and instilled in him. Many of Joseph's words to me were exactly of that same content." Father Pasquale took a short breath and anxiously continued on. "Father Catrone, those identical words were coming from the boy's mouth. This is unbelievable," he said with a face filled with awe. "The DeFalco boy speaks the same words that are right out of the Old Testament of the Bible. Almost everything that God instructed to Jeremiah, Jeremiah repeated to Joseph."

"Frank, are you sure?"

"I am positive! Make no mistake about that! Jeremiah spoke to the boy in the Hebrew dialect and the boy understood it all like he was a Jew himself. "

"I see. Are there any clues that signify the medallion's mission and direction?"

"Just two," Father Pasquale said. "Hold on a second, Father, let me get the exact verses for you." Father Pasquale reached for the Holy Bible that lay on top of the wooden desk. With his hands shaking, he carefully scanned through the thin pages of the sacred book for a word for word reciting. With his fingers leading the way, he quickly found the words that Father Catrone was looking for. "I found them!" he proclaimed. "They are Chapter I, verse 14 and Chapter I verse 16."

"Please read them to me."

"Out of the North an evil breaks forth upon all the inhabitants of the land. The next one says, you will utter my judgments against them touching all of their wickedness."

"Interesting, very interesting," Father Catrone commented. "How is the young man reacting to all of this?"

"He is a little shaken by all of this. The boy is having flashbacks of biblical events that occurred 2000 years ago. To this day he is seeing spiritual images. He doesn't know who this visitor is, and I did not tell him. All of this is very upsetting to him."

"That's only normal," Father Catrone said. "Was there anything else?"

"He is very inquisitive," Father Pasquale responded. "You know, like asking a lot of questions. Other than that, he appears to be fine."

"Well, it sounds like this is another resurrection that we are about to see. One by one, our creator is sending his spirits and their prophecies upon us. Over the many centuries, there have been thirteen documented cases or sightings. Now, you must add Jeremiah to that list. Therefore, only two prophets remain, Daniel and Isaiah."

"Father Catrone," a fearful Father Pasquale said. "What does this all mean?"

"It means that once all the prophets have returned in spirit, then Jesus will walk this Earth again. And that will signify the end of the world as we know it."

"Armageddon?" a somber Father Pasquale asked.

"Armageddon, apocalypse, call it what you must," he said. "But yes, the final battle between good and evil will commence. The battle of all battles. From the sands of the desert the antichrist will rise. He will do battle with God's armies at Megiddo. Satan will soundly be defeated. When this antagonist is conquered, then rapture will arrive."

"Who is this enemy of Christ?"

"We have no idea," a baffled Father Catrone answered. "It is up to the last prophet and the last chosen one to find him. With that medallion leading the way, eventually they will find him. When this happens, the consequences will be much more severe. This happening will have a drastic effect on all of us. God help us all!"

"When will this happen?"

"That all depends on when the last two chosen ones are found by that medallion," the dismal sounding priest said. "There were sixteen prophets and sixteen disciples chosen by God to fight and thwart evil. It could take a year or another century before the final two are found. Then and only then will God's wrath on earth arrive. The future is imminent, it is etched in stone," he predicted. "So, Frank, the medallion is stimulated and has begun to react. So follow it closely, Frank, and never say a word to anyone. All indications state that the prophets of the Old Testament have spoken again. This time it is Jeremiah. There are no more words to be spoken. The rest will be said through the Medallion of Nazareth."

"I wonder where it is going to take him?"

"That, my good friend," Father Catrone honestly answered, "is a question that none of us will ever know. All we know is that the medallion is taking this young man Joseph somewhere north. It could be a mile or it could be in another country. We shall have to wait and see."

"Okay, Father Catrone. We will all wait for the outcome."

"I will reach out to you. It seems that another chapter of the medallion is about to be uncovered right in your own backyard."

"It's strange," Father Pasquale uttered. "After many years and many, many uncharted miles, it was here before me."

"It doesn't have a designated path. The medallion searches the continents for the chosen, and it doesn't stop until it finds them. But its wrath and fury will soon be upon the evil that dwells among us."

"I know, but the last time was over forty years ago. What was that man's name who saved all of those children at that burning schoolhouse?"

"Vincenzo Carlucci," Father Catrone said. "Vincenzo's journey with the Lord and the Prophet Ezekiel was all documented. As far as I know, the medal was still floating around in that family. Somewhere, there is a link attaching the Carlucci's and that DeFalco boy."

"There are a few Carlucci's over here in Brooklyn. The one that I am thinking of is wrapped up in organized crime. He is the head of one of the bigger families of the Mafia. This DeFalco boy was just released from prison. Do you think that the medallion was passed along to him through Vito, Vincenzo's grandson? I read a few years ago that Vito was in a federal penitentiary in upstate New York. Could this be possible?"

"Anything's possible," Father Catrone said. "If there is a connection, then the medallion is responsible for it. It drew the DeFalco boy into that penitentiary to meet Mr. Vito Carlucci. Then the exchange took place. The DeFalco boy was never responsible for his actions, the medallion was. But let's wait and see. I will notify the Archdiocese about the medallion immediately. The rest will be said and done through the voice of God and his Almighty Son, Jesus Christ!"

"Okay, Father Catrone."

"I will keep in touch with you."

"Goodbye, Father Catrone."

"Goodbye, Frank, and say hello to Father Mirra for me."

"Will do."

Father Pasquale gently rested the telephone receiver back onto its cradle. Looking stunned, he sat down in the desk chair that was positioned before him. Slowly he picked his head up and looked at the wall in front of him. The holy man then performed the sign of the cross. A pair of peaceful eyes watched. Those eyes were coming from a picture hanging a couple of feet above the desk. To the priest, the man in the picture had been awakened again. That man's name was Jesus Christ.

Chapter 11

JOB APPLICATION AFTER job application had been turned down. There was no need for an unemployed ex-convict who lived with his mother. Any job worth something had a requirement of being bonded. Once the fingerprints returned from the files of the unwanted, you were history. On an application if you told the truth you were politely turned down for employment. If you lied, your criminal past was quickly exposed. Either way you turned up a loser. There just were not too many people willing to give someone a second chance. Second chances were only given in fairy-tales, in real life there was no such thing. Even good friends ran from the footsteps of a convicted felon.

Joey's life consisted of menial jobs at minimum wage. First there was a job pumping gas which only lasted a day. Pushing hand-trucks up small ramps and onto tractor-trailers is what he had been reduced to with his next gig. His working peers were a bunch of illegal aliens who barely spoke the English language. This atmosphere did nothing for Joey's ego. Even the women who worked in the offices above the tile warehouse looked down on him. To them he was no better than the Mexican working right by his side. With his many encounters with these secretaries and office workers, he would bow his head in shame. He knew he was much better than this and so did everybody else in the place. At seven dollars an hour the bosses had a bargain: a guy who spoke English and worked his ass off. With some patience and hard work he knew that someday he could run this warehouse. But patience was not a virtue for him at seven dollars an hour.

Friday was payday, as his first check was handed to him. The Marino Brothers Imported Tile Company always kept the first week of your hard-earned money. So after two weeks of busting his ass, Joey's net pay was a whopping $190.00. Forty hours of work produced enough money for dinner and a Broadway Show. To make matters worse, the bosses had a smile on their faces when they handed you this pathetic paycheck. They acted like they were doing you a big favor.

Joey looked at his earnings with pure disgust and went straight to his locker. He then started to remove a couple of his personal belongings from the small metal container, quickly stuffing them into the pockets of his jeans. "Fuck this place!" he said to himself, while putting his jacket on. The disgruntled employee then proceeded over to the warehouse foreman and repeated those same words.

"Where are you going?" the foreman asked, pointing his finger at Joey.

"Stick this job up your fuckin' ass. I quit."

"You can't quit now," he argued. "I have no one to cover you."

"Watch me," Joey said. "And make sure I get the week's pay that you held back. All you motherfuckers do is take advantage of people who don't know any better. You work these people like fuckin' animals. For what, for this," he said holding up his paycheck.

"Why, are you any better than these Mexicans?" the foreman shot back as he pointed to the foreign work crew. "You're an ex con."

At that point Joey rushed up and got into the face of the belittling moron. The whole loading platform stood frozen waiting for something to happen.

"I don't think I'm better than anybody," said Joey. "But I know one thing." He then grabbed the large man by his dungaree jacket with both hands. "I know that I'm better than you."

"If you're better than me, how come you're the one pushing the hand-truck?"

"You just don't get it, do you? You stupid fuck," Joey said as he pushed the foreman away from him. "Make sure you put my check in the mail so I don't have to come back here. Because if I do, the next time I won't be so nice."

Joey walked tall and stood proud while exiting the building.

That evening Joey got a hold of Tony Salvo and set up a meeting at the Cosmopolitan Lounge in Bay-Ridge. This over thirty hangout was a fixture in Brooklyn for many years. The popular nightspot was like a meat rack in a butcher's freezer. All the locals would bounce in and out of their marriages and into this place. Walking into this nightclub you would see the same people that you saw ten years ago. It was like a parade, as the women circled around the bar to get noticed. The men would just stand there ogling at the wannabe spring chickens.

But for these neighborhood singles, this was their meeting place. Once a week, they met under the colorful disco ball and searched for romance. Romance would find some, but most left the place with an empty and lonely feeling.

As soon as Joey entered the crowded nightclub he noticed his old friend standing by the bar. It had been a couple of long years since they had last seen each other. Tony had not changed that much except for a few extra pounds and a slightly receding hairline. His wire-rimmed glasses gave him a look that seemed pretty mature for a 28-year old. In his own way, he kind of resembled a studious Harvard graduate.

"Hey," Joey said tapping his friend on his shoulder. Tony then turned around and the two shared a well-deserved hug.

"What's up, pal?" Tony said, trying to speak above the loud music.

"Nothing much," Joey said. "Man, this place hasn't changed much."

"I know, but it's still the easiest place in town if you wanna get your dick sucked."

"Yea, I know, some things just never change. But we are kind of young to be in here."

"That's why we always came here, for the older bitches," Tony said smiling. "Don't you remember?"

"How could I forget?"

"What are you drinking?" Tony asked, dipping into his pockets for some cash. "Do you still drink the same shit?"

"Yea, get me the usual."

The two well-dressed men stood by the large round oak bar surveying the atmosphere. There were women everywhere, each one of them were a drink away from hopping into bed with you. Joey stood poised with a cigarette in one hand and an Absolute on the rocks in the other. His tailor made, olive green, double-breasted suit, looked impeccable on him. Through all of his problems he managed to maintain his wardrobe, which happened to be pretty impressive. At least Wall Street left him something other than a criminal record.

In the rear of the medium sized nightclub, the dance floor was hopping. The light show was fading in and out as the dancers bounced around to the thumping music. Women were showing off their stuff, while the men just stood by the railing looking to catch someone's eye. Off to every corner there were some couples conversing with an excited look on their faces. After all, in a nightclub everyone looks good in the dark. And after a couple of drinks the look gets even better. It was like magic, a bottle of booze could turn an orangutan into Marilyn Monroe.

"So did you have time to think about my offer?" Tony asked, staring across the bar at a woman in her forties.

"Yea I did," Joey said as he leaned both of his elbows on the bar.

"Well?"

"Well I decided to take a look at the place."

"What made you change your mind?"

"Don't even ask."

"Why not?"

"Because you wouldn't believe me if I told you anyway," Joey said. "And I'm not about to tell you."

"It must have been something big."

"Bigger than you could ever imagine!"

"Anyway, I'll pick you up at your house at about ten, Monday morning."

"Bartender!" Joey yelled at the pretty brunette behind the bar. The scantily clad beauty quickly responded to the call.

"What will it be?" she said, with a big smile running across her face. The young woman was gorgeous; from top to bottom this cutie had it all. Her skin-tight outfit covered her perfect figure like a glove. Every bump and curve was exposed to each pair of delighted eyes that she put into a trance. It looked like her sexy attire was spray-painted onto her ultra-hot body.

"Give me another round!" Joey said, throwing a twenty on the bar. The barmaid then looked at Joey with her *fuck me right now* eyes. The flirting gesture flew right over his head as she took his order and slowly walked away.

"Did you see that?" Tony said, putting his arm around Joey. "Did you fuckin see that?"

"See what?"

"She wants you, man, go for it."

"Wants what?" Joey said, shunning Tony's blunt words of romance. "What the hell could I have that she wants?"

"You didn't see that look she gave you," he repeated. "Go for it and stop being an asshole."

"Go for what? I don't even have enough money to pay for these drinks."

"Just ask her for her number and forget about the money. She's the hottest thing in here!"

"Wining and dining a chick that looks like her is the furthest thing from my mind," Joey confessed. "A woman like that has money written all over her face. Let her go find another sucker for a free meal." Vito's words and thinking were now coming to the surface. Joey was using them well as he sized up the situation. "I might look like a million dollars, but in reality I'm broke. I don't have a fuckin' penny to my name."

"Man, have you changed, a few years ago you would have been all over that."

"I have changed," said Joey. "Prison has taught me a lot about what is really important in life. Spending some money just to get into somebody's pants just isn't worth it anymore. She might be hot and a nice girl," he said while pointing at her. "But she's not for me."

"You're 27 years old, not 90."

"But my thinking has changed a lot."

"I'm only saying that because it's probably been a long time since you got laid."

"It has been a while, but I take care of my own business in my own way. It bothers me, but I try not to think about it much."

The two stood in conversation for about another twenty minutes. Their voices struggled to overpower the loud music coming from the disk jockey's booth. They reminisced about the good old days growing up as teenagers. But this was a time in Joey's life to start getting serious again. There was no time for chasing women and idle chit-chat.

"Come on," Joey said. "Let's get the hell out of here."

"It's early. Where are you going?"

"I want to leave!"

"Why, you wanna go somewhere else?" Tony said, with a baffled look on his face. "There's another place on 88th Street that rocks."

"Nah, I just wanna go home!"

"Have it your way," Tony finally said. He gave up trying to persuade his friend to keep partying. Looking through his large bankroll, he took out a twenty-dollar bill and tossed it on the bar.

Outside of the nightclub the friends confirmed Monday's business appointment. The line to get into the club was almost the length of a football field. Street congestion was chaotic as people from all over were coming and going. Passing cars were beeping their horns and whistling at the ladies trying to gain access into the popular club. This was midnight on a beautiful cool evening, for club goers the night had just begun.

Tony waited patiently as his Mercedes Benz finally arrived to the front curb. The valet handed him the keys to the showpiece on wheels. The car was definitely an attention getter. Most women stared and wished they were offered an invitation to hop in. To them Tony was a symbol of money, for the first time all eyes were on him. Joey was just his sidekick as the two walked towards the shiny silver car.

"Come on, get in," said Tony.

"Nah, it's a nice night. I think I'll walk home."

"Are you crazy, we're five miles from your house!"

"That's alright, the walk will do me good," he said, while slowly starting to walk away.

"Come on, get in," Tony yelled above the noises of the Brooklyn streets.

"I'll see you Monday morning," Joey said, slowly starting to disappear into the busy night. "Goodnight!" he yelled.

"Whatever," Tony said, hopping into his running car. *"Man, that guy got weird,"* he said to himself.

Feeling out of place and a little bit like a lost soul, Joey started his long journey home. Walking through his old stomping grounds brought back many memories with each bar and grill that he passed. A few years back the men used to parade around these same streets without a care in the world. This was definitely not like old times. Just after the stroke of midnight the two were on their way home already. Two hours of the night life scene was enough for either one of them to take, especially Joey. At the ripe old age of 27, Joey was acting like a 50-year old man.

Monday morning arrived quickly as the alarm clock awakened him. There was only time for a quick shower and a shave. Joey wondered while applying the shaving cream to his face, what was in store for him now. His future was as cloudy as the steamy bathroom mirror in front of him. With his right hand he wiped off the vapor, exposing a face that even he did not recognize. The next hour or two would represent another change to his pathetic life. The changes were coming much too frequently for him to take. Stability was what he was looking for, and he would search high and low trying to find it.

The horn from the Mercedes Benz was beeping outside of Joey's house. This time he would step into the spanking clean car. In an envious way Tony represented a lot of things that Joey once had. Nice car, a beautiful home and money were just a few to mention. But he was happy for his old friend; he was not the type of guy who despised people who had more than he did. If so, it would seem that he would have to hate the whole world, because at this stage of his life Joey had nothing.

"Where are we off to?" Joey asked.

"Crown Heights."

"Where?" Joey said with a stunned look on his face. "Could you repeat that?

"You heard me," Tony said. "Crown Heights."

"You better take your fuckin' foot off the gas pedal, because we're not going anywhere."

"Why?"

"You know why," he answered. "Don't play me for an asshole or I'll wrap those fucking glasses around your neck. I can see right through you."

"Come on, pal, lighten up, the neighborhood ain't that bad. It's an area that is made up of hard working middle class people."

"Do you think I was born yesterday? That neighborhood is a combat zone sitting in a fuckin slum. I know the neighborhood; there's nothing but poverty, poor housing and crime there. It's like a part of Brooklyn that's lying right in the middle of Vietnam."

"Its not as bad as you think it is. Let's just take a ride and look at the pizzeria. Could you just do me that one favor?"

Joey just sat there not saying a word. His eyes turned towards his mother's house as he spotted her on the front terrace. Still sitting silently, he saw the enthusiasm on her face. Joey did not want to let her down again. He thought that he owed it to her to at least take a look at the pizzeria. "Drive," was all he would say to Tony.

The twenty minute ride to the eatery was filled with a one sided conversation by Tony, trying to sell his idea to Joey. It would take a lot of convincing, because at this stage Joey was dead set against it. Tony felt that Joey had the toughness, and he could think of no better man to run his already dead pizzeria. Even though they were good friends, the two were worlds apart in their feelings about this business venture. For Tony it was just a matter of trying to recoup some of his losses. To Joey, it was just a matter of survival.

As they slowly drove through the streets of Brooklyn, you could see the neighborhood change right before your eyes. It was very easy to see where the city's tax dollars are really spent. In high poverty areas even the potholes in the street seem bigger. A flat tire waiting to happen, drivers impatiently tried to maneuver around the king sized holes. This was driving at its worst; the bumpy roads would back up traffic everywhere. If the neighborhood weren't so unsafe, you would have been much better off walking.

Looking out the passenger side window, Joey just took in the unpleasant sights. Every house was caged in steel bars that covered every window and entrance-way. From white to black, to red, the colors of the window dressing didn't matter. People here lived no better than animals in a city zoo. They were kept trapped while their zookeepers roamed and terrorized the streets.

Living in an apartment building was no safe refuge either. The higher the floor the more secure one would seem to feel. That safe feeling evaporated when he or she had to take the long elevator ride up or down to their destinations. Joey sensed a definite loss of freedom from the area's residents. Helpless people were living in fear right here on the open city streets.

The Mercedes made a left hand turn down St. Ann's place and pulled over to the building marked 205 on the left-hand side of the street. The pre war building was approximately fifty yards off of the corner of Franklin Ave. It was a four-story building with a commercial establishment on the ground level. On the left hand side of the pizzeria, between two buildings, there was an alleyway that led to a backyard covered with weeds and waste. Anything from a bicycle tire to a front bumper of a car could be found. It looked like an abandoned junkyard that went out of business. The looks of this place offered less of an opportunity than an unkempt cemetery.

There it stood in all of its glory, the business that nobody else wanted. The front window of the pizzeria was boarded up with graffiti stained heavy plywood. A heavy metal pull-down gate covered the doorway and its small window. Every punk in the neighborhood seemed to leave his signature on every piece of brick that contained open space. This art that comes in a spray can vandalized most of the neighborhood. Even the elevated trains on New Lots Ave. were smothered with these distasteful paintings of identity. You could see the bright colors as the sun beamed down on the roofs of the subway cars, a couple of blocks away.

The hunter green canvas canopy above the plywood was full of holes and hanging off from its metal support rods. There was a long twenty-foot pizza sign that ran up the side of the building. Every letter and light bulb on the public placard was either burnt out or destroyed by rocks. There was a strong distasteful stench of urine coming from the floor. Every nook and cranny in front of building stunk like piss. So far just by looking at the outside of this pizzeria, it was very, very depressing.

Garbage and debris of all kinds littered the streets with filth. About four overflowing trash-cans lined the front curb for sanitation pickup. Cats or rodents in search of food had gnawed away the plastic bags inside the cans. To put it bluntly, this place needed a major overhaul and the two men had not even stepped inside the pizzeria yet. To put it even more bluntly than that: this place needed to be condemned, not reopened.

Joey and Tony just sat in the car in silence, with the radio pitched at a low volume. How ironic was it when the song, "Welcome to the Jungle," by Guns and Roses started to come out of the radio's speakers. The two men just looked and each other in total shock, then busted out in laughter. The sight before them was so sad that after a few minutes it became very comical. Even Tony knew that it was time to put the car in drive and vacate the premises.

"Let's get out of the car," Joey said as he reached into his pocket for a cigarette.

"Are you kidding me, let's get the fuck out of here. I'd rather burn the place to the ground than put you in there."

All of a sudden the clicking started. Tony was starting to get nervous and his body was starting to react to it. With every clicking sound came a shift that rocked his head to the left. The condition got so severe that he banged his head on the driver's side window.

"Will you calm the fuck down." Joey then placed his hand around the back of his friend's neck. "Come on, let's get out and take a quick look at the place."

Tony turned off the car's engine and they both stepped out of the vehicle simultaneously. They proceeded to slowly walk up to the front door of the unappetizing eatery. Tony started to fumble through a large ring of keys while Joey surveyed the surrounding area. There was something very strange about this neighborhood. Even though most of the younger kids were in school, the desolate streets resembled a ghost town. Occasionally you would see an elderly person carrying a bag of groceries, but that was the extent of it.

The only activity was coming from the park across the street. Playgrounds were supposed to be an outdoor recreational facility for children to amuse themselves. Not this one, in this park the population seemed to be 18 and over. They were all huddled around in circles drinking something that was covered with a brown paper bag. The loud music coming from their boom boxes muffled out all of the cursing and unruly sounds. The two Italian men were most surely out of their realm. Tony's trembling hands confirmed it.

Tony finally found the right key and bent down to open the conventional style lock. He then pulled up the rolling gate exposing the front glass door of the pizzeria. Hesitating for a moment, he finally put the key into the round cylinder to open up the front door. Joey stood right behind him waiting to enter the rundown eatery. A little boy approached the duo.

"Mister, are you going to open the pizza place today?"

Joey turned around and looked down at the hungry little boy. The kid could not have been more than five or six years old. Joey went down to one knee and looked into the eyes of the young Afro American child. "Why, do you like pizza?" Joey said, putting his right hand underneath the little boy's chin.

"I love pizza," the small visitor said. "But this place doesn't open anymore."

"What's your name?"

"Steven!"

Joey paused and stared out into the empty street. His attentions slowly focused skyward. Staring intently, something supernatural had saturated and smothered his existence. He felt it running rampant through his body, as his glazed eyes were fixated toward the heavens. Not a word was spoken; quintessential silence was doing all the talking. Only Joey knew the answers for he had just heard them. Tony stood there holding the front door open. The moment of truth had arrived, for a decision was about to be made. With a solaced look on his face, his brows dancing, Joey then turned his attention back in Steven's direction.

"Well, Steven, in a couple of weeks you come and see me and I will give you a free slice of pizza." Joey then rubbed the palm of his right hand over the top of Steven's tiny head.

"Oh boy!" he said joyously, jumping up and down. "You're gonna open the place up?"

"Yep, I'm going to open it up."

"Wow, I can't wait!"

"Where is your mother, Steven?"

"Down the block," he said in a low, sweet manner. "She's over there," the tiny black youth pointed.

"Go to her now, she is probably looking for you."

"Okay," he said. "Mommy, Mommy," the boy yelled. He then raced up the block to tell his mother the good news.

"Are you serious?" Tony said, with a deranged look on his face. "Tell me you're not!"

"You bet your fuckin' ass I'm serious."

"What changed your mind?"

"I just saw it in that kid's eyes that I needed to be here. For whatever the reasons are, and I can't explain them, I need to be here."

"You need to be here?" Tony asked, puzzled by the decision. "I think you're crazy. But I know you all of my life and nothing you do should really surprise me anymore."

"Let me in, I want to see what this place looks like," Joey said. "Tony, do you have a flashlight in the car?"

"Why, there is no electricity?"

"No, I keep fuckin' with this switch over here and nothing happens. I'm sure the electric and gas has been turned off."

"I have one in the trunk of my car, I'll be right back."

Tony walked hurriedly to his car to retrieve the needed light. Joey stood by the front door patiently waiting for his friend's return. Besides the boarded front window there was no access for any sunlight to enter. The only light came from the opening of the front door. The jolt of fresh air seemed to thin-out the musty smell of non-occupancy. By the smell alone, this place was in need of a big time bath.

"Here," said Tony handing him the flashlight.

"Man, this fuckin' place stinks like vomit."

"What did you expect, the scent of fresh cut roses?"

"Just give me the damn flashlight," Joey said with a smirk. "And cut out the wise cracks. That's all I need right now is comedy when I don't feel like laughing."

Joey and Tony entered the disheveled pizzeria and started to scan over its contents and condition. The small beam from the flashlight led the way.

Right by the left side of front door, a long counter ran right down the center of the place. To the right, five hunter green booths trimmed with an oak type finish hugged the wall that was covered with mirror and paneling. The dusty mirror covered the top half, while the wood grain panel ran to the beige tiled floor below. Little crumbs of pizza crust still littered the dirty tabletops. This place had not been cleaned for months.

"When did this guy walk out of his pizzeria?"

"He left on June 6th of this year."

"What?" Joey screamed, looking in Tony's direction. "When did he leave? Tell me," he said with a beseeching overtone.

"June 6th. Why?"

"Because that's the same day I got released from prison."

"Ain't that a coincidence?" Tony remarked, while the two men conversed in the dark. Only the flashlight provided the small glimmer of light. To Joey, that small light blossomed into a shining star.

"It certainly is, it's like it was all planned out for me."

"What do you mean?"

"I really don't know, but something got the last owner out of here. Whatever it was, it opened up a new door for me. This place was waiting for me to come here."

"How the hell do you know that? The last owner didn't even know you!"

"I know, but somebody else does."

"What the fuck are you talking about?"

"Forget it," Joey insisted. "Let's take a look at the rest of the place."

"Trust me, I'll forget about it," Tony warily said, shaking his head. "You're starting to scare me."

"Look at this!" Joey said, spotting some small, dark looking pebbles scattered on the floor. "They're the size of marbles!"

"What the hell is that?"

"Its rat shit, what did you think it is, milk duds!"

With the flashlight you could see all the rat droppings scattered about the floor. This was one problem that had to be rectified in a hurry. But judging by the size of the droppings, it would be no easy task. The whole building and the surrounding neighborhood were probably smothered with rats.

"Damn," Tony uttered with amazement. "I didn't know rats shit that big."

"They must be some big fuckin' rats!" Tony started to nudge closer to Joey in fear of the rats. Joey felt his hot heavy breathing on the back of his neck. Tony stood close to Joey for safety and comfort, but to Joey it was too close. "Will you get the fuck away from me. Your breath is killing me."

"I can't help it, rats scare the shit out of me."

"I don't mind you being near me," Joey said. "But your breath, what did you eat, garlic for breakfast? I can't breathe with you on top of me like this, back up a little."

"I had garlic last night."

"Damn, it's still in you," he replied. "The shit is coming out of your pores."

The two men then continued on with their inspection. About five feet away from the front window was a double pizza oven in dire need of a cleaning. Grease covered the huge baking apparatus from top to bottom. A filthy glass partition separated the customers from the working staff. Opposite the oven and behind the counter was where the pizza man would perform his magic. The marble tops provided the durable working area to pound and smoothly stretch his work of art. Underneath his work-station was a refrigerator that held all of the extras for making the pizza of choice. The display area for all of the Italian delicacies was to the left of his work-station.

Joey and Tony followed the thin line of light about another ten feet. They walked very slowly, observing everything from top to bottom. Cobwebs about ten feet long stretched from one end of the ceiling to the other. The threads of spun material were reminiscent of a room in a horror movie.

Tony took out a cigarette and stuck it in his mouth. He then leaned up against the nearest wall for support as he lit up. "You want a smoke?" he said, striking the match.

"No thanks," Joey said shining the flashlight in Tony's face. The flashlight exposed little insects running around on top of Tony's shoulder. Joey moved closer and started to inspect his friend's body. The closer he got the more apparent it became. "Oh shit," he yelled.

"What, what?" Tony answered, as his body became very jittery.

"You got cockroaches running all over your body."

"Get them off me," he screamed as his body started to itch from the repulsive thought. "Help me get them off!"

Joey started to bust out in laughter while he watched his partner's drama from three feet away. Tony's hands were flying in all directions as his lit cigarette fell to the floor. In a state of panic he moved closer to his friend begging for help. Joey just stood there doubled over in laughter.

"Get them off, get them off!"

"Come here," Joey finally said, putting the flashlight on the counter.

He proceeded to wipe him clean from the unwanted guests. Tony could not stay in one place, his body wriggled in sinuous motion. He had more moves than Jim Brown scampering through the line of scrimmage. Even in a barely lit room you could see his face changing colors from the outburst of panic.

"Okay they're all off of ya," Joey said. "You feel better now?"

"No, I don't," he said walking away.

"Where are you going?"

"I'll wait for you in the car."

"Oh would you stop being a big pussy and get over here. Just don't lean up against anything."

"That's easy for you to say."

"Easy for me to say," Joey retorted. "For three fuckin' months I slept with this shit. This is nothing, so get over here and let's finish looking around," he said, picking up the flashlight again. "Now come on."

"All right, but let's hurry," he said while scratching his neck. "This place just gives me the creeps."

"Calm down and I don't want to hear any of those annoying clicking sounds either."

Standing side by side, the boys continued their inspection. At the end of the counter, by the opened cash register, was the meeting place for the customers to pay for their food. Two round tables took up most of the rear of the small eatery. The back of the pizzeria was small, and there wasn't much room for anything else.

Up a couple of steps was a small bathroom. Joey opened the door and got hit with a blast of foul smelling air. A toilet and a sink occupied the six by six room. He then opened up the water faucet in search of running water. The liquid resembled chocolate milk with its thick brown density. It was so thick that even the drainpipe had a hard time accepting it for disposal. The small mirror above the sink barely showed a reflection of anything. The mirror reflected the atmosphere, and the atmosphere was dead.

Opposite the bathroom was a door that was locked from the inside of the store.

"Where does this lead to?" Joey said, pointing at the old wooden door.

"It goes to the basement."

"What's down there?"

"Nothing as far as I know. I think it was used for storage."

"So the basement belongs to the pizzeria?"

"Yea," Tony said. "The lease states that the pizzeria has the only access to it. It's included in the rent."

"That's good to know," Joey said. "Because judging by the size of this place, we could use the extra space."

Continuing on with their inspection led them through some swinging cowboy doors. Those doors provided some privacy to the cluttered but quaint kitchen. The cooking area seemed fully equipped. There was a six burner stove with a double oven in it, a microwave oven, a dough mixer and much more. Everything from pots and pans to dishes were neatly stacked on heavy metal shelves. For all the foods that needed to be refrigerated, there was a walk in box in the back of the room. There was even a stand up double door freezer for preserving certain foods.

"Man," said Joey. "This walk in box reminds me of when I was in solitary confinement. No one ever better close this fuckin' door behind me."

"Why not?"

"Because if they do, I will kick their asses," he warned. "It brings back too many bad memories for me."

They both entered the warm walk in box. A foul unused smell lingered through the dark air. The 8x8 metal cube bore a striking resemblance to the hole in prison. The flashback brought chills running up and down Joey's spine. For a moment he just stood there frozen in memory of the nightmarish experience. The intensely distressed look on his face told the whole story.

"You mean you were locked up in something that looked like this?"

"It was much worse than this, this is nothing compared to that."

"Shit, man, I got to hand it to you," Tony said. "I don't think I would have lasted three minutes."

"You learn to deal with it. But I will tell you one thing. I don't want to have to go through it all over again. The next time will definitely push me over the edge."

The walk in box was basically empty except for a few crates of rotten vegetables that were somehow left behind. Joey shined the flashlight in the direction of the boxes and moved closer to inspect their contents. A half case of lettuce, some eggplant and some tomatoes were all that remained. He pulled out the boxes and right in the corner laid a dead mouse. The little creature was trapped inside the oversized refrigerator. For even his small body could not squeeze through any opening of the tightly sealed walk in box. He died right there while snacking on a head of lettuce.

"Look at that!" Joey said, looking in Tony's direction. "Even the mouse couldn't find his way out of here!"

"This place is infested," Tony said. "What else are we gonna find next?"

"You're asking me? You're the pizza man!"

"I just sell the shit, I don't make it."

"I guess you have to expect this," Joey reasoned. "After all, the place has been closed down for a while. You wanna know the truth?"

"What's the truth?" Tony asked, still waiting anxiously to go home.

"I expected much worse. We have to wait and see what the nighttime brings out. That's when the shit hits the fan and all the little bastards come out to visit."

"Well you wait and let me know what happens, cause I'm outta here!"

"At least we know the walk in box is air tight," Joey said. "It will save us some money on the electric bill."

"Big deal," Tony said. He was definitely not forgetting all the other problems, especially the two-legged problems on the streets outside the front door. "Are we done looking around yet?"

Joey and Tony were pleasantly surprised that mostly everything was intact. All that was needed was an immaculate cleaning and a good paint job. There was nothing there that a good handy man could not tackle.

It was time to leave; the two men started their walk to the front of the store. Both of them turned around at the same time and looked at the dark pizzeria. They looked at each other and stepped out from the front doorway and onto the sidewalk. Tony started to lock the front door and pull down the rolling gate. There was another gate that covered the front window that needed to be repaired. Instead of repairing it, the old owner put a piece of plywood to protect the window from being shattered.

To the men's surprise, they heard a bottle shattering on the concrete walkway, thrown from the park across the street. The gang that was assembled inside the park was standing there, waiting for a reaction. From a distance of about sixty feet away, the war of stares was about to begin. Neither party said a word, but a message was sent.

"Joey, please," Tony pleaded. "Don't say anything, there's too many of them."

"Don't worry, if anything is gonna happen," he warned, "it's not gonna happen now. Just finish locking up."

The eye confrontation continued even as Tony and Joey were about to step into the car. The park gang knew that something was going on with the small pizzeria across the street. Anything that interrupts their daily activities was definitely against their policies. Persuasion to leave the neighborhood and never returning was on the top of their agenda.

A deep voice suddenly roared out from the park. The neighborhood gang had inched its way closer to the black steel picket fence that separated them from the sidewalk. About eight angry faces were seen in between the bars of the eight-foot high barrier. Each looked very eager to confront the strangers. Their ghetto look was intimidating as they were establishing their so-called territorial rights.

"Hey man," a voice yelled out. "Hey motherfuckers! What's your business here?"

Joey just stared in silence as he walked around the car to get in. With his right hand on the passenger's side door, he never took his eyes off of this bunch. Tony was already in the car ready to start the engine. The engine was fired up as Tony waited impatiently to depart.

"Get in," Tony said. Joey just stood outside the vehicle with his eyes fixated at the unruly crowd inside the park. "Joey, get in the fuckin' car. You're gonna get us killed."

Joey, looking somber, just shook his head in disappointment as he stooped down to get into the front seat of the car. For many strange reasons he got the feeling of de ja vu. Finally sitting in the car, Joey turned towards the open window. It was then that he actually realized that this was no illusion; this was something that he was experiencing for the very first time.

"That's right, that's right," the voice from the park said. "You better not say nothin'. Don't ever come back, man. The next time might be your last time!"

Another bottle flew through the air like a precision guided missile. The glass container smashed right into the passenger's side front quarter panel of the car. This time the bottle was filled with beer. Glass shattered as cheap malt liquor dispersed through the air, cascading down all over the Mercedes. Tony then put the pedal to the floor and took off. His tires squealed from the urgency.

"Are you sure you still want to go through with this?" Tony said, his right hand squeezing tightly around the steering wheel. He was expecting to hear a definite no.

"My mind is made up," he quickly answered in a steady and precise voice. "I'm ready to rock and roll."

"Are you fuckin' kidding me? You saw what just happened."

"I told you before, I don't know why, but I have to be here."

"What the fuck are you talking about, you have to be here?"

"I don't know what I'm talking about," said Joey, raising his voice a decibel. "Let's just leave it at that."

The car then stopped for a red light. Tony looked at Joey in disbelief. Only Joey knew this destination and why he had to be there. Something or someone was pulling him in. He knew it, but if he told anyone else of these strange feelings he would be committed to an insane asylum. That eerie night in his bedroom explained a lot of things to him but sill left a lot of questions unanswered. No matter what he felt or knew, Joey decided to leave everybody else out in the dark on this subject. At least for now.

"That motherfucker told me he had a gambling problem and I believed him," Tony said, talking about the last owner of the pizzeria. "He told me he needed money to renovate the place. What a crock of shit that was. That son of a bitch stuck me for fifty grand, now I know why."

"Now you know why he left his business," Joey said. "Nobody gives anything away that's worth something, including you. The way he milked you for credit, he probably fucked Con Edison and the gas company too. He probably left a long string of people that he owes money to. He or somebody else had it all planned long before he left. This guy walked away from the place with some money in his pocket," declared Joey. "You can rest assured of that."

"Joey, in a way I don't blame him. If I was in his shoes and had to work in this neighborhood, I think I would have done the same thing. You have to be the only sick motherfucker who would want any part of this place. Are you sure you want to go through with this?"

"I told you already, my decision is final!"

"Well, then there are a lot of things that we have to go over. Joey, let me ask you a question."

"What's that?"

"Do you have a set of wheels to get back and forth to work?"

"No, I planned on taking the train."

"Are you crazy?" Tony said, starting to scratch his head looking for an answer to this question. "Listen, I have an 84 Buick sitting in front of my house doing nothing. For the time being, I want you to use it. It's not much, but it will get you to where you want to go."

"Are you sure?" Joey said, with a bit of a surprised look on his face. "I would appreciate it."

"Yea, it's not a problem."

"Thanks, I could use the transportation. I don't think riding the trains out of this neighborhood at one o'clock in the morning, is safe for anybody."

"Even for a tough guy like yourself?"

"Even for a guy like myself."

"Let's go grab some lunch," Tony said. "I'm starving."

"There's a place right there!" Joey said, pointing to a run down luncheonette not too far from the pizzeria.

"If you don't mind, I would like to at least see some familiar faces before I sit down to eat."

"I thought you might be in the mood for some collard greens and black eyed peas."

"Would you stop busting my balls, I think I need a martini instead."

"Okay," Joey said laughing. "Let's go back to the neighborhood for some calamari."

"Sounds good to me, let's go."

"And knock it off with the fuckin' clicking," Joey said for the last time. "It's driving me crazy."

Chapter 12

THE NEXT FEW days the new business partners worked diligently putting everything together. Everything from recipes to hiring a work crew was discussed in full detail. Then there would be a trip to certain city agencies to file for all the proper permits and working orders to run a business.

The following Monday, Joey was back in school taking food protection courses. The one-week class would supply him with a certificate to operate a food eatery in New York City. The Board of Health thought you should know all the ins and outs of serving food in a safe manner. The recipient of that certificate had to make sure that he or she was on the premises at all times. Getting on the Board's shit list was not a good thing for any aspiring entrepreneur. Heavy fines and uninvited monthly visits were sure to follow all the violators. The pizzeria had some major violations, but nothing too serious that could not be quickly corrected.

It was 8:00 on a bright Tuesday morning. Joey hopped behind the wheel of the Buick Skylark. The blue two-door car was in need of a good detail job. Bird shit was all over the hood and windshield of the conservative looking vehicle. Though dirty, it did run pretty well. It definitely was not the type of car that would catch the eyes of any young females. But for what Joey needed it for, it was perfect.

The Brooklyn streets were busy with the rush hour traffic. Pedestrians were rushing to catch public transportation. Long lines formed at the corner bus stop on Kings Highway. Women were busy adjusting their morning makeup, while the men had their heads buried in one of the city's newspapers. It was a beautiful autumn day, everything felt crisp and clean.

For Joey it was a different kind of day; it was the day the clean up and renovation would start. Tony had made a fifteen thousand dollar infusion to get the pizzeria up and running. That money had to cover everything, from food products to scouring pads. A timetable was set, and the place would be opening its doors in about ten days.

While driving through the neighborhood streets, Joey noticed a large group of Mexicans congregated on a street corner. They were lined against a building in search of someone to come and call for their services. Cars and small work vans would pull up to the curb and be mobbed by the illegal aliens. They looked like hookers trying to sell themselves to the first John that came along. But the Mexicans were just trying to earn some money to put food on their families' dinner tables. From construction work to picking up dog shit in somebody's backyard, they did it all. When it came to work, they had no pride. The American dollar was all the pride they needed and they were willing to work countless hours to get it.

Joey's search would be a little different; he was looking for a tough but honest face. He was looking for a man willing to deal with all the elements of a decimated neighborhood. A man who would be in for the long haul and who had balls of steel. He knew what he was looking for, but would he find it on this street corner? Maybe the Marine Corps was the only place to find what he was looking for. After all, their motto fit all the needs that he required for employment. But there wasn't a Marine or any other American around who would be willing to take this job for the money he was offering. And Joey certainly knew it.

Sitting in his double-parked car and watching all the activity from across the street, Joey noticed a disturbance. It seems one of the hombres cut in front of his smaller countryman in search of an opportunity. The smaller man wrapped his short arms around his impatient counterpart and threw him to the concrete pavement. For this Mexican it was not about the size of the opponent, it was about survival. Joey knew that he had found his man.

Joey bolted from his car and raced across the street in pursuit of this man. All of a sudden the crowd started to disperse, and the Mexicans scattered in all different directions. Joey scampered through the street but kept his eyes focused on the small but quick foreigner. Then it finally dawned on him why this guy was avoiding him. *Must think I'm Immigrations,* Joey thought as he ran.

"Hey, hey, come here," Joey shouted, chasing the man down the block. "You're not in trouble. I just wanna talk with you."

The guy just kept briskly walking, never even turning around. Joey's trot would soon become a run as he started to catch up with the man. The Mexican just kept walking quickly, but never running. If he started to run, it was all over for him and he knew it. A Mexican man running down the streets in an all-white neighborhood spelled trouble for him, and the smart kid from across the border knew this.

"I just want to know if you wanna work with me?" Joey asked, yelling from the short distance between the two.

Halfway down the block the young man stopped dead in his tracks. He then turned around exposing his young face. He was not more than twenty. But he looked battle tested. A bit shaky, he just stood there as Joey approached him with the offer.

Finally coming within talking distance, Joey made his introduction carefully. "What's your name?" Joey asked, feeling a little winded after chasing the guy down a couple of city blocks.

"Marco," the young Mexican said. His shoulder length hair was blowing in the gentle autumn breeze.

"My name is Joey." Joey then extended his hand. Marco cracked a bit of a smile as he received the handshake with comfort. Joey's smooth and trusting face seemed to alleviate some of his fear. "Well, Marco, do you speak some English?"

"Si, me speak a little."

"Good, do you want to come work for me?" Joey's words were spoken very slowly and with a lot of hand movements. He was doing his very best trying to get Marco to understand his proposition. But to his surprise, Marco spoke and understood better than he anticipated. "I am opening up a pizzeria and I want you to work for me six days a week."

"Full time?"

"Yea, full time," Joey said with a smile. "I will pay you two hundred and fifty dollars a week to start. Do we have a deal?" Joey said, extending his hand out again. "Do we?"

"Deal," Marco shot back accepting the offer of full time work. "Me work hard for you."

"Well first things first, you have to get a haircut. Okay?" Joey put his hand on top of his head and grabbed a chunk of hair. He was trying to make the demand a little easier for Marco to understand. "Compendia?"

"Me comprende," he said.

There were no applications or social security cards needed. This job did not come with a medical or dental plan. There were no sick days or paid vacation time. You get paid when you work and for the hours you work, that's it. These were the cruel conditions forced upon every illegal alien in the country. But it was still better than working on some banana plantation back home for a fifth of the pay.

Most Mexicans lived with other immigrants of their own kind. Sharing a one-bedroom apartment with five or six others was not uncommon. All their expenses were split and they still had some money left over to send back home to their needy families.

Joey and Marco worked countless hours cleaning the place up. It was fourteen hours a day of backbreaking work for a whole week. Eventually things were starting to come together. From side to side and top to bottom they scrubbed and scoured vigorously. Every type of cleaning tool and abrasive cleaning agent was applied to the filthy components. The two men went through countless buckets of hot water, using sponges and heavy brushes. From dirty ovens to greasy exhaust systems, the pair hammered away leaving nothing but dripping sweat in their path.

Every morning at eight o'clock Joey picked up his new employee at the same spot. Joey treated Marco well; all meals were on him, along with the transportation. They entered the store at nine and sometimes they did not leave until midnight.

Marco was fearless, and anything from spider webs to rat droppings was not a problem. He did whatever he was told and he did it flawlessly. Every night after a hard day's work, Joey treated him to dinner and the beers of his choice. Corona was at the top of his list, his big brown eyes lit up every time that name was mentioned. Mexicans love their beer, but it was always up to Joey to decide when enough was enough. This kid would drink all night long if you left it up to him. In Joey's eyes, two or three was enough. It was the least he could do for a guy who devoted his life to his work.

"Marco, do you know a couple of guys looking for work?" Joey said; the sponge in his hand was dripping water to the tiled floor below.

"Yes, boss," Marco answered while picking his head up from behind the counter. "My friend is looking."

"What is your friend's name?"

"Orlando!"

"Is he a good worker?"

"He like me."

"Monday morning when I pick you up, make sure he is with you."

"Boss, I think he can cook, he work in pizzeria before."

"Good, every little bit helps."

"I tell him."

"Marco, explain everything to him. You can tell him everything in Mexican, he will understand better that way."

"Okay, boss."

The following Monday morning Orlando was introduced to Joey. Now Joey had two thirds of his work crew, all that was left was for him to find a reliable pizza man. With this position, the job had to require some experience. There is nothing worse than an unappetizing looking pizza. There was a lot of technique in the making of good pizza dough. From Neapolitan to Sicilian pizza, presentation was very important. If someone ordered a round or square pie, you wanted to make sure that's what he or she got.

A big truck pulled up in front of the place with Joey's first order of provisions. Everything from canned tomatoes to pizza boxes was delivered. Tony put together a pretty basic menu for the grand opening, which was a week away. The owners did not think that anyone in this neighborhood would be ordering any Linguine Carbonara. Most of the fancy Italian dishes would be non-existent in this eatery. Besides, who the hell was going to cook them anyway? The small staff was now in the experiment stages of cooking. Everything was being read off of recipes, it took a number of times before they got it right. The one thing that Joey had going for him was that he knew good food. He also knew what a good tomato sauce was supposed to taste like.

Inside the small kitchen it was like a comedy of errors. There was sauce and empty cans everywhere. Their once white uniforms provided by a linen service were covered with sauce. The two Mexicans looked like a couple of used Tampons. There was tomato sauce everywhere. Joey knew that it was not going to be easy, but this was ridiculous.

"Orlando, I thought you knew how to cook?"

"Me know, boss."

"You know! Your tomato sauce tastes like salsa. You have to drink a gallon of water every time you taste it."

"It's good, boss!"

"Good, maybe with a fuckin Dorito it's good. What the fuck did you put in this shit?" Joey said, looking into the oversized steaming pot. "The smell alone knocks me on my ass!"

"Chile peppers and Tabasco."

"Orlando, this is America. The people around here would kill us if we fed them this crap. This shit is lethal," he said grabbing the pot by the large handles. "Fuck, even the handles are hot. Get me a towel!"

"Boss, don't throw out," Marco said. "I take home."

"You want to take this shit home. If you take this home you'll be shitting for three weeks. Your asshole will be on fire."

"Me like, me like," Marco pleaded. It got to a point where the kid was practically begging for the bogus tomato sauce.

"You like, how can you like this? In a couple of weeks you won't have to eat any of this shit anymore. God only knows what you guys eat," Joey said with a disgusted look on his face. He knew that poor living conditions had forced many people into bad eating habits. Being a good-natured guy, Joey would see to it that his main men start to change their diets.

Joey grabbed the large cookware and disposed the ingredients. Minutes later he started the whole process all over again. But this time he took control, and after another case of plum tomatoes, they finally got it right. All the extras were added as he let the sauce brew for hours. Just from the smell alone you knew that he had struck pay dirt.

"Here, try this," Joey offered as he held out the wooden spoon for a taste test. Both men put their lips to the utensil, one after the other. The results brought big smiles to their faces. You did not have to be born in America or be the product of some Italian village to appreciate good food. The trio knew that they had a winner. "Eat your heart out, Momma Leone." This tomato sauce was definitely good to the last drop, and the consistency was perfect. All that was missing now was a good hot loaf of brick-oven Italian bread.

Before long, the whole neighborhood started to smell like Little Italy. The steam from the home cooked foods quickly exuded out from the overhead exhaust system and into the city streets. With time and a lot of hard work,

Joey felt that this pizzeria would be as good as any other. The ambiance might not be as good, but the food would be.

For the next few days everything from Eggplant Parmesan to meatballs was prepared. Joey used his mother's recipe for the round Italian delicacy. Chopped meat, hard bread soaked in water, eggs, grated cheese, breadcrumbs, parsley, garlic, onion, salt and pepper. That was the recipe for the best tasting meatball in the city. Fry them up and throw in a good sauce and you got it made. Little by little, everything was starting to happen. For the first time in a long time, Joey felt a sense of accomplishment. He liked the feeling of being productive and it showed in every aspect of his total being.

Joey, Marco and Orlando developed a good working relationship. Each knew what was expected from the other. The two Mexicans knew who the boss was and in turn Joey treated them with the respect that they deserved.

It was Friday morning three days before the grand opening. The outside temperature was starting to drop; winter was not too far away. The two workers and owner were busy inside the store preparing for opening day. There was a loud bang against the plywood window. The rapping sound grew louder and louder with each passing second.

Joey walked up to the front of the store to investigate. To his surprise he realized that he had a legitimate visitor.

"Who is it?" he said, waiting for an answer.

"I'm looking for Joey," the visitor said.

"Okay, hold on a minute." Joey then rolled up the gate and saw an older looking Mexican man standing there. "I'm Joey, what's up?"

"My name is Manuel. Tony sent me here to make pizza for you."

"Manuel, have you made pizza before?"

"Yes, for about ten years."

"Good, take your coat off. The kitchen is in the back. I want you to make a fresh batch of dough and some pizza sauce."

Manuel seemed like he was all business. He quickly removed his outer garments and put on a work shirt from off of the rack. His next move was into the bathroom to wash his hands. Little things like that matter in the eyes of any boss. When a worker takes control of his own work responsibilities, it gets noticed. Some people you have to tell them each and every day the same thing over and over. They always have to be told what to do. It's a pleasure when a worker takes it upon himself and performs the way he is paid to perform.

The following day it was time to taste Manuel's pizza. The pizza dough sat in the walk-in box overnight and was ready for testing. Manuel stretched and twirled the white lump of dough easily. His experience was showing as he laid the finished product on his pizza board. The rest of the ingredients were put on top of the pie and it was tossed inside the hot 500 degrees oven. After about eight to ten minutes it was ready for consumption.

"Manuel, this is great, man," Joey said, shoving the crispy slice in his mouth. From the nice thin crust all the way to the zesty pizza sauce, it was good. Orlando and Marco soon joined in to taste the first pizza pie. Everyone was in agreement that Manuel was a keeper. From his appearance all the way down to his mannerisms, the guy had it all. He was like a Godsend to Joey; finally he had a man with some experience.

So the stage was set, Manuel made the pizza, Orlando was the cook and Marco was the all around guy. Marco would do everything from dishes to deliveries. Most importantly the crew would work as a team, with each helping the other in all areas that needed tending to.

Saturday afternoon they put up a new hunter green canopy above the storefront. The bright white lettering exposed the name of the reopening pizzeria. "Joey's Place," was now introduced to the neighborhood. Like it or not, there were new tenants on the block. Whoever did not like it, it was too bad, they were here to stay. Tomorrow the plywood would be removed from the front window and the roll down gate would be repaired to cover it. It was just a matter of time before Monday morning came around and the front door would open for business.

Sunday was a beautiful day. Joey and Marco pulled up in front of the store. Joey handed Marco the keys to the shop and went to go park the car. Upon returning, he noticed Marco still standing on the walkway. His eyes were focused on the front of the store.

"How come you didn't open up yet?" Joey said, looking at him with a puzzled expression.

"Boss, look!" Marco said, pointing at the plywood covering the window.

On top of the plywood, big bold black letters were spray painted on top of all the other shit that covered the wood. The application was applied so thick that each letter had lines of dripping paint at the bottom of them. But these letters were a little different. The letters formed a word that was threatening to everyone who worked in the store. These ugly letters spelled out the gruesome word, "DEATH."

Joey started to touch the freshly painted threat, which was still moist. He turned around and started to scan the neighborhood with his angry eyes. The park across the street was the first place his inquisitive mind told him to look. But the night owls who ruled this public facility were absent, the park was vacant. He knew that someday trouble was going to come his way from across the street. When and how was the inevitable question that he was asking himself.

"Marco, you go inside and get to work," Joey ordered. "I'll be right back."

"Boss, I come with you."

"No, you go inside. I'm just going to check something out."

"Okay, boss," Marco said with a worried look on his face.

Joey then took the short walk across the narrow street. He walked to the entranceway of the park, which was at the corner of the block. Constantly looking over his shoulder, Joey entered the park. Each step warranted another peek.

Large maple trees surrounded the eerie looking park from the outside. Their naked branches had been stripped of the leaves from the change of the seasons. The more Joey looked around, the more he wondered how anything could survive in this neighborhood. Everything seemed to be stripped of its original character. The whole landscape looked dead. The look of desolation was everywhere.

It seemed that city officials had abandoned this piece of property many years ago. The upkeep was non-existent; every piece of equipment was in need of repair. The jungle gym that children once climbed was practically in pieces. Swings that mothers used to push their toddlers on were hanging from one chain. The slide was embedded with spray paint. Even the park benches were destroyed, their wood panels ripped right out of the long seat. This park looked like a deserted ghost town in an old Western movie. Garbage and debris littered the place. The punks and hoods who controlled this park had taken everything away from the residents. They had made this pig sty their home away from home. Little children were forced indoors in fear for their safety. Everyone knew what was going on here, but nobody did a damn thing about it.

Joey looked around in disgust and disbelief. There were hypodermic needles scattered around the grounds. Empty crack vials and tubes of airplane glue were wedged in the weeds up against the iron fence. These escapees from reality used anything and everything to catch a temporary high. Used condoms were pasted to the pavement below. Empty beer bottles and shattered glass was everywhere. Trash-cans were overflowing. From corner to corner garbage was thrown in a heap, creating a dumping ground. Defecation was evident, from animals to humans, the appalling stenches of urine and feces dominated the senses. Every step was another adventure. This park was a landscaper's biggest nightmare; to improve the appearance seemed virtually impossible. The next rainfall would provide the park with the only half-assed cleanup that it would get.

Over at the far end of the park a vagrant was in a sound sleep. The homeless man was covered from head to toe in old newspapers, the only source of warmth that he could find. To find security in a place like this meant one or two things. He was either still high from the night before or he was dead. Joey just stood his ground, not eager to find out the reasons for his overnight stay. This park was a haven for the junkies and the dealers who made money from them.

With every cautious step that Joey took, something else caught his attention. He walked slowly and noticed some stains on the pavement below him. Bending to one knee, he observed closely to notice the blemishing stains of blood. Whatever rituals or killings that went on here, there were gruesome reminders in every crack and crevice of the broken down park. Joey had seen enough. It did not take a Harvard graduate to figure out what was going on here. His investigation would have to continue at another time. For now, it was time to go back to his place of business and continue working on the grand opening.

"Hey you," the old man shouted at Joey. Joey looked over his shoulder. The staunch and well-built older man stood firm waiting for an answer. "You're the guy who is working across the street?"

"How do you know?"

"I see you comin' in and out of the store from time to time."

"Well then, that's me," Joey said, observing the old man walking with a cane in his right hand. "What can I do for you?"

"You better get out while you're still alive."

Joey looked at the prophet who was filled with these kind words of advice. The two men stood about ten feet from the opening gate that led into the park. There was nobody else around, which was pretty unusual for a sunny Sunday morning. The congestion in the street was light as a couple of stray dogs ventured out to cross the traffic free roadway.

"What do you mean?" Joey said

"You got some pair of balls comin' into this park."

"It's a public park, isn't it?"

"They know you're here. And if they catch you in the park," he said with a nod, "they will kill you."

"Who are they?"

"You'll find out soon enough," the old man warned. "Why do you think they call it Dead-man's park?"

"I guess because they kill people in there," Joey said. "It doesn't take a brain surgeon to figure that one out."

"It could have been you layin' in the corner over there." The ruggedly aged man was looking in the direction of the corpse that lay lifeless on the park bench. "Do you see what I'm talkin' about?"

"Yea, I see what you're talkin' about," Joey answered. "But I got a question for you. Once again, who is they?"

"They are called the Brotherhood. This is their park and their neighborhood. They run everything around here, from drugs to extorting money from every small business in the area. They have a piece of it all and everyone abides by their rules or they die."

"The Brotherhood," Joey said. "Well, listen, friend, you can tell the Brotherhood that all I want to do is operate my business in peace. I did not come here for trouble. I just came here to offer this community a service and I'm not about to leave."

"Well, I guess you got to find out the hard way. You see that store over there?" the old man said, raising his cane and pointing in the direction of the pizzeria.

"What about it?"

"Well, the Brotherhood shook down the man who used to own the place. It got so bad for him that he just got up and walked away from his own business. They will surely do the same thing to you to," the elder statesman vowed. "You wait and see!"

"They ain't getting a fuckin' dime from me and you can tell them I said so." Joey's voice started to rise with anger; he worked too hard over the past few weeks to start giving his money away. The front door was not even opened for business and already somebody had their hands in his pockets.

"I just thought I should give you a warning."

"Old man, thanks for the words of wisdom. But I am not going anywhere. So read my lips! Nobody, and I mean nobody, is pushing me out of anything that I worked so hard for." Joey then turned away and started walking back to his place of business.

"Have it your way," the man said. "Son?"

"What?" Joey asked, turning around one last time to look at him.

"Good luck!"

"Yea, thanks," Joey said. "And thanks for the encouraging words of advice," he sarcastically said.

The old man began to slowly hobble down the block. His side-to-side strut was the result of a gunshot wound during World War Two. He knew the neighborhood and he knew what he was talking about. For Joey it was just a matter of waiting on the Brotherhood to make their first move. He knew what he was in for as soon as that first beer bottle came crashing down at his feet. Joey knew that he could not let this matter get in the way of his thinking. He had a business to run and the clock was ticking down to the opening of his establishment.

That afternoon the disgusting plywood was removed, exposing the front window. The glass frame was in good condition, so all it needed was a good cleaning. All the other minor problems were quickly corrected and the boys were ready to roll. The foursome closed the store early that Sunday evening, because everyone had to be fresh and ready to go. Joey and Marco were the last ones to leave as they stepped outside to lock up. Joey felt the peering eyes coming out of the park like they were embedded on his body. Like cats, their eyeballs glistened through the darkness of the dimly lit park. He quickly pulled down the rolling gates and fastened the heavy locks shut. Marco looked anxious, waiting for his boss to finish the small task. The trouble

that awaited them had no timetable. Joey and Marco took the short walk
to Joey's car. Carefully, they watched their backs as the trouble lurked from
behind their shadows

Monday morning came around fast; Joey and Marco arrived at the
restaurant a little early. They were expecting a small delivery from Tony's
food distributorship. At 9 o'clock the truck pulled up right on time. This
was going to be a small delivery, just four cases of cheese, some flour and a
few other odds and ends.

"Marco," Joey called. "Leave the walk in box open so we can carry the
cheese right in."

"Okay, boss." Marco quickly raced to the back of the store and opened
up the heavy metal door. He then returned to the 18-foot truck that was
double-parked out front. The two men waited as the driver handed each one
of them a fifty-pound case of cheese.

"Do you want me to put the cheese on a hand truck?" the driver asked,
preparing to hand over another 50-pound box.

"Nah, there is not that much here. I'll just lay them on the floor and
bring them in one at a time," Joey said. After all the contents of the delivery
were unloaded, Joey signed the delivery receipt and the driver took off.

"Marco, put everything up against the wall of the building. After we
bring the cheese in, put the flour in the basement." Joey had set up the
basement to use as a storage area. Mostly canned goods and paper products.
Except for the flour, anything that was perishable was never stored down
there.

Each man picked up a case of cheese and started walking down the
narrow aisle towards the back of the store. Joey led the way, but for some
strange unforeseen reason he stopped dead in his tracks. "Holy shit, what the
fuck is that?" he said, placing the heavy case of cheese on top of one of the
tables. "Marco, look at the size of that fuckin' rat! It's the size of a cat!"

The oversized rodent just stood there holding his ground. The arrogant
creature with his dark gray overcoat was perched up on his two hind legs.
His large incisors were protruding from the opening of his uncommonly large
mouth. This was no ordinary rat; regular pesticides would have no effect on
this monster. There was not a glue board on earth that could stabilize the
mobility of this super rat. From his head to the back of his tail, he must have
been at least 18 inches long. The barrel of his stomach looked like a hearty
loaf of Italian bread. Joey looked stunned; he had seen rats before, but none

the size of this mammal. A hungry Pit Bull would have a hard time with this one.

All of a sudden out of nowhere, Marco raced up to confront this freak of nature. The rat retreated and ran up the two steps that led into the kitchen area. In hot pursuit Marco followed the rodent to the back of the store. The now disoriented rat ran right into the walk-in box. The fearless Mexican followed up his rear as they met face to face.

"Get him, Marco! Get him," Joey screamed, slamming the big refrigerator door shut. The Mexican and the beast were trapped inside the walk in box together. "Kick his fuckin' ass!" Joey shouted again.

You could hear young Marco scrambling around inside the refrigerator. Cans, bottles and holding containers were crashing to the floor. It was pure chaos, with each combatant fighting inside the square encased cubicle. Then there was a sound of a metal rack tipping over and crashing into the side of one of the walls.

"Marco, are you alright in there!" There was no answer. "Marco, answer me, are you okay?" Joey pleaded, still with no response. It was then that he decided to open the door and take a peek inside. "Marco, Marco," Joey said racing to the fallen Mexican.

Marco was buried underneath the metal rack. There was crap everywhere; everything from carrots to mayonnaise was strewn about the small box. Joey then bent down to lift the heavy rack off of his buddy. There he was, lying flat on his back covered with God only knows what. He looked like a Mexican salad, with dressing and the leaves of lettuce covering him, a broken jar of olives was by his side. Throw some tomato sauce on top of that, and he looked very colorful and appetizing. Most importantly, he had a big grin on his face. His pearly whites were shining in a proud manner. In his right hand were the remains of one big dead rat. Marco had squeezed the life right out of him, and it died with its eyes and mouth wide open. He then held up his prey in a show of triumph, feeling very excited about his accomplishment.

"Boss," he said holding up his prize.

"Get that fuckin' mangy looking thing away from me," Joey said, extending his hand to help the victor to his feet. "Put him in a bag and throw him down the sewer on the corner."

The two men exited the walk in box. Joey had one arm around Marco's shoulder. Marco had his right hand wrapped around the rat's throat. Joey stopped and looked at Marco and realized what being loyal was all about.

He then realized that this young man would go through a brick wall for him. This kid had genitals the size of basketballs - nothing seemed to scare him.

"Are you alright? He didn't bite you did he?" he asked his worker, examining his body for rat bites. "Are you okay?"

"Yes, I okay," the jubilant Marco said. "He no bite me."

"Tonight we drink Coronas," Joey said with joy.

"Viva Corona," Marco shouted, holding the dead rat in the air over his head.

"Marco, please, put that fuckin' thing in a bag and get rid of it. When you come back, make sure you wash up nice and clean. In a couple of hours we will be open for business."

"Yes, boss. Me go."

"Jesus Christ," Joey said to himself. "If the Board of Health could only see us now."

Within the next hour, Manuel and Orlando showed up for work. They got right to work preparing the delicacies of the day. Within one hour the pizza counter was displaying everything from spinach rolls to garlic knots. At noon the front door was open for business.

The day started slowly, just a few people entered the reopening of the neighborhood pizzeria. Some people came in for change of a dollar; others just wanted to use the restroom. After three or four hours, Joey realized that this block was taboo. It was off limits to most of the law-abiding citizens. Even flooding the neighborhood with menus and flyers did not help. No one dared to venture to the pizzeria that was right across the street from Deadman's park.

Around dinner-time, things started to perk up a little bit. The telephone started to ring off the hook. It was obvious the people wanted their favorite Italian delicacy delivered to them. For three straight hours, Marco was hopping on and off of his bicycle making deliveries. The new crew was pumping out pizza and pasta dishes as fast as they could make them. Joey then knew that this would be the focus of his business. If the people did not come to him, he would make sure that his food went to the people. Each delivery order was handled in a polite and courteous business manner. Every order was followed up with a phone call for customer satisfaction. On this evening there were no complaints, everyone received their orders piping hot and delicious.

The following morning, Joey had everyone in a couple of hours early. They flooded the whole section of Crown Heights with thousands of menus. Everything from local businesses to hospitals was hit with the paper menu and flyers. The advertising was well worth it as even the lunch business started to pick up. Slowly but surely the place started to resemble a fully functional pizzeria. Joey's Place was starting to develop a reputation of good food and service. Yet, even with all the advertising, the inside of the small eatery was still devoid of any dine-in customers. Correcting this problem, Joey knew, would not be worth the bloodshed it would cost. The park across the street effectively blocked out any success that may have come his way. The business he had now was just enough to pay the bills, but anything extra was virtually impossible.

One night following a not too busy day Joey just stood a few feet from the inside window looking out onto the street. He closely examined the activity that was conducted across the way. Every ten seconds another car would pull up to the curb, merchandise was then exchanged for some money. This went on all day long, except in the daylight the thugs were a little more discreet. The nighttime brought everyone out in full force. The streets and inside the park looked like a busy trading day on the floor of the New York Stock Exchange.

People came from all over town to cop their high for the night. Even the desperadoes who came staggering over by foot got what they were looking for. These addicted crack-heads couldn't even wait to get back home before they started their journey to their so-called utopia. The nearest broken down park bench was the site for their pipe lighting or injection. A half dozen people would sometimes share the same needles. Every shared needle dropped a small amount of tainted blood into someone else's body. To them it did not matter, it was the after affects and the illusions they were looking for. Disease was just an afterthought. They just kept pumping the drugs into their brittle and disintegrating bodies. For some it was so bad they looked like walking zombies.

The women of this brutal way of life even exchanged their bodies for a ten-dollar vial of crack. Every half-hour you could see one of them bending over or down on their knees performing some type of sex act. Their addictions were so strong that they sacrificed their own bodies to satisfy it. The members of the Brotherhood took turns quenching their hungry lust. They held the powerful element that all these addicted women wanted. This was their Disneyland, and to hop on a ride, there was a severe price to pay. There was one big difference: this theme park was the site for every possible impurity that man could breed. This was a cesspool, contaminated with the lowest form of breathing creatures in the world. All these adulterated acts would breed an inferno of wasted human life.

The Brotherhood had everything done systematically, and each corner had a lookout man who searched for cops. Before any smell of law enforcement was arriving, the gang quickly dismantled and disembarked from the scene. All the cops would ever find were addicts too stoned out to flee the scene. In most cases they were taken away to thaw out overnight. The next night the addicts were back in the same spot that they were picked up from. It was a revolving door to nowhere, even the cops knew it. Their efforts were futile as their appearance in this crack den was sometimes non-existent.

For the people who lived in this community, it was a way of life. They were too poor to move from these horrors. But most of all, they were afraid of the consequences if they over exceeded their boundaries. The good people of the neighborhood were taxpaying prisoners. They were paying for city services that were never rendered. They all needed a miracle from God to release them from the hold of the demons that ruled the streets.

One Thursday afternoon a small but expectant visitor entered the pizzeria with a smile on his face that overshadowed his appearance. The young boy had a partner who was about three to four years older than him. They both carried knapsacks on their small framed backs. It was three o'clock and the two young boys were returning home from school.

"Hi, Mister," the eager six-year old greeted Joey.

"Well look who it is, it's little Steven," Joey said, bending over the countertop to greet the little fellow. He then put out his hand for a welcoming handshake. The young lad took Joey's hand and furiously shook his right arm. "Who is this young man with you?"

"That's my brother Derek," he proudly boasted.

"How you doing, Derek?" Joey asked, extending his hand.

"I'm fine, Mister. Thank you."

The two brothers were very polite, and each one showed the respect that was instilled in them from two fine parents. Both of the boys were well groomed and their well-mannered behavior was light years ahead of their ages. To Joey it was a pleasant sight, that two young men brought up and raised in this neighborhood could somehow overcome the obstacles that surrounded them.

"Did you come in for your free slice of pizza that I promised you?"

"No, my mother said that I must pay for it," Steven said.

"She said thank you anyway, but we have to pay," Derek said reaching into his pockets for some money.

"Then you go and tell your mother that the man in the pizzeria said thanks. From now on, I want you two guys to call me Joey, okay."

The two boys shook their heads in agreement and took a seat. They patiently sat and waited for their small order. A few minutes later the two smiling boys were each munching on a slice of freshly baked pizza.

There was not a day that went by when the two boys did not raise their little arms to say hello. Like clockwork, every afternoon at ten after three they strolled by the store and said hello. It became a habit as Joey looked outside the window and noticed the boys rushing to get home. They stopped into the store about once or twice a week, but they never failed with their friendly greetings.

The cold November rain was falling as the wind battered the front window of the store. There were swirling sounds with each gust from Mother Nature. The weather's nasty disposition had no pity for the entities that dwelled below. It was a cold wet rain, and the best place to be on this miserable Friday was indoors.

Joey and his crew were busy preparing for the dinner rush.

Through the raindrops, three loud gunshots exploded outside the pizzeria. Pop, pop, pop, were the sounds. Joey looked up. Within three seconds, two more were heard. Loud screams followed, and then the terrified voices of women going into a frenzy. People scurried for cover. Fishtailing with screeching tire sounds, a black four-door sedan raced up the block. In its aftermath, the skid marks of murder were left behind.

Joey ran around the counter and bolted towards the front door to confront the agitated commotion.

"Marco, get out here!" he said before exiting the pizzeria. Marco raced out behind his boss.

There lying in the middle of the street was a little boy. His companion was draped over his lifeless body. There were a couple of helpless women who stood shocked, dumbfounded by the horror. Each stood by the curb, wet and stunned, their hands covering their terrified faces. From up above, residents on the second and third floors of their apartments exposed a quick peek to investigate. All others scampered for the safety of their front door. Fear and retaliation had put their concerns in a checkmate. Nobody else was around, the intended victim was nowhere in sight. All that was left was sympathy. No one came to the aid of the little boy.

Jesus Christ, Joey said to himself. *Nobody's helping this poor kid. They're all just standing around watching and doing nothing.*

Hard driving rain continued to fall, diluting the blood oozing from the boy's body. The blood slowly found its way to the curb and joined the other rainwater heading for the corner sewer. There was dead silence in the air, except for the battering rain and constant sobbing. His hysterical friend sobbed uncontrollably over the fallen victim, crying and grabbing at the motionless body.

Joey was ten feet from the scene before he stopped dead in his tracks. He was paralyzed and numb while staring at the sight before him. "Steven!" Joey shouted.

Steven's tiny body lay arched for he had fallen with his knapsack straddled on his back. The friendly youngster was unconscious and losing blood rapidly. Without any movement to his lifeless limbs, blood trickled down the corner of his slightly opened mouth. The rain had no pity as it battered and saturated his stagnant body.

Joey then proceeded the final ten feet to try and aid his little buddy. He quickly removed his apron and placed it over the body. It was then that he noticed a gunshot wound right in the center of Steven's chest. The bullet was buried deep into the chest cavity of the popular little boy. His body was ice cold. The color in his once beaming face had disappeared. Steven was slowly losing life.

"Marco, get me a blanket!" Joey said, his voice strained. "Somebody call an ambulance," he screamed. "What the fuck is wrong with you people? Somebody please call for help!"

"Joey, is my brother going to die?" Derek sobbed, grabbing tightly at Joey's arm. "Save him, Joey, please save him!"

Joey then looked into Derek's eyes; he had no words to relieve the young boy's pain and suffering. Tears were streaming down Derek's face.

"Help him, Joey, please help him."

"I'm here, Derek, I'm here," said Joey in a soft consoling voice. "I will help him." Looking up he screamed, "Did somebody call an ambulance?"

"They're on the way!" a woman shouted from a second story window. "I called them already!"

Marco then returned with a white blanket. Joey dropped to one knee and placed the wool fabric over the comatose body. He picked the sixty-pound body up and cradled it in his arms. The young boy's little head was limp as it hung lifeless over Joey's clutching arms. Raising his head, Joey looked into the murky sky above. The rain pelted his face, making him squint as he was searching for the reasons for this terrible mishap. The many tears coming from his handsome face were lost in the falling rain. The downpour treacherous, it looked like rapid machine gun fire hitting the tar pavement of the street. Joey's clothes now revealed the blood from the little victim's body. There was water and blood everywhere.

He didn't even begin to live his life yet, Joey pondered to himself. *He never had a chance. He never had the fucking chance.*

"Why, damn it, why?" he shouted, his deep and powerful voice reverberating between the tall buildings. "Why this little boy, God, why?" Joey put his head down in sorrow and looked at the helpless little boy cradled in his arms.

A powerful gust of the wet wind was the only response. Joey's head was now bent in sorrow, his angry attention focused on the empty park. With the look of a mad killer searching for prey, he stared into the vacant park. This was worse than anything that he ever experienced in his life. Hatred was running through his body that was being propelled by his overworked emotions. He knew where the violence was coming from; he just did not have the firepower to confront it alone. He also knew that he could not let his emotions get the best of him. Any retaliatory strike would send him back to the place he despised. The forty-foot-walls were just a misdemeanor away. Joey DeFalco was handcuffed as the strings on his straight jacket were being pulled tighter and tighter. But most of all, he knew that this was only the beginning of bad things to come.

"You motherfuckers," he screamed, still looking into the park. The sounds of police sirens and an ambulance wailed mournfully in the heavy mist. To most, Joey's ranting and raving was meaningless and just an after thought. It looked like the people here had witnessed this scene many times before. The residents on this block knew that it was just a matter of time before death strikes their doorsteps again. To them it was nothing new, it was just another page out of the same old story. They just sat in their apartments waiting for history to constantly repeat itself.

Marco and Joey hurried the helpless child into the pizzeria and waited impatiently for the ambulance to arrive. The paramedics rushed in and performed valiantly trying to revive the young boy. Over and over again, they tried heroically to pump the life back into Steven. But over and over again, there was no sign of life or the faintest response. Their efforts fell in vain. The emergency medical technician looked up at Joey; his eyes told the story. The young paramedic just bowed his head in sorrow, nothing more could be done. Steven was placed on top of a stretcher and was ready to be carried out the front door. They then threw a blanket over his dead body to symbolize that a young life was over. As of this moment, little Steven had just become another statistic of murder.

"Don't let them take my brother! Joey, please, stop them. Steven!" Derek cried, tugging at Joey's saturated clothes. Joey then grabbed Derek and hugged him in his arms. He bent down to one knee trying time and time again to console him. "Is he dead?" Derek screamed. "I want my brother."

"Derek, where are your parents?" Joey was trying to ignore his pleas, afraid to tell him that his brother was gone.

"They are at work," he said in a broken voice. Derek was rubbing his watery eyes with every word of distress that came from his trembling mouth and body. "I want my brother, I want my brother," he repeated over and over.

"Give me their phone number," Joey said. He decided that it would be he who had to tell Steven's mother and father the heartbreaking news. There is nothing worse on this planet Earth than telling a mother that her son is dead. That job should have been left up to the cops if they ever got to the crime scene. As usual, they arrived ten minutes after the paramedics. The murderers could have crossed the Canadian border before the police department finally arrived. That's the way it is in this neighborhood, the cops are either overloaded with calls or sleeping somewhere in a Dunkin Donuts parking lot.

For the next couple of hours, Joey just stared, fixated at the park across the street. The only barrier was the falling rain as it separated evil from his front doorstep.

Chapter 13

THREE DAYS LATER little Steven was laid to rest. Joey and Marco attended the wake and the funeral services. Maurice and Dorothy Greene were two wonderful parents who did not deserve a fate such as this. The family mourned peacefully showing respect and great restraint for their son. He was now in God's hands and his parents knew that for the very first time he would always be safe.

A six-year old life was just taken out by a senseless drive by shooting. The kid did not even begin to live his life before some animal unintentionally took it away from him. And he died for what? Turf, drugs, money, revenge, whatever the reasons, a little boy was buried six feet under the ground. His casket was not much bigger than a crate of vegetables. It all seemed so senseless, but not too many people in this neighborhood would lose any sleep over it. To them, he was just another casualty or statistic, and tomorrow would be just another day. The ones who did care stayed fearfully locked inside their homes. Fear had caused their tears to dry up many, many years ago.

For the next few days every punk in the dreaded neighborhood kept a low profile. Each was running incognito. Heavy clothing and even in some cases disguises were used to hide their identity. The cops were all over the place searching the area for clues. A bullet dislodged from Steven's chest, the automobile, some skid marks, and a possible plate number were all the cops hoped to find. There were not many other clues to go by. But of course, nothing turned up any evidence. Every doorbell and every knock on a front door fell upon deaf ears. Nobody knew anything and saw absolutely nothing. Even if they did, there was not a chance in the world they would tell the cops. Their safety and the safety of their families would be at risk. In a rough area like this, payback can be a bitch. Fear kept these prisoners of St. Ann's Place from telling the truth. The only other people who saw anything were Joey and the dead boy's brother Derek. They were the only two links to the truth, and the Brotherhood knew it.

The front door of the pizzeria swung open and hit the wall behind it. Two plainclothes detectives walked in looking for some answers. Everyone who had eyes knew who they were and what they were here for. The cops spent about thirty minutes grilling Joey. He gave them more than the two cops ever expected to hear. Slowly, he described the vehicle and the number of occupants in it. He gave them every single detail about the crowd that congregated in the park. Joey was not telling the cops anything that they had not already known. The police knew where to go if they had to find out the answers to all their questions. It seemed they were all trying to avoid the inevitable. These murderers would never be caught. Joey knew it, the cops knew it and more importantly so did the Brotherhood. Besides, in a week or two little Steven would become a distant memory. For a certain few, Derek's appearance would provide the fond memories of his dead brother.

Christmas Eve was here. The pizzeria was decorated nicely with ornaments and a small Christmas tree that stood on top of a table. On the outside, colorful lights adorned the window and around the doorway. The decorations brought some cheer to a very miserable year. Christmas had a way of making even the most dreadful memories seem a little bit more bearable.

On this night, the whole crew was looking forward to closing up early and spending the religious holiday with their families. At seven o'clock the doors were locked and the partying started. Joey broke out with a case of beer and a couple of bottles of champagne. The mood was festive. The four men sat around a rectangular table while polishing off holiday booze. Soft Christmas tunes played in the background. A few nice catering jobs made the day financially worthwhile.

Through all the confusion the telephone rang in the background. The ringing chopped through the loud conversation and soft music. Joey sat there amongst his workers debating whether to answer the telephone or not.

"Shit, let me get the phone," he said, urging Manuel to slide his chair in so he can get by. The telephone was on its fifth ring before Joey finally picked the receiver up. "Joey's Place," he said in a loud voice.

"Are you still open?" the sweet sounding voice said from the other end of the wire. "Please tell me that you are still open!"

"No Ma'am, I'm sorry, we're closed."

"Oh please, please help me!" the woman's voice said, with a sign of desperation. "I am here with my sister and her two young kids and some other place messed up our food order. We are stuck here with nothing to eat on Christmas Eve. I am not worried about myself, it's the kids and all."

"What's your name," Joey asked.

"Gloria."

"Listen Gloria, my crew is ready to walk out the door and all the equipment is shut down. Even if I wanted to help you, I can't."

"You're my last hope," she pleaded. "You know what it's like trying to get anything in this neighborhood delivered to your home."

"Believe me, I know what its like," Joey said overhearing two young children crying in the background. "Believe me I know!"

"So, will you help me, please!" Her voice was so pleasant and sexy that Joey had a hard time saying no a second time. He just stood by the phone scratching his head and smiling. There was a long pause, Gloria was waiting for her answer and Joey was contemplating a response. "Are you Joey?" she said.

"Yes I am."

"You sound like a very nice, understanding man," she said. Joey's mind was already made up. The cries coming from the background was enough for him. There was no reason to deprive those kids of a happy Christmas Eve. "Please Joey, do it for a future customer," the alluring voice said with a slight Puerto Rican accent.

"Okay, you win," he conceded. "What will you have?"

"Thank you, thank you, you're a doll."

"I know, I know, I'm a living doll," Joey said, as they both shared a laugh.

Joey took her order and told his crew to fire up the ovens. The men had some very dejected looks on their faces. Joey knew that he was asking a lot of them, but like troopers they all respected his command. He then took her address and telephone number.

"Joey, there's one other thing," Gloria said.

"What's that," he asked.

"Could you bring the delivery up yourself?"

"Boy, you want it all, don't you," he kidded, but he was excited about the invitation. "I don't know if I can, if you see a short Mexican at your front door, then you know it's not me."

"Oh okay, but I just wanted to thank you in person."

"If I can't make it, maybe you can drop by the store one day and say hello."

"Most definitely," the lovely voice said. "I would be looking forward to it."

"Alright, let me get started on your order, give me about forty five minutes."

"Joey!"

"Yea."

"Merry Christmas!" Gloria said, in the most seductive way imaginable.

"Thank you, and the same to you." Right then and there Joey felt his knees buckle. A tingle ran rampant throughout his body and settled where it usually does on a man, right between his legs. He knew the woman behind that voice was hot. The sounds coming from the other end of the phone told him so. That voice was too sweet and sexy for her not to be beautiful. She sounded very inviting, even if it was only over the phone. Joey felt something there, he just sensed it in his thumping heart. Even though the woman was just placing an order for food, he knew the harmony between them was real.

"Maybe I will see you later," Gloria said, her voice coquettish. He knew her game.

"Maybe," Joey replied as he hung up the phone.

Gloria's order was ready to be delivered about 40 minutes later. Everything was put into two pizza bags so it would be kept piping hot. The crew shut down all the ovens and equipment for the last time. A fast cleanup followed and soon they would all be on their way out the door. Everyone finished the last few bottles of beer. It was now time to drop off the delivery and then go home.

"This delivery is about a mile away," Joey said.

"I take, boss," Marco answered.

"I wish you knew how to drive a car!"

"I know how to drive car," said Marco with a smile. "Give me keys."

"You have a driver's license?" Joey said, surprised.

"Si," Marco said with a cunning look.

"You don't even have a fuckin' green card, and you have a driver's license? Get the fuck away from me," Joey said giving Marco a playful shove. "I know what we'll do! We will all get in the car and take the delivery. Then I will drive everyone home, let's go."

Everyone agreed as they all hopped in the car and took the small order to the waiting customers. Joey warmed the car up for about five minutes before they took off. It was a very cold Christmas Eve; the temperature was about twenty five degrees. The skies looked overcast; a White Christmas was not impossible.

T he blue Buick pulled up to the four-family Brownstone that was located in the middle of the block. A long flight of steps led to the entranceway of the neatly kept dwelling. Joey popped open the trunk and unloaded the two pizza bags containing the small catering order. His workers sat patiently in the car with rock and roll vibrating through the cheap speaker system. As soon as Joey slammed the trunk shut, Orlando hopped out of the back seat to confront his boss.

"Boss," he said trying to grab the two pizza bags. "I take for you, its cold outside." Orlando had a wide smile on his face; he knew there was no way in the world that Joey was giving up this delivery. It would probably be the first and last delivery that he would ever make.

"You ain't taking shit," Joey said. "Stop bustin' my balls and get back in the fuckin' car." The chubby Mexican laughed all the way into the warmth of the car. Inside, they all shared a good laugh; they knew what Joey was after.

From the corner of Joey's eye, he saw some movement coming from the vertical blinds covering the front window on the ground floor. It was too dark to see any facial features, but there was some long dark hair draping over the peeking hand. As soon as Joey turned his head to confront the onlooker, it disappeared. He then started his slow walk towards the front door.

Inside the two-bedroom apartment Terri ran into the kitchen to tell her sister their food and Knight in shining armor was here. Gloria sat at the kitchen table with her legs crossed. Her right hand had an emery board in it, the back and forth motion was furious. The grinding sounds were prepping her long fingernails before a coat of nail polish was to be applied.

"Gloria, he's gorgeous," she said to her sister. Those were the words that her heart yearned to hear from her divorced sister. To Gloria, what were the chances of a young looking Clark Gable ringing the front doorbell on Christmas Eve. She loved Joey's sexy sounding voice, but the chances of him being the total package were too much to ask for. Her sister's words encouraged her; she knew that she shared Terri's taste in men. Little did she know that fate would deliver her a 6 foot 2 handsome Italian man on her sister's doorstep.

At that moment, Gloria flew into the bathroom to make last minute preparations to her already beautiful face. Her hand fumbled in her makeup case looking for anything to enhance her beauty even more. Terri stood behind her, giving her baby sister some last second grooming tips. But there was not much time as the doorbell rang and their order was here. It seemed as of right now, that the delivery man got to be more important than the delivery. The two women were acting like schoolgirls. Terri knew that she saw something special in her sister's eyes. Even though it was just a phone conversation, she knew her sister felt an intense connection and warm feeling towards the man behind that deep voice.

"Who is it," Terri said over the intercom. She damn sure knew who it was, she just had to play the games that eager women feel the need to play.

"Food delivery," the voice said in a business like manner. Joey's voice sounded muddled as he had the delivery ticket between his lips and his hands full with the two steaming pizza bags. The buzzer sounded, Joey then pushed through the doorway and entered the clean hallway. He then turned to the right, the family name Perez hung right below the little peephole on the door.

"Just a second," the feminine voice said from inside the apartment.

"Okay," Joey said, while the delivery ticket fell from his mouth to the floor. He then bent down to retrieve the slip of paper as the apartment door slowly opened.

Turning his head, Joey saw a shiny pair of black boots that were tucked underneath a pair of neatly pressed blue jeans. His curious eyes slowly scanned their way up past the knees and onto a pair of magnificent looking thighs. Blue jeans never looked so good, the tight fitting pants looked like they were spray painted on her body. Every curve was exposed as the denim pants hugged her legs. A trendy black belt was wrapped around her small waist. The centerfold of a Playboy magazine would have had nothing over this Puerto Rican beauty. The only difference was that this picture was lacking the two staples holding everything together. Everything holding this lady together was put there by the love of God.

Joey's head continued to move upward, as he was still on one knee. The white blouse that covered the woman's upper body clung to her. Her bosom was as full of promise. She was an appealing package of sultry beauty and curvy womanhood. Silky straight jet-black hair covered her petite shoulders and ran down the sides of her breasts. The two finally made eye contact; Joey just stood there mesmerized by the angelic face. Everything from her high cheekbones to her small sculptured nose just fit like it was broken from a mold. Then it suddenly happened, her full bee stung lips parted with a smile that could span across the deepest of oceans. Her pearly whites glistened through her smooth olive complexion. She was the type of woman whose smile arrived before she did. Even the essence coming from her inviting body was enough to drive Joey crazy.

"Joey," Gloria said.

"Gloria," he answered back.

"You can get up now," she said smiling mischievously. "Come on in, you can put the food on the table in the kitchen."

Joey quickly rose to his feet and followed her into the small apartment. His eyes were fixated on her swirling buttocks. All he needed was some French fries to go with that shake. To Joey, there was a tremendous undertow. She was dragging him deeper and deeper under her alluring spell. He knew that his feelings were extraordinary, magical even. He just prayed that she felt the same way too. Her parents did a really fine job putting together this masterpiece. In Joey's eyes, it was up to God to put together the rest. Joey wanted this woman real bad.

Joey laid the food atop the table. The tension in the room was thick as Gloria and Joey stood there very quiet, each waiting for the other to make a move, each afraid of rejection. This scenario was not like a nightclub, where if you strike out you move on to the next. Here, there was no place to run, but out the front door. Besides, Gloria's sister Terri and her two young children were watching, full of curiosity. This was not the place to hit on a beautiful woman, especially on Christmas Eve and in front of her family.

"Joey, this is my sister Terri. These little ones over here are my niece and nephew, Ashley and Michael."

"Nice to meet you," Joey said, removing the food from the pizza bags and placing the small trays on the kitchen table. He then shook Terri's hand and smiled at the kids.

Terri was a pretty good-looking woman herself, in a motherly way. She looked like a divorced housewife who spends most of her time chasing her children all over the apartment. But there was a slight resemblance between the two women; you just had to look close to find it. For some reason, a bad marriage or divorce takes something out of a woman when it comes to her looks. The stress and the wear and tear can be overwhelming and a detriment to her physical appearance. After all, there was only five years that separated the thirty year old Terri from her younger sister. An abusive relationship made the age difference appear to be wider.

"Would you like something to drink?" Terri asked, reaching into a cabinet for a glass.

"Uh, no, no thanks. I have to run. I have a carload of hungry workers who I have to drive home. But thanks anyway," he said lifting the empty pizza bags. He then handed the food bill to Terri and put his head down. Joey would have loved to say that it was on the house. But with his business just struggling to survive, every last penny counted. Besides, when it came down to it, no matter what the circumstances, business was business.

Gloria nonchalantly moved off to the right side of the kitchen. She bent over the countertop to write something down on a piece of paper. Her sister Terri was busy reaching deep down into her handbag to pay the tab. Joey tried to make his hungry eyes nonchalant. Every chance he got, he took another peek at the dark-haired beauty.

"Here you go," Terri said handing Joey the money.

"There is ten dollars too much here," responded Joey, while scanning through the money.

"That's just a small token for putting you out of your way. I know it's not much, but take it anyway."

"Thanks, but give it to the kids, it's Christmas," Joey said, putting the ten dollar bill back into Terri's hand.

"Are you sure, I feel bad. You went out of your way for me and my family and I really appreciate that."

"You didn't put me out of my way at all," he said.

"Well then, I really don't know how to thank you."

"That's quite alright, the pleasure was all mine. I should be thanking you," Joey said, giving a wink from his right eye to Gloria. That was the opening he felt that he needed. Gloria received it very well and returned the same wink right back at Joey. The two smiled at each other, as the ice seemed to be broken.

This was love at first sight to the truest form. From the little flip of an eyelid, Joey's confidence was now soaring like a high-flying eagle. If it weren't for his work crew in the car, he knew where he would be spending his Christmas Eve. The invitation was right there before his eyes, but he knew that he had to leave. Nobody in the car had a driver's license, and three foreigners driving around town stinking like beer was a chance that he could not take. Those three men were his business; the temptation that love can bring would have to wait for another day.

Joey said his round of good-byes and headed for the door. Gloria followed closely behind to see him out. They both stopped by the doorway of the apartment as Joey's hand grabbed the doorknob. He opened the door and turned around to say goodnight.

"Merry Christmas, Joey, and thanks a lot."

"Merry Christmas to you too," Joey said bending down to give her a kiss on her cheek. His lips caressed her tender cheek and seemed to get glued to her. They both felt a burning sensation as their passions yearned for more. Joey dropped the pizza bags to the floor and slid his lips across her face towards her now open mouth. His left hand found its way under Gloria's long hair and around the back of her neck. He pulled her closer as their two bodies became one. Joey then kissed her inviting lips, her pleasant low sounding murmurs of emotion showed a boundless enthusiasm that the two seemed to share. Gloria then proceeded to put a piece of paper into Joey's right hand, making sure not interrupt the kiss.

"Mommy, Mommy, Aunt Gloria is kissing the pizza man," little Ashley said.

"Ashley, shut up and get over here!" Terri said, firmly scolding her eavesdropping daughter.

Joey just stood there with a smile on his face as he pulled himself apart from Gloria. He then looked above him and saw mistletoe hanging above the doorframe. To his surprise, he then looked at her for an answer.

"It works every time," she kidded.

"Damn," Joey said as he picked up the bags and headed out the door. "Damn," he repeated. He never took his eyes off of her until the door slowly closed between them.

Outside on the front steps Joey unraveled the paper that she put in his hand. The contents exposed the seven numbers that Joey was hoping to find. Besides the telephone number, was a small message that read, "Call me real soon, Gloria." Joey looked up into the overcast sky and noticed a light snow beginning to fall. The snow seemed to put the finishing touches on this remarkable evening. He was feeling like a man was supposed to feel when he first meets that special woman. He was acting like a young child who saw Santa Claus for the first time.

Joey raced down the flight of steps and entered the car that he left running. Smiling as he bent down to step in, he started to receive some howling and heckling from the guys. There was something very obvious on his face. Marco was pointing and laughing out some Mexican lingo as the others laughed along with him. Joey looked into his rear view mirror and adjusted it to a position to find out what the commotion was all about. Not to his surprise, Gloria's red lipstick was running amok across the right side of his face. Joey just looked at Marco and winked as he shook his head in a sign of machismo.

"Okay, I go!" Marco said, he then started to open up the front passenger side door.

"Go where?" Joey shot back puzzled.

"Inside la casa."

"What?" Joey did not know too much Spanish or Mexican, but he did know what casa meant. He was still looking at Marco tying to comprehend it all. "Go inside the house? You ain't going nowhere! What the fuck you think, it's a whorehouse? Shut the fuckin' door and stay in here."

"But boss, me have money," he said, exposing a fist full of dollar bills.

"Hey idiot, she's a customer not a hooker!"

"Boss, Orlando wants to go too. His wife no care."

The work crew had pulled a fast one on Joey's psyche. Orlando started to bust out laughing, and he then knew that Marco was just kidding. Joey then looked at Marco and placed his right index finger and thumb under his own chin, and just grinned.

"Son of a bitches," he said, putting the car in drive and pushing his foot on the accelerator. The foursome then drove off to spend whatever was left of Christmas Eve with their families.

Christmas Day came and went, the following day it was back to the same old routine. Only New Year's would differentiate and distinguish the start of a new month and year. Other than that everything else basically stayed the same. Business was relatively slow; people were too busy recovering from the holiday blitz. Pizza was just an afterthought as people were overloaded with leftovers from the holiday season.

The day after Christmas, the pizzeria was quiet. Just a few people ventured into the store for a slice and a cold drink. The phones were even quiet, only the people without family or mates called up for their usual small order. Joey had the crew cleaning everything inside the store, from top to bottom. In the restaurant business this was a customary thing to do when business was very slow.

Around eight o'clock that evening, Joey was scrubbing the top of the counter by the cash register. He moved the abrasive brush back and forth thoroughly and with precision. Never taking his eyes off of his work, a loud bang then interrupted his thinking. The front door flung open and smacked into the wall. In through the door rushed three very identifiable looking men. Like three bulls busting into a small China shop, they steamrolled in. Just by looking at them, you just knew that these three men were looking for trouble.

The nighttime visitors wore long leather trench coats about a foot below their knees. Their loose fitting black raincoats were reminiscent of the threads worn by the leaders of a rough neighborhood gang. For the first time in Joey's short tenure of operating his business, he was paid a token visit from the Brotherhood.

Joey stood poised behind the counter, never relinquishing his ground. The three dark invaders approached him from the customer side of the counter, right near the cash register. Each one of these clowns was wearing sunglasses in the dead of winter... that alone told you something about their character. That alone would tell any proprietor that as soon as these men walked into their shop, trouble was sure to follow.

This trio was hardly ever seen in the park; they lurked in the shadows overseeing their prosperous enterprise. They were the mighty intimidation behind the whole setup. The bulk of their responsibilities included the drop off of drugs and of course the picking up of the proceeds. They provided the muscle and the backbone behind this cruel and vicious business. Each one of them reported to one man and one man only, his name was Steamer. His buddies came up with that nickname when he shot three men in cold blood in a steam room at some neighborhood health-club some years ago.

Steamer had it all, money, fast women and cars. The jewelry that he wore around his neck alone would make even Tiffany's envious. This guy lived large and in the lap of luxury; the money was flowing into his deep pockets at a fast rate.

"You know what we're here for," the leader said. This guy looked mean, from the bottom of his black boots all the way up to the top of his bald head. He had a matching set of small gold hoop earrings hanging from each lobe. In his mouth was a glistening gold tooth that was not there for eating purposes. He glittered in any light.

"It better be a slice of pizza, because that's all you're gonna get from me!" Joey said, his voice dripping sarcasm. "We are barely making a living here."

"Hey man, that's your problem," he barked. "Right now you all are in our hood. We make the rules around here."

"Is that so?"

"Hey, this ain't no fuckin' joke, man. Don't make this hard on yourself," the tough looking black man said, fondling a gold chain dangling from his neck.

"I'm listening," Joey said, walking away and placing a slice of pizza in the heated oven. He knew what was about to happen, but he could not show his enemies any fear. Joey had learned in prison that fear is a sure sign of weakness.

"Each and every Friday we will be in here to get a small donation from you. Say around twenty five percent of the gross, in cash." He paused, looking around and sizing up the joint. "You can call it a small contribution to our organization and the community."

Joey just rested up against the handle of the pizza oven. He acted like he was contemplating the very intriguing offer. With his right hand, he opened the oven door to take a peek inside. A couple of seconds later, he closed the oven door and turned in the direction of trouble. "And what do I get out of it?"

"You got to pay the landlord so you can run your business in peace. Do you get the picture, my brother?"

"Ohhh, you mean like the last guy that owned this place. You protected him so good that he ran from his own business. Out of fear, he started borrowing from everybody and their mother just to feed your drug infested pockets. Did he get the picture too, my good brother?"

"Yea man," he said laughing as he looked at his crew. "That's it, just like him." Now he was serious.

"I see that you guys are dressed in black," observed Joey. "So there seems to be a small problem."

"What's that, man?"

"None of you guys look like nuns to me," he said. Joey opened the oven door one last time and retrieved the slice of pizza. He then shoveled it onto a white paper plate. "And those are the only people I ever make donations to." Joey then walked over to the counter and placed the hot slice of pizza on top of it. He then looked straight into the eyes of Mr. Steamer's man. "So like I said before, the only fuckin' thing that you're gonna get from me is this slice of fuckin' pizza. And you're going to pay for it too."

At that moment the leader of the trio picked up a salt shaker from the counter. He slowly sprinkled the spice all over the triangular slice. His two sidekicks stood, bracketing him, motionless with their hands buried deep inside of their trench coats. Joey was also intensely focused on them. He knew that their hands were in their pockets for a reason, and paying for the pizza was not the reason.

Marco and the rest were busy cleaning out the walk in box. They had no idea what was going on. Even if they came to Joey's defense, the four of them were no match for this trio of armed men. Joey was praying that they stayed put exactly where they were.

The ringleader then picked up his slice of pizza and started to walk towards the door. He took a bite and turned around to look at Joey. His two men stayed glued to their original stations right by the front counter.

"This is pretty good pizza, my man," he said through the crunching sounds of his teeth. "It's even better than the grease-balls' before you."

He then raised his right hand and tipped his sunglasses, exposing his devious dark eyes. That was the signal for his two comrades to go into action. Simultaneously, his two cronies whipped out their pistols and started blasting away. Joey saw it coming and quickly ducked behind the counter with his hands protecting the back of his head.

Bullets were flying everywhere as they destroyed the wall behind the counter. Everything from the two phones and personal pictures shattered. The crucifix between the pictures was practically blown in half. The invasion was focused in one area, but bullets were ricocheting everywhere. The mirrors above the wall paneling were taking a beating from the flying lead. Round circular cracks shattered around the small bullet holes in the mirrors. Ping, ping, ping, it was like a very loud version of popcorn bursting inside a microwave oven. The thugs just kept shooting and shooting until they emptied out the clips of their semi automatic handguns. This whole scenario lasted about ten seconds, but to Joey it seemed an eternity.

After the fusillade subsided, Joey picked his head up and peeked over the counter. Little did he know that he was going to be looking right into the barrel of a gun. One of the gunmen was waiting for him to rise from behind the counter. The ruffian held the gun two inches away from his forehead. Joey just looked into the gunman's shaded eyes, thinking that his life would soon be over. He just stared at the hoodlum, never pleading for mercy or giving in to their demands. The gunman started to slowly squeeze on the trigger of the dark gray weapon. His hand started to shake as the trigger was ready to fire. Joey just stared into the metal tube waiting for the inevitable. Within the blink of an eye, he pulled the trigger. Click, click, click, the clip was empty as the thug and the rest of his boys erupted with laughter.

"Shit Julius, I must have run out of damn bullets," he said to his leader. "Oh fuck, maybe next time." He then slipped the gun inside of his pants and closed his trench coat.

"I'll owe you for the slice," Julius said. "But if you're a smart white dude, I won't have to make a second visit. Be smart, my man, be smart!"

After the fireworks Marco had come rumbling down the steps. He had witnessed it all, but there was nothing the fiery little Mexican could do. He just bided his time and waited for the hailstorm of bullets to subside.

"Stay right there, little man!" Julius said to Marco, while his man impeded his progress. "One more move and you'll be back in Tijuana stuffed in a fuckin' taco shell!"

"Marco," Joey screamed. "Listen to him, don't move!"

Marco understood the violent English words. He stopped dead in his tracks and looked at Joey. In a way, he had the look of relief all over his face. Marco was ever so happy just to see his boss alive.

Julius and his two pals got a few laughs watching this 140 pound Mexican trying to come to Joey's rescue. The trio didn't really consider him a threat. They just smiled and started to backpedal towards the front door.

"We'll be in touch," Julius promised. "One way or the other, we'll be in touch." The three men then coolly walked out the front door.

"Boss, you okay?" Marco asked, running towards his friend.

"I'm okay," Joey answered, looking around the place. "This place is a mess. Look what they did to us."

A few seconds later Orlando and Manuel peeked out from their hiding spots in the kitchen. The Mexican men ventured down the steps. The two men grimly offered their condolences in the only way they knew how. Not only did they express their sympathy and sorrow, they also expressed their growing fears. The illegal aliens did not have to speak a word, as their trembling bodies and uneasy appearance did all the talking for them.

Joey was sweating profusely and his whole body was shaking from the close call. He anxiously paced back and forth, not knowing what to do next. Now he definitely knew that everybody's life was in danger and that his business was on the brink of disaster.

Marco walked closer to his Boss to try and calm him down. With every step of the way, his squinting eyes focused at the center of Joey's chest. He did not stop this peculiar movement until he satisfied his intuitive actions.

"Boss, look," he said, pointing at the medallion around Joey's neck.

"Look at what?" a bewildered Joey asked looking straight down at his chest. "What are you talking about?"

"Blood!" Marco said, pointing with a finger that was getting closer and closer to his chest. "The medal, there is blood on it."

Joey nervously ran his fingers down his neck and grasped tightly around the gold medallion. He pulled the medal outwards and bent his head in a position to see it. Looking closer and closer, Joey finally came to a conclusion that Marco was right. What he saw was very minuscule and almost microscopic, but somehow very *distinct*. The medallion was moist and blood was ever so lightly dripping from its pores. Some of the drippings left a very small red stain on top of his white tee shirt. The stain circled around the medallion like a halo.

"Holy shit. What the hell is this? I can't believe my own eyes," Joey whispered. "This is unbelievable. Where the hell did this blood come from this time?"

That's when Joey knew that he was not alone. It was then that he realized what Father Pasquale was trying to tell him, but kept a big secret. This medallion was unusual; it was acting like it was starting to come alive. In a way Joey perceived these unusual signs as a message symbolizing something. Whatever that was, he knew that it all tied into that mysterious night in his bedroom. Joey continued to stare at the medal in shock, not knowing what to think of this amazing development. He wondered to himself, *did this medal keep me alive? Whose blood is this? Is this the blood of Christ?* Joey had a look of puzzlement on his face. He just stared at the Mexican trio searching for answers. But at that moment, he had many other things to worry about.

The Brotherhood gave him plenty of warning signals that they would be back. Joey had no defense for their definite threats. He had to either give in to their demands or die. The only other alternative was to just close up shop and run for the hills in search of safety. These were the choices that he would have to make in the coming days. He was also worried about the safety of his crew. Joey was also concerned that he would lose them to fear. They each had families to worry about, and he would understand if they packed up their belongings and left.

Orlando was the most passive of the trio; for sure Joey knew that he would be gone. The three men looked over the mess and started conversing in their native language. What started out as mild conversation, erupted into an argument. There seemed to be some sort of disagreement about their futures in Joey's Place. Joey just walked away towards the front door in order to let them settle their differences amongst themselves.

About ten minutes later, Marco started walking towards Joey. He walked slowly through the debris, trying not to step on anything that was salvageable. Joey turned around to confront his most valued employee. He knew the fate of the pizzeria was all hinging on what Marco had to say to him. If one of them left, they could probably survive. But if two or more handed in their walking papers, it was all over.

"Boss," Marco said.

"What's up, pal," Joey sadly said.

"We stay, we no quit."

"Are you sure?" Joey asked. "Marco, it's okay, I understand if you and the boys want to leave me. It's very dangerous here."

"You are good boss, we like you. You are very good to us. We no leave, we stay with you," Marco said, with a smile from ear to ear on his small round face.

Manuel and Orlando started to walk towards the front of the store. The three men converged upon their boss and Joey started to thank them one by one. The thanks turned into hugs as they all started to embrace each other. It was made clear, at least inside the pizzeria that nobody was going to push them out of their own business. His three workers showed the courage of Marines on the battlefield, and Joey would be forever grateful to them.

Joey decided to cleanup the mess on the following day. The boys shut down the store early that night trying to put the nightmare behind them. Only in the morning sunshine would the reality become crystal clear.

The hunter green canopy above the storefront was torn down from its metal frame. The luminous canvas material lay atop the concrete pavement slashed into ribbons. The metal structure that the canvas envelopes looked like it had been run over by a truck. Each metal pole had been bent and twisted into different positions. The canopy that read Joey's Place, had been destroyed. This was just another expense that Joey could not afford to repair. He would just have to pick up all the loose pieces and try to continue on. In the meantime, his business was slowly falling apart. In less than twenty-four hours, what seemed feasible now seemed hopeless. Joey also knew that going to the police was not the answer; it would only percolate an already explosive situation. He was dealing with a pack of vicious marauders who had no mercy for their fellow man. The only love they had was for the dollar, and to get it there were no boundaries that they wouldn't cross.

Little by little the boys put the store back together. The most important thing was getting the phones working properly. That was the lifeline that kept the business still breathing and surviving. In order to try and limit some of the controversy, Joey decided to close the store at nine o'clock every night. Usually the doors would stay open until eleven, but the later it got the more dangerous it was. Besides, the less activity he saw coming from the park, the better off he was. His next option was to close the store on every Monday; this was an option that he would soon put into effect. Monday was a relatively slow day, but at least it helped to pay the bills. With all the overhead of running this business, he was definitely strangling himself. Minimizing hours and even days in search of safety would definitely hurt him. The three lives he was trying to protect were more important to him than his business.

T he Friday following New Year's Day was a very busy afternoon. Business was definitely better, as the deliveries were flying out the door.

"Marco, go downstairs and bring me up a bag of flour."

"Yes boss," he said.

A couple of minutes later Marco returned with the fifty-pound bag of flour. He had a very concerned look on his face as he approached his boss. Behind him he was leaving a trail of flour that went all the way to the basement.

"Boss, look!" he said pointing to the hole in the big bag of high gluten all-purpose flour.

"Jesus Christ," Joey said. "What the fuck is gonna happen next!"

It wasn't the hole in the bag of flour that concerned Joey; it was how the hole came to be. The rats in the basement had eaten through the heavy brown wrapper that contained the flour. He knew it as soon as he saw the bag and the type of tear in it. The rodents gnawed through the thick paper and feasted on the white powder and the proteins of the finely grated cereal grains.

"Are they all like that?" Joey asked, wondering if the rodents had desecrated all of his flour.

"Yes"

"Fuck, now we have to throw them all out." Joey knew that the rats had also contaminated the rest of the flour. With all the rat poison in the basement he was sure that some of it got into the exposed bags of flour. Besides being destructively annoying rodents, these rabies infected health hazards were laced with every kind of disease imaginable. These diseases were now running rampant throughout the ingredient which made a lot of the pizzeria's products.

The winter months brings all the furry creatures inside looking for shelter and warmth. When the weather heats up, they venture outdoors and become more of a public nuisance. Whatever the case was, eight bags of flour would have to be thrown in the garbage and a new storage place would have to be found.

"From now on we will keep the flour up here," Joey ordered. "Marco, I have a delivery for you."

Joey handed Marco the delivery ticket and reached up on top of the oven for the two pizza boxes. Marco placed the pizza bag on top of the counter and Joey slid the hot pizza into the bags opening.

"You don't need the bike," Joey instructed. "The delivery is right around the corner. It's $22.50 and the apartment number is 6C, okay."

Marco put on his winter coat, picked up the bag and raced out the door.

Right after Marco took off with the delivery, Joey went downstairs to check out the mess. There were little white powdery footprints all over the place. Joey followed the white trail of prints that led him to their safe haven. The little bastards ran under the walls, inside the walls, into the ceilings, under the steps, everywhere. The long tailed occupants ripped opened every bag of flour and munched away until their bellies were full. The scene was disorderly; there was flour all over the basement.

Not only did Joey have a battle outside the store going on, inside there was a much sneakier enemy that was harder to find and probably much tougher to get rid of.

Joey went back upstairs and noticed Marco had not returned from his delivery. This was unusual and Joey quickly became alarmed and worried. It was just after 3 P.M.; he had been gone for nearly a half of an hour. Another 15 minutes had passed and Joey decided to go out and look for him.

As soon as he headed for the door he heard little Derek screaming from the corner of Franklin Avenue. The kid was returning home from school and something impeded his progress. He saw something that was quite disturbing to him. He started running towards the pizzeria. "Joey, Joey," he yelled from the top of his lungs. Practically delirious, he raced down the block like a sprinter in search of the finish line.

Joey flung open the front door to confront his little friend. The boy was huffing and puffing as he finally came to a halt. Manuel was looking on from inside the store through the big front window. Joey grabbed Derek by his small shoulders to calm him down.

"Calm down, Derek. What's the matter?"

"It's…" he said trying to catch his breath. "Marco!"

"What about Marco?"

Steam was coming out of Derek's mouth as his warm breath hit the cold air. "I don't know, Joey, but there were cops all around the building and I just looked inside and," Derek paused, he had a hard time telling Joey what he saw. The sight must have brought back too many painful memories for him.

"What, what?" Joey demanded. "Tell me! What is it?"

"I think Marco is hurt," he said. His voice started to break down as the tears started to appear. "They said he was bleeding a lot."

"Who said?"

"The people who live inside the building."

"How do you know it was Marco?"

"They said he was a pizza delivery man," Derek sobbed. "I just know it was him, I just know it."

"Nooo! Don't tell me this. This can't be happening." At that moment, Joey looked up at Manuel and just shook his head with sorrow. The expression on Manuel's face was enough to make anyone cry. He knew that something wrong had happened to his working buddy. "Derek, go home now!"

The young boy nodded and said, "Okay."

Joey took off and raced around the corner. In front of the building on Franklin Avenue a large crowd had gathered. About four police cars were left unattended; the cops were all inside the large apartment building. Joey ran up the walkway and into the large lobby where there were hundreds of names and doorbells. To get in you had to be buzzed into the lobby by someone who was expecting you. His inability to wait patiently while someone either walked in or out of the building was irritating. His restless eagerness was apparent; he started to ring on every doorbell in the building. Banging and banging away at the large metal frame, his efforts were frantic. Finally his hysteria paid off. Joey heard a loud buzzer and he pushed on the heavy metal door until he was inside.

Like a thoroughbred blasting out of the gate at the Kentucky Derby, he galloped up a few steps and stopped for direction. In his peripheral vision, he noticed a commotion off to his left. He started to move hastily across the filthy marble floor and down the long corridor. The police hindered his progress as his forward motion was brought to a standstill. To the right of where Joey was standing were two elevators. The one closest to him was still in operation and working properly. It was the other elevator a little further down the hall that drew all the attention.

"Where do you think you're going?" the cop said, grabbing Joey by his left arm. "This area is off limits to civilians."

"Is there someone in that elevator?"

"Yea," the cop said sadly.

"I think the guy in that elevator works for me," a fearful Joey said to the thin cop.

The young looking officer just looked at Joey and shook his head. "Do you own the pizzeria around the corner?"

Those eight words just confirmed that it was Marco laying somewhere inside that elevator. Joey's body started to grow faint; all of the fears of the past few days have come true. All the strength and vigor from his defiant body went feeble. He then buried his face inside his balmy hands and started to roughly massage it. His own physical therapy ended as he ran both hands through his thick black hair.

"I don't know if you are up to this," the cop with the name-tag Kelly sadly said. "But do you want to identify the body? Let me warn you, this is bad, really bad."

He's dead, Joey thought. *Marco is dead.*

Joey looked up at the officer and nodded. He knew this was not going to be a pleasant sight. But he also knew that this was something he was growing accustomed to seeing. In the past year he had seen more blood than a blood bank during an epidemic.

The police officer then quickly conversed with his associates and slowly led Joey to the enclosure that was used to transport tenants to and from their homes. "I hope you have a strong stomach," Officer Kelly said. "It's not a pretty sight in there."

Joey was about two feet away from the elevator when he got hit with the smell of death. Before he even looked inside, he saw blood flowing out of the elevator and down its shaft. Now looking inside, he witnessed Marco slouching in a sitting position up against the wall of the elevator. Above his head, the blood was dripping down from beneath the handrail against the metal wall.

His once blue winter coat was now covered in blood from the three puncture wounds in his chest. Bloody fingerprints climbed up every wall of the elevator. All indications showed that there was a fierce struggle for the right to live. Marco had lost that right. Inside his palms were deep lacerations from trying to fend off his vicious attacker. The murder weapon was sharp; it almost severed most of his fingers from his small hand. Joey noticed some blood protruding from around Marco's neckline. He tried in vain to see as much of the gore as possible. It was then that he noticed that his worker and friend's throat had been slashed. The deep laceration went from one side of his mangled throat to the other. Slumped over was the position of his head, limiting the amount of blood that was oozing from that area. The poor Mexican's head was almost decapitated. He was left lying there until every ounce of blood drained from his body. Marco had been stabbed 11 times. Right at Marco's side was his empty pizza bag, saturated with blood. Marco died with his left hand clutching the empty pizza bag.

Even though he was not permitted to enter the elevator, Joey had seen enough. He ran to the nearest corner and started to puke. The loud sounds of his vomiting echoed throughout the lobby floor. He slowly dropped to both knees as he found it hard staying on his feet. Kneeling down as the vomit encircled around his weak knees, he started to cry uncontrollably and pound his fist up against the hard walls. It was then that he felt a soft hand resting upon his shoulder.

"Are you alright?" Officer Kelly asked, while looking down at Joey.

"No, I'm not okay," an angry Joey answered. "I loved this guy. This is hard on me, real hard."

"I understand," the caring officer said. "Come on, let me help you to your feet. Here we go," he said assisting him up.

"Thanks," Joey said, trying to compose himself. "Tell me something?"

"What is it?"

"What kind of fuckin' animal would do this?" Joey asked, slowly rising to a standing position. "Especially in broad daylight!"

"I know," Kelly said. "It's as vicious of an attack that I have seen in a long time!"

"Did he ever make it to the apartment where the delivery was going?"

"No."

"Did you check with the people in 6C?"

"He never made the delivery to that apartment."

"What do you mean?" Joey asked, flicking some of his bodily fluids off of his saturated knees.

"He was attacked in the elevator on his way up. It's apparent that he was followed into the building. We checked the phone number on the delivery ticket and it don't match up with the tenant's number who lives in that apartment."

"You talked to the tenant?"

"No one was home," Officer Kelly said, revealing some of his police work. "The superintendent of the building told us."

"If no one was home, how did he gain access into the building?"

"Probably the same way you did. Or maybe his killer or killers were waiting for him on the inside or followed him into the building."

"You mean to tell me this was a setup," Joey screamed.

"That's what I was about to tell you, I'm sorry to say, this was a cold and calculating plan."

"Did the motherfuckers that killed him also rob him?" Joey asked, in a much calmer voice.

"We don't know that yet, we have not touched the body."

"Well I'll tell you one thing!"

"What's that?" Kelly asked, adjusting his gun belt and holster.

"The pieces of shit that did this must have been hungry."

"Why do you say that?"

"Because the pizza bag beside his body is empty. Are his pockets empty too?"

"We know about the pizza bag, but we haven't checked the body yet. We don't want to contaminate the crime scene. We're waiting for forensics to get here. That's about all we have right now."

"I am having a very hard time dealing with this. Somehow I have this major cloud of guilt inside my body."

"Stop blaming yourself, this is the way life is around here."

"I should have dialed the number back, like I do on most deliveries. Jesus Christ, this is all my fault. I was just preoccupied with some other shit. I wasn't thinking, I mean, I can't..." Joey just stopped right there, he was about to fall into the world of what ifs and whys. What if I would have done this or why didn't I do that. All of the second guessing and second thoughts were starting to hit him hard.

"Don't do that, kid," Kelly said. "Or else, you'll never stop beating up on yourself. This is the way of life around here. There is nothing that you or anybody can do about it."

"We will see about that," he replied in a threatening voice. "Mark my fuckin' words. Soon, we will all see."

"There are a few plainclothes detectives over there who would like a word with you," the officer said pointing to the neatly dressed duo. Joey just shook his head and walked over to the investigating officers. He then answered all of their questions and cooperated to the best of his knowledge.

Marco was only in this country for a little over three years. He and five other Mexican immigrants rented a one bedroom apartment in the Park Slope section of Brooklyn. Whatever money they earned went to paying their bills and feeding themselves. By sharing his living expenses with five others, his paycheck was stretched out a little further. Whatever was left over was sent to his poverty stricken family in Mexico. This was a way of life for most of these illegal immigrants. Now instead of receiving Marco's hard earned money, his family would be receiving his dead corpse. All the money that they received from him would now have to be spent on a proper burial.

After answering some questions for the detectives, Joey aimlessly walked across Franklin Avenue. He reached unsuccessfully into his empty pockets for a cigarette. The delicatessen fifty feet away would solve the problem for his sudden nicotine fit. Feeling very distraught and looking like he was dragged through a pile of dog shit, he headed in that direction. Still feeling dazed he reached into his back pocket for his wallet. He finally pulled out the black wallet and opened it up, reaching in it for a five-dollar bill.

"Could I have a pack of Marlboro Lights," he said to the man behind the register. Still trembling and fumbling for the money, the clerk waited for the exchange to begin. His hands were still shaking and his mind was still focused on the butchery that he had just witnessed.

"A dollar eighty five please," the man said as he prepared to slip the cigarettes underneath the bullet-proof shield. This was the sad way that business had to be conducted in this jungle. Everybody in this community was just a bullet or a slashing away from their deathbed.

Joey finally retrieved the five out of his wallet and slid it underneath the plate of protection. During the exchange, a small blue lettered business card fell from his wallet and onto the ground. The small card had fallen end over end like it was floating down in slow motion.

Joey's eyes followed the slow moving card all the way down to the floor. He then bent down to retrieve the tiny card. Picking it up, he closely examined the blue lettering. The card read, "Fred's Car Wash." He then flipped it over to read the reverse side. In bold black writing was the telephone number of Vito Carlucci. Joey quickly turned around and walked out of the store. He stood outside of the doorway as the vendor was calling him to come back in.

"Mr., you forgot your cigarettes and your change."

Not even hearing or recognizing his voice, Joey just stared at the small card with the powerful presence. He slowly started to walk back to the pizzeria. About seventy-five feet away from the pizzeria he stopped and looked into the park. Feeling revenge and deep thoughts of violence, he then took a gander at the card again. He finally slipped the card back into his wallet and entered the pizzeria.

He now had to break the sad news to Orlando and Manuel. Derek was a different story; this situation would have to be told to him a bit more delicately. Joey DeFalco had turned into the Grim Reaper, spreading bad news wherever he was present.

T hat night Joey purchased a quart of Vodka and decided to get drunk. Manuel and Orlando ran the business while he drowned his sorrows with booze. He just sat in the corner thinking and guzzling the clear looking alcohol. There was no time and need for a glass; his dire needs came right out of the bottle. The Italian man had the right recipe, good hard booze and chain smoking on his favorite cigarettes. Up until closing time all he did was drink, smoke and recollect on his miseries and the loved ones he had lost. Little Steven and Marco were on the top of his list. All of these misfortunes made him forget about Gloria. She was the woman who was going to make him forget his problems, but it didn't work: the beast had beaten out beauty.

"Boss, are you okay?" Manuel asked already cleaned up and ready to leave. "We leave now!"

"Call car service and have them take you and Orlando home." Joey said, his voice slurring from all the alcohol that he consumed.

"Boss, what about you?"

"I am staying right fuckin' here, I have a lot of thinking to do." Joey had his elbows on the table and his face was buried into the palm of his hands. "Don't worry about me!"

"But boss, you can't stay here, it's no good. I stay with you."

"Do as I say and go the fuck home." Joey's face turned deadly serious, Manuel was in no position to defy his orders. Manuel quickly walked to the telephone and obeyed his boss's commands. Ten minutes later the cab arrived.

"Manuel!" Joey said.

Manuel turned around to look at his boss.

"Thanks, I will see you in the morning."

"Okay boss, tomorrow," he said, opening up the front door while letting a blast of the frigid air inside the store.

Joey finally arose from his chair and stumbled towards the front door to get some desperately needed fresh air. He watched as the car service pulled away with its slowly disappearing red tail-lights. Joey then looked in the other direction and into the empty park. The bitterly cold weather had driven all the elements out of the park and into a warmer setting for the night. Most of their illegal activities would have to be conducted from the comfort of a warm car. Joey just stood there looking, with both hands folded and locked underneath his armpits. In a matter of seconds he returned to the store to finish his badly needed drinking. He went straight to the small bookshelf radio and cassette deck and put in a tape to try and drown out some of his sorrows with music. The volume was pumped up to capacity; even the ringing phone in the background could not be heard. Nothing seemed to matter anymore; everything seemed to fall upon deaf ears. All the lights were turned off and he just sat there in the pitch black for the next couple of hours. The only light came from the strike of a match to the burning tip of his cigarette.

Tears started to fall from Joey's face as the Vodka started to intensify his anger. He started to think irrationally as his anger was growing to a boiling point. The demons in him were starting to work his body into a frenzy. The fear and apprehension had vanished - there was now only fight. In a sudden burst of anger he pounded the table, everything from the salt shaker to the napkin holder fell over. Joey got to his feet and headed for the front door in a no nonsense frame of mind. Suddenly, he turned around and headed back down the aisle and went behind the counter. Bending down with his long arm he reached for a Louisville Slugger. Joey picked up the 34-ounce baseball bat with the thin handle and wielded it into the air. Never thinking that any more trouble would send him back to prison, he walked towards and opened up the front door. He then looked out into the cold winter night and up into the endless star filled skies.

Reeking of alcohol he stumbled towards the park. Right on Franklin Avenue there was a car with a couple of occupants in it. Joey stared into the vehicle and saw a couple of familiar faces. This sighting did not impede his progress as he lifted the bat with a show of power and defiance. His determination kept him moving along, the cold temperatures did not seem to bother him, even without a coat. Now holding the bat with two hands, he stationed himself right in the middle of the dimly lit park. Joey's position was straight and tall, his legs were spread out about two feet apart. Slowly he raised the bat into the air with his right arm, while looking around for a confrontation.

"Come on, you motherfuckers," he shouted with his voice reverberating off of the surrounding buildings. "Come and get me! It's me that you want you pussy bastards. Now you got what you want, so come on, I'm here." Joey's loud voice carried throughout the still nighttime air. The steamy vapors rising from his calls lay suspended above him in the cold stale climate. Joey's heavy breathing gave the appearance of a sauna as his exhaled respiration hit the frigid air at a rapid pace. Even the residents were awakened by this outburst of frustration. Every so often you could see a light going on in the windows of the buildings that overlooked the park. Nervous inhabitants would take a peek to see what all the commotion was about.

Joey screamed and screamed to no avail, calling out to his enemies. His challenges were never met. He started to grow impatient looking around for something to use his bat on. In Dead-man's park, you would have to look awfully hard to find something that was not already destroyed. Joey started to go on a delirious rampage, swinging and poking at everything in sight. His wielding was mighty, his intentions to destroy.

The frigid air left a terrible sting to his hands as the bat vibrated off of everything that it came in contact with. The anxiety and stress that had built up in his body brought him to this uncontrolled emotion. Anybody who stood in the way of this rage and fury was sure to die. After all, as soon as he stepped into the park those were his exact intentions.

Finally starting to slow down from exhaustion, Joey walked over to the nearest broken down bench to take a seat. Struggling to maintain his balance he reached his destination. To his startling surprise he saw something that would change his life forever. Right beside him were two empty clay pizza boxes that were spread wide open. Just a few pieces of crust and some remnants of pepperoni remained. Joey intensely examined the boxes and reached for one of the lids in order to close it. He slowly flipped over the cover of the pizza box and discovered that his worst nightmare had come true. On the cover the words "JOEY'S PLACE" were neatly printed on the box in green and red colors. His suspicions were correct; the killers of Marco dwelled inside this once happy playground called "DEAD-MAN'S PARK." Marco's murderers had the gall to munch on his pizza right after they butchered and sliced him to death.

"These bastards," he whispered.

The whispers soon turned into screams.

"God help me! I want them all to die!"

This sighting made his hysteria erupt all over again. Now he finally was at the point of no return, for he had lost his edge on trying to coexist in harmony with his new neighbors. He was going to bring out the heavy artillery. It was time to give these blood-sucking thugs a dose of their own medicine. There was no turning back now and Joey was not going to relinquish a business that he was trying so hard to build. In the name of Marco and little Steven, this was not a time to give into intimidation and fear. This was a time to stand up and rightfully defend what was yours.

"Vitooooo," Joey called. A loud and tremulous echo followed. "Vitooooo," he screamed again. The young Italian stood valiant and erect with his legs two feet apart and the bright crescent moon shining at his back. The heavy fog like vapors coming from his body stood stagnant over his defiant posture. Each call for his mentor produced another blast of steam from his mouth. His pained bellowing must have been heard throughout the neighborhood. But it was not loud enough for Vito to hear himself.

Chapter 14

JOEY HURRIEDLY RETURNED to the pizzeria. He turned on the lights and lowered the deafening music. Reaching into his back pocket for his wallet, he pulled out Vito's phone number and starting dialing. With his fingers shaking, he slowly pressed the numbers on the touch tone telephone. After five lingering rings, the monotony was broken. The voice on the other end was a recording, but there was something strange going on here. It was not Vito. The voice on the recording was that of a little girl.

"We can't come to the phone right now, but if you leave your name and number we will get back to you as soon as possible." Then a beep went off and Joey was supposed to talk and leave his frantic message. Instead he slammed the phone back on the receiver.

That son of a bitch gave me the wrong fucking number, he said to himself. *I can't fucking believe this. After all we've been through, he fucking lied to me.*

After thinking of the numerous reasons why Vito might want to hide his identity and whereabouts, Joey tried to dial the number again. He dialed the same seven numbers and the same little girl was on the greeting of the answering machine. This time he waited for the recording to end before he went into his ranting and raving.

"Vito, it's Joey DeFalco," he nervously said. "Vito, you have to help me, I am buried in a pizzeria on St. Ann's Place and they are killing everyone around me. I need you here. Please Vito, help me, I know you said to never call you unless I was getting married, but I am next. They are going to kill me too!" Joey said while pacing behind the counter. "Please Vito, help me, I have no other way out. I beg you to please come down here. I am up against insurmountable odds. These people killed Marco and a six-year old boy and now they are trying to extort money from me. They shot up the place and spray painted the front of my building and tore down my canopy. I had to fix it with the money you gave me in prison." Joey continued on, his words were coming from his mouth at an unbelievably frantic tempo. "I am broke and I have nowhere else to turn to. Please help me, I am falling apart. I cannot handle all of them by myself. Please Vito, please. I am in total fear for my life. These people are cold-blooded killers. The address is 205 Saint Ann's Place in Crown Heights. It is right off of Franklin Avenue and…," at that moment the recording reached its time limit as the beep was set off.

Joey thought about calling back but he was not really sure that he was talking to the party that he intended to talk with. He sounded much different than the tough talking man who just walked out of the crime-ridden park. But even Joey knew that he had to sound very dramatic in order to get Vito here. Still, there was nothing that he told him that was not the truth. Now it was time to just give in to the Brotherhood's demands and hopefully wait for the arrival of his Italian army, known mostly by others to operate under a distinct and very recognizable name.

T he next Friday night, gophers for the Brotherhood came into the store and were given two hundred dollars. That was definitely not 25% of the gross, but Joey tried to see how much he could get away with. Besides, he was only pacifying them until Vito arrived. If Vito never came through, it would be time to pack up and leave this war zone. There was no way in hell that he was going to keep greasing the pockets of extortion.

Since Marco's death Joey had to revise his system again. All the deliveries that had to be made to residences, he decided that he would take. The outgoing orders that needed to be taken to business establishments would be Orlando's responsibilities. Joey had decided that the safety of the remaining crew had to come first. Anything that looked suspicious, he was ready to confront himself.

It was a very busy Friday night and Joey was soon feeling the need to replace Marco. After all, they were running the business shorthanded and his services were sorely missed. Joey tried to compensate Manuel and Orlando with a slight pay increase. The men deserved it; they were busting their tails for him.

"Orlando, take the bicycle and go to this bar called, La Casa De Loco. The address is on the ticket and I already confirmed the order." Joey said, preparing the five pie order for delivery.

"La Casa De Loco" was the Spanish name for the crazy house. It was a neighborhood tavern that catered to the locals in the Hispanic section of Crown Heights. The small tavern had a pretty respectable reputation and was a legitimate running business.

In a few minutes Orlando was out the door and on his way. About fifteen or twenty minutes later, he returned and looked into Joey's eyes with a dejected look on his face. The very sensitive Mexican looked like he was on the verge of tears.

"Orlando," Joey asked. "What's the matter?"

"Boss, they no pay!" he said. Manual looked on slacked jawed.

"What do you mean they didn't pay?"

"I don't know, they take pizza and no pay. They say for you to go there and get money."

"Me! I don't even know who the fuck they are! Why didn't they pay?"

"Me don't know!"

"Alright, don't worry about it pal. Everything is going to come back to us. I will just chalk the $55.00 as a temporary loss." Joey looked closely at Orlando's face; he sensed that something was still not right. "What happened to your face?" Joey asked, pulling Orlando over to get a better look. He looked even closer and noticed some physical abuse that Orlando must have went through. "Orlando, tell me what happened. Don't be afraid."

"They slap me and laugh at me, boss," Orlando said as a teardrop started to fall from his already watery eyes. Orlando felt that he had let his boss down, and later on that evening the proud Mexican offered Joey to take the money out of his wages.

"Orlando, tell me what this guy looked like?"

"Boss, he had pony tail and he was tall and skinny," he sadly said. "I no remember too good, boss."

Joey just shook his head and absorbed whatever Orlando was telling him. But he made sure that he would remember it all.

"That's it," said Joey. "From now on, I will make all the fuckin' deliveries that leave this shit-hole. Anybody that tries to fuck with me, they are going to die for their efforts," he threatened, while scotch taping the name and address of La Casa De Loco to the wall by the telephone. "Every one of these motherfuckers is going to pay up in one way or the other," he warned. There were four delivery tickets that were hanging from the wall. Each one of them at one time or another would be paid an unfriendly visit from this disgruntled business owner. "This is a promise that I am making to you guys."

Joey never sounded more serious in his life. Every time he stepped out of the store he was equipped with a six-inch switch-blade in his pocket. There would be no hesitation on his part to use it. From now on, anyone unwilling to pay for their food would get a taste of his vengeance. Anyone who looked at him the wrong way was a potential target for his little friend. There would be no more robberies and definitely no more non-payments for anything that left his pizzeria. Everything would be delivered by car as the bicycle was put in storage down in the basement. The remainder of his crew was not permitted outside the building except to come to work and go home. This was the new law as Joey started to run the pizzeria like a prison. Manuel and Orlando had to be watched very carefully, they were all he had left. Not to mention the fact that he cared for them very much.

A couple of weeks had passed by in rapid succession; still there were no signs of Vito. At this point Joey was about to give up on ever seeing his prison friend again. Any hope of trying to survive in this pizzeria was dwindling down to nothing. It was just a matter of weeks or maybe even days before he would close the establishment down for good. In addition to the fear that was pushing him into giving up, business was also terrible. The news of Marco's death had spread throughout the neighborhood like wildfire; the place had become taboo to most of his customers. Even his most loyal of patrons were afraid to have any contact with the once defiant restaurant. They knew that it was just a matter of time before the windows would be boarded up again.

About a mile away two women sat around the kitchen table having a cup of coffee. Once a week Gloria would pay her sister and her two kids a visit. The two sisters were as close as sisters could be; they were all that each other had. Terri had fled her native country with her boyfriend Hector. Four years later, Gloria followed in her older sister's footsteps, both of them searching for the American dream. It just took a couple of years before they both learned that this dream was not that easy to obtain. Many times they had felt like returning back home to their abandoned mother and father. But every time something had always held them back.

"You never heard from Joey?" Terri asked Gloria, holding a coffee mug in her right hand.

"No," Gloria said. Her eyes were staring right into her cup of coffee. The disappointment on her face was very noticeable to her sister.

"Don't worry, he will call you. Right now is probably a bad time for him. He just went through a horrible experience when they killed that poor kid."

"I know, Terri, but for some reason I am afraid for him. I don't even know this guy and I'm afraid. I just feel this special bond between us that I can't explain," she said. "But I do know that he is in deep trouble working right across the street from that park."

"Gloria, he looks like a strong guy. I am sure he will be alright. Why don't you just give him a call to see how he's doing?"

"You think that would be alright?"

"Sure, you like him and you are concerned. What's wrong with that?"

"When should I call him, now?"

"Yes, now. Go in my bedroom and make the phone call. His menu is in the top drawer over there," she said pointing to a drawer right next to the kitchen sink. "His number is on the menu. I know he will be very happy to hear from you. After all, it's been almost a month."

Gloria always took whatever her sister said to heart. She was always asking her for advice and always listened to the advice that was coming from her. She had great respect for her sister as Terri struggled raising her two children alone. Independence was not one of Gloria's greater strengths. She always would lean on her sister when her indecisiveness would appear. Gloria never felt too comfortable about living alone. She and Terri came from a tight knit family, and all those comforts of home flew out the window when they ventured to the United States.

Gloria reached for the menu and walked down the hallway to her sister's bedroom. Her head was thumping as she dialed the number.

"Joey's Place, how can I help you?"

"Hi," the sexy woman's voice said.

"Hi," Joey said, obviously unaware. "What can I do for you," he asked again. He was really not in the mood for small talk.

"You can meet me somewhere for a drink tonight."

"Gloria?" Joey asked, his voice growing a little excited as he finally identified the caller. "Is that you?"

"Yes it is, how are you? I have not heard from you and I just wanted to touch base to see if you're all right. I heard about what happened to one of your workers and I am so sorry."

"Thank you, honey, it has been very hard on me. I'm trying my best to cope with this and all the other bullshit that surrounds me over here."

"Just try and hang in there," she reasoned. "Everything will eventually turn out alright."

"I am trying, but things just seem to be getting worse with each passing day. You don't know how I feel, you just don't know." Joey sounded like he needed a sympathetic shoulder to cry on. He had the feeling that if he poured his heart out to Gloria, she would be gone for good. "I'm starting to feel like I'd be better off dead!"

"Don't talk that way, it scares me."

"I'm sorry, I'm just very depressed. Whatever could go wrong in a man's life, is going wrong with mine."

"Why don't you meet me tonight and you can tell me about it," she offered. "It might do you some good."

"Alright honey, I could use a drink. Where do you want to meet?"

"My sister's neighbor Ramon owns this little bar called La Casa De Loco. Did you ever hear of the place?"

"What?" Joey said, raising his voice a bit. "Uh...I mean, where?"

"La Casa De Loco."

"Sure I know the place," he said, his heart to racing. Joey was nodding while looking up at the wall. He was also looking at the unpaid bill in the amount of 55 dollars with that same name and address on it. "I certainly do know the place." Joey grabbed a pen and wrote the name Ramon across the top of the delivery ticket.

"Is ten o'clock okay," Gloria said while getting to her feet.

"Ten is fine." Joey said, ripping down the receipt from the wall and sticking it into his front pocket. "I'll be there at ten."

"Okay Joey, I will see you later. Bye, bye."

"Bye honey, and thanks again."

"Thanks for what?"

"Thanks for understanding and not forgetting about me."

"Thanks are never needed when someone genuinely cares."

"You are something very special, you know that."

"I want to feel that way to you and you only."

"I felt that way the moment I first set my eyes on you."

"Me too," she confessed. "Well, enough of this, we will talk later."

"Okay, honey. I'll see ya later."

Joey hung up the phone and tried really hard to figure out what this woman really saw in him. She could probably have it all; there was not a man in New York City who would not go out with her. Any relationship that he flirted with would surely bring any poor and unfortunate woman into his world of misfortune. All the untimely mishaps and bad fortune would surely be too much for one woman to endure, especially a beautiful and classy woman like Gloria. All these circumstances befuddled Joey; he felt that anyone who came into his life would surely suffer from it. There was not much for him to offer anyone. On the flip side of all this, there was not too much to take either. Joey, at this stage of his life anyway, floated somewhere at the bottom of a barrel. To him, there was no reason to drag anyone else into this pit of misery and violence.

Right before Joey left the pizzeria to meet Gloria, he took the medallion off from around his neck. With the Christ head now in the palm of his right hand, he looked at it and started to recollect about the days gone by. Vito's face appeared before his eyes like it was yesterday. The handsome gangster had the same smile on his face the day he handed Joey the Christ head and chain. Joey just shook his head and kissed the medal as he hid it in a safe hiding place under the counter. He knew that this night, which was supposed to be special, could end in violence. The last thing he wanted to do was to lose the last memory of his never forgotten friend Vito.

At 10 o'clock sharp, Joey walked into the dimly lit Spanish bar and café. The oak bar had an L shape to it. There were three bar stools to the right of him that hugged a narrow passageway behind the front window. Neon signs flickered from each side of the two windows that surrounded the front door. The rest of the wooden bar went down about another twenty-five or thirty feet, with padded stools lined up against the brass foot railing. For what it was, it was not a bad looking place.

To the left of the front door, there was an old-fashioned style juke-box and five cocktail tables. The small round tables were lined up on the opposite end of the well stocked bar. All the way in the back of the establishment were a pool table and a few pinball machines.

The place is pretty crowded for a *Thursday night,* Joey thought while looking for a seat. Patrons lined up the back end of the long bar. He looked to the right of him and noticed an old man huddled against the wall, the flickering neon signs casting a rainbow over the surface of his wrinkled face. It showed the effects of excessive drinking, his blotted face and bloated appearance just told you so. People like him just come to a place like this to find some companionship. Their home-life brings nothing to them, just the monotonous sounds of their television sets.

A bar-stool away from the sorrowful looking old man was a drink that was left unattended. Joey looked down at what appeared to be a vodka and cranberry juice. Right beside the drink was a folded cocktail napkin with some writing on it. On the top of the napkin it read, "Please open." Joey looked around the room as he started to flip open the little napkin with the simple instructions on it. He nonchalantly took a peek inside. "I just went to the ladies room, I will be right back! Love, Gloria," the note said. Right below her name in dark deep red lipstick was the shape of her lovely lips engraved on the white napkin. He then took a seat right behind the drink that was left at the bar.

"There is somebody sitting there, pal," the bartender said.

"I know, she's expecting me," Joey said, looking for his cigarette lighter.

"Oh, okay," he said acting disappointed. "What will you have?"

"Give me a Coors light."

"Bottle or draft?"

"Bottle!"

"You got it," the not well mannered, but groomed man said.

"Let me ask you a question," Joey said while lighting a cigarette. "Is there a guy named Ramon in here?"

"Yea, he owns the place."

"Is he here now?" Joey asked as he took a long drag from his cigarette.

"He's in his office in the back," the bartender said, now starting to look suspicious. "Do you wanna to see him?"

"No, it's nothing important, it can wait."

The bartender then went to the middle of the bar and bent down to the refrigeration unit below it. Each movement warranted another peek at the newcomer. Quickly he snatched a bottle from the ice-box and stood erect. He then twisted the cap off the long necked bottle and returned to where Joey was seated. "Would you like a glass?" he asked, placing the bottle on a small coaster.

"No, just the bottle will be fine. I'm gonna run a tab, is that okay?"

"No problem," the bartender said. "Should I put her drink on it?"

"Without a doubt!"

Joey picked up the cold bottle of beer and raised it to his lips. After surveying his surroundings for a couple of minutes, he swung the swivel bar stool around and proceeded to look out the window. The flashing intermittent light form the neon beer sign obstructed his vision to the deserted streets outside. His mind was definitely on another planet, and in a matter of seconds he drifted off to somewhere very far away.

About a month ago he was tickled pink over meeting a woman like Gloria. But it seemed like life had kicked the shit out of him to a point where nothing seemed to matter any longer. The death of Marco left everything irrelevant to him, even her.

Sitting there alone for five minutes, he had reached his destination. He was now on the planet called Pluto. The only difference was that he did not need a spaceship to get him there. Society gave him a one-way ticket and his return flight was on standby.

Gloria exited the ladies room from the back of the bar in style. Every single inhabitant stopped dead in their tracks from whatever they were doing. The pinball machines were put in a tilt mode. Putting the eight ball in the corner pocket would have to wait until she passed by. The rest of the Puerto Rican clientele made some hand gestures or howling sounds that resembled the calling of the wild.

Walking down to the front of the bar she spotted Joey. She practically tiptoed quietly through the soft Latin music coming from the jukebox. With the element of surprise as her motive, she then wrapped her arms around him. This sudden and abrupt gesture drew a temporary jolt to Joey's apathetic system. He jumped as if he was awakened from a bad dream. He then quickly threw her arms away from him, while getting to his feet to confront the sneak attack. All in one swift motion, Joey turned around ready to start swinging. The half-empty beer bottle was his weapon, while most of its contents were steadily streaming to the floor below. Now with the element of surprise behind him, Joey then recognized his passive attacker.

Gloria just stood there in shock, with the look of fear in her eyes. She was left stunned with her eyes wide open, not believing what was happening.

Was this the same man that she once kissed under the mistletoe on Christmas Eve? She thought, feeling the full force of Joey's erratic behavior. "Joey, what's the matter with you? Calm down! You looked like you wanted to kill me."

"I'm sorry, honey, I just don't like it when somebody grabs me from behind."

"Jesus Joey, couldn't you smell my perfume? I'm sure the people that you fear don't smell like me! Besides, you knew I was here."

Joey smiled as he embraced her hand and pulled her towards him. They then ardently hugged each other with all the warmth, emotion and desire that they had felt on that joyful Christmas Eve.

While hovering over Gloria's inviting body, Joey opened his eyes and discovered some angry stares coming from the back of the room. He did not know whether they were from his sudden outburst of anger or jealously. Whatever the reasons, their malicious leers were secondary to him. At this moment, all he wanted to do was enjoy the company of this lovely young lady.

The two sat closely together, only their rubbing thighs prevented the bar-stools from touching each other. It turned out that Gloria was a very good listener who possessed the fine quality of empathy. She just sat there and listened to Joey pour his heart out. It didn't take Joey long; all he ever needed was a soothing ear to talk into.

The drinks kept coming as they picked on some chicken fingers and mozzarella sticks. They sat there for hours as Joey opened up to her in a way that he never had before. The more he drank the more he told her; to him he knew that these confessions might scare her away. But he really cared for this girl, being up front and honest was in his mind the best approach. In the long run she would only find out anyway. Depending on her character, she would either run for cover or let true love find a way for the both of them to exist together. The decision was hers and hers alone to make. Joey held nothing back, he told Gloria everything. From Wall Street to prison, from Vito to Dutch, he held nothing back. He even told her about that powerful visitor from the unknown who made that phenomenal appearance in his bedroom. Joey didn't skip a beat with his confessions to her. The drive by killing of little Steven to the stabbing death of Marco, he told it all.

At times Gloria sat there in disbelief, thinking how could one person go through all this and still survive. But she saw something in Joey's eyes that others failed to see. She saw sincerity and a man who managed to maintain the morals that she adores. This traditional woman knew that there was something special buried underneath this giant wall he was hiding behind. The more he talked, the further he drew her into his world. She seemed to passionately absorb it all in, every word drew her in even closer and closer. After a while she must have felt like a saturated sponge floating at the top of his bucket of problems. With all the stories of heartbreak and violence, she never back-pedaled once. She hung in there like a state trooper trying to give a drunk a sobriety test.

At the back of the bar a man in a slicked back ponytail started to work his way over to the engrossed couple. By this time, Joey and Gloria were doing some petting and kissing. Time was not of the essence to them, as the once crowded bar slowly thinned out. Joey felt like he could stay in her arms for eternity.

"Gloria?" The voice interrupted their euphoria. A slightly built but handsome man said, "What's happening, baby?"

"Ramon, how are you?" she said, turning to him.

Ramon then took Gloria by her right hand and planted a kiss right on top of it. Joey just sat there and stared at this gigolo looking Latino charmer. This guy looked like some cocaine dealer out of the movie Scar-face. His button down shirt exposed enough jewelry to decorate a Christmas tree. The aroma of his cologne overpowered the sexy scents that surrounded Gloria. What bothered Joey most was his perception that this cocky individual had the hots for Gloria. Joey just watched this Ramon character as he raped her with his eyes. This schmuck had her clothes off even before he came over to say hello.

"I'm fine, baby. And may I say that you look ravishing tonight," Ramon said, nudging in between Joey and Gloria. "You sure do look fine."

"Oh man," Joey said silently, but loud enough for Ramon to hear. "What a crock of shit this guy is shoveling."

Ramon turned his head and looked at Joey with a slight sneer coming from his upper lip. These expressions of contempt would be magnified if someone did not step in. Thank God Gloria had the common sense to smell trouble before it even started. "Well Ramon, it was nice seeing you again. But it's getting late and we have to get going," Gloria politely said.

"Okay darling," Ramon answered. "But the next time you come to my place, make sure you are in better company!" the Latin Romeo said, helping her off of the bar-stool.

"Bartender," Joey shouted after hearing Ramon's wise crack. The barkeep looked up and turned to look in Joey's direction. "Check, please," Joey ordered, ignoring the sarcasm coming from this Ricky Ricardo wannabe.

The bartender put the finishing touches on the tab that Joey had run. He placed the thin cardboard check by Joey's pack of cigarettes that lay atop of the bar. Joey carefully examined the bar tab and started to shake his head. He then reached into his pocket and handed the bartender his method of payment.

"What's this?" the bartender asked, looking at some piece of paper.

"Well," Joey said. "The way I see it, my bar tab was $38.50 and that piece of paper says that you owe me $55.00. So according to my calculations, you owe me $16.50."

"This is a delivery ticket for pizza," the dumfounded barkeep said.

"Exactly, it's a delivery ticket for five pies that scumbag refused to pay for," Joey snarled, pointing at Ramon.

"Who you callin' scumbag?" Ramon shot back.

"You, you slimy spic bastard. I'm calling you a scumbag."

"What's going on here?" Gloria frantically asked, pulling at Joey's shirt. "Joey please, let's go," Gloria begged. "Don't start any trouble in here."

"Not now, Gloria," Joey said. "This prick asked for trouble by not paying me for the fuckin' pizza. I want my money!"

"Fuck you, and fuck your pizza," Ramon shouted. "You ain't gettin' shit back from me."

"One way or the other," Joey promised. "I'm gonna get my money."

"Fuck you!"

"Are you sure about this?"

"You ain't gettin' shit from me!"

"Alright, no problem, but there's just one more thing!"

"Kiss my ass, pizza man!"

"Well then, if this is the way you really feel about it. Then I got something for you!"

"What's that?" Ramon asked, vehemently defying all of Joey's requests.

"This is for slapping around my delivery guy." Out of nowhere, Joey threw a hard right overhand punch that hit Ramon right between the eyes. The impact sent him reeling back, right into the jukebox and slowly slumping onto the polyurethane wooden floor. The force of his body transmitted by the fierce blow shattered the large panel of glass covering the bottom portion of the music machine. It also temporally discharged the coin operated machine from playing any tunes. "Now give me my fuckin' change," he screamed at the bartender. "Give me the $16.50 that you owe me.

Gloria just stood there motionless, lacking any significant movement to her body parts. She stood open mouthed and speechless. She had no clue about what had just taken place

The bartender than ran to the back of the room to call for reinforcements. His calls were not needed; the small Puerto Rican army was on their way. Armed and fully equipped with a pool stick in each one of their hands, they raced to the front of the bar. Whatever and whoever was in that back room soon followed the trio to witness the impending fracas.

The old man who sat in the corner intoxicated suddenly came to his senses and fled from the scene. The impending violence seemed to straighten his ass right up. Everything started to pick up steam as the fast paced tempo flew into a rage.

"Gloria," Joey shouted. "Get out of here, now!"

"No," she replied, grabbing at Joey's arm and tugging at it to get him out through the front door. Her efforts were in vain; between the alcohol and his own fury, Joey's testosterone level was raging. "Come on, you're leaving with me"

Joey ignored her pleas to retreat. There was no way that he was going through that front door with anyone. He had only one thing on his mind and one thing only. To get back the $16.50 that he felt was owed to him. To him it was a matter of principal and fighting for what he thought was right. He was tired of letting this unruly neighborhood bully him with its self-governed unlawful acts. Too much pain had already been inflicted upon him and his workers. It was now time for the pain and bleeding to stop. No matter what happened, he was going to stand up for what he thought was right. There would be no more retreating, even if it was to save his own life.

The three wanting and able combatants had arrived at the scene. They looked down at the fallen and disgraced owner for instructions. Ramon just lay there with his right hand covering his badly bleeding nose. His self-image and Dapper Don appearance had been destroyed with one quick blow from Joey's right hand. His patrons had never seen him so vulnerable. The knockdown punch definitely put a dent in his tough reputation. No one had ever put this kind of shame and dishonor upon him, especially in his own place of business.

"What the fuck are you looking at me for?" he said, screaming at his so-called friends. "Go get the asshole and beat his fuckin' ass!" Ramon only picked his head up for a moment; he just sat there with his back leaning up against the jukebox. He just uttered the Spanish word calling Joey a fagot, and then put his head back down. The embarrassed Prince of Crown Heights was too ashamed to face any onlookers in the position he was in.

The cavalry came at Joey one after the other, each armed with a pool cue from the billiard table. One by one they attacked him and one by one the first wave went down in defeat. The shattered remains of the broken pool sticks were all over the floor. With his arms and with the help of a bar-stool, Joey blocked everything that came his way. One after the other, he fended off his attackers. Joey quickly disposed of them like insects hitting a spray repellent. In a matter of seconds, the Puerto Rican trio would join their friend still wriggling on the floor in pain. The seasoned and pumped up convicted felon smirked as his stimulated eyes scanned the barroom floor.

"Anyone else!" he screamed. There were no more takers.

He then looked at Gloria, but at this moment she would have no part of him. She knew that she was getting an ex convict, but what she did not know was how hardened he had become. Between prison life and the beating society was now giving him, for Joey it was time to fight back. For the understanding and passive Gloria, it was time for him to reform and move on. Revenge and one's own brand of self-justice were not part of her resume. She was a dove and a complete optimist, no matter how dire the situation might be. To her there was always a thoughtful solution to every problem. Joey's hawkish behavior disappointed her immensely, her face showed her dejection. She was a very liberal thinking young lady, where violence was never the answer for anything.

"Now give me the $16.50 that you owe me," Joey demanded from the bartender. "Now!"

The bartender slowly retreated to the cash register and hit the no sale button. The cash draw flew open as he dipped his hand into the kitty. Joey waited patiently, never taking his eyes off of the enemy. Gloria stood by the door in disbelief. Not only did Joey win the fight, he still had the balls to demand the $16.50 back. The damage he did alone to the bar was at least twenty times that amount.

The shaken barkeep placed the money on top of the bar. Joey stepped over a bar stool and approached the vacant area. He reached down for the green bills and started to pick up the lose change.

"Did you have to give me five dimes?" he said, complaining to the bartender about the small loose change.

"Jesus Christ, Joey, would you fucking let it go already," Gloria said. "Let's go, you got what you wanted."

Joey just looked at her and smiled, but he continued to retrieve every last penny that was owed to him. He then picked up his beer and finished it. Feeling victorious with a touch of arrogance, he turned back around and looked at Ramon. Walking slowly towards him, he looked down at him and sprinkled the loose change on top of his head.

"This is just a token for your fine hospitality," he said.

From the back of the establishment, someone threw a shining red pool in Joey's direction. The red blur struck Joey on the right side of his head. Standing there, temporarily dazed, he quickly fell to one knee and put a hand to his head. Blood started to rush through the head wound and down the right side of his face. What started out as a small round bump, the bruise started to mushroom into the size of a golf ball.

Ramon suddenly started to come to life; a window of opportunity had opened up for him. He briskly got to his feet and picked up the butt end of one of the broken pool cues. With one full swing, he cracked Joey right on the top of his back. The blow sent Joey falling face down to the floor.

"Pick this piece of shit up," Ramon ordered.

Two of his buddies rushed to each side of Joey and picked him up off of the floor. Each one of them grabbed and held him up from under his armpit. Still groggy, Joey was an open invitation for revenge. With his head down and feeling befuddled, Ramon started to walk towards him. He then grabbed Joey by the back of his hair to raise his head in an upright position.

"You're gonna pay for this," he said spitting into Joey's face. The saliva caught Joey right above his nose and slowly dripped down his face. The warm bath seemed to awaken him from his semi comatose state.

"Fuck you," Joey said as he returned the favor and spit right back at Ramon. "Suck my fuckin' dick, you spic bastard!"

Ramon went into a ranting and raving rage. Every explicit curse word in the Puerto Rican dictionary was thrown in Joey's direction. He slowly walked over to the bar and picked up a cocktail napkin. With his left hand he caressed his face with it in order to remove the moisture. Now smiling, he walked back over to Joey. He then started to work over his restrained and fellow neighborhood proprietor. This guy lacked the punching power of Bootsy, but he was efficient on everybody's scorecard. He slowly picked his spots, from the midsection to the top of Joey's head. It now took three men to hold the beaten Italian on his weak feet. Ramon took full advantage of every opening on Joey's body.

"No, Ramon!" Gloria cried, begging for mercy. Her pleas were ignored.

"Amigo," Ramon said to the bartender. "Give me a bottle of Jack Daniels." He then walked over to the bar to retrieve his special brand liquor for sterilization.

Ramon grabbed the bottle from the bartender's hand and twisted off the cap. Now feeling like much the hombre, he went back to his prey. Finally figuring out what was about to happen, Gloria rushed in between Ramon and Joey.

"Ramon, don't do this to him. You have hurt him enough. Let us leave, please!" she pleaded, but all of her begging for mercy was still ignored. "No Ramon, no!"

"Get out of my way, you slut," he said to her. "There are plenty of Puerto Rican men worthy of you around here. But no, you are much better than that. You even stink like an Italian and you are not worth anything anymore. You are nothing more than a whore! But now," he promised, "you are going to see some Puerto Rican justice. Look at your pizza man now!"

Ramon then shoved Gloria with great force as she fell to the floor. She never new Ramon's true colors and what a racist he really was. The extent of their relationship was always hello and goodbye. But she always thought he had a little more class than what he was now showing.

Even though he had a wife and three kids, Ramon would have bed Gloria down in a heartbeat. To lose this chance with her, especially to an Italian, burned him really bad. He relished this opportunity to get back at her through Joey's pain. Nothing would keep him from achieving that goal.

"Now meet my friend Jack," Ramon said, pouring the popular liquor onto Joey's open head wound. He poured and poured until half the bottle was empty. Joey screamed as the grimace on his face reflected the torture he was going through. The poor guy had seen torture before, but nothing of this variety. This stung more than a teeming beehive on the attack. Joey's pain lingered on and on as the 80 proof liquid ran through his bloodstream.

"Ramon, that's enough, man," one of his men said.

"Don't tell me when enough is enough, I will decide when this scumbag has had enough," he snapped, placing the bottle back on the bar.

At that point the three men holding Joey up decided to let him fall to the floor. Joey fell to the ground in a lifeless fashion, only holding onto the burning side of his head. Tears of terror ran down the beautiful face of Gloria. Her evening tryst had turned into a nightmare of epic proportions. The poor girl knew nothing about Joey and the story behind him. Now she got an earful and a small taste of the medicine that he has been getting. In her mouth, it did not taste too good either as she looked at her badly beaten boyfriend.

"Go through his pockets and get his wallet," Ramon said, and his men acted like hungry ants on top of a picnic table. Their hands were all over Joey's body in search of his money.

"Here," one of his men said. He handed Ramon the $16.00 and Joey's black leather wallet.

"Give me it."

Ramon feverishly scanned through the contents of the wallet, looking for whatever money Joey had in it. He had a disgusted look on his face when he learned the only money Joey had was the $16.00 that his bartender had given him. Right then and there Ramon knew that it was Joey's plan to beat him and try to recoup the money from the pizza delivery. Joey's plan almost worked, he just fell $16.00 short from achieving his goal.

"Get this fuckin' trash out of my bar," Ramon said, pointing at Gloria and Joey. "They're stinking up the place!" He then threw Joey's wallet into a trash container behind the bar. Two of his boys proceeded to drag Joey's body through the front door, while Gloria followed them out.

Joey was left lying on the cold concrete with Gloria hovering above him on both knees. She tried in vain to get him to his feet so she could wrap his coat around his freezing body. With extreme persistence, she finally succeeded with her mission. Gloria had one of Joey's arms around her small shoulders as one of her arms was around his waist.

THY WILL BE DONE

"I have to get you to a hospital," she said. "Just hang in there."

"No hospital," Joey answered. "Take me home!"

"Are you crazy? You need medical attention."

"Gloria, take me to my car. I will make it home."

"You're out of your fucking mind, if you're not going to a hospital you are spending the night with me."

"Whatever."

"I hope you're happy. You almost got yourself killed in there."

"This is not over yet," he said wincing in pain. "Mark my words, that bastard has not seen the last of me."

"Oh yes he has," she snapped. "If you see him, you can forget about ever seeing me again!"

"Is that a threat," Joey joked.

"You bet your ass that's a threat," she warned. "And it's a promise too."

Together they staggered through the dark desolate streets in search of her vehicle. Gloria carefully put him in her car and took him to her apartment. She tended and cared for him like she had known him her whole life. Like a registered nurse, she worked the graveyard shift and stayed awake throughout the night. Gloria applied some tender loving care to every badly beaten bruise on his body.

The next morning Joey had awakened to the fresh and pleasant smell of perking coffee. For a moment or two, he did not know his whereabouts in the daintily furnished bedroom. Joey did not remember too many things from the previous night. Unfortunately, the only thing he did remember was the terrible beating that was administered to him. How could he not remember, his swollen body was crying in pain.

With his head still on the pillow, he strangely looked around the neatly kept bedroom. The whole ambiance of the room was decorated in pastel colors.

Growing impatient and trying to raise his head from the pillow, Joey felt severe pain. His head was throbbing. He started to regain his senses as he dwelled on the nightmarish evening. More importantly, he was more concerned about Gloria and what he had put her through. Sure, his actions were somewhat alcohol related, but his drinking could not be used as a crutch.

He was fully aware of what he was doing and why he was doing it. The booze just ignited his fury like lighting fluid to a dimly lit barbecue grill.

Joey slowly pulled himself out of the bed and hobbled over to the dresser. Every kind of cosmetic available to women was on top of it, all neatly placed one behind the other by a person who loved to look good. From lipsticks to eyeliner, from perfumes to hand lotion, it was all there.

"Look at all this shit," Joey said to himself. "Damn, the Avon lady must love coming to this fuckin' house. I never saw so much wasteful crap in my whole life."

He then started to raise his head to welcome the sight that he dreaded to see. With his eyes closed he positioned himself in the dead center of the mirror behind the dresser draws. Struggling to open his eyes in fear of what he might find, he finally mustered up the courage. After staring at himself in disbelief, he put his head down in shame.

"Fuck me," he shouted and then grimaced in pain. "That motherfucker, I'm gonna fuckin' kill him."

From the kitchen, Gloria overheard the profanity and words of threats coming from her bedroom. She quickly put her cup and saucer on the countertop and raced into the bedroom. Overnight she watched Joey's bruises darken and become more profound. To her this was no surprise, but the swelling and coloration did seem to intensify. Gloria stared at him from the doorway. She then noticed her blood stained pillow that rested underneath Joey's head. The sight of the pillow and the scary sight of his face brought tears to her eyes.

Joey could not take his eyes away from the mirror. Years ago he would look into the mirror to admire his good looks. These days every time he took a gander at himself he despised the results. For the past year and a half he had been reduced to a punching bag in some men's gymnasium. This was so bad that not even Gloria recognized the man she was falling in love with. It got to a point that Joey could not control himself from busting out laughing. The more he looked in the mirror the harder he laughed. For some warped reason, to Joey anyway, the situation started to get a little comical.

"Now I know you're sick," Gloria said while looking at him. "You are definitely losing your mind."

"I just can't help it, look at me," he said, pointing to his face and arms. His muscular arms had welt marks running up and down them. "Did you ever see anything so pathetic?" he said laughing.

"What do you find so funny, please tell me, I would like a good laugh also."

"What do I find so funny? My face, my body, my life, my future," he said. "Do you want me to keep on going? I have been reduced to nothing."

"Don't say that," she said. "Because you are something."

"Yea I'm something," Joey snapped back. "I'm a fuckin' piñata. Every fuckin' time I turn around someone is either shooting at me or kicking the crap out of me."

"Well you can do something about that!"

"Like what?"

"Leave the pizzeria!"

"I can't leave now, I'm in too deep. I owe it to Marco and that poor kid Steven to make a go of it. If I quit now, then I won't even have my self-respect. And that's all I have left."

"Well, you have one other thing that you didn't have before!"

"Yea, this golf ball sitting on the side of my head."

"Is that all you can think of?"

"Well what else is there?"

"Me, me you idiot. You have me!"

Joey took a few seconds to recollect his thoughts and it finally got through his thick skull what she was talking about. Her confessions brought a wide smile to his beaten up face. He opened up his arms and motioned her to come forward into his magnetic grasp. Gloria openly defied his gesture, awaiting her chance to give him a good tongue-lashing.

"What's the matter?" Joey asked, sounding very naive and innocent. But those unworldly and ingenuous looks got him nowhere with her.

"What's the matter! You want to know what's the matter? Now where should I start?" Gloria said, with her engine running and the verbal beating about to begin. "Let alone that you almost got yourself killed last night over 55.00 fucking dollars, you almost took me with you. Then when you had the situation licked, you had to be a stubborn, macho Italian and demand the other $16.00."

"It wasn't about the money, it was the principal of the whole situation that mattered."

"The principal? What about my principals? Do you know the humiliation and embarrassment you have put me through? Every time I go to my sister's house I will have to put my head between my legs." Gloria paused for a few seconds waiting for Joey to say something. "Well?"

"Well what? Why the hell should you be embarrassed? I'm the one who took the beating, not you."

"Is that right? That guy Ramon happens to live right across the street from my sister!"

"Oh," Joey said. "He lives across the street from her, that's good to know."

"Shut up," she barked. "It's my time to talk. Yea, he lives across the street from her. Don't ever think that you are stepping another foot on that block again, because you're not."

"What if I have to make a delivery?" he said, grinning.

"Then tell them to meet you on the corner. Besides, it is not safe for you around there. Joey, you are making a joke out of this, but I have never been more serious about anything in all of my life."

"I am serious too, lately it's not safe for me to be anywhere. Is it safe in your arms? Or do you want to kill me too?"

"No, right now it's not safe," she said, trying hard not to smile at him.

"Come here," Joey said, opening his arms.

Gloria slowly walked over to her man. As soon as she got close enough, he engulfed her and drew her into his clutches. They hugged as much as his sprained body could stand.

Joey knew that he was wrong for misbehaving this way in front of her. But for the past couple of years she had not walked in his shoes. The rift between them, however, seemed to have melted away.

"Joey?" she said, looking up at him.

"What?"

"You have to promise me one thing?"

"What's that?"

"Promise me that you will never, ever, go into that bar again."

Joey paused and hesitated with his answer. He knew deep down inside of his heart that he wanted a return bout with Ramon, but at what expense? It was definitely not worth losing Gloria over. Maybe it was time to let bygones be bygones, and let the past fade away into the sunset. After all, the person that he had turned into the past couple of days certainly was not him. He let the anger and alcohol temporarily turn him into the monster that he had become. In prison it was a matter of survival. In the outside world there was always the option of walking away from your enemies.

"I promise," he said.

"Promise what?"

"I promise what you wanted me to promise." Joey said, having a really hard time swearing and promising to the vow in question.

"That's not good enough," she said withdrawing from his arms.

"Okay, I promise that I will never set foot in that bar ever again. Now can we go and have a cup of coffee?"

"Alright," she said. "But somehow I am having a hard time believing you."

Gloria led Joey into the kitchen, he painfully took a seat and she started pouring. She put the milk and sugar on the table and sat across from him.

"Gloria, what do you do for a living?"

"I do product design for a cosmetic company."

"Oh," Joey said. "That explains all the shit all over your dresser."

"That so called shit helps make me look the way I do."

"Come on, Gloria, you're a natural beauty," he said, reaching over the table to pinch her cheek. Gloria locked eyes with him and started to blush.

There is not one woman on the face of the earth who does not like to be told how good they look. If every man on earth repeated those words each and every day the divorce rate would be practically zero. But like everything else, relationships unfortunately become habit and the flattery disappears.

"Oh shit," Joey said, scanning the room for a clock. "What time is it?"

"It's after twelve," Gloria said, looking at her wristwatch. "Why?"

"Because I have to get going!"

"Where?"

"To the pizzeria, I have to help the guys open up."

"I already called Orlando and told him that you were not feeling too well."

"But without me, they'll be shorthanded."

"Don't worry," Gloria said. "He told me that he had a friend named Jorge looking for work and he would call him up."

"What time did you call him?" Joey asked, trying to make sure that the store was covered.

"I called him at ten and then I called him back a little after eleven. His friend was already there and working."

"You are amazing!"

"Why thank you," Gloria said, looking like she was waiting for a medal to be pinned on her. "Besides, you are in no condition to go anywhere. I took the day off so I could spend it with you. And that's exactly what we're going to do."

"I guess you're right, but I have to call them up to give them some specific instructions. Where's the phone?"

Gloria sprung to her feet and walked over to the phone hanging on the wall. She picked it up and dialed the number of the pizzeria and waited for the ringing to start. Then she walked back to the table and handed Joey the phone.

"Hello."

"Who is this? Manuel?"

"Yes," the Pizza man answered.

"Manuel, listen, this is Joey. I have something very important to tell you, so listen carefully! If the guys from the park come into the store for money, give them $200.00 dollars, okay."

"Okay, Boss."

"Did you understand what I said?"

"Yes, if the men from park come asking for money, me give them $200.00 dollar."

"Good, and if you have any problems you call me at this number," Joey said giving Manuel the phone number to Gloria's apartment. "I will see you tomorrow, okay."

"Okay Boss, see you tomorrow."

The couple spent the rest of the day in Gloria's tidy one bedroom apartment. Joey relaxed on her living room sofa watching movies all day long. This sensational woman tended and catered to his every passing fancy. Like a nurse in an emergency room, she re-bandaged his wounds every few hours. The over the counter medications she was using seemed to be sufficient.

To Joey this was like spending the day in paradise. Not only did he need the day off to mend, he also needed the company of a beautiful young woman. He was so fatigued and out of it, staying away from the pizzeria for a day was the best thing to do. Besides, Orlando and Manuel were just a phone call away. After all, it was just one day, tomorrow it would be back to the grindstone for him.

Saturday morning arrived very quickly, the day ahead beckoned as the sun slanted into the bedroom between the vertical blinds. Joey opened one eye and was hit with the blinding ray of light. He turned his head around, rubbed his eyes and saw Gloria soundly sleeping beside him. For five minutes, Joey just stared at her in wonderment. He studied her blemish free complexion as his nimble fingers caressed her face ever so gently. This woman looked just as good in the morning's hush as she did going out to a five-star restaurant. Joey continued to stroke her face until he saw her big brown eyes open before him. She gazed at Joey with a rather Mona Lisa like smile, not really happy, as she looked at his battered body. She then covered up with the quilt, her sweet shyness apparent. Joey just slid a little bit more under the covers to catch up with her. His strong arms encircled and held on to her like a lifeline. Joey knew what he had here, and he was falling deeply in love with her. For the next ten minutes he held her closely to him, never relinquishing his position. He heard her sighs, as she welcomed the comfort of his arms. But unfortunately, time was not on their side. Business was calling; Joey had to go to work

Joey struggled through most of the day, every twist and turn wreathed his face in pain. For the most part, he was just as good as useless. There was not much that he could do other than just oversee his business and maybe cook a few dishes.

Even though he could not afford him, Joey kept Jorge on board. He decided that if any more deliveries had to be made, Orlando and Jorge would take them. This method was used strictly for precautionary reasons. Joey figured with the both of them out there together, danger might look the other way. Keeping everyone alive and in one piece was his major concern. Besides, it was just a matter of weeks before the pizzeria would have to shut down for good. Only a major miracle could save this business from sinking into bankruptcy. With each passing week the bills kept piling up with no relief in sight.

It was another lackluster day of business; the pizzeria resembled a graveyard during a hurricane. Orlando and Jorge were out making their rounds with a couple of deliveries. Joey was in the back preparing a couple of baked ziti's for an elderly lady. The senior citizen sat in front of the store to avoid the disturbances coming from the back seating area. She waited nervously but patiently for her dinners to go. The poor Black woman needed to get back to her sickly, wheelchair bound husband at home. Without a telephone or anyone to escort her, she took the trip around the corner alone. With each abrupt shout and unethical motions coming from the back, she just flinched and shook her head in disappointment. Her food could not come out fast enough, even if she had to take it home undercooked.

These unruly and repugnant practices of the four teenagers in front of her were a disgrace. Food was flying through the air and the language coming from their mouths was appalling. Fountain soda was expectorating from their mouths in all directions. The three eighteen or nineteen-year old males were verbally abusive to the lone female with them. Many times the young girl tried to exit the booth, each time she was stopped and boxed in. In a matter of minutes they turned the pizzeria into a pig-sty. There was food and soiled paper napkins everywhere.

Manuel looked on in disbelief, too afraid to intervene. Joey was in the back kitchen, totally unaware. The music in the kitchen drowned out any noises coming from up front. Thank God it did, Joey was not in the mood or condition for another physical confrontation.

From the corner of his right eye, Manuel saw two sets of eyes peering through the front door. This sighting was unusual to him; these two guys were definitely out of their element. To him, there was something different about these two individuals looking in from the outside of the store. They were looking for something, but he had no idea what.

Suddenly, with great force the front door opened. The unfamiliar duo stepped inside. Manuel watched as the men started to walk to the back of the store. The taller man had on a fitted double-breasted business suit. His wingman followed directly behind him in blue jeans and a black leather jacket. In tandem, they went directly over to the table with the disobedient patrons. The insubordinate behavior coming from the booth was unacceptable to the strangers. For the little that they had seen, they had seen enough.

"Get up," the well-dressed man said to the teenager who had the girl trapped inside of him. "Come on, let's go, you're outta here!"

"Get lost, man, this isn't your business," the dark skinned teen said, staring straight at the older and respectable looking man. "Leave us alone, man!"

"For the last time, I said get up," he said again, with his colleague standing right by his side.

"Fuck you, man, go back to wherever the fuck you came from."

"Do you believe this fuckin' kid?" the European looking man said, turning to his counterpart. He then raised his right hand and started to slap the youth around. The visitor continued his barrage of minor blows. "There's a new Grease-ball on the block and you can tell all your fuckin' friends about it!" he said, pulling the defiant teenager out of the booth. "Now get the fuck out of here and take your buddies with you. But before you go, you're gonna clean up this mess!"

"I ain't cleaning shit," the arrogant teen mumbled. "Let the Mexican clean it up!"

"No. You're cleaning it up." He grabbed the youth around the neck and flung him to the floor. The man started to kick all the loose scraps of food at the sprawling teen. "Now pick it up or else I'm gonna shove it down your throat!"

The juvenile delinquent had heard enough. He started to gather up all the morsels of food and picked them up one by one. Every ten seconds or so, he would look up at this tough guy. But he never said a word to him. He just obeyed the orders.

"Now take it all over to the garbage pail and throw it out," he ordered. The youth was embarrassed. He just raised himself off of his knees and did what he was told. With his head down, he slowly walked towards the trash-can. He quickly deposited the unwanted garbage and looked up for his next set of unwanted orders. "Now take your two friends and get the hell out of here."

The tough-talking visitor just stood there watching as the youth's comrades slowly removed themselves from the booth. All three of the young men just looked at each other in silence, their jaws slack. The old lady by the front door was smiling and nodding. This unexpected action even brought the same glee to Manuel's round face. The visitors seemed to be welcomed with open arms by everyone who witnessed this form of civilized discipline.

"Honey, you can stay and finish your pizza!" he said in the direction of the pleasant looking girl. "Take your time, you're welcome here!"

"Thank you," she said with a tepid smile of thanks.

"If you like," he said. "I will see to it that you get home safely."

"I'm okay, I just live across the street."

"Move," said the man who looked like a biker.

To the tough talking man's companion the trio was not moving fast enough. He decided to help them move along a little faster. A swift kick in the seat of the pants was painfully applied to the youth heading up the rear. The three kept looking behind their shoulders as they were heading for the front door.

"Is there a guy named Joey here?" the suited man said to Manuel, looking around the store.

"Yes," Manuel said. "He in the kitchen, me go get him."

"No, let him be. We'll wait right here for him to come out."

Joey had just finished up the out going order and placed the two 9 inch trays inside a paper bag. He threw in some plastic utensils and a few paper napkins and closed up the bag. Throwing a few pans into the overfilled sink, he started to walk through the swinging cowboy doors. At the top of the steps, Joey stopped dead in his tracks. There was a sight standing before him that he thought he would never ever see again. He closed his eyes and reopened them, thinking this was all a dream.

Standing right by the counter in front of the cash register were Vito and Dutch. The both of them wore huge smiles. Joey on the other hand was a bit more sentimental. Tears started to fall from his battered eyes and down the side of his swollen face. He stood there motionless with the paper bag full of food in his hands. Vito and Dutch were having some sort of a discussion and they had not noticed Joey entering the room.

The men turned and started for the kitchen and they spotted Joey standing at the top of the small landing. Vito looked at Joey and shook his head. He saw the battered face, noticed the limp and bruised body along with the grimacing pain. Vito gnawed on the clenched fingers of his right hand in a gesture that was innately Italian. Following this display of dismay came the dangerous look in his eyes.

"Dutch, look at his face. Whoever did this to him will pay," Vito warned.

Joey walked down the steps and placed the brown paper bag on top of the nearest table. Vito and Dutch started towards him, the mood was very dramatic.

Every step closer brought more pain and agony Vito's way.

With great passion Joey and Vito hugged with vigor born out of love. With tears welling, Vito murmured into Joey's shoulder, "You will never leave my side again. This time I will make you that promise that I should have made to you over a year and a half ago."

"Has it been that long?" Joey asked a bit surprised.

The two men then separated as Dutch walked over and also embraced his once forgotten cell-block friend. Dutch always held a very special fondness for Joey. The wild Irishman was more than happy to be reunited with him.

But this short separation was not Dutch's doing. If it were up to him, this parting would have never happened.

"It's good to see you, kid," Dutch warmly said. "Welcome back."

"Thanks, Dutch, you don't know how happy I am to see you guys."

"Look at you, you're a mess," Dutch said, with both hands on Joey's shoulders. "I thought we taught you better than this?"

"Dutch, you're forgetting one thing? I didn't have Vito's miracle drug the other night. These guys were fully awake," Joey said laughing. "But that's all water under the bridge!"

"Say's who?" Vito shot back. "What do you mean its all water under the bridge?"

"I meant nothing by it. I just want to let it go."

"We ain't letting nothing go. Listen Joey, I'm sorry we took so long to get here," Vito apologized. "We just had to take care of some business down in Florida. We only found out about a week ago and then we flew right back up here as soon as we could. On occasion, I had a few of my guys scope the place out to make sure you were alright. I guess they missed this last beatin' you took."

"That's alright, Vito."

"Look at you," Vito said, looking at Joey's face and picking up his bruised and battered arms, "you're a mess." Vito shook his head from side to side. "Now who did this to you? And you better tell me the truth!"

"Vito, it's all behind me. I want to forget about it."

"Forget about it? Why the fuck do you think I'm here? Do you think for one minute that I'm gonna start flipping fuckin' pizzas? I always told you time and time again never to hide anything from me. Now tell me, who did this to you? I'll make sure that this guy pays for this for the rest of his life."

"Why can't we just forget about it and move on. I'm tired of all the violence and bloodshed."

"Once again, you tried it your way and you lost. Now it's time to do things my way again! Now, who the fuck is responsible for this?"

The friendly greetings were just about forgotten, Vito was now all business. There was no way in the world that he was not going to get this information out of Joey. He knew it. And most of all, Joey also knew it. His promises to Gloria were about to all fall apart. That solemn vow that he gave to her lasted less than two whole days. At this moment he knew that Ramon was going to get another visit. This time Joey was not going in there alone.

Ramon was going to get a visit from some customers he will never forget, all because of five lousy pizzas that he refused to pay for.

"Sonny," the old lady said. "Can I have my order now?"

"Oh, I am sorry, Ma'am," Joey said as he motioned her to the counter. He quickly took care of the nice woman and wished her a good evening. Even the old lady examined Joey very carefully with sympathy. She knew the pain behind those bruises; after all she was an inhabitant of this brutal neighborhood.

"Take care of those wounds, Sonny."

"Thank you, ma'am I will," Joey said with a smile.

"Next time, bring these two guys with you," she said, pointing at Vito and Dutch. "You look like you could of used some help."

"Thank you, ma'am," Joey said politely. "I'm glad you noticed that."

For some reason, Joey felt that she really did not have to give him those kind words of advice. For he already knew that those sarcastic words were already etched in stone.

"Now let's do this one more time,' Vito asked. "Who and where is the guy?"

Joey stood at a standstill. He knew he was about to be forced to give Ramon's name up.

"You better tell him, kid," Dutch offered. "Believe me, it's the right thing to do."

"I know it is," Joey said. "But I made a promise to someone that I would let this go."

"Promises won't protect you around here," Dutch replied. "But we will."

The front door swung open as the elderly women slowly hobbled her way out of the store. The young lady sitting in the booth quickly followed. Vito, Dutch and Joey then slipped into the vacated booth to talk about what occurred the other night. They went over every detail of that sorry night at La Casa De Loco. The more Joey talked, the angrier Vito got. It did not take much to get his dander up; Joey just seemed to push all of the right buttons. There was just one little thing that Joey had not told Vito, he failed to tell him about his Puerto Rican girlfriend, Gloria.

"Dutch, get on the horn and get Bear, the Roach and Jimmy over here first thing in the morning."

"You got it, Vito," said Dutch. He then pounded on the table before getting up to use the telephone. "Where's the phone?"

"Behind the counter," answered Joey. He then looked back over in Vito's direction. "I don't want anybody getting killed."

"This I will promise you," Vito said. "I won't kill any of those pieces of shit. But they will remember the name of Vito Carlucci for the rest of their lives. The first visit, nobody dies. If I have to go back a second time, I can't promise you anything."

With those threatening words, it took Vito all of twenty minutes to formulate a game plan. To Joey there was one problem; he was part of this mastermind's plot. He tried frantically to get out of it, but his efforts fell in vain. To Vito, Joey had to be there to put his plan in motion and identify the culprits. He instructed Joey not to get involved in the plan. As soon as the violence started he was to stay exactly where he was seated. Joey's orders were plain and simple; even a baby could have executed them. Deep down he had a feeling the price of redemption was going to cost him dearly. This time it was most likely going to cost him the woman that he had fallen in love with. For Vito there was no turning back on this issue, it had to be done. He came fully equipped with his own brand of justice. Besides, this is why Joey called him here in the first place. The predominantly black section of Crown Heights, Brooklyn, would soon be introduced to Vito's style of law and order.

"Where is the medallion?" Vito asked, noticing that it was not around Joey's neck. "Did those bastards take it from you?"

"Shit," answered Joey. He then put his right hand to his neck and noticed that he had not put it back on. "I took it off the night I went to that bar. I knew I was going to be in some kind of trouble. Something told me to just take it off that night."

"Well, where is it?"

"I got it buried someplace safe behind the counter."

"Go get it and put it back on right now! And I never want to see it off your neck again."

"Vito, what do you know about that medallion?"

"I know that it's 18 karat gold," he joked. "What do you mean?"

"I mean the history behind it."

"It's been in my family for a very long time."

"What about the history before then?"

"Let's just worry about the history ahead of us," Vito quickly replied, like he was trying to avoid the issue. "Now go get the medal!"

Joey rushed behind the counter and retrieved the priceless piece. He went back to the table and Vito stood up to help him put it back on around his neck. He took the gold from Joey's hand and kissed the familiar face on it. Opening the clasp, he looked at Joey as he placed it around his neck.

"Let this be the last time I put this around your neck. This medallion will never hurt you, it's the animals around you that it will protect you from."

"Vito, not to get you pissed off or anything, but so far it's not doing such a good job. Look at me!" Joey said, laughing a bit as he pointed to his sorry looking beat up face. The comment drew a chuckle from Vito as his eyes started to wander around the store.

"That's because you took the fuckin' thing off. If you would have left it on, none of this would have happened to you. Don't worry, in a couple of more days you will look like your old self again."

"I don't know, Vito, ever since I put this chain around my neck, strange things have been happening to me. Some of the things, I just..." Joey paused for a moment before he continued on. "I just can't explain them."

"Why, what are you going to tell me next? That you saw Jesus Christ?"

Joey just let the conversation die right there. He knew that he saw something in his bedroom that night. Whether it was Jesus Christ or the devil himself, he knew enough to just let the subject be put to rest. Telling the story to Gloria was a bit easier, and he got a little bit more understanding out of her. She believed in the hereafter and reincarnation, so she was quite more sympathetic to Joey's sightings. Vito on the other hand was another story, he might have taken Joey in to the nearest insane asylum for a lobotomy.

"Let me ask you a question," Vito said. "How the hell did you ever get involved with a place like this?"

For the next five minutes, Joey sat there trying to explain how he became involved with this pizzeria from hell. Vito just stood there trying to comprehend the logistics of it all. He knew that once Joey got out of prison, things were not going to be easy for him. But he never expected this. All he did was shake his head and rub his hands together. The more he listened, the more he became involved.

"So where is this so called partner of yours now?" Vito asked, knowing that the burden was all on top of Joey's muscular shoulders. "Where the fuck was he when you got the shit kicked out of you?"

"He doesn't come around, he's too afraid to."

"He's too afraid?"

"The guy is not the fighting type. Besides, he has too much to lose."

"What do you mean he's got too much to lose?"

"He has a big food distributorship to run."

"So he sits in his fancy office while you are literally fighting for your life to survive."

"I was down and out, Vito," Joey confessed. "At the time I had nowhere or no one else to turn to. Something just told me that I had to be here. It was like a premonition or something like that. Besides, I thought it might be a good opportunity for myself."

"What premonition or opportunity? This is not an opportunity or anything else that's on the line here," Vito lectured. "This is your life that's on the line. Nothing more or nothing less. If that partner of yours really cared about you, he would have never handed you those keys."

"Now I realize that," Joey sadly said. "I think I'm being used. What for, I have no idea."

"Well, when you get a chance, you get on the phone. You tell that prick that he is no longer your partner."

"Why not?" Joey said with an astounding look on his face.

"Because I am, I'm your new partner!! I am going to offer him a non-negotiable settlement to get rid of him. What is your stake in this dump?"

"I have fifty percent."

"I will offer him twenty grand in cash and even that is too much. I am doing this for you, not him. If he has a problem with that, then he will get nothing. We will turn this place around and I will decide when it will be time to leave. Then we will sell it to one of the locals and go home."

Vito went on with his sermon, while Dutch was still recruiting some of his men on the telephone. Vito could not understand how a friend could stick another friend into a position like this. Sure, it did not cost Joey any money, the only price that it could have cost him was his life.

"Vito, he's not a bad guy," Joey said, speaking of Tony, his so-called partner. "He even gave me a car to get back and forth to work!"

"Nah, he's not a bad guy. He's just protecting his own self-interests using you as his guinea pig. The safer you were, the safer his investment was. He only gave you that car to protect his number one investment."

"What's that?"

"Himself and this shit-hole," Vito said. "He couldn't give two shits about you!"

"He tried to talk me out of it, but for some reason I felt that I had to be here."

"It's obvious he didn't try hard enough, because you're still here!"

"Yep, I'm still here."

"How many people died so far? Two, right?"

"Yea, two," Joey sadly said. "Marco and little Steven."

"Did this partner of yours even come here once knowing that all this trouble was going on?"

"No."

"The next time you would have seen him, would have been at your own funeral."

"Well I'm not dead yet."

"No, you're here and I'm here with you. So do as I say and make that call when you get a chance. Let's resolve this issue quickly."

"Okay Vito," Joey said. "I'll call him."

"And tell your so called friend that the fuckin' car is part of the deal."

"What do you mean?"

"We're keeping the car too, that's what I mean," he went on while continuing his inspection of the pizzeria. "These bullet holes in the walls are from the guys across the street?"

"Yea, the guys from the park. I told you a little about that when I left you that message on your answering machine."

At that moment Vito started walking to the front of the store. He looked out into the dark night, his eyes steadily gazing into the park. The traffic outside the park was building up, addicts were coming and going as they copped a fantasy to start off their late night activities. Saturday night was always the busiest night of the week for the corner dealers. The world could be coming to an end and these degenerates would still be out there in full force. This brand of Saturday night fever would sometimes go on until three or four in the morning. God only knows what the summer brings out of hibernation from the cold winter that had just passed. Vito just stood there not believing what he was seeing. He then turned around and looked at Joey and Dutch.

"One thing at a time," he said. "We will take care of it, one thing at a time."

For some reason everyone present knew that these were words spoken from the heart. In Vito's mind he probably was already thinking about an antidote to the pollution across the street. One thing at a time meant that this problem that dwelled across the way had to be dealt with. The sooner it was taken care of, the better everyone would feel, but for now it was time for him to move in and make himself more comfortable. More important than that, it was time to make his presence felt throughout the crime infested neighborhood.

"Hey kid," Dutch said, hanging up the telephone. "Did you ever think of taking up karate?"

"What good is karate gonna do me?"

"What good? It's the oldest form of self defense known to man."

"It ain't older than running, is it?"

"No kid," Dutch said as he resurfaced from behind the counter with a smile on his face. "It ain't older than running."

"Come on, Joey," Vito said, joining in on the small laugh. "Take us on a tour of this fuckin' dump."

Chapter 15

VITO AND DUTCH had workers down in the basement cleaning it up and preparing it for their own personal use. All day long technicians were coming and going. Vito emerged from the dark cellar and walked around to the front of the store. He stopped to talk to an installer who worked for the phone company. Joey was looking on from inside the store trying to tend to his own daily business. He was watching Vito go into his pockets and hand the telephone company employee some money. Something was not right and Vito had to bribe the guy in order to get things done his way. For some strange reason, Joey knew that the basement would never be the same again. God only knows what those two guys were up to. Vito then started to walk towards the store as the front door swung open.

"Do me a favor," he said with an aggravated look on his face. "Give me something cold to drink."

"What do you want?"

"Ah, I don't know. Give me a Coke or something."

"What are you doing down there?" Joey asked, filling a cup with ice.

"I'm redecorating your storage room."

"Thanks, maybe after you're done I could put the flour back down there."

"What flour?"

"I had to bring the flour upstairs because of the rats."

"What rats?"

"The rats in the basement, they were eating through my flour bags."

"Joey, stop, we are both on the wrong fuckin' page here," Vito cracked, picking up the cup of soda. "The basement is gonna be my playpen. I'm gonna conduct some of my business down there. You thought I was fixing it up so you could put some flour bags down there?"

"I just thought…" Joey started saying, and then he was cut off as he started to speak.

"Whatever you thought, you thought wrong! And what's this shit about rats?"

"The basement is loaded with em, they're this big," Joey said, holding his hands about a foot apart. "I'm just surprised that you haven't seen one yet?"

"Yea well, this is this big," Vito answered back, removing his .38 caliber pistol from his pants. "And this big will fuck up that big!"

"I guess you're right, I never thought of it that way."

"Listen, speaking of rodents, I got these three guys comin' over here. When they get here," Vito paused. He proceeded to take a large sip of soda to try and quench his thirst. "Send them downstairs."

"Alright, I'll look out for them."

Joey did not have to ask for their names, he knew who they were. They were part of Vito's crew, the part that wasn't in jail anyway. Joey finally put it all together and realized that Vito was going to operate some of his illegal businesses from the basement. The accommodations were not plush but for his intended purposes they need not be.

A couple of hours later, members of Vito's crew started to funnel into the community. One by one, their presence was immediately felt. From a distance, Joey heard some Frank Sinatra wannabe belting out a tune outside the store. His music was heard minutes before his body even appeared. This guy was singing Italian melodies right in the middle of the tough predominantly black neighborhood. Walking all the way up the block, he never missed a beat. Most of the residents just knew that this wise guy had to have a few screws loose.

The pizza owner just cracked up laughing as the well-built stocky man took a bow outside the storefront window. Someplace, somewhere there is a stage for this guy, but unfortunately it's not on St. Ann's Place in the middle of Crown Heights, Brooklyn. But until fame and fortune arrived to rescue him, this member of Vito's crew needed some kind of sedative to slow him down. His talents were definitely in his mouth, there was no doubt about it. Besides his voice, this wise guy could talk a prison guard into handing him over the keys to his cell, believe it, he has done it before. He was once busted for fraud and embezzlement, spending 4 years behind bars. The brazen gangster put his name on somebody's last will and testament. The funny thing about it was that he wasn't even a close friend or a member of the family. During the reading of the will this jokester even had the balls to show up. For whatever its worth, he was that good.

He sings pretty good, but he's fuckin crazy, Joey said to himself, as the guy walked through the front door.

"Are you Joey?" he said now tapping a tune on top of the counter with his fingers.

"That's me, I'm Joey," he said, extending his hand as the two men introduced themselves. "What's up?"

"Hey Joey, I'm Jimmy, I'm here to see Vito."

"You know, Jimmy, you sing pretty good."

"I'm better than good, kid, someday you'll see."

"I'm sure I will," said Joey. "I'm sure I will."

"Well where's Vito?"

"Go back out the door and make a right and then another right up the alley way. There's a door on the right hand side that leads to the basement. He's down there."

"Okay kid, I'll catch you later!"

The front door closed behind him. Jimmy continued to sing all the way down the alley and into the basement.

Twenty minutes later a Ford van pulled into the driveway and two more of Vito's soldiers exited from the white vehicle. The enclosed small truck had no windows. In the business that these guys were in, the less anybody sees the better. God only knows what was being transported in that vehicle. The inside was fully equipped with a garden hose, pitchfork, a couple of shovels and a toolbox. You would think that these guys were in the landscaping business. But the looks of them told you quite a different story.

They walked in tandem right into the store and wasted no time asking who they were looking for. This duo was definitely more serious than the character that just left. These two individuals were all business; the looks on their faces just told you so. As soon as they walked through the doors of the pizzeria they looked like they wanted to kill somebody. You could just tell that these two had no conscience and never would feel any remorse for their actions. They both looked like they hated living and had some sort of grudge against the whole world.

Talk about muscle, one of them was Vincent "The Bear" Matteo. This mountain of a man looked like he dined on steroids three times a day. He had more protein in his body than a Bumble Bee Tuna factory. Talk about lumps, there wasn't a portion of his upper body that did not bulge from his swelling torso. The guy was built like a brick from head to toe. His hands were the size of cinder blocks and even had the same coarse look. The gold ring on his right finger was big enough to fit around a young lady's wrist. Like everything else on his enormous body, nothing ever seemed to look right. His clothes always looked like they were a couple of sizes too small. Day after day he looked like he was getting bigger and bigger. His head had a hard time keeping up with the rest of his body; it looked like it didn't belong on the top of his broad shoulders.

Vinny arrived at this nickname in a quite peculiar way. They say he killed a bear with his bare hands somewhere in the Adirondack Mountains while burying a couple of dead bodies. He then took the animal and threw it into the back of his van and took it home with him. The proof is now stuffed and mounted on one of the walls in his den. Just by the looks of him, you would not find this story hard to believe.

Ricky the roach was another story all in himself. This guy got his name from being all over everything he touched. Like a cockroach, he did his best work at night. If you looked at him, he had the same flat body of his nocturnal namesake. Without a shower for two or three days he looked just as raunchy. After dark, Ricky was unbelievable; he could get in and out of things without anyone even knowing he was there. He just had a knack of finding things that others thought were impossible.

Ricky did have at least one fine characteristic, his mustache. The hair on top of his upper lip was perfect in every shape and form. It looked like a brand new push broom without a bristle out of place. There was no way that he did not have this mustache of his professionally groomed. It was too perfect not to be.

These were the final two pieces to Vito's puzzle of maladjusted looking misfits. But make no mistakes about it; this trio was as tough as they come. They served a purpose for their leader and served it up on a silver platter. Each one of them was excellent for what they were needed for.

So the birth of Vito's crew was born in a neighborhood where seeing too many Italians in one spot was not a familiar sighting. The only Italians who ventured out this far were some city employees or morons like Joey. But to Vito, he could kill two birds with one stone by being here. To him, it was clever thinking operating his business in a neighborhood infested with Blacks and Puerto Ricans. Nobody would ever think of coming to look for him in this section of Brooklyn. The added bonus was that he could keep a watchful eye over Joey. So to him, it was a temporarily perfect setup. The neighbors were not his type but nobody said that he was going to be borrowing a cup of sugar anytime soon.

T he weather started to warm up a bit as a warm front from Canada smothered the Metropolitan area. Whatever snow and ice remained from the last snowfall quickly evaporated and slowly flowed into the nearest corner sewer. Every drainpipe in the neighborhood was leaking in the aftermath of melting snow.

Slowly but surely things started to change for Joey, the Brotherhood had not made an appearance in weeks. Their weekly pickup was almost forgotten since Vito's arrival. The gang noticed Vito as soon as he stepped out of his late model Lincoln. The Brotherhood now knew that Joey's Place was well protected and their services were no longer required. Joey's protection came from his own kind now, free of charge.

Joey's relationship with Gloria grew stronger with each passing day. He spent many nights with her. These rendezvous usually lasted until the following morning. Joey always kept her away from the store in fear of her safety. Most of all, he kept her away from Vito. She knew of him all right, but what she did not know was what Joey was trying to keep from her. He dreaded her finding out that Vito was conducting his business right below him, in the basement of his store. Gloria was totally against everything that he and the mob stood for.

To make matters even a little bit more complicated, Vito had no idea that she even existed. Joey kept the relationship a secret from Vito, knowing how he felt about being with anyone but his own kind. His Godson having a Puerto Rican girlfriend or wife was just out of the question. Sooner or later they would have to both find out about each other. But right now, in Joey's mind, he was not in a position to lose either one of them. He loved them both. He was not about to put either one of them against the other or against himself. There had to be a simple solution to all of this, or so he thought.

To make matters even worse, the following day Vito came into the pizzeria ready for him and his boys to go to work. It was Monday, and Vito knew that this was the slowest business day of the week. The fewer the patrons, the quicker they can get in and out and still retain most of their anonymity. At 9:00 that night Vito would be ready to pay that promised visit to La Casa de Loco.

V ito, Dutch, Jimmy and Joey piled into Vito's Lincoln Town car. The Bear and Ricky the Roach followed right behind in the Ford van. Vito gave Joey some last minute instructions before he entered the bar. His last minute pep talk infuriated Joey even more. He had a way with Joey when it came to making the kid see things his way. Vito even pointed out the bruises on Joey's face to try and incite him just a little bit more. After all, like Vito, Joey had the same Italian blood in him. It didn't take too much to get either one of them overly excited, sometimes over things not worth mentioning.

The two vehicles pulled up about ten feet from the front of the neighborhood bar. Vito stuck his hand out the window of the car and waved the white van to go ahead of him. The van went to the corner and whipped a U-turn and parked directly across the street from the bar, facing north. Both vehicles then had their engines turned off as they now rested on the wide two way street. Everybody just sat and waited for Vito to make his move.

"Remember," Vito said to Dutch and Jimmy. "No shooting. Leave your guns in your pants or wherever the fuck they're hidden."

Vito never drove his own car. He always had one of his boys chauffeuring him around. But this time was different; he had to be in control of the whole situation. He just sat there like a rattlesnake ready to gobble up any unsuspecting field mice. The four men just waited and waited for the time to be ripe. Finally, Vito summoned the move. It was time to strike.

Without saying a word, Vito disembarked from the car and started walking towards the tavern. He walked slowly and took out a cigarette from his overcoat. Stopping by the front door, he paused and took a few extra seconds to light it. Now looking in both directions out of force of habit, Vito adjusted the collar on his overcoat and entered the bar.

Ten minutes later it was Joey's turn, but Joey was not as nonchalant as Vito appeared to be. This time his body was alcohol free and his apprehension was showing, big-time. He was totally against this, but he had no choice. At this time and at this moment, there was no turning back. He picked his head up and took a real deep breath before he entered the bar.

Upon entering Joey saw Vito sitting about ten feet away from the front of the oak bar. His tailor made overcoat was draped over the back of the wooden barstool. By design, Joey was to sit in the same seat that he occupied on his previous visit. Acting a little hesitant while checking out the surroundings, he decided to sit. Not to his surprise, he looked up and saw the same bartender on duty. The bartender had a look of ultimate surprise on his face. His facial expressions represented a sight that he never thought he would ever see again. He walked over to the stubborn customer and offered no condolences.

"You know that I can't serve you here," he snapped at Joey. "So why don't you pick your sorry ass up and get the fuck out of here."

"I just wanted a beer," Joey replied. "I didn't come here for trouble. I came here to make amends with everyone, including you!"

"Well, whatever you came in here for, you better forget about it and leave while you still can. You're not wanted in here, so get the fuck out."

"Is that anyway to talk to a paying customer?" Vito said from a few feet away. He was closely monitoring the whole conversation. "The kid doesn't look like trouble to me."

"Mac," the barkeep said. "Mind your own business! This guy is not welcome here, and he knows it."

"Why, what did he do?"

"Never mind what he did," the tough talking bartender said. "He's outta here!"

"Come on, give the kid a beer!"

"If you don't stay out of this, you'll be joining him."

"Is that right?"

"Yea, that's right. So like I said before, mind your own business."

"Here kid," Vito said, sliding his beer in Joey's direction. "I just ordered this, take it."

"Thank you, sir!" Joey said, never taking his eyes off of the angry bartender.

"Now I'll have another one," Vito said. "And that's a fuckin' order! Now do your job like a good bartender should, and get me another beer."

The angry bartender listened to the instructions coming from the older patron. He quickly hunched over and retrieved another beer from the refrigeration unit. It did not take the barkeep too long before he vacated the premises. Not more than a minute later, he sneaked into the back room.

"He's going to get him, he's going to get him," Joey whispered to Vito from a few yards away. "Ramon hangs out in the back office most of the time."

"Just keep your cool and follow the instructions that I gave you."

Vito and Joey took a small peek into the rear of the tavern. The back room had the usual crowd of deadbeats hanging out back there. Most of the faces looked very familiar to Joey - so did their pool sticks.

Not more than two minutes later, Ramon appeared. He had an arrogant grin on his face and was walking with the swagger of the Heavyweight Boxing Champion of the World. Just seeing his face made Joey want to hop off his barstool and rip his fucking head off. But this was a different chapter of the story and a totally different set of circumstances. Joey had to stay put.

"Here he comes, this is him," Joey said, without moving his lips. "Just look at that piece of shit. He thinks who the fuck he is."

"Sit tight and try to relax," Vito whispered back. "He's comin' your way."

Ramon walked right past Vito and towards Joey. The whole way over, he had that stupid looking grin on his face. Even his sidekicks were notified of the unwanted guest. From the back room, they all started to inch their way closer to the impending confrontation. Now standing under the archway that separated the two rooms, they patiently waited. Like before, they were heavily armed with pool sticks. The bar whores who hang out with this group were snuggled up right behind them.

Ramon put his left hand on the bar and looked directly into Joey's eyes. He just stood there shaking his head and laughing. Joey never said a word to him. He just waited for Ramon to make the first move.

"You are one stupid and stubborn grease-ball," Ramon said. "What the fuck are you doing here?"

"What does it look like I'm doing? I'm having a beer. And I don't appreciate the racist remark either."

"I thought you were smart enough to never come back here."

"I am," answered Joey.

"Then what the fuck are you doing in my place of business? Did you come for another beatin'? This time I see that you don't have your slut bitch Gloria with you. That's a mistake, you should have brought her with you."

"Why?"

"So she can peel you up off of the floor again."

"Nah, I left her home tonight," Joey said, trying real hard to obey Vito's orders. "She didn't have a good time the last time we were here."

"You didn't answer my first question yet."

"The beatin' you gave me the last time I was here keeps giving me memory lapses. What was the question again?" Joey said, toying with Ramon. "I forgot!"

"What the fuck are you doing here? Pendejo!" Ramon asked again, this time calling Joey an asshole and raising his voice.

"I got permission to come here," Joey said.

"From who?"

"From him," Joey said pointing to Vito.

"And who the fuck is that old man?"

"That old man," Joey said, "is my gangster!"

Ramon slowly turned around to see the friendly host who was inviting unwanted people into his place of business. He looked closely and saw the well-dressed man in his late forties just sipping on his beer. Tentatively, he started to inch closer to Joey's so-called gangster. His suspicions started to grow a little weary of the whole situation.

"And who the fuck are you, his Godfather?" Ramon asked, from about three feet away.

"The kid already told you who I was."

As quick as lightning strikes, Joey picked up his beer bottle and propelled it right in the direction of the front window behind him. The fierce velocity from his powerful throwing arm sent the heavy bottle crashing right through the neon sign. It was lights out for the colorful flickering sign as it fell off of the hooks that held it in place. The bottle shattered the window behind it and crashed onto the street along with flying shards of glass.

Caught by the element of surprise, Ramon then turned around to confront the sudden burst coming from the broken glass. Startled, he then was just about to charge in Joey's direction. Vito started to rise off of his barstool. With his right hand, he picked up his now empty beer bottle.

"Where the fuck are you going you Spic bastard?" Vito said, walking in Ramon's direction. Vito grabbed the back of Ramon's shoulder and spun him around. With one fast and furious swing, he smacked his beer bottle right over the top of Ramon's head. The bottle shattered into a hundred pieces, leaving only the neck in Vito's right hand. Ramon dropped straight to the floor and definitely was feeling the effects of being incoherent. The blood from the impact of the blow started to appear underneath his head. It quickly oozed out and formed a circle on the wooden floor. Vito continued his assault, stomping and kicking the fallen man.

Ramon's boys rushed to their fallen man armed with pool sticks, just as they did the last time. By the time they arrived, the front door flew open and three other very angry men confronted them. Ricky the Roach stood outside as the designated sentry.

Vito's timing, like almost everything else he did, was perfect. Each one of his boys was armed with baseball bats and whatever other concealed weapon they needed. This time the Puerto Rican gang's pool sticks were outmatched by their enemies' heavier lumber. They stopped dead in their tracks and slowly started to retreat. The looks on their faces alone told you that they were not taking another step forward. Ramon's boys knew that this time they were in way over their heads.

Leading the way, Dutch and the rest of the boys were relentless. Every step they took, they destroyed whatever crossed their way. The scene looked like a batting cage on an early Saturday morning. They were swinging at everything within their sights as they relentlessly pursued their prey into the back poolroom.

The poolroom was now the sight of a one sided rumble. Joey just sat there as instructed; taking the whole thing in. He never left his bar-stool. Deep down, Joey did not want any of this to happen. But there was nothing he or anybody else could do to stop it.

The Bear picked up his smaller foe straight over his head, then heaved him on top of the pool table. The thunderous vibration traveled throughout the small and now chaotic bar. Bear swiftly jumped on top of the overmatched man and just kept punching and punching with horrific hostility. He would not stop until his opponent was not showing any spark of life. The green felt carpet on top of the pool table was now changing to a dark deep red. The first drop of blood was spilt; unfortunately it was a sad beginning of things to come.

Finishing his first victim off with remarkable ease, Bear searched and found his second opponent not too far away. Now setting his eyes upon him, he hopped off of the pool table like a cat. His unpredictable pursuit led him chasing the retreating foe into a small kitchen. What went on behind that closed door, only God knows. But from the sounds of it, you just knew that there was no mercy involved. The only sounds were coming from a broken English voice begging for his attacker to spare his life. But his crying for leniency was never heard. Bear's wrath showed no signs of ever letting up. It was only when he exited from the kitchen that you knew that he had disposed of another hapless victim. This strong and powerful man had made short work out of two overmatched combatants. .

Joey's eyes scanned the dimly lit tavern, he next focused across the room on one of Vito's other goons. There, he noticed Jimmy's bat strangling another guy by the throat as he had him pinned up against the wall. The singer held his Louisville slugger by both ends as he put all his weight and strength into the gasping throat of his opposition. In a matter of seconds the man slowly fell helplessly to the floor with his tongue hanging from his mouth.

Like leaking water, he hugged the wall all the way down to the naked floor. With the bat still in his hands and around the guy's neck, Jimmy followed the descending body until its unconscious head slumped over the top of the bat. With no more oxygen, the Puerto Rican patron's brain had no other choice but to respond in this manner. To make sure that his victim was soundly defeated, Jimmy smashed the butt end of the bat into the motionless man's face. The blood gushed like a fountain, splattering out in all directions. Now hovering over his prey, Jimmy turned in the direction of Vito. He stared at the under-boss waiting to be noticed for his good deed. Vito would just nod his head in agreement of a job well done.

Dutch, on the other hand, never stopped using his bat; the Irish maniac was having the time of his life. His victim was unconscious, but that did not stop the beating. He must have broken every bone in his opponent's body, but he was not finished.

The madman then fell to one knee and reached into his back pocket. From where Joey was sitting, he could see the luster coming from the concealed weapon that he pulled out and exposed. Now brandishing a sharp knife, Dutch grabbed the screaming and immobile man by his right hand. With one stroke of the sharp blade, he dismembered his pinky finger from his left hand. This was not in any way unusual behavior for Dutch. Whatever trouble he was involved in, he always had to leave his mark. For the faithful friend of Ramon, he would now be scarred and handicapped forever. He will also remember this night for the rest of his life, if he ever gets through it.

The horrified girlfriends and acquaintances of this unfortunate foursome just cried in silence. They just witnessed a horrendous beating administered by a group of fearless and heartless men. Looking around the room, they just pinned themselves against any open space they could find. They stood erect, hoping and praying that they would not be next. Each one of them possessed the alarming awareness of fear. They were never touched by Vito's crew, they were just administered a small sermon to forget whatever they saw. This little speech never fails and always gets its point across. The people hearing it never respond, they just listen very carefully while shaking in their shoes. This warning was only given once to the potential victim. Consequences or another visit were hardly ever needed. The message was always heard loud and crystal clear. It never fell upon deaf ears.

Vito waited patiently for his boys to finish their business. He hovered over Ramon's body like he was guarding a bag of money from some bank heist. In a matter of seconds, one by one, his ruthless crew returned from their mission leaving bodies, some deadly still and others twitching and crawling all over the barroom floor. They all gathered around their leader waiting for his next set of instructions. Still looking down at Ramon, Vito then turned in Joey's direction. "How much did you say this prick owes you?"

"$16.00."

"Hop over the bar and pop open the register and take what belongs to you."

Joey jumped over the shiny wood bar and onto the rubber mat that covered the floor. To his surprise, there was the bartender sitting in a hiding position, crouched under the bar like a little child. The frightened man was left untouched as he was shaking as if he had Palsy. He also knew that any information that he leaked out would have great reprisals pointing in his direction. Joey just looked at the disgraced man and shook his head. To him, there was no need to harm the middle-aged man. There was enough damage done already. Anything further was totally unnecessary and foolish. It's a shame that Vito and his people thought quite the opposite.

Joey hit the no sale button and the cash register popped wide open. He took out a ten, five and a dollar bill from the cash drawer. He then turned around to Vito as he put the money in his pocket.

At that same time, Jimmy hurdled over the top of the bar with his bat still in his left hand. He walked around observing the choice liquors that were neatly lined on the wooden shelves.

"How much is in there?" Vito asked, starting to compose his suit to its proper attire.

"I don't know, but by the looks of it, I'd say about four or five hundred," Joey answered, flipping his fingers through the larger bills.

"Why don't you take some more money for all the pain and suffering you went through," Vito said, with his right foot putting pressure on top of Ramon's twitching and wiggling body. He just looked at Joey waiting for him to react to his offer. "Go ahead, take it!'

"The 16 dollars is all I came for in the first place," Joey said, shaking the green paper bills. "What do you think I'm a thief?"

"You might not be, but I am," Jimmy quipped, pushing Joey aside and emptying out the register. "Move over and let me in there!"

"Hey Bear," Vito said. "Give me a hand getting this piece of shit to his feet."

Bear placed his bat on top of the bar and walked over to Vito. He then placed both of his enormous arms under Ramon's armpits and quickly raised him to a standing position. Bear then threw the top part of Ramon's body on top of the bar. The beaten Puerto Rican used the bar as a crutch to stay on his feet. His head was lying in a sideways position right on top of the bar's counter.

"Joey, come here," Vito ordered. Joey approached Vito. Vito picked Ramon's head from off of the bar by his ponytail. "You see this kid?" he said to Ramon, looking straight at him. "You see him?" he said again, tightening his fearsome grip around Ramon's hair.

Struggling to see, Ramon then barely opened his eyes. He raised his head from Vito's vice like grip and looked at Joey. The two mortal enemies just stared at each other. Only one was victorious. "Yes, I see him."

"If you ever fuck with this kid again, I will come back here and kill you myself. Do you understand me?" Ramon just winced, not saying a word. But Vito kept on going with his words that were filled with threatening content. "Say it God damn it!" he snarled, raising the tone of his voice. "Say it!"

"Yes."

"Yes what?" Vito asked again, wanting a full answer to his question.

"Yes, I understand."

"Good, because if you ever forget the understanding that we now have," Vito slowly scanned the room, looking at everyone in attendance. "You will definitely understand the pain that you will be going through," Vito said, giving a nod to Bear.

Bear then grabbed Ramon's right hand until he located his thumb. He put his massive hand around it and bent it backwards until it fell limp. Ramon's thumb was now dangling like a branch hanging from a dead tree. The cracking sounds of his bones gave chills to all the squeamish present. Joey and the women trembling in the back of the tavern winced at this violent application. The rest couldn't care less. Ramon almost passed out from the pain; his high pitched screams wailed throughout the tiny bar. The uncontrollable sobs were unbearable to hear. The pain was so bad, that tears soon followed. The once proud and insolent Puerto Rican man had now fallen from grace. He was reduced to nothing more than a crying baby in search of a feeding.

"You should have took his thumb off," Dutch chimed in. "Let me in there! I'll take care of this fuckin' scumbag!"

"That's enough, Dutch," ordered Vito. "I think he got the message. Alright Joey, come on," Vito said. "Hop back over on this side of the bar. Let's get the fuck out of here."

Joey quickly jumped over the bar and walked to the front door. Vito gave a nod to Jimmy to go into action. Jimmy put a bottle of Johnny Walker Black on top of the bar. He then turned around and picked up his idle bat. With both hands tightly wrapped around the handle, he went into action. Like a little kid waiting for his first pitch from his father, Jimmy started swinging at everything around him. He kept swinging and swinging without ever thinking of stopping.

Jimmy worked his way from one end of the bar to the other. His aim was perfect as he destroyed everything in sight. Every single bottle that lined the shelves in a decorative fashion was destroyed. The mirrors behind the bottles shattered from the explosive impact of force coming from the flying glass. There was liquid everywhere and the bar stunk of it.

"Okay Jimmy, that's enough." Vito said, ordering Jimmy to stop his rampage.

Jimmy walked back to retrieve the bottle of Johnny Walker he placed on top of the bar. He picked up the bottle and walked over to the opening to exit the serving area. There he saw the bartender still cuddled up in the corner of the bar. He quickly delivered a knee to the head of the innocent man before he exited the area. The fierce blow knocked the employee backwards and into dreamland.

"I'm fuckin' thirsty," Jimmy complained. He then twisted off the cap of the famous scotch and took a long swig. "Ahhh!" he said, wiping the booze from running down the corner of his wet lips. "That felt good. Anybody want a shot of this shit?" There were no takers.

"Now look what you have left," Vito asked Ramon. "Was it worth not paying for those five pies?" Vito then grabbed Ramon by the ponytail again, waiting for an answer. "Was it?"

"No," Ramon muttered, barely able to get the word out.

Upon that answer, Vito raised Ramon's head by his hair. With great intent, he smashed his face right into the bar. All that was heard was the loud crunch of Ramon's bones grinding against each other. His whole face mushroomed from the devastating impact. Once Vito let go the sudden jolt sent Ramon falling to the floor beneath him. There was not a sound in the room, only the moans and groans of the battered victims.

Vito picked his coat up from off of the barstool. He neatly dusted some of the glass that flew over the bar off of his coat. While putting the long gray overcoat back on, he was looking around for a mirror. His appearance was important to him, and he never wanted to look disheveled while out in public.

"Did you have to break every mirror in the place," he said to Jimmy. "Ah, the hell with it."

"There's still a big piece right behind that bottle of vodka over there," Jimmy said, pointing behind the bar. "I think it's big enough for your head."

"Don't be such a wise ass, Jimmy. Okay boys, let's go," Vito said walking to the front door. He then turned around and looked at Ramon for one last and final time. "There's just one more thing I forgot to tell you, Ramon. Every Friday night, like clockwork, you will order five pizzas from Joey's Place and you will pay for them. If you decide not to pay again, the next time I will come back to pick up the money. And I don't think you would want that to happen. Do you?"

"No," was the faint reply from Ramon.

"Oh, and there is one more thing I forgot to tell you. Always remember that the toppings are $2.00 extra," Vito said as he and the rest of his boys busted out laughing. They all walked out the front door the same way they entered, as one.

Their mission was accomplished as they left behind something that resembled a war zone. But the message Vito's crew sent was loud and clear. The next day it would be heard throughout the Hispanic part of the neighborhood. Crown Heights had a new tenant, and his name was Vito Carlucci.

"By the way, Joey, who's Gloria?" Vito asked, before he stepped into the car.

"Tomorrow, Vito, I'll tell you all about her tomorrow."

Chapter 16

THE NEXT DAY, Jimmy dropped Joey and Vito off in front of the pizzeria. Vito went directly to the basement using the entrance in the driveway. Joey did not even put the key into the front door when he heard the phone ringing from inside. In a hurry to answer it, he opened the door and raced towards the telephone. It was pretty uncommon that the phone would be ringing at 9:30 in the morning, it was definitely someone he knew, and he thought he knew exactly who it was.

"Hello," he said.

"It's me," the familiar sounding voice said.

"Me who?" Joey joked.

"Me, Gloria."

"Oh," he said acting surprised.

"Don't oh me, you know exactly why I'm calling."

"You're calling me because you love me?"

"Don't be an asshole, Joey."

"Then why are you calling me?" Joey said, absolutely certain of the reason.

"Where were you last night?"

"I was out!"

"Out where?"

"I was with a few friends," Joey said, then paused. "Playing cards!" He was trying to choose his words very carefully. "The game lasted for about twenty minutes."

"Did you win?"

"Yea, I won. I won sixteen dollars!"

"That number sounds familiar."

"It does, doesn't it?"

"You were supposed to come over to my house last night. Don't fucking lie to me, where were you last night?"

"I told you where I was."

"You're a liar!" she said, through tight lips, her voice now picking up a little steam and tempo.

"Don't call me a fuckin liar. If I'm a liar, then you tell me where the hell I was. Because I have a strange feeling that you already know."

"My sister called me up at seven o'clock in the morning yelling and screaming at me. It appears you and a few of your Guinea friends went into Ramon's bar last night and destroyed the place. His wife was ringing my sister's doorbell at 6 o'clock in the morning screaming and yelling at her. Ramon and a couple of the other guys are in the hospital! You and your animal friends beat them up pretty bad. God, Joey, this is not good. A couple of them are in critical condition. Ramon needs plastic surgery on his face and some other guy lost a finger and was beaten so bad that he is in a coma."

"Oh," he said. "Good news travels pretty fast in this neighborhood, doesn't it?

"It doesn't stop there. A guy named Marcello, who my sister also knows has a broken neck. This is bad Joey," she lamented, "really bad."

"Wow, we did a better job on those scumbags than I thought. What hospital are they in? I want to send them some flowers and a couple of "get well soon" cards."

"Joey, would you stop it with all this macho Italian bullshit!"

"Oh, Okay," he said. "Now it's an Italian thing. You know for a fact that somebody was gonna kick the crap out of Ramon sooner or later. Besides, how do you know it was me anyway?"

"What's the matter, Joey, did you forget that Ramon lived across the street from my sister? Ramon told his wife that it was you. And his wife told my sister. It appears that you did not cover your tracks too well."

"Well, did that bitch go over to your sister's house when I got the shit kicked out of me!" he said, going on the offensive. His lies and his alibi had fallen apart; it was time for the excuses to start rolling out.

"That's not the answer I was looking for Joey!"

"Then what is?"

"You lied to me, you told me you would never step foot into that place again."

"I didn't put a foot into that place, I put two feet in."

"Joey, stop trying to be funny, because I'm not laughing. I am at work now and I can't talk too loud. For the second time. Why did you lie to me?"

"Gloria, you don't understand. I had to go back, it was a personal issue between me and that prick, Ramon."

"Why couldn't you just let it go like you promised you would?"

"Because every time I look into a mirror I see my beaten up face. Every time I look in the mirror, I see that little boy Steven with a bullet hole in his chest." Joey then paused to catch his breath; his temper was rising. "Because every time I look in the mirror I see his Brother Derek crying over his dead body. Because every fuckin' time I look into the mirror I see Marco lying dead inside that elevator. I also see Orlando crying after he got smacked around by Ramon. And most of all, every time I look in that fuckin' mirror, I see a man who did not do shit about any of it! Does all this answer your question, Gloria?"

"So what did you run all the way back to Bensonhurst and get all of your little Italian friends? Is this an Italian thing, Joey? You had to get back some of your Italian pride?"

"Again with that Italian thing. Will you stop it with that Italian bullshit," he demanded. "But I am going to answer your questions in the same order that you asked them."

"I'm waiting," she said while shuffling some papers on her desk.

"First of all, I did not run back to Bensonhurst, they came to me. Second, they were three Italians, an Irish guy and a Jew. And finally number three, it had nothing to do with Italian pride. What I did separated the difference between right and wrong!"

"Violence never separates the difference between anything."

"Maybe to you it doesn't! But if it reaches down and bites you in the ass a couple of times, maybe then you will feel differently about what was done here. But I can promise you one thing."

"What's that?" Gloria said.

"It will no longer be open season on me," he promised. "Picking on Joey DeFalco will not be a choice or an option any longer. The whole fuckin' neighborhood will find that out, one way or the other. Yesterday, Ramon was the first one to find that out. But I promise you, there will be others."

"What are you and your friends going to do?" she said. "Keep beating people up until you kill somebody."

"If they leave me no other choice, then yea."

"Well maybe I made the wrong choice!" Gloria said, casting doubt on their relationship.

"Well then, maybe you did. Maybe Vito was right. I should stick with my own kind. You'll never understand it and you most certainly will never understand me! Go find yourself a nice Puerto Rican man like Ramon. Maybe you will understand him a little better," Joey said, then slamming the phone against the receiver on the wall. Joey just stood staring at the wall in silence. He felt terrible about what had just transpired with Gloria. But her way of thinking about non-retaliation was ridiculous to him. After a while any man with any sort of pride would have to fight back. Even if it meant costing him the woman he loved.

A couple of minutes later, Vito walked through the front door. The second Vito laid eyes on Joey; he knew that something was wrong. Vito knew next to nothing about Gloria or her relationship with Joey. He only heard her name come out of the mouth of Ramon. Gloria knew everything about Vito, but she had no clue that Vito was even in the neighborhood. It was just a matter of time before Vito asked about her again. It was time for Joey to put all his cards on the table and resolve the certain issues that he tried to hide. The time seemed ripe for another heart to heart conversation with the Mafia Kingpin.

"What's wrong now?" Vito asked, walking to the kitchen to put up a pot of espresso. "You look like you just lost a good friend."

"I did," said Joey. "Vito, we have to talk!" He then followed Vito to the back of the store.

"About what, Gloria?"

"How did you know?"

"I know everything!" Vito said, putting a couple of scoops of the Italian coffee into the strainer. "When are you going to get that through that thick head of yours?"

"How did you know I was talking about her?"

"We ran the phone wires down into the basement. Remember? We both picked up the phone at the same time. I heard your whole conversation with her."

"That was pretty sneaky!"

"I know," Vito said. "But it is for your own protection. Everything that goes on up here, I want to know about it down there," he said, pointing to the basement. "It's pretty sneaky but it has to be done."

"When you knew it was her, why didn't you hang up?"

"Because there is more to this than you want to know."

"Like what?" Joey asked, impatiently waiting for the answer.

"Like her, that's what. Why didn't you tell me about her before?"

"I was going to tell you about her today. But I guess you found out in your own way."

"So, she's a Puerto Rican?"

"Yea, she is. How did you find that out?"

Vito went over to the sink and started to run the cold water. Three times he ran the cold running water in and out of the coffee-pot. Joey was anxiously waiting for his response, but Vito just tended to the making of his coffee. He watched as Vito put the pot on top of the burner and raised the flame. Then still in silence, he went into the walk-in box and took out a lemon. Closing the door behind him, Vito reached for a knife and cut the lemon into little wedges.

"Her accent, when she gets excited that characteristic is more profound in her speech. And at the end of your argument you mentioned about her finding a nice Puerto Rican man like Ramon."

There was a pause.

"Well aren't you going to say anything else?" Joey asked, expecting to be berated by the impurity that he committed. The impurity that seemed to be alive in Vito's eyes anyway. "Say something?"

"Listen to me, I told you all you needed to know when we were in prison. Obviously you did not take my words of advice to heart. Now look and see where it has gotten you. Look in that fuckin' mirror and look at your face."

"She had nothing to do with this."

"She didn't?"

"No, she didn't."

"Did it ever occur to you that your Puerto Rican girlfriend was the reason why you got beaten out of those five pies? And did it ever occur to you that Ramon wanted to meet you face to face?"

"What the hell are you talking about?"

"It seems to me that your friend Ramon had a thing for your little Gloria. He's been trying to bang her for years. Once he found out that he could not have her, he went after you. You being Italian just made matters worse. So he placed the order and refused to pay for it." Vito placed a cup and saucer on the stove, beside the burning flame. "Ramon knew damn well that you would soon go in there to collect your money. You fell right into his fuckin hands."

"Are you saying that she set me up when I met her there?"

"No, that was coincidental. She had no clue at all about what was going on. That night Ramon did not expect to find you and her together. He thought that when you would go to see him, you would go alone. He was very surprised to see the both of you at the same time. That night, he didn't want any trouble from you because she was there. He didn't want her to know what a scumbag he really was. But you forced his hand."

"How did he find out about me and Gloria?"

"He got all the information about you and Gloria from his wife. It seems that his wife and her sister are the best of friends."

"Holy shit! That's right," Joey said, in disbelief. "I can't fuckin' believe this crap. No wonder why Orlando came back and said that they wanted me to go and collect the money. I can't fuckin' believe this," repeated Joey again. "First Marco gets set up, now this!"

"Whatever happened to Marco," Vito warned, "we will take care of very soon. But what happened with Ramon, you better believe it. Because it's all true. When he saw you sitting at the bar with her, it just intensified his jealously for you. The rest, my good friend, is history."

At that moment, Joey just looked at Vito like he was Nostradamus. Vito had this uncanny knack about finding out everything. But this was unbelievable; everything he told Joey seemed to fall into place. He was not going to second-guess Vito and his source of information. His reasons had to be true; they made too much sense not to be. The amazing thing about all of this was how he found everything out so fast.

"So you're not mad at me for going out with a Puerto Rican woman?"

"I just give you advice, I can't control you. You seem to like finding things out the hard way. I would rather see you with a nice Italian girl from the neighborhood. But if this is what your heart is telling you to do, then go with your instincts."

"So I have your blessings?"

"Yes, you have my blessings. But if you ever have a son and you name him Pedro, I'll fuckin' kill you!" Vito said, pulling out his gun and jokingly pointing it at Joey.

"Thanks Vito," Joey said. He then embraced Vito. "Thanks."

"Besides, I heard that she's a good looking piece of ass."

"Yea, Vito, that she is. She is beautiful and I do love her," he said. "Vito, what does it matter what she is or where she came from?"

"To some people it does matter. I heard that she is a wonderful and dedicated woman. She is a far cry from what I have experienced. Just be prepared to hear all kinds of shit from assholes like Ramon. Do you think you could handle it?"

"I know I can handle it."

"I hope so."

"I know so."

"Good, but the next time, at least wait until I get there before you go up against five guys. Now go get ready to open up your store, I want to have my coffee in peace."

Joey seemed very surprised on how delicately Vito took to his going out with Gloria. Whoever his informant was, he must have passed her with flying colors. Anything else but straight A's would not have been acceptable for him. But for Joey this was only half of the battle, he still had to win Gloria back. The battle would only be tougher with the arrival of Vito and the deceit that Joey had set in her mind. This was a true blue woman, and dishonesty and violence were not part of her distinguished resume. How was she ever going to accept that the man of her dreams is like a son to a notorious gangster? All she did was get a little taste of something that she did not even know Vito was involved with. If she had the slightest clue of Vito's involvement, the romance would surely be over.

Up to this moment, Joey was stunned how no one even mentioned Vito's name when it came to the brutal beating of Ramon and his friends. But sooner or later the truth would all be exposed. It was up to Joey to tell Gloria before she found out on her own.

Joey exited the kitchen area and heard some loud grumbling going on outside. He strolled out to the sidewalk and noticed a small commotion going on at the corner. Jimmy was in an argument with some overweight meter maid. She definitely did not look like lovely Rita the pretty meter maid from the famous Beatles song.

Joey opened the front door and stuck his head in to call Vito. Vito was already sitting down smoking a cigarette and enjoying his cup of espresso. Jimmy's yelling was so loud that Vito had to be hearing his complaints.

"Vito, come here," Joey called.

"What the fuck is it now?"

"Jimmy has a problem on the corner."

"I know, he's been arguing with that fat bitch since I came in here. She keeps giving him parking tickets."

"For what?"

"For anything, she got a hard on for him. Wherever the poor bastard parks, that gorilla tickets him."

Vito got up off of his chair and walked outside to join Joey. The two of them just stood there laughing. Jimmy was up in the heavyset black woman's face. In his right hand he had a bunch of unpaid fines. He just kept on berating her while she had her head down writing up another summons.

"Every fuckin' time I park my car I get another fuckin' ticket," he screamed. "If it's not the meter it's the fire hydrant. If it's not the hydrant, I'm too close to the corner. I got ten fuckin' tickets in the past two weeks. You fat bitch, you're making a living on me alone. I'll fix your fat fuckin' lard ass," he warned as he stormed away from the scene. "I'll fix your ass!" The nervous woman never said a word. She just went about her business like he was not even there. Her nonchalance made Jimmy even more aggravated and dangerously infuriated.

Jimmy started walking towards the pizzeria talking to himself. By this time the whole crew had arrived and they joined in as onlookers. Joey and Vito just looked totally entertained by this comical scene. To Jimmy it was not to funny at all, his face was beet red with anger. He just walked straight up the block and made a left hand turn up the driveway of the pizzeria.

"I'll fix her fuckin ass! I'll fix all their fuckin asses," he warned, talking to nobody but himself. "They want to fuck with me? Okay, now it's my turn to fuck them back."

That same night at around two o'clock in the morning, Jimmy got a hold of Bear and they walked up the block together. A couple of minutes later the Ford van pulled up with Ricky the Roach behind the wheel. One by one, they ripped down every parking meter on the left side of the block. One by one they threw the money machines into the back of the van. They were just equipped with a sledgehammer and Bear's brute strength. This was Jimmy's way of getting even with the meter maid and the city. To him this was better than spending a long day in court trying to beat the fines. Pleading guilty was out of the question, he was a part of Vito's gang. None of them were ever guilty; their actions were always justified with illogical reasons. Those reasons made sense to no one but themselves. Instead of being a little bit more careful on where he parked his car, Jimmy had to be pig headed. The streets were his, and he parked wherever he pleased without using any discretion at all. He didn't feel that he had to pay for something that belonged to him. His stubbornness defied reason. Putting a penny into the meter was even way too much.

Slowly but surely everything involving the pizzeria started to stabilize. Joey's Place seemed safer than a baby Pit Bull being nursed by his mother.

Even the rats seemed to disappear; it seems that the exterminator got tired of having them for lunch. The crew actually held the poor slob down and stuck a dead rat down his throat. The guy's life was on the line if another rat was ever seen running throughout the building. Like all other repairmen when visiting requires a fee, the exterminator just kept milking money from Joey. He was always doing something, but never doing enough. Vito would have none of that. Either the exterminator corrected the problem or his family would be dining on rat meat also. The problem was quickly rectified.

Eventually Manuel got his driver's license and was ready to motor. Joey gave him the blue Buick under no conditions for repayment, but one. Manuel had to be responsible for driving Orlando and Jorge to and from work every day. The proud pizza-man did not mind at all. He would have driven them to Guam if he had to. It was the jubilation of receiving his first car for nothing that made him happy. To most, it was nothing more than a second hand used car. But to Manuel, it was a Bentley.

Derek's life also started to change upon Vito's arrival. Every day the kid would come into the store right after school and do his homework. He always sat in the same booth in the back of the pizzeria. Joey was like his tutor, always giving additional help and remedial instructions on the little deficiencies that he may have had. Once in a while Vito and his crew had him running some local errands around the neighborhood. The dry cleaners, florist and the delicatessen around the corner were the extent of his small walks. Besides, it put a few bucks in the kid's pocket. Both of Derek's parents loved the idea that their only child was spending his afternoons with Joey. They felt safe knowing that their son was in good hands until they arrived home from their livelihoods. Little did they know that Joey's protection came from the most powerful organized crime family in the city.

Everything just seemed to be falling into place since Vito settled into the basement. Everyone felt safer as the pressures of intimidation seemed to subside. There were no visitors from the park venturing into the pizzeria. Even the stares coming from the recreational facility were at a minimum. Overall, things just seemed too quiet, too good to be true. It couldn't have been this easy; an Italian guy walks into a neighborhood and changes the chemistry and complexion of it? Or were the Brotherhood just biding their time and waiting for the right moment to continue their destructiveness? Whatever the case may be, everyone involved in the store enjoyed the newly found peace and quiet. But the gang across the street was still there doing their thing. Day in and day out, they were still there conducting their business as usual. It was only a matter of time before a major confrontation erupted. The Brotherhood knew it was coming and Vito would make sure that it did.

Joey and his small team of foreigners just chugged along the same grind. Business was not great, but it did seem to stabilize. Whatever funds were needed, Vito would fork over the cash. Little by little, all the minor problems were soon taken care of. The place was now starting to be run like a real business. The only problems were business related and related to the business only. Occasionally a screaming customer would be bitching about the food being too cold. Or sometimes an erroneous delivery would be sent out. But that was the extent of it; to Joey these problems were minor. Vito's presence made everything seem like it was heaven on earth. Every function of the restaurant was running smoothly and efficiently.

On paper the pizzeria was Joey's, lock stock and barrel. Vito was just a presence that never mingled in on the operations and decision making. But he was a silent partner; after all it was his twenty thousand and his name that brought everything to a head. Tony Salvo hopped on the money like a hungry waiter receiving his first tip. For him, he killed two birds with one stone. He recouped some of his losses and got rid of a major headache. But no matter how Tony felt about it, he really did not have a choice in the final decision. The offer was put on the table, take it or leave it. Either way he was going to lose the pizzeria. There was no negotiating, so Tony just took the money and bowed out peacefully. The two childhood buddies remained friends and spoke to each other on occasion. Joey still purchased all his provisions from Tony, but one thing stayed the same. Every product or item was given to Joey at cost. For Tony, there was no mark up, and he did not make a dime from Joey's account. Also, he had to make deliveries at least twice a week. Tony was a shrewd apple and businessman, but this was one force even the sharpest of minds could not conquer. Tony knew that Vito was calling all the shots, like it or not, he just ran with the program. These were all part of Vito's demands, nobody ever said they had to be fair.

Down in the basement was another story. One would never think that it was once a storage room for the pizzeria. The place had all the earmarks of a full staged gambling operation. There were four wooden desks that formed a square cube rubbing up against each other. Each desk had a pair of black phones with access to all the other lines. Twenty four hours a day, seven days a week, those phones were constantly ringing. A couple of feet away from the desks was a round card table where the boys amused themselves every once in a while. A good poker game always seemed to lighten up the atmosphere. It was their soothing tonic to eliminate some of the stress in their lives.

From horse racing to cricket, from soccer to tennis, anything where there was competition, they took bets. If there was any action in a bingo hall filled with all elderly people, the boys would take a bet on it. This was just one of the many businesses that were run from this small basement

There was a full-fledged operation above the green, commercial carpet that was installed. Six televisions were suspended from any available wall space. Each set was wired to the satellite dish on the roof of the building. The remote control gave them access to it all. Action was taken from all over the country. You name the racetrack and they took the bet. From first base to the fifty-yard line, the action was everywhere. It really didn't matter, when it came to money, every bet to be made was on their board. On occasion, Joey would see strangers going down the basement. These visitors would just be hired to answer the phone lines and take bets. From morning till night, all they did was take bets and relay the spreads.

Loan sharking and racketeering were just a few of the other businesses to add to Vito's impressive resume of organized crime. Their best clients were the degenerate gamblers who were in way over their heads. With bad credit and no assets, these morons had no credibility with any legitimate bank or lending institution. So to pay off their gambling debts, they would go right back to the same source that they were indebted to. But this time, the stakes were much higher. Broken limbs, death threats and even going to their jobs for payment was the price of failure. Whatever the means, if that method brought back results, the mob went with it. Vito and his crew did not care where the money came from, so long as their clients covered their lost wagers or borrowed money. A client would only be cut off when all possible ways of getting their money back had been exhausted. Some lowlifes would borrow a couple of thousand dollars and continue to pay the vig for the rest of their lives. Each week, the vig had to be paid no matter what the circumstances were. If you did not come up with the whole amount all at once, there was never an ending in sight. The higher the interest rates were on bank loans, the higher the vig was. In a way they sort of worked hand and hand with each other. Some losers would lose their jobs, their families and their reputations. But they would always come back for more.

This addiction called gambling did not travel through the bloodstream. This was an external addiction that had to do with the thrill of it all. There must be some sort of excitement when you lose all of your possessions and loved ones. But the excitement turns to fear when you have the mob on your heels for payment. They run, but there is no place to hide. The job, the wife, the kids...the addicted gambler is shunned by everyone. The only person they now know is their bookmaker and the bone-breaker. With the mob, you do not have to have good credit to do business with them. Your life was the only credit they needed. There were no such laws as bankruptcy or Chapter Eleven in their rule-book. The only way that they became insolvent was when they were in a casket and buried six feet under the ground. That was the only time an addicted gambler was safe. The more they gambled the deeper they got. I guess you call it digging your own grave. But this digging did not require a shovel - pure stupidity and irrational thinking broke up the earth. All it took was a little shove to push them into this self made hole.

Chapter 17

WINTER SLOWLY PASSED and a new season appeared. The temperatures started to finally rise, leaving an unforgettable winter in its memory. Cold weather, death, destruction and a love that seemed lost were Joey's miserable reminders of the past few months. Maybe the changing of seasons would blow in much calmer winds.

Almost a whole month had gone by and Joey had not heard from Gloria. Not a minute went by that he was not thinking about her. His phone calls to her job were screened and were repeatedly ignored. At home it was no different; her answering machine did all of her dirty work. Many days had gone by with Joey thinking and wondering what would it take to win her back. Maybe a visit to her home? How about a surprise appearance at her place of business? Chocolates, flowers and his many apologizing phone calls were just not getting it done. It was time for more drastic measures; it was time for some real romance.

One Wednesday evening at around closing time, Joey reached for a pen and a writing pad. He walked over to the front door and locked it from the inside. Sitting down thinking, he started to write some sayings that he never thought he was capable of. For two straight hours he hammered away trying to put something from the heart together. Time and time again, nothing was making any sense. The meaning was there, but not to his liking. The tiled floor became littered with paper. Over and over again he tried. The persistent Italian worked diligently until the words from his heart were starting to take shape and make some sort of sense. Never in his life had he ever resorted to these desperate measures. But never in his life had he ever been in love like this. If this didn't work, then he was out of options. He would have to put her behind him and move on.

This was not a five or ten-year relationship, but it was love. There were no photo albums or any other special things of remembrance. Just the vivid memory of her beautiful face and caring ways evoked these lifelike images in Joey's brain. Everything he touched reminded him of her. Every time the phone rang he was praying that it was her voice on the other end of the line. It got so bad that even the women walking in the street started to look like her. Many times he would take a peek outside the store hoping that she would be heading up the block to see him. Once in a while he would drive by her house to see if she was at home. The one thing that he feared was that the love of his life had found someone else. So visits down her tree lined block, were very infrequent. It would have killed him to see her in the arms of another man. Rejection was not a very good attribute of his; he would rather wait and hope.

Joey finally finished his work of art. He picked up the completed version and held it in his hand to read it. There weren't any big words where a dictionary would be needed. His words were short, but right to the point. Nodding with approval, he felt that he finally had gotten it right. Her face came before him as he pictured her reading his words.

That same night, Joey sat behind the wheel as he and Vito were heading home. Vito was in a very talkative mood, but his driver wanted no part of it. Always the one who could spot when something was wrong, Vito just looked at his Godson shaking his head. He had seen Joey's mood swings many times, so to him this was nothing new.

"Alright, want to tell me about it?" Vito asked, now staring at the envelope that Joey placed on top of the dashboard.

"Tell you about what?"

"Tell me about what the hell is bothering you. You're not a hard guy to figure out, kid. So come on, let's have it."

"It's nothing."

"It's about the broad, isn't it?"

"No."

"Don't lie to me," Vito said, getting a little annoyed with Joey's short choppy answers. "I see the envelope over there with her name on it."

"Yea, she just don't seem to want any part of me. I guess my actions just scared the shit out of her. In a way, I don't blame her."

"Women are funny, they can turn their fuckin' emotions on and off like a light bulb. When that switch goes off they can just disappear like they never existed at all. It's amazing," he went on. "They can wake up one morning like they never knew who the fuck you even were."

"I thought we had something a little bit stronger than that. I guess I was wrong," Joey said, never taking his eyes off the road. "I guess I was dead wrong!"

"Listen Joey, don't do too much chasing. If she really cares, she will come back to you. If she doesn't, well then you know that her love was not that strong. Besides, what the fuck did you do? You didn't lay a hand on that prick, I did."

"I know, but I swore I would never go back there."

"Like I said before, if she loves you, she will be back. You didn't do nothing to deserve this kind of treatment. You were just defending your own ass and dignity. Now everybody knows who the fuck you are and what the price is for fuckin' with you."

"I guess you're right."

"No more!" Vito screamed, looking straight into Joey's eyes. "From now on we will deliver the pain. When somebody rings our bell, we will answer in the only way that we know how. There are no more free rides for anyone. The fuckin' party around here is all over."

"I hope you're right."

"Don't hope, just believe. You know sometimes its funny how things can happen."

"What do you mean?" Joey said, turning left.

"I mean, this guy Ramon living across the street from her sister and all. That guy set it all up to pull you two apart, and it worked. All the odds were stacked up against you."

"Maybe, but when we went back the second time, that was the straw that broke the camel's back."

"So what are you supposed to," Vito asked, "get beat out of money and have your worker slapped around? Then you go there to get what belongs to you and you get the shit kicked out of ya. So what are you supposed to do, nothing? If you would of acted like a pussy they would have laughed your ass right out of the neighborhood. You defended your rights and honor. You have nothing to be ashamed of. When she comes to terms with this, she will come back to you. If she don't, then you are better off without her."

"She just thinks that I took it too far."

"That's because she was not the one taking the beating."

"Whatever, Vito. All I know is that I miss her badly. I don't know what the fuck to think anymore. To make matters worse, I don't even think she knows that I went back to Ramon's with you."

"Well who the fuck does she think that you went back there with, Popeye the Sailor?"

"She knows about you, but I don't think she knows that you're here with me now."

"Whether she likes the fact that I am with you or not, it's too fuckin' bad. I'm here and I 'm gonna stay here until I say that it's time to go. And when I go, you're comin' with me! Do you hear me?" Vito said, looking right at Joey waiting for an answer. To Vito there was no way that any woman was going to pull them apart. No matter how much Joey was hurting, he was not going anywhere.

"You're right, Vito, the hell with it. And if she feels that way about you, the hell with her. But I will mail this letter and give her the benefit of the doubt."

"Joey, I could give two shits if this broad likes me or not. I just want to see you happy."

"I really don't know how the fuck she feels about you. But judging by my actions and how she felt about them, I have a feeling that she's gonna hate your fuckin' guts." Joey then started to bust out laughing and Vito soon joined in. The sharp looking gangster then lightly slapped Joey on the back of the head. Vito slid his left hand and rested it on top of Joey's shoulder. Joey was now Vito's son, and would have it no other way.

The car finally pulled to Vito's Colonial style home in the Dyker Heights section of Brooklyn. Vito reached for a cigarette from his suit jacket and pushed in the cigarette lighter of the car. Never taking his hand off of the lighter, he impatiently waited for it to pop out.

"Listen, tomorrow I want you to pick me up a little early," Vito ordered, talking with the unlit cigarette in his mouth. "I got a couple of tables and chairs that are being sent over to the store."

"Table and chairs for what?" Joey said, wondering what he was up to now.

"For the outside of the pizzeria, the weather is getting nice. People might want to sit outside while they eat their pizza."

"Oh yea, this way they can take in the sights of Disney-Land across the street. Should I hire a waitress and start taking reservations?"

"Don't be a fuckin' wise ass. I might want to sit outside once in a while myself. And I'll bet ya a grand that before we leave that neighborhood for good, those tables will be full of people eating their lunch," he said, finally lighting that long awaited cigarette. "Do I have a bet?"

"It's a bet," Joey said. Then he extended his hand to make it official. The two men shook hands as Vito was about to step out of the dark four door sedan. He finally exited the car and poked his head back into the opened door.

"I'll see you about eight thirty."

"Alright, eight thirty sharp."

"Are you alright?"

"Yea, I'm fine, don't worry about me, I'm okay."

"You want to stay over and talk for a while?"

"Nah, I'm just gonna go home and go to bed."

"Don't worry, everything will turn out fine. You're a good man, and she knows that. You're a little rough around the edges, but that's nothing. Jesus Christ, she could be going out with a guy like me. Then what would she do?"

"Commit suicide!" Joey said, with a smile. "Who the fuck could live with you?"

Vito laughed, and then slammed the car door shut. He flicked his cigarette to the curb and headed up the driveway to his home. Joey waited a couple of minutes until Vito entered his home safely. He slowly drove off looking for the nearest mailbox.

Vito's home was magnificent. This five bedroom Colonial style home was overpowering in looks and style. There were two columns that ran up both sides of the mahogany door that was decorated in brass. The columns gave some support to a balcony that hung overhead. This awesome brick structure overlooked a sprawling circular driveway. The landscaping alone was something to be proud of. The manicured lawn all the way to the expensive shrubbery was stunning.

Nine o'clock sharp an 18-foot truck pulled up to the front of the pizzeria. The driver kept honking on his horn until Vito came outside to greet him. Vito went over to the driver and exchanged some words and of course some money. Another man exited from the truck and went around to the rear and pushed up the back door. They quickly started to unload Vito's delivery of patio furniture.

"Put one table here and the other one right next to it," said Vito. The driver and his sidekick quickly obeyed his orders. Then they placed the eight chairs onto the concrete sidewalk. There were four chairs to each table. Then the moment of truth had arrived. Out of two long narrow boxes Vito removed two umbrellas that would be placed in the center of both tables. But there was something different about these umbrellas. Both of them adorned the colors of red, green and white, the colors of the Italian flag.

Vito himself had to be the one to have the honors of standing and opening the umbrellas up. He placed his hand on the bottom of the pole and slid the pole through the little round opening on top of the metal table. Now fastening the pole to the heavy weight underneath the table, he was ready to open it. Vito placed both hands on the collapsible frame and pushed up until the umbrella was in full bloom. The same process was repeated with the other table. He took a few steps back to admire his work. For some reason, Joey had a notion that these two tables with their colorful umbrellas, were not there for protection from the sun and rain. Vito and his devious mind were trying to send a message. The people working the morning shift in the park across the street seemed to get it. Vito kept looking in their direction making sure that they did.

"Look at this, Joey, it makes the whole place look better. Now all we need is some Italian music!" Vito said, being very serious about his latest idea.

"Where the fuck do you think you are, in Little Italy?" Joey asked, knowing that Vito was going to upset a lot of people on the block. Joey was never so right, the mischievous locals could attest to that. They had a major problem with some Italian guy coming in and staking a claim on their territory.

"This is nothing, this afternoon I am running these same colors from this telephone pole all the way across the street to that light pole."

"Oh God help me," Joey said.

Later on that afternoon Vito kept his promise. Two more men with ladders and the same colors ran the streamers to three connecting poles. Two of the telephone poles were on the same side of the pizzeria about forty feet apart. The other pole was across the street by the park. The triangle shaped decoration looked pretty good, as it definitely added some personality to the block. Except these colors were not the colors that the neighbors had in mind. To them there seemed to be a slight discrepancy with one of the colors. The red and green streamers were okay. It was the other color that stirred all the commotion. That color separated the cultures of two very proud ways of life. That other color was black.

Vito, Dutch and Bear were going to have some lunch outside the store on this bright and sunny day. They mostly talked business as they were waiting for their sandwiches. Vito was sipping on an espresso spiked with anisette, while the other two drank sodas. Dutch sat slouched in his chair, while chewing on a toothpick. Even though the weather was only in the sixties, Bear was exposing his whole upper body. How he fit into his sleeveless undershirt was a mystery. Breathing alone had to be tough; the tee shirt looked like it was choking him. Vito as always was the fashion plate of the crew. His olive green double-breasted suit was tailor made to fit his body perfectly. The natural tan on his face alone signified a man with class. Not a stitch on his clothes or a hair on his head was out of place.

It didn't take too long for things to heat up a little bit. Vito and the rest of his crew were involved in an angry stare down with the guys in the park. For almost an hour, they just sat around the table and focused on all the activities across the street. But no one said a word - then again, nobody had to. Both sides knew where and what the other was all about. In was just a matter of time before they would all start to mingle and find out a little more about each other.

"Son of a bitches," Bear fumed. "Look at em, a bunch of fuckin' degenerates. Let's go across the street right now and clean that fuckin' park out. Let's kill them all, Vito!"

"Fuck those guys," Vito said. "They know that we're gonna be breathing down their necks soon."

"The sooner the better," Dutch said. "I can't stomach lookin' at em any longer."

"Don't let them spoil your appetite," Vito said. "Here comes our lunch!"

"Shrimp Parmesan?" Jorge asked, holding three plates in his hands.

"Over here," Dutch said, putting his hand out for the sandwich.

"Chicken cutlet, lettuce and tomato?" Jorge asked again, while Bear reached across the table for his hearty looking sandwich.

Jorge placed the last sandwich in front of Vito. The three men started to have their lunch. This was not the French Riviera or even the boardwalk at Atlantic City. But it was the best this pizzeria had looked in years. Just the few repairs and certain changes that Vito made added a big difference to the appearance of the place. Everyone seemed to notice, even the residents who dared to venture outdoors.

Dutch grabbed his sandwich by both hands and started to take his first bite. Out of the corner of his eye he noticed a black limousine slowly making its way up the block. Dutch pulled the sandwich away from his opened mouth and signaled to Vito. "Vito get a load of this!" he said, as Vito picked his head up to see what was going on. "You're not expecting anyone are you?"

"I got a doctor's appointment but I don't think he makes house calls in this neighborhood," Vito joked.

"For some reason," Dutch shot back, "I don't think your doctor is in that fuckin' car."

The luxury car stopped at the fire hydrant right in front of the store. It stood motionless for about thirty seconds with its motor running. The limo looked like a Preppie in a hobo camp. Vito and his men stood poised and ready to accommodate whatever the visitors had in mind.

From inside the store, Joey saw the long black vehicle and quickly walked to the front door. He slowly opened the glass door and saw Dutch's right hand slip into his belt, exposing his revolver. Dutch just sat there motionless, waiting for some sort of movement coming from inside the car.

"Joey, get back inside," Vito said to him, without turning his head. "There's nobody in that car coming to see you!"

Joey obeyed his orders and closed the front door, but stayed stationed right behind it. To nobody's surprise the black tinted window of the limo started to slowly open. The face behind the now opened window was only familiar to Joey. For a good minute, nobody said a word to each other, and then it happened.

"You got a fuckin' problem?" Bear said, quickly rising to his feet. "You don't want any of this, pal."

"Stay, don't move," Vito said to Bear, placing his hand around the big man's wrist. "Be patient."

"I just wanted to say how nice you decorated the place," the visitor said. "It brings out a nice homey feeling."

"We're so happy that you approve," Bear said, as his veins were popping out of his thick neck. "You said what you had to say, now get the hell out of here."

"Hey, motherfucker, this is my hood. Don't go pushing your shit on me, big man. I make the rules around here."

"Not anymore you don't; there's a new Mayor in this town. Your rules mean dog shit to us. You want to find out what we do to dog shit like you?" Bear threatened, while Vito and Dutch sat quietly enjoying the verbal exchange. "Get out of the car, fuck face!"

"Hey big man, you want to get down?" the unwelcome visitor said to Bear. "Then come and get some."

Bear just sat there and was still being put in check by Vito. To Vito this was not the time and place for a gang war. Dutch, knowing the way Vito operated, knew it too. Bear had a hard time accepting the lasso that Vito had placed around his neck. The invitation to break this guy in half was mighty appetizing to him.

"I thought so, man," the black man in the car said. "I thought so."

"You thought what?" Bear retaliated. "You're too fuckin' stupid to think."

"We will see when it all goes down. In time, my brother, it will all go down."

"When it goes down, that's when me and you will dance," warned Bear. "And I'm not such a good dancing partner. I might get your shoes dirty."

"That's right, big man, we will dance. But we will be dancing to my music."

"Vito," Bear said. "Let me pull this motherfucker out of the car and beat his black ass."

"Not now, relax," Vito ordered. "Not now."

"Vito, this fuckin' clown has no idea who the fuck you are," Dutch whispered. "He's clueless."

"That's good, Dutch, cause when I kill him it will just make things a little easier for me."

Joey had seen and heard enough. He shot through the front door. At that moment, he and the black man locked eyes for the second time. Suddenly Joey turned to Vito and offered his advice. "Vito," Joey said loudly. "This guy's name is Julius. Him and two other guys are the ones that shot up the store and demanded money from me."

"Pleased to meet you, Julius," Vito said.

"Like wise," Julius answered, laughing as he started to raise his back seat window. "I'm a couple of weeks behind on my pickup. I will send somebody in for the money. Maybe I'll just stop by for another slice of pizza myself. It's good pizza!"

"Any time, pal," Vito said. "This front door is always open for you. But the next time you won't be so lucky."

"Is that so, old man?"

"Yea, that's so. The next time you won't be leaving the fuckin' store alive," he threatened, with his hand covering the handle on his revolver.

Julius cracked a small smile. The power window of the limo hissed as his face disappeared behind the tinted glass. The car slowly took off down the street. Vito and the rest of the crew angrily watched without saying another word. Bear just sat there with a stunned look on his face. The hulking man was in a rage that he let this guy talk to him that way. Dutch just sat there smiling and eating the whole time, he knew that this was nothing to get excited about. To the man with the brass balls, he knew that one day he would have a rendezvous with this character named Julius.

"Vito, why didn't you let me break his fuckin' neck?" Bear said, glowering at Vito.

"Because, this has to be done diplomatically," Vito quietly said. "It has to be done slowly and very, very carefully."

"How?" Bear asked.

"By cutting their balls off," Dutch characteristically said.

"We will cut them off where they breathe," added Vito. "Once they feel smothered, then and only then, we will go in for the kill. We won't stop until every single one of those motherfuckers is off of that corner."

"What do you mean where they breathe?" a bewildered Bear asked, looking at Vito and Dutch for an explanation.

"Dutch," Vito said, looking at his right hand man. "Do me the honors and explain all of this to him. I want to finish my lunch before I lose my appetite."

Still chewing on his shrimp Parmesan hero, Dutch grabbed a napkin and wiped the red sauce from his mouth. "We're gonna cut off their drug supply and cripple them right where it hurts," Dutch said.

"Where's that?" a clueless Bear asked.

"Right in their pocketbooks," Dutch said. "When there is no more drugs, there is no more traffic. When there is no more traffic, there is no more business. Then one by one, we will hunt them down until they get the message."

"Who are they?"

"We already know who runs this operation. His name is Desmond Hammons. His women call him Desi," Dutch added, while stopping a second to take a sip from his soda cup. "To his gang members and associates, they call him Steamer."

"Who the fuck is this guy Julius?"

"He just runs the streets for Steamer. Steamer knows who we are, but this guy Julius does not have a clue. Steamer has no idea that we are here. But soon they will all know that we mean fuckin' business."

"Vito, why don't we just pack up and get the fuck out of here!" Joey chimed in. "At first I wanted to stick it out, but now I had enough of this place."

"So why didn't you leave before we got here?"

"Every time I want to leave, something just keeps me here. I can't explain it, it's like someone is holding me down and not letting go."

"You're sure it ain't Gloria?" Vito said, looking up at Joey.

"No, it's something deeper than that. It's something that I just can't explain," he said, as an unexpected and abrupt chill just ran through his body. "I just want to get the hell out of this neighborhood!"

"Why?"

"Because I'm afraid!" Joey screamed. "And I'm not embarrassed to say it either."

"Afraid of them?" Vito asked him, pointing into the park.

"Fuck them! It's much more than that."

Joey then looked down at the medallion and started to wonder if it had anything to do with all of this. After all, it was only after Vito put it around his neck that he started to experience all these weird occurrences. But he was not about to tell Vito anything about them.

"Well, whatever this shit is that you're talking about. Me and Dutch have some long standing and personal issues to resolve with Steamer," he said. "When the smoke finally clears, we will all pack our bags and get the hell out of here."

"What issues? What are you going to do, kill him?" Joey asked, picking up Vito's empty cup of espresso.

"No, probably not," Vito said. "That would cause too many problems, it has too many ramifications. But we are going to destroy his business."

"I know you're not doing this just for me," Joey said. "Why then?"

"You're part of the reason, the other reason has to do with Dutch. How do you think this guy got the name Steamer?"

"I don't know."

"He shot three guys in a steam room over the control of this park right here," Vito said, pointing across the street. "One of those guys was Dutch's cousin, Danny. As kids we all hung out together, so to me it's a little personal also."

"Are you kidding me?"

"No," Vito said. "I'm not kidding you, but that's all you need to know. But I will tell you one thing, it is kind of weird how all of this shit came together. I mean you, me, Dutch and all this other crap. It seems like there is someone out there putting all of these little pieces together. In a way Joey, you're right!"

"I know," said Joey. "It's weird, I wish I could explain it."

"Sometimes there are no explanations," Dutch offered. "But one thing is for sure! We are going to give this park back to the people in this neighborhood."

"Why is this park so important to you guys?"

"Because when we were kids, me and Vito used to hop the train while we were playing hooky from school. Danny and the both of us spent many days in there just fuckin' around and having fun. Danny never left the neighborhood after his mother died. He died trying to defend this park from all these scumbags who now occupy it."

"Oh shit, Dutch," Joey said. "I'm sorry. But who were the other two guys in that steam room?"

"They were just there, they were nobody to Danny. They just happened to be at the wrong place at the wrong time. It's because of you, kid, that we're here. But it's so ironic that you are right across the street from this park."

"Where did Danny live?"

"Up the block, his address was 248 Saint Ann's Place," Dutch said, sliding his plate to the center of the table. "When Vito let me hear his voice mail with you calling for help, I almost fell off of my fuckin' chair."

"How long ago did this happen to Danny?" Joey asked, continuing his barrage of questions. Bear just sat there in silence.

"About eight years ago. Danny moved back in with his mother after he got divorced. There were only a few white families left on the block at that time. A couple of years later his mother died and left him the house. Then he got shot and killed, and the house was left to the State. He had no will, or any existing relatives. So the house went into probate for a while and fell into the hands of the State."

"What about you?"

"I was rotting away in jail at the time. As far as they were concerned I did not even exist. In the State's eyes I was as good as dead."

"Can you get the house back?"

"Nah, it's a dead issue. Who the fuck wants it anyway." Dutch then looked across the street and into the park. His mind had obviously drifted back to his youth. After a minute or two he started shaking his head in disbelief. He returned his focus to Joey. "You know what they call this park?"

"Yea, Dead Man's park."

"How did you know that?"

"Some old man who lives on the block told me."

"Well the park got that name after they killed Danny. He died defending that park from all these fuckin' dope dealers. This used to be a lively block, look at it now. It looks like a morgue, there's not a person on the streets. It's time for things to change around here. And it's going to change, we're gonna do it for you and Danny. But most of all, it's going to happen for the people in this neighborhood. Coming back here was always in the back of my mind. Now I'm here and fate has brought me back. It's time to take care of business."

"How come the cops never arrested Steamer for killing your cousin?"

"Oh, they arrested him, but he beat the rap. It seems there was not enough evidence to put him away," Dutch said, rolling the toothpick around in his mouth. "To this day, the case is still open. They know that it was him that murdered Danny. Someday, when I had enough of this fuckin' business, I will kill him myself. Out of respect for this man," he said pointing to Vito, "for now, I keep my distance from him. But there will come a time when this damn earth will swallow one of us up. Mark my words, kid," he warned. "I want that motherfucker real bad. I will kill him."

You had to take Dutch's words very seriously, even though many years had passed after Danny's death. The memories of his cousin were still fresh and the wounds were deep. In his youth he had spent a lot of time with Danny. Together the pair happily frolicked the streets of Crown Heights. He spent many a weekend sleeping over Danny's house with his Aunt Peggy. His ties ran pretty deep with emotions when it comes to St. Ann's place. Not to mention the animosity and anger that brought him back here to seek his revenge.

For Vito it was just a matter of helping his buddy out after many, many years of loyal friendship. After all, all he really had to do was just grab Joey and drag his ass out of this cesspool. But Vito would never forget the day that Dutch saved him and his son Eddie's life. He was forever grateful for that one colossal deed.

Using their powerful connections, Vito and Dutch started their drug embargo against Steamer. Every supplier in the Tri-State area was cut out of his reach. Whatever he had in stock was basically all the drugs left in his dwindling supply. Within a matter of weeks, Steamer could not even buy a dime bag of weed off of a hungry crack head. He was basically being squeezed out of the business by the balls. The harder Vito squeezed, the louder Steamer was heard screaming. Even his so called friends and other drug traffickers shunned him. To other dealers, this guy was poison, associating with him would only bring about trouble.

The other street dealers who were once his competition were rejoicing. They had nothing to complain about because all of Steamer's clientele were running to them. To them, Vito was the Second Coming of Jesus Christ. Sales and profits were up big time, there was no reason to complain or help

Steamer out. If they did, they would be hit with the same deadly wrath. The word was out and everyone was abiding by it. If they didn't, the welfare line was just a couple of weeks away.

Even the traffic inside and outside the park was definitely lighter. Right from the start of this prohibition, you could see the stunning effects. Day by passing day, the thugs and society's unwanted seemed to be disappearing. People would drive up for their usual prescriptions, only to be turned away or sent to another part of town. The addicts who used their feet for transportation finally started to realize that the park was not worth the journey any longer. The demand was there, but the supply ships just could not make it through the enormous blockade. On a busy night, Steamer used to have eight dealers working the park alone, he was now down to one or two. A week after that, there were none, they were all gone. There was not a drug dealer in sight. If there was, they were quickly escorted off the corner by Vito and his crew. The dealers had a choice to leave peacefully or die with the dwindling dime bags of crack cocaine still in their hungry pockets.

Everyone in the neighborhood noticed the difference, but the residents were still leery. They did not know what to expect, or for that matter what was going on. But whatever was happening, the good residents of the neighborhood were feeling it. Little by little, they started to unlock their doors and venture outside. What started as a peek behind the steel caged windows soon became a full bloom appearance. Even the breathing around this fearful community seemed to get ingested a little easier, the density disappeared. Everyone now felt that the large, dark cloud which had been smothering them for years had finally been lifted. The once repugnant air smelled cleaner, for the stench coming from the park appeared to be gone.

One evening, a late model BMW pulled over by the park and Julius exited the vehicle. He looked at the once thriving business and shook his head with anger. Then his eyes slowly turned in the direction of the pizzeria. To him it looked like there was some kind of party going on inside the store. He noticed people coming and going and a different ambiance to the once ghost town of a neighborhood. The change was that drastic, that even he had to do a double take. It suddenly occurred to him that it was all over, Steamer and his boys had lost their dominance over the park. More important than that, they had lost whatever rule they once had over this impoverished neighborhood. The people and Vito's crew had taken back control of the predominantly black community. For Julius, it was time for him to call Steamer and raise the white flag. His drug business was dead and by the looks of it, would never be awakened again. The masterful run was a very lucrative and profitable one, but like all other good things, it came to a sudden end. The power of command had now shifted hands. The jurisdiction was now in the hands of a couple of vengeful characters from yesteryear. There was no way that anybody was going to try and buck their authority. The Game started the day Vito and Dutch returned to this freedom-starved neighborhood. It ended just a few months later.

Julius ran across the street, while dodging a few cars. He settled upon a pay phone to call up his employer. Constantly looking in the direction of the restaurant, he started to make that dreaded phone call.

"What's up," the deep sounding voice said.

"It's me Julius!"

"Was up?"

"Listen man, it's over," a dejected Julius declared. "In a little more than a couple of weeks that motherfucker put your fat ass out of business."

"It's time to abandon ship, man," Steamer admitted. "Sooner or later we will work ourselves back in there. That fuckin' dude can't stay there forever, and he knows that."

"Steamer, listen man, I don't know why this Carlucci guy got it in for you. But it seems to me that you just fucked around with the wrong Italian! Let me tell you," said Julius, putting another dime into the phone company's pocket, "it all started as soon as that kid opened up that pizzeria."

"It goes back further than that, Julius. He got some Irish prick with him named Dutch. Way back I filled his cousin's ass with lead, so that lily white prick has it in for me too. How the fuck was I supposed to know that the kid running the pizzeria knew those two motherfuckers?"

"Well, whatever man," Julius said. "It's too late to start dwelling on all this shit. It's all over, man."

"Is it?" Steamer asked, never thinking that anything was over. "Nothin's over!"

"What do you mean it ain't over?" Julius asked, noticing a big man right across the street sizing him up. "There's nothing here, man! This place is fuckin' dead. We don't want any part of Carlucci; he's too big, man. He'll destroy us, Steamer. We still have the other locations."

"I know, but I got a plan that's gonna eat Carlucci up from the inside out. I'm gonna hit him where he least expects it. We're gonna hit him close to home, Julius. There's some shit I know about him," Steamer warned. "And what I have in mind is gonna stick him right in the fuckin' heart. Our business over there might be dead, but what he is doin' to us is gonna cost him big time."

"What is it, man?" a bewildered Julius asked, still with his eyes fixed across the street. "What do you got on your mind?"

"Get your ass over here, there's work to do!"

"I'll be there on a dime." Quickly hanging up the phone, Julius started to scamper across the street en-route to meet Steamer. About ten minutes was all it would take for him to listen to this ingenious plan that his boss had in mind. Whatever the plan was, Steamer was never in doubt that it would not work.

This was not the only location that Steamer controlled that was hurting. But because of this park, he was dying all over. He had two easy choices to make. Either abort his once profitable business on Saint Ann's Place or be completely run out of the market of selling drugs. This was a hard pill for Steamer to swallow, but he knew that he was a beaten man. Going up against Vito Carlucci and the powerful Italian Mafia was more than he could handle. Any defiance from Steamer would be disastrous for him.

If it were up to Dutch, he would rather just chop off Steamer's head and call it a day. But that solution had too many implications for Vito to burden himself with. After all, when operating at full tilt, Steamer was quite the earner. He put a lot of food on many dinner tables. For Steamer to be taken out of the picture completely would hurt a lot of people. Some of the people were even business associates of Vito. But if Steamer did not play by the set of instructions that were given him, it might leave Vito no other choice. Vito just wanted him to abandon the park and leave the terrified community forever. Steamer had to make a vow never to relocate here or any place near it. Disobeying that vow would mean his downfall or possibly his death.

Seeing his drug business slowly dying, Steamer quickly started to pick up and intensify his extortion activities. But Vito was one step ahead of him at all times. Every merchant in the neighborhood was paid a visit from the Italian family. From seventy to seventy-five fed up proprietors, they were all offered Vito's services for free. In return Vito was given the time and day that Steamer's boys would pay them a visit. Just to make sure that he had the manpower; Vito imported another twenty family members to Crown

Heights. This small army would make sure that the protection was secure. Each was armed and ready for combat. This area had not seen such an infiltration of Italian men since the 1920s. The whole neighborhood was set for a bloody gang war.

For the merchants there was just one small hitch involved for protection. Each one of them had to do business with Joey's pizzeria. Whether they lived in the neighborhood or not, this was an offer they could not refuse. Besides, by ordering pizza, sandwiches or pasta dishes, they were still getting something back for their money. Nobody seemed to complain, because the food was very good. But like every thing else in this world, you get nothing for nothing. Everything worth something had a price tag that you must pay for in return.

One by one, Steamer's crew of extortionists were tracked down and severely beaten. From sunup to sundown the streets became a bloody battlefield of open warfare. Dutch led the way as they followed the shake down artists into each place of business. Day after day, they were stalked and ruthlessly attacked by the thirsty mercenaries. Idle threats were followed up by beatings to the once powerful ghetto gangsters. Many times Steamer's boys were seen leaving businesses with blood pouring from their battered bodies. Some were even thrown to the curb while still unconscious. Store owners watched in horror as racks of food and beverages were turned upside down from all the violence. From flowers to laundry, depending upon the nature of the business, it was not a pretty sight. Occasionally there was some serious gunplay, but the victims were never seen. After business hours they were shrewdly carried out a back door and dumped into a waiting van. Mostly, a bullet in the leg or arm would suffice. Vito had the enemy running scared all over the neighborhood. The Mafia used any tactic that they had to, as long as they got their hard driven point across.

Steamer's crew was mostly just a bunch of gophers not hardened criminals. They were not highly trained thugs; most of them just lived off of the reputation of their employer. The smart ones just ran for their lives, never to return. The ones who suffered some sort of learning disabilities bore the brunt of the violence. To the ones who got away, a return visit by one of these pretenders would spell out death. There were no second chances given, just one warning and one warning only. Some of the defiant ones just needed to be dealt with a little more severely.

There still were a couple of dangerous guys out there, and Julius was one of them. Defeat went down a little harder for him; after all, he was one of Steamer's best. Besides Steamer, Julius took the hardest hit when it came down to dollars and cents. But the two men both had something in common. Both of them had two names written across their tombstones whether they died or not.

Part of Steamer's misfortunes was that he had a psychopathic Westie after him, hungry for revenge. Dutch was one man who Vito could not control at all. His twisted and sick mind could snap at any moment and revenge would soon be his.

For Joey, business was never better. Besides the local merchants and Vito's enlarged crew ordering food, a lot of different residents started to do the same thing. From lunchtime way past the dinner bell, the place was rocking and rolling. The cash register turned out to be a non-stop money machine. Money and food were going in and out of the place at an uncontrollable rate. From sunup to sundown, the action never stopped. Joey's crew never worked so hard, but it was all well worth it to them. Those guys had seen it all, from the best and worst of times. For Joey and his dedicated unit, the past seemed like it was all behind them now. Each one of them would be rewarded handsomely for their courage and dedication towards Joey and the business. Even Vito greatly admired them for the tenacity and the will and desire that they displayed. Joey just wished that Marco and little Steven were around to see and enjoy all the incredible changes that had taken place. After all, it was those two who were responsible for all this good fortune. Their untimely deaths just paved the way for Vito and Dutch to arrive on the scene. Unfortunately they had to lose their young lives for these events to occur. Somewhere in the heavens above, Joey would sometimes wonder if both of their smiling faces were looking down on him. He constantly saw their facial expressions in front of him. Somewhere up above, Joey had a strong inclination that that those two were watching his every move. Joey knew for a fact that Marco and little Steven were dancing on the doorstep of heaven. How could they not dance, some of this revenge belonged to them.

People from all over who were never seen before started to show their faces. It was like night and day, the difference was amazing. No more extortion, no more intimidation, no more hatred and racism. Every tactic used for fear by the Brotherhood was all but forgotten. House by house and block by block, everyone started to see the light as their restraints were slowly released. From dawn to dusk, the whole neighborhood was starting to venture towards the freedoms that were rightfully theirs.

People were starting to take pride in being alive. To be reborn after many years of captivity was ever so inspiring to them. From young school kids to senior citizens, everyone was breathing much easier. Pedestrians were walking the streets again without fear. Mothers pushed infants in the strollers that were never used before. Every business in the area was thriving, each one supporting the other. It was like a new community that was constructed overnight.

It actually got to a point where customers were buying food and sitting in the park across the street to eat it. Wherever they could find a seat they sat, it did not matter if the park was run down and filthy. They just enjoyed the fact that they had their park back again. Even a hot dog vender set up shop right by the opening of the park. Small lunch crowds would form a circle around his colorful umbrella. People now started to have a choice about how they lived their lives. They dictated to life now, instead of having life dictate to them. Vito was right all along when he said that before long, people would be sitting outside at his table and chairs. Every afternoon there was a not an empty chair in sight. The delighted customers even enjoyed the Italian music blurting out of the outdoor speaker system.

For everyone in the neighborhood, there was only one thing left to see. Children utilizing the facilities that were once called a playground. For this to happen there would have to be major renovation and an infusion of money. Thugs and drug dealers had destroyed all the amenities that a crowded playground should have. From the teeter totter to the swings, everything was in shambles. This dream would take time, but with Dutch and Vito behind it, this dream would come true.

Dutch put together a "save the park" program and everyone was a part of it. Money started to come in from all over town. Vito used his tremendous power and influence to get nice contributions and donations from everywhere. Everyone from union officials to illegal aliens was anteing up into the kitty. This program would take a while to complete, but unless the world came to a sudden end it would be completed. A new name was also going to be given to the resurrected park. The name symbolized the turnaround of the once terrified neighborhood. "Victory Park" would soon be hanging bold letters signifying its name above the front gate. The new park would be under constant supervision. It would open at 7:00 in the morning and close at 9 p.m. The heavy steel gates that were already there would finally be utilized.

Chapter 18

FOR SEVEN DAYS a week and fourteen hours a day, Joey and his crew busted their tails. Business was up one hundred and fifty percent. The pizzeria was now opened every day at ten o'clock and sometimes the doors would not close until after midnight. Orlando, Manuel and Jorge had found a new home away from home. They did not seem to mind the long tough hours. Money talks and they were making it.

The only addition to the crew was Derek, who became the local delivery boy. Any delivery within a block or two of the pizzeria was his to make. The longer trips were given to Jorge and his bicycle. Everyone's confidence was at an all time high. There was not a chance in the world of anything bad happening ever again. The word was out that Joey's Place had protection and everyone seemed to abide by that word. Unless you lived on Mars, you knew that this place was off limits to all kinds of thievery or robberies. The wrongdoers would be hunted down and pay for all of their evil acts. The ironic thing was that the customers felt safer than anyone else. They knew the setup and to them it was like a breath of fresh air.

It was eleven forty five one Thursday evening. Joey was sitting in a booth counting the receipts for the day. Money was all over the table as he was trying to balance the cash drawer to the register's final tally. This was a daily chore, but as the business grew the balancing got tougher and tougher. Months ago when the activity was so light, it was a simple matter to tally up for the day. But now with three people who constantly had their hands in the register, things became a little bit more complicated. As the expenses grew, so did the meticulous ways of running a thriving business. Joey's Wall Street experience came in handy when it came to balancing numbers, but when the money was not there, no magic or brain power could make it reappear.

"Boss, we go now," Orlando said. "Everything shut off and clean."

"Alright guys, I'll see you in the morning. Get some sleep, tomorrow will be a busy day," the boss said while patting Jorge on his back.

All three of the men said goodnight to Joey at approximately the same time. In tandem, they simultaneously walked out the front door. Joey sat down for another five minutes and finished his paperwork. He put all of the big bills into his pocket and left a two hundred dollar drawer for the next day's business. He neatly stapled all of the paperwork together and stuffed it into a small envelope, and dated it. Walking over to the register, he slid the drawer back into the pocket of the machine that tabulates all the sales. Pushing the drawer shut, he turned the key to lock it up for the night.

Looking around the pizzeria to make sure that everything was up to par, Joey noticed something strange outside the store. He felt something leering at him from a short distance. Joey's eyes took a quick gander outside the front window. Standing across the street was the figure of a man. Struggling to make the image out, Joey slowly walked towards the front of the store. The only distinct-able trait that he could make out was that the shadowy person was a white male. From behind the counter Joey just stared him down. The slightly built man across the way stayed focused and never relinquished his position. Fixated, the stranger stood next to one of the few trees that decorated the block. The tree and its branches cast him in shadow. The suspicious looking man had both hands in his pockets and stood partially erect, leaning up against the thick dark trunk of the tall tree as he carefully watched the store.

Joey had seen enough; he raced around the counter and headed for the exit of the pizzeria. It was time to get acquainted with this night stalker and ask him what he was searching for.

Opening the front door and landing on the concrete sidewalk, Joey gazed across the street. To his amazement the man was gone; he wasn't anywhere in sight. Joey rushed to the tree and searched everywhere. His examination came up with nothing, there was not even a scent left behind. The mysterious night crawler disappeared faster than a bank robber after a successful heist. Joey just stood there, hands on hips, confused. The outsider had left him feeling jittery and somewhat alarmed.

With his failed search concluded, Joey headed back towards the store. His wandering eyes kept searching for this elusive predator with every step that he took. Now standing in front of the store, he gave one final look. But to no avail, his thorough examination turned up empty. Saint Ann's Place was very quiet, only the wind and certain sounds of the city's wildlife could be heard.

J oey sprayed the disinfectant over the toilet seat as he wiped down the stains of urination that were all too common in the restaurant business. Most men were too lazy to even pick up the toilet seat. The women were even worse. Some of them would go through a whole roll of toilet paper after they only took a small tinkle. Everything from sanitary napkins to paper towels was stuffed down the toilets. The waste paper basket was right in front of them, but they never used it. Women always had to hide their anonymity when it came to having their monthly visitor. Many times Joey had to unclog the toilet. The stuff he used to find in there was just amazing. From tampons to disposable diapers, it was there. Nobody seemed to care; after all, they were not the ones who had to clean the mess up.

Dipping the mop into the plastic bucket, Joey was almost finished mopping the tile floor. This was only a ten-minute job but everybody hated to do it. But to him it was of great importance, the bathroom must be spotless. His mother always told him the bathroom in your house was a reflection on how people perceived you. A clean restroom was a sure sign of your character and reflected the appearance of your business. But to Joey, the people who were using these rest rooms could care less about the cleanliness of it. They would relieve themselves on a busy Times Square street if they knew no one was watching.

Finally finishing up, Joey heard a slight noise by the front door. Expecting Vito at any moment, the noise was nothing to worry about. Vito had a lot of work to finish up on down the basement. It was not uncommon to see

Vito popping in and out at all hours of the day. But when it came time to go home, he was usually right on the money.

"Vito, I'll be right out," he said. "I'm cleaning the bathroom!"

Joey waited a few seconds and received no response. That was very unusual not getting any answer from Vito; he never liked to be kept waiting. When he was ready to go home, home you went, no matter what you were doing. Nobody ever kept him waiting and nobody ever wanted to.

"Vito, are you there?" Joey called, with still no answer. He opened the bathroom door that was shut behind him and exited from the now spotless facility. Dragging the bucket into the kitchen, he slowly dumped the contents into the large metal sink. With both hands, he wrung out the dirty mop head and put it into the empty bucket. Reaching for some soap, Joey started to wash his hands and arms. To his surprise, he started to feel something strange coming from his chest cavity. He was getting a very weird sensation from underneath the medallion. Something was throbbing causing a light pulsation against his chest. He tugged and groped at his tee shirt to eliminate this peculiar sensation. But the throbbing was stubborn, it would not disappear. Nothing he could do would eliminate it. Joey wearily looked down at the medal and decided to continue on with his business.

Beyond the sounds of splashing water, Joey again thought he heard some movement from up front. He called, "I'll be right out!" Never picking his head up, he stood at the top of the landing. It was only then that he noticed that Vito never entered the store. It was then that he noticed that he was looking down at the barrel of a gun.

Standing two steps below him was a thin perilous black man waving a dark looking handgun at him. By the front door was his counterpart, probably his lookout man. The two men were acting very jittery; they seemed like they were lacking total confidence in what they were doing. To Joey this spelled out danger from the very start. Any slight movement or disturbances would definitely trigger the pistol that the hoodlum held in his right hand. This guy looked like he was going through some sort of drug withdrawal. Either that or he was just a novice in a world of professional crime. Sweat was profusely dripping from his shaking body. He looked like a walking time bomb ready to explode. This was the worst kind of thief, very unprofessional and afraid of what he was doing. Panic and any delay of what he wanted could spell death.

"Not again," Joey said in a low voice that only he could hear. "God help me!"

"What?" the man said loudly. "Give me the fuckin' money!" he said, constantly looking over his shoulder and towards the front door. "Come on, move, man," he gestured, shaking his head towards the register. "Open up the fuckin' cash register!"

"What money?" Joey said, holding the towel over the bulge in the right pocket of his pants. "There's no money in the register. The money is already at the bank!"

"Don't fuckin' play with me, man. I want the money, man!" he said, waving at Joey to come down the two steps. "Come on, man, let's go. Open the damn box up. You know the routine, man. I ain't got all fuckin' night."

Joey quickly walked down the steps and started his way towards the almost empty cash register. He would be happy to open it up and give the thief what he wanted. The real money was in his pocket, and the thug never had a clue that it was there. Joey's biggest nightmare was to have Vito walk in now and walk right into some gunplay. He prayed that Vito would stay down the basement just a little bit longer.

"Open it up, come on, man. Open the motherfucker up," the impatient thief said, all the while pointing the gun in Joey's face. Joey started to unlock the register and popped open the drawer. He then looked below the counter about two feet away from his right foot. There he saw the baseball bat that he kept there for special moments like these. There were only two options to choose from, and violence was not one of them. He decided to hand the contents of the drawer to the stickup man.

"Here, take it and get the hell out!"

"That's it?" the gunman said, gaping at the meager haul. "There ain't even two hundred bucks here!" he said, scanning the money in his left hand.

"That's it," a visibly shaken Joey said. "We had a bad day."

"Bad day my ass. Where's the real money?"

"I told you already, you have it all."

"What's that around your neck?"

"What?"

"The gold, man, the gold!"

Suddenly the front door flung open and his lookout man came calling for him.

"Come on, man, let's bolt!" the lookout man cried. "People are comin' up the block. Come on, you're taking too long, we're gonna get nailed. Do him up, man," his panicking partner ordered. "What are you waitin' for? Waste the motherfucker!"

The man with the gun started to look in both directions as he made a motion towards Joey's neck. He wanted the medallion badly; he knew that the gold chain was worth at least five times the amount that he was holding in his hand. Enticed by the gold, he raised his left hand and started reaching for Joey's neck. Joey then back-pedaled a foot or so to make his attempt a bit more difficult. In his mind there was no way in hell that he was ever going to give up that medallion; he'd rather die first.

Joey put his right hand over the medallion and felt this strange emitting heat coming from it. To the startled pizzeria owner, the medal seemed like it was alive. It felt like a burning charcoal briquette that was throbbing inside the palm of his hand. Joey just kept his feelings and thoughts to himself and concentrated on the trouble before him.

Panicking, the punk seemed even more rattled as his nervous system kicked into full gear. His buddy kept calling and calling, a move in one direction or the other had to be made.

The moment was intense, for Joey a miracle was needed.

Strangely and uninvited, a dark grayish eerie image started to develop in between Joey and his attacker. The cloud like visitor loomed suspended in the air. Boldly, the translucent phantom stood defiant as its powers were being released. The supernatural visitor acted as a shield as it defended Joey from the potential danger in front of him. The specter was only visible to the thief as Joey felt its presence and oddly looked on. The threatening apparition haunted and intimidated the senses of the street thug as his eyes wandered around the small eatery looking for answers.

"Turn back evil and wicked one," the powerful apparition said in a demanding voice. "Turn back, turn back, turn back."

"Fuck," he hurriedly said looking around the room. "What.... what the fuck is that? Shit, man. Who are you? Get the fuck off me." The thief looks around the store for answers and starts to swing wildly at the ghost like figure before him. "Let go of me," he said while trying to pull his gun arm from the grasp of the hazy orb. "This place is fuckin haunted. Fuck this shit, man. I'm outta here. Dude, you must have a Guardian Angel."

"He's back! It's all real," Joey thought to himself. *"Damn...it's all real."*

The panic stricken thug scampered towards the front door. Never looking back, the two men fled down the street running as fast as they could. Their small heist was semi successful, but most of all it was easy. They got off with a quick two hundred bucks in the matter of a couple of minutes. The only thing that they left in the register was the change. To these two punks, it was enough money to get them through another day or two.

Joey leaned over the counter and buried his face into the palms of his hands. He thought that all of the danger was behind him since Vito entered the picture. But the violence would never end; it followed him wherever he went. It got to a point where he started to trust everyone who entered the store. All the peace and quiet had put him into a tranquil lull. That's when he started to get soft and let his guard down. With all the stuff that he'd been through, he should have known better.

A few minutes later, Vito appeared.

"Come on, let's go home," Vito said. "It's been a long day."

Vito walked up to Joey and pulled on his right arm. Joey pulled his arm back and kept it where it was. He was embarrassed to show Vito the look of defeat that was written all over his face. Vito knew something was wrong with his Godson. Every time Vito came for him to go home, Joey was ready. This time was much different, he just stood there with his face buried deep into the palms of his sweaty hands.

"What's wrong?" Vito asked, this time in a more stern tone of voice. Still nothing was coming out of Joey's mouth. "Answer me, what's wrong with you?"

Joey slowly picked his head up and looked into Vito's eyes. Vito stood before him undaunted and impatiently waiting for his answer. "I just got robbed! Two guys just came in here to kill me."

"What? Who wanted to kill you?"

"These two black guys that just robbed me!"

"When?"

"A couple of seconds before you came up the steps."

"Where are they?" he said, heading for the door. "Which way did they go?

"It's too late, Vito, they're gone."

"Son of a bitches," a seething Vito said. "Are you kidding me?"

"No, I'm not."

"I should have come in from the outside. God damn it," he fumed.

"They had guns, Vito, I'm glad that you just missed them."

"Are you alright?"

"I'm okay, just a little shaken up. This shit just don't seem to want to stop. I'm getting so fuckin' tired of it. I work my ass off for what? For two pieces of shit to come in here and take my money?"

"How much did they get away with?"

"Less than two hundred. I had the bulk of the money in my pocket."

"That's it?" Vito said with a smile on his face. "Don't worry about it, we'll get the bastards."

"That's not the point. I'm tired of people pointing guns in my face all the time. I'm tired of getting the shit kicked out of me every other month. I just want to get the fuck out of here and go home. I've been here for almost eight months and it feels like eight years. And I'm still stuck right in the same spot where I started from. I seen more than I ever wanted to see over here, I have had enough."

"Look at all the progress you made, business is great and the people over here love you."

"Love me?" Joey said, looking at Vito like he was walking around with three heads on his shoulders. "Love me? It's you that they love, you're the one they look up to. You saved their homes and their neighborhood. I had nothing to do with that."

"You're wrong, it's because of you that I'm here. I could not give two shits if this whole neighborhood burned to the fuckin' ground."

"You care, Vito, I know you do. Dutch cares and so do you."

"We both care for different reasons! My major concern is you, and you have come a long way. This place is a money maker now."

"That's all because of you also. You know it just as well as I do."

"Maybe so, but you're the one who is making it all happen. You're doing a great job running this business. I have nothing to do with the food, the food is great. The people keep coming back because you put out a good product and you respect them. And in return, they respect you. So stop feeling sorry for yourself and put all this fuckin' shit behind you."

"It's easy for you to say that."

"You'll do it, I don't like quitters."

"I'm not a quitter," Joey snapped back with a roar. "I never was and I never will be!"

"Good, now make me proud and just hang in there for a while longer. In another couple of months we'll be out of here. Are you sure you're alright?"

"I'm alright, but I'm not going to let these animals get away with this," Joey said. He then started to walk to towards the telephone to make a call.

"What are you doing?" Vito asked, observing Joey's aggressive behavior.

"I'm calling the cops!"

"The cops?" Vito said with a surprised look. "While you're on the phone with them, ask them if they want to place a bet on the third race at Aqueduct. Better yet, maybe one of them wants to borrow a couple of grand. Tell them that we will send Bear down to the precinct once a week to pick up the vig money."

"What are you talking about?"

"Hang the fuckin' phone up!" Vito yelled, losing patience. "What the fuck is wrong with you! That's all we need is the cops sniffing all around this place. I thought I taught you better than this," he grumbled. "With all the shit we got going on here, they'll close us down in a heartbeat. And I ain't going back to prison over some stupid shit like this. If I'm going back, it will be for killing the rotten bastards that robbed you. So never ever call the cops, do you hear me?"

"I just lost my head for a second, I wasn't thinking clearly."

"Never call the cops!" Vito screamed, standing on the outside of the counter. "I can't believe this shit!"

"I hear you, I hear you," Joey said. "Jesus Christ."

"Good, and don't use the Lord's name in vain."

"I'm sorry already. So what are we going to do, let them get away with this? Those two fuckin' guys were going to kill me!"

"Don't worry, these clowns will be back," predicted Vito.

"Why do you say that?"

"Because you were an easy target. They went in and out of here untouched. Mark my words, they'll be back."

"Thanks, that makes me feel a whole lot better. Maybe the next time they will put a bullet in me, I can't wait."

"Stop being a jackass," snapped Vito. "The next time, we will be ready for them."

"And how the hell are you gonna do that?"

"Leave it to me," he said. "Just leave it to me."

"You know, Vito? Right before I got robbed I saw this strange looking character just staring into the store. I went outside to confront him and he was gone."

"He was probably casing the place for the other two. Why didn't you call for me when you saw him? If you did, this would've never happened."

"I don't think he had anything to do with them. This guy was after something else, besides he was white."

"So what the fuck does that mean? Just because he was white means that he was not involved with them? They probably used a white guy to throw you off guard. If a nigger was standing across the street you probably would have called me in a second. They out smarted you, these three stupid hoodlums played you for a fool."

"I still think you're wrong; this guy across the street had nothing to do with them. He just gave me an eerie feeling, he was looking for something else."

"Maybe he was just hungry and wanted to see if the store was open."

"From across the street?"

"What the hell do I know. Next time just get a whole of me and I'll be right up. And why the hell did you have the front door opened when you were closed?"

"I was waiting for you."

"I came into the store through the inside because I knew you were closed. I thought you would have enough sense to lock the front door."

"You always come in from the outside, I never thought that this time would be any different."

"That's because you never think ahead, that's your problem. This is the big difference between me and you. I'm always thinking ahead, that's why I never get fucked. You on the other hand seem to get fucked coming and going. You trust everybody and everybody takes their turn fucking you. Be smart and start thinking ahead. Always be prepared for what's going to happen the following minute or even the following day. Always expect the unexpected. Now get your keys and let's get out of here."

Vito put his arm around Joey's shoulder and they walked out the front door together. Even though Vito verbally bashed Joey, he loved him more than anyone on earth. His fear for him caused the fierce admonishments. His affection was obvious with his hugs and when he looked into his eyes. Sometimes he got a little bit too harsh, but this was Vito's way of getting his point across. He was not a gentleman by any means; society had bred him that way. Besides the robbery, now there were these unexplained supernatural acts coming from the gold chain wrapped around Joey's neck. Joey just picked up the medallion from off of his chest and stared at it all the way out the front door, never taking his eyes off of it.

"What are you looking at?" Vito asked, noticing Joey's strange behavior.

"Nothing," Joey answered. "If I told you, you would never believe me."

The following day, Vito kept to his promise. When he said that the next time anybody tried to rob the store they would be ready, he meant it. He also was getting pretty tired of seeing everyone taking pot shots and abusing his Godson. To Vito, the latest episode was the final straw that broke the camel's back. Even though the neighborhood was a lot safer now, Joey's safety was the utmost of importance to him. Vito could tell that Joey had enough of getting beat up and pushed around all of the time. What bothered him even more was the fact that this latest robbery happened right under his nose. He didn't show it, but underneath he was furious. To show any disrespect to someone else was one thing. But to disrespect him when the people know who he was, was quite another thing. This was something that he would never ever let happen again. Pity the poor fools who robbed the pizzeria. If they are ever caught, Vito silently vowed, their whole family tree will feel their pain.

Around noon time a couple of guys came into the store and started to run wires everywhere. The wires ran from under the cash register down to the basement. Holes were drilled underneath the counter into the walls and through the floor. Each small opening was meticulously hiding the wires from being seen. In the kitchen, the same method was used. Vito's new brainstorm had a bell and a button applied to each end of these wires. One button was placed right under the cash register and the other by the opening into the kitchen. Down the basement was a bell that was installed and placed on the wall by the poker table. Obviously these were just a couple of precaution items put in to signal for help. Not in any way were they any type of deterrent to a would-be robber.

But Vito was not finished. He brought in two brand new security cameras and took them out of their boxes. One was installed showing the whole aisle and the walkway up to the front door. The other was placed right behind the back wall showing the cash register and every patron that paid for their food. Every movement would now be monitored down in the basement on two 13" television sets. Both sets were also wired to a video cassette recorder. From open to closing, all activities would now be taped and reviewed by the gangsters who occupied the basement of 205 Saint Ann's Place. An intercom was also set up from the basement to the pizzeria. This little walkie-talkie device was placed right by the two telephones hanging on the wall.

The new technology brought one problem along with its installation. Every time someone suspicious looking walked through the doors, either Joey or one of his work crew was ringing the bell. The alarm had all the boys racing up and down the steps at all hours of the day. Even if they had a Roman orgy going on in that basement, they had to stop whatever they were doing and run upstairs. Three men would come in from the outside, and two from the basement steps. The Italian gangsters came charging to the scene like a hungry fat man hearing the sounds of a ringing dinner bell.

It got so ridiculous that Manuel rang the alarm for a man pushing an old lady in a wheelchair. The Mexican pizza man thought that the old lady was sporting a wig and brandishing a firearm under the light blanket that covered her legs. It was only a matter of time before Vito would put an end to these illusions.

One evening Vito came rushing through the front door with shaving cream all over his face. There was a commotion going on in the store, but nothing that could not be rectified without sounding off the alarm. The ado was only over a couple of dollars of change. A customer said that he had given Joey a ten-dollar bill, when in fact it was only a five. Joey went around the counter to settle it and give the patron the difference. Orlando saw it differently and summoned for help downstairs.

"The next time one of you idiots ring that fuckin' bell, I'm gonna stick it up all of your asses. Are you fuckin' morons forgetting that we have a camera downstairs?" Vito continued, with his tirade just beginning. "Jesus Christ all mighty, you rang the damn bell over an old lady in a wheelchair. The other day you had my boys running up and down the steps all day long. What was it?" Vito said, pausing to think for a second.

"I know what it was," Joey said. "You don't have to repeat it." He had a feeling that he was going to hear it anyway.

"Oh yea," Vito said ignoring Joey. "A kid and his father came in here with a bat in one of their hands. Joey, the fuckin' guy was just taking his boy home from baseball practice. They came in here to have some lunch. We scared the shit out of the kid and his father. I saw the father the other day and he told me the kid does not even want to play ball anymore. He thinks that every time that he picks up a baseball bat, five Italian assholes are going to come running after him with guns in their hands."

"I'm sorry, Vito, that was a bad scene," Joey said. "My men are just a little afraid after all the shit they have seen and been through."

"I understand that, but sooner or later someone is going to get hurt."

"I'll have a talk with them; it won't happen again."

"Make sure that it doesn't, because if it does I am holding you responsible."

"Oh yea!" Joey said, mocking Vito in a joking manner. "Ooh, I'm shitting in my pants."

"You son of a bitch," a smiling Vito said. Vito then ran around the counter with his double-edged razor in his hand. He trapped his Godson by the pizza ovens and proceeded to wash out his mouth with shaving cream. "Now come on, tell Orlando to make me something to eat."

"What do you want the usual, linguine with red clam sauce?"

"Nah, no fish today, why don't you surprise me!"

"Alright," Joey said. "Go finish shaving, I'll ring the bell when your food is ready. But leave the razor and gun downstairs."

On his way out the door, Vito just turned around and smiled at Joey. "Hey ball-buster," he said. "You ring that bell and I'll kill you myself. Let me shave in peace, since I came here my face is all scarred up with cuts. The ladies at the club aren't finding me that attractive anymore."

Vito had gotten his message across and he was so right. Joey, soon after his discussion with Vito, sat everyone down at a table. He quietly relayed the significant message and the meaning behind it, which they all understood loud and clear. After all, the boys were only abusing something that was supposed to benefit them. But making a mockery of it only abused the protection that the bell was supposed to give them. After a while, every time the bell rang, nobody would have taken it seriously anymore. Everyone has the potential to look suspicious, but you have to wait until they make that first move to provide the faintest of evidence that the suspicion always hides. Sometimes it might be too late, but just suspecting it was not enough at all.

Chapter 19

JOEY WAS PUTTING the finishing touches on a pie that he just prepared.

"So you did it!"

With flour all over his body, he quickly picked his head up to see the caller. "Hey, how the hell are you?" Joey said, not even knowing the older gentleman's name.

"I'm fine. Every winter I sort of stay low. The cold weather is kind of rough on my old bones," he said, leaning on his cane. "Makes them hurt too much."

"I hear ya," Joey said, placing the raw pizza in the oven behind him. "You know I never did get your name. What is it?"

"Gus, and I guess you're Joey!"

"That's right, how did you know?"

"The name is outside on your canopy. Ain't it?"

"It sure is, Gus."

"Well, I would have never believed it, but you did it."

"Did what?" Joey said, brushing any excess of flour from his arms and hands. "Survive?"

"Exactly! You know what? I always watched from my bedroom window. I see everything that goes on around here."

"Then you must have seen a lot."

"Sure have. Thank God you did not listen to my advice. You would have packed your bags a long time ago."

"Gus, when I met you in front of the park that morning, you scared the shit out of me. But you kept me on my toes."

"I didn't mean to scare you, son, I just wanted to warn you. I didn't want to see you get hurt. I saw the graffiti they printed on the front of your store. The word death only means one thing to me."

"What's that?" Joey asked, even though he knew what was going to come out of the old timer's mouth.

"Death! I also saw how they treated that poor Italian man who was here before you. That poor slob was borrowing money just to pay the Brotherhood off."

"I know all about it."

"But you, you came a long way. Look at this place, you did a fine job here. Thanks to you and your friends, life seems a little easier around here."

"Thanks Gus, that means a lot to me."

"So where is your buddy?"

"What buddy?"

"The older guy, I see you always hanging around with."

"Oh, that's Vito."

"I always see him outside ordering people around. That man is a sharp dresser."

"That he is old timer. That he is."

"Joey, put a slice in the oven for me!"

"I got a fresh pie coming out in about five minutes. Have a seat, Gus."

"At my age," he said. "When I sit my ass somewhere, sometimes I have a hard time getting up."

"At your age?" Joey answered, rubbing his sore back. "I have the same problems now. Every bone on my body hurts."

"If it's bad now," Gus predicted. "Wait until you reach my age."

Gus slowly hobbled over to the nearest table and placed his cane against it. He slowly slid into a small booth and sat there quietly. Gus was the first person Joey had met upon arriving into this snake pit. Always full of advice, all of his warnings turned out to be true. He was not a fortune-teller, just an old man who poured his heart out while reliving experiences of the past. This was the first time that he ever entered the pizzeria while Joey operated it. His life would just consist of a daily visit to the corner grocer for the basic necessities he needed to survive. The Brotherhood had also held him prisoner to fear. Even though he was a World War II veteran, old age had stripped him of all the fundamentals to fight. He was now only beginning to explore his new found freedom. Gus only wanted to pay his gratitude for this change of life that was brought to him and a lot of his close friends.

Business was moving along at a rapid pace. It seemed to reach its peak or maximize its potential. But after all, how much can be produced out of a small place like this. There was only a staff of four people and they busted their asses to get this far. The sales seemed to outpace the staff and the equipment to go any further. More business was out there, but nobody went out of their way to go after it. Things just seemed to settle in and everyone just ran with the program. Mostly everyone seemed content, more important than that, all the workers seemed very happy. They were all benefiting from the sudden explosion of business. Every Sunday evening they all walked out of the store with smiles on their faces. It was not going home that made them so happy- it was the money in their overstuffed wallets, all in cash.

There wasn't a Mexican alive who was on the payroll in the pizza or food business. To the Internal Revenue Service these hard working illegal aliens didn't even exist. They knew they were there but it was too much of a problem to try and rectify. But to the owners of these establishments, having Mexicans was the only way to survive. To put them on the books and paying payroll taxes was just too costly for most small businesses. Therefore, health benefits and a few of the other amenities were totally out of the question

Nobody ever used a credit card in this neighborhood, not too many people had them. From a slice of pizza to a tray of lasagna, everything was paid for in cash. And the cash register kept ringing and ringing to the tune of about ten thousand a week. Ten thousand a week less expenses put about $8,000 a month in Joey's pocket, tax-free. This was not chump change, this was hard cold cash. Earning it was a very hard chore, but to Joey the money seemed meaningless. He had seen this kind of money before. Everyone else seemed overjoyed but him. He was not happy; something was still missing in his life.

An unexpected heavy rain was passing over the city one dreary evening. Hiding under an umbrella, a young lady dashed to her car. Finally reaching her car, she reached into her long black raincoat for the car keys. Fumbling for a moment, the classy looking woman opened the car door and gracefully slid in. Pulling at the rear view mirror, she gazed into it to check her freshly applied makeup as she ran her fingers through her thick black hair.

For the past six weeks, Gloria did a lot of thinking and soul searching. The Puerto Rican beauty spent many nights crying and missing Joey. She spent most of her time in introspection, scrutinizing everything from her emotions to her moral objectives. After countless hours of thinking and examining the situation, the good seemed to outweigh the bad. Searching for every possible reason in the world to get out of a relationship that seemed wrong to her, love finally overcame her resistance.

Acting nervous and erratic, Gloria reached into her handbag for a cigarette. Pushing on the cigarette lighter, she finally started the car's engine. Letting it idle for about five minutes, the impatient woman pulled out of her tight parking space.

The wipers were thumping away to keep up with the downpour. Visibility was obstructed, so she turned on the car's defroster to clear up some of the fog that had formed on her windshield. The heavy rain kept battering the car as it slowly crawled through the flooded streets. After about twenty minutes, she reached her destination. Reaching for the wet umbrella, she hurried out of the car, opening the umbrella as she went. Gloria walked the long block to pay Joey an unexpected visit, dodging and side stepping puddles every inch of the way.

Finally settling under the store's canopy, she shook out the water from her umbrella before closing it. Like a child going to school for the first day, Gloria was very nervous. Taking one last deep breath, she entered the pizzeria.

Looking all around, Gloria spotted Joey in the kitchen straight ahead. She studied his every movement as he assisted Orlando getting a large order ready for delivery. The swinging cowboy saloon doors partially took away some of her vision, but she did not seem to mind. Amazed at his kitchen know how, Gloria just smiled and continued to watch. With snail like movement, she continued to creep forward to the back of the store. The boys downstairs watched her every step. The camera gave them a very vivid description of the gorgeous young lady.

"Hey Bear, get a load of this!" Jimmy said, his eyes fixated on the small television monitor. Bear stood from his desk and walked over to join his partner in crime.

"Holy shit! Where the fuck did she come from?"

"I don't know where she came from," replied Jimmy. "But I know where I'm going."

Jimmy then raced out the side door and down the dark wet alley. Bear was in hot pursuit, right behind him. The two were acting like they had never seen a woman before. In a way they had every reason to feel this way. Being out of their element and always focused on business, Mama Cass could have even gotten a rise out of them. It did not take much to arouse these two guys, especially when Vito was not around.

"Can I help you?" Manuel said from behind the counter to the woman in waiting.

"No, I'm waiting for Joey."

"I go get him."

"No, let him finish what he's doing. I will just wait here for him."

"Are you Gloria?" Manuel asked.

"Yes I am," she politely said. "You must be Manuel!"

"Yes."

"Nice to meet you, Manuel," Gloria said with a smile and an offering of a handshake.

No more than two seconds later, Jimmy and Bear came steam rolling through the front door. Their maniacal behavior and excessive enthusiasm made them look like a pair of bumbling lunatics. Making this loud entrance only exposed their clown like tendencies in order to get to know a beautiful woman.

In their haste, Jimmy's back heel clicked with Bear's front shoe. The contact pushed him stumbling forward down the slippery tile floor. His wet attire just made his short trip a little smoother and quicker. The wannabe singer landed right at the feet of the hysterical woman.

"Can I help you," she asked, looking down at him. Always trying to control her emotions, this happening seemed just a little too much for even her to maintain. "I never had anybody fall for me this way before."

"You're even more beautiful from down here!"

"Why thank you. That was quite an introduction, nobody has ever fallen for me in such a manner. I am very flattered," she added.

"Well then how about we skip all the preliminaries and run right to City Hall?"

"Oh no, I want a big wedding!"

"Don't worry, honey," he said. "Just trust me, it will be big! With me, you will be hearing wedding bells every night for the rest of your life."

"You sound very sure of yourself. Are you?" Gloria said, looking down at Jimmy who was still lying flat on his back. She was so innocent that Jimmy's sexual overtones were going right over her head.

"Back where I come from, they call me the king of romance."

"Oh," she said, starting to smarten up a bit. "So then you must do everything on your back?"

"You got it," he said, flipping her a wink.

"There is just one problem here."

"What's that, babe?"

"I'm in love with the man who is in the kitchen."

"Who, Orlando?" he kidded.

It did not take a brain surgeon to figure out whom she was talking about. Even so, that would never stop him from making a play for her. He had no clue that he didn't even have a shot. All of his excessive and insincere compliments would get him nowhere. But nobody would ever blame him for trying so hard. Trying was in his nature and no one would ever take it away from him. Jimmy was the type of guy who would hit on every woman in a nightclub until he found the one who would go home with him. He was not afraid of rejection. A lot of women found him very attractive, his boyish behavior and sense of humor always brought a smile to their faces.

Bear on the other hand was shy and much more laid back when it came to the female gender. Besides, his massive size would scare most level-headed women away. Having him on top of them was not something a woman would dream about. This guy was like a big concrete slab. There wasn't any softness to even the lightest of his touches. One caress out of his monster-like hands could break a woman's cheekbone. Talk about a bull in a china shop, this guy had the same effect in the bedroom.

Unaware of the comical events taking place, Joey quickly strolled down the steps and went straight behind the counter. Both of his strong arms carried the assortment of different entrees in a cardboard box. The delivery was the only thing on his mind and he hardly ever strayed away from tending to his business. Placing the large box on top of the counter, he turned around and went over to the calculator next to the telephone. Running his fingers swiftly over the keys, he quickly tabulated the total amount of the bill.

Gloria just watched his every move. Joey had no idea that she was even in the store. She watched proudly as she started to realize how much pain his absence has put her through. Her heart was pounding in proportions that she had never felt before. She also knew that right before her stood a good man with all the values that she would ever hope to find.

"Jorge!" Joey said, yelling for his delivery-man. "Come down here, the delivery is ready."

Jorge ran down the few steps and Joey gave him the delivery instructions. The young Mexican quickly took the large box and headed towards the front door. Joey then ran his fingers through his thick black hair and took a deep breath.

"Excuse me," Jorge said to the small crowd that was cluttering up the narrow passageway. With those words Joey picked his head up to see what was impeding his delivery boy's progress. He stuck his head out past the counter and saw Jimmy still lying on the floor in deep conversation. The overpowering image of Bear stood behind Jimmy looking dumbfounded. Slowly, Joey maneuvered his eyes upwards and closely examined the female before him. His jaw slackened and his eyes went wide.

"Gloria," he said in a low voice. "Gloria!"

Gloria stood there with a bright smile on her face. She then placed her umbrella down and secured her handbag under her armpit. Jimmy kept talking at a machine gun rate but all of his sweet talk was falling upon deaf ears. Joey rushed out from behind the counter and in moments swept her into his arms. Their lips met with a tender expression of love.

Joey's right arm was wrapped around Gloria's small waist while his left hand caressed her delicate and smooth face. He finally lowered her, feeling the buckle coming from her understandably weak knees. Joey steadied his grasp around her waist and gazed into her eyes until he was lost in them.

"I am so happy to see you," he murmured into her perfumed hair.

"I feel the same way," she whispered. "I had to come here, I couldn't take it any longer."

"I'm so sorry for what happened, I promise I......" At that moment Gloria placed her finger on top of Joey's lips prohibiting him to speak.

"There is no need to apologize, I now know everything that went on. I was the one who was wrong," she went on. "I had no idea what you were going through. I was being very selfish and only thinking about myself."

"But I," at that moment Joey looked down to the floor. There was Jimmy, laying there listening to every word that was exchanged. Jimmy looked like he was watching the season ending finale of *"As The World Turns."* All he needed was a handkerchief to wipe away some of those tears.

"Excuse me," Joey said to Jimmy. "I forgot to ask you this before, but what the fuck are you doing down there?"

"He was just keeping me company while you were busy," Gloria said protecting whatever lie was going to come out of his mouth.

"Yea," Jimmy said. "I was just keepin' her company."

"And I suppose Bear was just holding your hand?" Joey said. "Jimmy, come on, get up."

"You mean the show's over?" Jimmy said, slowly rising to his feet.

"For you it is," Joey said. "Anyway, Gloria, this is Jimmy. Jimmy, meet Gloria."

The two began to shake hands very cordially. But what started out as a simple handshake turned into something much more. Jimmy quickly tried to pull Gloria into his awaiting arms. But he did not succeed in getting that far. Joey quickly interrupted.

"Damn it! Would you knock the shit off," Joey said. "Sometimes you can be a real pain in the ass."

Joey was not mad at Jimmy at all, he was so elated by the moment, that there was nothing that even Jimmy could do that could spoil it. He knew that Jimmy was the biggest ball breaker on earth. But everything that he did was in pure clean fun. Sometimes you had to put an end to it or he would continue on all night long.

"Gloria, this is Bear."

Gloria then turned around to greet this tree-sized character. She extended her petite hand and it slowly vanished into a sea of moving flesh. Her dainty fingers were just swallowed up by his intimidating looking hand. The poor girl just looked up at him and never said a word. All she wanted was her hand back, in one piece of course.

"Pleased to meet you," Bear shyly said.

"Likewise."

"Come on, honey, let's go sit down." Joey grabbed her by the hand and led her to the back of the store.

"God, Joey," she whispered. "I never saw a guy that big before!"

"I know, he's huge, but he's harmless. Unless you get on his bad side, then watch out," Joey warned. "But I don't think you're capable of doing that."

"I better be good to you, the last thing I need is that guy chasing me all over town."

"You better be," Joey said with a laugh

Jimmy and Bear ordered a slice of pizza before returning to the basement. Once in a while when Vito or Dutch were not present, the two of them would stray from their work and horse around a bit. They always had Ricky the Roach to fall back on and pick up any loose slack that they left behind. Ricky on the other hand was never the womanizer. How could he be? His mother told him how ugly he was the first day she laid eyes on him. That brutal assessment would live with him for the rest of his life. This guy couldn't get laid in some cheap whorehouse with a handful of hundred dollar bills. With no sexual potential or self-esteem, he lived for two things and two things only: Vito Carlucci and his finely manicured mustache.

"Come here, honey, slide in and sit over here."

Joey had Gloria slip into the small booth at the rear of the store facing the street. He quickly hopped in right opposite her, not getting as close to her as she wanted him to.

"Oh no," she said. "I want you to sit right over here next to me!" Joey obliged.

For the next half-hour they just sat and talked about how much they had missed each other. Joey kept trying to explain his actions that night at Ramon's bar, but she would have none of it. Something made her start singing a different song. Whatever it was, Joey was glad that she started to see things a little bit differently. All the news about what was going on in the neighborhood traveled swiftly. Being the inquisitive one, Gloria never went a day without being informed about what was going on in the pizzeria. She was so proud of Joey and all the things that he had accomplished. She even wanted to meet Vito, the man who made this all happen.

Joey sent his work crew home about an hour early. The business would not suffer one bit, if it did, that was too bad. He just wanted to focus on Gloria and enjoy the company that he had been missing so badly. He'd waited for this night for the last couple of months. Nothing in the world could ever spoil this moment; it was too special to him. Even though they were just sitting in his place of business, he had hoped this magical moment would last forever.

"Joey," she whispered lightly in his ear. "I have to use the ladies room."

Never taking her raincoat off, Gloria wiggled out of the small booth looking a little confused. She got to her feet and kissed Joey on the cheek. Walking by him, she left a scent that would linger long after she was gone. In Joey's mind, her smell alone exuded a scent that radiated from her like a promise. Joey took a deep breath; his need for her was almost overwhelming. The old familiar stirring left him no choice. He wanted to eat her up alive. No woman had ever made him feel this way before. He was breaking out in a sweat just thinking about her. Granted, it had been several months since they had had sexual relations. But this was something totally different. It was true love and honest desire.

After a few minutes, Joey walked over to the bottom of the steps and waited patiently for her return. The bathroom door slowly opened and she finally stepped out. Gloria stood on top of the small landing looking even more ravishing than when she entered it. For a whole minute they drank in each other silently.

"You know what I was doing in the bathroom?" she asked him, while pulling on the belt of her raincoat to open it.

"Yea, fixing your makeup." Joey then put his right foot on the bottom step, inching his way closer to her.

"Besides that," she said with a smile.

"What then?"

"I was reading the letter that you sent to me. It's been months since I last read it. I'd forgotten that you could be so sensitive. The way you poured out your feelings gave me goose bumps and brought tears to my eyes. God, I love you so much," she murmured.

He placed both of his hands inside her raincoat and fastened them around her tiny waist. He hoisted her off of her feet and carried her to the surface below. Joey then released her at an arm's length distance, never relinquishing his hold from around her midsection. His appetite for her was growing more powerful with each emotional second that passed. He knew that she felt the same way as he drew her closer and closer. The breathing started to get heavier even before their first passionate kiss.

Taking charge, Joey then went for her soft velvet neck and started to caress it with his wet lips. Gloria did not say much; she didn't have to. The vibrant tremors running all over her body left her breathless. She arched her head back and let his lips and tongue gently stroke the left side of her neck. Joey's hands slid down around her firm round buttocks and with intense feeling, he squeezed. His roving hands managed to find their way up her short black skirt. It was then that he felt as well as sensed her desire. Never letting go, he drew her in to the point of no return. Gloria was now pressing up against his aroused manhood. With her right hand, she gently searched for an opening and stroked his throbbing organ. She let out a small murmur, her body now vibrating with excitement. Their hungry lips finally met. Their lips parted and hot, wet tongues swam back and forth. Gloria was ready. This smoldering Latina needed him and left no question about how much. It did not matter where she was. All that concerned her was who she was with. Suddenly he released her.

"Oh Christ," Joey said.

"What's the matter?" Gloria muttered, looking confused. After all, her passions were just snuffed out like a burning cigarette in an ashtray.

"Hold on a second!"

"Joey," she then repeated. "What's wrong? Where are you going?"

Like an Olympic runner, he raced to the front of the store. Peeking his head out of the front door, he looked in both directions. Seeing that the coast was clear, Joey stepped outside and reached for the metal pull down gates. He quickly pulled both of them down and crawled underneath the one that covered the front door. From inside the store, he pulled it down the rest of the way. Not taking any chances, he locked the door from the inside. Joey then raced up the aisle and right past Gloria.

"Where are you going now?"

"Just give me one more minute," he said as he passed by her.

He then ran up the two steps leading to the bathroom and kitchen area. Before he got to the kitchen, he made a sharp right hand turn. Finally reaching his destination, Joey placed his hand on the deadbolt and locked the basement door. For the first time in his life, he did not want any unexpected visitors popping up from down the basement. Letting out a deep sigh of relieve, he thought he had all angles covered and his privacy safely secured.

"Are you finished?" Gloria asked, hoping that this delay did not spoil the moment.

"Yea, I'm done," he said with a big smile on his face. "I'm all yours now."

"Good, now come on down here and sit right in this chair!" Gloria cooed, her right hand on the handle of the wooden chair.

Joey just followed her orders and sat where he was told. Gloria then removed her raincoat and dropped it to the floor. She wasted no time. Fully clothed, with her skirt riding up her legs, she mounted him. Wrapping both of her legs around his midsection, Gloria tightened her grip on him. Joey then placed each one of his hands on one of her thighs. He slowly took the smooth journey, riding his large hands all the way up her shapely legs. His magical fingers kept probing her yearning body, with each stroke intensifying his lust for her. Taking his time, he maneuvered slowly and masterfully. Her excitements grew wilder and wilder as he found her erogenous zone. He gently tugged on her pink laced panties as Gloria let out a heavy sigh. Breathing hard she rocked back and forth, thrusting with wild abandon. Joey started to gently glide both of his hands up and down her shapely round buttocks. Using his free hand he pulled the back of Gloria's hair, jolting her head backward. He then ran his tongue from between her round breasts all the way up her moist and scented neck. The passion was wild and ready to explode.

With his eyes wild with lust, his body sweaty, breathless and satiated, Joey's gaze lazily followed the wall. It was then when he noticed a potential nightmare. He was looking straight into the eyes of the surveillance camera. The lens was staring right at Gloria's backside and into his face. For some reason he knew that he was being watched.

"God damn it," Joey screamed. "Those two sons of bitches!"

"What's the matter now?" Gloria said as she got tossed off of him like a rider from a bucking bronco.

"The camera, Gloria," he said. "The fuckin' video camera!"

"What about it?" she said, adjusting her clothing and long black hair.

"What about it?" he screamed, while pointing at the piece of equipment behind the counter. "I forgot to turn the thing off. There is no doubt in my mind that those two pieces of shit down there are getting an eyeful of all of this. That fuckin' Jimmy probably has his prick in his hand right now!"

"No," she said raising her sculptured eyebrows. "They wouldn't do that."

"Yes they would," Joey fumed. "I could see the looks on their fuckin' faces right now."

"Why would they do something like that?"

"Because Vito and Dutch are not here," he said. "Jimmy lives for shit like this. He's probably rolling all over the floor right now. Well the show's over, we should have never started anything in here in the first place."

"Well it's too late to start second-guessing ourselves," she said. "We just got carried away a little. I'll be right back, I'm going to straighten up in the restroom."

"Are you alright?"

"I'm fine, don't worry about it," she falsely admitted. "I just feel a little embarrassed, that's all."

"I'm sorry," Joey apologized. "It figures something like this would have to happen now. It's just the way my luck has been lately."

"Oh stop it," she said walking towards the restroom. "Maybe they didn't see anything at all."

"Yea right, I would bet my life on it that they did."

Gloria walked into the bathroom and closed the door behind her. Joey immediately held up his middle finger and pointed it at the camera. "Fuck you!" he screamed. He knew that someone had gotten an eyeful. Deep down he also knew who the two characters were. He was just praying that Jimmy and Bear had enough common sense to turn off the camera and respect his privacy

But of course all of Joey's intuitions were right. The two guys were glued to the little monitor watching every little detail. To make matters worse, they were enjoying it immensely. Ricky the Roach was the only one who strayed away from all the shenanigans. He just answered the phones and diligently prepared his paperwork. To him, seeing this was no big deal at all. At his home he had a stockpile of pornography buried from top to bottom inside his bedroom closet. The Roach had every type of broad in the world at his beck and call. All he had to do was pop the cassette into the VCR and all the lewdness in the world was his. Whatever type of sex he wanted was there for him. Inside of his closet was his Disney World, filled with all the lustful and sinful characters that he desired. From Asian to French, the Roach had women from every continent on the globe. To him, watching sex on a television set was not a big deal at all.

What the other two guys did not know was that Vito and Dutch had quietly entered the basement right before the show was over. For about forty seconds they were standing right behind them. They bagged the two clowns gawking over Gloria's body and sexual prowess. They both stood there silently, until they had seen enough. Vito then flew into a violent rage, verbally abusing the two grown men. He knew who the young lady was on the other side of the camera. He also knew that she was not some cheap hooker that Joey had pulled inside from off of the street. What enraged him even more was the fact that Joey's special moment had been ruined. Vito felt bad knowing how special this occasion was to his Godson and how much it meant to him. This beautiful moment was ruined by a couple of amateur peeping toms in search of some cheap thrills.

Rushing over to the intercom, Joey was about to release his verbal tongue-lashing. He pushed down on the speaker button, but Vito beat him to the punch.

"Joey, you there? It's me Vito!"

"Vito, when did you get back?" Joey answered, with his hand on the speaker button..

"A couple of minutes ago."

"Are those two pieces of shit with you?"

"They're here."

"Did Jimmy and…" Joey was interrupted right there.

"Yea, the two idiots saw everything. Don't worry about them, I'll take care of the both of them."

"You always told us to keep both of our eyes on the camera at all times," Jimmy was overheard saying in the background. "Well that's what we was doin'."

"Shut the fuck up and get back to work," Vito ordered. "Or else you'll be picking up horseshit at Belmont Park for the rest of your life. Just remember who I know there, I can make it happen!"

"Vito, you know if it were someone else, I wouldn't give two shits about it. But with Gloria, it's different. How do you think she feels about all of this? Every time I'm around her something happens."

"I know, just relax and stay there. Give me a couple of minutes with these two morons and I'll be right up."

"Alright, but come up through the basement entrance, I locked the front door."

"I just have to take care of some shit down here first," an angry Vito said, all along looking straight into the eyes of his two loyal confidants, Jimmy and Bear.

From the main floor of the pizzeria, you could hear Vito's violent tongue-lashing directed at Jimmy and Bear. The diatribe was not too pretty. He tore into the juvenile men like he would a juvenile delinquent. This mission on St. Ann's Place was not intended for fun and games. There would be serious business to be done here. Once Vito got his point across and everyone was in compliance, he started up the steps to enter the pizzeria.

Joey and Gloria just sat in a booth listening to whatever their ears would allow them to. Gloria seemed a little ill at ease with herself, knowing what just had taken place. What made her even more nervous was that she was about to meet Vito for the first time.

"Joey, I feel so cheap all of a sudden."

"Don't worry about it. Whatever they seen was very little anyway. You had all of your clothes on."

"Yes, but your hands were underneath my skirt, lifting it up," she lamented. "They had to see something."

"We are both making way too much out of this."

"I hope so," she said. "I certainly hope so."

Not making much of an entrance, Vito approached the two. His dark gray designer suit was neatly pressed, with not a wrinkle on it. A slight hint of some soft smelling cologne clung to him. Vito was not very hard to look at. For a mature man, he was very soft to the eyes of the opposite sex. Even Gloria appeared impressed when the gangster hovered over her, waiting to be introduced.

"Gloria, this is Vito," Joey said, starting off the introduction process. "Vito, this is Gloria."

Gloria extended her long thin arm in a welcoming gesture. Vito smiled at her and accepted her friendly handshake. Joey never expected to see this. He always knew the choices that Vito had hoped that he would make when it came to love and companionship, were Italian. But this time Joey just sensed that Vito was going to make an exception. Vito knew what stood before him. It appeared that he liked what he saw. The beauty that Gloria possessed was almost overpowering. By just looking at her, you were forced to like her. In fact, many Italian women looked at her with envy. In a way, if it were not for her slight accent, she could pass for a grease-ball. Even Vito adored her looks, you could just tell that he seemed to be taken by her in a paternal way.

On the other hand, Gloria was not the type at all to be running around with gangsters and mobsters. Deep down she knew that Joey was not one of them, or so she hoped he wasn't. She quivered when the word violence was even mentioned. But somehow she decided to try and find the good in everyone, even when it came to Vito. His actions in cleaning up the park were admired by Gloria in a very special way. In the meantime, some of the horrifying stories she had heard about him left her speechless. But somehow she had to come to the realization that this man was always going to be a part of Joey's life. Like it or not, the two would never ever be broken apart again. This she knew and this was the major concern that she had to come to terms with. All of these obstacles were all thought out very carefully before she made her decision to return to him. Love prevailed above all, even though one of the city's most notorious gangsters stood right before her, holding and shaking her hand.

"How are ya, honey?" Vito asked, looking down at her. "This guy over here was absolutely right about you."

"Why is that?"

"Because you are stunning," he said. "Any guy would flip his lid just to talk with you. I got a couple of assholes downstairs who make my point bona fide."

"Thanks, Vito, but they were a bit much," she replied. "Especially that Jimmy character."

"Don't worry about him, he really means no harm." Vito adjusted his neck-tie and said, "He's just a jokester who don't know when to quit."

"Vito, sit down and I'll get you a cup of coffee," offered Joey.

"I can't, I have to go to the club and meet some people. You two want to join me?"

"Nah, I think we're just going to go to her house and watch some television."

"I got a better idea for you. Why don't you take a couple of days off and go somewhere. I have a friend of mine, his parents run a bed and breakfast place upstate," he offered. "I think the both of you should pack a light bag and get the hell out of here for a few days. What do you say?"

"That sounds great!" Joey said with an enthused look on his face. Gloria knew exactly what Joey was thinking, she quickly nodded in agreement.

"I will call you later with all the details. Okay?"

"Thanks, Vito," Gloria said. "Thanks a lot. Gloria looked at Joey and put her arm around him. "He could use the rest."

"Good, so it's finalized. Besides, it will give you two a chance to get reacquainted with each other without any shitheads around," Vito said, winking at the both of them.

"What about the pizzeria?" Joey asked, wondering how Vito would cover his absence. "It's a lot of work."

"Don't worry about it. Your crew is fully capable and I'll stick Jimmy in there to just oversee things."

"Are you sure?" Joey asked, slipping out of the booth and getting onto his feet. "Jimmy ain't gonna like that!"

"He'll like it. If he has a problem with it he knows where he's going."

"Where's that?"

Vito started to laugh a little thinking about Jimmy and his new career. He also knew that Jimmy liked the ponies. But to what capacity was an entirely different story. "Let's just say that there's a union card waiting for him at the stables in Belmont Park. That guy likes to throw his shit around. Well, it's about time he starts picking some of it up."

"I could never picture him picking up horseshit!" Joey said, grinning and grabbing a hold of Vito's arm. "But then again!"

Of course, this was nothing more than idle chit chat. There was no way that Jimmy was going anywhere. Besides being a great worker and earner, he was loved by the whole crew. Jimmy's antics were just part of who he was. But when it came down to business, he was one dedicated and mean son of a bitch.

"Come on, let's get the hell out of here," Vito said. "I'll wait for you to lock up."

Vito waited outside, while Dutch sat in the driver's seat, ready to take the ride to Staten Island. Vito leaned up against the car and put a cigarette to his mouth. He hurriedly lit the tobacco stick and took a deep heavy drag on it. It was a matter of minutes before Joey and Gloria appeared. Gloria stood idle as Joey locked the front door and pulled down the heavy metal gates. After all was locked and secured, Joey turned around and flipped Vito the keys to the pizzeria.

"I have a set," said Vito.

"Take them anyway, just in case."

"Gloria, come here, darling," Vito said. "I want you to meet my right hand man."

The new woman on the block walked over to the running car without hesitation. She went straight to the driver's side window to meet Vito's companion. Dutch sat there quietly buffing out his black leather jacket.

"Gloria, this is Dutch!"

Dutch stuck his short arm out of the window and greeted the young woman with a handshake. His voice was trying to overpower the loud music coming from the cars stereo. "Hey Gloria, how you doin?"

"Fine, Dutch, it's so nice to meet you."

"Hey Joey, it looks like you picked a winner," he said shaking his left hand in an up and down motion. To most Italians and Dutch, that hand gesture meant something like the word awesome. In other words, all Dutch was trying to tell Joey was that he approved and consented to his fine choice of a lady. All three men shook their heads in agreement, while Gloria stood there blushing and flapping her eyelids. "Gloria, you and Joey look like you belong in Hollywood."

"You think we make a handsome couple?" she asked, turning to look at her man.

"Yea I do! You just gotta make sure that he don't get the shit kicked out him all the time. It's starting to ruin his features."

"Thanks Dutch," commented Joey. "I'm glad you noticed the difference."

"Any time, kid," he said smiling. "Vito, come on, we gotta get out of here."

Vito hugged Joey and gave Gloria a kiss on the cheek. He then ran to the passenger side of his car and was about to hop in. Looking at Joey one more time, he paused and asked him one last thing. "Remember, have a good time and if you decide to stay longer, just give me a call."

"You got it, I'll be gone two maybe three days' tops."

"Listen, when you get to the place, give me a call and let me know how it is. And always stay in touch with me just in case something comes up."

"Alright," promised Joey. "I will!"

"Gloria, where is your car, honey?" Vito asked her, while bobbing his head in her direction.

"It's right down the block," she answered, pointing in the direction with her closed umbrella. "On this side of the street."

"You want a lift down there?"

"Nah, the weather cleared up now," Joey said. "We'll just walk to her car."

"Okay then, have a good time, kid. If I was in your shoes, I know I sure would. And when you get back, I have something for you that you're going to like."

"What is it?" asked Joey, while moving closer to Gloria.

"It's a surprise, I'll tell you when the time is right."

With those parting words Vito did his usual thing before hopping into the car. He looked in both directions and behind his back until he felt safe enough to enter the car.

Joey put his left arm around Gloria's shoulder and the pair started their short walk to her car. Within an hour's time, Gloria met the whole crew. Well, almost the whole crew. The only missing misfit was Ricky the Roach. He was the only missing ingredient from the fabulous five. The last thing she needed was to see this unkempt vagabond, especially right before bedtime.

St. Ann's Place was lively, even at 10:30 in the evening. Traffic was flowing at a steady pace up and down the once desolate street.

"Hi Joey!" the man watering his garden said, waving his free hand.

"How are you, sir?" Joey responded, waving his right hand. "It turned out to be a nice night!"

"It sure has," the neighbor said.

Every step Joey took he was recognized by the people on the block. From little children to the handicapped in wheelchairs, they all knew him. The greetings came from the windows six stories up and even from vehicles motoring down the street. It was amazing, but Joey took it all in stride. He felt that he was just a small spoke in a gigantic rolling wheel. He just thought that somebody from the heavens above had put this all together. The more he thought about it, the more realistic it became. He had this weird sensation that he was on some kind of mission. From Vito on down to the Roach, the whole crew was a part of it. In Joey's mind they were a group of missionaries sent here to perform some charitable work in some foreign territory. But the more Joey thought about this, the more he started to believe it. It started the moment he put that medallion around his neck.

"Joey?" Gloria said, squeezing and clutching to him around his waist with her right arm. "It's unbelievable what you guys accomplished around here."

"I know it is," he started to say before pausing a bit and looking over his shoulder. "It's like all of this was planned or something. I can't put it into words."

"What do you mean?"

"I can't explain it, but I feel that someone is watching over me."

"Does this have anything to do with what you saw that night in your bedroom?" she asked, never breaking her stride. "To me, it sure seems like it does."

"I don't know, Gloria, but I never told anyone about it. The only other person who knows is Father Pasquale at my local parish. Besides, no one would believe me anyway."

All of a sudden Gloria stopped walking and pulled on Joey's left arm. "I believe you," she said to him. Joey then hugged her as she felt the powerful embrace of his loving arms.

Out of the blue, Joey felt some slight heat coming from his chest cavity. The burning sensation stunned him, though it was definitely a feeling that he had felt once or twice before. But this time the burning was just a tad more intense. He knew it was not Gloria's body heat; it was something much more than that. It was something similar to heartburn or indigestion. Only it was coming from the outside of his body. Joey withdrew from her grasp and looked over his shoulders and all around him. Struggling to see anything unusual, he knew something was out there staring at him.

"What's wrong with you?" a dumbfounded Gloria asked, starting to get a little worried. "Why are you acting this way?"

"There's somebody watching us, I can feel it."

"Joey, you're scaring me."

"Come on, let's hurry to the car."

The couple then picked up the tempo and headed straight for her car. Gloria got behind the wheel while Joey stood outside waiting for her to pop open the passenger's side door.

"Pull out of the spot," Joey ordered. His eyes were all over the block searching for the predator. After Gloria pulled out of the tight spot, she opened the door to let him in the car.

"Come on, get in," she hurriedly said, swinging the door wide open.

The quick thinking Joey just pretended to crouch down and get into the car. With his head halfway in, he swiftly reversed his motion and sprung to his feet. He knew that there was something out there stalking him for reasons why, he did not know. He would try anything to see that his intuitions were correct. This little maneuver worked to perfection, the guy's stealthy behavior was now exposed. It was then that Joey saw a figure that looked somewhat familiar to him.

What he saw was the head of some white man peeking out over the top of a parked car about fifty feet away. Joey just held his ground and stared at the stranger of the night. It was definitely the same guy that he saw the night the store was robbed. But this time Joey was right and Vito was wrong. This stalker had something else in mind. He was definitely not a part of the duo that robbed him the other night.

"Joey please, get in," pleaded Gloria. "Please!!"

"Alright, I'm coming."

Both men refused to give up one inch of ground. But Joey was not in a position to start chasing this guy all over Brooklyn. Gloria would have no part of his violence and his irrational behavior ever again. She was only back in his life for a couple of hours, so the thought of going after this lunatic was out of the question. He then succumbed to her wishes and hopped into the car.

"Honey," he said to her. "Take me out of this city for a couple of days, I'm starting to see things that just aren't there," he lied.

"I know you need some rest. And I am going to make sure that you get it."

"That's not all I need!" he said, playfully sticking his hands between her warm legs.

Joey was not going crazy at all. These nighttime images that he was seeing were not figments of his vivid imagination. He just told her that to ease her mind. But this man was definitely out there, somewhere. Joey was not seeing things, what he saw was most certainly real and very dangerous to him. And so were the warning signals that were coming from around his neck.

Chapter 20

THE WEATHER COULD not have been any nicer for a long drive up north. Their destination was Green County in upstate New York. For Joey, all the ingredients were there for a nice short vacation. He had his toothbrush, some toothpaste and Gloria. What more could a young man ever ask for out of life. Sure he packed some other necessities, but he wasn't planning on using them. They would be lucky if they ever stepped foot out of the bedroom.

The ride up was full of conversation and plans about the future. Both of them were thinking way ahead of themselves, but sometimes love makes you start walking even before you crawl. There were times during the three-hour drive when Joey would lapse off into a semi coma. Major portions of this drive brought back very bad memories for him. It so happened that the last time he traveled up the New York State Thruway, Justin O'Leary was sitting by his side. Every so often Gloria had to slap him on the arm to break him away from this spell that he was temporarily under. Prison life has a way of never letting go of you. One might walk out of the front gates towards freedom, but the bad memories linger on forever. They stay confined and indented inside your brain like the prisoner that you once were.

After a couple of stops for breakfast and a trip to the restrooms, they finally pulled up to a serene and pristine looking Manor. The oversized house was the perfect setting for retirement and old age. There was not a sound to be heard for miles. Even the birds seemed more at peace within themselves. Everything looked and smelled so fresh and clean. This was nature's bounty and it could bring out the country boy in all of us.

The couple removed their bags from the trunk and stood there staring at the tranquil house and its scenic setting. They slowly walked up a couple of steps and onto the veranda. The wooden porch was very rustic looking with all the fixings for rural living at its finest.

Overhead, the roof extended from the outside of the building protecting the quaint porch from all the elements of Mother Nature. A couple of rocking chairs and an oak love seat was all that furnished the outside platform. But for whatever it was, it was going to serve its purpose. There was not much more you could do up here besides enjoy some peace and very special quiet moments.

Joey put his suitcase down and took a seat on one of the rocking chairs. His eyes wandered across the paved road into the magnificent landscaped backdrop beyond the towering trees. There sat a beautiful six-acre lake shining brightly with its entire luster. The soft reflection resembled a clear sheet of ice without any movement to mar its picturesque view. A mother duck and her six ducklings floating in unison right behind her created the only motion.

"Come on, honey, let's check in," she said to him holding a small black duffle bag.

"You know, Gloria, somehow how I feel that I can get used to living like this," admitted Joey. "Being up here just makes you forget all your problems. Right now it seems that I don't have a care in the world."

"I know," she said looking quite comfortable. "This type of atmosphere does tend to put your mind at ease."

Later on that same afternoon Gloria and Joey spent their time doing absolutely nothing. Making love and watching some television were the extent of their daytime activities. They fell asleep the same way they entered the bedroom, together. After all, the three-hour trip had knocked both of them out. The marathon lovemaking just made sleep come a little sooner than expected.

For a couple of hours the next day the happy couple went row boating and took a stab at catching some wide mouth Bass. The manmade lake across the way provided the perfect opportunity to bring out the fisherman in the city dwellers. Neither venture was too successful; they both looked like bumbling fools. Joey was not that bad, but dealing with his girlfriend on a rowboat was more than he could handle. Everything she touched made her faint and feeling very dirty. There were no fish to be caught on this beautiful lake. Joey would have had a better chance of catching a great white shark in the deep blue sea. Instead he got stuck with a prissy Puerto Rican woman and an empty fish bucket.

"Come on, honey, let's go back to the room," Joey said. "When we get home I'll buy you some goldfish."

But all in all, it was a wonderful few days that Joey and Gloria enjoyed together. This was not Rome or the French Riviera, but it was what they were looking for. Peace and quiet was on the menu and peace and quiet was what they found. Sometimes to get what you are looking for you have to give something up. What they forfeited was the miserable city life for three whole glorious days and three wild and sensuous nights.

For some reason, when their stay ended they could not wait to get back to the city. They could not wait to get back to the dirt and filth, back to the degenerates and molesters, back to the muggers and thieves. But most of all, back to the place that they called home. What Joey failed to realize was that there was something else luring him back into the city. This something had surreal powers that were invisibly calling him back. Like a magnet, it pulled and pulled him back to where it thought he belonged. That something was hanging right around his neck.

The car pulled up in front of the pizzeria at about 9:30A.M. Vito and the rest of the crew were all out there sitting around the tables drinking coffee and eating Italian pastries. They were carrying on like they did not have a care in the world. Each one of them behaved like they owned the neighborhood, and in a way they did. All the threats were just a thing of the past. These guys had everything under their thumbs and under control. The power they displayed was simply awesome; nobody would ever take the chance to go up against it. It was immovable and quite devastating when it was aroused. They knew it, and the people in the community knew it.

"Hey, look who's back!" Dutch alerted everyone as Gloria's car braked to a stop in front of the pizzeria. Dutch quickly ejected himself from his seat and started moving towards the late model Chevrolet.

One by one each one of the boys got off of their chairs and came over to the car to welcome back Joey. They all acted like they had not seen him in years. The kid was only gone for a few short days, but to them it seemed much longer than that. The way he was greeted made him feel like he was just released from prison all over again. He never felt that anyone besides family and Gloria could ever miss him so much. The affection overwhelmed him, especially coming from a bunch of ruthless gangsters.

Joey just stared at Vito from inside the car as all the boys were inching closer to greet him. All of them made the short trip, except Vito. The messiah of St. Ann's Place just sat planted in his chair underneath the colorful umbrella. But he did share in the jubilation of the moment. A tepid smile was almost hidden on his tanned face. That's the way Vito was, he never went over to anybody just to say hello. Like it or not, if you wanted a greeting from this handsome Italian man, you would have to go to him.

"How was your trip?" Dutch asked, observing a smiling Joey and Gloria through the open driver's side window of the car. "You both looked like you had a good time!"

"It was quiet," said Joey. "Real quiet."

Now leaning against the front car door, Dutch shook Joey's hand. "Good, you both look like you are well rested."

"Yea, but after a while you can go out of your mind up there," said Joey. "It's good to be back!"

"And how are you, doll?"

Gloria slightly pushed her neck forward to look at Dutch from the passenger's seat. "I'm feeling just fine, Dutch," she said in a shy manner, "I was in very good company."

"How are things over here?" asked Joey, observing the surroundings that he seemed to miss. "Do I still have a business to run?"

"Barely, Vito had Jimmy running around like a chicken without a head. He's been bitching about running the store ever since you left," Dutch went on. "There's no more singing coming from his mouth, just complaining. He claims that he lost ten pounds from all the heat from the pizza oven."

"Hey Jimmy," Joey called to his temporary replacement. "No wonder why you look happy to see me. You probably never worked so hard in your life, you lazy bastard!"

"Yea, I'm happy to see you."

"I bet you are!"

"I'm so fuckin' happy, that you just gave me a hard on," Jimmy said. "Now get out of the car and come over here and take care of business," he added while grabbing his crotch.

"Not in your wildest dreams," Joey said.

"I wasn't talkin' to you, I was talking to…" he started to say before he was interrupted.

"Don't even go there," Joey warned. Joey knew that the next few words out of his sick mouth were going to be spoken in Gloria's direction.

"Just get out of the car and put this fuckin' apron on," he added, slowly untying the strings of the white garment from behind his back. "No more vacations for you!"

"Why, I think you look kind of cute in white, the color becomes you. You look like a fag in it!"

"Kiss my ass," he said to Joey's sarcasm. Jimmy then rolled the apron up into a small ball and threw it at Joey who was still sitting in the front seat of the car.

"This fuckin' apron is spotless. Don't go telling anybody that you were busting your ass in there. I know you probably had my men running ragged. Did they all quit on me?" Joey asked. "Looking at this apron, it doesn't look like you did shit anyway."

"Enough with the fuckin' apron already," a deep voice from the back ordered. "Joey, never mind him," said Vito. "Get out of the car, I want to talk with you."

"Let me go," Joey said, turning to Gloria. "The king has spoken."

"Will I see you tonight?" she asked, waiting patiently for an answer. Joey then rubbed his eyes with his right hand. For a few minutes he pondered about the invitation before giving his answer.

"Probably not, God only knows what I am going to find in there. Jimmy probably left the store a mess," he said. "My guys work so hard all day long that sometimes they get lax when it comes to cleaning up before we close for the night."

"Okay," she whispered close to his ear. "I'll call you later."

"Come by tomorrow night about eight o'clock. You can eat here and then I'll go home with you."

"Ok, honey," she said, kissing him on the cheek. Joey then opened the driver's side door and slipped out of her car. Gloria then hopped over the stick shift and sat behind the wheel of the car.

"Be careful driving?"

"I will, I'll talk to you later," she said, adjusting the rearview mirror of the car. "Okay?"

"You got it," Joey said, giving her another kiss before she left.

"I had a great time."

"So did I, honey."

"Bye!"

The white car then pulled away down the busy street. Joey's eyes followed the car half way down the street then turned and headed in Vito's direction. He paused for a few minutes to shake a few hands as he realized he was back to the real world. Vito stayed seated sipping on his espresso, waiting for Joey to take a seat next to him. Walking with his right hand extended for a greeting, Joey bent down, shook Vito's hand and kissed him on the cheek. The rest of the boys disembarked into the basement to take care of their daily activities. With the baseball season in full gear, the phones would be ringing off the hook with customers ready to place their bets on Saturday's games.

"Sit down," ordered Vito. "How was your trip?"

"It was nice," he said, while falling into a chair. "It felt good to get away for a few days."

"That's why you went. Sometimes a few days away from the real world can clear up a clouded mind."

"Well now I'm back," Joey said. "There's something that I want to talk to you about also."

"What is it?" Vito asked, as a light wind riffled his hair and moved the umbrella overhead.

"Remember I told you about that white guy who was staring at me from across the street?"

"That was the day the store got robbed, right?"

"Yea."

"What about him?" Vito asked, still feeling that the observer was always part of the robbery.

"The night before we left to go upstate, he followed us down the block."

"Are you sure it was the same guy?"

"Without a doubt, he kept hiding behind parked cars and trees. But then I got a full view of him and it looked like the same guy."

"Are you sure?"

"I would bet my life on it."

"So what did you do?"

"Nothing, I had Gloria with me. I was not about to go chasing this guy all over the neighborhood."

"What does he look like?" Vito asked, continuing his small barrage of questions. "Is there anything you can tell me about him?"

"It was dark, I couldn't really make out his face. But he seemed to have the same clothes on that he was wearing the first night I saw him."

"Was he tall, short, fat, skinny, what?"

"He appears to be thin and seems to be around six feet tall."

"I'm gonna talk to the boys and see if there were any suspicious characters hanging around here lately."

"Vito, I just know that this guy was not a part of the robbery that night."

"And how do you know that?"

"I just have a feeling that he is here for something else, that's all."

"Well what could he want from you?"

"I don't know, I don't have any enemies who know my whereabouts. Shit, besides the guys in the park I don't have any enemies at all."

"What about from your days on Wall Street?"

"Nah, those guys aren't the type for revenge."

"Well then forget about it. Maybe he's just a homo who likes the way you look."

"Would you stop making a joke out of this!" Joey said, pulling out a cigarette from a freshly opened pack. "The only other person I could think of that had a problem with me, would be Ramon."

"Ramon, forget about that spic bastard. That guy is still shitting his pants. He gets skid marks in his underwear every time he hears my name. Once a week I send one of my boys into his bar just to keep his memory fresh," he said, putting his lighter to Joey's unlit cigarette. "He's still ordering the pizzas from you, isn't he?"

"Every Friday night he orders five pies."

"That guy will still be ordering the fuckin' pizza from his grave, that's how fucked up he is."

Well then if it's not Ramon, I don't know who the fuck it is, Joey thought.

"It just gives me a funny feeling when you have to keep looking over your shoulder. I don't like it."

"Join the club," Vito said. "There's not a single moment of each and every day of my life that I don't constantly look over my shoulder. After a while you kind of get used to it."

"Well I don't want to get used to it. This is not how I want to live my life, Vito," Joey nervously said. "I want to get out of here."

"Soon, kid. We'll all be leaving very soon."

Vito started to go into deep thought; he was thinking and hoping that someone was not after Joey to get back at him. He knew his Godson was not the one to make up stories like this. Knowing the feeling of being stalked gave him great concern for Joey's safety. But he did not want him to worry about it too much. To Vito, this had now become an issue to be severely dealt with. At all times, either he or one of his boys would always be keeping an extra eye on Joey.

"If you ever see this guy again, you call me," Vito said, with a very concerned look on his face. "It don't matter where you are or what you're doing, you call me. Do you hear me?"

"I will, but I hope that I'm wrong."

"I hope that you're not seeing things either. This could be very dangerous, sometimes innocent people could get killed. So make sure and don't assume anything about this guy."

"I'm pretty sure."

"Pretty sure is not good enough. You must be 100 percent positive about this."

"Okay," Joey softly said. "I'm a 100 percent positively sure."

"Lately you keep telling me about all this weird shit that's been happening to you since you put that medallion on. I'm starting to think that you're seeing things. Tell me about these so called things that have been happening to you?" Vito asked, while moving his hands through the air. Just by his hand movements, Joey knew that Vito did not believe him at all.

"It's nothing, I just get these weird feelings that's all. Like someone is trying to direct the fate of my life."

"Who?"

"I don't know," Joey answered, taking a peek at the gold chain dangling from around his neck.

"And you think that it has something to do with the medal?"

"It's probably just coincidental, that's all. I wish I had the right answers for you."

"Well, obviously I think that you're assuming again."

"I don't know what to think anymore."

"Do you know the history behind that medallion?"

"Not really, other than what you already told me. But when I went to have it blessed, a priest told me that it was a very old and rare piece."

"What else did he say?"

"Nothing much, he was just acting very silent," Joey explained. "Like he was hiding something from me. I know there was something that he wanted to tell me, but for some reason he couldn't."

"Like what?"

"I don't know. But little by little I am starting to understand why."

There was no way in hell that Joey was going to get too technical with Vito about this, at least not now. He felt that there was no way he would believe him. Whatever was discussed between Father Pasquale and Joey would have to stay secluded from others, even Vito. But deep down, Joey thought that Vito knew something that he also was not revealing. It was about time for Vito to come clean and tell him what he really knows.

"I know you know something about this medallion. So tell me."

"What makes you say that? Did Dutch say anything to you?"

"Dutch never said a word about anything to me."

"Alright then," Vito confessed. "There is something that I failed to tell you."

"I knew it!"

"Be quiet and let me tell you a little story about that medallion," Vito said. "In prison, I also told Dutch this same story. He thinks that this medallion has some kind of powers or something strange to that effect," Vito chuckled.

"What do you mean?" asked Joey, starting to show grave concern on what was about to come out of Vito's mouth. "What powers?"

"Well, now he just thinks that all the coincidental stuff that brought us here has a reason behind it. When I told him the story that I'm about to tell you," Vito paused a second to light a cigarette.

"So, go on!" Joey said, acting very anxious to hear the rest. "What did he think?

"It just gave him some crazy thoughts. That's all."

Looking very mystified and puzzled, Joey wasted no time with his next question. "What's so crazy about his thoughts? Sometimes these premonitions can be very real. Tell me the story."

"Well, many years ago back in Palermo, Italy. My grandfather was doing some masonry work on a school in some small village right outside the city," he said looking straight into Joey's eyes. "A mysterious fire broke out inside the school with a bunch of school kids trapped inside the small building. When he saw all the fire and smoke pouring out of the building, he raced inside," continued Vito. "My grandfather saved each and every one of those eleven kids who were trapped inside their classrooms and brought them to safety. Two at a time with one child under each arm, he carried them out and went back in to look for more."

"Did he find any more kids?" Joey asked, glued to his seat.

"He didn't stop until he rescued them all." Vito then paused to light another cigarette and then quickly went back to his story. "The ironic part of the whole story was later on the authorities found out that these kids were abused by the caretaker of the school. It turned out that this idiot was the last one who was trapped inside the building by the surrounding flames. This fucking degenerate screamed and screamed, but he could not get out. My grandfather heard that bastard's screams coming from inside the weakening and damaged schoolhouse. The roaring fire had that piece of shit trapped inside one of the classrooms. One last time my grandfather went into the school to save this scumbag from death. He was almost overcome by the smoke, but he continued to look for this guy. Thank God all of the little kids were outside because the fire was intensifying with each passing second. Suddenly the roof caved in falling right on top of him." Vito kept on going, even though a small teardrop was seeping out the corner of his right eye. "It took them two days before they were able to dig him out of the rubble. When they finally reached his seared body, he was unidentifiable. They knew who he was, but the medallion proved his true identity. He was found with his right hand clutching to that gold piece. My grandfather died with that medallion in the palm of his right hand. That pervert bastard was lying right below him, covering the bottom of his legs. He probably dropped him when the roof caved in on top of them. Once he saved those children from the fire, it was all over for him. Someone did not want him to exit that building with that pedophile on his back. They say he was struck down by something even mightier than the fire. Some kind of spirit or something," he said with a low whimper.

Holy shit, Joey thought. *I saw that spirit.* Was *it the same one?*

Vito took a few seconds to compose himself, and then continued on. "He did it all for what, to protect someone that deserved to die?" Vito asked, with a confused look on his face. "Funny thing about the whole story was that he was not even supposed to be by that school that day. His boss had a change of plans for him when somebody called in sick. The boss took him off of another job site and placed him at the school." Vito was now showing sure signs of compassion, his voice and teary eyes were proof of that. "My Pop, may his soul rest in peace, thinks that Jesus Christ sent his father on this mission."

"Do you?"

"No, I just think that it's all just a coincidence and that's it."

"But your family thinks that it's much more than that."

"So does the whole town that they come from," Vito calmly said. "That day some of the people claim they witnessed all kinds of weird crap."

"Like what?"

"Earthquakes and lightning and all kinds of shit. They say something biblical happened that day. The people over there are still talking about it."

"Man!" Joey said, shaking. "This gives me the chills."

"It gave everybody the chills. In Italy, the Carlucci name is next to sainthood. They turned my grandfather's grave into a shrine."

"So you must have been proud to wear this medallion around your neck, I know I am."

"Not really, somehow I feel that I have ruined the image of my own family. All of my rotten ways have disgraced my family name. That's why I have always felt that I did not deserve to wear that medallion."

"Wow Vito, but that's some story," a startled Joey said. "You must be very proud of your grandfather."

"I am, he was some man. I never met him, but I always felt that he lived inside of me through that medallion. That's why that piece means so much to me. Do you understand what I'm telling you?"

"I do," Joey said. "But where did your grandfather get the medallion from?"

"Back in 1908 my great-grandfather Alfonso, found it. There was a major earthquake outside the city of Cantania. He dug it up while he was searching for bodies. The medallion has been in my family ever since."

"This story gets spookier and spookier to me."

"Never mind all that," Vito warned. "Just make sure that you take care of that medallion. It's very special to me."

"I promise that I will never take it off of my neck ever again."

"Good," Vito said, rubbing Joey's head. "Let's get to work, you have a lot to do. And I don't ever want to hear anything about weird happenings or spooky feelings ever again. I know that sometimes certain things appear to be strange, but everything is coincidental. Sometimes situations appear to be the same, but they're not. Let's just say that everything happens for a reason, and leave it at that. There is nobody planning or arranging your future or your fate. You are the only one who is responsible for the outcome of your life, nobody else."

"I know but….," he started to say but his mouth was quickly covered by Vito's right hand.

"I said that's enough, go to work."

"You're probably right," Joey falsely said. "I will put it behind me. Hey Vito, what about the surprise you promised me before I went upstate?"

"When the time is right, I will tell you."

Joey knew that Vito was wrong. He also knew that there was some kind of spirit or presence lingering over him. What it wanted from him, he did not have the faintest idea. All he knew was that it was alive and it was watching every one of his moves. There was no way in hell that Vito would understand or believe any of this. This matter was better left unsaid or untold when it came to him. But deep down, Joey had a feeling that Vito knew something was strange or suspicious when it came to this medallion. He just was not coming clean with whatever he felt or knew. Maybe his tough guy image would never let him reveal the truth.

"Listen, I have all the paperwork and money from the last three days downstairs. I'll bring it up to you later."

"How did we do?"

"Good, the business now runs itself. Even Jimmy couldn't fuck it up," a laughing Vito confessed. "You got a bunch of good workers in there, they really respect you."

"I know, they are the best."

"One other thing I forgot to tell you," Vito said. "Tomorrow night at eight, we're having a big poker game downstairs. Make up a couple trays of food for me and the boys."

"You got it. Anything special?"

"Nah, just throw any shit together."

"No problem, what time do you want the food?"

"Have it down there before we start the game."

"You got it, I'll see you in a little while, let me go inside."

That little story that Vito had told Joey sent chills up and down his spine. The feeling was so strong that it took him over half the day to temporarily release it from his mind. Joey came ever so close to telling Vito about the episode in his bedroom that late summer night. Vito never would have believed him anyway, or would he? Joey thought that he knew Vito well; he also knew all the idiosyncrasies that the man possessed. Sometimes his peculiar behavior and stubbornness forced him into not believing anything. But Joey still decided to stay mute about the whole situation, at least for now. A little premonition from up in the sky must have told him to.

Sunday night came very quickly as the boys geared up for their monthly poker game. Five men would sit around a round table entrenched in their seats for at least 12 to 24 hours. Each one of them took this event very seriously. Besides Jimmy, there was not too much clowning around at all. But he did tone it down a bit, especially when he was winning.

Vito's facial expressions never changed, winning or losing, he never revealed any emotion. He was much the competitor and he played cards the same way he lived his life, dangerously. Most of the time, he would just try to scare someone right out of a hand. Even if the player opposite him had a full house, Vito did not care. There was never a limit to his betting or raises when it came to playing cards. He either won big time or lost his pants trying to bluff everyone at the table. Sometimes his strategy worked, but most of the times it didn't. Everyone believed that he just played for the excitement of it all. When money or anything else of value was on the line, Vito seemed to get aroused. The higher the stakes the more excited he got. Of course these feelings were kept hidden underneath his stoic poker face.

The food was there right on time as Joey promised. There was a tray of chicken Marsala and some pasta in marinara sauce. Everyone ate like animals before they decided to sit down and finally play cards. Dirty paper plates littered the small basement. They all ate standing up, for eating at the poker table was a mortal sin. The table was only used for cards, money, ashtrays and cigarettes. Occasionally a can of beer or another type of beverage would find its way to the table, but nothing more.

After an hour, Vito was losing big time, and he was in for over a thousand bucks. Jimmy was also getting pounded as his theatrics were starting to surface. Dutch just coolly sat there with no expression on his face at all; so far things were going his way.

Holding his own was the Roach; he was like any other Jew when it came to money. This guy could have been sitting with four aces and he would still think twice about throwing money into the pot. Even with the best hand in the world, you couldn't get a dime out of him. That's how careful he was with his money, but that's how careful most Jews were. They would look at the same dollar bill one hundred times to make sure that it was not a ten. His procrastination made everyone nuts, most of the time this behavior got everyone at the table furious. If the Roach did not like his opening hand, 99 percent of the time he bowed out. Never willing to risk his money on what the rest of the deck had in store for him. But there was one thing for certain, down in his mother's basement, where he lived, somewhere there was a closet full of money.

Bear was another story altogether; he was too stupid to realize anything. This guy would stay in a hand just because someone else told him to. He was very easily coaxed into situations or favors by the other players. This activity enraged Vito to the bitter end. But this was his crew and these were the people that he played cards with. Many times the Bear's ignorance made him a winner. And that infuriated Vito even more. Bear was not a rocket scientist, that's for sure. But he wasn't as stupid as everyone thought he was.

"Come on, come on, deal the fuckin' cards," an anxious Vito said to Jimmy. "For once I wish that you would shut your fuckin' mouth and just play cards."

"Hey Vito," Jimmy said. "What do you call two niggers in a shoe box?"

"I don't know, just deal!"

"A pair of loafers," Jimmy said, in a fit of laughter. His antics practically threw him off of his own chair. It seems his racist joke only got a rise out of Bear, the rest just concentrated on the hands in front of them.

Jimmy slowly started to deal the cards around the table. Each man slowly picked up their play and examined it closely. One by one, the playing cards landed in front of each player. This game was called draw poker and each man received five cards. After the task of dealing all the cards, Jimmy started up with his shenanigans all over again.

"Vito?"

"What is it now?"

"What do you call an Ethiopian with sesame seeds in his head?" Jimmy said intently at Vito. He really knew how to get under Vito's skin. He also knew that Vito was not in the mood to hear any of his stupid jokes.

"What?" Vito quickly answered.

"A quarter-pounder!"

The second joke brought out the same responses as the first. But this time even Dutch managed to crack a small smile. It was hard to tell what he was laughing at, Jimmy or the joke.

"All right, that's enough of the jokes," Vito ordered. "This is a card game, not a fuckin' comedy club."

"One more," Jimmy pleaded, with laughter. "One more."

"It better be the last one or you'll be sailing to Ethiopia first thing in the morning."

"Okay, ready for this one, this is a killer!"

"Go ahead," Dutch said to Jimmy. "But make sure it's the last one, he's getting pissed." Dutch then used his head pointing to Vito who had his eyes buried in his cards.

"How do you get a nun pregnant?"

"Be careful with this one," Vito warned, but never taking his eyes off of his cards. But his warning did not affect Jimmy at all. He went right on telling the joke.

"You dress her up as an altar boy."

Vito picked his head up away from his cards. He just stared at Jimmy with a look on his face that could kill. Vito really did not have to say anything, but this time Jimmy got the message. The show was over and it was back to playing cards again. Jimmy was always a fun guy to be around, but he just did not know when to quit. The only thing that slowed him down was the ire on Vito's face. When he saw that his boss was ready to explode, then he quickly backed off. It was either that or really going on a one way trip to Ethiopia. Jimmy opted to do the right thing and just stay quiet for a while.

Another hour had passed by and Vito was sitting with an ace high flush. The name of the game had been changed to seven-card stud. Everyone but Jimmy was already out of the game. There must have been about two thousand bucks sitting in the middle of the table for the winner. This time there was no joking around as the two players tried not to show each other any emotion. The mood was very serious; each move was made with ultimate precision.

"I'll see your hundred and raise you another hundred," Vito said to Jimmy.

"Here's fifty," Jimmy said, throwing fifty dollars into the pot. "And I'm going light on the other fifty."

"No, no, no, no, no," Vito said. "No money, no play."

"Come on, why not?"

"You know the rules in which we play by."

"Those are bullshit rules."

"They might be bullshit rules when you don't have the money," answered Vito. "And it appears to me, that you ain't got the money."

"After I win this hand I will pay the pot back."

"No dice, Jimbo."

"Come on, just this one time."

"Nope."

"Bear, lend me fifty!"

"No borrowing on this one, pal. And you're only in this fuckin' hand because the Bear plays like an asshole. I know you and him are cheatin' me. He keeps kicking you under the table."

"That's bullshit!"

"That's bullshit? You're bullshit. Now just put up the money or else say goodbye to the money in the pot."

"I got the fuckin' money," said Jimmy, rising to his feet. "I'll be right back!" He then walked into the back room.

"Where the fuck is he going?" Vito asked Dutch.

"You think I have a clue about anything that guy does?"

Bear and the Roach just sat there quietly trying to hold in their impending smiles. Both of them knew what Jimmy was up to, but either one was about to give him up. About a minute later Jimmy reappeared with a sarcastic look on his boyish round face.

"What the fuck are you doing?" a stunned Vito asked, in disbelieve.

"Here's my money," Jimmy answered, holding two parking meters, one under each arm. He then dropped one meter on the floor and took out a hammer from inside of his belt that was fastened snugly around his waist.

"This is no good."

"Why not," Jimmy said, hammering away to crack open the city meter.

"Because there is no silver allowed in the game."

"Using coins was never discussed as a rule, and you know it."

"If silver is good so is lead!" Vito shouted, removing his gun from his shoulder holster. "I can't believe this fuckin' guy."

With a final blast from the hammer, Jimmy cracked the parking meter wide open. Quarters went flying all over the card table. There was no way that there were fifty dollars in coins there, and Jimmy knew it.

"Bear, while I'm counting this shit, crack open the other one."

Vito just sat there seething. He was never in a card game with such inane playing tactics before. He was mad, practically snarling at Jimmy as he hovered over his quarters.

With one swift strike from the hammer Bear nearly broke the sturdy parking meter in half. The explosion sent coins flying all over the basement floor. Jimmy and Bear went quickly to their knees to retrieve the coins. Dutch and Vito looked on, incredulity written on their faces. They exchanged a troubled glance and shook their heads in disbelief.

"Dutch, could you please tell me what the fuck is going on here?" Vito asked. "This fuckin' guy is unbelievable!"

"Vito, let him count the change and get it over with," Dutch reasoned calmly, while getting ready to deal out the last card. "You probably got him beat anyway."

"Look at these two fuckin' clowns, sometimes I'm embarrassed to say that they even work for me."

"Hey Jimmy, there's one over there," Bear yelled out from underneath the table. His long arm then pointed to the corner of the room where a few quarters managed to land. "Vito, could you move your foot?"

"How would you like my foot up your fuckin' ass?" Vito said in disgust, never moving his feet. "That's enough, I had it now. Both of you get the fuck up now!"

Jimmy and Bear ignored Vito's orders for a few seconds trying to gather up as many quarters as they possibly could. Their pace just picked up a little speed as they tried to grab every last cent. Jimmy rose to his feet with a big smile on his face. Bear just kept his head down in embarrassment, never looking in Vito's or Dutch's direction. It then took another five minutes to count all the quarters before Dutch was to deal the last card of the hand.

"I got fifty eight dollars and seventy five cents," Jimmy declared. He then pushed the 200 quarters into the center of the table. Leaving the rest of them by his side. "I see your hundred," he said looking at Vito.

"Do you have anymore parking meters in the back room?" asked Vito, his tone belittling.

"Why?

"Because you fuckin' idiot, there's still one more card to be dealt."

"Shit," he said in a loud and angry voice. "No, there's no more. I cracked the other ones open a few days ago"

"Don't think for one minute that you're going to go outside and rip down every parking meter on the block."

"Come on, Vito, cut me some slack here!" Jimmy pleaded, practically begging Vito for mercy. His facial expression was very hard to refuse, even to Vito.

"I'll tell you what," Vito began to reason. "Let Dutch deal the last card and the winner takes all. I will check the hand to you. You call, and then we will reveal our cards. I had enough of this shit. Next time you two clowns pull this shit with me I'm gonna break both of your fuckin' necks. Do you understand me?"

"Yea, I do," Jimmy nonchalantly said.

"Okay then, let Dutch deal the last card and the best hand wins."

"Okay," said Jimmy softly. Besides, Vito was growing very impatient with this hand of cards. Never in his life has he ever seen a hand of cards take so long to finish.

"Deal the cards, Dutch," ordered Vito.

For some reason Dutch was off in dreamland looking in another direction. Vito's words to deal the cards flew right over his head. All the boys just sat there waiting for him to deal the last two cards, but the cards never left his hand. His eyes stood focused on something else other then the card game.

"Dutch, deal the fuckin' cards!" Vito demanded again, again with no response. This time Vito looked at him and saw his eyes fixated at something beyond the round table. The boss followed Dutch's eyes. Vito slowly moved his head to the right of him and right into the video monitor that led up to the pizzeria. At that moment all five members of this cut throat poker game sat frozen and watched what was slowly transpiring upstairs.

What they saw was a mangy looking character standing in front of the counter conversing with Joey. Behind the intruder sat Gloria acting very nervous, her head was looking in two different directions. The boys then turned their focus on the other camera, which captured the short aisle of the small eatery. It appeared that an accomplice was standing by the front door, holding it open. This nerve-racking suspense was growing stronger with each passing second. Everyone was watching tensely as Joey and the "customer" were engaging in some kind of conversation. Slowly but surely, they silently watched Joey's right hand slide down his side and rest on top of the button that would summon the troops. The gang waited and waited, but they got nothing. They continued to watch, anxiously waiting for the call that would require their response, still nothing. In the background they saw Gloria bury her face in the palm of her hands. From her angle she must have gotten a whole different perspective of the situation. It was almost time for the gangsters to react.

"If he's in trouble, why isn't he ringing the fuckin' bell?" Dutch asked, hoping his premonitions that a robbery was about to take place were wrong.

"I don't know," Vito answered. "But I don't see a gun."

"Come on, kid," Dutch said to an unhearing Joey. "Tell us something. Ring that damn bell!"

"There it is," Jimmy said. "There it is!"

In the heat of the moment, the villain raised his right hand over the top of the counter. This movement revealed what the boys were looking for. Everyone's worst nightmare suddenly came true. A small revolver was now in full view of the video camera. Without hesitation, the five card players quickly jumped to their feet, poised for action. Playing cards were flying everywhere, exposing both hands of the two final players. As it turned out, Jimmy had nothing better than two pairs, kings over deuces.

"Dutch, you and Jimmy go up the back steps!" Vito barked while reaching for his pistol. …"Bear, you come with me. These two assholes just signed their death warrants."

"Come on, Jimmy," Dutch called. "Let's bury these motherfuckers."

"Dutch, move quietly," Vito informed him. "As soon as you get a good shot, you take him out. Just kill the bastard. We'll get what we need to know from the other one standing outside the store."

Everyone listened to their orders and responded without hesitation. Dutch and Jimmy started to quietly and slowly climb up the basement steps. The old and decrepit wooden steps started to sing a tune with every movement of the duo's feet. Every board on each step made an aggravating squeaking sound. The sounds were definitely an alarm for the intruders upstairs.

"Take off your shoes!" Dutch said to Jimmy, while bending down to take off his own pair.

"What," Jimmy said in a loud voice.

"Be quiet, you fuckin' idiot, or they'll hear us." Dutch hissed. "Do as I say and just take off your shoes."

Jimmy did not have to be told twice, the men silently removed their shoes and started up the old staircase. Meanwhile Vito and Bear raced outside and down the alleyway to the front of the building. Coming to a complete stop, they started to inch their way towards the front door.

"You stay here," Vito said quietly. "You're too clumsy. Just stay here and watch my back."

Vito then spotted his prey with one foot in and one foot out of the pizzeria. Inch by inch he crept closer to the target, never exposing his presence. Within the blink of an eye he raised his pistol and made his final move. He stuck the barrel of his gun right in the back of the surprised hooligan. With his left hand he covered the mouth of the wild and potentially destructive criminal.

"Don't make a sound or I'll blow your fuckin' brains out," Vito gravely warned. "Now slowly drop the gun and don't turn around."

"Okay man," he said. "Don't shoot."

The tall thin black man offered no resistance as he obeyed Vito's orders. Bear quickly rushed to Vito's side and picked up the silver revolver from the pavement and stuck it in the waist of his tan trousers. Relentlessly, Bear then grabbed the nervous lookout man and pulled him away from the position he was guarding so carefully. Then with one fast and furious thrust, Bear hoisted the bewildered foe and tossed him to the concrete floor. The other hoodlum in front of the counter turned quickly to observe the whereabouts of his cohort. In a matter of two seconds, gunfire rang throughout the small eatery followed by female screaming.

The young lady, blanched white with terror, turned her head away from the perilous scene. Gloria sat mortified, crying and shaking as she buried her head in the palms of her trembling hands.

The gunshot had a tremendous impact. At close range, it perforated a gaping hole right through one side of the suspect's skull and out the other. The predator was most certainly dead. A .38 caliber bullet blew a hole through his brain. He fell face first to the tiled floor below. The tainted bullet lodged in the wall, adjacent and a few feet behind Joey. The glass partition that covered the food was splattered with blood and unidentifiable body parts. Blood and gore were everywhere. This guy had no chance - he never knew what hit him.

Standing in the background was Dutch with a big smile on his face. His .38 caliber revolver, still smoking was propped up about six inches from his right shoulder blade. Right next to him was a relieved Jimmy, who stood erect with his pistol by his side. Behind them the three Mexicans, with their eyes darting, looked on horrified. They all huddled around standing very close to each other frightfully watching the events unfolding. But it was not over yet, as there was still one other punk that had to be dealt with.

"Bring that motherfucker in here!" Vito said to Bear, holding the door open and waving him inside the store with his gun. Bear walked through the front door holding his victim around the waist and a few feet off of the ground. He then sent the helpless thug hurling to the tiled floor. The lookout man crashed down hard, not knowing what to expect next.

Joey and Gloria just stayed silent, waiting for more bloodshed. To Joey, this was the last thing that he ever wanted Gloria to see. He knew that these atrocities would surely scar her for life. Never in her young life would she ever be exposed to such wickedness.

"Bear," Vito said. "Bring down the front gates."

Hurriedly, Bear ran outside and pulled down the heavy metal grate covering the front window of the store. He then stepped inside and pulled down the other grate that shielded the front door. This move secured Vito's privacy from any witnesses or passersby. Everyone inside the store knew what was about to happen. Some of the occupants enjoyed these rituals, and others just cringed with just the thought of it.

"Gloria honey," Vito said. "Go into the bathroom, darling, and cover your ears. I'm very sorry you had to see all this."

The poor girl was in shock, she looked at Joey sobbing hysterically. Like a zombie in a comatose state, Gloria did as he suggested. Joey was distressed realizing that this was his fault. He had thought that maybe, just maybe, peace had finally arrived. But he was dead wrong. It seemed that there would never be the absence of hostilities on St. Ann's Place.

"Get on your fuckin' knees," Vito screamed at the man. "You heard me, get on your fuckin' knees!"

Slowly he picked his body up off of the floor and got onto both knees. He was shaking so much that his pants were quivering. Perspiration started to bead on his forehead. It was now finding its way into his eyes causing him to squint. His white tee shirt was now transparent as it clung to his wet, sweaty body.

With the evil of Satan possessing him, Vito started to take a couple of steps closer to the disgraced suspect. Now hovering over him, his total being became so intensified; his eyes looked like they were changing colors. All of his composure was gushing from his over eager body. Vito abruptly took a look over at Joey and then shook his head in a loathing fashion.

"Are these the same guys that robbed you the last time?" Vito asked Joey, impatiently waiting for an answer. "Come on, give me an answer!"

Joey carefully examined both of the men before him. He knew that he had to be 100 percent sure of his finger pointing. To be wrong in a situation like this could wind up more tragic than it already was. He took his time as he scanned back and forth between the two hoodlums. Joey finally reached his awaited decision. For the truth must be told.

"The one on his knees, he's the one," Joey forcefully responded. "This one over here," he said, pointing to the dead man. "He was the lookout man the last time. They probably switched positions thinking that I would not recognize them. But yea, this is them."

These circumstances always brought out the worst in Vito. To him, these two thugs showed a total lack of respect for him and his crew. Plus the fact that they threatened the one person in this world he truly loved. Not to mention the woman who truly loved his Godson. For these were acts that would never be tolerated and go unpunished. These actions had to and would be dealt with in the most severe and extreme way possible.

"Look at me," Vito sternly said as the man looked up at him. "Who sent you here?"

"Nobody, man," he cried in vain. "We just needed some money."

"That's bullshit," snarled Vito, with his gun two inches away from the guy's mouth. "For the last time and you better tell me the truth. Who the fuck sent you here!"

"I'm telling ya the truth, man, you gotta believe me!"

"Tell me," Vito repeated over and over. "Tell me, or I'll fuckin' kill you right now. Who the fuck do you think you're dealing with?" an irate Vito said. "What do you think, that I'm one of your homeboys! Do you know who I am?"

"No, and no one sent me," the screaming black man said. "I don't know what you're talkin' about, man. We just needed some cash to cop some dope and that's all."

"You're lying to me you piece of shit. I'll get the truth out of you if it takes me all fuckin' night."

"I don't know nothin'," he cried again. "Please don't kill me! Please...I don't want to die!"

The lost soul frantically searched around the room for leniency. His begging eyes were wide open as he pleaded for mercy. But no one would hear his cries. The small pizzeria and its inhabitants were deaf to his urgent requests for clemency.

"Bear, get over here and make this fuckin' eggplant talk," Vito harshly demanded. "Jimmy, go into the bathroom and bring the girl downstairs. Have the Roach take her to her car and then come right back up here."

"You got it, Vito," Jimmy replied.

Jimmy knocked on the bathroom door to summon Gloria. All Jimmy heard was the sound of running water and the continuous flushing of the toilet bowl. The frightened woman was desperately trying to drown out the horrific sounds coming from the pizzeria. Finally getting her attention, she slowly opened the bathroom door and peeked out. Jimmy then grabbed her by the hand and escorted the silent Gloria down the basement steps. She always kept her eyes looking toward the floor, afraid of what she might see if she picked her head up. Joey shook his head and sadly watched his girlfriend being removed from the premises.

"Vito," Dutch said. "I got a better way to make this guy talk. Give me a minute, I'll make him talk."

Dutch then ran into the kitchen area looking for a metal container. The three Mexicans scattered like field mice that just heard a bulldozer coming their way. Dutch searched on every shelf and behind every appliance in the kitchen. Like a wild famished dog searching for food, he started hurling everything from plastic containers to eating utensils all over the kitchen. The Mexican trio were looking at him like he was nuts. None of them would even dare to ask him what he was looking for. After what they just seen, they were all better off just keeping their mouths shut.

Finally Dutch came across a small coffee pot. The empty four-cup metal container was perfect for what he had in mind. He grabbed the silver pot by the thick black plastic handle and twisted the cover off. The deranged Irish mobster then walked over to the deep fryer and looked down into it. Not knowing the temperature of the brown liquid, Dutch expectorated right into the oil and watched his saliva explode into tiny effervescent bubbles. With his mind now satisfied, he dipped the coffee pot into the scalding hot frying oil. The hot cooking oil must have been peaking at a temperature of over 450 degrees. Dutch then filled the pot three quarters up and fastened the lid back on top of the small opening. He then grabbed a white dish-towel off of the counter top and stuffed it into his back pocket.

"Oh," he said to Orlando. "When was the last time you changed this oil, it's filthy."

"Me change yesterday," Orlando meekly answered. "We cook a lot. We very busy."

"It don't matter anyway, clean oil is too good to waste on that piece of shit over there."

Walking down the tiny aisle over to where all the commotion was, Dutch stepped over the dead body like it wasn't even there. His footprints left track marks of blood that followed him to his destination. Joey and the three Mexicans were peeking out of one eye to see what was going to happen next. Vito didn't even know what to expect. Dutch's way of thinking was that sick. He was the master of torture, he would use any method to try and get someone to talk. If nothing in his bag of tricks worked, death would always be the next best alternative.

"Bear," Dutch said. "Take his shirt off."

Standing right behind the thug, Bear bent down and grabbed hold of the young man's shirt. Instead of pulling it up, he ripped the white cotton tee shirt right off of his back. Bear then threw the sweaty and smelly material into the face of the dead man laying a few feet away.

Seeing his opening, Dutch proceeded to walk over to the helpless body. He inched closer and closer, every step of the way the eyes of the victim grew wider and wider. Afraid to move, the culprit just stood on his knees awaiting his punishment. Steam emitted from the shiny metal pot, this potion was next to lethal. Hot coffee would have been a breath of fresh air compared to what was going to come out of that pot.

"Hold him down, Bear," ordered Dutch. "And make sure you keep him on his knees."

Bear planted his huge hands on top of the poor soul's shoulders. He then buried his thick knee into his spine. Now driving his knee inward, Bear pulled back on his shoulders, thrusting the immobile man's chest forward. This application exposed his hairless upper torso.

Reeking with fear the man never stopped pleading for his life. Even though he knew that some type of torture was awaiting him, he never told the gangsters what they wanted to hear. It was now time to see if he could withstand the ultimate in pain and torture. This was worse than losing a finger or getting your arm broken. Only the upcoming horrible screams could justify the pain that would be running rampant on this unfortunate character's body.

Dutch stood directly above the sobbing man ready to pour the hot oil over his naked upper body. With not one ounce of compassion or remorse in his cold-blooded heart, Dutch looked over at Vito one more time.

"This is your last chance," warned Vito. "Tell us what we want to know."

"I swear to God, man, we came alone. Nobody sent us here," he said, never taking his watery eyes off of the small coffee pot. Right then and there the captured thief knew where his punishment was coming from. "Don't do this, man, please don't do it!"

"Vito," Joey chimed in. "Maybe he don't know anything and nobody sent him here. It could be he's telling you the truth."

"Stop being so God damn soft and shut the fuck up," he said to Joey. "Nobody's talking to you. Did you forget why you called me here in the first place? I guess that stretch you did in prison did nothin' to toughen you up. Or maybe you already forgot the way they butchered Marco and gunned down that little boy in the street."

"I didn't forget any of it. I just wanted to say..." Joey was then cut short of saying anything more.

"I said shut up," Vito bellowed. "I'll handle this my way. It's an eye for an eye now. If I want your damn advice, I'll ask for it."

"Vito, don't do it," Joey begged as all of his pleas for mercy were ignored. "Please Vito, it's not worth it."

"For the last fuckin' time, shut up!"

"Here," Dutch said to Bear, taking the white towel out from his back pocket. "Stuff this in his mouth."

Bear took the dirty linen from Dutch and forced it into the man's mouth. They knew that this was going to be very painful. The last thing they wanted was for the whole neighborhood to hear the screams and unbearable pain coming from their woeful victim.

Vito then shook his head in an up and down motion, giving Dutch the go ahead to let this deplorable persecution begin. Slowly he lifted the silver can over the dark thin chest of the coerced and abused suspect. His mental anguish was about to turn into a physical torment of the worst kind.

Joey and the three Mexicans just cowered and watched in awe from different locations. With their mouths open, all four men dreaded what was about to happen. Suddenly the phone started to ring to break this flow of madness. Joey turned around and looked at it and then turned to Vito.

"Don't pick up that phone," Vito ordered. "We're closed for the night."

The telephone was relentless as it kept ringing and ringing. But nobody had the balls to pick it up and answer it. It merely delayed the sacrifice until it finally stopped ringing. Upon that cue, Dutch then slowly tilted the can and patiently waited for the thick piping hot oil to drip out. The honey colored liquid started to ooze from the small spout of the old coffee pot. Everyone watched as the vegetable solvent landed on the chest of the disgraced human being. Then the smoldering oil made contact with the expectant outer layer of skin.

"Ahhhh!" he screamed, underneath the towel stuffed down his throat.

The black man screamed in excruciating pain as the hot dirty liquid pierced his now scathing skin. His sobbing never stopped as he cried. But the torture was unyielding, it was being applied in a steady and persistent manner. The top layer of the human covering formed smoking bubbles of blisters with the very first drop. The crest of the erupting outer layers of skin started to transform into a lighter color. This devastation followed the path of the running oil all the way down his body. His top layer of skin swiftly blistered and swelled up with watery matter. The elevation and swelling caused by the scalding and irritating oil was about a half inch thick and ran about a foot down the middle of his chest. Some of the heavy liquid even seeped inside of his pants causing even more pain to his groin area. His skin was actually baking and turning colors. The burning was so bad that you could smell his skin frying like a piece of raw meat; it was not a very appetizing smell. It was only a matter of time before the tortured man would pass out from the excruciating pain. This modern day crucifying was not a welcome sight for anyone who was squeamish. It was enough to make anyone vomit.

Vito then removed the rag from the mouth of the nearly passed out man. He grabbed him by the hair and tilted his head in his direction. "Did you have enough?" he asked, ready to let Dutch give him another dose of the cooking oil.

"No, no more," the man on his knees said. "I beg you, no more!"

"Who sent you?"

"Steamer," he finally said. "Steamer sent us here!"

"Who?" Vito asked, although he heard the rat the first time.

"Steamer!"

"You hear that, Dutch!" Vito proudly boasted, then turning to give Joey a look like, I told you so. "Why did you come back here a second time?"

"He wanted us to kill this guy named Joey," he said, loud enough for everyone to hear.

"Why didn't you kill him the first time you were here?"

"Because I panicked, I wasn't too sure who Joey was. This time they pointed him out to me. I knew who he was."

"So you came back to kill him this time?"

"No man, I just wanted some money. I was never gonna kill him. That's why my man over there went to do it for me," he sobbed. "I never wanted to kill him. I just couldn't pull the trigger, something was holding me back. It was weird, man, but someone was telling me no. It told me to turn back!"

"Who?"

"I don't know, man," he started to reveal. "I just heard voices. When I looked at Joey I saw someone else. It was a dark face of an old man. A ghost. It scared the shit out of me."

With a strange look on his face Vito turned to Joey and then back at his prey. "Don't lie to me you piece of shit," Vito said, growing angrier at each word coming from the paid assassin's mouth. "Tell me the truth God damn it!"

"I'm not lying," he said with his words fighting through the streaming teardrops. "It was yankin' on my arm and screamin' at me. It wouldn't let me shoot that dude, Joey. It was protecting him. I'm tellen' ya the truth, man," he cried. "I'm tellen' ya the truth. Fuck Steamer! I know what I saw and I don't want any part of killing."

Joey stood wide eye, visibly shaking and perplexed. *Who is this old man?* he thought.

"Are you two the only ones," Vito demanded to know.

"No, there is some white dude out there."

"Who is he?"

"I don't know, man," he retorted. "I swear to you, I don't know. You have to believe me," he stammered as he grimaced in pain. "I just don't know."

"Vito," Dutch said. "If he knew anymore he would have told us. He don't want another shot of this shit! I practically emptied out the whole pot on him," he said, holding up the coffee pot in his right hand. "Look at his skin. It's bubbling up all over his body! I'm surprised that he hasn't passed out yet."

"Stay on your fuckin' knees and make sure you keep your head down facing the floor," Vito ordered the quivering stool pigeon. "Bear, tie this towel around his head and make sure you cover his eyes."

"Alright Vito," Bear said. "Come here you piece of shit."

"You ruined my fuckin' card game," grumbled Vito, before striking a kick right into the midsection of the helpless intruder. "I had an ace high flush you son of a bitch!"

Somewhere wherever Jimmy was standing, he had to be smiling when he heard that news. These severely punished and ill-fated characters just saved Jimmy a lot of money. The poker hand and the money definitely belonged to Vito.

Bear quickly blindfolded the wannabe hit man and shoved his head against the cold tile floor. Everyone stood frozen, and most of them didn't know what Vito's next move was going to be. Vito slowly looked at every face in the small pizzeria and pulled out his gun. The malice in his eyes said it all. There was no turning back for Vito, and the smell of another death was imminent. Vito raised his left hand and performed the sign of the cross, kissed his fingers and raised them into the air. He then put his head down for a moment of silence. Turning, he then looked at Joey to speak.

"Joey," he boldly said. "It's time to put this to rest!"

"Vito no," Joey screamed. Again his cries for leniency were being totally ignored. "Vito please! For God's sake, for me, for us, please don't do it!" Joey just stood there helpless. "Damn you, Vito! Damn you! No!" It was much too late, Vito was already in motion to carry out his final deed.

"THY WILL BE DONE, Joey," Vito blurted out loud. "THY WILL BE DONE!"

Vito then knelt down and extended his right arm outwards. He proceeded to stick the barrel of his gun right into the temple of the blindfolded and bewildered man. A slight whimper was heard as the dazed and humiliated suspect knew what was about to happen next.

"Nooooo! the humbled ruffian screamed.

The pizzeria suddenly grew somber as death was knocking on its doorstep again. With one decisive pull of the trigger it was all over. Vito blew the guy's brains out. With his limbs shuddering from the blast, his body succumbed to death. In a split second and not even knowing what hit him, another human being was dead. The bullet shot right through the skull of the vertebrate and sent a large mass of gray nerve tissue spraying out from the other side of his head. His thinking organ and guts went scattering across the floor in all different directions. Bone fragments from his shattered cranium were everywhere, the tiny pieces floated down the aisle in a current of blood. Blood splashed across the floor like a paintball hitting a hard surface. There was blood, clumps of guts and gore everywhere as the silver dollar sized hole in his head discharged all of its contents. Now, the two dead bodies were connected by a river of blood. In the matter of minutes the pizza place was the scene of a real bloodbath at some slaughterhouse. The only thing missing was a couple of meat hooks and some sharp butcher knifes.

"Now take these two pricks out the back way and throw them in the van," Vito said. "Take them to Butchie's place out in Staten Island. Dutch, you go with them. You know what to do with the bodies."

"Vito," Dutch said. "Did you ever think that I would let them go without me?"

"No, but there's one other thing."

"What's that?"

"Make sure they turn the van around and back it into the driveway," Vito instructed. "We don't want anyone around here to see us dumping two dead bodies in it."

"I already got the Roach doing that," replied Dutch. "Vito, relax, everything is under control."

"I won't be relaxed until every one of these motherfuckers is dead."

"There's one more out there," Dutch predicted.

"There's three more," Vito replied. "You forgot Steamer and Julius!"

Jimmy and Bear each grabbed one of the dead men around the ankles. They slowly dragged the dead bodies across the blood soaked floor and up to the entranceway that leads to the basement. Every inch of the short journey was followed by a wide trail of blood and whatever else that was pouring out of the corpses. One by one, Jimmy and Bear pulled the bodies with them down the basement steps. Their heads thumped on the wooden steps as they were being towed away.

"Joey," Vito called. "Get your guys to clean up this fuckin' mess."

"Vito, I can't ask them to do that," he answered firmly from behind the counter. "They don't have the stomach for this. I'll clean it up myself."

"Make them do it right now."

"I'll help them then," offered Joey, from behind the counter. "I can't believe all of this shit that's happening to me. I should have stayed in fuckin' jail."

"What did you say!"

"Nothing, Vito. Nothing. I just can't believe you did this."

"Believe it, because the proof is right before you."

"I had enough of this."

"You had enough of this," Vito said approaching the counter. He just looked at Joey and shook his head. "It could have been you laying on the floor you fuckin' idiot."

"I don't care anymore. Maybe I'm better off dead. I just want some peace in my life," he pleaded. "Is that too much to ask for?"

"Whatever, I'm really not in the mood for this right now. You better get your head screwed on right."

"It is on right, I'm just tired of all the violence."

"Sometimes there's just no other way."

"There's always another way. Death is always your only option, it's not mine."

"Have it your way," Vito decided. "This conversation is over for now."

"Is it?"

"Yea it is," he declared. "I don't want to hear another word about it."

"Fine."

"Make sure you put all this shit into a plastic bag and bring it downstairs to Dutch," Vito directed, pointing to all the blood and guts still lying on the floor. "They'll be leaving soon."

"Okay," Joey said. "Where are you going?"

"I'm going downstairs to check out what they're doing. I'll be right back, I want to talk to you."

"Vito, could you give me five minutes before you go?"

"I said the conversation was over."

"It's not about that," Joey professed. "It's about something else."

"Yea," he said practically standing in the mess on the floor. "Hurry up. What is it?"

"I hate to keep bringing this up," a shaken looking Joey said. "But this medallion is starting to give me the creeps."

"What happened now?" he asked, impatiently.

"Now I'm convinced that this thing has some kind of mystical or supernatural powers."

"Joey, please," he said. "Not now! We have to get this mess cleaned up."

"It's alive, Vito, the medallion is alive!" Joey said, blanching. "This thing is breathing around my fuckin' neck, I can feel it. Sometimes it throbs so much that I feel like it's choking me!"

"What the fuck do you mean it's alive and breathing? Listen, if this piece......" Vito paused for a moment before recollecting his thoughts. He rubbed and rubbed his forehead looking for some relief to all of Joey's problems. "If that medallion is going to fuck you all up, don't wear it anymore. You're starting to go crazy."

"No, I will never take it off my neck but," he said, looking down at the top of his chest. "It has become a part of me that I can't break free from. There is something that keeps it clinging to me. I feel like it is glued to me and I can't get it off. What's really crazy is that it seems to sense when danger is coming." Joey knew that the medallion had a Biblical past, but he never expected anything like this to happen. "I am not wrong on this, Vito, you have to believe me. You heard what the guy you killed said."

"That guy was fuckin' delusional, but anyway why do you say that?"

"Because it heats up the closer danger comes to me," he offered. "The last time these two guys came in here to rob me it only got warm. This time, the heat was much more intense. I felt it go right through my tee shirt and into my chest."

"Now I am convinced that you are losing your mind. Did you hear voices or see something also?"

"No, but I felt something come between me and the dead man. And the blood Vito, on my hands, coming from my nose, what about that? The damn medallion was even bleeding. That was not my blood!" professed Joey. There was a slight pause. Both men gawked at each other. "Anyway... how do you explain this?" Joey then said, lifting the gold tablet from the top of his chest. With his left hand he pointed to something that was absolutely amazing and unbelievable to the naked human eye.

Vito's eyes moved in to examine what Joey was talking about. He then motioned Joey forward to a point where he was leaning over the front counter. What he saw left him stunned and slack jawed.

"Holy shit," Vito said. "What the hell is that?"

"You tell me!"

The 18 karat gold medallion had made its presence felt in a remarkable way. The gold piece generated so much heat and energy that it transmitted its exuded radiance onto Joey's white tee shirt. A scorching dark gray and black discoloration left a burnt image on the surface of his undershirt. This phenomenal occurrence was embedded with the same characteristics and visual effects that were left on Joey's bedroom wall. More remarkable than that, even the eerie colors were the same. Except this time, the elusive image was a little bit more profound. The features were not profound enough to make a positive identification, but they were becoming much more focused. Something was there, but neither Vito nor Joey would have enough courage or intelligence to pinpoint exactly what it was.

"Are you sure that you were not around anything that could have heated it up," Vito asked.

"Yea Vito, I stuck my whole fuckin' body inside the pizza oven," he sarcastically said. "It happened when that guy had his gun in my face. I felt it burning me. Jesus Vito, it even burned the skin on my chest. Look!"

Joey lifted the tainted shirt up, revealing a small round sensation and the truth.

"It looks like a welt," proclaimed Vito.

"It's not a welt. But no matter how it got hot, how do you explain the face or what ever the hell it is on my shirt?"

"Maybe the gold is starting to tarnish!" Vito said, fishing for answers to the one million dollar question. "It could also be dirt."

"Gold don't tarnish and dirt would come off," Joey shot back. "You couldn't get this off with a scouring brush."

Vito started to look even deeper into this strange happening. He definitely saw what was before him, but he would not commit to what he thought it actually was. His eyes started to squint as he pulled Joey closer and closer to him. With a handful of Joey's tee shirt, his right index finger made a move to gently caress the face of this supernatural image. With each passing second his patience grew thinner. Vito started to rub harder and harder to try and remove the appendage from the white undergarment. To no avail, his efforts fell short, the stain could not be removed.

"There is definitely a face in there!" Vito predicted, examining the material like a laboratory scientist. "I can see something but it's blurry, I'm not sure."

"What else do you see?" Joey curiously asked, not knowing what to expect and hear next. "This is unreal! Do you see anything else?

"Take the shirt off," Vito said. "And give it to me."

Joey proceeded to unpeel the undershirt off of his lean upper body. He then handed it over to Vito who placed it on top of the counter. The shirt was now stretched out to its maximum length, taking up about two feet of counter space. Both men drew in closer and closer as their peering eyes were looking for answers to all of these mysterious questions. Being only a round inch in circumference, their findings would become very difficult to achieve.

"I can't see it that good," Vito said. "It's too small."

"I'll be right back," Joey said.

"Where ya going?"

"I have a magnifying glass in the kitchen!" Joey declared, racing up the steps and into the back room. Ten seconds later he reappeared behind the counter handing the large lens to Vito. "Here, use this."

Vito bent his head forward and put the round shaped glass up against his left eye. He drew closer and closer to the small image desperately trying to make something out of it. Picking his head up to rub his eyes, he quickly submerged himself again into the magnifier.

"God damn," he said in a startled voice.

"What is it?" Joey asked, ever so curious. "Tell me, what is it?"

"I can see the shape of a face," he whispered. "It has an eye a mouth and a nose. There also seems to be some facial hair."

"Let me in there," Joey insisted, actually pushing Vito out of the way.

For about 60 seconds, Joey stood motionless with his head buried into the contents eerily lodged on top of his shirt. He constantly adjusted the magnifying glass to get the best visual effect possible. To the human eye, this was a sighting that only could be described in Biblical terms. This unearthly feature would have no accountable or natural explanations behind it. There was definitely something sacred about all of this, at least Joey thought so.

"Vito," Joey said, picking the shirt up off of the counter. "I know this might sound premature and you might think that I'm a nut. But this face looks like the face of Jesus Christ. It looks like the same face that's on the medallion!"

"Stop it right there," Vito sternly said. "Don't even go in that direction."

"But you see the same things that I see. I know it's not that clear, but look at the outline and the facial features."

"All I see is something that resembles a face, nothing more," he said, before giving Joey a warning. "And don't ever make it out to be anything more than that."

"I know what I see, and nothing you tell me is gonna make me think otherwise."

"Believe what you like, but keep all this shit to yourself. I don't want to hear another word about it."

"You know it's all starting to come to me now."

"What is," asked Vito.

"Everything, from your grandfather all the way down to this."

"You're going fuckin' crazy, you know that. You just flipped your lid!"

"Did I?"

Deep down Joey knew that Vito felt the same way that he did. He also knew that there was something very special and cryptic about that medallion. Vito would never relinquish his true thoughts, no matter what he saw. He just put everything behind him and went into the kitchen like nothing ever happened. Joey went in the other direction, he opened the front gate and slammed it shut behind him. He then stepped out into the street and looked up into the never-ending skies. Silently he searched for something that he knew was becoming a part of him. He knew that there was somebody up there; the glistening stars had just told him so. He also knew that there was somebody down here who wanted him very much dead. But Joey had no idea about either one of them. One seemed to dwell somewhere beyond the stars, the other on the streets of this big city.

Before Vito went downstairs into the basement, he had a few choice words for Joey's Mexican crew. Walking slowly up the few steps that separated the pizzeria from the kitchen, Vito carefully adjusted his clothing. He then proceeded on into the kitchen area where he confronted the three men. "You guys didn't see anything, right?" Vito asked, his jaw set grimly as his eyes leveled a chilling glare at all three of them. "Right," he asked again.

"No Vito," Orlando said, quaking in his boots. "I no see nothing, I was making pizza sauce."

"What about you, Manuel?" he then asked the pizza man, with the same tone of voice. "Did you see anything?"

"No Vito, I no see nothing either."

"Good, Jorge you didn't see nothing either?" Jorge just shook his head in a negative direction. "Make sure the three of you keep your mouths shut about all of this. Do you understand me?"

"Yes, Vito, yes," they all said in tandem while shaking their heads in an up and down motion. "We will. We understand."

"Now go outside and cleanup that fuckin' mess out there," he ordered them. "And make sure you do a good job."

The Mexicans started to clean up the mess from the massacre. Vito and his crew were waiting for the rest of the dead men's remains in the basement. This cleanup was not for the squeamish or anybody with a weak stomach. The massacre was only twenty minutes old and already the remains started to emit some kind of distasteful odor. These three Mexicans were in way over their heads. They worked in a pizzeria not a slaughterhouse. But after all, these two assailants faired no better than a doomed steer on some cattle ranch.

Jorge starting vomiting as Orlando swept the blood and guts into his awaiting shovel. Manuel was patiently waiting with the mop in his hands. These poor guys had seen enough violence to last them a lifetime. To them America was supposed to be the land of opportunity, not a graveyard. Vito and the rest of the boys exposed them to a whole new world of life. But to the Mexican trio, this still beat working in their country for basically nothing. No matter what they had seen, they knew not to open their mouths. All three men liked Vito, but they feared him even more. In some cases, fear can breed affection. It cloisters the senses while it incarcerates the soul.

Chapter 21

"**H**ERE'S YOUR PLASTIC bag!" Joey said, holding the black bag in his right hand.

"Take it outside and throw it in the back of the van with the bodies," ordered Vito.

Vito had been giving last minute instructions to his crew of gravediggers before Joey interrupted him. These guys were always the masters of deception when it came to disposing of corpses. There was no way in hell that anyone would ever find these bodies, in one piece anyway.

The card players cleared off the tables of what was rightfully theirs, and it was off to Butchie's place. Butchie ran a private sanitation carting company in Staten Island. This business was fully owned and operated by the Mob. There were two businesses that served these guys all their needs of disposing any unwanted materials or bodies, garbage and concrete. These guys had people buried everywhere, from foundations of buildings to landfills. Whether it by land or by sea, they used up every inch of God given or man made element at their disposal.

"What are you gonna do with the bodies?" Joey said, after closing the back door of the van and returning to the basement.

"Let me put it this way," said Vito. "Don't be eating any bluefish for a while."

"That's gross."

"That's life," Vito retorted with a loathsome look on his face.

"You guys are heartless." Vito just shrugged and walked away.

Vito's little hint left Joey a little premonition that the bodies were going to be dumped at sea.

Dutch, Jimmy and Bear crammed into the front seat of the white van. Jimmy was behind the wheel, and Dutch was sandwiched in the middle, between Jimmy and Bear. They finally pulled out of the dark alley and started their short trip to the small borough of Staten Island.

After fifteen minutes of driving through the streets of Brooklyn, the van entered the Brooklyn Queens Expressway. It was only a matter of ten minutes of highway driving before they were about to cross the Verrazano Bridge. There was only one way of gaining access into Staten Island from Brooklyn, and this was it. There was a ferry-boat, but the popular ferry had to be boarded from lower Manhattan. Besides there was too much danger involved driving a van with two dead bodies onto a ferry-boat. If they ever got caught, there would be nowhere to run. The only option was to throw themselves overboard to escape the law. Out of the three, Jimmy was the only swimmer, so the other two would have been as good as dead. On land, Dutch and Bear were two of the toughest sons of bitches on Earth. In the water with all its tricky currents and undertow, an infant had just as good of a chance at surviving.

"Man, it stinks in here!" Jimmy complained, driving with his head halfway out of the window.

"We're almost there," Dutch said, always looking cool calm and collected. "Relax and just breathe through your mouth."

The trio finally crossed over the long span of the bridge and settled behind a few cars waiting to pay the $2.00 toll. Bear and Dutch waited quietly as Jimmy tapped away to the tune coming from the van's radio. Foot by foot and inch by inch the van crept closer and closer to the toll-booth. The Port Authority cop collecting the money took a quick peek at the van before it came to a stop right by his small window.

"Oh shit," Jimmy complained. "I need two bucks!"

Jimmy frantically started to look everywhere for some money. He stuck his quick moving hands into the mound of change that was inside of his right pocket. With one quick release, he withdrew a handful of quarters. One by one, he started to count them out. . The cop had a funny look on his face; his nose was definitely sensing something was not right. He was sniffing and not admiring the scent that was flowing out of the vehicle. The officer was moving his head back and forth trying desperately to peek inside.

In the back of the van by the double door, blood was dripping onto the roadway. The red drops started to form a small puddle between the van and the car waiting behind it. This was not a good situation for the boys to be in. And there was no way that blood could ever be confused with transmission fluid.

There was another cop who started to walk in the direction of the cargo van. He hurriedly paced between the van and the Ford Taurus behind it. In his left hand he carried a change box as he held up his right hand to halt the oncoming motorists. This moron stepped right into a tiny puddle of blood and tracked it across the pavement below him. He left about four or five vivid footprints until his tracks faded from the thinning out red liquid. The cop was in such a hurry to get to his awaiting toll-booth that he didn't notice anything.

"Here," Dutch said, finally getting to his wallet and pulling out a twenty dollar bill.

"Thank God," Jimmy said to himself, while throwing his quarters onto the floor mat of the van. He snatched the twenty from Dutch's hand and in one continuous motion handed it to the toll collector. The cop took the money and started to make the change.

"What's that smell?" he inquisitively asked, still feeling a bit uncomfortable.

"My buddy over here has his shoes off officer," Jimmy smilingly said. "The fuckin stink is killing me to."

"I had a long day, Sir," answered Dutch. "This is a genetic problem, my father's feet used to stink the same way. For years him and my mother slept in separate bedrooms."

The cop just smiled and shook his head; the idiot seemed to believe the whole story. He then handed Jimmy back his change and wished the killers a good night. Jimmy quickly stepped on the accelerator and pulled out of the potentially dangerous situation. They left a small puddle of blood and an untraceable trail of droppings of the thick red liquid in their aftermath.

"Give me my change," Dutch demanded. Jimmy without hesitation handed Dutch the money that got them out of a possible heap of big trouble.

"Damn it, Bear," an annoyed Dutch said. "Move the fuck over, you're killing me here!"

"What?" the big man fired back. "What do you want me to do?"

"I don't know. Open the door and stick one foot out. Do anything, just move over a little." You could tell Dutch was growing very impatient and irritable sitting in between Jimmy and Bear. The sooner they got this job over and done with, the better he would feel. It didn't matter where he was, Dutch never liked the feeling of being smothered or cramped in. His only other alternative was to throw Bear in the back of the van with the two dead bodies. Luckily for Bear, Dutch liked him. So that option was never even an issue.

Going up and down the winding roads of Staten Island led the boys to the Port Richmond section of town. This was mostly a commercial section that was built for industry. The streets at nighttime were very desolate, only the drunks and the homeless roamed these parts at night.

Turning up Bridge Street, the small truck finally came to a stop in front of a large gate with barbed wire resting on top of it. Inside the gate, on the left side of the large lot was a trailer that was converted and used as an office. A dim light was flickering out of control inside the decaying make shift office. The front door to the movable facility suddenly swung open and a short stocky man emerged. This ex convict had tattoos running up and down his powerful looking arms. A pot-belly appeared just above his belt buckle, expanding his waistline a few inches. This battle scarred warrior showed all the effects of criminal life. His every movement seemed to be hampered with pain. He slowly wobbled down the three steps and onto the gravel pathway, kicking up dirt and small rocks with every step of the way. Dangling a bunch of keys in his hands, he nodded his head and started to open the front gate to let his comrades through.

"How you doin, Jimmy?" Butchie asked. He then looked at Dutch and Bear and shook his head in a positive motion.

"Same shit," Jimmy answered. "Just a different day."

"I see that you have some more bird food for me," Butchie said. "Bring it on in."

"Nah," Jimmy said as he moved his head from side to side. "This pile of shit is going to the fish. The last time those fuckin' birds at the dump shit all over my car. It was way too messy. No more sanitation dumps for me."

"What's up, Dutch?" he then asked Vito's right hand man. Dutch said nothing as he acknowledged Butchie in silence.

"Come on," Dutch said. "Let's get this fuckin' thing over with."

The van crept through the front gate and up the rocky driveway. There was nothing but darkness covering the foul smelling lot. The only brightness was coming from the headlights of the murderous transport van and the fading flickering light of the trailer. Jimmy just followed the head-beam of the van. He knew exactly where it would take him.

The radial tires made small crunching sounds while maneuvering through the grayish gravel. Each spin of the tire kicked up the small pebbles that were used as a pavement for the narrow passageway. Crawling past the trailer, he made a left turn and kept driving another fifty feet to what looked like a wood chipper. Jimmy pulled to within ten feet of the slicing and dicing machine and came to a halt.

"Get the bodies out," ordered Dutch. "Stop dragging your fuckin' asses and let's go!"

Reacting quickly to Dutch's heated words, the boys exited the vehicle and walked quickly to the back of the van. Opening the wide double doors exposed the two morbid bodies and all of their foul smelling odors. One by one they started to drag the remains out from the back of the vehicle. The cold blood was everywhere as it started to form a dry crust all over the dead bodies. Tugging them over the hard gravel and through the debris lifted pieces of flesh from their faces. Heartlessly, the boys placed the corpses behind this landscapers piece of equipment.

These two unfortunate victims were going to be prepared for a different kind of cremation. They were going to be grinded down into mulch. But the remains were not going to be sprinkled around some rich man's sprawling garden. The gangsters had something else in mind for their final resting place. The two cold bodies would be buried at sea in more than a million pieces. Their almost liquid existence would be spread over the oily water like the chum that is used to attract fish on a deep-sea adventure. Whatever the fish didn't eat, the filthy water would always consume any other parts of their ill-fated anatomy.

Right up the block from the private carting business were the polluted waterways that separated Staten Island from New Jersey. This was a very convenient location for whenever Vito and the rest of his crew had to dispose of any dead bodies.

The long wooden pier turned the oceans into a cemetery of the forgotten. This disgusting burial sight made Potters Field look like the Garden of Eden. The smell of death seemed to linger off these oceans like the rising vapors on a hot summer day. The dead bodies would soon be joining the world of the unexplained mysteries of the deep.

"Did you get the bags," Dutch said to Jimmy as he turned the machine on.

"Yea, there right here," Jimmy said, pointing to the floor.

"Well, hold it up and cover the opening or else you're gonna get this shit all over you."

"Butchie," Jimmy said. "Give me a hand, hold this end over the hole."

"Come on, Bear, let's do it!" Dutch ordered, with a cold and calculating look to his demeanor. "Pick this guy up first."

Jimmy and Butchie held the heavy bag up over the rear end of the wood chipper. On the other end, Dutch and Bear easily hoisted one of the lifeless bodies and slowly maneuvered it into the large metal opening.

The deafening sounds of the machinery's motor drowned out every other sound of the large temporary dumping ground. Head first, one body was jammed through the blades as the chipper started to do what it was intended for.

With its gears meshing smoothly together, the wood chipper had no problem absorbing the limp lifeless cadaver. It quickly sucked the dead corpse into its hungry tunnel. All the friction in the world could not stop this high-powered piece of equipment from bearing its teeth down on the dead carcass.

In went the first body. The grinding and crunching sounds were horrible. The head, limbs and torso were crushed and chewed into fine particles. Bones, organs and whatever other parts that made up the human body were blended into one. The chipper smoothly ate up the human flesh and bones and spit it out on the other side where the large heavy plastic bag was waiting. Not one drop of blood hit the floor from the minced body; this macabre ritual was performed flawlessly.

The gangsters repeated this process one more time with the same successful results. When this bizarre expedition was finished, they systematically hosed down the inside of the van along with the wood chipper to eliminate any scent or sight of foul play. The boys had this cleanup down to a science, as this was not the first time that these procedures were performed. To Vito's pack of savage marauders, it was all in a day's work.

Back at the pizzeria Joey and Vito just sat around talking about the future of Joey's Place. All of the workers had already gone home as the pizza place closed early for the night. The two men had decided that it was just about the right time to sell the place to one of the locals in the neighborhood. Vito had some people already interested in taking the place over. The price, on the other hand, had not been determined yet.

Judging by the amount of business that the pizzeria was pumping out, Joey was sure to get at least five times the amount he paid for it. But it was not the money that was forcing Joey to leave the place that he became so attached to. He had enough of the killing and blood. There were just too many painful memories. From Marco and little Steven, all the way down to the events that just took place.

Besides, Vito and Dutch had just about accomplished their own mission. They had won the rebellion to take back the park that Dutch's cousin Danny had died for. The park across the street was just about a few weeks away from being totally renovated. The good people of Crown Heights had gotten their neighborhood back.

In Joey's mind, he figured that he had accomplished something himself, no matter who sent him here. He just thought that he was a big part of all the extraordinary and unusual events that have taken place. In his eyes, this was a manifestation of a divine and supernatural power. Even though many had suffered, these circumstances to him were starting to be considered as some kind of miracle. These miracles often left him with feelings of admiration, awe and wonder. Others might disagree with his projections, but the others had not felt this great presence from beyond the earth's atmosphere. This realm can only exist somewhere very far away in a kingdom not known to the breathing man. The more time that had elapsed, the stronger the phenomenon appeared to grow in strength and affliction. The more this perception kept growing inside of his believing body, the more he believed. Joey knew that he was on a collision course with something that reigns supreme to most of the spiritual believers around him. Whatever fate awaited him, he did not know. But what he did know was that he had been sent to St Ann's Place to put together this minor miracle. Like Father Pasquale had told him many months ago, "You are a chosen one." Those were words that he definitely believed.

The people of St Ann's Place could also attest to the fact that something miraculous had just taken place. They had suffered for a very long time with nowhere or no one to turn to. Their lives had been marked by tragedy, heartache, disappointment and death. A brighter day had come for these people as all of their insurmountable fears had finally subsided.

"Vito!" an anxious Joey said, while removing his dirty apron.

"What?"

"So what's up with this surprise that you have been telling me about?" Joey asked, finally calming down from all the brutality that he had just witnessed.

"In a couple of weeks you'll find out," Vito promised. "I decided to wait a while before letting you know."

"Give me a hint!"

"Nope, just wait it out and be patient," Vito said. "Listen, in two weeks the park will be ready to reopen."

"I know, the construction guys come in here for lunch and they keep me posted on its development."

"Well, that Saturday we are going to have a block party to celebrate the opening of the park. We're gonna supply everything to make it happen," a tired looking Vito said.

"What do you mean by everything?"

"I mean from the food, drinks to the music, everything."

"I guess I'm making the food?"

"No you're not, I'm going to cater everything, from Italian food to barbecue," he proudly said. "On that day you, your girlfriend and the Mexicans will just relax with me. The store will be open, but not for business. We will be closed that Saturday and Sunday. So tell Gloria and your crew about it."

"Oh shit, Vito, Gloria!"

"What about her?"

"She must be a nervous wreck," he frantically said. "After what she saw, who wouldn't be? I have to get over there right now. Will you give me a lift?"

"Now?"

"Come on. Please!"

"Alright. Let's go."

"Just let me call her and double check the store to make sure everything is turned off."

"Meet me down the basement," Vito instructed. "We will walk outside together."

In about ten minutes they arrived at Gloria's apartment. Joey removed himself from the late model sedan and Vito exited from the other side. Vito carefully watched his Godson open the small gate that led to the steps of the three family building. He stood by the driver's side door as Joey rang the doorbell.

"I'll pick you up at nine and make sure you don't go anywhere," Vito said. Joey just shook his head in agreement, not saying a word. "Do you hear me," Vito loudly asked. "Make sure you don't go anywhere!"

"Don't worry, we're staying in," he promised.

"Who is it?" the sexy voice said over the intercom. Joey put his head up to the box and then pushed on the speaker button.

"It's me, let me in."

Joey waited patiently for his girlfriend to buzz him inside the building. Once he heard the annoying sound, he pushed on the door to gain access, then turned around and nodded at Vito. Vito then jumped into the driver's seat and took off.

Joey did not know what to expect when he finally entered her apartment. After what happened in Ramon's bar, he vowed to himself that would be the end of the violence. Boy, was he wrong. He often wondered how much more this poor girl could take before she dumped him. After all, it seemed like she took a liking to Vito and all of his buddies, she just detested their ways.

"How are you feeling?" Joey said, running his fingers through her damp hair. "You don't look too good!"

"I'm okay, I just took a long hot bath."

"I'm sorry about what happened tonight," Joey said with an apologetic look on his face. "But that guy was gonna kill me."

"Joey, I know, Dutch saved your life," she said. "Why are all these things happening to you? I don't understand it. Why?"

"I don't know, honey, but in a couple of weeks it will all be over with."

"Why is that?" Gloria asked, tightening the belt on her white satin robe.

"Because we are selling the place and getting the hell out of there."

"But you worked so hard to make it a success."

"I know, but my life is worth so much more to me," he confessed. "And more important than that, you are worth more to me than life itself."

"I'm so afraid for you, Joey," Gloria said, hugging him as tears started to rain from her swollen eyes. "I never want to lose you."

"You won't, in a couple of weeks this will all be behind us."

"You promise," she asked.

"I promise," he said. "No more killing, no more gangsters, it will be just you and me."

"Have you told Vito that?"

"No, Vito will always be a part of my life, but not like he is right now."

"He loves you so much."

"I know he does," Joey said. "But I also know he would understand my decision. He's the one that wanted it like this in the first place. He doesn't want me being a part of his lifestyle, he never did. I'm the one that reached out for him. Without him in my life right now, I would surely be dead. At the time I had no other choice, I had to call him. You have to understand that!"

"I do understand and I am very grateful to him."

"Gloria, he saved my life behind bars and he also saved it on the streets. Without him, there would be no you and me."

"I know, honey."

"Gloria, I have changed!"

"What do you mean?"

"My priorities are not what they used to be," he said. "Before, all I thought about was money, it ruled my fuckin' life. Now things are different, I see things in a different light. I just want to live a normal life, that's all I ask for, nothing more or nothing less than that," he said. "I now know what it's like to struggle and I feel the pain of other people. I've learned to work side by side with people that I never thought would be possible. In all of my life, I never thought it could be possible."

"What do you mean by possible?"

"What I am trying to say is that I love those Mexican guys, to me they are family," he confessed. "I bust my ass for 14 hours a day, seven days a week and I know what its like to earn a dollar the hard way. And those guys are right by my side. They never failed or disappointed me once. With those guys it's not about money, it's about them and me."

"I know," she replied. "They are very dedicated to you."

"On Wall Street I used to earn off the hard work and sweat of others. I really never knew the value of the dollar. Now I am no different than anybody else, and I am proud of it."

"I'm proud of you also," she fondly said. "You're living proof of something I have always treasured in a man. You have finally found yourself. Now you know who you truly are."

"Maybe so, but even my customers who live on the block," he continued, "I realized that they are no different than you and I. It broke my heart to see the way they were living, that's why I never left." Joey looked around the room, pondered for a moment and then turned back to her. "I knew that I could make a difference in their lives and with the help of others, I did. I just knew that it was up to me to put all of these pieces together. No matter how I did it and how violent it got, it had to be this way."

"Why do you say that?"

"I don't know, I just don't know. I just feel like I was appointed by someone to be here."

"Maybe you were," she added. "But you were not appointed to die for them either, were you?"

"I don't know that either," he said. "But I just couldn't leave, Gloria, these people needed me here! But now something tells me that it is all over, it's time to go."

"Why?"

"Because now is the time for me to find some peace in my life."

"You deserve the peace and you will find it."

"I hope so. Maybe leaving the pizzeria will help me find it."

"And how do you feel about that?"

"I'm very tired, honey, my heart wants to stay, but my body tells me to go. The violence has gotten the best of me. I just want to go. Something keeps telling me that it's time to move on. What I really came here for was accomplished."

"I understand, Joey."

"No you don't, you don't understand. There's some other intangible involved here."

"What, me?" she asked, looking right at him.

"No, you are coming with me wherever I go. It's something else that I can't explain right now. It's out there somewhere, it seems to be directing every move that I make."

"What is it?"

"Now is not the time, honey."

"Does it involve that medallion?"

Joey then looked at her and grabbed her left arm. He never mentioned to her anything about the special powers leaking from the gold around his neck. All she knew was that Vito gave him this medallion; she knew nothing of the life that was buried inside of it.

"What makes you say that?" he asked, with a raised brow.

"Because I always see you clutching and holding on to it," she said. "You keep acting like it is telling you something."

"It's just special, Gloria," Joey said. "That's all it is, and let's just leave it at that." He was not going to go into details about all the unusual happenings and cryptic feelings he was experiencing. The poor girl had been through and seen enough already. From the Mafia to the blood of murdered men, this was more than enough for one person to bear. There was no need or room for anything else to frighten her any further. "Gloria, you don't look so good to me, you look kind of pale," said Joey. "Are you sure you're alright?" Joey asked, putting his right hand under her hair and behind her damp neck.

"I feel kind of weird, my stomach keeps churning," she confessed. "Maybe I'm coming down with something."

"It's probably all the shit that you saw tonight that's making you sick."

"No, this is something different," she said. "I can't describe it, I never felt anything like this before."

"Maybe you're coming down with the flu or some kind of stomach virus?"

"It could be, but I doubt it. If I feel this way in the morning, I'll go see a doctor."

Joey went into the kitchen and ignited the flame under the tea kettle. Gloria took a seat on the sofa and turned the television set inside the wall unit on. He was very worried about her, she did not seem the same to him. To him, her face appeared to be fraught with peril and confusion. There was an easy way out of this for her, but love had conquered all of her fears. This was definitely the type of woman that the words, "till death do us part," were written for.

The red tea-kettle was whistling as Joey turned off the flame and poured the boiling water into the awaiting cups. He added the remaining ingredients and slowly walked towards the coffee table in the living room. Placing the two cups on top of coasters, he looked at her and shook his head.

"What's the matter," she asked him with a smile on her face.

"You're so beautiful, I don't ever want to lose you."

"You won't," she innocently said. "No matter what happens, you will never lose me. I can practically feel you inside of me right now."

"What do you mean?" a worried Joey said.

"I don't know, Joey," she said, fondling the teaspoon in her tea-cup. "I just feel so consumed with you. I mean, I never loved anyone or anything so much in my life. But this is something different; I can't explain it. Jesus, Joey, please don't think that I am crazy. But I feel like you are growing inside of me."

"But I feel the same way, it's called love."

"I know it's called love. But this is something more than that." Gloria looked at the medallion around Joey's neck and reached out for it. Now touching its radiance, she felt a spiritual connection. "It's this piece," she confessed. "I feel like I'm a part of it. Like I'm a piece of this whole puzzle. Somehow, I feel something possessing me."

Joey looked on stunned, then brushed it off. "Nah, it's just your emotions. Love has a special way of making people feel unusual."

"I don't know," she wearily said. "Are you saying that I'm lovesick?" she asked him, with an angelic smile on her face.

"That's exactly what I'm saying. Now, just relax and let's watch a movie," he said, trying desperately to make her forget about these strange premonitions.

Gloria and Joey just sat on the floral print sofa for the next hour melting in each other's arms. Never were the two so close as they had now become. Joey knew this and he was seriously thinking about making a full time commitment to her. It was now time to look towards the future and all it had to offer. Joey's future did seem a bit murky. But whatever the consequences may bring, he did not want to face them without her. The loving couple had become consummated into one. It was just about the right time for Joey and Gloria to start living their lives that way.

Holding the remote control in his hand and flipping through the channels, the medallion around Joey's neck started to react in a peculiar way again. The familiar heat was there, but this time he felt something much, much different. The round gold piece was vibrating, sending its signals running throughout his body. Joey's chest cavity was pulsating as if his heart was popping out of his rib cage. He slowly looked down and noticed the slight movement coming from his upper torso. Like a heartbeat, it just kept going, thump, thump. thump, thump. With each passing second, the movement and the feeling accelerated.

Joey was convinced that this medal had a life all its own. It was living and breathing inside of his being, trying desperately to come out. Quickly, he covered the strange abnormality with his right hand and stared straight ahead in astonishment. This was definitely a happening that was unknown to scientific logic and procedures. This event and all the others were totally unexplainable.

"Joey, I feel warm," Gloria said. "Could you close the window and turn the air conditioner on." Joey just stood there not even acknowledging her request. "Joey, did you hear me," she asked. "I feel warm, turn on the air conditioner."

Joey snapped out of his daze and put his left hand on top of Gloria's forehead, feeling around for any excess heat. He kept his hand there for a few seconds and said in a shaky voice. "You do feel kind of clammy to me."

He slowly got to his feet and walked the short distance to the opened window on the left side of the room. Pulling the curtains to one side, he stooped a bit and reached for the white aluminum window. Putting both hands on the thick framework, he started to drive the window downward to a closed position. Suddenly his motion came to a dead stop. With the window still not totally closed, Joey then reversed his movement and reopened it. He pulled up the screen to take a peek outside. Joey knew that something was out there, the medallion had just told him so.

Nervously sticking his head out the window, Joey stared across the street in shock and disbelief of what he was seeing. The fearful chill paralyzed his senses momentarily, reality then brought them back. Standing about sixty feet away, right before his eyes, was the same man who he now knew was looking to kill him. He was positive it was the same man as before, this maniac's limited wardrobe had stated that fact. The light brown hair and frail body were two other reminders that he was the man Joey had seen twice before.

The two men just sized each other up and down with steady and wide-eyed gazes. Still not close enough to get a positive identification; Joey looked for other strange characteristics that might help him identify the stalker. But his faltering eyes failed him.

Into the night air, he just stared and stared at his assassin, never saying a word. Joey was looking straight into the eyes of the man who wanted him dead. Neither man would yield an inch to the other's stare. It became a fight of the defiant, with either man unwilling to back down.

"Fuck me," Joey said to himself. The profanity was only loud enough for his own ears to hear. "This son of a bitch! How the hell did he follow me here?"

"Joey," Gloria called. "What are you doing?"

"Nothing, honey," he lied. "I'm just trying to get some fresh air, that's all."

"Well, come on," she insisted. "Shut the window and put the air conditioner on."

"Okay," he said, as if nothing happened. "What's on television?"

"I don't know, let me look."

Joey did what he was told. He quickly shut the window and pulled the curtains together. He walked over to the air conditioner and turned the power on a low setting. At that moment he felt like making a B-line right out the front door to confront his enemy. He knew that he couldn't, his love had rendered him immobile. He felt like he was shackled at the hands and feet by some heavy steel chains. But in his heart he also knew that running after this nut was not the right thing to do. There was no way in hell that he wanted Gloria to go through any more stress and violence. Any additional emotional pressure might really push her over the edge. This was a chance that Joey was not willing to take. He then decided to keep this current episode in his sick life away from her eyes and out of her mind. What really troubled him was the fact that the stalker now knew where Gloria lived. Fearing for her safety, Joey was afraid that he might harm her to get to him.

Sitting side by side again, Gloria became engrossed with some women's movie on the Lifetime channel. Joey was just running his mind off in another direction, pretending that he was watching along with her. All the while, he was just biding his time until she fell asleep. The clock kept ticking and ticking, but still there were no signs of drowsiness. He had to get to the telephone to call Vito, but he had to wait until she would be totally unaware of what was going on.

Finally about another half hour later, Gloria's head started to droop as she was now fighting sleep. Still sitting erect, her head would drop into a sleeping position, then she would snap it right back up. This went on for another five minutes, until she finally passed out. Her slim body settled on the cushioned sofa as her head peacefully rested on one of its soft pillows.

Joey pulled out a light bed sheet to cover her. His next move was fixated on getting to that telephone hanging on the kitchen wall.

"Hello," a sleepy sounding Vito said.

"Vito, it's me, Joey," he whispered, while pacing back and forth. "Are you there?"

"This better be good," he warned. "You just woke me up!"

"Listen carefully, I can't talk too loud," Joey softly said. "A little while ago I saw that guy standing across the street from Gloria's apartment."

"Did he see you?"

"Yea, I got up to shut the window and he was staring at me from across the street."

"What did you do?"

"Nothing, Gloria was sitting right behind me. I wanted to run down the steps and kick his fuckin' ass."

"Are you crazy, the guy probably has a gun. You did the right thing by not doing nothing, it's way too dangerous." In the background you could hear Vito yawning as he tried to spit out his next words. "Does she know he was there?"

"No, I kept it from her." Joey turned around to look at his girlfriend on the sofa. She was still sound asleep.

"Good, the girl does not have to be frightened any more than what she already is."

"Vito, what am I going to do?" Joey pleaded, knowing that he and his girlfriend were both in a dire situation. "He knows where Gloria lives."

"You're going to tell your girlfriend to pack her bags and that she's going on a vacation for a couple of weeks."

"To where?" Joey asked, still frantically pacing like a battery operated toy.

"You and her are spending the next two weeks at my house."

"What?"

"You heard me," he said. "Tell her to take some vacation time away from her job. She can relax by the pool or do whatever the hell she wants. There will always be someone there to watch over her."

"That's a good idea, at least I know when I'm working she'll be safe."

"You're not working either."

"What do you mean?" Joey said, raising his voice a little. "I have a business to run."

"Your pizzeria days are over," ordered Vito. "At least in that store anyway."

"Vito," Joey shot back. "I'm not going to run away from this."

"You'll do as I say," he demanded. "I don't want anything happening to you. The only time that you will ever set foot on that street is at the block party in two weeks."

"But…," Joey tried to say, before he was cut from speaking any further.

"It's final and I don't want to hear anymore about it. I will send a couple of guys over there to sift through the neighborhood and look for this punk. And there will be another car sitting right in front of her house throughout the night."

"Vito, there's one other thing I have to tell you!"

"What's that?" Vito said, raising himself and now sitting up on his bed.

"Now don't get mad."

"I won't."

"You promise?"

"Joey!" he said, raising his voice to an angrier level. "It's two o'clock in the fuckin' morning. Tell me already!"

"The medallion gave me the warning that someone was outside," Joey quietly said.

"How?" Vito asked, acting not too surprised.

"It heated up again, but this time it did something that it never did before."

"What did it do now?" asked Vito, in a "here we go again" type of voice.

"It started to vibrate inside of my shirt."

"It was probably your nerves," reasoned Vito, like he was some kind of medical doctor. "Your heart is probably overworked from all the shit that's been going on."

"No, no, this time you're dead wrong."

"Have it your way, we will talk about this tomorrow."

"You don't want to hear it, because you know I'm right."

"Think what you want, but it's late," Vito said, trying to cast this aside like nothing ever happened. "I had enough of this talk already. At the moment we have more important things to worry about."

"Yea, okay," Joey sarcastically said.

"Now, I want you to get some sleep and I will pick you up at noon," he said. "And don't worry about the pizzeria, it'll be fine."

"Alright."

"Go take care of your girlfriend, she is more important than pizza and that medallion. And don't call the cops, we'll take care of this son of a bitch our own way."

"Okay Vito, I won't," a dejected Joey said. "I'll see ya tomorrow."

"Make sure you get some sleep."

"I'll try, goodnight."

There was no way that Joey was ever going to get any sleep under these conditions. With a killer wandering around the neighborhood, sleep was the furthest thing from his mind. He just put up a pot of coffee and stood vigil over Gloria. If his nervousness did not keep him up all night, the caffeine would. Joey constantly got up from the kitchen chair to check out the activity going on outside. His uneasiness forced him to smoke cigarette after cigarette as he was letting his emotions get the best of him. The only time he started to relax was when he spotted Vito's men parked right outside Gloria's front door. Joey felt a little better knowing that their safety was a bit more secure. But tomorrow would bring another day forward and another set of circumstances to worry about.

The following morning Joey had to break the news to Gloria in the most discreet way possible. Telling her everything that went on the night before was not easy. He had somewhat of a hard time convincing Gloria to agree with Vito's plan. But after her intense scrutiny of the situation, she finally agreed to put her whole life on hold. Everything, from her job to her family life had to be cast aside for a short period of time. She agreed to discard everything for the safety of the man she loved. She knew that she was doing the right thing for him and herself. But she also knew that even she would be guarded and protected like a Mafia Princess. Never in her wildest dreams did Gloria ever think that she would fall into a situation like this. To her, all these principles and Italian rules were definitely against her Bible and her way of thinking. This was a lifestyle that she dreaded, but this was a lifestyle that love had taken her to. And love would only determine the outcome of her impending destiny.

The noontime sun had perched right outside Gloria's bedroom window. Like a laser beam, it shot through the crystal clear glass of the glistening window. It boldly crept inside the bedroom, brightening and absorbing everything that surrounded it.

Gloria's two black leather suitcases were neatly packed and fastened, ready to be taken off of the queen sized bed. Next to the large pieces of rectangular luggage was a duffel bag filled with all of her cosmetics and toiletries. She was only going away for a couple of weeks, but she seemed to think differently. She packed enough things to last her a decade. She packed her bags like she never ever expected to return to the place she once called home.

Outside, Vito's horn was beeping as an unknown man was standing by the driver's side door. Vito stood erect on the other side of the car, waiting for the arrival of his passengers. Joey hurriedly took down the overstuffed suitcases and placed them into the empty trunk of the car. He took a quick peek at Vito and ran back upstairs to retrieve some of his belongings. A few minutes later, both he and Gloria appeared on the front steps.

With tears in her eyes, Gloria locked the front door and turned to look at her new landlord. Holding Joey's hand, she started descending down the five steps and through the black front gate of her home. Joey kept watching every move she made; dejection was the makeup of her face.

Gloria just passed the first few days at Vito's home mostly reading. She was an avid reader, sometimes even knocking off a book or two inside of a week. All she did was sit on a reclining lounge chair and read her romance novels at poolside. Occasionally she would get up and dip her manicured toes into Vito's built in swimming pool. But mostly, she just moped around looking gloomy and depressed. Her once vivacious and bubbly personality was reduced to a shadow of its former self. Everything she wanted was at the end of her dainty fingertips, except her freedom. The confinement of being not able to come and go as she pleased was eating away at her. This whole situation had drawn her in as a potential target, nobody felt safe anymore, especially her.

Joey's time was mostly spent watching over his girlfriend. He also relaxed poolside as reading was also a part of his agenda. His reading consisted of something of a much different nature. The Holy Bible and its content was his order of business. Flipping pages at a furious rate Joey searched and searched for the answers to his many questions. He felt compelled to find out who this mysterious "old man" was and what the reasons for his coming were all about.

There were always a couple of Vito's men walking in and out of the large house. Not a day went by where there was not a strong arm watching over them. Whatever the couple wanted, the hired staff quickly brought to them. They felt like they were living in the lap of luxury inside of a prison. All the money and modern conveniences at their disposal meant nothing to them. The things that they wanted most were not available to them anymore. You can not buy freedom or your health, and these were the two things they desired most.

Vito's backyard was magnificent with all the trappings of a tropical resort paradise. This landscaped wonderland had it all. Lounge chairs circled the blue water of the oversized swimming pool. Spanish bricks covered the earth with lavish style. Off to another corner was an authentic brick-oven and a barbecue pit that was overlooked by a fully stocked wet bar. Vito's backyard had more appliances and amenities than most homes did. This was outdoor living at its finest.

Back at the pizzeria, Vito and all of his forces were searching the streets for this potential assailant. They were also in hot and heavy pursuit of Steamer and Julius. They put money all over the street to try and buy the intelligence that would help find them. His men visited every crack den and hangout in which Steamer had any affiliation with. All street corners and every nook and cranny that resembled an alleyway turned up empty. The gangsters practically turned the city upside down, still to no avail. Either nobody knew anything or people were just not talking. For this night, Steamer and Julius could sleep peacefully. Vito's crew didn't even have the slightest of scents concerning their whereabouts. This dynamic duo was nowhere in to be found. They high-tailed it to another location as soon as they found out that Vito had ordered a hit on the both of them.

Construction workers were active erecting a small stage where the live entertainment would be performing. The city was also notified for permission to close down the street to traffic on Saturday, August eighth. Policemen were busy unloading barricades that would thwart any traffic from entering St. Ann's Place. The facelift for the once demolished park was finally completed.

"Come on, Honey," Joey hollered, from the hallway leading to the bedroom. "Are you ready yet, Vito is waiting outside for us."

"I'll be right there!" Gloria replied, from one of the many bedrooms' private baths. "I'm just putting on my lipstick."

"Can't you do that in the car?" he asked, having already waited almost an hour for her to get ready. "We're running late."

"You want me to look good don't you?"

"Yea, but I don't want to grow old waiting for you."

"I'll be right out," she said. "Just give me a couple of more minutes."

"Are you feeling any better since you went to see the doctor?"

"I feel fine, honey, better than ever."

"Are you sure, because if you are not up to the party, we can skip it and just stay home." Gloria then stuck her head out of the bathroom door and looked at Joey. She had a smile on her face from ear to ear. Joey just looked at her, wondering what this turnaround in her behavior was all about. As of yesterday, she went from sulking and feeling depressed all day long to this. A couple of trips to the doctor changed everything about her demeanor. Whatever the doctor had given her seemed to work to perfection. The turnaround was so stunning that Joey wanted some of whatever she was taking for himself.

"Just give me a couple of more minutes," she said again. This time actually laughing like something was funny. Joey looked puzzled; he just shook his head and walked back into the hallway and on his way down the steps.

Over the past few months, Vito had developed a strong liking towards her. Ever since Joey and Gloria were staying at his house, the bond between him and her grew stronger. She was now treated like the daughter that he never had. And in turn, she started to trust him and looked up to him in her own special way. Gloria even started to like her new surroundings. It's not too hard for a woman to get used to living in a multi million-dollar home. Though she appeared to settle down a bit, she was still very tense and nervous about attending this block party. Gloria felt very uneasy, even though the couple would have more security around her than the President of the United States of America.

Chapter 22

$\mathfrak{G}$LORIA AND JOEY looked fabulous as they sat in the back seat of the fancy limousine that Vito had supplied from one of his businesses. Both of them were sporting tans like they just arrived home from Hawaii. Gloria never looked better in her white pants suit and black accessories. Joey was wearing a blue double-breasted suit that looked like it was tailor made to fit his body. They looked like a couple of movie stars going to some premier in the theatre district on Broadway.

The limo slowly drove through the removed barricades on Franklin Ave. and rested about fifty feet from the pizzeria. The driver quickly opened the door to let Vito out of the car. He then raced to the other side and politely reached for Gloria's hand and assisted her out. Joey soon followed and quickly adjusted the jacket on his expensive looking suit. Gloria did the same as they both looked at each other and smiled.

From the moment they exited the limousine they were confronted by a half a dozen bodyguards. This protection could not be found in the Yellow Pages under the heading of, "Security." These were foot soldiers of the Mafia, each one of them were packing enough heat to defend a small city. To Joey, this was not a welcomed sight at all, but there was nothing he could do about it. Vito had recruited these guys to watch over him and Gloria for their own safety. Quickly, a huddle formed around the new arrivals as they were whisked off to their awaiting table.

Dutch, Jimmy, Bear and the Roach occupied the half empty rectangular table. They each were in the company of beautiful women who looked like they were paid escorts. These broads just kept quiet and mingled only when they were spoken to. But they did what they were paid to do - they looked good. One look at the beauty sitting at this table would raise more than an eyebrow.

Vito, Joey and Gloria were led to the table and each took a seat as the festivities had already started. Seated right next to Joey at another table was his work crew with their families. Orlando, Manuel and Jorge smiled at Joey as each one of them got up to shake his hand and hug him. They missed Joey dearly the past couple of weeks. For the Mexican trio, things were just not the same anymore with Joey gone. Their greetings told Joey more than just a hello. No words were needed; the tears he witnessed were saying goodbye also. Joey knew that this was it, this was the last day that he would ever step foot on St. Ann's Place again. He wondered if the Mexicans knew what was going on. The way they were acting seemed to tell him that they had accepted the fact that it was all over. None of them said a word about it. The future, for now anyway, was put to rest.

To the left of Joey, at another table, were Derek and his parents. Even though the young boy did not come by the pizzeria that much anymore, he was still a favorite in Joey's eyes. There was just too much danger for him to be around anymore. After all, his parents already lost one son to murder. Losing another would almost be suicidal to them. Totally unaware, they practically sat right on top of the spot where little Steven was murdered.

There was a bodyguard standing at each corner of the crowded table. And there were two men standing on each corner of the long block. Everyone was checked and almost patted down before they could even enter the party. The only thing missing was a metal detector to walk through. If Vito could have installed one, he would have. All the security guards were peering into the crowd looking for suspicious characters. The White House had a better chance of letting someone through its doors on this evening. The security was tight, it was tighter than a crab's butt, and that was waterproof. The bodyguards all knew what they were looking for; they just didn't know what it looked like. For anyone to go on the offensive on this night had to be crazy. They would be shot dead before they came within fifty feet of Joey. But no matter how tight the security and protection was, nothing was insurmountable anymore. Even the Berlin Wall came crumbling down to pieces.

St Ann's place was packed to capacity on this beautiful evening. Everyone willingly participated in the festivities with eagerness and joy. The residents lined the streets with tables and chairs right outside their homes. From one end of St. Ann's Place to the other, they decorated the crowed block with happy party-goers.

The pleasant aromas of the many types of food lingered with the soft summer breeze. The smoke from the roaring barbecue created a haze that drifted thirty feet above the ground. This was one giant sized buffet and barbecue, whatever satisfied your pallet was there.

Directly across the street from the pizzeria, a bandstand was erected. This makeshift platform was where all the ceremonies would take place. The temporary structure would accommodate the disc jockey, live music and the Master of Ceremonies. Vito anointed Jimmy as the emcee of this memorable event. He also warned Jimmy that this was to be taken seriously and there was no room for clowning around. Vito threatened to shoot him dead right on the stage if he saw any of his lunacy or foolish antics.

Joey just sat there in awe; he was silenced by the change he was seeing in the people of the neighborhood. From the prosperity of small businesses all the way down to the complexion of the atmosphere, everything had changed. It was like something bigger than life was looking out for these people. Joey was starting to comprehend what this was all about, no matter what Vito chose to believe. He knew that an existing power was responsible for this unbelievable phenomenon. Vito and himself were just a piece of the puzzle to make it all happen. He also realized that this mission was coming to an end. In his eyes, he was mysteriously led here for a reason, and the reason was unfolding right before him. In less than five hours, he would be taken from this mission for good. Joey would be starting a new chapter in his life, though it still remained unknown to him.

An hour later, Jimmy introduced himself to the crowd as they assembled around the stage. The five-piece band stood poised behind him ready to rock to the tunes of yesteryear. This was Jimmy's stage and you could see it in his face that this is where he wanted to be.

The large audience took to him as he gave a brief description of what the festivities for the night would be. This guy was born for the microphone, his persona coolly blended into the spectators with ease. His delicate style was captured by most of the swooning females in the audience. Everything from Motown to Italian melodies was flowing from Jimmy's soothing voice. His chosen medley of music was perfect.

With Jimmy singing in the background, Vito's table was buzzing with good conversation and laughs. Business was put on the backburner for this special night. Everyone was having a good time except Gloria. She just sat there in her own little world with the look of complexity all over her face. There was something that wanted to come out of her full lips. It seemed that she was just waiting for the right time to say it.

"What's the matter, honey?" Joey asked, trying to find the reason behind her strange behavior.

"Well, I guess now is as good a time as any other," she said. "I can't wait any longer."

"What do you mean?"

"I didn't want to tell you any sooner because of the party and all."

"Tell me what?" Joey asked, turning her around and looking directly at her. "Is everything okay?

"Joey," she nervously said. "We're going to have a baby," she whispered. "I'm pregnant."

"What!" he cried raising his voice up a couple of notches over the loud music. "Did I hear you right! You're gonna have a baby?"

"Yes, that's why I have not been feeling too well," she explained. "The doctor told me the other day."

"Why didn't you tell me sooner?"

"I knew that I had to find the right time and place to tell you. I was going to wait until after the party was over with, but I couldn't keep it a secret any longer. It was killing me to not tell you. I couldn't wait another second."

"Oh, honey," an elated and beaming Joey said. "This is so fantastic. I'm so grateful to you," he said still looking astonished. "You're gonna be the mother of my child!"

Joey then grabbed Gloria as they both had risen to their feet. They hugged and kissed, their eyes welling with tears. Their jubilation was apparent, everyone at the table just stopped whatever they were doing to notice the happy couple.

"They took a sonogram of me and the doctor told me that everything was fine," she explained. "He said it was too early to determine the sex of the baby. But if it is a boy, we're going to name him after his father. Joseph DeFalco Junior."

Joey was too emotional to speak any further. This great news had strangled his vocal cords shut, preventing him from speaking any further.

The special sentiment in his heart and the teardrops on his face rendered him speechless. The news had given him a feeling that he had never experienced in his whole life. Gloria had seen it and she loved what she was seeing. There is nothing greater for a woman to see a proud expecting father looking so exhilarated and honored in this time of joy.

"Do you want to see it?" she asked, reaching down for her oversized handbag. "I have it with me."

"I know you have it with you," he said. "But how am I going to see it?"

"Not the baby, silly."

"What do you mean then?" Joey said, looking confused.

"The doctor gave me a copy of the sonogram to take home."

"Oh!" he said, feeling a little relieved. "For a minute I thought you were having another bout of morning sickness."

"Well, do you want to see it?"

"Hell yea, I want to see it."

Gloria pulled her black handbag apart from the small buckle that was holding it together. She reached inside with her long fingers and retrieved a large yellow envelope. Slowly opening the wing type clip, she slid her soft hand inside and pulled out a dark shiny piece of paper. Gloria then looked up at Joey and smiled as she handed the proof to him.

Joey examined the dark photo but was having trouble finding what he was looking for. He searched and searched but he kept coming up empty. There was some kind of development that was there, but he couldn't find it. He turned the sonogram every which way but backwards. Joey held it down pointing at the floor, still nothing. He raised it above his head, still with no success.

"Here," Gloria said. "Let me show you."

"It figures," Joey said. "I have a baby somewhere in this thing and I can't even find it."

"Here honey, here it is," she said as she pointed to the little head that was barely visible. "Do you see it?"

"A little bit, it's kind of dark out here," he said, while straining his eyes to catch this miracle gift from God. "Let me go inside the pizzeria, the light is much brighter in there. I'll be right back. I want you to tell Vito the news."

"Maybe you should do that."

"No, I want you to do it."

"Okay, if that's the way you want it."

Joey just shook his head in agreement and raced into the pizzeria. Both of his arms were swaying with motion. With the sonogram in his right hand and the yellow envelope in his left, he smiled brightly as he raced towards the light. Two of the bodyguards followed him inside, watching his every move.

"Will you two guys excuse me?" Joey asked. "I want to be left alone."

"But Mr. Carlucci said for us to never take our eyes off of you," this big strapping looking character said. "And that's exactly what we're gonna do."

"Well then watch me from the door, you don't have to come all the way inside."

The two men back-pedaled all the way out to the entranceway of the store. Each one of these two mean looking men stood beside opposite ends of the narrow doorway.

Joey leaned over and placed his elbows on top of the pizza counter. He began to examine the welcomed black and white photo. He first saw what looked like a beam of light. From left to right, the light grew in size as it traveled through the womb. Inside this light, everything faded. The characteristics were somewhat bleak but distinguishable. He slowly focused on the unformed embryonic fetus ingrained at the bottom of the photo and nodded in agreement. There he saw his child's tiny head and what appeared to be a body amongst the mass of cloudy tissue that floated around it. Joey looked harder and harder and could not believe that the object before him was his own flesh and blood. The smile on his face was evidence that he was a very happy man.

Picking his head up, Joey then went to slide the sonogram back into the large yellow envelope. Putting it three quarters of the way in something made him stop dead in his tracks. He quickly withdrew the whole sonogram back out of the envelope.

Little by little, his eyes and whole face inched closer to the sonogram. Profusely, he stared until he saw something totally unusual and surreal. There was something unrealistic hovering above the fetus of this explanatory medical photograph. It was then and only then, did Joey realize that all of his perceptions and premonitions were very, very real.

There was something other than the baby living and breathing inside the body of his girlfriend Gloria. Even more than that, it was alive and breathing inside of her developing womb. Joey saw it as plain as day as the face of this phenomenon was looking down at his unborn child.

The right side of its forehead was partially revealed as long and overflowing hair covered the left side. The facial image was tilted in a downward position with its eyes staring straight down at the growing embryo. The bushy eyebrows lay a top of a pair of eyes from which teardrops appeared to be falling from. There was a hint of sadness and sorrow coming from the facial expressions of this embedded apparition. It appeared like the emerging figure in the sonogram was coming here for a very special reason. He alone knew the reason… for he had been here before.

There were traces of a thin mustache that resided below a long, crooked battle scarred nose. The lips were perfectly formed from top to bottom. Each lip rested peacefully, one on top of the other. Though cloudy, a shadowy beard provided the finishing touches to what appeared to be a perfectly chiseled face. The oval shape was in full blossom as it lovingly looked down upon this innocent gift from life. All of this was erected right on top of a pair of broad shoulders covered with a shroud. The shabby material of the cloak looked spotty and imbued with blood. This strange and unbelievable happening was carrying this unborn young fetus securely in his arms and snuggled against his warm and safe chest. The bottom of the dark photo revealed more of this inexplicable event. There were minuscule images of young children just staring into the sky of the sonogram. They all seemed to be waiting for some kind of arrival or presence. These faint sightings of the young started to slowly fade out the closer they got to the right side border of this remarkable photo.

"Oh my God," Joey whispered to himself. "He is holding my baby. Gloria, you're a part of it all."

Joey stood there frozen like a block of ice in the cold Artic waters of Alaska. His shaking body started to sweat with abundance from this alarming and unnatural incident. He then turned and looked out of the pizzeria's window at Gloria. These unforeseen events left her clueless to what was really going on. She just sat there in a deep conversation with Vito. Joey kept staring at her and then his attention went back to the sonogram. Back and forth he went, each time with this stupefying look on his face. He stood in awe of what he was seeing. But the respect he was seeing was laced with fear.

"Get Vito in here now," Joey screamed. The two bodyguards at the door didn't move. They just stood there looking at Joey and each other. "Did you hear what the fuck I said," he shouted again. "Tell Vito to get in here!"

Finally one of these big oafs got the message and walked over to Vito and whispered something into his ear. Vito excused himself from Gloria and slowly got out of his chair. Vito whispered something back to the two big men, and they stayed put. Each one of them waited outside watching over Gloria and her unborn child.

Puffing on a cigarette, Vito walked through the entranceway of the pizza parlor. He had his arms extended wide open ready to embrace Joey as he walked towards him. "Hey, hey," Vito said. "You're going to be a father, you little son of a bitch. Get over here and give me a kiss!"

Joey did not move, he stayed glued to the surface below him. He did not respond to Vito at all. His whole body was numb from head to toe. The look on his face alone set off smoke signals to Vito telling him that something was wrong.

"What's wrong?" Vito asked, now standing right next to his Godson. Joey stood there silent, tears started to stream down his once happy face. "Tell me what's wrong," Vito asked again. Still nothing, Joey just continued to look at Vito. His body was anchored with total shock.

Vito dropped his lit cigarette and suddenly grabbed Joey by both shoulders. He violently shook him with a short jerky movement to awaken him out of this state. Vito continued until he started to get some sort of response from the traumatized Joey. These abrupt ruffled motions brought some life back into Joey as the blood started to freely flow back into his brain.

"Now tell me God damn it, what's wrong?"

"Vito," Joey nervously said. "Take a look at this." Joey handed the blemished sonogram to Vito.

"Yea, so," he said. "Gloria told me about it, I know what it is!"

"No you fuckin' don't," Joey yelled. "You don't have the faintest of clues of what the hell I'm talking about." At that moment, Gloria turned around to notice the commotion going on inside the store. She stayed seated; she knew that she should never get in between Joey and Vito, especially during an argument.

"Calm down, and don't you ever talk to me that way," Vito shouted. "I'm not one of your fuckin' buddies hanging out on some street corner!"

"Well, for once, could you just do what I ask you to do?"

"What do you want me to do?"

"I want you to sit down and look deeply into that," Joey said, pointing to the sonogram in Vito's hand.

"Okay, I'll sit down right over here. Is this alright," he said sporting a saccharine smile.

"Vito, for once in your life, will you take me serious on what you're about to see."

"I promise, no jokes, I will be dead serious."

"This is the baby, right over here," Joey pointed. "Do you see it?"

"Kind of."

"It's here," he pointed again. "Do you see it?

"Yea, I see it."

"Well, look above that!"

"Yea, so."

"What do you see?"

"Nothing."

"Look harder!" Joey demanded. "Look around this area," he impatiently pointed out one more time.

Vito sat there for about a minute, trying desperately to find something inside the sonogram. He never picked his head up as he relentlessly searched for something that he did not know what he was looking for. But to make Joey happy he pursued the issue, even though his patience was growing very thin.

"Do you see anything?"

"No," an undaunted Vito said.

"God damn it, Vito," he yelled. "Hold it up to the light."

Vito got to his feet and held the sonogram up over his head. He placed it right underneath the fluorescent lighting running down the length of the store. Moving the photo closer to his face and then sometimes further away, he then struck pay dirt.

"I see it, Joey," he said, stunned with what he was looking at. "I see it."

"What do you see," Joey asked.

Vito slowly turned to Joey; he had a very flushed look to his olive complexion. His eyes alone told Joey exactly what he wanted to know. The tough mobster just looked at Joey in disbelief and discomfort. Vito knew that there was no logical explanation to all of this. But he did know who and what he just witnessed. This was no aberration or deviation from the normal. This was reality; the time had come for Vito to fess up to the truth. There was nothing distorted or tarnished about this picture. His eyesight was not blurry and there was no need for reading glasses. Even though the photo was a bit obscure, it was time to put all the excuses to rest, there weren't anymore. It was time for Vito to become a believer.

"Vito," Joey asked again. "What do you see?"

"I see a face," a stunned Vito started to say.

"Whose face do you see?" a relentless Joey demanded.

"I see the face of….," he whispered with a tinge of fright in his voice. "The face of…., I see the face of Jesus Christ."

With great precipitation, the overhead fluorescent lights started to flicker in and out. The powerful surge of current made snake like noises as it traveled its way through the electrical system of the store. In and out the lights fluttered, bringing everything inside the store to a temporary halt. The electricity was dancing with emotion, blowing out everything in its destructive path. After a couple of seconds, a loud bang and the smell of burning wires were detected. Every circuit breaker in the pizzeria was tripped, causing complete darkness. To Joey this was nothing new; he had seen this electrical path of destruction before.

The bodyguards rushed through the front door with their pistols ready and poised for gunplay. They rumbled to the scene expecting the worst, but not able to see much. Gloria was held back from entering the store as a crowd assembled around outside. Over the microphone Jimmy tried to calm everyone down with his soothing voice. Everyone was overreacting and expecting the worst.

"Everyone just calm the fuck down, it's just the lights," Vito said. "Go find the circuit breakers in the kitchen and flip the power back on," Vito ordered to one of the bodyguards. "Here, use this to find your way." Vito handed one of the men his cigarette lighter.

"Vito, what's going on," a scared and bewildered Joey said.

"The breaker box was just overloaded. We're pulling a lot of power from the store, that's all."

"That's bullshit," Joey said. "He's here, Vito! That was his way of telling us that he's here!"

"Who's here?"

"Jesus Christ!"

"Will you stop it," Vito said. "The electrical system was just overloaded from the party outside. Don't make this out to be anymore than what it is."

"He's here! I can feel him all around us. I tell you, his spirit is here!"

"The only thing you feel is fright," Vito insisted. "Enough already!"

A couple of minutes later one of the bodyguards restored the power. But not until he stated that there was definitely something strange going on in the kitchen. It seemed that all the confusion and minor destruction had left its mark on the wall behind the circuit breaker box.

"Thanks," Vito said to the bodyguard. "At least all the power is back on."

"Yea but if you saw the smoke back there," he said, shaking his head, "it's a wonder how you have any power at all."

"Nothing was on fire?"

"No, but the whole wall behind the box was scorched," the burly bodyguard said. "I can't believe that you still have power in here. Judging by the explosion and smoke you would think that the whole fuckin' kitchen blew up. But the breaker box and the wires inside it were untouched. I never saw anything like it in my life."

"You see," declared Joey. "I told you so!"

"Alright, enough you," Vito said. "Let's go take a look."

Vito and Joey took the short trip into the kitchen, fighting their way through the thinning smoke. Vito then stepped up to the breaker box and opened it up. His man was right, not a wire was touched. The system looked like nothing had ever happened to it. Everything inside the small metal container was as clean as a whistle. It seemed Vito was having a hard time believing how the breaker box and kitchen remained untouched and immaculately clean. *Where the hell did the smoke come from?* he thought. He examined it some more and came to no final conclusion on how this could have happened.

"Holy shit, Vito," Joey screamed. "Look!"

"Look at what?"

"The wall, Vito, the wall!"

Vito stepped back a couple of feet to where Joey was standing. They both looked up at the wall with their eyes wide open in disbelief. A large dark feature had melted its way into the wall around, underneath and above the breaker box. The enamel painted, white plasterboard wall was covered with a thick darkish gray residue. The once dense smoke had breathed some life into something of a surreal nature. The blemish had a head and the limbs from a whole torso attached to it. If you looked hard enough, you could find a remarkable resemblance to the other images that were left before. Each arm appeared to be open like it was welcoming somebody. This sighting was much different than the others. This cloudy figure embedded in the wall possessed something that scared the shit out of Joey. It was something that he never saw before in each one of his other sightings. Unlike before, this unbelievable configuration had a pair of legs that were now touching the ground. Instead of just the torso or face, this time the whole body made an appearance.

The indistinct vapors that made up the outline of this revelation were massive. To Joey, this meant that Jesus' spirit was finally here walking the same earth that he was. From head to toe, Joey saw what he thought was the whole body of Jesus Christ. The smoke instilled body stood stagnant on the wall inside of his small pizzeria. This sighting was even more profound than the face found in the sonogram. To Joey it was something that he knew all along. Joey stared and stared. With arrested senses, his whole body was consumed with apprehension. Vito looked over at Joey and decided that they had both seen enough.

"Come on, snap out of it, it's all over."

"It's all over," he said. "It didn't even start yet."

"Listen," Vito said. "At first it startled me too. But you have to realize that it's just smoke."

"Where the hell did the smoke come from? And if it is just smoke, then go over there and try to rub it off the wall."

"Why?"

"Because if it is just smoke, it will come right off. I'll bet you any amount of money that you can't clean that off the wall."

"Don't be ridiculous," Vito responded with a cocky voice. "I'll show you."

Vito went over to the metal sink and retrieved a thick scouring brush. He ran it under the hot water for a few seconds and sprinkled some abrasive detergent over it. Without hesitation, he walked directly over to the stained wall. Vito started to scrub and scrub with a mighty vigor, not once looking to see the results. Joey just stood there watching as all the soap and water was dripping to the floor. Vito scrubbed so hard that he was taking the paint right off of the wall.

"Just as I thought," Joey said. "It's not coming off."

"That's impossible," shouted Vito.

"That's not impossible," declared Joey. "Look and see for yourself."

"I have seen and heard enough," he said. "Let's go back out to the party. We will talk about this later."

"Will you look again," Joey said. "You took the paint right off of the wall. But it's still there!"

"Come on, everyone is waiting for us. I said we will talk about this later."

"Later, what later," he snapped back. "I want to talk about this now. Later might never come for me!"

"I told you time and time again to stop talking like that," reprimanded Vito. "I will have none of it."

"Then explain this all to me."

"I can't."

"Well I can, but you don't want to ever hear what I have to say."

"That's not true."

"So then stay here and listen to my reasoning behind all of this!"

"Alright already, go ahead for crying out loud and say what's on your mind."

"I'll begin where it all started from," Joey said. "First off, you give me this medallion. Is it an ordinary medallion? No! It does dances around my neck and almost chokes me every time something happens. Not only that, but it practically sets my body on fire with the heat coming from it. Every time it happens it leaves me with some reminder of its presence," he said ranting and raving. "Besides the medallion, I got this fuckin' madman chasing me all over town trying to kill me. But wait, Vito, it gets even better than this," Joey said, now on a roll. "We look into a sonogram and see that Jesus Christ is living inside the womb of my girlfriend. And if that's not enough for you, then the lights start going in and out until there's complete darkness. The breaker box blows up and there's smoke everywhere. But no, there's nothing strange going on. We only come back into the kitchen to see this!" Joey ended, pointing at the wall. "But this time it's the whole body. Do you want to hear more?"

"No, I've heard enough. In a couple of hours it will be all over with," Vito tried to reason. "We're all getting out of here."

"This isn't going to stay here, Vito," Joey said. "It's going to follow me wherever I go."

"That's bullshit, you don't know that for sure."

"I do know it, I can feel it."

"You're wrong, once we leave here all this shit in your mind will disappear."

"I doubt it," predicted Joey. "But now Gloria is getting dragged into this whole mess," Joey cried. "Besides her, now I have to worry about the baby. Vito, if I die, you have to make sure you take care of them."

"Stop it right now, you ain't dying," assured Vito. "So stop talking so foolishly. Whatever the reasons are for all of this, I'm sure Gloria, the baby and you, will be alright. All I could say is that if any of this is true - and I am not saying it isn't - but if it is all true then that baby is in the arms of Jesus Christ. And there is no place on earth that offers more love and safety then where he is right now. So let's calm down and think this out rationally."

"Think what out," retorted a frantic Joey. "You still don't believe that this is all happening. You seen it," he went on. "You seen it on my tee shirt, you see it in here," he said flicking the sonogram into Vito's face. "And you see it over there," Joey said pointing in the direction of the newly found blemish in the kitchen. "Do you want to come to my mother's house so you could see it embedded in that damn wall too?" Joey was now getting very irate, never before had he ever talked to Vito in this tone of voice. "This thing is growing and growing, each passing day it becomes larger in life then the day before. What are you going to tell me next, that I am losing my fuckin' mind?"

"No, but what you are trying to tell me is that this all started to happen the day I put that medallion around your neck."

"That's what I have been saying all along," Joey explained. "But you never once wanted to believe me," he said. "I'll be right back."

"Where are you going now?"

"I'm going to get that damn tee shirt."

"This kid is driving me fuckin' crazy," Vito said to himself. "I can't believe this shit. I'm getting too old for all this crap."

Joey took the short walk around the counter and bent down right under the cash register. He pulled out a shirt box where his tee shirt was neatly folded and placed into. Holding the box in his hand he returned to where Vito was standing at the bottom of the steps. Joey then placed the box onto a table and opened it up. Never hesitating, he quickly removed the contents and spread it out all over the top of the bare table.

"Look Vito," he said. "You've seen this just a couple of weeks ago." Vito knew what he was looking at, and he also knew the striking resemblance between the two images. "Now look at the likeness of the two," Joey went on. "For God's sake, they are practically twins. Except the face in the sonogram is much more vivid and profound. What are you gonna say now, Vito, that Gloria swallowed this medallion before she went for her pregnancy test?" Joey blasted out his proof, practically pushing the medallion into Vito's face. "Vito, it's all here. The signs are everywhere. The wall in that kitchen just finalizes everything. What are you gonna say now?"

"I'm not going to say anything," he said. Each word out of his mouth was getting louder and louder. "What the fuck do you want me to say, that I brought this whole thing on top of you myself?"

"No, I don't want you to say that. But you are a big part of this, and so is Dutch. I just want you to believe me and believe the fact that this is all happening. Vito," Joey said as his voice silenced up a bit. "When I got out of prison a spirit out of the Bible came to me."

"What are you talking about now?" he asked, not being able to take anymore of this Biblical and spiritual stuff.

"I saw him above my bed, right before I was about to fall asleep."

"Did he look like this?" Vito said, pointing to the sonogram.

"I couldn't make out his face, but I now know that it was not him. It was not Jesus."

"Then who was it?"

"It was Jeremiah."

"Who the hell is Jeremiah?"

"He is one of the prophets of the Old Testament. He speaks by divine inspiration and expresses the will and commands of God."

"What did he want from you?"

"He wanted me to follow him. He said, will you come with me," Joey remembered. "He issued some commands from the scriptures of the Bible and sent me on this mission. And then he just disappeared into the wall," Joey softly said, giving Vito only a brief description of what really took place that unbelievable night. "Jeremiah is my protection. He is here amongst us. But the image in the wall is not of him, it is of Jesus Christ. So are all the other images. When Jeremiah leaves me," Joey paused, his eyes piercing, "then Jesus will come for my soul."

"I can't believe this is all happening to you."

"Believe it, because it's all true. If your grandfather was still alive, I am sure he would have the same story to tell you."

"Do you think that he saw Jeremiah also?"

"There is no doubt in my mind that he saw something," a confident Joey said. "Your Grandfather saw the prophet Ezekiel. He was on the same kind of a mission as I am."

"What mission?"

"You know what mission," Joey said. "He rushed into that burning schoolhouse to save all those little children from a most certain death. He prevented many more years of abuse that those poor children would have been suffering through. He was sent there to dispose of the evil once and for all. That's why he died with the sex abuser at his feet. Ezekiel would not let your Grandfather carry that man out of the burning schoolhouse alive. That is why the roof caved in on the both of them. Once that was all accomplished, he was then called by Jesus Christ. Now your grandfather rests in the arms of his savior. But before it all took place, I am positive that he was getting the same premonitions that I have been getting."

"What is your mission?" Vito tentatively asked, knowing very little of Joey's destiny.

Joey started reacting like he was just consumed by a trance. He drifted off somewhere very far away. His eyes were wide open as he just stared with an emotionless detachment from his physical surroundings. All of his senses and movements had come to an abrupt standstill. This hypnotic or cataleptic state touched Vito very deeply. He just listened and looked into the glassy eyes of his dazed Godson.

Vito's eyes starting flapping like the wings of an eagle. He slowly inched closer to Joey. Now totally fixated, he noticed an impression permeated inside the eyes of Joey. Glowing in gold, Joey's body had absorbed the medallion and transmitted its image to his organ of vision. Jesus was now looking out of the windows of Joey's eyes. From the inside corners of Joey's eyes, threads of blood evolved. Slowly the blood trickled down both sides of his nose and onto his lips. Refusing to believe, Vito kept shaking his head from side to side. His adherence to the truth was in denial.

No, no, no, Vito thought to himself, *this ain't happening.*

"I know now that the prophet Jeremiah came to me in spirit that night in my bedroom. He instructed me through God that my mission was to be here with you. But I am the one who will be sacrificed for this good deed, not you. I have been set apart from all others and appointed as a disciple from someplace very far away. Wherever I go, I say and do as I am commanded," Joey softly said. "Vito, I bleed the blood of Christ!"

A stunned Vito just listened; he couldn't believe these ancient prophetic words that were coming from his Godson's mouth. But he did see the blood.

"I feel like I'm giving up my life for the good people of this neighborhood. With your strong arm, this mission was accomplished. All the evil was uprooted, tore down and destroyed from this area, never ever to return," lamented Joey in a soothing voice. "They have fought us, Vito, but with you by my side they could never overthrow or conquer us. With your help, we have reseeded and planted a new life for the unfortunate ones. The neighborhood was given back to the people. Do you now see, Vito? I was commanded to be here, and now it is time to go. Just like your grandfather, soon it will be my time to leave. Please don't ask me how I know all of this, I just know. And I also know that this story has all been told before. This has all been written and saved in the Scriptures of the Old Testament. Read it, Vito, and one day tell it to the world. Now is the time to make all the non-believers believe. So you see, Vito," he went on with his sermon. "Your grandfather was no different than me!"

"But my grandfather died, Joey."

"Exactly, he was taken right after his mission was completed."

"If this is true," he asked. "Why you, and why my grandfather?"

"I don't know for sure," he tried to explain. "But we were both chosen. I am just a man and I have no idea how I fit into all of this. But I do know that it has something to do with this medallion!" he said, holding the medal in his hand. "A priest once told me that many people are called, but only a few are chosen. Somewhere, there is a reason behind all of this. Vito, these words that I speak are not of my own choosing. I am speaking through the spirit of Jesus Christ!"

"For the first time in my life I am at a loss for words."

"I know that this is all hard to believe," Joey said. "But it's all right here in front of you. What happened tonight, writes the final chapter!"

"So what are you trying to tell me, that you're living on borrowed time?"

"I don't know, Vito," Joey said shaking his head. "But I am not afraid any longer. I know that Jesus is with me and he will rescue me from all of this."

"From all of what?"

"The pain and suffering that has been put upon me. For the first time in my life, I am at total ease within myself."

"Nothing is ever going to happen to you," promised Vito. "With all my power and resources, I will make sure of it."

"Vito, you are not bigger than God! Nobody is!"

"I know, kid, I know," Vito said, soon realizing what he was up against and what he had said was foolish. "But I don't want anything to happen to you."

"It's too late," Joey declared. "My fate is already etched in stone! So believe me when I speak these words. For I am not a fool," he said. "But if and when something does happen to me, you must remember it and tell it all!"

Joey suddenly stood silent; a transformation was taking over his body again. He appeared to be snapping out of whatever possessive state that had swallowed him up. He quickly shook his head from side to side trying desperately to awaken himself. In a matter of seconds, he looked at Vito not knowing where he was or what he was doing. But to Vito, this awakening was a welcomed sight. Even he was swept away by these final words of wisdom.

"Welcome back."

"What?"

"Never mind," Vito answered. "It was nothing." Vito was not about to reveal the past series of verbal exchanges to him. He was positively sure that Joey did not remember a thing. At least he thought he didn't.

"Vito, Gloria is getting suspicious out there, she keeps looking in here. Please, not a word of this to her," said Joey. "Vito, I don't want anything to happen to her and the baby."

"Nothing will happen to them, I can promise you that," Vito swore, wiping the beaded sweat from his forehead.

"Please Vito, you're the only one that can see to this."

"I will, Joey, I will," he vowed. "Now before we go outside there is something that I feel I must tell you. It's been bothering me for months."

"What is it?" Joey asked, in a very inquisitive nature.

Both men started to walk slowly back into the main section of the pizzeria. They both looked outside the eatery and saw that calm had been restored. Vito then turned to Joey with a very uneasy look on his once confident face. "Maybe this is not the right time, but it is something that I have been meaning to tell you for a long time."

"What?" Joey asked again, while turning around to look at Gloria. He then raced to the front door and said to her, "We'll be right out, we're just going over a few last minute details." Gloria just shook her head in agreement. "Okay Vito, what is it?" he said, rushing back over to him.

"I guess there is no other way to tell you than to come right to the point. I'm your Godfather," he unexpectedly blurted out. Vito was always to the point, never beating around the bush with anything, even this.

"Yea so, you're everybody's Godfather."

"You don't understand, I baptized you as a baby."

"What?" Joey yelled out with his eyes wide open. "Say that again!"

"You heard me right the first time."

"It sounded like you said that you were my real Godfather."

"That's what I said," Vito confirmed. "Me and your father were best friends growing up as kids. When your mother got pregnant with you, he asked me to be the Godfather of his baby boy. I was at their wedding and everything."

"Get the hell out of here," Joey said, turning away from Vito to walk out the front door. "Don't play with me like this, Vito!"

"Turn around and look at me," Vito demanded. Joey slowly turned his head and looked dead straight into Vito's eyes. "I'm not playing, it's all true."

"So you know my mother?"

"Yes, and she knows me. And she knows everything about me."

"But Vito, she never mentioned anything about you to me."

"She was never too thrilled about the way I lived my life. Your mother was only too happy that me and your father never stood close friends," Vito sadly said. "In a way, I don't blame her. There were many times that I tried to offer your father a piece of any action that I had going on."

"And he didn't take it?"

"No, your mother fought him tooth and nail not to. She is a strong woman, Joey. If not for her, your father would have been part of this scum ridden lifestyle of mine."

"Why didn't you ever tell me this before?" a dazed Joey asked, looking directly into his eyes. "You knew all along, but yet you never told me. Why?"

"Because I wanted you out of my life," he said looking down at his black leather shoes. "I knew that I was no good for you. My lifestyle was not the lifestyle that I wanted for you. Your mother did not want it for your father, and I really don't think that she would want it for you either," he sadly said.

"From the time you were born until the time I left you in prison, I felt that the less you knew of me the better off you were."

"You didn't have to stay away from me."

"I know I didn't. But at the time I thought it was best for the both of us. Now I realize that I was wrong."

"Is this the reason why you protected me in prison, because I was your Godson?"

"Yes, that's true. But we had our eyes on you anyway. We knew that you were Italian, but at that point you were no different than anybody else. When I found out what your last name was, it all came back to me. I guess you could say that I was a bit over protective of you."

"This is so fuckin' unbelievable, are there anymore surprises for me?" Joey asked, shaking and scratching his head. "What the hell is next?"

"I'm sorry, kid, I never thought that it would come down to this. How all these circumstances are coming together is really hard for me to believe."

"Believe it, Vito," Joey warned. "Because everything is so true, and what you are telling me now, is just icing on the cake. We were meant to be together again. This medallion," he said pointing to the piece, "has brought us back together again. Vito, when you baptized me, were you wearing the medallion around your neck?"

"Of course I was, why do you ask that?"

"That's when the connection was made between me and the medallion. Many years later, its powers brought us together in prison."

"That's ridiculous."

"Is it?" he asked. "Now I know why I committed those crimes. That person was not me. I found my way into prison to get to you and this medallion. That is when the transfer was made. Everything was planned out since the day I was born. This was all meant to be. It could be no other way," he firmly stated. "So you see, Vito, I was chosen at birth. The graces of God have waited many years for me. Now my destiny has been conceived."

"Joey, enough of this for now. Come here," said Vito.

Joey moved closer. Vito then wrapped his arms around him and refused to let go. He hugged him as if he had just been relieved of something that was lying on his chest for years. The burden of not telling Joey who he was must have been killing him. But it was all over now; the truth always has a way of finding its way to the surface.

"Joey, stay still," Vito said. He reached into his pocket for a handkerchief and pulled Joey towards him. "You got some dirt on your face." Vito lightly wiped the red blemish from both sides of Joey's face until it was clean. "There, I think I got it all." Turning away from Joey, he then looked at the fancy white rag. The blood was gone. Astonished, Vito did a double take and came up with the same empty results. *I must be losing my mind,* he thought. *This is all some kind of a dream. Am I starting to see things now?* He paused a second or two. *Nah, it's probably nothing.* Vito shrugged it off like nothing ever happened.

"Vito, I don't know about you," Joey said to his Godfather. "But I need a fuckin' drink."

"You can say that again!" Vito answered, while they both walked out the front door together.

Gloria welcomed them back.

Chapter 23

$\mathcal{V}$ITO AND JOEY returned to the party. Gloria never mentioned his absence. Her silence was good news to Joey, as he was not about to tell her anything anyway. This was the exception to the rule when it came to telling the truth. This new revelation could wait before it hit her ears. Sooner or later she would find out everything anyway. Destiny will do all the talking.

Jimmy was just about done with the first singing engagement of his aspiring career. Like a true professional, he focused the rest of the night on the park. After all, that is what the people really came to see, Jimmy was just an added bonus. But he was quite a surprise to everyone's ears; he was sensational.

"Ladies and gentlemen," Jimmy said, calling to the audience. "Can I have your attention, please." Most people turned towards him. Many started to slowly rise off of their chairs and walk up towards the stage area. "This is the moment that we have all been waiting for," he said. "But before we christen the opening of the brand new park in your honor, Vito Carlucci and the rest of us want to thank each and every one of you for attending this affair. It is now time for all of us to drop whatever we are doing and take a walk to the corner of the block."

At that moment, the large crowd started to cheer in the direction of Vito. Mostly everyone had put their hands together and showed their gratitude with a large eruption of applause. The clapping went directly into a chant,

"Vito, Vito, Vito, Vito," the crowd repeated. Vito just sat there in silence, practically hiding behind Joey who was seated next to him. The one thing that Vito did not want was any recognition and notoriety. He would have preferred to stay somewhat anonymous, but that was probably asking for too much. Everyone here knew who he was and what he had done for them. He should be standing tall for what he has accomplished here. But that was not Vito's style, his business was his own business. And that's the way he wanted it to stay, like it or not. He was flamboyant in style, but subdued, personality wise.

"Go ahead, Vito," Joey said, pouring himself vodka. "They are calling for you, stand up. You too, Dutch, stand up!"

Dutch hopped right to his feet and soaked up all the attention. He quickly started to wave back to the people like he was a celebrity on a Hollywood stage. Dutch was very quiet and well reserved when it came to his mannerisms, but he loved attention. Showing off and killing were two of this Irishman's best attributes. And he was not shy about it either. He did not care who knew about him or what he did. Dutch just performed everything in a quiet way. But he always wanted the attention for any feat that he was responsible for. He was quite the ham when he had all eyes upon him. To Dutch, this was his spotlight and nobody was going to take it away from him.

"Come on, Vito," Jimmy said over the microphone. "Take a bow for the people."

Vito then looked up at Jimmy like he wanted to kill him. He pointed his finger at Jimmy, shaking it vigorously. But then Vito cracked a smile and laughed it all off. It was then that he realized that Jimmy had to bust his balls in some way before the night was over.

"That son of a bitch, he did it to me again," Vito said. "One of these fuckin' days," he said laughing.

"Never mind him, he'll be breaking your balls up until the day you die," said Joey. "But right now get up, please Vito, they want you, so stand up," Joey said again, this time practically nudging him out of his chair.

"If I stand you stand, deal?" Vito said.

"Deal," Joey agreed.

Vito and Joey got out of their chairs and joined Dutch who was standing proud on his feet. They looked at each other as both men recognized the explosive ovation coming from within the large crowd. The clapping and whistling sounds swarmed all around them, even deafening them at times.

It was a continuous reception that had amassed closer and closer to them. Handshakes and pats on the back were soon to follow, that's how appreciating and delighted these people were. Never in his whole life had Vito seen this much gratitude for something that he considered not that big a deal. Quite the opposite of Dutch, Vito preferred to stay out of the public eye. He was not the type who wanted anything in return for any good deeds that he happened to dish out. To him, this gratitude was not necessary. As for Joey, he just went along for the ride. He had more important things to worry about than basking in the glory of somebody else's standing ovation.

The scene quickly shifted to the corner of Franklin Ave. Joey and Gloria along with their entourage of bodyguards remained at the table. Joey continued drinking trying to temporarily forget about his problems. He knew that once the alcohol wore off, the problems would reappear. But ask any alcoholic or junkie, any temporary escape from this mess would be well worth it. His brain needed to be released from being held captive by all this madness.

Vito and Dutch worked their way through the crowd on the corner. The rest of the boys followed suit right behind them. The crowd waited with great anticipation as they all looked up to the waterproof canvas that covered the entranceway of the park. The heavy drop cloth covered the archway and the front gate leading into the park.

The residents of the neighborhood knew there was something hidden underneath the thick green tarpaulin. What it was protecting from being exposed, they had no idea.

Suddenly, the bright lights over the park were radiating with the full force of current. The powerful beams of manmade sunlight lit up the skies and everything around it. Everything in the park was now revealed to the delighted crowd. Those children who managed to stay awake jumped up and down with enthusiasm. Most of them were trying to break free of the tight grasp of their parents' hands. Their anticipation had finally arrived, the childlike glee written all over their young faces told the whole story.

Two men then approached and stood underneath the high arch hanging above the front gates. Each one of them grabbed the tarpaulin from both sides. Within the blink of an eye, they violently tugged at the heavy material, pulling it down from the steel supports up above. Another beam of light suddenly appeared shining directly at the large black letters spreading across the archway. There marked the opening of the people's brand new park.

Standing there boldly was a name that fit this neighborhood to perfection. There stood the lettering that spelled out, "VICTORY PARK."

One by one the people started to enter this state of the art facility. It had everything from a sprinkler system to a jungle gym. From slides to swings, the little kids would have no problem trying to stay amused. For the sports enthusiasts, the space was very limited. But there was enough room for handball and shuffleboard courts. To the far left, a couple of backboards were installed for shooting hoops. But the most important factor was that this was all placed inside a world of beautiful shrubbery and trees. The peaceful and serene setting was perfect for the elderly to spend their lonely afternoons outdoors. There was a little bit of something here for everybody. But most of all, there was peace, serenity and safety.

Peace, serenity and safety were three commodities that mostly all of these people were not accustomed to. They would always cherish the opportunity to enjoy those three fine qualities of life.

After the festivities were over, most of the people were busy saying their goodbyes to the gangsters they now considered family. There were even teardrops falling from those who could not control their emotions. Like brothers, even though they came from different sides of the tracks, the Italians were lovingly embraced. From Jimmy all the way down to Ricky the Roach, they were all accepted. Everyone reveled in the excitement, for they all knew what they had accomplished here. The impossible had been achieved. Little by little, Vito and his crew of roughnecks instilled life back into this dying neighborhood. This life was now breathing and functioning with a throbbing heartbeat. These people of the community now had a soul that was built on this foundation. This strong foundation could never ever be shattered again, for it was built from the soul on up. These people would not let it be destroyed, for they now stood united like never before.

The crowd slowly followed Vito back to the table where Joey was seated. Instantly the crowd gathered around Joey and started to remove him from his seat. In triumph, they hoisted him above their shoulders while parading him through the merry streets. Each step along the way was another signal of the joy and jubilation that was acknowledged by the party-goers.

Joey absorbed it all in, it was then that he realized how many people of a different color really cared about him. Within a flash of the moment, Joey remembered yesterday and how much pain that everyone had suffered through. These painful thoughts would never disappear for him. They would linger on as the memory of the dead still breathed within him. Not only was the crowd carrying him, Marco and little Steven also came along for the ride. But now it was time to dwell on tomorrow and the uncertainties that it brings. Tomorrow would soon arrive, just an hour away.

It was now time to lock the pizzeria up for the last time. Joey made sure that he took all of his personal belongings with him. Inside the store he looked around one last time before it finally set in that it was over. In a way he felt very proud of himself that he never did give up. It was a continuous struggle as he defied the odds and survived.

Through all the mishaps, he did manage to find a love that would certainly last him a lifetime. Through this love there was a life that would soon come into this world. Along this very turbulent trip, he also made many friends in which he grew to love dearly, from residents on the block to his dedicated work crew. He would sorely miss Orlando, Manuel and Jorge. For those three had struggled every step of the way with Joey. Each one of them endured all the pain and made the ultimate sacrifices for him. Joey bowed his head for the last time and said a prayer for Marco and little Steven, because they were the ones who paid the ultimate price. Their untimely deaths made Joey realize that for anything good that has to happen, struggle and misery had to precede it.

Turning out the lights and putting the key into the door for the final time was rough. Vito and his crew, Gloria and all of the Mexicans were there to witness this sad event. While turning the round cylinder to lock up, Joey turned around and looked at everyone. The look on his face alone told the whole heartbreaking story.

"Well, this is it!" he said, with a hint of a teardrop falling from his bloodshot eyes. Bear then pulled down the rolling gates and locked them for the last time. Joey then flipped the keys to a waiting Vito who would hand them over to the new owner.

Walking with his head down, Joey reached out to hug and kiss his work crew. He said his goodbyes for what he thought would be the final time. The Mexicans seemed to take it well, although there surely was inner turmoil. Even they held some deep sentiments towards this place. After all, they flourished in this tiny pizzeria and they knew it. This hole in the wall eatery provided a better life for them and their families. They worked extremely hard and deserved everything that came to them. Joey always got his money's worth from this hard working bunch of illegal aliens. They were paid more than others, but they were worth every penny of it. Throughout all the good and bad times, they would never forget about "Joey's Place."

"Don't worry, guys," Joey said to them. "I will find work for all of you."

"Thanks, boss," they all said, one after the other.

"I will never ever forget about any one of you," he promised. "And you too, Marco!" Joey shouted as he looked into the sky above.

All of them noticed the dejected look on Joey's face, but no one said a word. This was just a very fragile moment, where nobody knew what to say anyway. But it was now time to move on; this chapter in everyone's life was over. It was time to turn the page and see what the unstable future brings.

Chapter 24

$\mathcal{V}$ITO AND DUTCH hopped into the front seats of the dark blue Lincoln. Joey and Gloria comfortably settled into the back. For some reason Dutch was driving very slowly back to Vito's house. These two guys had something else on their minds. They were acting very peculiar and Joey noticed it right away.

"Dutch," Joey said. "Why are you driving so slow?"

"Just relax, kid," he answered, "and enjoy the ride."

Joey didn't reply. He just put his head back and looked out the window. With one hand holding Gloria's, the other was gnawing away at whatever fingernails that he had left. Joey looked over at Gloria and noticed that her eyes were shut and she was off into a semi deep sleep. A few minutes later Joey put his head between the two gangsters again.

"This is not the way to your house, Vito," he said. "Where are we going?"

"Would you just relax," Vito said. "We're going to Staten Island."

"Vito, it's late, why the hell are we going out there?"

"You'll know why in a little while. Now sit back and get some rest," Vito insisted. "And stop asking so many fuckin' questions."

This time Joey did what he was told; besides he was too tired to do anything else. He just put his head back and tried to join Gloria in dreamland. But it was futile, there were too many things racing through his mind. For the next twenty minutes, Joey just stared up into the roof of the car and listened to Dean Martin singing on Vito's stereo cassette player.

"Make this light, it's a long one," Vito said to Dutch.

"This guy just spent 8 years in prison and he's worried about waiting a few minutes at a traffic light," Dutch answered back.

Dutch zipped through the yellow light and made a left hand turn. Suddenly the car slowed down and veered off to the right hand side of the road. Vito lowered the music and turned around to look at Joey and Gloria.

"We're here, Joey," Vito summoned. "Wake your girlfriend up."

"Where are we?" Joey asked, while gently trying to awaken Gloria.

"Gloria, honey," Vito said. "Are you awake yet?"

"Yes, Vito, I'm up."

"Good, because I want both of you to take a look across the street," Vito said, motioning his head.

Joey and Gloria then looked out of the left side window of the luxury sedan. What they saw left the both of them astonished while witnessing this unexpected surprise. Gloria was practically lying on top of her boyfriend, desperately trying to get a better view. Together they captured the moment of every man's dreams.

"Do you like it?" Vito asked, sporting a smile the length of the car.

"Like it," Joey responded. "I love it."

"Did you see the neon sign running across the top?"

Joey's eyes then scanned the top of the flat building. To his amazement, his signature was flowing thirty feet across the beautiful brick structure. The bright green neon sign had his penmanship down to perfection. It had looked like Joey had climbed a ladder and inscribed his name himself, it was that good. The name *"Joey DeFalco's"* was beaming across the skies for the entire world to see. Joey finally had gotten his name up in bright lights.

Underneath the sign was a long hunter green canopy that hugged the length of the stylish building. Below that, crystal clear windows took up most of the remaining space that was entrenched in a stucco finish. Each window exposed the beautiful décor and peaceful ambience of the fancy restaurant. The setting was perfect and the atmosphere could not be described with words alone.

"Joey, it's beautiful," Gloria said, throwing her arms around him.

Joey looked at Vito and just shook his head. He then looked over at Dutch who was smiling at him. Practically jumping out of his seat, he grabbed the two gangsters around the neck and drew them in closer to him. With all three heads almost touching each other, Joey squeezed on his grip harder and harder.

"Okay, okay," Vito said with a laugh. "You're choking us."

"Vito, I can't believe this!"

"Well, this you can believe," he promised. "Cause this is real. Come on, Dutch, let's go inside."

Dutch put the car in drive and slowly maneuvered it towards the large eatery. He drove into the huge parking lot on the right hand side of the brand new restaurant. The four of them scrambled out of the car. They stood in the parking lot as the soft breeze of the ocean's waters stroked their bodies. Crashing sounds could be heard from the rear, as the waves were striking the rocky shoreline. Each sound left the scent of nature as the under-toe pulled the frisky water back into the deep blue sea.

"I love that fresh ocean smell," Vito said, taking a deep breath.

Grabbing Gloria's hand, Joey took off towards the rear of the building. It was there that he saw a sight so breathtaking, that he had trouble breathing.

The backyard of the restaurant was overlooking a beautiful bay that fed into the Atlantic Ocean. A large cedar deck was wrapped around the whole back of the contemporary building with style. Tables and chairs adorned the deck; each patron would have a view that was alone worth the price of admission. Enormous French doors opened up from the dining room and out onto the wooden deck. There was even an outdoor bar that strictly catered to the romance that this spectacular view provided.

"Come on," Vito shouted. "Let's go inside."

Joey and Gloria rapidly walked towards Vito and Dutch. Joey's body was pumping with adrenaline, and his thumping heart was racing at an uncontrollable tempo. All of this excitement was just too overwhelming for him; you could just see it in his eyes.

"Here," Vito said, flipping Joey the keys. "It's all yours kid."

"Vito, why did you do this?" Joey asked, never once did it cross his mind that this was the surprise that Vito was talking about.

"When I give something, I never ask for or tell the reasons why I did it."

"But this is just not something, this is unbelievable! I can't accept this."

"It is unbelievable and you will accept it," he said. "It's a gift from me to you."

"Vito, nobody gives out gifts like this," Joey said. "I could never repay you."

"The whole damn place, lock, stock and barrel is yours," he explained. "There is nothing to ever repay me for. Just make sure that I get the first dinner that comes out of that kitchen."

"No problem," Joey said. He then wrapped his strong arms around Vito, practically squeezing the life out of him. "You're one of a kind."

"Now get out of here and open the front door."

Joey raced to the front of the building with enthusiasm. He could not wait to get inside to see what the rest of the place looked like. Trying to peek through the wooden and glass doors got him nowhere. The only light coming from the inside was from a pastry display and a few other dimly lit apparatuses. There was only one way to satisfy his curiosity, and that was to enter the building. He started to desperately search for the right key to open the door. Each one that he tried turned out to be the wrong one. Fumbling so much with the keys, the rest of the gang had caught up with him.

"Calm down," Vito warned. "You're going to give yourself a heart attack."

"Vito, which key is it?" he asked, growing impatient by the second.

"This one," he said.

Joey quickly inserted the right key into the round cylinder and turned. Everyone standing behind him waited quietly for him to gain access to the place. The transition went smoothly as the cylinder turned with ease. He then pulled on the brass doorknob of the large wooden door and held it open. Dutch grabbed the door and pulled it all the way back as everyone followed Joey into the restaurant.

"Surprise!" everyone screamed as the lights were suddenly turned on. People were crowding around Joey from everywhere. The happy mob swarmed all over him with a show of delight. At first, Joey did not know what hit him, this event took him totally by surprise. When he finally came to his senses, he saw a lot of familiar faces in the buzzing crowd of people. The guests all did a miraculous job of hiding their identities. Their cars were nowhere in sight, they must have parked a mile away from the place. The restaurant's parking lot was empty and there was not a scent of any visitors to be had.

From his Mexican crew to some residents of St. Ann's Place, they all wished him the best. Nothing, except for the arrival of his baby, could have made him any happier. One by one, Joey sifted through the friendly faces and thanked them for attending this moment of joy. Everyone was patting him on the back as the handshakes were plentiful. Now looking around the place, Joey saw some people sitting in the corner of the large dinning room. Seeing these people just brought more tears to his already drowning eyes.

"Ma," he called from across the large room. His mother had heard his call; she just sat there with a pleasant smile on her face. Seated next to her was his brother Louie with one of his many girlfriends. Across from them was the apple of Joey's eyes, his sister Michele. It had been a while since Joey had seen his all of his family together like this; he really enjoyed and relished the moment.

Joey went over to his mother who slowly rose to her feet. He grabbed her around her sunken shoulders and planted a big kiss right on her cheek. Then he turned to the rest of his family and exchanged hugs and kisses. Joey stood proud, for he had come a long way since he walked out of those prison gates over two years ago. His whole life had now changed in an extraordinary way.

"Joey," his sister Michele said. "This place is spectacular!"

"Is it?" he asked, not even having the time to look it over yet. "I haven't had time to go through the whole place yet."

"Good luck," she said. "We're all so proud of you."

"Thanks Michele, but none of this would have been possible if it were not for that man over there," Joey said to his sister, while looking in the direction of Vito.

"Who, Vito?" she asked.

"You know about him?"

"Mommy told me a little about him."

"Well whatever she told you, it's all true."

"Joey, everybody knows about Vito Carlucci."

"That may be true," he said. "But everybody doesn't know him the way that I do."

"Just be careful."

"Michele, if it was not for that man, I would be dead right now. So there is nothing for me to be careful about."

"I know Joey, I know," she said. "But Mommy is worried about you, that's all."

"I couldn't be in better hands than I am right now," he reassured her. "I'm not a part of any of his other shit. Once this place takes off, I am on my own."

"I know you are going to make it," she said crying. "We all love you so much."

"How did you guys find out about me being here?"

"Vito went to see Mommy the other day."

"And?"

"He promised that once you get started in this restaurant, he will have nothing to do with it. But he also said that he will always be a part of your life," Michele explained. "He loves you very much, Joey."

"How does Mommy feel about all of this?"

"I guess she's alright with it. She's here isn't she?" Michele said, taking a quick peek at her mother to make sure that she was not overhearing the conversation. "Vito gave her his word that you will not become a part of his business, and she believes him."

"I won't, Michele, you can trust me on this one."

"I know I can, Joey," she said. "There is one other thing."

"What?"

"Don't say anything about this to Vito."

"Why?"

"Because he wants us to trust him. I think he wants us to be the family that he never had. He told Mommy that he loved you like a son!"

"I won't say a word to him." Joey said. "He's a good man, Michele."

"Only time will tell," she worriedly said. "Only time will tell."

"Trust me on this one," he said. "Hey, did Vito mention anything to Mommy about prison?"

"No, she never said a word about any of that. As far as I know she acts like she has no idea that you ever went away."

"That's because I disgraced the whole family and she's embarrassed by my actions. I think it's best that everyone put it behind them."

"Don't worry, it's forgotten as far as I'm concerned."

"Thanks, Michele."

"Joey, later I want to get a few pictures of everybody."

"That's a good idea," he said. "I have an office in the back room that I haven't even seen yet," Joey cracked. "I'm sure I can find some room on the desk to put some pictures. Later I want you to take a picture of me and Vito."

"I already took a couple when you first came in."

"Good, I will put one of them on the desk."

"Maybe we should go and take a look at that office of yours?"

"That's a good idea," agreed Joey. "Let's go!"

Gloria arrived at the large round table and conversation between Joey and Michele was suddenly cut short. Gloria had met all of Joey's family a few other times, but never all at once. The pregnant mother to be gracefully took a seat at the table and started to mingle with her future mother in-law. She fit in perfectly with the Italian family that accepted her as one of their own.

"Gloria," Joey said. "Me and my sister are going to take a look at my office, we'll be right back." Gloria just shook her head in agreement, that's all that she could do. Joey's mother had a hold of her ear and was refusing to let go.

Minutes later, Joey and his sister sifted through the crowd and arrived at the untouched office. This place looked like it was suited for the Chairman of the Board at some fortune five hundred company. The desk looked like it had been buffed out with a whole case of furniture polish. It had everything from a personal computer to a gold plated pen and pencil set resting on top of it. This fancy office furnishing had an extending shelf off to the right that sported a fax machine and printer. On the left hand side, a telephone with a built in intercom took up the remaining space of this sprawling desktop.

Visitors would not encounter any problems finding a seat in this spacey office. Two fabric chairs sat right in front of the impressive desk. Off to the right side, a comfortable black leather sofa fit in nicely occupying most of the remaining footage.

From a television set to a stereo, this office had it all. Off to the far corner of the room was a wooden cabinet that must have had at least eight security monitors inside of it. Every part of the restaurant was visible and under surveillance at all times. To run his business, Joey did not even have to get up out of his chair. From where he was seated, he could see it all. But since he was a hand on owner, staying put in his office was just not his style.

The clock ticked past the 2A.M hour of the early morning, but that did not stop the festivities. Champagne bottles were popping like it was New Year's Eve. The lively crowd consumed bottle after bottle of the French sparkling wine. Everything was on the house, from liquor to appetizers. People were just standing around listening to some good music and enjoying all the amenities that this restaurant had to offer. This party was not open to the public; you had to have a very familiar face to get in. If someone even looked suspicious, the ocean's dangerous waters were only about a hundred feet away.

Tropical plants and flowers lined up the front wall of the place with congratulations and good luck signs wrapped all around them. The restaurant smelled like a florist, there was greenery everywhere. But it was the thought that counted; each plant had a special card inside a small envelope. Most of the gifts were coming from people that Joey did not even know. The anonymous donors just happen to be mob associates of Vito Carlucci.

The restaurant finally emptied out a few minutes before 4 o'clock in the morning. Now it was time for Joey to look over his new establishment with a fine-tooth-comb. His excited journey took him into a room situated on the left side of the building. Inside the room, Joey examined the dark mahogany bar with its entire luster. The wood had such a deep shine to it that you could practically see your face in it. The top and bottom of this gorgeous bar were decorated and lined with brass. From the trim along the top to the footrest at the bottom, it glistened with the shiny yellowish metal. The liquor shelves in back of the bar were empty, but that did not take away from the beauty of this masterpiece.

A couple of dozen black leather stools were neatly placed all along the bar and around the small curve at the other end. In the back of the quaint bar area was another set of those beautiful French doors. They also swung open to take in the fresh air and the panoramic vista of the Atlantic. To the right of the bar were a few tables set up for the unsociable. Patrons who wished to drink in peace or in the private company of a loved one, this was the place.

Joey walked out of the bar area and headed for the dining room on the other side of the restaurant. Once there, he carefully examined the setup. There must have been over 40 tables, seating anywhere from two to eight people. This was a topnotch operation at its finest, only a five star rating would give this place its due. Anything less would be a disgrace to its décor.

Every wall in the place was brick; from top to bottom the colorful rectangular block of clay lined the walls. Even the fireplace in the middle of the dining room adorned the classy looking baked material. The gas-burning fireplace recessed from four sides, never cheating any patron from the sight of its burning embers. The restaurant had a very cozy look to it for such a big place. The soft ambience would make all customers feel right at home.

Joey slowly walked through the set of French doors and onto the veranda for a breath of fresh air. He stared out into the dark brackish ocean with a mind filled with wonderment. His eyes focused on the sunlight that was slowly rising above the horizon. The line where the sky and earth meet seemed never-ending to him. It brought out the mysteries of the unexplained and the unknown. He was mesmerized as the sun started to reflect off of the choppy water. The stimulated sea-foam was effervescent, dancing on top of the ocean's crest. The morning's hush came quietly as the tiny bubbles faded away. There was not a cloud in the sky and everything looked tranquil and serene. The crystallized stars were slowly evaporating with the outbreak of daylight. They sluggishly faded into the open sky. Each God-given mystery told Joey of another story in time. People that he once knew seemed to disappear in the same manner. These continuous motions of the sea and sky seemed to drift him into yesterday, and tug him back into the world of tomorrow.

Suddenly, no more than 50 yards away, the ocean began to tremor with a mighty fury. A vapor like steam emitted and hovered above the percolating blue water. The sea virtually looked as if it was on fire. There was eerie fog and blinding haze everywhere.

Joey stood stagnant. His body would not let him move as he looked on in awe.

From the oceans depths, something unfathomable was ascending from the quaking waters. It kept rising and growing in size as it violently pulled the now restless sea with it. This spherical and eruptive force was fighting to free itself from the rising flume of water in which it was trapped inside of. With one powerful surge the breathing and porous globule exploded ejecting large cascading raindrops back into the turbulent sea. The glowing phantasm, now free of the reins that surrounded it, expanded in size as its mighty presence started to rise towards the heavens. The gray image was intimidating and powerful as it floated effortlessly towards its destination. It looked down on Joey, never wavering its purpose or true identity. The image looked very familiar to Joey. It was the same spirit that he had seen before. It was the spirit of Jeremiah.

"It's Jeremiah," Joey whispered to himself. "He's going home."

Twenty minutes later, Vito walked out onto the back patio. "What are you doing?" Vito asked while sitting down at one of the outdoor tables.

"I'm just thinking, that's all," Joey said, still slightly dazed. "I'm thinking about all the shit that's happened to me."

"Well, stop thinking. This week we have a lot of work to do here, are you ready?" Vito asked while Joey just kept staring out into the crisp ocean water. He had both arms leaning up against the wooden railing of the cedar deck. "Would you get your head out of the clouds and wake up."

"I heard every word that you said, I'm ready," Joey said, still looking out into the open waters. Everything on his body stood motionless as his eyes stared in one direction.

"You're acting like you're fuckin' hypnotized again. Will you turn around and look at me," he ordered. Joey then quickly did an about face and looked at his Godfather. "We will shoot for next Saturday night as the grand opening."

"We can't do it sooner?"

"No, there is too much to do," he said. "We're gonna invite all the people we know," Vito said. "But things are going to be different now."

"Why's that?" Joey asked, fighting weariness, his eyes half shut.

"Everybody pays, that's why. Last night at the party, everything was on the house. But the free rides are over. Now, my son, you will see more money than you ever dreamed was possible."

"I know, business is business."

"Exactly, we will pack this place with customers," he boasted. "And we'll have live entertainment."

"Jimmy?"

"Yea, he did a great job last night. This is going to be the hottest spot on this whole island. Before you know it, you will own half of it."

"Vito, I'm just happy with what I have."

"I know you are, kid, but there is nothing wrong with trying to be the best, is there?"

"No, but I don't know if my guys could handle this," Joey nervously said. The atmosphere and the awesome surroundings seemed to intimidate him a bit. "This is fine dining!"

"Do you think for one minute that I would let a bunch of Mexicans run this kitchen?" Vito asked, while slowly starting to break out into laughter. "Listen, I like your guys, but they are in way over their heads here. I have a whole new crew and concept coming in here."

"I'm not getting rid of those guys."

"I never said you had to. They will just do odd jobs around the place until they pick up what's going on. In a matter of time, we will make first class chefs out of Orlando and Manuel. Jorge can be their understudy. The bottom line is that those guys are not going anywhere," Vito said. "They will all be here with you."

"Thanks, Vito," said Joey. "They mean a lot to me."

"I know they do, but shit, this is your place. I'm just trying to get you off on the right foot, that's all."

"I'll follow your lead."

"And don't worry, you will be safe here," he promised. "Nobody knows you're here and I have men all over the Island."

"I know, I am starting to feel better already. Maybe this place will be a new beginning for me. Maybe all that other shit will all be left behind me."

"It is," Vito promised. "Besides, my club is only five minutes away. Nobody is going to fuck with you here. We're too powerful! And another thing, since the business is here, I suggest that you get your girlfriend and move out here."

"That's a good idea."

"Good, I'm glad you agree with me. Once the restaurant gets rolling, we'll start to look for a house for the three of you."

"The three of us?"

"You're having a baby, aren't you?"

"Oh shit, I forgot," he said with a slight grin. "Vito," Joey said. "Speaking of Gloria, next Saturday night I want to get engaged to her. I want her to be my wife!"

"That's great, it's about fuckin' time," Vito said, while nursing on a cup of coffee in a white mug. "I will send one of my guys over to see you and you could pick a ring out. Now get over here and give me a hug!"

Joey walked over to Vito and accepted his sincere congratulations. The embrace lasted for about a minute before the sound of sea gulls awakened the two from their merry bliss.

"What is this guy gonna come here with a suitcase full of diamonds?"

"Yea," a smiling Vito said. "Something like that." Vito then took another swig out of his coffee cup and asked. "Is this supposed to be a surprise?"

"Without a doubt, she has no clue."

"That's good, we'll find something real nice for her."

Real nice was an understatement.

A couple of days later this guy walked in with a valise full of diamonds. The Jewish looking character walked right into Joey's office and laid the piece of hand luggage right on top of Joey's desk. Joey just sat back on his leather recliner and watched this guy spill the small hard rocks all over his desk. From small to large, from white to blue, in every shape and size, it was there. Whatever Joey wanted for his bride to be, it was just a matter of picking it out. He studied the jewels real hard and wanted something suited for Gloria's personality. The decision was not too tough at all. Joey opted for a 1.50 karat, round white diamond stone. This gorgeous stone was practically flawless. The white crystalline form of carbon was a gem that any woman would be proud to wear. If you talked about cutting glass, this beauty put a laceration in you just by looking at it. It sparkled from a thousand different angles, with each angle looking more magnificent than the other.

This salesman even came fully equipped with a bunch of gold and silver settings. The only thing that was not available was the finger that the ring would be placed on. To Joey, this was shopping the way it ought to be. He never had to leave the comfort of his office chair. This whole transaction took no more than twenty minutes. He knew that if he were to do this with Gloria, it would have probably have taken up to three days. But the element of surprise was much better. Not only did it take out the window shopping it also saved a few days of driving him absolutely nuts.

Carpenters were banging away, trying to meet the deadline. Saturday night was just a couple of days away from the grand opening. Everybody from the gas company to the Maytag man was at the restaurant. Slowly but surely, things were starting to shape up. Things had to shape up; Vito was watching every hammer and nail that was being applied. After all, he practically had every union in the city in his back pocket. If these guys had to break union rules and work around the clock, they would. To put it bluntly, they really had no choice.

Once the mechanics of the restaurant were up and running, it was time for all the stock to be delivered. Choice liquor and beer boxes were stacked from the ceiling to the floor. Each box waiting to be emptied out and either placed on top of the shelves of the fancy bar or cooled off in the refrigeration unit. Kegs of all different brands of beer were rolled in and ready to be tapped into. The plentiful bar had 10 different types of draft beer on tap. For the stressed out or thirsty consumer, this was the place to be. There was some sort of alcohol or beverage for all patrons, even the ones on the wagon.

From lobster to porterhouse steaks, this first class establishment skimped on nothing. The provisions kept coming and coming through the front door, each delivered by a different vendor. The amazing thing about it was that they all knew Vito. From fish to meat, from fruits to vegetables, from plastics to paper products, he knew them all. He claimed that he was never in the restaurant business before, but he could have fooled anyone. The Under-boss appeared like he owned a chain of fancy restaurants all over the country.

Chapter 25

$\mathfrak{I}$T WAS 5 o'clock early Saturday evening. Cars were pulling up to the restaurant one after the other. The valets were keeping themselves very busy. Everything from a Mercedes Benz to a Cadillac filled the busy parking lot. The oversized lot looked like a showroom at some expensive new car dealership.

They came from all over; someone of importance represented each borough. From Connecticut to New Jersey all the way down the turnpike to Pennsylvania, they were all there. The license plates bearing their state names were the only things that exposed their identities. Three quarters of the people in attendance Joey did not even know. All he knew was that they were friends or business associates of Vito, that plus the fact that they had mountains of cash lining their pockets.

The restaurant reeked of money, and everyone had a different way of showing it. Everything from their attire to their personal vices looked very lavish. Some of the cigars that these pretentious men were smoking even looked expensive.

Everyone was beautifully dressed, it was when they opened their mouths that you could tell where they came from. It was the underworld that had gotten these socialites of organized crime all of their prized possessions, not Harvard Law School. But this was now Vito's world, even if it was for just one night. These were his friends and they had to be respected, not for whom they were, but for whom they knew.

The cream of the crop and anybody who was somebody huddled around their associates and talked business. In every corner of the restaurant, three or four gangsters hunkered around each other discussing their secret playbooks. Once in a while, but not often, you would see some clowning around. If the Feds ever wired this place, there would be enough information on those tapes to put most of these characters away for a very long time.

Some of these mobsters were so old, that if the restaurant was not handicapped friendly they could not even get a foot through the front door. Most of them seemed to be suffering from one type of ailment or another. From wheelchairs to hearing aids, from emphysema to Alzheimer's, you name the sickness it was there. The place looked like the emergency room at King's County Hospital. Most of these elderly Capos looked like they were just a short trip away from their family mausoleums. But with all the illnesses that these old men had, or said they had, they were still dangerous men. Some of them even faked sickness to avoid court hearings or prison time. But when you put them with one of their own, they were as sharp as a tack. In front of the Feds though, you could get more out of a hospital patient in a coma. Most of these proud old-timers always suffered this prolonged "unconsciousness disease" when it came to telling the government anything. But whatever ages these guys were, you could not take the gangster out of them. Most of them start out young, and then age slows down their physical prowess. Throughout the years, though, their mentality seemed to never change. Don't ever let their ages or illnesses fool you. These men would kill you for just looking at them the wrong way.

If you scanned around the room, then you would come across the young stallions. These born without conscience men would kill you just to cover up their own loose lips. There was a world of difference between this new breed of gangsters and the old-timers across the room. They lacked the pride and business skills of their counterparts. Quick thinking and the quick buck was their way of running the show. The modern day gangster was ruthless but most off all vain. He could be digging a ditch while he was burying a murdered body, but he would have his Rolex on while he was digging it.

After busting his tail for over six hours, Joey had noticed that the crowd was starting to slowly thin out. He impeccably ran the restaurant like he was doing it his whole life. Everything from the kitchen to the service was run in a flawless manner. There were no broken dishes or glasses, no complaints and everything was cooked to perfection.

Opening night was a major success; the people kept coming and going all night long each leaving an expensive tab upon their departure. Most of it was cash; whoever knew a gangster who whipped out his American Express card to pay a bill? The only thing they never leave home without are their guns and the attitude that goes along with it.

"How did we do?" Vito asked, after walking into the kitchen. He already knew that the night was a huge success. "I think maybe I should get a job here."

"I know, the waiters did great," Joey said. "If I had to give you an educated guess, I'd say about 17 to 20 grand."

"That's a good way to start for only one night's work. It's only going to get better."

"Damn, I can't imagine it getting any better than this," Joey answered, trying to get some tomato sauce off of his white dress shirt.

"Oh it will," Vito vowed. "It will." Vito was looking all over the place, but couldn't spot who he was looking for. "Where's Dutch?"

"He's out on the deck in the back!"

"By the way, did you give her the ring yet?"

"No, I'm going to give it to her after everybody leaves. I'm going to need about twenty minutes alone with her."

"When I leave, I will send someone back here to pick you up."

"Okay, we should be out of here in about a half an hour."

"Good."

Vito walked out of the kitchen and towards the back doors that led out onto the cedar deck. Dutch was sitting down by himself enjoying a cup of Irish coffee.

"You know it's really beautiful out here," Dutch told Vito." I could sit out here for hours."

"Yea, it is pretty."

"I don't know," he said holding the cup in his right hand. "It just makes you think and rehash the past. It kind of separates you from everything else that's going on in this fucked up world out there."

"It does put everything into perspective."

"Are you gonna sit down or what?"

"Nah, I gotta get over to the club."

"You got everything arranged?"

"Yea, the people are starting to pile into the club now. Make sure you get him in there before midnight if you can, twelve thirty the latest."

"Did Joey give her the ring yet?"

"He's gonna do that when everybody gets out of here," said Vito. "So disappear for about fifteen to twenty minutes. He wants to be alone when he gives her the ring."

"No problem," Dutch said. "How many friends of his are coming?"

"I got a hold of everybody that he used to hang out with. Counting their wives, and some of Gloria's people, I'd say close to a hundred and fifty."

"Man, is he gonna be surprised."

"Joey doesn't have a clue about what's going on."

"Hey Vito, how come nobody ever did these things for us."

"Because we got no fuckin' friends, that's why. Who the fuck would ever throw a surprise engagement party for us?" Vito asked, smiling down at Dutch. "Better yet, who the fuck would ever want to be engaged to me and you?"

"She'd have to be one sick twisted bitch, I'll tell you that."

"You're right," he conveyed. "Anyone who would marry us you know is in it for the money."

"You got that right," Dutch laughed. "Vito, you know, I have been walking in and out of the restaurant all day long. Something is just not right. There's something strange going on here."

"What do you mean something strange?"

"I can't put my finger on it, but things don't seem right to me."

"Why, what's wrong?"

"It's coming from out there," Dutch said, pointing to the briny body of water. "Before when it was light out, I looked over the railing and saw about a couple of hundred dead fish laying by the rocks down there. They were floating lifeless as the waves were kickin' them around. A little while later I saw a flock of seagulls flying out of control like they were running from something. Vito, something is gonna happen and they know it."

"What are you trying to tell me?"

"I don't know what I'm trying to tell you. But the waters have been very choppy and turbulent all day. Look at the waves, they are four feet high. This is a bay, Vito; the waters here never get this rough. Even the clouds have been acting strangely. All day long they have been moving in a circular motion, banging violently against each other," he quietly and eerily continued. "I never saw anything like it in my life. The winds have been picking up steam with each passing second. All of this just gives me the creeps. I tell you, something is about to happen and the creatures of nature are reacting to it. They can sense it and maybe they are running from whatever it is that they are afraid of."

"Are you starting to get like Joey on me?"

"No, Vito, but maybe the kid is right. There is something going on here and I wish I knew what it was. Last week I saw some smoke or steam rising out of the water. The water looked like it was on fire, steam was everywhere. Something came out of the water, like a big bubble. A few seconds later it blew up. Then it formed into a giant image of what looked like an ancient old man." Dutch looked at Vito in disbelief. "It just floated into the sky until it disappeared. The kid saw it also, he didn't see me cause I was inside the restaurant."

"Joey never said anything to me. It probably was some mist or something," Vito explained, he always had an answer for everything. "Dutch, will you cut the shit out!" Vito then looked up into the night and saw nothing but an overcast sky. Dutch was right, the weather had taken a drastic turn for the worse, but that was all. Other than that Vito saw nothing so unusual about anything else.

"I don't know, Vito, it wasn't mist. The fuckin water was on fire and I saw what I saw."

"That's crazy!"

"I know it sounds nuts but I figured I needed to tell you this."

"The only fuckin thing that you might need if you hang out here too long is an umbrella."

"What about the fish down there?"

"As far as the fish go, maybe a fishing boat lost its net or decided to dump the catch. Who knows," he reasoned. "Besides, I wouldn't eat anything coming out of this water, would you?"

"Not really," Dutch said with a smile.

"So come on, let's forget about all of this supernatural shit. And for God's sake, Dutch, do not mention a word of this to Joey. He seems to be forgetting about whatever he thought was happening in the past. That's all I need now is to send you and him to some fuckin mental hospital for evaluation."

Both men shared a final laugh before Vito walked back into the restaurant and out the front door. Dutch hung around, still staring out into the open sea until he finished his coffee. It was then that one of the strangest things that ever happened to Dutch took place.

A beautiful white seagull flew up the coastline and perched himself precisely on the wooden railing of the restaurant deck. With full plumage and pure white feathers, the bird expanded its wings and looked into the eyes of Dutch. The wingspan of this graceful bird was enormous, at least four feet long. The two just looked at each other. It was like this bird was a friend and he was trying to tell Dutch something. Dutch just sat patiently waiting for the warm-blooded visitor to just fly off into the night. But what he then saw was something quite the contrary. The pretty bird with the long beak just roosted, as it kept opening his eyes wider and wider. It was then that the gull's dark black eyes started to make a drastic transformation. Slowly they started to revert to another color that was glowing in the darkness. Dutch was gripped as pure drama unfolded before him. The bird's eyes evolved into a garnet red color. It was the same color as human blood.

The gull squealed at Dutch. Within another second or two, the seagull started to wildly flap its wings while still staying defiantly perched. The white creature looked at Dutch for a final time and flew off over the rocky seas. Within seconds it disappeared into the night.

Dutch just sat there stunned, for all his premonitions that he told Vito now seemed believable. This brief visitor had just confirmed it. These feelings that he was receiving, were no aberration. There was a message coming from somewhere, somewhere very powerful and very, very far away.

Never one to forget about the business at hand, Dutch just took this all in stride. About five minutes later, he removed himself from the chair and all of his eerie feelings. Now walking back into the dining room, Dutch turned around and looked into the choppy body of water. He shook his head in a negative direction as he closed the French doors behind him. Looking like nothing ever happened, he proceeded into the kitchen to find Joey.

"I'll be back in a half an hour to pick you up," Dutch said.

"Why does he want me at the club anyway?" Joey said, acting a bit suspicious. "I'm tired, I just wanted to go home."

"He just wants to hang out a bit and discuss some business. I don't think it will take long."

"Oh, alright, I'll be ready," Joey said. "Where's Gloria?"

"She's out in the dining room."

"Before you go, Dutch, tell her that I'll be right out."

"Alright," Dutch said. "Joey, how do you feel?"

"I feel great! I'm just a little tired, why?"

"Nothing," Dutch strangely replied. He then drew Joey close to him and gave him a hug before he walked through the kitchen door. Joey looked at him and just shook his head wondering what the hell that was all about.

A few minutes later, the work crew had just about finished up their cleaning chores. One by one Joey said goodnight to all of them and congratulated them for a job well done. Just his Mexican crew remained; they were responsible for the major cleanup. They would not leave the restaurant until every crumb and drop of food was cleaned up. These guys knew that, and were super-conscientious about Joey's interests.

"Goodnight Boss," Orlando said. "All finish, we go home now."

"You cleaned everything?"

"Yes, place clean."

"Good, I will see you guys tomorrow."

"Goodbye," Manuel said.

"Goodnight, guys, thanks."

After washing his hands Joey looked around the kitchen for a clean white rag. He picked up the linen off of a counter top and proceeded to dry his hands. Never stopping his motion, he then went directly into his office to put on his suit jacket. Checking the left side pocket, he found what he was looking for before he slipped the dark blue jacket on. Hastily, he turned to look into a small mirror and ran his fingers through his thick black hair. After coming to an agreement with his appearance, he finally exited. Realizing that he had forgotten one last thing, Joey turned around and went back inside the office to put the stereo on. This out of control man then ran out through the kitchen and poked his head out into the dining room.

"Gloria," he called. Joey walked over to Gloria and sat beside her. A candle was burning in the middle of the round table. The candlelight was flickering, throwing shadows off of the brick wall a few feet away. Gloria was sitting quietly staring at the flame. The light smoke from the candle was rising into the relaxed mood of the moment. "Are you okay?" he then asked her, before caressing her cheek.

"I couldn't be better," she said. "I feel much more comfortable here."

"You know something, so do I. It just feels like we left everything behind and started a new life."

"I know, I feel the same way," she confessed. "Everything just seems too good to be true."

"Sometimes a change of scenery can work wonders on a person's mind," Joey said, "I feel so at ease here. It's like I was meant to be here."

"I'm so happy for you, Joey"

Joey's timing could not have been any better than this. Right after she spoke those last few words he rolled into action. The song that he had purposely waited for was about to come out of the stereo's speakers. The king of rock and roll, Elvis Presley was about to play a major part in both of their young lives.

"Come on honey, let's dance," Joey asked, taking her by the hand and in between the row of tables.

Gloria, wearing her colorful sundress, quickly obliged. She moved towards Joey as he was lightly tugging her into his clutches. Joey nestled her tightly, with both arms settling around the bottom of her tiny waist. He rested his yearning lips right at the top of her eager ear. She reciprocated likewise, holding him tightly. Her head was snuggled comfortably up against his powerful chest. The slow-footed duo was drowning in each other's love on the makeshift dance floor.

"But I can't help falling in love with you," he sang in her ear.

Each word out of his mouth forced her to squeeze tighter and tighter around his muscular back. She said nothing, but her tight grip told him a story of epic proportions. Joey then reached into the left side pocket of his suit jacket and pulled out the ring. Nonchalantly, he took a step back and pressed a soft kiss on her lips. Gloria held her head up as her left hand slowly relocated to the top of his chest. Joey then spotted her bare ring finger and gently slid the gorgeous gem around it. The ring slid over her thin long finger like it was tailor made for it.

In total bewilderment, Gloria withdrew her hand from off of his chest. With a numb gaze, she looked at her finger and then looked up at him. She then retreated a bit, putting about 12 inches between the two. Joey just lovingly gazed into her inviting eyes knowing that now was the time to propose.

"Will you marry me?" he asked.

With tears starting to cascade down from both sides of her face, Gloria stood there paralyzed. She lovingly gazed at him as the tears continued. Her accelerated heartbeat was now working overtime as she vehemently tried to compose herself. "Yes, yes, yes," she cried, her voice husky as she threw her arms around him again. "A thousand yeses!"

They shuffled about, melded together, moving mindlessly to the soft music. They were no longer of this world.

"Joey, the ring is beautiful."

"That it is, I knew you would like it."

"I love it."

"Honey, I hate to break this up," he said. "But Dutch will be here in about twenty minutes and I still have to count the cash drawer."

"Can't you do that in the morning."

"Yea, I guess I can. But let me double check everything and I'll put the money in the vault."

"Okay, I'm going into the ladies room. My face must be a mess."

"Gloria, I love you, honey," Joey sincerely said. "But do me a favor, don't take an hour in there."

"Will you stop it, I never take that long to get ready."

"That's because you're not the one waiting, sometimes it feels like two hours."

"Oh stop it," she said as she started for the ladies room. Gloria stopped all at once and quickly turned around. " Joey!" she called one last time.

"Yea?"

"I love you!"

"I love you too. This is only the beginning, honey. Me, you and the baby have the rest of our lives together."

"I know we do, I can't wait." she said as she looked at Joey one last time.

Walking towards the front door, Joey reached into his pants pocket and pulled out the keys to the front door. Getting ready to lockup, he was interrupted by a ringing telephone. Quickly he reversed his direction and raced to the nearest phone.

"Hello," he said.

"It's me, Vito."

"What's up?"

"Are you ready to go?"

"I just have to put the money in the vault and lockup. I'll balance the drawer in the morning."

"Alright hurry up, Dutch will pick you up in fifteen minutes."

"Vito, what the hell is the rush?"

"There's no rush, I just want to talk with you a little about the business."

"You're at the club?"

"Yea, come on, get going."

"Alright, I'll see you in a little while."

"Bye."

"Vito...," Joey said. But it was too late. Vito had already hung up. *I just wanted to say thanks for everything and, and that I love you*, Joey said to himself and the dial tone of the telephone.

Joey walked over to both registers and unlocked the cash drawers. One by one, he emptied both of them out. There was not that much cash left in the register. During the course of the evening the drawers had been emptied at least a couple of times before. With a wad of money in his right hand and a stack of receipts in his left, Joey walked towards his empty office. Inside the office he placed everything on top of his desk and took a seat behind it. He then heard some very indistinct movement coming from outside the door of the office.

"Gloria, is that you, honey?"

He was met by a chilling silence. Joey then looked up and saw a shadow lurking outside of the opened door to his office. Looking at the floor, Joey knew that it was a man. The outline of the body was partially blocking the light behind it, causing its fuzzy image to run across the floor in front of his desk.

"Orlando," Joey called. "Are you there?"

Still there was no answer. Joey's neck muscles tensed up. There were now no moving sounds coming from behind the partially opened door, just heavy breathing. He then looked into the security monitors and saw nothing, each monitor came up empty. The shadow started to move very slowly. *Was he going to make a move?* It was then that Joey decided to jump out of his seat to confront the intruder.

"Fuck," Joey said, loud enough for his visitor to hear. "I forgot to lock the front door. Damn it, how could I be so fuckin stupid?"

"That's right," the sickly and gaunt looking visitor said while entering the room. He then pointed a 38 special at Joey's head. "You did forget to lock the front door. But I was already in the place watching your every move. That's one fine looking lady you got there."

"You touch her and you're gonna need more than that gun to stop me from killing you."

"Calm down, tough guy, you ain't killing nobody. Oh, by the way," the sarcastic intruder said. "Congratulations."

"Congratulations about what?"

"About your engagement, that was a very touching moment that I saw out there. How big is the ring?"

"None of your fuckin business."

"Alright, Cary Grant, sit the fuck down, you ain't going anywhere."

Joey then returned to his seat, but he never took his eyes off of this nervous looking young man. The guy was sweating profusely, perspiration was excreting from every open pore on his body. The moisture was exuding through his button down shirt at an uncontrollable rate. He was suffering from some sort of withdrawal. Judging by his vital signs, he was in dire need of another hit of whatever he was addicted to. The track marks running up and down his arms told Joey that it must have been heroin. This sight was so sad, that this addict had used up every possible vein on his upper body that he could have exposed a needle to. It was like his arms were full of tattoos.

"Who are you?" Joey said, struggling to identify his unexpected and unwanted guest. "And why the fuck have you been stalking me for the past month?"

"Never mind who I am," he shakily said, while walking around the desk. He now was in a position to see Joey's whole body. "Just keep your hands where I can see them."

Joey eyes were steadfast; his beady glare never wavered from this strange looking character. There was something about him that he recognized, but he couldn't put his finger on it. He knew that he had seen him on the streets, but he also knew that he had seen him someplace before that. He just couldn't figure out where or when. Now struggling with his memory, Joey's focus turned towards Gloria. That's all he needed was for her to walk through the office door and get caught in the middle of this. He silently prayed that this time she would take forever to refresh herself in the ladies room.

Whoever this guy was, he was a walking time bomb. The slightest of movements would cause his trigger finger to react. Joey knew this, so he proceeded with caution.

"What do you want?" Joey said, to the swaggering man. "Why don't you just take the money and get the hell out of here."

"Just shut the fuck up and slide the money down to this end of the desk."

Joey did as he was told. He carefully stockpiled the money and slid it down to the left hand side of the shiny desk. The hoodlum then picked up a picture frame that was standing on top of the desk. He carefully examined it, and then in a fit of rage he slammed the framed photograph against the wall. Joey just looked at him, wondering what significance the picture had. This out of control character looked like he was about to explode, his total being was intensified with anger. It now seemed that his anger and lack of drugs to feed his hunger, made him erratically unstable. Looking irresolute, the intruder wavered and was having trouble standing on his feet. The pitiful sight then put his left hand on top of the desk searching for balance and stability. After a second or two, he recouped and proceeded on.

Suddenly the robber was concentrating and focusing on the medallion around Joey's neck. He inched closer and closer. With taut eyes and a slacked jaw, he struggled to identify the object. With the gun still pointing at his head, Joey was rendered immobile.

To Joey, the weird thing about all of this was that the medallion was failing to react. It sat peacefully where it belonged, not having the usual effects when danger was present. There was no heat or any of the lively movements coming from the medal. This dumbfounded and scared him as he looked down with complete puzzlement all over his face. It was then that Joey knew that this time he was all on his own. For the first time he knew that something was different, the medallion was not protecting him any longer. Jeremiah had gone home.

"Where did you get that?" the thug said, pointing the gun in the direction of the medallion. Joey stayed seated, still trying to desperately remember where he knew this guy from. He now was sure that he had seen him somewhere in his past.

"Get what?"

"Don't play stupid with me," the intruder said. "That medal around your fuckin' neck!" he snarled, pointing this time with his left hand. "Where the fuck did you get that?"

Joey stared at the left hand pointing in his direction. There was something very familiar about it. "Shit," Joey shouted. "I know..."

At that moment the thief lunged at him reaching for the medallion. Joey at the same time reacted to protect himself. The two men struggled for the possession of the medallion. With the assailant now on top of a seated Joey, the tug of war continued. Each man was yanking on the chain from a different direction. The constant pulling of the chain ripped the medal from around his neck. Joey and the perpetrator were now in a mighty battle for the possession of the rare gold piece.

Joey then decided to use his free left hand as a weapon. He desperately was trying to connect with a couple of fierce punches that might end this violence. But from the seated position that he was in, his punches would lack the power that was needed. This drug-infested villain felt no pain as he relentlessly pursued his conquest. The two men violently struggled on. It was a life and death battle for the medallion. Then the inevitable happened, "pop, pop," like firecrackers the assailant's gun went off. The assailant jumped off of his prey.

"Oh my dear God," Joey cried.

Each pop dug another deep hole into Joey's stomach. Joey clutched desperately to his now bloody stomach. Stunned, Joey looked down at his bullet-ridden stomach in disbelief. With his left hand he put pressure on his wounds. But the pain never subsided and the blood never stopped flowing. It was now pooling around his feet.

The ruffian was now in full panic. Blindly he grabbed the money and then turned to look at Joey for the last time. Showing no remorse, he was about to fire one last bullet into the severely damaged body.

"Die, you piece of shit, die!" he muttered, before he fired another round. Joey's moans told him that he had made another direct hit. He then bolted for the front door, leaving his victim to die.

Joey's body lunged backwards as it absorbed another piece of lead. This third bullet was lodged in his chest. The final blow was so devastating that it rocked the black leather chair back and forth. Joey's body was now almost lifeless; he felt his young life slipping away. His whole life started to appear right before him, with every loved one flashing before his eyes. It was then that he saw the smile of his dead father coming to life. Inside this sighting, Joey saw the spitting image of himself. There was no fear in his eyes or body. These pretentious feelings had been lifted from him not to long ago.

The tremendous loss of blood was starting to hit Joey's vital signs with great impact. Struggling and trying to get to his feet, he started to grab onto anything around him. With each faltered step, he managed to stay on his feet. Leaving a trail of blood in his wake, he headed for the front door in pursuit of his attacker. Knocking over chairs and falling on top of tables and whatever else got in his way, he proceeded on. Finally reaching his destination, Joey stumbled forward crashing through the front door and falling to the pavement below. The blood would not cease from pouring out of his weakening body. For Joey, it was only a matter of time before it was all over. His maker awaited him.

Back inside the restaurant, Gloria had just existed from the ladies room. She immediately sensed that something was wrong. The music was still playing and she noticed some of the chairs that were in disarray all over the floor. It was then that Gloria saw the blood splattered tablecloth spread out right before her.

"Oh my God," she screamed. "Joey, Joey!"

With her heart thumping in her chest, she rushed into the office looking for her fiancée. With every step, she came across more blood. There was blood everywhere, on the floor the walls and all over the office door. Afraid of what she might see and intensely shaking, she peeked into the empty office, but nobody was there. She walked around the desk and saw that her worst fears had come true. Joey's black leather chair was covered in blood. It was then that she knew that it was Joey's blood all over the restaurant. Now panicking, Gloria picked her head up and looked into the security monitors and saw something that she would remember for the rest of her life. Right there, in one of the monitors marked number six, she saw Joey sprawled out in front of the restaurant in a semi unconscious state. The black and white image was very vivid to her; she did not need to know the color of the liquid that was surrounding his body.

"No," she screamed again. "Somebody help him!"

Gloria raced out of the office and into the dining room. Now hysterical, she searched everywhere looking for someone to help her. Every corner that she peered into turned up empty; everyone had gone home for the night. With nowhere or no one to turn to, she ran out the front door. It was then that her life almost came to an end. It was there that she saw the same man who was plastered all over the monitor. This was not an illusion; Gloria's eyesight was not failing her. The dreaded image lying helplessly below her was that of Joey. She sunk to both knees and frantically cried over him.

"Noooo," she wailed, her voice pitched with grief. "Joey, please, please don't die!"

The blue Lincoln came to a screeching halt right in front of the restaurant. Dutch and Jimmy jumped out of the car and ran over to the sprawled out body. Gloria was now in an uncontrollable state of mind. She kept tugging at the lifeless body for some kind of response, but there was nothing. The only response was a slight hint of breathing, as the body was gasping for air.

"Don't leave me, Joey," she cried. "I love you, you can't leave me this way. Dutch, please help him, he's dying! Oh my God, he's dying, Dutch!"

"Jimmy, go inside and get Vito on the phone," Dutch ordered. "Tell him to get over here now. Gloria," he said grabbing a hold of her. "Try to calm down and go call an ambulance, honey."

Jimmy and Gloria quickly ran to opposite ends of the restaurant. Both in a desperate race against time to try and save the life of a wonderful man, a man who was on the verge of finally enjoying his life. It was certainly not his time to go; his calling arrived way too soon. But this is life, not some fairy tale. Sometimes others determine one's fate, either in a positive or negative way.

"Hello," the voice on the other end of the line said.

"Who's this, Nicky?" Jimmy asked.

"Yea," the bartender at the crowded club said.

"Nicky, get Vito quick. Joey's been shot."

"What?"

"Get Vito, God damn it, now!"

With the loud music blaring in the background, Jimmy waited impatiently. A few seconds later, Vito was on the other end of the phone. "This better not be a joke."

"Vito, get over here fast, the kid don't look like he's gonna make it."

"Son of a bitches!" Vito screamed. "Keep him alive, Jimmy, please keep him alive."

"It don't look too good."

That's all Jimmy had to say and the phone conversation was over. Jimmy ran back outside and tried to assist Dutch. He looked down at Joey who was still clinging to whatever life that he had left. Joey managed to open his eyes to only shadows, his vision along with everything else was failing him.

"Jimmy," Dutch said. "Stay here by Joey, I'm going inside to look things over."

"Whoever did this is long gone."

"Just stay here," Dutch ordered.

With his gun drawn, Dutch followed the trail of blood that was still moist on the floor. The gory path led him into the office. Like a detective, Dutch started to look for some clues. He bent down to pick up the picture with Vito and Joey in it. Looking intensely at the bent frame, he placed it back on the desk. While standing the picture upright, he noticed something very unusual. He saw some fingerprints that were embedded into the wax of the shiny mahogany desk. Dutch examined them closely and went into his pants pocket and pulled out a handkerchief. With the white cotton fabric in his hand, he started to remove all of the prints that were splattered across the desk. He also noticed a gold chain lying underneath Joey's leather chair. The chain was missing the proud medallion that gave it all of its splendor. Bending down to retrieve the gold link chain, Dutch then placed it into his pants pocket.

The fiery Irishman slowly walked over to the surveillance equipment and popped out the video-cassette that was recording everything. Hurriedly, he slipped it into the breast pocket of his suit jacket. He replaced it with a blank tape and shut off the equipment. For whatever his own reasons were, he also did not want to leave any clues once the cops got involved. This tape had more than just Joey's attacker on it. It also possessed the faces of mostly all of the notorious gangsters that dwelled in the City of New York. There was no way that he could let the cops get a hold of this tape. Dutch had arrived at his own conclusions even before he viewed the tape, and only he knew what they were. Over and over again, he kept searching for more evidence, but time was running short, it would bring his clue hunting to a rapid end. But in his own mind he had seen enough to tell himself who the perpetrator was. Quickly, Dutch raced back outside to be by Joey's side.

In a matter of minutes, Vito had arrived at the scene. He quickly raced to the fallen body and fell to his knees. The anxiety and panic in his eyes brought out the fear that was running through his whole body. His usual calm, cool demeanor was gone. Seeing Joey in a pool of blood destroyed his very essence.

"Come on, kid, open your eyes, try to stay with us. You got too much to live for, don't give up on your right to live," Vito pleaded. "Fight, God damn it, fight. Where the fuck is the ambulance!"

"They're on their way," Dutch said.

"Did you check the place out?"

"Yea, there's nothing; the prick got away."

"Don't leave us now, wake up," Vito continued to plead. "Please, Joey, hang in there. Breathe, kid, please breathe!"

Joey's cold body was starting to turn colors, most of his blood was already spilled. He was unresponsive to any of Vito's pleas. His existence was slowly fading away as the last few ounces of blood poured out of the wounds to his torso. The once strong heart was running out of the blood that his veins were unwilling to provide. Still gasping for air with a face seething in pain, his agitated body was about to lose its fight for life. Suddenly Joey opened his eyes for what appeared to be the last time. He saw nothing but blurry shadows, but he saw enough to recognize who was hovering over him. Squinting with almost blindness, he saw his Godfather in total distress.

"Vito," the weak voice said. "It wasn't supposed to be like this," Joey cried, as he struggled with every word. Showing remarkable strength, he tried desperately to continue on. "Take...," he paused for a precious breath of air. "Take care of Gloria and the baby, tell.... tell her that I love them with all of my...... heart."

"I will, kid, I will," vowed his Godfather. Teardrops started to pour off of Vito's pain racked face. Never before had Vito ever felt anything like this. The tough and fearless gangster had a human side after all. His love for Joey was genuine; there was no one on earth who meant more to him. Gloria stood in the background, mortified and covering her pain with her hands. Jimmy had his arms around her, trying to prevent her from falling. The girl was too shell shocked to do or say anything more, she was on the verge of collapsing.

"My mother and sister Michele, try...., try to explain to them that," Joey then painfully gasped for more air. His breathing was becoming heavier and heavier, each breath looked like his last. His lungs were not cooperating; they just were not taking any more air into them. "That I will never forget them and please send them my love."

"You tell them, because you will be alright."

"It hurts so much. It's.... it's over, Vito, it's finally over."

"Don't say that."

"It's only a matter of time now."

"It's never over."

"I feel cold, Vito," Joey said. His body was sweating profusely as he broke out into a cold sweat. "I'm very cold."

Vito quickly removed his suit jacket and covered the bloody body. He then dug into his pockets for a handkerchief or tissue to wipe away some of the perspiration. Frantically, he searched and searched but came up with nothing. Vito went through every pocket in his expensive suit, with the same empty results.

"Here, Vito, use this," Dutch said, handing him a handkerchief. Vito snatched the white linen from Dutch's hand and slowly ran it along Joey's saturated brow. He patted the cloth on top of his forehead until most of the moisture was absorbed. It was only then that Vito and Dutch knew that something very strange was starting to happen.

"He's sweating blood," Dutch alerted. "The sweat is turning into blood!"

"What?" asked Vito, picking his head up to look at Dutch. "What the hell are you talking about?"

"Look at the fuckin' handkerchief; there's blood all over it. He's sweating blood, Vito! There's blood coming out of every pore of his body!"

Now with a face fully drenched in fear, Vito looked at the square piece of cloth and opened it up. Dutch was right, there was red blood all over the once clean material. Once the clear salty liquid had hit the fancy rag, it turned all of Joey's perspiration into blood. This miraculous event was happening all over his body.

"Holy shit," Vito said in a total state of confusion. "I can't believe this all happening to him. Dutch?" a frantic Vito called, not knowing what to do next. "Help me, what's going on here?"

"I don't know, Vito, I don't know. But I told you so."

"Told me what?"

"That something was gonna happen."

"Damn you, Dutch, we never should have left him here alone."

Almost unconscious, Joey then turned his head to another shadow that he assumed was Dutch. He just looked at Dutch and cracked a small smile. But his eyes told Dutch something quite different. Dutch sensed it right away and he knew what Joey was trying to tell him. Joey then reached out to grab Dutch by his hand, but his strength had failed him for the very first time. His left hand fell limp as Dutch reached out to grab it. Too tired, and struggling to keep his eyes opened, Joey succumbed to the gunshot wounds. He then appeared to lapse off into a coma as he shut his eyes for what seemed to be the final time.

"Don't worry, kid," Dutch said to the unresponsive body. "I will take care of whoever did this to you. I promise you that I will have no mercy on his soul."

Out of nowhere, a voice was about to beckon down upon Joey's struggling body. The time was now - his salvation was about to arrive. With a heartbeat that was barely ticking, he was just a matter of seconds before death. He then heard the voice that would give him eternal life. The voice that had come for only him, the chosen one.

"Will you come with me," a sonorous, yet peaceful and calm voice said to Joey. The voice echoed for millions of miles through the endless skies. These were words that Joey had heard before, but this time they had a much truer meaning to them. This time these calling words would have an ultimate effect, an effect that he would never return from. From up above, only Joey heard this message. But everyone crying over his body heard his response.

"Yes, I will come with you," Joey feebly uttered, after opening his eyes one last time.

Those strong and meaningful words were said with his last dying breath. Amazingly, his left hand slowly started to rise into the air. Joey reached and reached, trying desperately to touch something that others did not see. He devoutly struggled with each fingertip, trying and trying again to reach his purpose. Joey's shaking fingers were thrusting with movement, as his long limb was extended to its fullest capacity. He tried in vain with whatever effort he had left in his faltering body. Joey's body would not assist his desperate hand, there was no life left in it. Every ounce of life that he had left was exerted in his extended arm. He would not stop reaching until he felt the salvation that he was searching for.

Finally fulfilling his needs, he answered and touched the command from up above and accepted it. Then it was all over, Joey's arm had come tumbling down and crashed on the concrete pavement. He then lost consciousness forever as his eyes faded away and closed for a final time. Joey's head slowly tilted to the right as he died with his mouth wide open.

He had peacefully come to terms with whomever he was conversing with. His mission in life and the feat that was before him had been accomplished. It was now time to rest with the indescribable peace that had just taken over his body.

Vito just looked down at him confused, wondering what these words, "I will come with you," meant. He heard the words out of Joey's mouth before, but now it was much different. Those chilling words were finally taking place to fulfill their meaning. The believing Gloria understood it all; she knew what was happening. She also had a very hard time accepting it. Gloria was caught up in the crossfire of two colliding worlds. One of those worlds was taking something that meant everything to her. She knew what it was, but she had not yet come to terms with it, or herself.

"Noooo!" Vito screamed. "Don't die, God, please don't take him from us." In the background Gloria was heard crying and not believing that this was all happening. Jimmy was trying in vain to console her, but nothing was working.

"Vito, help him," she screamed. "Don't let him go, I can't live without him!"

Now acting out of control, Vito tried everything within his power to resuscitate Joey. He started to pound on his chest to revive him, but got no response of life. Vito then grabbed Joey around the mouth and lowered his head. With his lips wrapped around Joey's, his powerful lungs tried in vain to give him his life back. But that method failed also. It was then that Vito had realized that he had run out of options. Joey had already gone into cardiac arrest and died. It was too late to do anything.

"You're not supposed to die," Vito sobbed, shaking the dead body by its shoulders. "God please….," he painfully wailed. "You're not supposed die!"

Vito then put his head to Joey's chest and felt nothing. He then checked for any signs of breathing and got the same results. It was too late; it was all over. Joey DeFalco was dead.

"He's gone, honey," a stunned Vito said to her. Each word out of his mouth produced another tear-drop. "He's really gone."

"Joey," Gloria called out in a delirious voice. "Joey."

"Jimmy," Vito said. "Take her inside."

"No," she said balking. "I'm staying right here. I don't want to leave him, Jimmy, let me go." Jimmy never released his hold on the hysterical woman, he held on trying to control her outbursts.

"It's all over, Gloria, his suffering has passed," Jimmy said. "And he would not want to see you this way."

"I know, Jimmy, it's just so hard," she cried. "I loved him so much. Why him, why did it have to be him?"

"I don't know, Gloria, I wish I had those answers for you."

Still down on their knees, Vito then looked over at Dutch with venom in his eyes and with the look of Satan on his face. "Whoever did this to him," he viciously warned. "You find him and bring his fuckin head back to me in a duffle bag. Do you understand me!"

"Are you giving me a green light on this?"

"Yes, no matter who it is, you have a green light," he said. "I don't care if it takes you the rest of your fuckin' life. You find him, kill him and bring him back to me in pieces," Vito ordered. "Do you hear me?"

Dutch looked at Joey and then picked his head up and looked at his longtime buddy. "You have my word, Vito," he promised. "I'll find him, you can count on it. I will find him. This motherfucker will pay for this. He's as good as dead right now!"

In Mafia terms, once someone is given the green light to kill, it must be done. It doesn't matter who it is or where they come from, the hit or contract must be carried out. Dutch kept looking at his boss and shook his head in sorrow. There were no further discussions on this subject. Both men knew what had to be done.

Dutch then looked at Joey's corpse and noticed something very strange happening. He thought he was seeing things, but then he realized what was happening was real. "Vito, look," Dutch said pointing to Joey's body.

Vito followed Dutch's finger and picked up on what he was talking about. All the blood Joey was laying in, and the blood all over his body, was having a mysterious reaction. Little by little the deep red liquid was slowly drying up and disappearing. It started from the concrete floor and worked its way to Joey's ice cold body. Vito looked up at Dutch, not believing what he was seeing.

"What the fuck, Dutch, what's happening here?" the startled Italian said, continuing to look on in wonderment. "His blood is disappearing!"

"His blood is being taken from his body," Dutch proclaimed. "It's like he's being cleansed!"

"Dutch, look at it, it's practically all gone," an astonished Vito said. "The blood is gone." Vito then looked at his hands and all over his clothes. The blood had disappeared off of his garments and once stained hands. He then looked over at Gloria in disbelief, the same thing was happening to her. Every ounce of blood that poured out of Joey's body had evaporated into thin air.

Vito frantically grabbed Joey by the hand and watched this Biblical event unfold right before his eyes. For Vito was told of this prophetic event a few weeks ago. Whether or not he chose to believe it was another story. Now he had no choice in the matter as it was unfolding before his eyes and all around him. Alone with his thoughts, it was then that Vito also noticed something very significant. Joey's right hand was clenched in a tightly closed fist. There was something in his hand that he was holding onto for dear life before he died. Vito struggled to open the vice like grip that Joey had applied. Finally, one by one, he opened up the fingers on the dead body. Stunned, Vito saw the medallion cradled up against the palm of Joey's hand. He reached for the gold medal to pull it from Joey's dire clutches.

"Shit," he cried in pain. "This thing is as hot as a branding iron. Look at it, Dutch, it has the color of a burning ember. I can't pick it up, it's too hot."

"Use the handkerchief to pick it up," Dutch said. "It's right next to you!"

Vito picked up the scorching medallion using the white handkerchief that was once covered with blood. The intense heat from the medal quickly shot through the rag, forcing Vito to lay it down on the floor. With every motion that came from his dazed body, Vito was left in awe about all that he was seeing. While holding Joey by the hand, he raised the lifeless limb closer to his face. He looked deeper and deeper into the palm of Joey's hand. That's when he made the most remarkable discovery imaginable. The medallion had left an amazing imprint of the face of Jesus Christ right in the middle of the palm of Joey's right hand.

The Mark of Christ.

"Dutch, you have to take a look at this."

"What is it?"

"It's all true, Dutch," Vito cried. "It's all true."

The Irish mobster slowly bent his head down to examine what Vito was talking about. The sight left him with his eyes wide open. He just looked back at Vito not knowing what to say. "Vito," he paused for a second. "The kid was right all along."

"I know, Dutch, and I always doubted him," he sobbed. "I'll never forgive myself, Dutch; I should have believed what he was trying to tell me all along. I knew strange things were happening, but I never foreseen anything like this." Vito then looked across the body and into his buddy's eyes. "Dutch," he shakily said. "My grandfather died with the same imprint in the palm of his hand as this one."

"You never told me that."

"I know," he admitted. "I never told Joey either. When my father told me this story many years ago, I never believed him. But now I see that it's all true. Damn me!"

"I guess you believe the kid and your father now."

"I do, Dutch," a somber Vito said. "But my heart is full of guilt."

"Vito, there is no explanation for all of this."

"Yes there is, Dutch," he answered while looking into the sky. "Yes there is."

"Joey died for that medallion, Vito. He knew how much it meant to you."

"I know," he said shaking his head in disgust. "I should have never gone to the club. Maybe this would have never happened."

"Vito, judging by the signs, it would have happened anyway. There was no way to prevent any of this."

"I guess you're right," he replied. "Where's the chain to the medallion!"

"Here," Dutch said, reaching into his pants pocket and handing it to Vito.

"Where did you find it?"

"I found it in the back office."

"What else did you find back there?"

"Nothing, it was clean," he falsely said.

"What about the cameras?"

"Joey didn't turn the machine on. I guess he figured it was in our best interest to leave the tape off," he lied.

"I know, there were a lot of people here tonight."

"Vito, put the medallion back around his neck," Dutch said. "Let him be buried with it. It's time to put this legacy to rest."

"No," Gloria interceded. "I want it, Vito, put it around my neck!" she said, unafraid of the power behind the medallion. "I will give it to my baby."

Vito then looked down at his Godson to try and ask him for forgiveness, but it was too late. Whether Vito believed Joey or not, nothing would have prevented this from happening. Joey said it all along, that his time on earth was limited. Unfortunately nobody wanted to believe him.

For what might be for the last time, Vito bent down to kiss the almost blue body on the forehead. The loss of all its blood had turned Joey's face and the rest of his body into a pale blue color. The corpse was ice cold like it was laying in a freezer. His limbs were rendered immobile, stiff. Vito then said a few words to himself and performed the sign of the cross over the dead body. It was all over, everyone was just waiting for the ambulance to arrive. He picked up the medallion, got off of his feet and slipped the chain through the gold loop. Never taking his eyes off of her, he walked over to Gloria and placed the still warm medallion around her neck. Vito kissed her on the cheek and held her closely. They both cried in each other's arms as destiny unfolded right before them.

Suddenly, without warning, the winds started to pick up steam. The mighty breezes were swiftly moving parallel to the ground, forming a whirlpool around them. The heavy gusts were sucking up dirt and debris, sending it skyward. The tenacious gale forces whipped witnesses into a shocking frenzy. Moments later, the robust fury subsided.

Everyone exchanged troubled glances. An ominous silence descended over the world.

The moon turned black. The darkness turned darker.

There was wild movement overhead, the mourners looked on petrified.

"Look," Vito said, pointing to the sky.

"Oh my, God," Gloria uttered in silence. "He's really coming for Joey."

The dark clouds above them were reacting in a turbulent fashion. The odd and agitated forces were undisciplined and violently disruptive. Like an eddy, the gloomy mass started to react against its natural current. These visible masses of foamy particles were colliding against each other, causing a massive eruption in the dark night. Something with incredible power was trying to break through. Amazingly, an explosion was heard, opening up a highway to eternity. Now, the raw opened wound of the galaxy was exposed.

Everyone looked on stunned.

Beyond the clouds, from four corners of the earth, peals of thunder rumbled and lightning cracked the sky in a shaft of violence, turning the darkness bright, throwing fear into the stoutest souls. The stars, like fireballs, were blazing across the night sky. This beastly confrontation caused deafening explosions that lit up the skies with fury and might. The sounds, like echoes of war, littered the atmosphere. Above the clouds, the whole celestial foundation was being disrupted.

Like a scroll, the sky receded.

There was a dead silence again.

The tumultuous looked on in awe.

Abruptly, the earth started to tremor. Tremendous jolts opened up seams of pavement in the Earth and the cities. Destruction was everywhere. Glass windows shattered as lights flickered in and out. Mountains crumbled, buildings tumbled, mighty fires roared. Oceans, with their 30-foot surges, rumbled and gobbled up the shorelines. Chaos and destruction ruled the universe. What seemed like hours was just a matter of minutes. Then, calmness reigned.

Mother Nature never reacted like this before; every element of her power was being utilized. Whoever was coming or whatever was happening, no one has ever witnessed an incredible fury like this.

This was no aberration.

"Is it over?" Vito asked. The others just stood mute.

Finally freeing itself, a high-intensified light started to crack through the murky sky. For everything had separated, leaving a wide-open eternity to the heavens. The miraculous parting exposed the atmosphere and everything else behind it. What started out as a soft shimmer, the flickering and tremulous light was growing to epic proportions, descending rapidly. This beam of radiation was quickly blossoming in size, and blindness was imminent. The powerful earthbound light drew closer and closer to Joey's dead body. It did not stop until it rested upon his illuminated corpse, forming a tunnel around him.

Call it a phenomenon, but this happening of brightness must have been billions of miles long. The laser of brilliance was no more than ten feet wide, but glistened throughout the world. The beacon of light stood supreme to the very darkness that surrounded it.

Now aware of the sensation of perception, everyone was glued to the sky. They stood paralyzed, not knowing what to expect. For the first time in their lives, Vito and Dutch were very afraid. Even they have never witnessed anything close to this before. Jimmy and Gloria were numb; to them it was like the world was coming to an end.

What seemed impossible turned inevitable. Only the dead could witness this next spectacular event. Because spirit can only see and talk to spirit. For no eye will see and no ear will hear.

The visitor was about to enter the Earth's atmosphere.

Slowly, an overpowering figure started to descend through the immaculate brightness. Closer and closer, the final confrontation was about to commence. What seemed like millions of miles away, in reality was just a short distance to Joey. Miraculously, the coming drifted easily and lightly as it floated downwards toward its subject. With each second that passed, it grew more profound in facial image, never hiding its true identity.

The visitor finally rested within Joey's internal sights and thoughts. It now looked down on the fallen body ready to react. From Joey's dead body, his spirit had seen a glowing face with all the characteristics that he had seen before. This time the image was bright and profound, there were no more illusions. This was no mystery or surprise to Joey; he knew who was coming for him.

With his spirit still stagnant inside of his cold dead body, Joey waited patiently. But what hovered above him appeared to be a bit more enthusiastic. His remains started to react in a very unusual way; something was tugging away at them. Throbbing and jerking all over the floor, Joey's body was going through some unearthly transformation. The pulling and powerful suction sent his dead body into a convulsive reaction. This agitating force would not let go of the dead body. It was trying to pull something from it, and it wouldn't stop until it was released.

"He's alive," barked Jimmy. "He's alive."

"What the hell is happening now?" a stunned Vito said as he rushed to Joey's side. He then planted himself on his knees, opposite Dutch. "His body is going crazy!"

"Its okay, Vito," Gloria calmly said. "He is going home."

Within a Biblical second, Joey's body started to levitate. It started to slowly rise off of the deathbed of concrete. Inch by inch, it floated higher and higher. Vito and Dutch looked startled as the floating corpse slowly rose over their heads. It did not stop until the mighty vacuum had gotten what it had come for. There was no resistance or defiance, just the willingness of a wanting soul waiting to be emancipated. Now hovering about 48 inches above the ground, his body finally gave in and discharged its soul. Released from the almighty clutches that were pulling at him, the empty corpse came free falling down to the same spot that it had risen from. A loud thump was heard, as the painless body crashed back onto the pavement. Joey's spirit was now free, away from his painful past.

Joey is going to another world that is unknown to the living. The life giving principal of his living being was now gone. It was now free from all the pain and heartaches caused by this immoral society. It was free from the confinement and restraint that man had wreaked so much havoc on. Joey's soul was now taken from the dead body that belonged to him, never to be shattered again. His spirit was going to another world that was unknown to the living, but renowned to the chosen dead.

Gloria was overlooking these astonishing revelations, as Jimmy held on to her tightly. Vito and Dutch remained on their knees, continuing to stare at each other in disbelief. The foursome had just witnessed a miracle that unfolded right before their eyes. Each one of them had their own reasons for the events that had just taken place. But in reality, the only explanation that mattered, had already spoken. He only needed to speak once; the believers or non-believers would have to come up with their own conclusions.

Without anyone noticing but Jimmy, Gloria suddenly grew faint and fell down to both knees. Jimmy stopped her from injury as he broke the fall by grabbing her before her body crashed against the hard concrete pavement. He then gently rested her shaking body and laid it flat on the floor. Vito and Dutch hurried to their feet to help the fallen angel. Gloria just looked at all three men and smiled.

"Are you alright," Vito asked. He then placed his right hand behind her head and lifted it a little. "Why the smile, honey?"

"I just felt Joey's soul enter my body," she revealed. "He was inside of my womb, Vito. I felt him inside of me."

"What did he want?" Vito asked, returning the smile.

"He wanted to see and hold his baby before he left."

"Is he gone?" Vito asked.

"Yes, he was called to leave and he just floated away from me," she said. A teardrop shed from the corner of her left eye. "I heard the voice calling for him!"

"What voice?"

"The voice of," she paused trying to regain some of her composure. "The voice of Jesus Christ. Vito, I heard Jesus calling out Joey's name to come to him."

"What did he sound like?"

"He sounded very strong and yet so calm and peaceful."

"Did Joey say anything to you?"

"He called out my name and he said that he loved me," she uncontrollably answered. "He also said that he will forever wait for me until we are reunited again."

"Where did Joey go?"

"He went back into the light," she uttered. "He was only permitted to visit for a second or two." Gloria then put her head down, this occurrence absorbed every ounce of strength she had left. Jimmy peeled off his suit jacket and placed it underneath Gloria's faltering head. She now seemed to be resting peacefully knowing the unexplainable truth. "Joey's gone, Vito," she faintly said. "But this time he is gone forever. He is never going to come back to us. But one day we will all go to him"

Inside the tunnel of light, Joey's spirit laid, waiting to be taken. The never-ending tube was narrow by the earth's crust and grew in dimension the further it traveled into the night sky. His spirit started to rise as it ventured into the safety of Jesus' arms. The further he ascended, the more he was at peace within himself. The peace that passes all understanding was almost upon him. The soul did not stop rising until it confronts the almighty spirit of Jesus Christ. This divine intervention was at the altar of its final conception.

There he was, dressed in the finest of white linen. The immaculate robe and undergarment were flowing through the gentle breezes. A sign of purity was his penetrating aura as he glowed from every angle of his striking appearance. He waited with opened arms for his new arrival to come to him.

Jesus Christ was welcoming this chosen soul of Joey's into God's Kingdom. His piercing brown eyes provided the windows to which Joey's soul was to enter from. Long dark brown hair adorned a chiseled face covered lightly with hair. The thin mustache and beard slightly covered the olive complexion.

Jesus then looked at Joey and opened his arms even further. Joey in turn extended his hand to his savior, never relinquishing his sight. The two then locked eyes as Christ reached down with his right hand. Inside the palm lay scars just like the ones that we have been taught to know. Those were the same nailed scarred hands that hung him to be crucified on the cross. Both hands, inside and out, showed the suffering and pain that was inflicted throughout his body. His naked arms bore similar blemishes of pain from the repeated strokes of the punishing whips. These stigmata's were clear indications of the pain and torment that was suffered during his crucifixion.

It was truly him, Jesus Christ, the holy one who sacrificed his life for all of us. The one who laid down his life for us, the chosen one. No one took his life, for they did not have the power. He gave his life and bore all of our sins, even though he was sinless.

Joey then looked into the eyes of Christ and saw a love that he had never known. An unconditional love based on total acceptance. Joey was in such a glorious state of peace that he forgot the past and left it all behind him. His total existence on earth was wiped away and forgiven, and all that was left is peace and love. For he had accomplished and obeyed what God has asked of him. Now was Joey's time to receive his long awaited solace. There was no need to worry about Gloria and the baby. Just looking into the eyes of Jesus told Joey that everything would be all right. No more words were spoken, as the rest would be said through the spirit.

"Well done my good and faithful servant!" Jesus said to Joey.

"I come before you, my Lord," said Joey.

"Don't cry, my son, for I will wipe every tear from your saddened eyes!" Jesus said, waiting for his new arrival. "I am the resurrection and the life; he that believes in me, though he were dead, yet shall he live." Jesus continued to look down upon Joey's accepting soul. "And those whoever live and believe in me shall never die. I am the Alpha and the Omega, the First and the Last, the Beginning and the End." Jesus then reached down for Joey's willing hand. "Reach unto my finger and behold my hand. Be not faithless, but believing. Your time to join me has come."

Spirit to spirit and soul to soul, they became one. With Jesus leading the way, the window of souls was now open. Now taking Joey's hand, he lifted him through the window and out of the tunnel of light. Within a heartbeat, the fascinating light had disappeared like it was never even there. It vanished into the same night sky that Joey did.

Only the destruction remained.

The gates of heaven were open. The Lord waited with opened arms. Jesus welcomed this chosen soul into God's Kingdom. In God's Heaven, Joey appeared dressed in the finest of white linen, just like Jesus. Both Jesus and Joey bore the wounds and scars of their life on earth. God's entire kingdom was structured in solid gold and pearls. The atmosphere glowed in a stunning aura of peace and love.

Joey DeFalco was now home.

Chapter 26

THE DEAD BODY was laid out for the customary three days in his neighborhood's funeral parlor. During visiting hours, the place was packed with tearful mourners. They came from all walks of life, some knew him well and others had wished they had gotten a chance to know him better. Besides Joey's immediate family, everyone from childhood friends to paying customers came to pay their respects. Every mobster in the metropolitan area paid homage to the distressed family. Whether they knew the kid or not, they paid their respects with sincerity. At times it looked like someone very influential was being laid to rest, not some kid from the streets of Brooklyn.

It was non-stop; the grieving kept viewing the open casket in disbelief that Joey DeFalco was really gone. All of them but four had no clue surrounding the death and its aftermath. Murdered in cold blood was all that everyone was told, nothing more.

There he was, comfortably laid out in a beautiful mahogany casket with all the brass trimmings. Vito loved that tropical American tree that produced the hard, reddish brown wood. The coffin sat in front of a large bed of flowers that kept coming in all day long. From roses to carnations, the scented flowers bombarded the large room with their sad fragrances. There's just a different smell exuding from a flower when it sits behind a dead body. The collage of aromas, just appear to bring out the scent of death.

The body in the dark blue suit and black shoes lay peacefully in the white interior of the casket. Lacking the pallor of death, his head rested upon a fluffy pillow as his eyes were in a sleeping position. Both of Joey's hands were folded together above his waist. A string of rosary beads with a gold crucifix dangled from the still hands. For the first time in his young life, Joey looked at ease and in total peace within himself. For God had preserved him well, he looked perfect on his final resting bed. Joey showed nothing from the turbulent struggle in order to maintain his life. The young man lost his life, but even death could not take away his good looks from him. His heart was the only thing that changed; it stopped beating. The only thing taken from him was his soul, and even that reigned supreme.

Sobbing and delirious cries of disbelief flooded the room with sorrow. Joey's immediate family sat up front, all of them trying passionately to console his grieving mother and sister. The most people could do was say that they were sorry, there was not much more to say or do. Most people are always at a loss for words when something this tragic takes place. In most cases the less said, the better. Only time will heal some of these wounds, but time would never wipe out the fond memories of this human passing. Only death will have them reunited with the man that lay before their eyes. Soon, the casket will be closed permanently and Joey's handsome face would be lost forever. Only the memories will now remain. To some they will be short lived, to other they will last a lifetime.

At the cemetery, it was pretty much of the same thing. Everyone formed a circle around the huge hole as Father Pasquale performed his religious eulogy. Most people just stared at him, numb, knowing that this was the last time that they would observe the closed casket. The color black was everywhere, to Italians, it is the color of death. Long after the body rots, the black clothing is sometimes worn for years. In a lot of families, it is a superstitious ritual that mostly all Italians truly believed. To break that belief, would most certainly bring hardships and show major disrespect towards the dead. Some wives or mothers adorned the color black until they finally died, never easing up on their mourning for a loved one who had passed on.

Each mourner tightly held a rose. Those roses would be gently placed on top of the coffin after the final eulogy. Joey's final resting place would be right beside his father in the family's plot on Staten Island. It was only a matter of time before his body was lowered and placed inside the concrete container and covered with dirt.

The sun was blazing hot and was emitting heat around all of the mourners. Death and the suffocating weather were two obstacles for all of Joey's loved ones to endure. Blinding rays were beating off of the top of the coffin as the haze just floated around them. Many were having a hard time standing on their feet, as the grueling last few days had taken everything out of them. The hot weather had no mercy and made all the severe conditions even worse.

When the sermon was finally over, a loud burst of tears echoed throughout the quiet cemetery. Now the grieving would truly start, it was now that reality was finally sinking in that Joey would not be around any longer. His mother and sister had to be practically pulled away from the burial site; they did not want to leave.

Gloria, on the other hand, understood everything as she looked down at the gold medallion. She knew that the only man she ever loved and possibly would ever love, was in good hands. But she didn't know what fate awaited her. Never without tears, she was now without Joey and the yearning comfort of being in his loving arms. Even though she was dying inside and missing his touch, she knew that she would never see him again on this Earth. To her, she now knew that Joey had made that final crossing.

To get to heaven he had to leap that final hurdle. Joey DeFalco had crossed over from death to eternal life. Joey had escaped the world of darkness and stepped into the light. The light and the darkness have nothing in common, just as evil has nothing in common with good. Gloria knew that Joey was good, he had to be to step into the light. Everyone who loves evil hates the light and will not enter it. They fear that all of their bad deeds will be exposed, and rightfully so. But those who always live by the truth and righteousness will never abstain from entering that strong glow of brightness. For he has nothing to hide, his goodness will be exposed through the eyes of God. Where Joey is now resting there is no sun and moon, God is the light.

Nightfall was soon to be setting in, the recessed sun had settled in behind a mature oak tree. Everyone who paid last respects to Joey had left the cemetery a long time ago. There was only one man left who decided to pay his respects in his own way. He just stood about twenty feet from the opened grave just waiting for the gravediggers to finally lower the body. This was not normal behavior for most mourners, it was against cemetery rules. But Vito had decided not to leave the spacious graveyard until every last grain of earth was covering Joey in that 6 foot deep hole. He just stood there, hour after hour just thinking and waiting. No one asked him to leave the closed cemetery... no one had the nerve to.

After three or four hours and a pack of cigarettes, Vito observed a small truck pulling up the narrow passageway. Out jumped four diggers with a shovel in each of their hands. They placed the shovels one on top of the other and moved towards the casket. The union workers slowly started to lower the casket into the cement box below. In a matter of seconds the lid would be placed on top as the concrete container was sealed. The four of them quickly retrieved their shovels by the handle and proceeded to work. Simultaneously, they all scooped up large portions of dirt from the large mound that lay a few feet away. You could hear the dry soil banging off of the concrete box below. In a few more minutes, the box would be completely covered with dirt and rocks.

Vito just looked on, never saying a word. Then for the first time in over three hours, he started to move. He carefully walked over to the mountain of dirt and with his bare hands scooped a handful of the brown soil up. Walking towards the hole, he stopped about a foot away. The four men just looked on, while their work temporarily came to a halt.

"Here's to you, Joey," he said while preparing to throw the dirt on top of the coffin. "Please forgive me and always remember that I love you. I know you're in a place that you always wanted to be. God bless you, kid" Vito looked down into the large hole and sprinkled the soil on top of his Godson. He started to choke up as the tears were cascading down his face. Now looking into the eyes of the gravediggers, he just turned and walked away. Returning to the spot that he was originally standing on, he turned to the grave again and just stared at the on going procedures.

The door to the black limousine opened up as Dutch exited the air-conditioned luxury car. He trampled through the freshly mowed grass never breaking his short stride. Occasionally, he looked over at one or two tombstones, but he continued on. He finally arrived at the spot where his boss was standing and placed his right hand on his shoulder.

"Come on, Vito, it's all over," he said. "It's time to go."

"How the hell did this happen?"

"I don't know, but I will tell you one thing. I will never forget any of it."

"He's gone, Dutch, the kid is really gone."

"I know, we will all miss him."

"But it's not all over," Vito insisted. "You know what you have to do!"

"It will be done by tomorrow," Dutch promised. "You have my word on this one! Hey Vito, did you ever wonder what this dark secret behind that medallion is all about?"

"I don't know," a stupefied Vito said. "Joey told me about some of it, but if it takes me the rest of my life to find out the answer to that question, I will."

"These mysteries are kept hidden for a reason," Dutch implied. "You can't mess around with the powers of God."

"I know, but there is more to this story than we think there is. That medallion goes back hundreds and hundreds of years. I only know what happened to my grandfather and Joey. But I'm sure there is much more to find out than what I already know."

"Why do you say that?"

"Because, did you see the way Father Pasquale was staring at Gloria today?"

"No, why?"

"She was wearing the medallion around her neck. The guy looked like he was gonna have a heart attack. I just saw the frightened look on his face and the fear in his eyes. There is something buried somewhere and he knows what it is."

"Well, whatever he knows he's not gonna share it with us."

"One day we'll just have to see about that," Vito vowed. "One day we'll pay him a little visit and we will see what this is all about!"

"And what if he don't talk?"

"Oh, he'll talk," Vito promised. "He'll talk."

The two men then slowly started walking towards the limousine. The driver then hopped out of the car and opened the rear passenger side door. Both men then looked back at the gravesite for the final time. They then looked at each other shaking their heads in sorrow. One after the other they entered the black vehicle as the driver closed the door behind them.

Chapter 27

HIS HANDS WENT through drawer after drawer cleaning out the mahogany desk in Joey's office. All the envelopes and paperwork was thrown on top of the spacious desk. Vito looked around and picked up the small picture that lay right in front of him. The photo was taken only ten days ago, ten days later Joey was dead. In a matter of ten days, Vito could still not believe that this had happened to him. Seeing death was nothing new to Vito, it just never hit him so close to home. There was one thing for sure, he definitely did not like the taste of it. For even he and his loved ones were not immortal, death shows no favoritism.

Vito decided to open an 8x10 yellow envelope and he noticed that it contained all of Joey's personal documents. From a high school diploma to a poem written to Gloria. He continued to sift through the personal papers and discovered something very disturbing to him. Picking the item up, he drew it closer so his fading eyesight could catch a better look.

Where the fuck did he get this? he thought to himself, trying to remember the place where Joey could have gotten what he was holding in his hand.

A sound was heard out front by the dining room area. Vito took a peek at the surveillance cameras and noticed Dutch and Bear coming towards the back office. He quickly threw whatever he was looking at into his back pocket and awaited their arrival. The two men looked very anxious and disheveled. It looked like the both of them had not gotten any sleep in a day or so.

"What's up, Vito?" Dutch asked, standing with Bear in front of Joey's desk.

"I'm cleaning out the kid's desk," a depressed Vito said. "We're gonna sell this place. There are just too many bad memories here."

"That's a good idea. Every time I walk through the front door, something just scares the shit out of me."

"I know what you mean," said a pale looking Vito. "Man, you two guys look like dog shit. Where the fuck have you been?"

"Here," Dutch quickly replied, raising a black duffle bag and throwing it on top of the desk. "This is where we've been." Dutch then adjusted his black leather gloves and went into his pants pocket while callously looking up at Vito. "Here's your fuckin killer and here's the money he stole," he said while placing a wad of cash on the desk.

Vito stood there with both of his arms leaning down on the desk. He looked at the bag and then back over at Dutch. "Where did you find the prick?"

"He was shacking up somewhere in Brooklyn. But I also found something else out."

"What's that?" Vito asked, before he was about to take a seat.

"You were next!"

"What?"

"Do I speak French," Dutch sarcastically said. "You heard me right the first time. I said that he was going to kill you next."

"This motherfucker," a steaming Vito said. "Who the fuck did this cocksucker think he is.? Give me that fuckin' bag."

Vito pulled the black duffle bag towards him to open it up. Dutch and Bear took a step backwards from in front the desk. Dutch stopped after retreating about two feet, Bear kept on going until he nearly hit the wall. They both watched an incensed Vito go on the warpath and never stopping until his hands reached the zipper of the black bag. For the first time in his life, Vito was shaking with fury. He could never imagine anyone having the balls to try and kill him. Not only was killing Joey bad enough, but this piece of wasted life wanted him dead too.

He fumbled with the zipper, desperately trying to get it open. Vito pulled and pulled, but his nervous hands would not stop shaking. His right hand was holding the duffle bag firmly, but the left hand was so out of control.

Finally after tugging irrationally for a few seconds, the zipper gave in. Inch by inch, he pulled from right to left exposing some of the contents inside the blood soaked bag.

"Do you want my gloves?" Dutch asked, knowing that the bag was drenched with blood. "It's kind of messy in there."

"No!" Vito violently screamed.

Vito continued on like a rabid crazed wild animal. He knew what was inside that bag, but that didn't stop him from opening up his present. Looking into the soiled bag, he noticed the back of someone's blood stained matted head laying face down in it. Dried blood was running throughout the hair of the killer, caking each strand together like some adhesive glue. Now more focused then ever, Vito opened the bag all the way. He then switched hands, his left hand held the bag while his right hand reached into the small carrying case to pull out what was inside.

Grabbing the head tightly by the hair, he slowly raised it out of the duffle bag. Some blood was still dripping off of the face and from the perforated and chopped up neck of the decapitated head. Blood was all over Vito's hands now, but he did not seem to care. His wrath and ire was too overpowering, he had to see who the killer of his Godson was.

Raising the head to eye level, he snapped his wrist turning the head in his direction. Vito now stood face to face with Joey's killer. Reality was about to stick a dagger right through his heart. Suddenly, Vito's whole body started to tremble with a fear. Rendered numb, he became faint as he received the almighty shock of his life.

"Ahhhhh," he screamed. "Oooh my God!" he ranted and raved while dropping the morbid head to the floor. The head bounced off the carpet and rolled a couple of feet away from him. When the momentum of the rolling body part came to a halt it landed face up looking at the ceiling. "Noooo, noooo, this can't be happening to me. God help me," he pleaded. "I don't deserve this, help me."

Acting very unstable and emotional, Vito could not stand on his feet. He reached for the leather chair behind him and rolled it underneath his weak body. Carefully sitting down, he then buried his face into his bloody hands.

"What did I do," he asked himself hysterically. Now looking up at Dutch he said, "Dutch, what did I do? Oh my God, what did I do?"

What Vito saw was enough to give anyone a nervous breakdown or heart attack. The blood stained face was bloated, gruesome and gory. Both eyes of this butchered head were wide open. His mouth bore the same feature, for it too was open to capacity. Blood had discolored whatever teeth he had left in his mouth. There were black and blue welts around each battered eye to go along with a severely split lip. Running dried up blood was dripping out of both nostrils of the badly broken nose. Large open seams of flesh ran up and down the strangled and mutilated neck. Before they dismembered him, it was evident that this guy was inflicted with severe pain and torture. But to Vito, he saw something much more than that. He saw the butchered and battered head of someone who was once very dear to him. He horrifically saw the slaughtered and decapitated head and pulverized face of his biological son Eddie. Vito had ordered the direct hit and death of his own son. He never dreamed that Eddie Carlucci would be the killer of Joey DeFalco.

"How do you know it was him?" Vito asked Dutch, still sobbing in emotional pain.

"His fingerprints were all over the desk."

"What fingerprints?"

"The prints on his left hand."

"You butchered and cut my fuckin' son's head off because you saw some fingerprints on top of this desk," Vito yelled.

"All the prints that I found had a missing index finger just like yours."

"You fuckin' idiot," Vito blasted at his friend. "I was in this damn office all day long the day Joey got shot. They could have been my prints!"

"There's more, Vito!"

"Like what?"

Dutch pointed at the desk and then looked up at Vito. "I found that picture of you and Joey up against the wall," he explained. "Apparently Eddie got annoyed when he seen it."

"That's it, a fuckin' picture."

"Now listen, Vito?"

"No, you listen," he demanded. "You better have more than what you're giving me."

"What about the medallion? That piece of shit ripped it off of Joey's neck," Dutch answered, pointing to the head on the carpet. "He wanted the medallion back. Don't you see all this?"

"The only fuckin' thing I see is my son's fuckin' head on the floor."

"Well then look fuckin' harder," Dutch screamed, never backing down an inch. "He was jealous of the relationship that you and Joey shared."

"Assumptions, all you are giving me is assumptions."

"I hoped and prayed that it would not come down to this," Dutch screamed back. "But you're in fuckin' denial! You can't face up to the fact that Eddie killed Joey."

"You're wrong!"

Dutch reached into his back pocket and pulled out a videocassette of the whole incident.

"Am I? It's all on here," he said.

He flipped the black tape onto the desk in Vito's direction. You could cut the tension inside the office with a knife, both men were furious. Each one of them had their own reasons for defending their argument.

"What is?" Vito asked, while picking up the tape.

"The murder that was committed by your precious boy Eddie."

"You told me that Joey shut the surveillance equipment off."

"I lied," Dutch screamed back. "Do you think for one fucking minute that you were the only one that loved that kid Joey, we all did."

"But Eddie was my son!"

"Fuck your son, he meant shit to me. You can disown me too if you like, but I had to do what I had to do. Besides, you gave me the fuckin' order to kill him."

"You should have come to me first."

"Why, so you could have called off the hit?"

"No, that's not why," a furious Vito answered. "I would have dealt with him my own way."

"You had all these years to deal with him and you never did. So I did it for you. If I would have come to you first Eddie would still be walking the streets. For years you knew there was a problem with him, and for years you neglected it. And because you neglected it, Joey is dead."

"No, you're wrong."

"I'm not wrong God damn it," Dutch shot back. "And you fuckin' know it." Dutch continued with his verbal assault, knowing quite well that he was the only guy in the world who could get away with it.

"You know how it is, Dutch," Vito insisted. "When it comes to family, it's off limits and you know that."

"It's off limits?" he asked, knowing that Vito was only acting this way out of guilt. "What about you? You were next on his hit list, and then what, maybe me?"

"How do you know all this?"

"He sang like a canary before we killed him. He was working for Steamer and Julius. Eddie killed Joey for some heroin and money. Nothing more than that."

"So Eddie was the one who was following Joey all over town?"

"You got it."

"He was working for those two rotten bastards!" Vito yelled, slamming his fist down on top of the desk. "Where the fuck are they?"

"I even got that out of him," Dutch said. "I know where they are."

"Good," Vito said, while digging into his back pocket. "I have to ask you something, Dutch."

"What?"

"Where did Joey get this from?" Vito asked, handing Dutch a photograph that was in the yellow envelope.

"Where did you find that?"

"It was in this envelope buried in the side drawer of the desk."

"He got it off your bunk the day you were being released from prison. I told him to put it back, but I guess he didn't."

"Did you tell him who the kid in the picture was?"

"Yea, I did."

"So Joey knew who Eddie was before he died."

"Yea."

"Before Joey died why didn't he tell me that it was Eddie who shot him?"

"I guess he was worried that it would have destroyed you. He probably never wanted you to know that your son shot him. That poor kid loved you more than you'll ever know," confessed Dutch. "But that was him and this is me. I felt that you had to know who killed Joey. My conscience had to bring him back to you this way."

"Why?"

"Because it was the only way," Dutch professed. "The rest of the body parts of this piece of shit are over at Butchie's place. I cut him up like a side of beef. After I was done with him, I pissed all over his body."

"Don't talk to me that way!" Vito screamed, not believing the hatred Dutch was showing for Eddie. "You're way out of line, Dutch!"

"Nothing is out of line here, it was meant to be this way. That damn medallion started it all. From the moment you put it around Joey's neck. There was no way to stop any of this and you know it."

"Do you think that Eddie killed him over that medal?"

"He was gonna kill him anyway, seeing the medallion around Joey's neck just sealed the deal. The two of them had a fight over the medallion. Joey won the fight for the medal, but lost his life over it. Your son confessed everything to me before he died."

"It was jealousy."

"For Christ sake, Vito! It was more than just jealousy," Dutch said. "Come on, Vito, wake up, will you."

"Then what was it?"

"It was fate, Vito, or whatever the hell else you want to call it. Joey told you all this a couple of weeks ago and you still fail to see it."

"I know, Dutch," Vito finally confessed in a softer tone of voice. "I didn't ever want to feel responsible for all of this. So I tried to hide it even though it was happening before my eyes. Joey kept telling me over and over again. Each time I made him think that he was crazy. I knew there was something buried inside that medallion. What is was, I swear," Vito looked dead straight into Dutch's eyes, "I had no idea. I never believed anyone, even my own father. Then what happened outside the store just confirmed what he was trying to tell me all along. I feel so guilty for trying to hide something that he felt so strongly about. I should have believed him from the very start. I just feel like I am responsible for his death because I gave him that medallion. "

"You're not responsible for anything," he said. "That medallion would have found its way to Joey in another way. You have nothing to be ashamed of and you are not responsible for a damn thing. The medallion was meant to be around Joey's neck. The rest is a history that we or no one else could ever change."

"I guess it was destiny," Vito said. "I never thought of it that way. I just can't believe that this is all happening to me."

"To you! Damn it, Vito! What happened outside the other night affected us all. I still can't sleep at night. It was a story that you only see in the fuckin' movies. So you better believe it, because it happened and this is the only way that it could ever be. And don't ever forget that."

"I won't. I could promise you that, I won't." Vito then turned to look at the head laying only a few feet away from him. "How much did Eddie suffer?"

"He suffered up until the point where we got what we needed to know. The ending came quick for him. He didn't even know what hit him."

"Dutch, take the head and put it with the rest of his remains," Vito ordered. "I want to at least bury him with whatever dignity that he had left."

"No problem," the tough Irishman said. "I'll bring everything back to you."

"Now and only now, my good friend," Vito said. "Revenge is finally yours. You, Bear and Jimmy go find those two filthy niggers and kill them. You kill them slowly, but make sure that you inflict more pain and punishment than is imaginable. I want the both of them to suffer the same way that Joey did. I want to feel their pain from here, God damn it." Vito then jabbed his finger into the desk and started to poke it harder and harder like a jack-hammer. "And make sure that they know that Vito Carlucci is responsible for killing them."

"What about their bodies?"

"You do what you do best with them," Vito ordered. "When you come back we will finish this discussion. It's still not over yet."

"Consider it done," his warrior said, while stuffing Eddie's head back into the duffle bag. "Come on, Bear, we have work to do."

Dutch did not have to be told the same thing twice as he and Bear headed out the door. Vito sat down in the chair again and then picked up the videotape. He carefully examined the tape while shaking his head from side to side. Slowly rising from his seated position, he walked over to the cabinet with all the equipment and looked at the idle TV and VCR. His right hand searched for the power buttons as he slid the evidence into the empty slot of the recorder.

"Nooo!" he screamed, shaking his head violently. "Nooo, I can't do this," he cried out again. "What am I doing?"

In a fit of rage, Vito quickly withdrew the tape from the video equipment and held it tightly in his possession. Proceeding on, he then walked out into the dining room and opened up the glass doors to the fireplace. He turned the gas on high and waited about a minute before he threw the tape into the fire. Now all alone and shedding tears, Vito watched the tape disintegrate as the intense flames melted it down to nothing. He followed the black fumes all the way up to the chute of the fireplace. Shaking his head with sorrow, he kept observing until the dark smoke drifted into the mysterious skies above.

Now feeling broken shattered and all alone, the Mafia under-boss walked through the front door of the restaurant. He stopped and stood over the spot where Joey had died. Vito then looked down to see if there were any bloodstains that were embedded on top of the concrete walkway. But there was not a trace of crimson anywhere. He went down on one knee to examine it closer as he rubbed his hand along the warm walkway. He then kept rubbing and rubbing as if he was trying to feel for something that just wasn't there. Out of nowhere, Vito thought that he heard a voice calling for him from up above.

"Vitoooo,"............ the hollowed, echoing voice called. "Vitoooo."

With the look of astonishment all over his face, he looked up into the endless sky. There he saw a deep bodied red sun with the same extraordinary characteristics of blood. The sun was bleeding Joey's colors for the final time. Even the surrounding clouds were affected; their saturated rich tones absorbed the divine radiance of the majestic sun. The believers call it "The Star of Jesus."

This miraculous manifestation was as full and round as it has ever been. With its soft glow gently touching the horizon, Vito then knew that it had symbolized tranquility to him. This star was very easy to look at; it was not hard on his eyes. It was a star that he knew was there, but a star he would only see once in his lifetime. He then looked up into the soft light and performed the sign of the cross. Vito's newly found wisdom left him with an understanding of something that modern science could not ever explain. There was something that existed billions of miles away in a place the believers called heaven. There is a purpose, Vito now knows, a destination for every beginning and first breathe of life.

Still on one knee, Vito proceeded to lower his head in agony. He knew that he felt his Godson's aura looking down at him. Vito finally realized what Joey had been searching for all along. Once Joey found and attained those precious gifts, there was no way he was ever coming back. Those precious gifts that were promised to him many, many years ago were called eternal peace and love. It was the appointed time for Joey to receive these priceless amenities from the mighty God who dwelled in the heaven up above us all.

Spellbound and now feeling the emptiness, Vito returned his focus to the open sky. Fond memories drifted back with visible images of the past. A checkered past that will linger on, never letting go.

"Joey, I know you can hear me," Vito softly whispered. With tears falling from his heartbroken face, the mollified gangster voiced his sentiments one last time. "You made me proud, kid," he uttered. "You made me proud."

Vito again made the sign of the cross. In agony, he then lowers his head one final time.

A higher power had spoken.

"Behold, I am coming soon!
My reward is with me,
and I will give it to everyone
according to what he has done."
REVELATION 21:20 VERSE 12

The End

Printed in the United States
48488LVS00005B/61-255

9 781420 897333